*The*
First Ward

by Richard Sullivan

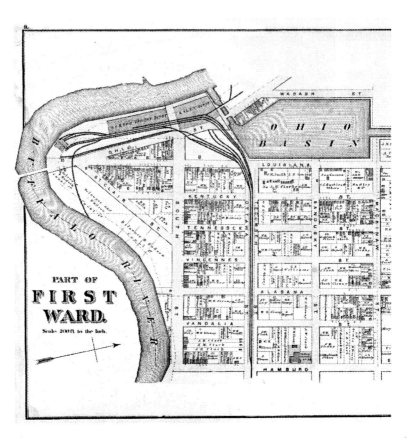

visit www.mutualrowingclub.com
for photos and information on
the Mutual Rowing Club.

Other Books
by Richard Sullivan:

The First Ward II: Fingy Conners & The New Century
Driving & Discovering Hawaii: Oahu
Driving & Discovering Hawaii: Maui and Molokai
Reclaim Your Youth

The First Ward
Volume I
by
Richard Sullivan
Third Edition, Revised
Copyright © 2011, 2012. 2013 by Richard Sullivan

Montgomery
Ewing

This book is dedicated to my sister,
Barbara Sullivan,

and to my friend,
Samantha Payne

Grain Elevators Along The Buffalo River, 1880s

ACKNOWLEDGEMENTS

This novel, heavily based on actual events, is a scrapbook of sorts, made up of disparate parts: family geneaology, historical facts, antique photos, yellowed news clippings, family legend and lore, and a bit of imagination.

I wish to honor and pay tribute to the forgotten and mostly nameless photographers whose riveting images herein provide a true-to-life window into the very people and events chronicled in The First Ward, as well as to the dozens of anonymous news writers of their day whose colorful accounts of events and unique prose have been incorporated into this novel, woven like weft into the warp of my family's story.

No one short of a time traveler from this period, and a very literate time traveler to be sure, could even come close to duplicating the jargon, phrasing, sentence structure and colorful definitions and descriptions for which these wonderful anonymous authors are hereby gratefully acknowledged.

PS 30 at Louisiana and South Streets in Buffalo's 1st ward, 1900.

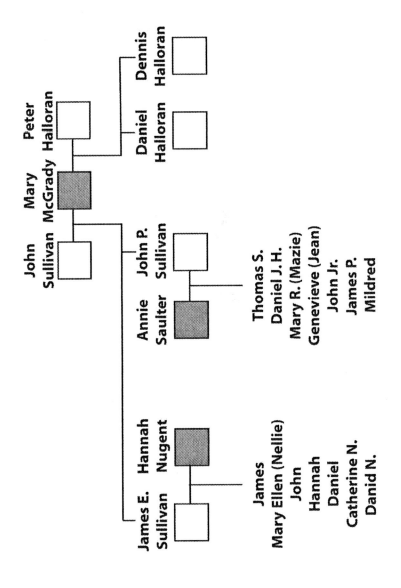

❧

1850
Welcome to New York

"Nigger!"

Sweet Mary McGrady felt a sharp sting...then the sickly, sticky, stinking stench of rotten egg running heavily down her face. It slithered under the collar of her dress like a muculent slug crawling toward her left breast—as if she didn't already feel wretched enough.

"Go back to where you come from, nigger!"

The men on the pier were shouting at her and at those around her as the victims of their insult cowered, trying to fend off the attack and find their way safely off the ship.

A piece of slate roof that could have sliced a man's flesh wide open flew past, and then a stone, and after that, rotten vegetables and a shower of slimy browned pear cores. Those who got within range were spat upon.

"There ain't no more room left for you colored in New York! Why don't you get the hell out of here!?" shouted the Native.

"Ask me arse, caffler!", one of the newest of Americans hollered back.

Mr. Tweed turned around from his complimentary restaurant set-up and bellowed at the hooligans to stop their barrage or he'd have his police friends crack their heads wide open. The hurling of objects then ceased, but not that of epithets.

Mary McGrady was dazed and weak from the difficult five-week journey. Addled she may have been, and English they seemed to have been shouting, but there were words in their volley she had never heard before.

"Nigger?" she said to the woman in front of her. "What is that blarney they'll be callin' us, now?"

Mary McGrady had risked everything by crossing the ocean on her journey to escape a hopeless future, famine, and the despicable English, not being exactly sure which of the three was less tolerable. She had an older brother who awaited her arrival upstate, in Amsterdam N.Y. James McGrady had preceded her in his emigration by five years, and Mary was anxious to finally be reunited with her favorite sibling.

She had witnessed the deaths of half a dozen of her shipmates on what her fellow passengers had rechristened The Coffin Ship on its month-long journey. Their bodies were slipped into the sea from a polished wooden litter tilted at an extreme angle. They slid cleanly under the surface with nary a splash. Sharks soon appeared and while others watched fascinated, Mary had to turn away. She wondered all during the undulous voyage if she herself would make it out of the ship's hold alive. She huddled in fear with like-minded families onboard for the protection that numbers afforded against lurking predators.

There were 250 passengers on the ship England, most of a very decent sort. The voyage was extremely rough, and the specter of shipwreck was always looming.

Storms were frequent and the ship was driven mightily back from its course by thrashing gales. One night a great terror prevailed. The storm caused the sailors to shut all the hatches upon the passengers, and Mary feared that the crew were about to abandon the ship leaving her and the other passengers to their fate. She prayed to the Saints, then to the Holy Mother, and finally to God as well, not having wanted to bother Him unless absolutely necessary. The vessel rocked and groaned, and gales roared fearfully. Panic took hold of all aboard. Mothers clutched their babies with one hand and their rosary with the other.

The England's shipboard food allowance was two quarts of water, a pound of pork, bread, and potatoes or rice as one might choose. Passengers cooked for themselves in a place called the galley. People fought over whose turn came next when seas were calm, but when seas were rough the galley was empty. Everyone was up on deck vomiting. Previous to boarding in Liverpool, Mary had laid in some provisions to supplement the ship's monotonous fare. These didn't last long. A thief stole her cache of carrots.

The relief and joy she felt the moment she walked out and away from her floating jail cell and down the gangplank onto the solid ground of South Street was spoiled somewhat by the shower of curses and offal raining down upon all the newcomers. She stooped in the shelter of a dray until the fusilladiers ran out of ammunition, then stood upright to gain her bearings. Her destination was Orange Street, in a place called The Five Points.

She asked for directions, but was shunned. Two men on the wharf were offering soup to the new arrivals for free, along with exhortations for someone or something called "Tammany". She was hungry, so she queued up. When it came her turn, the well-fed full-bearded Tammany man, Mr. Bill Tweed asked, "Who's yer man?"

Mary didn't have a man, and was prepared to say as much, when the red-haired young man in line behind her interrupted in his Ennis accent.

"She's my woman."

Mary McGrady turned, surprised. The gingered Irishman shot her a look that said do not speak. The Tammany man handed Mary her soup. When she tried to take it the man refused to let go of the tin bowl. The tug of war was designed to force her to meet his eyes with hers. When she did he gave her an obscene smirk.

She wanted to hit him.

Women did not have the vote, thus a lone woman without a man was of no value to Tammany Hall in their trolling for balloters, and therefore received no soup. The two new friends ate their free lunch together, grateful for it. The man from County Clare introduced himself.

"Me name's John Sullivan, from Ennis," he smiled.

"Meself, I'm Mary McGrady, from Limerick."

"Limerick! So, we used to be neighbors, practically," said he.

John Sullivan had become dejected and disheartened by the failure of the Young Ireland Insurrection of 1848 that sought to free his homeland from British tyranny. Reeling from the horror of the Irish famine, he decided that America might hold for him the promise of a better future than Ireland.

"Did ye just step off a ship?" she asked.

"No, me, I arrived two days ago, but I soon discovered that I'd been taken in royally by a bloody grifter sellin' me lodgin's that don't even exist."

John produced a hand-drawn map from the man in Ennis who had pre-sold him his lodgings on Cross Street, located in The Five Points.

"When I finally arrived to this address," he said, "there was an old brewery there, but not a sign of me promised lodgin' house."

Mary was suddenly concerned, and took out her hand-drawn map. They compared. Hers had been drafted by a different hand. She was relieved.

"To make things worse, a second grifter had also taken me money for a position of employment waiting for me here, with a certain Mr. Selpho. But when I arrived, there was not only no position waitin' fer me, but this Selpho brute despises all the Irish, and kicked me rear end down the steps!"

"Oh, that's terrible Mr. Sullivan!" Mary was now becoming worried. "What're ye plannin' to do now then, if I might ask?", she inquired kindly.

"I secured passage on a sloop," he said, "leavin' tomorrow from right over there."

He pointed a few slips eastward through the forest of masts and rigging.

"I'll be travelin' up the Hudson River to Albany, where it meets the Erie Canal to Buffalo. It's a journey of four weeks or more, I'm told."

"Aye, that's the route I'll be goin' meself. Me brother James is awaitin' me arrival in the town of Amsterdam, near Albany," she revealed. Then she pulled back, wondering if it were wise to divulge intimate details to a perfect stranger.

A lad on the ship Anna Tift had told John Sullivan about Buffalo, of the plentiful work available to newcomers aboard the Erie Canal barges headed west. The lad himself was going, as had many of his former Irish neighbors who preceded him. His people had a situation waiting for him there. The lad suggested to John that he might consider Buffalo. Believing he already had secured a position in New York, John thanked him for kindly sharing his confidence anyway.

"There are hundreds of new Irish comin' down these gangplanks into New York each and every day, Mary. There are no jobs, much less anywhere decent fer 'em sleep."

Chills ran up Mary's spine hearing this, despite the early autumn heat. She worried for those she'd met onboard who were certain that a wonderful new life awaited them in America. She was relieved she had her brother to rely on. Mary was the first in the family to join him in America. She would stay in New York City only as long as it took her to arrange passage to Amsterdam.

"Listen, if it pleases ye Mary, I'll accompany ye to the Five Points and we'll see what ye have waitin' fer ye there. It's a long walk. Ye really shouldn't take it alone. We'll have us a dander, if yer willin'?"

Mary McGrady nodded her acceptance of his offer, and they set off through the muddy streets amid the stench of excrement, the growls of starving dogs and the squealings and snorts of pigs running loose. Mary couldn't say exactly what she had expected, but she had never imagined New York to be anything like this.

They walked with care. Mary recognized that other passengers from the England were also heading in the same direction she and John were. The Five Points seemed a popular destination. There were bills pasted to the walls and fences they passed, one advertising a museum of oddities, another calling for the people's support of Tammany. And one in particular caught Mary's attention: a ghastly drawing of an ape-like creature in Irish regalia.

"They don't think we're human here in New York," said John, as she inspected it. "That's how they view us, like monkeys. They don't believe Irish are white people. They claim that we're coloreds, like the blacks."

Mary was confused by this. To most people, Irish were basically indiscernible from the English, so how could they think the Irish were not white?

The pair were sufficiently irritated by people who continually collided into them along their way. Rude, these Americans, they agreed. Luckily, neither carried any valuables in their pockets for the hands of these unsubtle churlish cutpurses to pick.

The smell of the docks was bad enough all right, but as they approached their destination in the Five Points the air became positively nauseating. Sewage ran in fetid streams across the muddy streets, Mary trying her best to keep her long skirts out of it. She was puzzled by all the unaccompanied children in rags that she saw, many scores of them along the way. One girl of about seven held the hand of a boy of three, as she pulled a crude wagon with an infant lying in it, the baby silent, though looking quite distressed. Mary, troubled to see such a tiny baby being pulled about by such very small children, stopped the girl.

"Good mornin'. Could ye tell me, darlin', where yer mother might be found?"

"Why'd ye be wantin' t'know?" shot back the little girl, aggressively.

"Their mother's been dead a week now, I'd say," shouted a delicate young man wearing feminine clothing. "Ye want 'em? Have 'em! They're all yours!"

The he-she cackled uncontrollably at her own heartless humor, and when Mary turned back, the urchins had been absorbed into the crowd.

Upset, she proceeded to go searching after them.

"Mary, ye haven't even gotten yerself settled yet. Ye can't save all these people. Look around ye. Just look! It's a nightmare, nearly."

He was right. Children of every age, looking sick and listless, swarmed every which way. Very thin nine-year-old Irish girls posed in doorways trying to seduce any man willing to pay, whether with coin or something that might fill an empty stomach. Mary plodded ahead, disturbed, eyes down. She remained quiet for some distance. After a while she becalmed herself again, but until then John Sullivan said nothing. Finally she resumed speaking once more. The two talked of their lives back home and the acquaintances they might have in common.

She liked him. He liked her.

When they reached Orange Street, John Sullivan said, "I'll be escortin' ye t' yer lodgings if ye don't mind, t' see to it that yer settled. I should have asked ye before this, but can I call ye Mary?"

"Yes, please," she replied.

"Will ye be callin' me John?"

She nodded yes.

At home in Limerick she might have considered such easy familiarity a provocation, but by herself in this strange new place she thought it best not to be rigid about the old country ways.

Mary McGrady could not quite read. She knew her numbers well enough, and some vital words, but not nearly enough of them. To indicate the location of her lodgings her map was marked with an X and a drawing of an orange fruit with a house number written next to it as her guide.

With their bundles held close to safeguard them from intruding hands, the couple searched for Mary's "guaranteed safe for women and children" boarding house, arranged and paid for in advance in Limerick. She was horrified to ultimately see on the banks of a flowing stream of ordure a ramshackle nightmare edifice four floors high, leaning dramatically at a troubling angle, seemingly only prevented from toppling by the adjacent rickety tenement it leaned against. This human chicken coop could not possibly be the place, she thought. There was no sign posted on it, nor any name to be seen. But upon John's inquiring about it, she was told to her horror that this was indeed her destination. She was frightened by the cheap, dirty, aggressive women loitering out front. They stared at John with hungry eyes.

Upon her initial footfall into the seething hovel, Mary McGrady was nauseated. The slum was crammed with manky Irish from back home. Sick panicky babies crawling with nits screamed unattended. The rooms were mainly windowless, stinking of shit and rotting dead vermin, of noxious garbage, of disease, of vomit. Except for a solitary angelic child's face that she momentarily paused to gaze upon, a tragic silhouette with sweet, brilliant blue eyes reflecting what little light seeped between the cracks in the wallboards, she observed only horror. Mary, now almost paralyzed with fright, grabbed John's hand when offered. She had paid for three days' lodging in this hell, thinking that should be long enough to arrange passage up the Hudson to continue her journey.

He asked her to go out from that place, to walk and talk together with him. She refused to leave her belongings, so John Sullivan hoisted both their sacks on his shoulders. They felt their way blindly down the three jerry-built flights and emerged outside.

"Let's take a walk back to the water, the air is a bit fresher there," he said. "I can't leave you here."

John told Mary he had arrived on New York's South Street secure in the notion that pre-arranged employment awaited him with Mr. William Selpho, creator of artificial legs and arms, "The Best The World Affords." Celebrated for his unique artificial leg, Selpho worked for years on his revolutionary artificial hand. Selpho's advertisement read, "An entirely new and useful substitute for a lost hand, arranged so the wearer can open and shut the fingers, & c. by means of the remaining stump."

Arriving to claim his employ, Selpho screamed at John, vowing "There ain't no work for no wiggers in my establishment!", and let him have a good swift one in the arse.

After Selpho dashed John Sullivan's hopes and dreams he recalled the advice of his Anna Tift shipmate. With nowhere to live and nowhere to work in New York, John Sullivan decided that perhaps Buffalo, rather than Manhattan, might prove itself a more promising destination after all. He inquired on the street for where the sloops headed up the Hudson River might be found. He wasn't able to locate his friend from the Anna Tift, but he did find a sloop loading up at Pike Slip that was in need of a laborer. He had arranged to work on the ship all the way to Albany for a greatly reduced fare. This pleased him enormously since he had so little money to begin with.

John gazed intently at Mary as they walked together, his eyes revealing to him a lovely girl alone, who if allowed to remain on her own might not survive this demonic place long enough to make it to Amsterdam. He could not abandon her. He asked her if she might wish to have him for company as far as Albany.

Desperation was no stranger to Mary McGrady nor to any other immigrant whose life was wretched enough to risk the horrors of an open ocean crossing just for a whiff of a promise of an improved existence. Quaking, Mary surveyed the unforeseen abomination of her present surroundings and recognized the value of the security afforded by her acceptance of John's proposal. He had lovely blue eyes, and a polite and kindly manner, and despite her reservations she said yes, "I will come with you."

Mary was fearful she may be trading one frightening prospect for another only slightly less so, even though she'd been assured upon learning they had acquaintances in Clare in common. Both had fled from desperate circumstances only to arrive in a foreign place hardly less dire than the one they'd left, one teeming with unfriendly calculating hordes scrambling in frenzied competition to merely survive.

They walked together back down South Street toward Pike Slip to the anchored sloop Honora McKenzie on which John was scheduled to depart the following morning. He boarded to see if he could arrange passage for his new companion. There was no work to be had for Mary on board. The captain's wife did all the cooking and the cleaning of passengers' tiny sleepers. Mary would be obliged to purchase a full passenger fare.

Despite his lack of resources, John helped purchase her passage without hesitation. Mary protested. It was not his place. She did not want to be obliged to this stranger. But when the full price of her ticket was revealed, she acquiesced, as it would have taken nearly half her money.

Once agreed upon, they asked to be allowed to sleep aboard on deck that night. They were told it was not allowed for passengers to board until the scheduled hour the next morning, so they looked for a safe sheltered spot on the docks to rest and wait.

They were hungry. The Tammany Soup man was long gone. A boy came by hawking pears from the Stuyvesant Orchard. An old man peddled earthy-smelling roasted chestnuts. John bought two pears and two scoops of the roasted nuts. They huddled up against the brick wall of the Townsend warehouse using their bundles for pillows, a crate blocking the cooling wind. The starch in the chestnuts would fill their stomachs, so those were eaten first. Then, as they began to trade their histories with each other, they slowly bit chunks from their fruit, savoring the sweet juice and trying to make the pears last.

John told her as much as he dared about what had brought him to this place, but his humdrum tale was no match for Mary's colorful account.

She delightedly related the saga of her brother James McGrady and his amazing success in Amsterdam N.Y. She had been enticed to America by the vividly portrayed prosperity as chronicled in James' letters home. He had left for America five years earlier. The young Irishman, tramping the Mohawk Valley in search of a pot of gold, paused at a magical palace called Guy Park.

His evident native ingenuity induced a Mr. James Stewart to employ him there, she said, and being a carpenter of no mean ability, James McGrady quickly learned to make himself a useful man about the place where there presently existed many evidences of his superior handicraft. She proudly boasted that her brother, a true son of Erin, was lavishly endowed with the national characteristics of his race—deep superstition, ready wit, a jovial manner and glib tongue. He wrote her of the many hours passed merrily most evenings in the big kitchen below stairs at Guy Park as he regaled his new world bearers with his wonderful stories of the Emerald Isle. He drew from the stores of his vivid imagination with impunity and apparently his patrons had rewarded him handsomely for it.

He had induced Mary to emigrate, telling her of his beautiful home, his servants, his fine horses and beloved Irish pigs; where money grew on bushes in his garden on the banks of the beautiful Mohawk River upon which he sailed his own ships.

The vividly drawn picture of James McGrady's prosperity had the desired effect, and his pretty young sister set sail as soon as she was able for the Promised Land of the Mohawk.

John Sullivan felt uneasy hearing this yarn, for Mary related it as if she thought it all to be true. At the very least, if her brother had his own ship, why wasn't one here waiting for her to take her to Amsterdam? He couldn't decide if she actually believed her brother's tall tales, or just delighted in the retelling. He wanted to ask, but began to doze before he could have his chance. After they finished their last bit of core, conversation fading, Mary McGrady fell asleep against the shoulder of this perfect stranger, as much for security as anything else.

It proved to be a lovely Indian Summer night. The two were gratified to awaken warm and dry the next morning after only being startled periodically by unfamiliar movements here and there in the dark. A block and tackle were already in motion lifting cargo onto the deck of the Honora McKenzie. John hopped athletically onboard to report for duty. Mary was shown to her minute cubicle below decks, which contained a tiny fold-down table, four coat hooks and wooden shelf-bed with no blankets and just a mattress of straw. She was relieved that the door had a strong lock at least. She would make do.

John's labors on the Honora McKenzie would prove more burdensome than expected, the journey taking longer than advertised, its progress dependent as it was on the wind and tides. Heavy cargoes of timber, nails, wool and lard, the principal freight, were taken on to be loaded off all along the ship's route to Albany, with some crockery and Virginia tobacco trade as well, at places nestled along the Hudson with names as lovely as the countryside they were snuggled in: Sleepy Hollow, Croton-on-Hudson, Poughkeepsie.

On their first evening, supper finished, Mary retired alone to her cubicle, but the night was hot and still, and mosquitos were devouring her. She took her blanket and climbed up on deck where other stifled passengers too were settling in to dream, cooled by the Hudson breeze. She found John dead asleep, exhausted from his first day's work. She gently woke him and asked if she could sit by him. She wanted to talk. He wanted to sleep. Mary had observed the crew working and wondered, considering John was paying the captain a partial fare, why he was having to work as hard as the paid help did.

The moon was brilliant enough that good eyes could have read by its light. The orb would be full in four or five days. There lingered yet a faint luminosity in the sky at the western horizon, its hue a deep violet. Mary leaned back, snuggling as close to John as she dared. She craned her neck and looked upward, her eyes tracing along the towering mast and the rope rigging that led to the top where the stars sparkled, feeling suddenly the desire to climb up there to experience the view. And then she fell asleep.

John was awake at first light. He pointed out at Mary's urging that he was working the same long hours as the crew. The captain acquiesced and acknowledged his hands would be needed full time after all, and a wage would be paid. The sloop was being met dock side at every stop along its route by anxious businessmen having unforeseen shipments to send. The opening of the Erie Canal had created new markets and eager customers for every sort of goods. The captain found himself overwhelmed, ecstatic for the boom in business but caught off guard without opportunity, plan or scheme to accommodate all the new customers. At Yonkers, Mary posted a letter to her brother James in Amsterdam, telling him that she was on her way up the Hudson.

Mary found herself delightfully bored. She was quite intrigued by that notion, since she had experienced ennui so seldom during her hard-working twenty years. She soon found though that she didn't take to being idle, so once again she inquired of the captain if she could make some arrangement for work. Mary was good with numbers and possessed excellent organizational skills, so she was given to assist in the complicated inventory involved in the boon in onloading and offloading of cargo along the route.

At first she worked five or six hours and her passage was reduced by a third. But by day three of her employ, the ship almost capsizing with unanticipated shipments, she worked from sunrise until sunset, and her full fare too was refunded. She was happy to have her task, one that she excelled at, as well as having her money returned. The Captain was happier still to have happened upon Mary and John's capable hands, referring to them as his "lucky Irish pennies."

Mary unburdened herself by returning John's loan, reclaiming her independence once more. She thrived in this newfound adventurous life that was both welcomed and unexpected. While they waited for sleep to come, huddled together on deck for warmth as the nights grew chillier, they laughed about their bone-weariness and marveled at how their lives had so suddenly and completely changed.

"Mary?"

"Yes?"

"Pardon me fer askin', but if yer brother James is so wealthy now, as he says, and he lives in that grand mansion, why didn't he arrange for you to ride the train to Amsterdam?"

"I wrote and told him I had booked passage on the England," she responded without hesitation, as if it all made perfect sense to her, "and about what day the ship was supposed to arrive in New York, but I hadn't received his response by the time my ship set sail."

That didn't fall into place as far as John was concerned. She appeared to want to offer no further insight, but the more he thought about it, the more he wanted to meet this James McGrady with his supposed cache of riches. Even compared to the tallest tale-teller in Eire, his were stretching things beyond their limits.

The nights turned abruptly colder as the bucolic interval of Indian Summer passed, but the couple continued to sleep on deck, other passengers preferring the shelter of their berths below. They moved closer. John admired Mary's sweet nature. She possessed a tenacious spirit and an unwavering dedication to keeping her word. Mary admired that John worked with bleeding hands not only without complaint, but with a smile. She also saw that he watched over her around the clock, and at night, she melted into him to sleep more soundly than... well, she couldn't actually remember the last time she'd slept so peacefully.

Their third night sleeping on deck, they'd kissed. Their fourth, their hands went under the blankets, and the fifth, under each other's clothes.

The journey proved a joyful odyssey during which their optimism multiplied with each passing day. As the sloop worked its way upriver, they would stand together on deck to behold the spectacular and quite startling transformation in the colors of the foliage. The cold nights had applied dazzling color to the landscape for as far as the eye could see. Neither had ever witnessed anything like it. The endless limitless forests of upstate New York were ablaze with orange and crimson and gold right to the horizon. The sky took on an unfathomably cerulean hue in the brilliant sun, the air and water absolutely transparent. Neither Mary McGrady nor John Sullivan would have dared to dream just a week previous as they sloshed through Five Points' filth that they might be sailing through the beautiful Hudson River Valley over crystal waters beneath the arcs of afternoon rainbows, and falling in love.

The ship's offloading at Rhinecliff stood out as especially laborious. The captain was in a rush to quickly set sail again, as the money was flowing into to his coffers more swiftly than the Hudson current. A keg of iron nails tipped over, landing squarely on John's foot. At first it was thought the appendage had broken, but since he was able to eventually flex it, relief was experienced by all, especially the captain. He was scurrying at a furious pace and he needed John Sullivan indispensably.

This new country's relentless construction and the fabricating materials required for such a vast undertaking were escalating month by month with no let up in sight. The captain offered John and Mary full time employment on the sloop Honora McKenzie. It was a tempting proposition. They were each enthralled with the beauty of the place, and for a few hours they reflected on the captain's proposal, giving special consideration to what the difficult winter's work might be like.

Nights on deck were frigid now, but still they preferred topdecks to below. Up there they could be alone to follow the progress of stars migrating across autumn's ebony sky. They borrowed blankets to supplement their own and fashioned a mattress of burlap bale. They snuggled and kissed and considered the pros and cons of the captain's proposal, as well as their future together, and before either was fully aware of its initiation, they were making love for the first time.

The Erie Canal had opened the new country to settlement and trade to an extent never even dreamed of by its foremost imaginer, New York Governor DeWitt Clinton. Every possible kind of staple, luxury, and building material was loaded onto the Hudson River sloops and steamers heading upriver from New York to Albany. From there the cargo was transferred to an armada of canal boats and barges heading west for Buffalo. There it would be either offloaded for the expansion of that boomtown or transferred to lake ships to be transported even further westward to every town and harbor along the thousands of miles of Great Lakes shoreline, fodder for the ongoing creation of these ever-expanding inventions called America and Canada.

Rather than accept the captain's offer, John and Mary decided to keep moving west. The more he heard about Buffalo, the more John believed they could find real opportunity there. Mary hoped instead that John might just find the opportunity he was searching for in Amsterdam, so that she might not have to leave her brother.

With the unloading of the sloop McKenzie completed in Albany, John gave their regrets to the captain. He and Mary visited the swarm of barges tied up along the Hudson at its joining with the Erie Canal. Docks and warehouses crowded the area, jammed with goods and the loading and unloading of canal barges and packet boats. John Sullivan was heartened to have a number of options from which to choose, as quite a few were hiring, and were partial to workers like him who were willing to make the entire journey along the canal's length to its terminus in Buffalo.

"But John, we'll be stoppin' in Amsterdam, to be with James and his new wife. Yer not plannin' on goin' directly to Buffalo, were ye?

"Why, sure, Mary. That's where the opportunity is."

"I can't just sail past Amsterdam! My brother brought me here. He bought me passage. I love me brother, I miss me brother. I have to spend some time there with him."

A feeling of horror suddenly overcame her: John had no intention of making her his wife.

He saw the look on her face and realized what she was thinking.

"Of course we'll stop in Amsterdam, Mary. I wasn't thinking correctly. We can see what Amsterdam has to offer, and then together you and I, we'll come to a decision afterward."

The barge Van Planck carried both passengers and freight. The owner had offered Mary a discounted passage for her help in the galley, as three meals a day for twenty people had to be prepared. Mr. Van Planck made this consideration based on John's pledge of working all the way to Buffalo. The heavy cargo of timber and kegs of iron nails made John's back ache just looking at them. Mary was happy to reach a working arrangement. The Van Planck was the only canal boat with work available for both of them, and so they signed on. They were just three days out of Amsterdam now.

John's hands were torn up. He had them wrapped in rags as he worked,. He found the scenery a beautiful distraction, counterbalancing his pain somewhat. The first night, as they lay on deck in the October chill and the clop-clop of the mules on the towpath as they dragged the barge along inspired a rhythm, Mary stopped him as he reached under her dress, and revealed her fears.

"John, what kind of future might I be havin' with ye?"

He knew the time had come.

"Why, you'll be my wife, if you'll have me. You will, won't ye Mary? Do me the honor of bein' me wife?"

"Yes, John. Of course I will be your wife," she giggled contentedly. "But when? And where?"

John had already been considering Amsterdam.

"Day after tomorrow, me darlin' girl. After unloadin' in Amsterdam. When the task is done, we'll first go find yer brother James, and then soon thereafter a priest."

Mary was thrilled. She hadn't really doubted that John would want to marry her, but she had some nagging fears that she may have made a mistake by surrendering herself to him before they'd even planned a future, together. And so, their intentions agreed upon, they concentrated on making a baby.

Mr.. Van Planck was not at all happy with the unexpected change in John Sullivan's plans. Rather than just jumping ship, John felt honor-bound to tell

Van Planck that he was going to disembark with Mary, and that he and Mary were going to wed. He supposed they would remain in Amsterdam until they had a chance to make further arrangements.

"I still want to go to Buffalo Mr. Van Planck. Maybe on your next go-round we could join ye, and I can make good my original agreement?"

"That, my boy," snarled Van Planck, "depends upon whether I can find a replacement for you in Amsterdam!"

"Honest, Mr. Van Planck, we just decided this last night. I have to make an honorable woman of 'er, don't I?" John maintained with a big smile.

Van Planck recalled back to his own youth, and as much trouble as this change in their agreement might cause him, he himself was familiar with such a circumstance. But he wasn't going to give Sullivan the relief of letting him off the hook easily.

"We'll see!" was the only response that Van Planck could bark at Sullivan's unexpected change in tactic.

With Sunday's coming Van Planck knew just how anxious John and Mary were to disembark and locate her brother, yet they both finished up their work completely to his satisfaction. Their commitment to their word impressed him.

Eight eager replacements waited on the docks, competing to take their positions. Van Planck quickly found a good man half again the size of John Sullivan, and whatever lingering hard feelings he may have harbored quickly dissipated.

"The Van Planck might be comin' around again this way once more before the canal freezes, John Sullivan. Check the schedule at the locks, it should be mid-November. I can't make you any promises. There might not be any work for you then. Or the canal might freeze over early."

"I understand Mr. Van Planck. I do apologize sir. It was not an intentional plan."

The two shook hands. Van Planck wished the couple well and waved goodbye as they headed toward the river.

John and Mary crossed the Mohawk on a two-penny ferry and climbed its embankment. As they gained elevation from the river's edge, they stopped a number of times to rest, and to survey the beautiful hillside town.

"Can ye tell me where I might be findin' Wall Street?" Mary asked a citizen. He pointed toward a red brick building overlooking the river, a ten minute walk distant.

"It's right there where that red building is. Right there's the end of Wall Street."

Upon reaching the edifice they saw a welcoming "Wall Street" sign painted on its one side. Mary's heart was racing at the prospect of seeing her brother for the first time in five years. Nowhere in the vicinity did John see anything resembling mansions. A small wooden house with a porch crowded with pots of spent flowers had caught their attention when suddenly from its darkened doorway they heard the shout, "Mary! Is that you?"

James McGrady came lumbering out onto the porch and down the plank walk, immediately followed by Margaret, his new wife, both twenty-two years old. The siblings threw themselves at one another and became so lost in their reunion that Margaret and John were made to feel ill at ease.

Then James McGrady of the Mohawk ships and the money bushes cast a withering look toward John Sullivan.

"James, this is my fiancée, John Sullivan."

"Fiancée? When did this happen?" asked James suspiciously.

"We're hopin' that ye and yer lovely missis would do us the honor of standin' up for us at our weddin', James." John quickly offered, making his intentions known before things could turn awkward.

Margaret squealed and hugged Mary, thrilled at the prospect, while James McGrady reluctantly shook his brother-in-law-to-be's hand. Mansion horses and Irish pigs indeed, thought John.

The little McGrady house was of simple construction with solid details, the crackerjack finishings the work of James McGrady himself. Sawmills outside of town, McLaughlin's Mill and Finhout's especially, kept the lumberyards full, he claimed, and the boom created by the opening of the Erie Canal provided opportunity enough that McGrady had set his sights on purchasing this very house.

More a cottage than a true homestead, it had been made ready for guests upon the delivery of Mary's letter from Yonkers three days previous. Margaret apologized for the humble abode, but John and Mary were happy to have a warm and cozy place on solid land to lay their heads, no longer surrounded by strangers. John searched for any sign of disappointment in the accommodations in Mary's features. There was none.

Less than an hour after they'd stepped onto the porch, the newcomers having barely caught their breath, James gathered his wife, his sister and her fiancee and hustled the group off along the Mohawk. John Sullivan noticed no McGrady fleet of ships on their march to Church Street. They turned inland toward Main Street and the awaiting Father William McCallion, pastor of St. Mary's Church. Mary was embarrassed by her brother's rush to get them legitimized, making no attempt to disguise his obvious anxiety over their unmarried situation.

The mission of St. Mary's was a young one, having opened in 1844, and James McGrady expeditiously escorted John and Mary straight to the priest's house behind the church. Father McCallion was an immigrant from Ireland as well. His priest's house was in disarray, much to the consternation of the parish ladies who volunteered there to keep things neat and organized. McCallion was scattered in his thoughts and his manner as if he had never performed a marriage ceremony before. He asked few questions, and seemed to look to James McGrady as if for guidance.

Mary's letter from Yonkers stated that she was traveling with a man. It was clear that James had paid Father McCallion an earlier visit and had gotten all the preliminary details out of the way so as not to hold up the nuptials. He was worried for his sister having been with this lout in close quarters for the past weeks, and feared she might be already pregnant.

The couple stood before God, Mary clutching a small bouquet of chrysanthemums from Margaret's yard that she had been protecting from the night cold with piles of fallen maple leaves. They were united in the Catholic ceremony and kissed in front of their relieved gathering of witnesses.

The married couple penned their marks in the church registry, just as had James and Margaret McGrady a few months before. St. Mary's register was no more than a gathering of unsecured pages. The priest apologized for the lack of a proper bound volume in which to record the sacred ceremony, "but we're a new mission, ye see, and still quite poor. But don't fear. These pages will be affixed into a proper ledger just as soon as we can arrange for it."

The next day, Margaret McGrady began to prepare a wedding meal for her new relatives. James had arranged for a cured ham, and Margaret baked sweet potatoes and a beautiful pumpkin. Mustard and dandelion greens were cooked in bacon fat, and a tray of buttermilk biscuits was popped in the oven right as the ham came out. There was honey for the biscuits, and beer and lemonade, and a bottle of wine for toasting the bride and groom. It was a feast, and everyone was effusive.

James McGrady couldn't take his eyes off his sister, so terribly had he missed her. What a miracle that he and she both had traveled across the ocean and landed safely here, and now they were both married as well. He had experienced no such happiness or tranquility back in Ireland. He was a fervent convert to Americanism.

As the merriment subsided and the alcohol lulled, John asked James about what opportunities might be available for him in Amsterdam.

"We'll make a walk of the town tomorrow and you can see for yourself, brother."

As the wine and beer took full effect James took back his boast that his finishing business was robust, admitting he was also doing farm labor to make ends meet. The knitting and carpet mills in town paid poorly and worked the people hard. James confided that he had come to America with the intention of making a far better life for himself, but as yet had been unable to find his way to riches. He confessed after his last gulp of wine that he was disappointed and anxious about what might lie ahead.

"Have ye given any thought to goin' west, to Buffalo, or further? Everybody crowding New York seemed to think that Buffalo is the new place of opportunity. The Erie Canal is makin' it the largest port on the great inland lakes and new industries and jobs are springing up there every day, they say. Do ye know of these lakes, James, that they say they're truthfully as big as a sea?"

James shook his head. "I've heard these same stories about Buffalo and about Toronto as well. But I'll be promisin' ye this, Johnny. I'll never be goin' back under the yoke of the English ag'in. I've learnt me lesson in that respect! I wouldn't go to Toronto no matter what vows they'd be swearin' to me. Ye can't never let yerself be taken in and be trustin' the English. No Irishman can, that's fer certain."

As the days passed, and the couples got to know and grow fonder of each other, James in his heart knew he could not encourage John and Mary to stay, even though he had only just found his sister again. He was uncertain about his own future in Amsterdam, and was fearful that if he insisted that John and Mary Sullivan give Amsterdam a try, that he might have to become responsible for them if things didn't work out. He didn't tell them this, but his lack of optimism about a future in Amsterdam spoke for itself. John and Mary decided to keep heading west.

The next morning, John was back at the canal, offering his labors to bargemen and packet boats. He and Mary had gathered their things in anticipation of the first opportunity. They couldn't wait for the Van Planck to come this way again, for the canal might freeze over before then. It was getting very cold and they were anxious, once they'd made up their minds, to be on their way.

The following day John was successful and returned to the little house on Wall Street to collect his bride and their things. Saying their goodbyes was more difficult than they'd anticipated, and the couples promised to visit each other once they were established.

Mary held her brother in a long embrace.

"I'll not spend five years away from ye ever ag'in, James. I missed not havin' me big brother to lean on."

As the barge cast off and the mules dug their hooves into the towpath, Mary McGrady Sullivan stood on deck and marveled at how far she had journeyed, and what their next destination might hold for her. In a little more than two and a half weeks' time, their Erie Canal journey would end right in the heart of the city of Buffalo.

Migrating Irish had been filling the Erie Canal's barges, and the couple found along their journey some welcome cordiality. The Director of Tolls at Little Falls, Mr. Luther Chase, very kindly provided directions for both a friendly Irish neighborhood and a clean boarding house, owned by his sister, in Buffalo's waterfront district, the First Ward. The house was located on Ohio Street, at No. 28, and Mr. Chase told John there might be work for him at the nearby Phoenix Iron Works.

"And if the lady will be workin'," said Chase, "the Mansion House is the finest hotel in the city. My sister might be able to provide an introduction there."

As John and Mary Sullivan entered Buffalo city proper, vast numbers of other barges choked the canal, making further progress almost impossible. Arguments, shouting and angry oaths were heard everywhere, and men hopped from barge to barge to challenge with fists and clubs those blocking onward movement. The Erie Canal towpath was a desperate narrow tangle of mules, towlines and agitated handlers. Their barge was headed toward a destination near the very termination of the clogged canal system, at Louisiana Street, along Buffalo's Main-Hamburgh Canal in the city's First Ward.

After much stress, shouting between barges, and outpourings of frustration, the ultimate destination was finally reached. When John had completed his contract, the newlyweds bid goodbye to their canal craft and together they walked down Louisiana Street toward the lakefront to their Ohio Street boarding house and a new life together.

They found the air in the First Ward begrimed and caustic despite the strong clean breezes off Erie, the gargantuan fresh water lake the district faced. The combination of industrial fumes and organic smells was at times almost suffocating. People were scurrying about everywhere, Irish people mostly, and a few Germans too. Within two days, following Luther Chase's recommendations, John & Mary Sullivan had jobs and a place to live. Fearful of the infernal furnaces at the Phoenix Ironworks, John took work there anyway. Mary followed up on the recommendation and was given an introduction to the management at the Mansion House. It proved less difficult to become settled than either had anticipated, thanks to Mr. Chase. In the coming months as they explored the city they were surprised at how beautiful a place it was, especially Delaware Avenue.

"Someday, we're goin' to be livin' on Delaware Avenue, Mary. You and me, and our ten wee ones," he promised, with a wink.

❧

July 16, 1853
Rescue

Within months of their arrival, John and Mary Sullivan had found a tiny house on Louisiana Street to rent, one they shared with paying boarders they'd taken in, mostly new arrivals from Ireland. It may have been small but it was well-made against the wind, with tightly laid pine flooring and plastered walls. The stove heated the entire place, so it was comfortable in winter. A taller, larger house to the south shielded theirs from cruel winter blasts off the great lake. John had escaped the fires of the Phoenix Furnace in favor of less dangerous work on the docks. When the baby came along in 1853, after two unsuccessful pregnancies, Mary cherished finally having a strong healthy infant, as well as time off from her job. They named him James, after her brother.

"We've got to have James baptized," fretted Mary as she cradled her day-old infant in her arms.

"You just stay in bed, Mary, like Doc Greene said. When yer stronger, we'll be havin' James baptized then."

Mary wasn't about to wait, for she was a true believer, and dreaded limbo almost as much as she feared the fires of hell.

Catholics were instructed to believe that if a baby died before being baptized, the soul of that baby would be banished forever to a non-existence in limbo—as if not getting baptized was somehow the fault of the child. John Sullivan thought that this precept was ludicrous and typical of the nonsensical fraud that was the foundation of the Romish Church.

He had become increasingly non-Catholic as the years progressed, so offended was he by these distressing Church contrivances designed to keep the faithful locked in a permanent state of fear and dread—inventions like limbo, and original sin, and a bounty of other cruel hogwash. John Sullivan refused to believe in a God who would intentionally set his children up for failure from the moment of their birth.

"We'll go tomorrow, John. After mass. Did you ask Tom Riley to be godfather?"

"Yes," John replied. "And who's the godmother to be, again?"

"I asked Mary Maguire, and she was truly honored, since we don't know each other all that well, in truth. But she would be an ideal person to, if... well, you know."

Mary shouldn't have been in such a hurry, having lost substantial blood during childbirth, but nightmares of limbo were keeping her awake. Tom Riley was asked to be godfather because he was a friend of John's from back home in County Clare. They rediscovered each other one day passing on Ohio Street, neither knowing that the other had emigrated. The other reason was that Riley had use of a carriage, and that greatly eased the journey downtown to St. Joseph's Cathedral.

The baby fussed all through Mass, and Mary was feeling faint, so John took them outside to revive in the March chill. He looked up at the architecture of the Cathedral, admiring and condemning it at the same time. If all that money and effort had been put into the community of people who were praying inside, rather than answering some pissing challenge from the cathedral's neighboring Protestant congregations, think of what might have been accomplished, he thought.

Mass finished, the worshippers poured out and the family returned inside to await Father John O'Donnelly as he prepared to administer the sacrament.

Mary smiled with relief as the water splashed atop James' head. She could finally relax. Her disembodied baby's head wasn't going to be flying endlessly around limbo on gossamer wings after all. If God decided to take him, he'd go straight to heaven.

As the summer of 1853 approached, dock work slowed down and John Sullivan began to panic. He had a new baby to support. He had stood on line every morning for ten days in a row at the freight houses, then on the docks as incoming ships anchored, and at the lumber companies in the First Ward, trying to get himself hired. He had no luck. Mary was frightened.

Their Louisiana Street neighbor Thomas McNamara collared John as he left the house.

"John. I'm workin' at Niagara Falls come Tuesday, and they're lookin' fer another good man or two. Would ye be interested?"

John was ecstatic.

"Lad, would I ever! What will be expected?"

"They're building a tourist hotel by the river and they need men with lumber experience, like you and me. Can ye come along with me now? I'll introduce you to the boss."

John had been on his way to stand line at the Erie Freight house but was happy to change direction. McNamara introduced him to the foreman.

"It's five weeks work, more or less. We'll be sleepin' there. In a tent. Bring all the blankets you can, and a rain slicker if ye have one. And some changes of clothing. Even in summer, if you get wet, you can still catch yer death of cold," the boss instructed.

Mary was very unsettled at the idea of being left alone with an infant, but John reminded her that both Shea families were just down the street and their good friend James Stanton was right next door. John had never been on a train before, nor even seen the Falls of Niagara, nearby as they might be.

The men were worked hard at Niagara, but the whisky bottle was passed at supper at day's end and the company proved agreeable. The foreman had chosen a fine group. Not a trouble-maker in the whole caboodle.

As exhausted as he was, the roar of the Falls awakened John Sullivan many times during the night. Others found it calming, they said, especially compared to the clamor and jolting noises in the First Ward with all its ships and industries. But the rumbling sound's newness and unfamiliarity was unsettling to John at first. By the third night however, he began sleeping quite soundly. The steady thunder now lulled him to slumber.

On the morning of July 16 there arose a great ruckus and the men were called outside loudly at first light.

"There's a man stranded on the rocks right above the brink, and they need help rescuing him!" shouted the foreman. "Let's go!"

The group took off with ropes, running across the bridge leading to Bath

Island.

Standing at Prospect Point upon his first arrival, John had been more terrified than awed. McNamara went straight to the edge and balanced himself inches from death.

"Come on, Sully! It's fantastic!"

John Sullivan's balls retreated painfully upward in horror and fear as to McNamara's foolish act, his friend teetering on the brink. John couldn't look. He turned and marched in the opposite direction, quickly.

Now, it seemed they were being asked to, what? Go into the river to rescue some pitiful drunk who should have known better? There was no way he would ever join in doing that, not with a wife and baby waiting at home.

The tragedy had its beginning with three foolish men who'd been working on a dredging scow anchored in the Niagara River off Goat Island, and after a few too many swigs of whiskey after supper decided they wanted to go ashore for some entertainment. The only transportation available to them was a rowboat. As darkness fell, the extreme nature of the rapids alone should have been sufficient to cause at the very least one of the idiots to entertain a second thought, but that was not the case. The trio piled into the rowboat together and cast off, not crossing from Goat Island as intended, but instead hurtling downstream under a furious velocity toward the brink of the mighty Niagara falls.

Panicked, they tried to control the oars, but the violent bouncing of the rowboat caused it to capsize, and two of the three were thrown in and swept over the precipice. Samuel Avery, the third man, was able to grab some mighty tree roots just off miniscule Chapin Island, located only fifty yards from the brink halfway between Prospect Point and Bath Island. There he held on for dear life. No one saw him. It was nightfall. His screams could not be heard over the din of the powerful cascade. He spent the entire night there, arms entwined inextricably around the tree roots.

He had managed to wedge the craft precariously between two substantial appendages and dared not release his embrace. By daybreak he was cold and thoroughly exhausted. Tourists who arrived to enjoy the sunrise discovered him there, and immediately alerted others in the vicinity.

Hastily-assembled teams of would-be rescuers rushed to the shores flanking both sides of his situation, trying to figure out a way to reach Avery. It was decided to release a boat toward him from the Bath Island bridge. John said, "If you let that boat go free, it will just crash into him and knock him into the drink!"

John was overruled. The boat was released. It was captured by the furious current and zoomed past Avery too distant for him to catch, even if such a thing had been wise, or manageable. John wondered what kind of morons he had fallen in with, as more and more men with grand ideas assembled on the bridge. They brought more boats to set loose, all of which passed their target. Then a raft was released.

"How could he make use of a raft even if he were able snag it? Where would he go except over the edge?" John reasoned to them with exasperation in his voice.

No one was interested in his logic concerning the situation. They were scurrying around themselves like rats on a sinking ship, nobody thinking clearly.

"Sullivan," the foreman ordered. "We're going to tie a rope around you and tether you to the bridge. Then we'll guide you downstream to where you can grab him, and we'll pull you both back."

John Sullivan was aghast.

"Have ye lost yer mind, sir? I can't even swim!"

"You don't need to be able to swim!" the boss concluded. "We'll have you safely on the end of the rope!" and with that the men began to tie the rope around his waist.

"Fuck! Get off me right noo, ye fools! Go and snag the caffler yerselves if yer willin'!" said John, pulling the rope off himself, and pushing the men away from him.

"Sullivan, you'll do as yer told!" shouted the foreman over the roar of the water. "Or else you're fired!"

"Fired? Yew bugger! I quit!"

The men glared at him with disgust, even as no one volunteered to step forward and fill his place.

Another boat arrived from the Bath Island side, and this time it was tethered to the bridge as had been the plan for John Sullivan. The boat was guided downstream, bouncing wildly in the rapids until it reached Avery. A cheer went up from the men on the bridge. Hundreds of the curious now lined the shore on both sides of the river.

Samuel Avery had the delicate task, whilst in a physically depleted state, of letting go of his tree roots and quickly climbing into the wildly undulating rescue boat. Somehow despite his fright and fatigue the man managed to do this, whereupon the craft immediately capsized, throwing him into the murderous current. Resigning himself to what fate lay just a few seconds in his future, he threw both of his arms up toward the sky in final surrender, and disappeared from sight over the brink into Niagara's mists.

John Sullivan was blamed by all his mates, with the exception of his friend McNamara, for the death of Samuel Avery. He was shocked beyond comprehension at their shunning, as if it were he — and only he — who might have pulled the man from his nightmarish perch. All his efforts to shed his Irish accent collapsed with his upwelling of rage.

"Noone of yew cowards would go into that river, and yet ye've got the balls to make me the guilty one? Instead of sich blarney, ye'd better kape shady!' he screamed at them. "Take yerselfs aff noo, and lave me alone!"

He stalked away to collect his things at the campsite, and demanded his pay. Coins were tossed on the ground at his feet in a display of loathing, and he was made to scurry after them.

It would take fully half his pay to buy his train ticket back to the First Ward.

Once Mary's strength returned she applied renewed effort toward improving their modest house so they might attract a better, higher-paying class of boarder. She and John had constructed a large vegetable garden at the rear, keeping a wary eye out for neighborhood thieves who might wish to raid it.

A short walk up Louisiana Street from the house revealed the beginnings of a massive construction project, the excavation of a ten acre inland harbor meant to relieve the explosion in Great Lakes boat shipping and canal barge traffic. The city had been unprepared for the massive gridlock initiated by the great success of the Erie Canal, and there was a frenzy of new feeder canal and slip construction afoot in response. The new basin would take some years to complete, they estimated, providing John with the promise of steady dependable work.

The excavation process was grueling. Armies of men with hand shovels, buckets, and deeply calloused hands dug and carted off the earth mined by the great steam shovels. John had never seen a machine such as this, able to do the work of scores of men in a tenth of the time. He had joined the team as a track man, laying rail to accommodate the steam shovel. The track had to be picked up and moved multiple times daily as work progressed. After it was securely in place and the giant black smoke-belching machine went to work, the men shoveled the dirt and rock it removed into drays to be carted off to fill local areas prone to flooding.

The steam shovel employed a railway car chassis upon which an imposing shovel arm was mounted at one end and a massive boiler to the other. In summer the boiler radiated unbearable heat as workers toiled in the cruel sun and suffocating humidity, but in the cold of spring and fall its effect was welcome indeed.

On Sundays, freed from John's labors, he and Mary strolled the neighborhood in the afternoon with the baby along Buffalo Creek as it lazily wound its way toward Lake Erie. They traced its route westward, marveling at the impossibly tall grain elevators that were being erected, a few towering almost as high as the city's highest church spires. Sometimes they would walk along the construction site from their house and John would point out to Mary where he was currently toiling, and explain the progression of labor on the Ohio Basin, newly named for Ohio Street located at its southern end.

In winter the digging work would halt often when blizzards dumped so much snow on the city that it made excavation impossible. For a number of winters he had secured work with Mr. David Clark of the Buffalo Ice Company harvesting ice out on frozen Lake Erie. This too was heavy toil; scoring, cutting, steering, chopping, harvesting and hauling blocks of ice weighing three hundred pounds. John had a healthy fear of falling into the freezing open water after witnessing one of his crew mates who arrived to the job drunk tumble in and immediately disappear in the opened channel, dragged under by his water-logged layers of heavy winter wool clothing.

The bucolic shallow sandy-bottomed tree-lined Buffalo Creek that their neighbor Mercy Abbott recalled from her youth was nowadays alive with the clanking of heavy dredging equipment deepening the channel far upstream to allow access to larger ships. Even before its completion the Ohio Basin was ringed by the construction of those businesses that would best take advantage of direct access to barge traffic, especially lumber yards. The Basin screamed with activity six days a week, but come Sunday all was quiet. John and Mary cherished the infrequent opportunity to slumber late and make love.

Katie Hanson

One Sunday afternoon as they had a ramble 'round the Basin, John and Mary each holding one of their curious five-year-old's hands, a strange character approached. Dressed as a male with short cropped hair parted on the side and having male mannerisms contradicted by delicate facial features of a decidedly feminine nature, this individual stopped and politely asked their assistance.

"I was told that this is where the steamships that sail between Buffalo and Duluth tie up, but I don't see any ships here. Do you know where I might find them?"

This stranger's voice was high-pitched, but with an obvious effort expended to attain a rougher timbre. A rifle on a leather strap was slung 'round one shoulder. It was as if this person were attempting to look older and appear stronger than was actually the case. Little Jimmy stared upward from the perspective of his short stature with great curiosity, hypnotized by the stranger's large vivid violet-colored eyes. His father had blue eyes, his mother had green. He had never before seen eyes so entrancing or of such a strange color.

"What happened to your eyes?" little Jim asked innocently.

"What do you mean, lad?" the stranger responded, smiling.

The little boy just continued staring, not responding, while at the same time reaching around to scratch an irritation between his buttocks.

"I believe my boy means the color. It's very unusual," complimented Mary, fascinated.

The stranger knew exactly what Jimmy meant, but basked in the attention that the violet eyes attracted from people. It was a life-long subject of conversation, sometimes winning new friends and once in a while a promising opportunity or two.

"This isn't Buffalo's harbor, lad. It's the Ohio Basin," said John. "The big steamships pull in further down river. If ye continue along this street, ye'll reach Ohio Street at the southern end of the basin. Turn right and follow it along the river, and eventually ye'll see the big steamships that go up the lakes sittin' there near the big grain elevators."

Again little Jim asked, "What happened to your eyes?"

The stranger replied "I was just born this way, lad. I was lucky, I'd say."

Turning to John and Mary the stranger said, "Thank you very much for your assistance. Good day." then hurried away, head down.

Still fidgeting, young Jim looked up at his parents and asked innocently, "Was that a boy or a girl?" John and Mary burst out laughing, both having wondered the exact same thing themselves. His mother told him, "We honestly don't know what to tell ye, Jimmy."

Katie Hanson made her way down Ohio Street and along the river for almost an hour to where the Union Steamboat ship lay at anchor. She called up, asking permission to board and meet with the steward. Captain George Tremaine stepped out on the deck instead, noting the somewhat odd appearance of this visitor.

"Who calls there? asked the captain.

"The name is Michael Smith, Captain. I am an excellent cook, having worked in the finer hotels of Pittsburgh, Pennsylvania," lied Katie, "and I was told that you were in need of a boy with just such a skill."

The captain looked the character up and down, appraising. He beckoned the prospective cook up the gangplank. He bellowed, "You'll come aboard and have a look about the galley, and in one hour's time either serve me a wonderful lunch, or you'll be left standing there on the dock as we depart, young man," sternly challenged Captain Tremaine.

Katie nodded her agreement and followed the captain into the ship's galley. There she was introduced to the chief steward, and calling upon habits wrought by her experience, she went quickly to work. Katie Hansen had never seen such a variety of meats, fish and vegetables before—having not been the least truthful about her hotel experience—and she began assembling chicken to fry and potatoes to slice and brown in butter.

"Can ye bone and filet a sturgeon?" inquired the steward. "We catch a lot of sturgeon."

"Yes, of course," replied Katie with pluck, never having even seen one before. It can't be much different from a trout, she thought to herself.

"I'll be leavin' ye here for a moment. I shan't be gone more than five minutes," said the steward.

Across the chopping block lay an issue of the Buffalo Courier newspaper. As she moved it out of her way to set to work, a small heading toward the bottom of the sheet caught her eye: MISSING PENNSYLVANIA GIRL. She turned and looked to make sure the steward had departed the galley. Then she read.

"Katie Hanson, the daughter of Mr. and Mrs. Elija Hanson of Tioga County, Penn. went missing last week, disappearing into the woods near the family home..."

Katie was aghast. The story went on, telling of the family's inconsolation, followed by a physical description: "Miss Hanson is seventeen years old and of rather masculine appearance and attire, with short dark hair. Her most unusual feature are her large, striking violet-colored eyes."

Katie swallowed hard. She never dreamed they'd go to such lengths as to put notices in newspapers so far from home. She crumpled up the newspaper and stuffed it into the stove, waiting to make sure it caught fire.

She didn't take another normal breath until the captain belched his satisfaction and approved her boarding the Buffalo-Detroit run. "Very, very fine, young man. We'll see if you continue to do as well before I make any final decision about you joining our crew for the duration.

"In the meantime, I'll have steak for my supper."

With an economic depression gripping the country, the Sullivan family could only attract two paying boarders of late, and Mary no longer cooked for these because the rent they paid was so low. As the economy continued to decline employment was harder to come by. With so many men competing for jobs, wages were reduced. The family struggled to get by.

On Sunday evening, Mary Sullivan had only boiled potatoes and root vegetables from the garden to offer her family for supper. It had been two days since they'd had a single egg to share, almost a week since they'd had meat, and that was a squirrel. She had sneaked up and whopped it with a bat as it distractedly buried an acorn in one of her flower pots.

They had been warned never to eat fish from the Buffalo River, so polluted were its waters. "Especially don't feed any river fish to the young ones," they were cautioned. It was over a two hour walk northward to the Niagara River, or three hours of fast walking to get far enough upstream on the Buffalo River to the south, past the furnaces and iron works and city sewage, to find water clean enough to snag any eating fish. The water along the lakeshore wasn't much cleaner. But Mary would rather eat turnips than to have her husband absent all day long every Sunday, hoping to snag something.

Good news came none too soon in the form of new public transport. The city had recently initiated streetcar service; a Main Street Line and a Niagara Street line. This meant that now on Sundays after church the family could go to the Niagara River together and spend the afternoon fishing. John Sullivan could barely contain his excitement as he traded information with equally enthused neighbors.

The first Sunday after the trolley service began the family boarded the streetcar with their fishing poles. In the fall, king salmon moved up the river to spawn. From November until April there were steelhead and brown trout. In summer, bass. John wondered whether his pole could support a twenty pound thrashing salmon but could hardly wait to find out. He wasn't disappointed when he'd snagged two large bass in succession that first Sunday.

No matter what happened to be on the menu, John nevertheless sat down to Sunday evening supper exhausted, dreading work again the following morning. He fretted about how he might get his family out of the downward spiral that entrapped them. He worked twelve hours a day, six days a week. Sometimes more. He couldn't read or write much. He was not acquainted with anyone of influence. He had not yet discovered a way to change his situation so that he could make more money, short of committing a crime. Although at times he had encountered an opportunity for unlawful profit, he quickly turned and walked the other way, knowing he could not take the chance of being sent to the workhouse or prison, leaving his family to starve. Turnips and potatoes and a lucky Sunday fish would have to remain their staple until he could find some solution.

Mary lay in his arms that night, and just as he was ready to drift off to sleep, said "John, I think I'm going to have another baby."

1859
Man On A Tightrope

Neighbor and friend James Stanton rushed up to the front door with his seven year old son Ed and knocked excitedly. As John Sullivan opened it, Stanton shouted, "We're going to Niagara Falls to see Blondin!"

Blondin's fantastic upcoming feat was the talk of the entire city.

"Well, that's just grand Jim. Good for you two."

John was genuinely happy for his friend. It was good to see him smiling again after the loss of his wife.

"No! Good for us! David Clark is taking all his employees and their families on the train, as his guest, and he sent me to invite you and Mary and little Jimmy! He's paying for everything."

John was shocked. He had only worked for Mr. Clark intermittently during the past two winters, cutting ice as he was needed. Stanton worked for Clark full time mostly, all throughout the year.

"Are you sure he wants to include us?" John asked doubtfully.

"Indeed! He just told me an hour ago. We're going to all meet at the depot on Thursday. Can ye make it?"

John desperately needed the money he would lose if he were not in line at the docks on Thursday morn. He thought quickly. But Mr. Clark might take offense if he didn't accept, and might not hire him again this coming winter.

"Yes, of course we'll go. We wouldn't miss it for the world."

"That's grand!" exclaimed Stanton. "Got to get back to work now. I'll be talkin' to you again later." Little Ed waved goodbye as father and son disappeared down the street.

John went inside and told Mary, who immediately grew very excited.

"Jimmy!" she squealed to her son. "We're goin' to see the Niagara!" She had been quite depressed since she'd lost the baby, and this might be exactly the tonic she needed, thought John, to put some happiness back in her life.

That evening, the Buffalo Ice wagon pulled up in front of the little house on Louisiana Street again, and James Stanton knocked once more.

"Johnny, lad. Mr. Clark now says that he is going to have everyone to his mansion for a breakfast at 9 o'clock, before we leave on the train! Have you seen that place? He's got four hearths in it!"

"No, I haven't. My God, Jim. Whatever will we wear? His servants will surely be dressed better than us!"

"I'm no better off than you, John. We'll just put on our church clothes. Mr. Clark knows we're just laborers. He won't expect more than that."

John became lost in thought with all kinds of concerns suddenly running through his head. He was nervous about being a guest in such a grand home. How would he act?

"I will come by with the ice wagon and pick ye up at 8 o'clock Thursday morning. He lives pretty far up along Niagara Street, at Prospect Hill."

Tourists enjoy Prospect Point at Niagara.

Sam Avery, snagged on a tree branch above the brink at Prospect Point, awaits rescue.

"That'll be grand, Jim! Thank ye, Laddie. Thank ye for being such a good friend to Mary and me. Give our love to little Ed."

James Stanton's wife Frances had died of diphtheria two years previous, and whenever they could John and Mary cared for little Ed and helped out in other modest ways. The well-behaved little boy had grown very quiet since losing his mother. Mary lavished attention on him whenever he was in her charge. Ed soaked up her mothering like a parched sea sponge. The two little boys got along famously.

Thursday morning broke bright and warm, with Mary in a nervous state, worrying about the impression she might make. John could not calm her because he was even more nervous than she. Stanton knocked on the door with young Ed in tow. Forty-five minutes later, after talking and laughing together, the group was relaxed and calmed. They arrived at No. 799 Niagara Street and headed up the walk to the front entrance.

A servant girl swung open the heavy door before they reached it, and the group entered to the sound of laughter and chatter. David Clark and his wife Catherine glided over to greet them with welcoming smiles. The house smelled heavenly.

"John, I am so glad you could join us! I would like to present to you my wife, Mrs. Clark."

"Honored to meet ye, ma'am," said John, hat in hand. "Mr. and Mrs. Clark, please may I present my wife Mary, and our little boy Jimmy."

"How do ye do, sir," sang Jimmy unself-consciously., thrusting out his tiny paw Both of the Clarks laughed and took Jimmy's offered grasp.

Within minutes a dinner bell rang, and Mrs. Clark invited everyone to enter the dining salon where a massive table occupied most of the length of the room. The table sat eighteen, easily accommodating the entire group.

John and Mary tried to disguise their wonder at the beautiful table settings and the sheer variety of food. There was egg, bacon and tomato pie, warm berry muffins, two kinds of bread—brown bread and Irish soda bread—corned beef, sausages, buttermilk biscuits, peach preserves, apple butter, coffee and tea and lemonade. It was a feast the likes of which they had never been served. Mary was fascinated by the egg pie, for she had never seen eggs prepared in this way, and it was delicious.

"It's French," said Mrs. Clark, brightly. "They call it quiche!"

Neither Jimmy nor little Ed was able to contain himself, since at no time previous had either boy been tempted by so much exotic food. When their embarrassed parents admonished them, David and Catherine Clark overruled the adults and ordered the boys to eat as much as they liked. The boys obeyed without argument.

After the spectacular meal, the Clarks asked the group to follow them as they gave a tour of their grand home. Mary was starry eyed, astonished to think that people actually lived like this. Room after room revealed wonderful treasures arranged with Catherine Clark's sophisticated taste, and after exploring the upper floor, Mr. Clark said, "I want you all to see my aerie."

A narrower, less ornate flight of stairs ascended from the second floor to a wondrous single room of generous size on the roof, completely ringed with large windows on all four sides, providing magnificent views of the city, Lake Erie, and the nearby Niagara River.

"Look here everyone. Far in the distance — can you see it?" They all looked

The iceman David Clark.

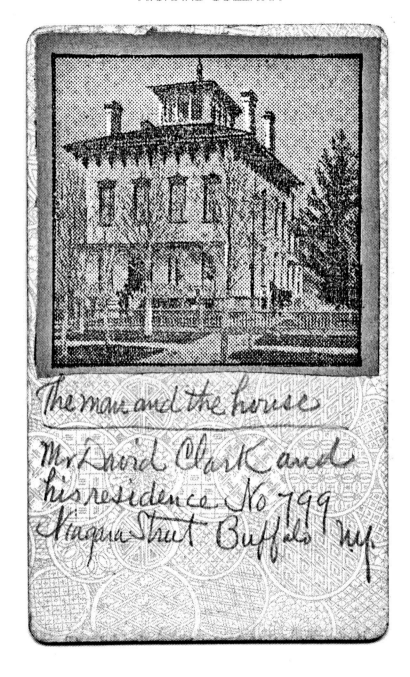

The man and the house

Mr David Clark and his residence No 799 Niagara Street Buffalo NY

Iceman David Clark's residence.

to the North and saw it, but it took a few seconds before James Stanton realized, "Is that the mist rising from Niagara Falls?"

"Yes! Isn't it grand? Old-timers tell me that before all the church spires and grain elevators and the factory smoke that everyone in the city could see this sight. But these days it's a rare thing indeed. Some days the smoke is so thick, we can't even see across the river to Fort Erie!"

The group slowly traced the perimeter of the large room, whose only furniture was a single leather wingback chair, a small French desk, and a covered basket.

"Beginning every autumn I bring my morning coffee up here and survey the lake, checking to see how well the ice is forming, chomping at the bit to get out there and begin cutting."

He looked directly at John when he said this, which John interpreted hopefully. David Clark paid a good wage as well as a bonus to the hardest workers. John dreamed of working for Mr. Clark full-time. But Stanton had told him that with the economy the way it was, even his own position was precarious, as he was the newest man hired. Stanton told John that he had let it be known to Mr. Clark that John would very much like the chance to prove himself on a more regular basis.

"Mr. Clark has been thinking of expanding into the coal business," James Stanton had enthused during the wagon ride, "and that could mean new opportunity."

The tour finished, Mr. Clark addressed the group.

"We'd better be on our way, or else we'll miss the train."

John and Mary Sullivan each hoisted one of Jimmy's hands as they alighted from the bottom step of the Niagara Falls Railroad car right below the suspension bridge.

The railroad tracks followed the course of the Niagara River, providing passengers a thrilling view of the churning whirlpools. A vast construction of wooden benches stepped up the slope, having been erected especially for this astonishing occasion, the temporary seating capable of accommodating many thousands of paying spectators.

Beneath the bridge and along its entire length, awnings were stretched to prevent, as much as possible, clandestine gazers from getting a full view free of charge. The company that owned the bridge reserved the right to take on a thousand spectators at twenty-five cents a ticket, and every spot had been sold within an hour. The owners immediately regretted not charging a half dollar. Rooftops were filled with people hoping to witness a catastrophe. In all, a total of 100,000 people were gathered to observe the spectacular feat.

The scheduled time for Blondin to cross the two and a half inch-thick rope wire was 4 o'clock, but last minute adjustments prevented his departure until 5 o'clock. Blondin, fancifully attired, stepped out onto the wire to the excited applause of the vast gathering. His cap, festooned with many ostrich plumes dyed various bright colors, fluttered in the wind. He wore brilliant yellow tights and a beaded tunic, reminiscent of the Indian style, his arms and neck bare.

Blondin's cool unwavering self possession removed from the gathered masses any feeling of dread or horror which ought rightfully be experienced under the

1859: Blondin crosses the Niagara Gorge on a high wire.

circumstances. Indeed, his great skill and ease diminished fully half the thrill that such a feat has every right to engender.

The rope was 1300 feet long, tethered 230 feet above the madly rushing watery aggregate at its highest point, dipping 60 feet lower than that at its lowest.

Without any hesitation Blondin ran full speed down the manila rope with pole in hand for some four hundred feet or so, when suddenly he halted, threw out one foot and stood balanced motionless on the other. The wind swayed the rope, but he was unbothered. Women gasped. Men shielded their children's eyes. The young ones loudly protested, immediately pulling the offending digits away from their faces.

The diminutive Blondin again touched the wire with both feet and scurried not unlike a harbor rat climbing up a ship's anchoring tether onward another few hundred feet. There he stopped again, sat down, and settled the pole across his knee. He rested, took off his feathered cap and waved it wildly at the spectators in both countries as multiple tens of thousands cheered from every possible vantage point. Almost immediately, he was up on his feet again, running further toward Canada, only to stop once more and lay down completely prone on his back, the pole resting across his chest.

He arrived on the grateful Canadian side seven and a half minutes after his start, complaining about the lowering sun being in his eyes the entire way. He relaxed for a bit and enjoyed a lemonade before commencing his journey back to the United States, carrying some unrecognizable apparatus on his back. Midway across the wire, he stopped and unloaded his burden, which turned out to be a small cooking stove. He set it up and affixed it to the narrow wire. John, Mary and Jimmy were unable to see exactly how—so far away was Blondin from everyone—but soon enough smoke rose from the stove as the wire walker began to cook a meal.

"Jesus, Mary and Joseph!" blasphemed Mary softly into her husband's ear, "I don't believe that rope is fire proof! What ever will he do if it catches a flame?" The Frenchman apparently did nor share Mary Sullivan's apprehensions, for when he had finished preparing this grub, he placed the meal neatly in a pail and lowered it with a rope two hundred feet or more to the Maid Of The Mist sightseeing boat, which was fighting the current in the middle of the river. Thick black coal smoke belched from the Maid's smokestack as it labored mightily to remain sufficiently stationary to catch its prize.

Expertly, the Maid's passengers snagged the pail, waved their thanks from far below the showman, and enjoyed their meal as the valiant Maid continued chugging upstream to thrill her excursionists furthermore by transporting them right up to the foot of the thundering cascade and thoroughly drenching them under its famous mists.

With the boat safely upstream, M. Blondin discarded the cooking stove. As it plummeted into the abyss the crowd gasped, not realizing the act was intentional. Then, he retraced his steps backward for a hundred feet or so to thrilling effect, and from the same sack that had held the stove, he produced a large camera. He set about making photographs of the spectators while at the same time a stereoptic photographer made photographs of him from the bridge. Finally, he scurried along to finish at his starting point on the American side.

The cheers and applause of the hundred thousand echoed across the chasm, bouncing off the ramparts of the Niagara Gorge as M. Blondin took a dozen or more deserved bows, with the retiring Mme. Blondin — looking completely unfazed — by his side.

Mary Sullivan was troubled by the disenchanted faces and the comments she kept overhearing as hundreds slowly walked past her family.

"Why, these people seem disappointed that Mr. Blondin didn't fall and get killed!"

Her husband chuckled. A little part of him was hoping for that too, but decided to keep that thought to himself.

"I'm hungry." Jimmy whined, and the group, headed by the boss, set out to peruse the bounty of foodstuffs for sale by an army of vendors who had descended upon the event solely to serve this need. Jimmy wanted corn on the cob, which was only just this week coming to harvest from the sheltered inland valleys, impaled on a stick and dipped in melted butter and covered in salt. Everyone enjoyed sandwiches, crab apples and lemonade, all courtesy of the generous Mr. David Clark.

As they rode back to Buffalo on the train, most in the group fell asleep from the effect of full stomachs and the excitement of the day. John Sullivan rose from his leather seat as Mary and Jimmy dozed, and approached Mr. Clark, who was gazing out the window at the darkening sky.

"Sir?", John said.

David Clark snapped out of his daydream, turned and said, "Yes, lad. What is it?"

"Mr. Clark, sir. I wanted to thank you for including me family on this wonderful excursion, even though I've worked for ye only a few weeks during each winter. It was generous and delightful beyond expectation sir, and we—me wife and boy and meself—we will never forget this day."

"Don't mention it, John," said Clark gently. "I'm hoping we'll enjoy an early winter so that I can take you on again this coming season, that is, if you're available."

John Sullivan had received the answer he had hoped for to the question he was too afraid to ask, and again he shook Mr. Clark's hand enthusiastically, saying, "Yes sir, Mr. Clark. Whenever I might be of service to ye, sir, it would be me honor."

"Where are ye from, lad, back home I mean?" Clark asked. "The Clarks, we're from Limerick."

"Gosh, Mr. Clark," exclaimed John excitedly," me Mary's from Limerick! And meself, I'm from just over the line, in Clare, right outside Ennis!"

The men laughed at the revelation that they had been neighbors, practically, only to finally meet three thousand miles from home.

John backed away with a smile, wondering if he had been too supplicant, or maybe not supplicant enough. But having been in the employ of mostly heartless brutes during his life, John Sullivan felt blessed to have stumbled upon the grand kindness of Mr. David Clark.

He was able to see a glint of a future now, something to look forward to rather than worrying endlessly about how he might feed his family. He sat back down and put his arm around his sleeping Mary. She roused just enough to burrow her head deep into his chest. The click, click, click of the train wheels as they hit the seams between laid rails had a calming effect, and John too fell asleep.

October 1860
The Wide Awakes

It was a warm and sunny October day when James Stanton stopped by the little Sullivan house on Louisiana Street with his son Ed in tow.

"Mr. Clark lent me a carriage for tomorrow evening to attend the rally for Abraham Lincoln. Why don't you and Mary and young Jim come down to The Terrace with me and little Ed?"

John looked to Mary for any sign of interest.

Stanton had just the week before asked them to accompany him and his boy to Fort Erie, directly across the Niagara River in Canada to see England's Prince of Wales on his eagerly anticipated state visit. Fort Erie had been at a fever pitch with excitement for weeks. Stanton's goal, as a loyal son of Eire, was to pelt the Prince with rotten eggs. The Sullivans thought it best not to accompany him.

Mary was seven months pregnant and not feeling well. She would be grateful for time alone for a couple of hours, to perhaps visit with her friend and neighbor Mercy Abbott, or just to nap. Mary had begun working at the American Hotel down on Main Street shortly after she learned she was expecting, and she was bone tired.

"Go on, John. It will be good for you and your son to do something together."

Mary wasn't much aware of the Wide Awakes, or she might have been a little more hesitant.

The following evening, Stanton and son arrived bundled against the chill to pick up the Sullivans and head downtown. Stanton outlined his strategy for their remaining in the carriage so that they could have a viewing platform from which to oversee all the action, and to get a good look at Mr. Abraham Lincoln from Illinois. But in truth, it was David Clark's proviso for lending a Buffalo Ice Company carriage to Ed Stanton that he not leave it unattended for even a second.

They approached as closely as they could the great convergence of young rowdy men in their black capes and black visor caps, the national uniform of the 400,000-strong national Wide Awakes movement. It was a noisy, testosterone-fueled gathering of mostly unmarried male youth, whose families were more grateful than wary of this newest outlet for their sons' bottled-up rowdyism.

The nation was alive with dozens of clubs milling about the country's elections, but the Wide Awakes group was the largest. Its distinguishing features were militarism, youth, and the members' cultivation of handsome goatees. The organization's structure included ranks, duties and uniforms, though their intent was not a violent or physically aggressive one. The ambitious upstarts proclaimed themselves the new-found voice of the young voter. The Wide Awakes served as political police, escorting party speakers and preserving order at public meetings. The young men were superbly drilled in impressive marching steps and each carried a six-foot-high torch, with a few of the lights of the higher ranking teetering atop 12 foot poles. They presented a spectacular display.

The previous week in Chicago, 10,000 Wide Awakes had marched in a three mile-long procession in support and celebration of Illinois' native son Abe Lincoln, and it was the talk of the entire city for days thereafter. The account of the event in the Chicago Tribune occupied a full eight columns, and the recent New York City demonstration was said to have attracted 12,000 Wide Awakes marchers or more.

In downtown Buffalo there was much noise and confusion to accompany the high spirits. Wide Awakes held aloft their banners picturing as their symbol a giant human eye wide open, the marchers ready to set out on their procession through the city streets ending at the rally in the open square at The Terrace.

"Where did all these Wide Awakes lads come from?" asked an astonished John Sullivan. "I never heard of 'em before."

"Me, I'm not entirely sure, John. But I first saw 'em here in June while on my rounds at some Republican to-do when they ratified Lincoln's nomination. Those smelly black capes were swarming all over the place. Their numbers have only grown since."

The Wide-Awakes were ridiculed by the local Democratic press, which tried its utmost to diminish the movement's popular influence. The Buffalo Courier described them as Luciferian, "...a band of rather dowdy looking young men who have been singularly destitute of taste in the choice of a costume. Their uniform, if that name may be given to it, consists of a black glazed cap and an extraordinary, shapeless tippet, or short cloak, which is also black, of the deepest dye—tar dye, if we may judge from the odor, which 'smelt to heaven' as they passed. They bore lamps on sticks in their hands, and altogether carried on expression in their faces as if they had tarrily decked themselves for a holocaust and were going very shortly to set fire to themselves."

It could readily be said that if the impressive Wide Awakes in their daunting numbers were an invention of the Democrats rather than the Republicans, the Courier might have sung an entirely different tune.

John admired the sea of goatees, at least on those lads who were old enough to grow fine specimens, and stroking the red stubble on his beardless face with his rough hand, wondered how he'd look with one.

The meticulously arranged parade and torch-light procession was a splendid spectacle. The night was conveniently dark, the wind favoringly lulled. As the long glittering line drew itself up Main Street, it was difficult to refrain from making the most extravagant calculations as to its size. Enthusiastic Republicans thought their predictions as to six or eight thousand torches verified.

Several buildings on Main Street were elegantly illuminated, the newspaper offices of the Buffalo Express and The Commercial extensively so. The Express building was beautified by two of the splendid illuminated stars which had just recently shed luster on the arrival of the Prince of Wales in Toronto. A central transparency was illuminated from behind and bore the Wide Awake eye and a motto. Along with a string of Chinese lamps, this flourish made up altogether a fine effect. The Commercial building displayed yet another of the second-hand Canadian stars, and more Chinese lamps.

There were several interesting floats in the procession. A stalwart darkey carried on his shoulders a large wooden effigy of Abe Lincoln The Rail Splitter which, by a double action lever contrivance, was made to ply a mallet. Democrats saw the heroic representation differently than the Republicans intended, interpreting it as a representation of the "irrepressible negro" carrying the weight of Lincoln on his shoulders, working the machinery of the Republican party.

In another display, Lincoln's early history was shadowed forth by a crew of rough and tumble young gentlemen in a flat boat mounted on a buckboard, going through the motions of rowing.

Yet another wagon featured a Lincoln impersonator tirelessly splitting real rails.

In between were inserted two marching bands, including the Union Cornet Band. A flurry of fireworks, rockets and roman candles to rival those of any 4th of July were set off continually along the way. But it was the thousands of torches comprising a living river of fire that truly made the spectacle.

In the open square of The Terrace, at the intersection with Main Street, thousands more people had collected to await the candidate's arrival. The smoke from the torches, most fueled by kerosene, burned and watered the eyes of the assembled, and a sea of glistening tears borne of the fumes sparkled in the flame light like moonbeams reflected off Lake Erie. Some of the guests staying at the Mansion House hotel across the street from The Terrace closed their windows against the caustic vapors, while others less offended gathered on their balconies to witness the magical illusion of thousands of torches drifting by. Wardwell, Webster & Co. had been advertising their "Superior Oil For Torches" in the Buffalo Courier, "used extensively by the Wide-Awakes of Buffalo and vicinity."

Suddenly, The Man was called forth with much fanfare and cheering, and the very tall, gaunt-faced, clean-shaven figure of the Republican candidate for President, Abraham Lincoln, appeared on the dais. The throng went wild, and the sea of torch-light revealed that every upper-story window and rooftop was crowded with local residents gawking to capture the spectacle.

Stanton's borrowed carriage could not get close enough to Lincoln to clearly hear his speech, but they were able to catch bits and pieces after the candidate flashed a friendly smile and calmed the boisterous crowd.

"I understand this demonstration. But in order that you may hear a tired voice which has been vigorously exercised for five weeks, it will be necessary for you to hold your tongues and open your ears," quipped Lincoln.

The crowd laughed, and then settled down. Periodically the two friends were able to hear the sound of Lincoln's voice, but little of what he was actually saying. At intervals great roars of approval welled up from the crowd immediately in front of Lincoln in response to his remarks. The night was uncharacteristically still, with only the slightest of breezes blowing, and every once in a while that breeze favored their catching a few syllables here and there as it shifted in their direction and carried Abe Lincoln's utterances briefly toward them.

The city was wild that night in the hours both before and after Lincoln's speech as throngs marched up and down the streets cheering and waving their torches and banners. John Sullivan and James Stanton both noticed that the promise of all these young men parading by had the consequence of drawing out the city's prettiest young ladies to survey and appreciate the masculine spectacle, like ants to molasses.

The youngsters Jim and Ed were entranced by the entire demonstration, neither having ever witnessed any gathering so large, nor any sight so dazzling, boisterous and memorable.

John Sullivan sat with his left arm around his son. With the other hand he gently knocked his son's noggin three times.

"Keep your eye on Mr. Lincoln, Jimmy," his father admonished when he saw his seven year old's curiosity favoring the crowd. "'Tis a night you will never want to forget, the night you and your Papa came to see the next President of the United States, Abraham Lincoln."

1861
The American Hotel

It had been a warm, lean winter for the Sullivans.

By early February, normally prime ice cutting season, Lake Erie ice had barely attained a thickness of seven inches, a little more than half the density that was usual by this time of year.

Iceman David Clark had only summoned John Sullivan for work sporadically. Even John's friend James Stanton, a full time employee of Mr. Clark's, was apprehensive. John did find some daily work at the Erie Railroad freight house at the end of South Street, just a two minute walk from the Sullivan house, showing up every morning at seven o'clock to stand in line, clamoring to be chosen.

Mary Sullivan had just recently given birth on December 9th, but had held her job at the American Hotel until the end of the day December 7th, at which time she experienced the initial pangs of labor while scrubbing a floor in the Michael's home.

Mr. John Michael owned the American Hotel and his family lived in two houses to the rear, facing Pearl Street, connected to the hotel by a corridor.

A guest had criticized Mr. Michael upon seeing the very pregnant and hard-working Mary Sullivan going about her duties in the hotel, telling Mr. Michael he should be ashamed of himself for making that poor woman work so hard in her condition. But it was Mary's decision that she work as long as she could, since John had not been able to find daily employment.

They were struggling to even eat well.

When Mr. Michael told hotel proprietor Mr. Hodges about the complaint, Michael suggested Mary take her leave until after the baby was born. When Mr. Hodges relayed the message to Mary, she begged him to allow her to stay on. She suggested perhaps she could exchange places with Rosie Platt, the housekeeper who kept up both Michaels homes in the rear, where she would be out of sight of guests. John Michael agreed. Mary worked right up until the moment her water broke. Mr. Michael had the hotel coachman quickly drive her home, fetching Doc Greene along the route.

The baby's birth was without complication, and Mary was gratified when John Sullivan Jr. was born healthy and robust. But her happiness at being home with her newborn was diluted by the apprehensions of her no longer bringing in a wage. She took in laundry. The work was difficult and paid little, and clean water was harder and harder to procure. Mary's older friend Mercy Abbott recalled a time when she could wash clothes right there in the Buffalo Creek, now fetid with industrial pollution and human waste.

On the morning of February 12th, Mr. Hodges paid a visit in the American Hotel's crested carriage to Mary Sullivan at home, asking her if she might be able to return to work for two or three days. President-elect Abraham Lincoln was going to spend two nights in Buffalo at the American Hotel that weekend on his way to his inauguration in the nation's capital, and they needed her.

"Mary, you're one of our best workers, and the new girls don't accomplish half as much as you do in the same amount of time. I know you do not want to be away from your new baby, but is it possible for you to come in for the days preceding the new President's visit? We need to have the hotel spotless and for everything to run smoothly. I cannot afford to have anything go wrong."

Mary was very happy with Hodges' proposition, and agreed even though she had not consulted her husband. When he came home she told him of Mr. Hodges' visit and the two set to work formulating a plan to care for the baby so that she could work. They went round the corner to Mercy Abbott and asked, if John had to work on one or both days, could she care for baby John? Mercy was delighted to. In truth, Mercy Abbott was alone far too much of the time, with her husband off captaining aboard the Great Lakes Steamer Alliance. She jumped at the chance to have purpose, to feel like a mother once again.

The American Hotel was a handsome five-story structure on Main Street at the heart of downtown, located on the same side of the street as Mary's much-loved Van Velsor's Bakery. The Van Velsors baked breads and other goods for the hotel dining salon, and Mary was often dispatched there to fetch what was needed above and beyond the day's normal delivery.

Barbara and John Van Velsor had grown very fond of Mary on her almost-daily visits, and regularly gave her day-old breads that hadn't sold by closing time to take home to her family, as well as stale bread for grating into bread crumbs, and periodically, fresh treats like Scottish shortbread, squash pie, apple tarts or fried doughnuts.

Lewis L. Hodges, the hotel proprietor, was in a quandary as Mary stood silently waiting in the hotel reception area for his decision. He was befuddled about where to install the large Lincoln party. He studied a plan of the hotel and the Register of Guests. Many of the hotel guests were permanent residents who occupied apartments, and deciding on suitable vacant quarters, appropriate for both the President's needs as well as his exalted status, was a challenge.

"Mary, you go and take care of Mrs. Sherman for now, and I will send for you when I resolve this," said Hodges.

Mary knocked on the first floor suite door of Mr. and Mrs. Richard J. Sherman, whose apartment during her regular employ she had cleaned twice a week. Mrs. Sherman was a kind woman, and during Mary's pregnancy made sure that she was not overburdened.

Mrs. Sherman liked to tidy up right alongside Mary so they could gabble and prattle. She took each of the leather-bound books in her luxurious library lovingly from the shelf one by one and with a soft cloth, wiped each volume down. Mary sat on the floor, applying beeswax polish to the beautiful mahogany pedestal library table, which must have weighed two hundred fifty pounds if it weighed an ounce. The table sustained an Irish cut-glass vase of elaborate accomplishment. The bustling crowd outside animated the obscure corners of the Shermans' library with their dancing shadows as they scurried past the windows overlooking Main Street. The sunlight slanting through the windows collided with the vase, fracturing the white light into projections of jeweled tones that lent a chromatic effect to the lambent apparitions of the passers-by. The women enjoyed their chatter together, and Mary, in confidence, subtly revealed to Mrs. Sherman what was going backstage at the hotel, much to the delight of both. They pretended they weren't gossiping.

43

"Mr. Hodges is beside himself because he can't settle on appropriate lodgings for the new President," said Mary as she buffed the grand table's supporting column. "There are plenty of single rooms upstairs, he told me, but nothing grand enough fer Mr. Lincoln and his family, it would seem."

Mrs. Sherman's apartment was the most stately quarters in the American Hotel, and she and her husband, who was presently away on business in New York, had been enthusiastic supporters of Abraham Lincoln. The Shermans took great pride in their collections of furniture, rare books, and artifacts from Europe, including an ancient marble bust of Roman Emperor Nero. Mary was fascinated with it, wondering how a man who lived nearly two thousand years ago could look not any different from people did today.

"Mary?" said Mrs. Sherman, "I wonder if I might suggest to Mr. Hodges that the new President stay here, in my apartment. I could move upstairs for those few days."

Mary was dispatched by Mrs. Sherman to go fetch Mr. Hodges. Thrilled was the only suitable word that could be used to describe his relieved reaction, as the splendid Sherman quarters would be ideal, and Mr. Hodges' problem would be solved.

"I will put the entire staff at your disposal, Mrs. Sherman." he promised. "Thank you, thank you!"

Mrs. Sherman was certain that her largesse would have its own rewards, the least of which would be elevating her status even further in the community. She was also titillated by the idea that the most powerful man in the country would be sleeping in her bed.

"We will need to remove all my clothing and personal items so that the Lincolns will feel at home. Can you provide the hands I will need for that task, Mr. Hodges?"

"I certainly shall, Mrs. Sherman. I will assign you a room on the second floor, and an adjoining room for the temporary placement of your beautiful belongings."

"Very well, Mr. Hodges. I will begin to gather my dresses immediately. Can you send some staff in to begin transporting them, shall we say, in one hour?"

Hotel manager Lewis Hodges was like a man afire once he set about organizing the move. Even the coachman was pulled off his regular duty and the complimentary American Hotel's guest carriage service suspended for the day so the driver could pitch in.

As the little army descended on the Sherman suite, Mary took charge, supervising the careful transport of fragile personal items, and especially Mrs. Sherman's elegant brocaded gowns and French millinery. With Mary Sullivan coordinating Mrs. Sherman's directives, all proceeded smoothly, and the move was concluded sooner than expected. The transfer complete, Mary, Mrs. Sherman, and Rosie Platt, along with two friends of Mrs. Sherman, Mrs. Holt and Mrs. Clarke, both permanent hotel residents, all set to work. Like a whirlwind they cleaned, dusted and polished every inch of the already spotless apartment into a state of unprecedented perfection all day long on Friday. There was not even time for small talk, so focused were the women on their toil.

Mary awoke Saturday before dawn, exhausted. She breast-fed and took care of the baby John's toilet needs. Normally she would give him a bath, but that task would have to wait until the following morning, for this day she had to return to the hotel for last minute duties. The new President and his family were due to arrive around five o'clock in the afternoon.

An enthusiastic Mercy Abbott arrived at the door fresh and perky almost at dawn to take charge of the house while Mary was away. John departed to stand his place in line outside the freight house. Seven-year-old James was home from school and had a list of chores to complete before he was allowed out for Saturday play.

An hour later John returned home, dejected at not having been chosen for work. He tried to dismiss Mercy Abbott, but she seemed so disappointed at not being needed after all that he reversed himself, and set to work fixing a lovely broken chair that Mr. Clark had given him.

Early in the afternoon, when they had all eaten a lunch of bean and carrot soup and Van Velsor's bread, young Jim asked, "Pa, can we go see Mr. Lincoln arrive at Ma's hotel?"

John didn't have to think about it for much more than a second before asking Mercy if she might mind staying a little longer than planned. Mary had promised to arrive back home at approximately four o'clock, if last minute preparations didn't detain her later at the American Hotel. Mercy was only too happy to spend time alone with the baby. She cradled his tiny form in her arms and sang to him as she rocked in Mary's rocking chair.

"Wash up, Jimmy, if ye'll be goin' to see the President," his father said. They took turns at the wash basin after heating water on the stove. They combed their hair and changed into clean shirts. John stood his son before him and brushed off his coat, a bit ashamed at the collar's unraveling edges which he tried to hide with the scarf Mary had knitted him for Christmas.

He was feeling bad for not being a better provider.

1861
Lincoln's Inaugural Visit

Saturday was one of the gala days of Buffalo history. For the week of the past, Old Abe Of The West had been rolling hitherward out of the heart of the prairies, and the intermittent clicking of the telegraph which recorded his triumphal progress had served to quicken expectations almost as if the sound of his approaching chariot wheels had been borne here on the West wind.

—Buffalo Courier Republic

On Saturday, February 16, 1861, Abraham Lincoln relaxed as best he could within the luxury and comfort of the splendid rear railcar of the special train that bore him and his family on a circuitous route from Springfield to his March 4th inauguration in Washington D.C. The President-elect was surrounded by his loved ones; wife Mary Todd Lincoln and sons Robert, age seventeen, Willie, age eleven, and Tad, age seven. The name of the engine that drew the family's train was Rocket.

Lincoln was already quite fatigued, and the long journey was not even half complete. He had been hiding the disturbing threats of assassination from his wife so as not to worry her further. His beloved Mary Todd sat across from him, with young Tad next to her, his head in her lap. He was playing with a miniature toy carriage. Willie sat next to him, studying a map of their itinerary.

The train had stopped in every major city along the way, including Indianapolis, Cincinnati, Columbus, Pittsburgh and Cleveland, with brief stops in many a small town and village along the route. At every stop, admirers expected a speech, but his voice was almost gone. Lincoln was weary. Buffalo was his next destination.

Over-enthusiastic crowds began assembling at the Exchange Street Station hours before Lincoln's arrival to welcome the family back to the city. Abe and Mary had first visited in 1848, primarily to see Niagara Falls. They'd stayed at Buffalo's then-finest hotel, The Mansion House, located just a few blocks from the same depot that was again their destination. On that earlier trip, Congressman Abraham Lincoln had made his way down to the harbor to book first class passage on the palace steamer Globe to carry him, his wife and baby son Robert from Buffalo to Chicago on their way home to Springfield.

The Lincoln family's train was scheduled to arrive in Buffalo at 4:30 o'clock in the afternoon. A mile out from the station, excited crowds lined the track, some getting dangerously close to the speeding cars.

Abe Lincoln observed with concern.

An inept effort had been made to keep the Exchange Street train depot closed to the public until Lincoln's train arrived. The doors had been barred, but the train entrance was left wide open, so people simply walked around the depot buildings to the tracks and entered the platform and depot building from that direction. The crowd was extremely dense and excited, and when Lincoln's train finally approached the station, the scene turned alarming.

Lincoln looked out the window, and foreseeing trouble in the crowd's mad behavior, turned to his bodyguard, Colonel Ward H. Lamon. Lincoln asked Colonel Lamon if he might move his family to one of the cars further up the line toward the engine, as he feared that the unruly crowd would most likely swarm the presidential car. Believing his primary duty was the protection of the new President himself, Lamon asked Lincoln's brother-in-law and personal physician Dr. W. S. Wallace to take charge of Mary and the boys. Mary Lincoln was alarmed at the sudden urgency, but tried not to show any emotion as she gathered her sons and their toys. They quickly arose and made their way from car to car toward the head of the train.

The Light Artillery had been stationed on Michigan Street to signal the approach of the awaited train. Cannonade fire boomed the train's arrival at the depot. People stood in open freight cars and on tops of idle railcars and on the roof of the depot building itself, and occupied every other conceivable viewing place. A tremendous volley of cheers swept through the assembled, and behind and alongside the arriving train ran the crowd, pouring forth from all directions toward the center of attraction, grabbing the railing of the rear car platform and dangerously tripping along the ties with the iron behemoth until it finally came to a halt.

The unsettling reality was that those in Buffalo entrusted with making arrangements for the President-elect's arrival had failed woefully.

Only a handful of military and a smattering of police were on hand. Nearly 10,000 citizens were present, at least a third of whom were crammed into the depot building itself, most now whipped into a frenzy. A current of imminent tragedy coursed through the air. To say that those entrusted with arranging for a safe welcome for the new President had proven incompetent would be a gross understatement, for it was deplorably apparent that they had applied little thought or planning toward the matter at all.

Lincoln's visit was the opportunity of a lifetime for most people, the chance to see a President of the United States in person. They had descended in droves from all parts of the city, its surroundings, and from as far away as Toronto.

Abraham Lincoln was appalled. There had been no such disorder in any of the previous stops. He scanned the throng and saw but few military present. As the train halted, among the legions he was relieved to see the friendly face of former President Millard Fillmore, looking quite calm amid the maelstrom. The first to exit onto the car's rear platform were Lincoln's four-man military escort, Colonel Summer, Major Hunter, Captain John Pope, and Captain George Hazard.

The mob swarmed over and climbed onto the train, and tried to enter the President's car itself. A battle ensued between the horde and the train officers, and even the civilian members of the President's party, with the most extreme physical efforts having to be employed to keep the invaders out.

Calm restored, in due time Mr. Lincoln accompanied by the committee and his suite stepped out onto the rear platform of the car and the hero of the day was met there by Millard Fillmore, with whom he exchanged hearty greeting. The former President in a few words congratulated Lincoln on his safe arrival and welcomed him to the Queen City of the Lakes. The party then made its way toward the gateway, when began the Great Crush.

We are not prepared to locate the blame for this part of the
performance upon any one in particular, but blame certainly
rests somewhere, for it was a flagrant piece of mismanagement.
That it was not attended by terrible and fatal results was no
virtue of the reception authorities.
—Buffalo Courier Republic

The quick few words of greeting and introduction having been exchanged,
a perfectly indescribable scene of chaos ensued. The enthusiasm of the crowd
was frightening. Lincoln was forced to keep bowing his acknowledgements of
the plaudits while at the same time asking Fillmore, "Who is in charge here? We
could end up being killed in this."

Fillmore looked sheepish, for he had assumed the police and local military
had taken all necessary precautions, but now the former President saw that he
was wrong. Finding himself engulfed in the mob, he grew fearful for his own
life as well as that of Mr. Lincoln.

"I do apologize, Abraham. I was assured that all safeguards had been put in
place. Just remain close and let us allow these soldiers to get us onto the carriage
intact."

The small contingent of military men were physically imprisoned by the mad
crush of the crowd and virtually powerless to do their duty. The few members of
Company D who were able to move finally accomplished holding back enough
people to open a passageway from the President's railcar to the depot exit. That
accomplished, Lincoln trepidatiously sallied forth, grasping the arm of former
President Fillmore, followed closely by Buffalo Mayor pro tem Bemis.

The Presidential party was surrounded by the soldiers, bayonets at the ready,
as the incessant compression of the surrounding sea of humanity grew by the
second. A wave through the crowd pushed Lincoln nearly off balance, and just
as abruptly, a counter surge from the opposite direction nearly toppled him
again. As the soldiers expended a Herculean effort to move the Presidential
party forward, the physical pressure against the bodies of Lincoln, Fillmore,
and indeed all present exceeded the merely dangerous.

"Soldier!" Lincoln cried. A soldier's bayonet came within inches of Lincoln's
eye as the wave of humanity compressed and overwhelmed.

"Sorry, Your Grace!" exclaimed the discombobulated enlisted man, who in
reality, had to use all his strength to keep his weapon from hitting the President,
or even himself, so overpowering was the might of the crowd.

"Where's Robert? Bobby? Bob!" Lincoln called, unable to locate his eldest
son.

"He's right there behind us, Sir, being taken care of," lied Colonel Summer,
trying to keep the new President's attention focused on the escape.

Mary Lincoln and the two youngest Lincoln sons were anxiously peering out
the window of the first rail car. Mary was unable to see her objective because of
the crowd, and worried aloud for the well-being of her husband and son.

"Mother, what is going on? Why are all these people acting like this?" a
frightened Willie Lincoln exclaimed. He was having his very first glimpse at the
negative side of being the son of a President.

The instant that Mr. Lincoln got fairly out into the depot and before more
than half of his attendants had made good their exit from the railcar, the vast

multitude on both sides made a blind tremendous rush after him for the door. The passageway that had been laboriously opened by the soldiers closed up instantly, and the two files of military men were broken into as many pieces as there were men in them. In vain the military struggled and threatened and resisted. The crowd was deaf, blind and relentless.

The mob was now out of control. All were determined to get a better view of the President-elect. In the crush there was threat of suffocation. Women fainted but did not fall to the floor, as the pressing bodies of those surrounding them kept them vertical. The soldiers were overrun and their bayonets were pointed in the horizontal.

The specter of calamity loomed.

The entryway of the depot acted as a sort of huge human sausage-stuffer into which hundreds who already in their opinion had assumed their most minimum proportions were forced by the circumstances to demonstrate the ultimate pressure their bodies could possibly endure and still survive. Some little boys were only saved from death by being held aloft in the arms of soldiery. Strong men grew white in the gills and were doubtful about their prospects of ever getting out of the frenzy alive.

An especially macabre threat was incurred from the bayonets of the soldiers, some of which had been immobilized, wedged by the crowd into a horizontal position, threatening to impale innocent victims. In the thickest of the compression, one gun was horizontally affixed against a man's chest directly in line with his heart, steadily and heavily despite a dozen or more strong arms trying to control the weapon. Desperate appeals were made to the crowd, but it was merciless and bore down with the weight of a thousand tons. An anguished scream exited the man's throat as the steely tip broke through his skin, and only the preternatural coordinated effort on the part of many saviors finally angled the point of the weapon out and past the man's breast.

Lincoln's son Robert, together with Ohio Governor Dennison's son Neil, was almost pushed to the ground and trampled, just barely escaping. Major Hunter, of the presidential suite, was crushed against the wall and cried out in an unsoldierly but thoroughly excusable manner. So forcefully was he slammed that it was believed he had sustained a severe injury. It was thought at first his arm was broken, but a serious sprain and bruise of the shoulder were later pronounced as the extent of his injury.

The heavy portal of the depot was broken down by the pressure of those being crushed against it, and scores of the crowd tumbled out into the open air scarcely able to stand upright from exhaustion.

As he was inched toward the open door, Lincoln's heart beat faster, anticipating his freedom but fearing it might not be his to have. As the cold February air hit his face, he knew he'd almost made it, and suddenly no longer confined by the depot walls, the soldiers fiercely returned the push of the crowd. President Fillmore and Colonel Summer physically elevated Lincoln up into the carriage when at last they reached it, and for a moment the two presidents sat there depleted, and thanked the Almighty for their safe deliverance.

"I never!" exclaimed Fillmore.

"Where's Bobby? Where's my boy?" Lincoln called out.

"Father! I'm here! Look!" Bob and Neil had been brought out right behind Lincoln and were being loaded into the carriage directly behind. Abe was relieved. He counted his men. He didn't see anyone missing, except his Mary and the boys. Before he could ask, Colonel Summer said, "Mrs. Lincoln and the boys were taken off the car while the crowd had its attention on us. They're on their way to the hotel as we speak."

Lincoln nodded his thanks and patted the Colonel's knee affectionately, like he might have his own sons'.

Meanwhile, inside the depot, the crush continued to prove terrifying, and once out of the terminal every man and woman able to extricate him or herself uttered the phrase "Thank God!" for the preservation of their lives. Others were carried away with broken ribs. Another had sustained a serious stab wound in the back from a soldier's bayonet. Fainting women recovered under a free use of hydrant water. Those who had not been assaulted were immediately reinvigorated with new energy, eager to be in full view of the cortege as it passed, adding a new round of urgency to the tumult.

Lincoln did not speak to the crowd, but after catching his breath he did stand up in the open carriage so that those far away from it might see him, which helped satisfy the crowd's need to view him and perhaps precluded them from having a reason to continue their surge forward.

The Lincoln cortege swept down Exchange Street toward Main Street, then turned right onto Main, heading straight for the American Hotel located at the intersection with Eagle Street. Lincoln's safety was foremost now, and the four horses drawing the carriage were charged though the crowd, some of whom were attempting to impede the Presidents' quick escape. Little regard was shown for these determined aggressors, but there were no reported injuries.

When other members of Lincoln's party were finally able to make their way out of the depot they found that the carriages which had been provided them had been appropriated in a most cozy manner by Buffalo reception committees, and some of the President's suite were forced to walk a mile to the American Hotel carrying their heavy suitcases.

Captain D.W. Bailey, a member of the Buffalo City Guard commanded by Major Bidwell, had the duty as one of the bodyguard to jog opposite the left front wheel of Lincoln's carriage. The President-elect was now closely guarded by all those soldiers who were able to extricate themselves from the depot crush, as well as some detectives in civilian clothes. Having successfully escaped the lunacy of the crowd, the party was now able to proceed at a less frantic pace. Citizens lined the route, and thousands of handkerchiefs were waved, creating a roiling sea of white. The Union Cornet band preceded the presidential carriage, playing rousing airs. As he periodically looked back at the new president, Captain Bailey could not help but notice some relief on the face of the still-shaken Lincoln.

Abe was smiling now, and waving back to the crowd.

Bailey could not understand how some folk could ever call Lincoln ugly. He thought Lincoln was far from it. He had a kind face and a gentle demeanor. Why, he looked to Bailey like a saint more than anything else—a man for the times—and everyone along the way, cheering and waving with great smiles on their faces, seemed to worship him.

The cortege moved up Exchange and Main, the latter street presenting a coup d'oeil which must have made quite an impression on visitors present. The sidewalks were thronged and every available point of vision at windows, from the first stories to attics was filled with ladies and gentlemen, the former apparently predominating.

"That's him, there's Old Abe!"

"There's the arms that split the rails!"

"Oh, won't he give Southk'liny Aleck!", were the exclamations of individuals, the most enthusiastic of which were the recently extinct Wide Awakes in their black capes and visored caps who crowded in the get a sight of their hero. Lincoln was not allowed to shake hands with anyone, nor was anyone allowed to run alongside the carriage that he shared with the former President. Even upon his arrival at the American Hotel, he shook hands with but a very few.

The excited crowd at the depot was duplicated at the American Hotel. A gay scene it was, to be sure, every window on the block as well as those of the Arcade Buildings opposite, holding its own group of cheering onlookers, Under the windows of the Young Men's Christian Union rooms was stretched an inscription, which in view of Mr. Lincoln's recent Springfield speech, did not lack appropriateness. It consisted of the words We Will Pray For You.

The new building being erected on the Clarendon Corner, farther down, was crowded at every beam and aperture from top to bottom with cheering construction workmen, appearing like some great masted sailing ship against the sky with all its riggings manned.

The assembled crowd that awaited in front of the American Hotel included John Sullivan and his young son Jim. The throng parted after some rough coaxing by the soldiers accompanying the cortege, allowing the Presidents' carriage to pull up to the main entrance. Lincoln left the carriage, dusty hat in hand, waving it to the cheering crowd as he alighted. John Sullivan felt electricity course through his body with the excitement of again seeing this great man.

Lincoln and Fillmore entered the hotel between two files of escort and very quickly thereafter Lincoln appeared on the second floor balcony, with the former President just one step behind. The President-elect's appearance was the signal for the most enthusiastic cheering, helped out by a continuing salute of booming artillery in Clinton Street. The balcony of the hotel was festooned with American flags and red white and blue draping.

John Sullivan and his seven-year-old Jim steeled themselves against the crush in front of the hotel. Jim rode his father piggyback so he could see, but when Lincoln appeared on the balcony to great tumult from the crowd below, John put his son on his shoulders, more for safety than anything else. Among the crowd, not far from him and his son, stood a young twenty-three year old lawyer who was just as enthralled as they at seeing the new president. His name was Grover Cleveland. At that moment gathered in the same place were a former president, a president-elect, and a future President of the United States.

Having seen candidate Lincoln just four months previous, young Jim had remembered his clean shaven look.

"Pa, look. Mr. President's got a beard now!"

John recognized one of the men behind Lincoln on the balcony as the Buffalo Express reporter who had interviewed ice man David Clark just the previous week. His name was J. N. Larned.

Larned had followed Lincoln and ex-president Fillmore out onto the balcony to greet the citizens, and was impressed with the new President's ease and his kindly manners, and especially his height. Larned stood as far behind him as the small space would allow, his back pressed flat to the wall. Lincoln towered over everyone in the group, and Fillmore was himself a tall man. As Lincoln stepped forward to speak, he handed his hat—the high, queerly shaped style so popular among gentlemen—to the reporter. Larned held it in his hand, looking down at it with surprise, as did the others present, for they were interested that the new President would be wearing something so battered and dusty.

The brief speech Lincoln gave was extemporaneous. Although situated fairly close below him, the fidgeting and voices of those around them kept John Sullivan and his son from hearing its entirety. Lincoln's voice was stronger as he began, but quickly it lessened in volume due to his fatigue. As the new President spoke, his gracious opening statement disregarded the pandemonium experienced at the depot that had engulfed him just minutes before.

"I am here to thank you briefly for this grand reception given to me, not personally, but as the representative of our great and beloved country. On our journey to Buffalo from Springfield, it is true we have had nothing so far to mar the pleasure of the trip. We have not been met solely by those who assisted in giving the election to me, but by the entirety of population of the country through which we have just passed. This is as it should be. It is an evidence of the Constitution, the Union and the perpetuity of the liberties of this country."

The crowd below and across the way responded with great cheering.

"I am unwilling, on any occasion, that I should be so meanly thought of as to have it supposed for a minute that these demonstrations are tendered to me personally. They are tendered to the country..."

Lincoln's voice trailed off as he turned to face the crowd north, then a few moments later, as he turned once more in the direction where father and son stood, his words picked up again.

"Your worthy Mayor has thought fit to express the hope that I may be able to relieve the country from the present, or should I say, the threatened difficulties. I am sure I bring a heart true to the work."

The interruption of tremendous applause was the crowd's response to the man's confidence and sincerity. The country had been hoping for a true leader, and as far as Buffalo was concerned, they had found him.

"For the ability to perform it, I must trust in the Supreme Being, who has never forsaken this favored land..."

Again Lincoln's voice trailed off again, and the noise of the crowd picked up. John surveyed the scene, anxious to be one of those early in the queue that would file past the new president and be received. He looked closely at the new President as he spoke, observing, wishing to remember this day by preserving Lincoln's image in his mind. He observed his extremely tall, gaunt form, the queer angular movement he made with his arms while speaking—peculiar flailing movements.

Later that evening, the respects of the people were paid to the President-elect in the American Hotel's main hall, on the second floor at the head of the left stairway. Mr. Lincoln stood on a slightly raised platform surrounded by a few friends while a bodyguard selected from Company D kept the crowd admitted from below queued into a line which passed him up the right stairway and down the left. Soldiers outside the entrance to the hotel stood by large pails, seeing to it that every man dispose of his plug of chewing tobacco before entering.

Lincoln, as he received his admirers, simply bowed his acknowledgement to the greetings and kind wishes expressed, shaking hands intermittently with only a few ladies or children who mingled with the crowd.

Notwithstanding the great exhaustion necessarily incident upon a public reception of this kind, the President-elect stood his ground manfully for three long hours, responding to the hearty greetings of his fellow citizens. A kindly smile lit up his genial face and his fatherly attention to the children and gallant bearing to the ladies won their hearts. Many of the little girls were lifted up and kissed by the president and some of the mothers suddenly wished they were a child again.

In line, a few feet ahead of the anxious and excited John and Jim Sullivan, three tittering ladies, finely attired, awaited their turn. After being presented to the President-elect, they moved on. One of the group turned around and looked over her shoulder, and seeing Lincoln kiss a baby girl exclaimed, "The dear soul! Oh, how I should like to kiss him!"

"Come on then!" boomed Abe of the West. Mr. Lincoln had overheard her plainly and responded that he was not averse to such labial inflictions. The women giggled uncontrollably, but settled quickly to receive their kiss: the ceremony was duly performed on all three of the blushing belles.

John Sullivan felt a little dizzy as his turn approached to be acknowledged by the great man. He walked toward the new President, his son in front of him, both his hands on the little one's shoulders. Young Jim was enthralled by the excitement of the occasion, the great emotion that filled the room from those who were experiencing the thrill of meeting their new President face-to-face. He hinged his little neck backwards to fully take the man in, because not only was Lincoln the tallest man he had ever seen, but since the statesman was standing on a platform, that just expanded his height further.

Lincoln nodded his acknowledgement to John Sullivan, who said, "Tis is a grand pleasure to make yer acquaintance, Mr. President. Our kindest wishes to ye, sir." Lincoln then looked down at young Jim's star-struck expression, smiled, and bent over awkwardly at the waist, extending his giant hand out to the little boy. Young Jim placed his miniature paw into the giant's grip, and shook it gently.

"And what's your name, young man?", Lincoln inquired.

"Jimmy Sullivan!" was the boy's excited response.

"Pleased to meet you, Jimmy Sullivan."

And with the smile still on his face, Lincoln turned his attention to the next person in line as the flow of the crowd conveyed father and son past the President. John Sullivan was over the moon that Lincoln had taken his son's hand in his own, and regarded it as a sign. He glanced back over his shoulder for a final look.

There burned a fire in Lincoln's eye that blended with an impressive kindness in his face; the man was genuine in his sincerity. All in all, Abraham Lincoln gave full promise that he was the man for these troubled times. John Sullivan's introduction that evening confirmed to him the providence of Lincoln's election as President.

As father and son descended the stairs, they looked into the Ladies' Parlor where Mrs. Lincoln stood with her oldest son Robert greeting guests. John observed the First Lady's beautiful blue silk dress with hoop skirt and fitted bodice, and long gloves. What caught his attention most remarkably was that she had a number of rings on her fingers, but was wearing them on the outside of her gloves.

When they exited the building, despite being very weary, John wanted to join the line that was formed to be received by Mrs. Lincoln as well. But when they went to the end of it two soldiers informed them that the line had been closed and that the Lincolns' reception would soon end.

Though he was disappointed, John Sullivan felt blessed that he and his boy had been provided the occasion to meet Abraham Lincoln. He didn't even want to think about how badly he would have felt, after waiting so many hours in the cold, if the doors had been closed on them before they had ever reached the President.

Once the doors were shut, the German delegation was allowed to read an address to the new President. It was an arrogant sort of presentation, indicating they regarded themselves as deserving unique treatment apart from all the other groups that comprised the citizens of the United States.

Lincoln immediately responded:

"Mr. Chairman, I am gratified with this evidence of the feelings of the German citizens of Buffalo. My own idea about our foreign citizens has always been that they were no better than anyone else, and no worse. And it is best that they should forget that they are foreigners as soon as possible."

The Germans were quite taken aback that their modest demand be responded to so harshly. Lincoln was not xenophobic by any means. His mission and goal as president was to keep the Union together. Faced with the direst of circumstances ahead, he had no patience with the idea of yet another entitled group placing themselves apart from the mainstream.

There would be no special accommodation made for the Germans or any other ethnic or religious group that came to this country, Lincoln believed, for this was the United States of America, not the disassociated states of special interests. Lincoln's message was clear—assimilate, or else consider going back from whence you came.

The Lincoln family retired to the sumptuous suite provided by Mrs. Sherman. The German singing societies followed, the Sangerbund serenading them from the hallway outside their door, and the Liedertafel from out on the street. Lincoln said his thanks and goodbyes to Millard Fillmore. As the former President left the suite he diplomatically approached the singing society in the hallway, thanked them profusely, and asked them to be on their way so the Lincoln family could sleep.

Outside, John Sullivan wanted to tarry a bit to hear the Liedertafel's offerings, but young Jim was collapsing, so he scooped his sleepy son up into his arms and headed toward home.

The two walked into a darkened house, save for the embers burning in the stove. John threw more wood on the glowing remains against the cold night, and put young Jim to bed. The baby cooed softly in his cradle, and John Sullivan felt his infant son's cheeks and tiny hands to make sure he wasn't cold as he gazed lovingly at his newest, John Jr., eight weeks and three days old.

Mary slept the sleep of the exhausted, and never stirred as her husband slipped under the blankets, put his arm around her waist, and drifted almost instantly off to sleep.

There had been rumors and counter rumors as to which church the Lincolns would attend Sunday morning. The consequence was that more than one local pastor found himself facing a congregation of phenomenal numbers. Mr. and Mrs. Lincoln ultimately joined former President and Mrs. Fillmore quietly for services at the First Unitarian Church, located at Franklin and Niagara Streets. Afterward they retired to the former president's sprawling residence, known locally as "The Castle," located just across Niagara Square opposite the church.

Later, Abe relaxed with his family, and played leap-frog in the hallway of the American Hotel with his sons and the children of hotel employees.

The last event during his visit to Buffalo on that historic Sunday was likewise interesting—the President-elect's visit to St. James Hall, as the invited guest of President Fillmore and acting mayor Bemis. The meeting was conducted under the auspices of Father Beeson on behalf of the Indians. Lincoln listened attentively to Father Beeson's passionate lecture on the plight of native Americans. There were many empty seats.

The following morning, D Company arrived at the American Hotel at 4:30 o'clock in readiness for their duty. Horace Greeley had joined the Lincoln group shortly before it arrived at Buffalo to report on the President's journey to New York City, and along with Mr. Lincoln and his retinue was escorted to the depot. Half a dozen carriages constituted the cortege. The Union Cornet Band, directed by Peter Cramer, led the way with a patriotic quickstep, and D Company, the escort, with the gallant Captain Bidwell as its head, followed. Jim Stevenson drove Mr. Lincoln's carriage.

As Mr. Lincoln passed down Main Street, an earlier fire continued to rage at Townsend Hall, one of the city's largest buildings, located at the corner of Swan Street. It had begun at 11 o'clock the previous night. Firemen succeeded in rescuing the valuable libraries of the law offices that occupied the structure, as well as the inventory of Matthews' Pharmacists and Dresser's Jewelers. The department was promptly on scene but the streams could not seem to reach the fire with any efficiency. The steamer Jones was able to keep two streams playing vigorously on the blaze, but the Chandler Wells did not work with any steadiness or force. However, the firefighters had prevailed in keeping the fire contained as it sought to spread to the structures adjacent to it.

John Van Velsor was a member of Eagle Hose Company No. 2 and responded to the fire call from his apartment above his bakery located just a few doors down Main Street from the American Hotel. Feeling that the fire had mostly done its destruction, he joined his fellow volunteers in forming a line of honor as Lincoln's cortege passed the inferno, and all saluted and cheered him. The gathered crowd of civilian fire-watchers cheered too, as the new President passed. Lincoln waved to the men, but was concerned with the size of the still-consuming blaze, questioning the wisdom of firemen interrupting such pressing duty to acknowledge him.

Van Velsor had heard a rumor that the fire had been set intentionally by Southern sympathizers, but he felt that was just a canard attributable to the excitement of the times. Upon investigation, the baker found that the blaze had begun in a pile of wood shavings in the corner of the Slaght Billiard Hall on the fourth floor, ignited by someone's lit cigar, discarded.

Upon Lincoln's arrival at the depot, the train left immediately at 6:30 o'clock. The Presidential party left Buffalo over the New York Central Railroad. Mr. Lincoln stood on the rear platform of his car, bowing to a considerable crowd, loudly cheering. He was greatly relieved that there was no repeat of the chaotic scene he had encountered upon his arrival in the city.

A small group stumbled along as they ran down the tracks behind the train as it pulled away, reaching out to him, and until the gathering speed became dangerous, Abe Lincoln returned their reach.

August 1861
Off To War

Two days before John Sullivan was to report for duty, the family was already moved in and settled, with fresh clean food in the cupboard of their two room flat on the top floor of the large Kentucky Street house they shared with two other families, afforded by the $75 bounty John was provided for joining the Union Army as a volunteer. The rooms came furnished with a narrow bed for the two boys to share, their very first. The large heavy carved oak bed Mary had inherited five years previously from her first friend in America, Noreen McLeary, when Noreen decided to return to Ireland, was transported with some effort from their Louisiana Street quarters.

John was heartened by the kindness of the German couple with whom they shared the second floor, Gustav and Ines Krupp, and the protectiveness of the Geary family, who occupied the entire ground floor below them. The Gearys owned the home, bought with an inheritance from Mrs. Geary's mother, Hannah Geary of Concord, New Hampshire. The Gearys had nine exuberant children, having lost two. Mary Sullivan looked at all those children with longing in her heart for the continuously mourned babies she herself had lost. Tears welled up in her eyes with sadness caused by her remembrances, along with a wee bit of happiness and relief as well, for the family's improved situation. The Krupps were strangers in a strange land indeed, finding themselves now surrounded by nothing but Irish, doubling the discomfort of their expected uneasiness about their emigration to America. But despite the ethnic isolation they felt here in Eire by The Erie, they instantly grew protective of Mary and the boys.

On his last night in their new home, in their comfortable bed on the top floor, where the open window cut the sticky air with welcome cooling breezes off the lake, John Sullivan at very long last slept the peaceful sleep of a dutiful man. He knew he was doing the right thing by his family. He believed he would be gone no more than the nine months promised on the recruitment pasters. Probably less. He would be sending most of his $18 monthly wage home, living on as little as possible. For the first time since his oldest Jim was born, he felt like he was finally providing sufficiently for his family.

The morning John Sullivan left was one of anguish and stomachs entangled in knots. Doc Greene, who had delivered baby John in December, and was a staunch Union Army supporter, insisted that his carriage take John and Mary and their two children down to the Exchange Street station, to help make their goodbye a little less terrible.

"It's the least I can do," he said forthrightly.

When Doc Greene's carriage pulled up to the Kentucky Street house, seven year old Jim ran out just ahead of his parents so he could stroke the doc's beautiful new colt, Chestnut. The ride to the depot was unexpectedly quiet, as sadness and dread had stolen everyone's words away.

Mary rode with her head on her husband's shoulder, their baby in her arms.

As they stood on the platform among a chaotic scene of uncontrollable tears and sadness, and a few brave smiles, emotional goodbyes were exchanged and before anyone was ready, the 49th Regiment New York State Volunteers was herded quickly aboard. The locomotive spewed gritty black smoke into the air, making it hard to breathe and impossible to know if their waving handkerchiefs could be seen by the heroes as they went off to make quick work of this war.

It then dawned on Mary that in the bedlam and rush of moving and making arrangements they had forgotten to arrange a visit to the Bliss Photography Gallery to have a likeness made. She had no photograph of her husband, nor did he have one of his wife and sons.

"I'll be back before you know it" were the last words John Sullivan's wife and children ever heard him say.

Jimmy Sullivan was one very tired nine-year-old.

His new job as a lamplighter boy earned him desperately needed money to help support his mother and baby brother. The pay his father sent home from the army was very erratic, and it didn't amount to much. Private John Sullivan was supposed to be paid every two months, but six desperate months stretched between the two most recent payments. His mother had been frantic. Working seven days a week, doing all the chores at home, keeping the garden up, and going to school was a heavy burden for a little boy his age. He wanted to quit school and work full time, but his mother would not allow it.

He had become the man of the house in his father's absence and took the role dead serious. He was now proficient enough in literacy that he could read the newspaper aloud every morning at breakfast to his mother. He always found a discarded copy somewhere along the way while on his rounds, and rarely was he more than a day late in his knowledge of what was going on in the world, especially about the war. The 49th New York Volunteers was somewhere in Virginia according to the latest report in the Buffalo Courier. Jim was eager to contact his father but didn't have a proper address for him.

The lamplighter job worried his mother, for it required her son to begin his rounds at dusk and continue until he completed the task of lighting all the lamps in their district in the First Ward, then repeating his route at dawn to extinguish them. Mary Sullivan worried about her boy's safety, about him being set upon by toughs or falling into the Basin, but she was proud of him at the same time.

Like his wife, Private John Sullivan could neither read nor write with any proficiency. He was ashamed of this fact to the extent that he did not reveal it to any of his comrades in the regiment.

One night in Virginia, Harrison Sheldon confronted John as he cleaned his musket by lamp light.

"Sully, you never write any letters. You never get none neither, despite the fact you have a pretty wife and two fine sons. I figured you have some trouble with reading and writing. It's nothing to be shy of. Half the regiment can't."

John Sullivan remained silent. He turned a bright shade of red that was visible even in the dim lamp glow, which made Sheldon press all the harder.

"I can write one for ye, Sully. Just tell me what to write and I will put it down on paper. Your family needs to know you're fine. They must be worried about ye for sure."

Young Jimmy Sullivan was aware of how lucky he was to be attending school and to have a job that allowed him the opportunity to do so. Some of his friends were not enrolled in school at all, but were working full time in dangerous factories, or were newsboys, awake from sun up until past midnight, peddling papers on the street, on streetcars and in the rowdy saloons. Others went out into the country in July to harvest crops, not returning until mid-October, making them very late for school. And thus, many didn't even attend anymore, so far behind had they fallen.

The lamplighter's tool of the trade was a six-foot-long pole with a wick, a snifter and a hook on its end. Some of the district's lamps were of the old fashioned oil kind, but the newer ones were of gas. Jim first used the hook to turn on the gas. He then brought the pole down, lit the wick, and raised it back up to ignite the gas, or as the case may be, the oil wick. Periodically he had to tote a ladder to change all the old wicks as they burned down and replenish oil. Then, at first light, he had to return and use the snifter to extinguish the oil flame or the hook to turn off the gas.

As he lit all the lamps that ringed the perimeter of the Ohio Basin he sometimes found dropped coins outside the saloons. It was an important job, one he enjoyed, as he got to know people all over his district, and it didn't require heavy exertion, except on ladder days. But he did have to be alert to thugs, whether those in the guise of criminals or of Niagara Frontier police officers.

His hooked pole was his protection.

Lamplighter boys served an additional function as neighborhood watchmen, observing and reporting any problems to the police. Perhaps because the lamplighter boys were often more diligent than they, or the police resented having to respond to the boys' reports of disturbance, the police hassled and harassed the lamplighters, and often mistreated them. Jim had been slapped hard across the face just that week by a drunk Niagara Frontier policeman who knew that his father was absent. The copper's only excuse was that Jim was in his way.

But Jim suspected that the copper somehow believed that it was he who had written the letter. When she saw the bruise, he told his mother that he had gotten into a friendly scuffle with a young neighbor. He didn't want her to fret about him any more than she already did.

One of the first projects Jim Sullivan took on after learning how to write well enough was to compose a letter of complaint to the editor of the Buffalo Courier.

He was tickled to see his very first letter in print.

A LAMPLIGHTER AFTER THE POLICE

A plucky little lamplighter boy who while traveling his dreary rounds at night sees many things that some folks would not like him to divulge, is indignant at the Police "going back on him." Having no one to defend his case he boldly stands up for himself, and sends us the following communication, by which it will be seen. He is after the Niagara Frontier Police "with a sharp stick." We give the communication as received, without any alteration in spelling or matter:

Young Jim Sullivan

Mr. editor of the courier.
I have noticed an article in last evenings paper. something about the
Police. they have been after the lamplighters. I am a lamplighter and
it is many a time I have seen them when on duty, comming out of
saloons drunk and have seen them sleeping under sheds. if they are
going to be so hard after the boys they will report them. I hope you
will please give room in this evenings paper. I am a subscriber and
a lamplighter.

Private John Sullivan swallowed his pride and admitted to Private Harrison
Sheldon that yes, his suspicions were right. And so, there by lamp light under
the Virginia stars, John Sullivan dictated his very first letter to his family.

Dearest Mary, Jim and Baby John,
My friend Harrison Sheldon is writing this for me. I want you to know
that I am fine, and that I have seen very little in the way of battle.
I miss you all very much and I think of you all day and all night,
wishing I could see you again. The war is taking longer than they said
it would. I hope you are receiving my pay if not ask someone you
know who is able to write to send me a letter at this address with an
explanation and I will fix the problem with the paymaster. I know my
little man Jim is watching over the family but I trust you are asking
James Stanton or John Hanavan if you ever need anything. They
promised to watch over you. I read in the newspaper that families
are trying to send boxes to soldiers. There is no use in sending a box
it would not come to me if it did the stuff would be spoiled it would
be so long on the road. As for sending you a likeness, I want to do
this but there is no way to get it made yet. As soon as I get the money
I will send you some money and you can go to Main Street with the
boys and have your likeness made for me. That is what I want most
now. I hope I shall be home in time to eat some of the stuff that you
are growing in the garden. You must write often now ask Hanavan
to write the letter as you dictate to him I will write often too now that
Sheldon is helping me. My address follows.
P.S. I think Hanavan knows how to read and write ask him or if not
ask someone else.

"Sign it here." Sheldon said. John made his mark with a rudimentary J.
Harrison Sheldon was troubled that John didn't even know how to write his
name.
"I'm out of practice." John explained.
"Here, I can teach you in less than five minutes," replied Sheldon.
Sheldon wrote LOVE, JOHN in block letters and said, "Just copy this."
John awkwardly held the pen, his hand unable to as neatly duplicate the eight
letters. Sheldon took John's hand in his own and guided it, over and over until
John had written LOVE, JOHN twenty times. Then he let go and had John try

again. This time the letters were much improved. Then John signed the letter.

"Keep this paper, and practice signing your name every day until it comes second nature. Tomorrow I will teach you how to write your address. You need to learn to write your home address in New York, as well as your Union Army address. All right?"

"All right. Thanks t' ye, Sheldon."

John had not wanted to write the truth to Mary, that the previous Saturday they had a little skirmish with three men killed and more wounded. They had been as close as 40 miles to Richmond, and there had been a fight just the day before as well, but their regiment had gained that day with no losses.

For the time being, they were in the rear and relatively safe, resting, eating fresh cherries and apples. Some of the men did receive boxes from home, but their excitement turned to disappointment at unpacking insect-infested pies or cakes, broken glass jars of put-up fruit, or dried meat that had gotten wet and molded. The weather was splendid and they were sleeping on the ground every night without any need for a tent. Rations were short, but they were getting by, and whatever extra they could find locally they were grateful for. They were in rich farm country. The wheat was coming along fine and corn was high enough to hoe, and it wasn't even June yet. All the regiment's time was taken up with duties.

John had been very sick for an entire month, and had been confined to the camp hospital tent. He was still feeling poorly, but his kin back home didn't have to know that. They would worry enough as it was believing he was perfectly fine. No need to make it worse.

John Sullivan had already seen the best and the worst in men during the ten months he had been a soldier.

"Sheldon? You asleep?"

"Nope."

"I never realized the value of a letter as much as I do now. I regret not learnin' to read and write."

"I'll help you. I will."

"Sheldon?"

"What?"

"Thanks, lad."

"Don't mention it, Sully."

John paused a bit, then spoke as much to the stars above as to Harrison Sheldon.

"I believe we should all degenerate into savages, if this war should continue fer another year."

Jim rushed into the Kentucky Street house and up the stairs calling to his mother.

"Ma! We got a letter from Pa! We got a letter!"

Mary had been crying while she rocked baby John in her arms as he breast fed. She pulled a blanket up to dab her tears and then over herself for modesty as Jim raced in. He handed her the letter.

"I've got me hands full, Jimmy. Do ye think ye kin read it, son?"

"Sure I can!"

Jim opened the envelope and began slowly deciphering the words, reciting them one by one slowly, but proud that not one of them tripped him up.

When he was done, he began again from the beginning, this time reading in a less halting and more natural manner, and for the first time in many months, he saw his mother smile.

"Kin ye write him back, Jimmy? If I tell ye what to say?"

"I'm sure of it, Ma. Let's try!"

Harrison Sheldon had written John Sullivan's return address on the letter and on the envelope too.

Jim was excited as all get out, to not only hear from his Pa but to be able to write back to him directly.

Mary dictated her words, editing herself so that Jim would not be upset, nor to worry her husband. She had a few questions for him, but most of all she needed just to tell him how much she missed him. It was a relief to get the words out, knowing he would hear them.

Jim patiently reprinted his mother's dictation to look neater, and folded the sheet, placing it in the envelope. Then he went out to light his lamps. When he returned, his mother had bread and porridge for him for his supper. Afterward, Jim said he was tired and wanted to go to bed early, but in fact he wanted to write his own letter to his father.

He took the candle lamp to his bed, and when his mother was asleep, he struck a match and lit it. Then he began writing.

> Dear Pa,
> I learnt how to write now. I am very happy we got your letter. It is very lonely without you and Ma cries a lot. She thinks I don't see. The baby is fine and I am teaching him to walk atop my feet. He can almost walk by his own now and its funny.
> I have a job. I am a lamp lighter boy. I am careful don't worry. Mr. Stanton brings food sometimes last week some eggs. I give my money wages to Ma and sometimes pennys I find outside the saloons.
> I am doing good at school. My big wish has come true. I can write to my own Pa now. I love you Pa and wish the war would be finished soon. Write again very fast.
> Your son, Jim

He stuffed his letter in the same envelope with his mother's, then sealed it. He opened his pouch and saw that he still had eleven pennies, hoping it was enough in case he had to buy more postage for the extra weight.

Peter Halloran

Peter Halloran had set his lecherous eye upon Mary Sullivan for years, watching her from afar on those Sundays when she and her husband John gathered their children and mingled with the neighborhood. He would pass them as they walked on the riverfront or along the Basin, admiring her, coveting her. Once, John Sullivan shot Halloran a threatening look after catching him gazing at his wife with far more than casual interest.

Peter Halloran by an interesting circumstance had a half-brother with the exact same name, Peter Halloran, who emigrated from Ireland and joined his namesake half-sibling, who was living in Fonda, N.Y., in the area of Amsterdam, Montgomery County, in 1847.

The two brothers Peter Halloran lost affection for one another at some point and parted ways when the one turned to criminal acts and lost his religion altogether, and the other mended his drunken ways and found a new religion. Opposites in every regard, the newly arrived half-brother had by 1862 become a teetotaler and a Protestant, and then lost his eyesight. He had gained local renown in the county as a famous Protestant preacher known as Blind Peter.

Peter Halloran the saloonkeeper scoffed whenever he read the preacher Blind Peter's name, which was appearing increasingly in the newspapers' religion notices. Blind Peter sighed whenever he was read a notice under the newspapers' Police Court heading about the latest grievance committed by his namesake.

John Sullivan was one of the first Buffalo volunteers in the Union Army, joining the 49th Regiment soon after the war began, and thereby thoroughly puzzling saloon-keeper Halloran, a fellow Irishman. How could a man closing in fast on forty years of age up and leave an infant of just a few months, an eight-year-old son, and a lovely defenseless wife, all alone? And to fight in a war for an adopted country? When considering war, with its inevitable ripped flesh and spilled blood, shouldn't a man's very own flesh and blood receive his first allegiance?

John Sullivan had been gone almost a year when on July 17th of 1862 Peter Halloran heard the news from young Patrolman Steven Whelan that Mary had been arrested with her baby in her arms for stealing food.

Peter recognized his chance, and rushed up Louisiana Street to the police precinct on the corner of Elk, where Mary sat with her crying toddler John Patrick, and her morose young son Jim.

Peter Halloran approached the constable and inquired about Mary, revealing that her husband was a brave fighting man defending his country, and fibbing that he was a friend of the family. He lied and said that upon departing to muster in, John Sullivan had asked him to keep a watchful eye on his wife and children for him.

The police already knew about Mary's difficult plight, as they were charged with giving special attention to the families that Buffalo's brave Union Soldiers had left behind. Mary had been arrested by the patrolman reluctantly. It was clear she was stealing only food, nothing more, and that she had her hungry children with her at the time. Patrolman Steven Whelan did not want to take her in, but the law, and the fruit vendor, compelled him to, and he, a family man with four children of his own, was grateful for his secure job. He had no recourse.

Arrangements were made for Peter Halloran to pay Mary's fine of $2. Other arrestees whose names embarrassingly appeared in the Buffalo Courier the following day along with Mary Sullivan's were given $5 fines for a similar offense, or sent to the workhouse. Peter was glad to pay, for the chance to be the knight in shining armor.

"Mrs. Sullivan, Ma'am?" he asked as he approached.

The baby had stopped fussing, and eight year old Jim Sullivan was munching on a piece of stolen apple given him by the patrolman. Mary looked up from the bench that she occupied, appearing a little dazed and quite ashamed.

Surveying the room to make sure no one was within hearing distance he said, "Me name's Peter Halloran. Patrolman Whelan has requested that I escort ye home, ma'am."

"What's going to happen to me?" she asked, desperation in her voice.

"Nothing, Missis. It's been resolved. I can accompany ye and the lads home now."

Little Jim was happy to be out of the building, and desperately missing his father, soaked up the attention that Peter lavished on him. As they walked along the Ohio Basin toward the Sullivan home, Peter gave most of his attention to Jim, and Jim reciprocated. Mary Sullivan did not feel much like talking.

"Thank you Mr. Halloran," she demurred, "but the boys and I can find our way now."

"Sorry, Missis, but the patrolman said I must walk you to your door. It was one of the conditions."

"Conditions? What conditions?"

"Why ma'am, the conditions of your release. You were released to my custody, and I am obligated by law to make sure you get home safely," thus lied the brazen manipulator.

Mary Sullivan was embarrassed, depressed, and exhausted by her futile efforts to care for her family. She was infuriated with her husband for abandoning her, leaving the family at the mercy of a frightening and stressful world through which she must now navigate without him. Word of her arrest had spread around the basin, and passers-by gave her looks, one or two scornful, but most sympathetic, for many others had recently been in Mary's shoes as well, or close to it. The war had sent prices skyrocketing. They were all feeling the pinch.

Mary didn't argue. She was anxious to return home. It was only noon, but already two drunks were feuding outside Peter Conners' Mariner's Home, a Louisiana Street saloon that faced the basin with rooms to let upstairs, mostly to itinerant sailors. A boy of about five years with a strange face having a squashed-in quality about it tussled aggressively with a smaller boy out front.

"Jimmy Conners, ye stop yer bullyin' right now!" a female voice shouted at him from within.

Peter Halloran thought to himself, what must it be like having to live so close to that? His own saloon could be rowdy for sure, but no platoon of worthless misfits was sleeping it off upstairs at Halloran's.

They turned left and followed the Erie Railroad tracks one block to Kentucky

St. As they stood awkwardly at the gate in front of the house Mary and her boys shared with the Gearys and Krupps, Peter Halloran tried his best to extend the moment, but Mary was anxious to go inside so she could cry.

Peter tipped his silk stovepipe hat, which he wore for the deceitful illusion it implied of his being a gentleman, and avoiding looking him in the eye, Mary said, "Thank ye, Mr. Halloran. I am very sorry to have put ye through such an inconvenience."

"It was no inconvenience a' tall, Missis. Please let me know if there is anything I can do for ye. I realize with yer husband away, servin' his..."

Mary had already turned to walk into the house. Peter watched her for a moment, and when the door shut resoundingly behind her and the baby, he looked down at young Jim, sitting on the stoop. The little boy waved goodbye to his new friend. Peter waved back and said in his light Irish brogue, "I'll be seein' ye, Jimmy Sullivan, me lad," turned, and began walking toward South Street. The sad youngster watched him intently until he disappeared.

After reaching the corner, Halloran turned left and completed the five blocks along the river to the corner of Hamburgh Street, where his saloon stood. Heavy black coal smoke drifted over from belching steamships passing, their horns screaming, the noise and soot of wartime industry filled the air of the First Ward.

As he walked into his saloon, a family, one of the three who boarded there in the large house at No. 16 with him, emerged and said good day.

Peter Halloran

The Notice

His lamps extinguished, young Jim Sullivan headed home in the early September morning heat with a newfound penny in his pocket and a purloined copy of the Buffalo Commercial. He read as he walked along. He especially liked reading the Police record that told of brawls between women.

His heart nearly stopped as he saw the name J. Sullivan on the short list of wounded. He halted and read very carefully, trying to convince himself he had misread. or that this particular J. Sullivan was not his own Pa.

ADDITIONAL NAMES OF WOUNDED
IN THE BUFFALO REGIMENTS
—We glean the following additional names of members of Buffalo regiments injured in the late battles, from the New York papers:
J. Sullivan, Co. E 49th Regt—arm

Jim counted fourteen names on the list. J. Sullivan was at the very top. It had to be him. No, maybe not. J. Sullivan is not at all a rare name. Surely there must be others in the 49th.

James Stanton, his father's friend, was driving toward him down Louisiana Street in the Buffalo Ice Co. wagon. Young Jim, panicking, waved him down, but Stanton had already begun to slow, when from a distance he recognized Jim with his distinctive lamplighter pole. He spotted the newspaper in Jim's hand as he drove up, and was prepared not to say anything, but then he saw the anguish distorting Jim's face. Jim spoke first.

"Pa's been hurt!" Jim cried, his voice cracking. A cloud of grief wrinkled the boy's expression.

"Now Jim, we don't know for sure if that's him, and even if it is yer Pa, it is just an arm injury. It could have happened in any of a hundred ways."

"How do you know it's just his arm? Do you think he got shot?"

"No, no. Maybe a horse wrenched it, or he hurt himself cutting wood. Come on, I'll take you home. Climb aboard."

"I have to tell my Ma!"

Stanton was silent. He was contemplating. There it was, right there in the paper, so surely someone would be telling Mary soon enough, if they hadn't already.

"Jim, we'll go tell your mother together."

Peter Halloran called on the Sullivan family at their flat upon reading the opportune news of the wounding of Private John Sullivan. Peter Halloran was, like Mary and John Sullivan and ninety per cent of the neighborhood, Irish-born. He was an older widower with no children, as far as anyone knew.

Mary Sullivan noticed that there was no scent of alcohol on his breath, and was impressed with that, his keeping a saloon and all. She caught the essence of his loneliness, and interpreted his intentions as those of one who himself was familiar with loss and grief. Peter Halloran politely extended an offer of whatever assistance Mary Sullivan and her sons might require.

Suspicious of everyone, even the kindly Krupps at times, Mary was polite but chilly to him, as both the social requirements of a married lady of the day, and her instincts, dictated. She was still mortified about his having to step in to save her just a few weeks before, when she was arrested for stealing fruit.

Mary was so exhausted by the long months alone, struggling to raise her boys while their father fought the country's war, that she often said to people, had she known war would be in their future, she never would have left Ireland.

The financially bereft dock laborer John Sullivan had been lured to the life of a soldier by the lucrative-sounding bounty offered for volunteering; allowing for his family to secure safe, clean new lodgings in a much better house, away from the lurking sailors, staggering drunks and suspicious characters who loitered along Louisiana Street on the Ohio Basin quay. Their new flat was located on the next block over from Louisiana and the dangers posed by the Ohio Basin, on Kentucky Street. It was located five doors away and upwind from the noise and smoke of the Erie Railroad's tracks, almost directly behind their former house on Louisiana Street.

Sadly, John Sullivan wasn't the only First Ward father and husband desperate enough to view fighting in a war as an opportunity to better his lot.

As troubling a prospect it may have been to leave his beloved wife and sons behind, he had every confidence that this war would, as advertised, be over in just a few months, allowing him to return to an improved situation and a more secure future for his family.

John Sullivan had been optimistic. He felt relief in those last few late August days before mustering in. He had signed up with Buffalo's 49th regiment on the 21st of August, to muster in on the 28th, just three days after resettling his family.

He had despised his miserable itinerant existence scrambling for the city's toughest jobs, competing with the negroes to see which group, the Irish or the blacks, would accept the lower wage, just to put scraps of food in their babies' bellies.

Most of the negroes in Buffalo were American born, and deeply resented these destitute white nigger immigrants for invading their city and taking away the opportunities they had waited so long for, worked so hard for, opportunities that were only now finally beginning to present themselves.

The negroes were happy about the war in more than just one respect. For colored Buffalonians, it meant less competition for what few jobs were available.

For the first time in his married life, immediately after collecting his signing bonus, John Sullivan was able to spend entire days and nights with his wife and sons. He and Mary had been married almost eleven years. He was finally experiencing what it was like to provide properly for the family he loved and had long promised a better life to, but whom up until the previous week, in his opinion, he had been failing miserably.

Mary had pleaded with him when John Sullivan first approached her with his radical and frightening plan.

"Please, John, no!"

Up Harewood Road

John Sullivan felt a sharp thwack! followed by a deep pain in his forearm. He was advancing, running fast as hell, tripping forward full speed toward the cover of a tree with his adopted regiment under fire at Bull Run. While in the tent hospital with his stubborn illness, the 49th had moved on without him. The musket ball that caught him caused him to drop his weapon. He lay there in the mud defenseless. It hurt more than he'd expected it might, and all he could think of was "They're going to cut off my arm." It was at the very least broken, that was certain.

With every month that passed spent in the Union Army, he had crossed off each interval on his little calendar, glad to have made it safely through another without a major scare. He'd passed the one year mark since mustering in just a week back, surprised and disheartened that there seemed to be no end in sight for this war. Now here it was the last of August, and he had to go and get himself shot. Well, he almost made it safely through another month.

He hit the ground hard. He was lying on his back on top of a sharp rock. What to do now? He'd have to find his way back somehow. Crawl. His musket was nowhere around and it was useless anyway since he was left-handed and they got him in his left arm. He managed to turn himself over and began to slither back to the unit's original position as other advancing soldiers just jumped over him in their attempt to win ground. Fifteen minutes later, he was exhausted. A screaming wounded man lay in his path.

"I'll send someone here to get ye, if I'll be makin' back myself. Hold tight, soldier."

"Please hurry, sir. I'm dyin'. I just know it," cried the boy, not much older than fifteen years. He looks just like me own Jim, John Sullivan recalled thinking later.

Ten minutes further on, John Sullivan's face scraped and bloody from arduously dragging his wounded weight through the dirt and scree, he came upon a motionless man. The soldier appeared to be dead. He tried not to look, wanting to just get past him, but his progress was excruciatingly slow. He glanced over. Bounteous blood had flowed from the man's eye. He'd been shot with a musket ball right in the eye socket. John suddenly gasped.

"Oh, dearest Jesus!" he cried out.

It was Harrison Sheldon.

"Oh God, oh God, oh God..."

He began to panic. I can't stop. I can't be cryin' now. I'll cry later, if I can make it back, he thought to himself.

He reached out to squeeze Sheldon's hand, and despite his depleted state blurted out with voice cracking, "Goodbye t' ye, me grand good friend!"

It took two hours before he was able to come within view of someone who could help. He didn't realize he was in shock. He was overcome with alarm about what might happen to his wife and children, terrified that he wouldn't make it back to the regiment in time to receive aid, scared he might die right there in the dirt, yards from salvation, and be left there to just rot. He was desperate to hold his Mary and his sons.

Having been so ill during May and June had badly weakened him, and he was more affected by his wound than he thought should be usual. From a distance men saw him crawling. They ran out to fetch him. He was never so happy to see negroes in his entire life. "Thank you, gentlemen," he blurted, sincerely grateful. "Thank you." Once assured he was in safe hands, he allowed himself to pass out.

It took three days for the ambulance to traverse the thirty-or-so miles to Washington, where Harewood Hospital had just been opened. A campus of hastily-built wood dormitories dotted the hillside property, and although feeling very poorly, John Sullivan was up and around and socializing with other men who were in far worse shape than he. They were missing arms and legs and eyes, and he quickly realized how fortunate he was.

They wanted all who were able to line up outside Building B for a photographer who had arrived to document the newly-opened facility for the government. He remarked to John how pretty the environs were, and how the area's pleasantness would be a help to the men in recovering faster. John remained in his bed until prodded to get up. The others were waiting. He stood on the little porch with his arm in a sling and joked with a couple of the men who like himself were also not badly wounded. But they were surrounded by so many others whose lives would never be the same again, for they had been injured so grievously.

The group was instructed to remain motionless for a full two seconds on the command of the photographer, "or else yer all just gonna be a blur."

The man made three exposures.

Then John high-tailed it right back to his bed. It was hot and he was dizzy and sweating. Almost immediately he fell asleep.

A few evenings after his arrival at Harewood he began to feel much more ill, burning with fever and suffering nosebleeds and a miserable headache. Within days he was prostrate and experiencing periodic hallucinations, mostly involving him being at home in his wife's bed with his children at his side, caring for him. He heard his young Jim say, "Pa, you just lay there and rest. You'll feel better in no time at all. I'll take care of you." His devoted boy carefully placed a cool wet cloth on his dear old Pa's burning forehead. It felt wonderful.

"Thank you, son, " said John Sullivan, lovingly.

The nurse looked down at him and smiled knowingly. Then she soothed, "You're welcome, soldier."

Mary was busy baking bread and as good as it smelled he just wasn't hungry right now. Maybe he'd take a sandwich later on. His parents were there too. Funny, he didn't remember them telling him they were coming all the way over from Ireland, but no matter. As long as they arrived safe and sound. Later on they should all take the streetcar down to the Niagara River and fish for pike. Then visit the Falls.

John reached down and felt his painful abdomen, its size so large that he laughed thinking how similar it felt to Mary's when she was pregnant with the boys. But it hurt to laugh, so he stopped himself.

And as the fever consumed him and he experienced periods of euphoria and other men's bodies were first covered, then removed from his vicinity and dehydration played havoc with the electrolytes in his system, he ceased to be

FIG. 705.—Excised portion of ulna. Spec. 69.

CASE 1920.—Private J. Sullivan, Co. E. 49th New York, was wounded at the battle of Bull Run, August 30, 1862, and admitted to Harewood Hospital, Washington, September 5th. Surgeon T. E. Mitchell, 1st Maryland, noted: "Excision of three and a half inches of right ulna, upper third, September 14, 1862, for gunshot compound fracture of forearm." The patient died September 18, 1862. The excised portion of the ulna was contributed to the Museum by the operator, Dr. Mitchell, and is represented in the adjoining wood-cut (FIG. 705). It is described by Assistant Surgeon B. Stone, U. S. V., as "a section of shaft of the right ulna extensively comminuted by the impact of a conoidal musket ball."

Harewood Hospital Washington DC, 1862 interior.

aware.

Four negroes lowered him into the ground adjacent to Harewood Road along with other patriots the likes of him. Lots of others, unfortunately, in boxes, stacked and waiting. The captain filled out the form accounting for a fallen man's valuables.

He wrote in the space provided:

Private John Sullivan.

Date of Death and Burial: September 18, 1862.

Memoranda:

1. 1 Pr. pants.
2. 1 Pocket Comb
3. 1 pocket Glass
4. 1 Handerkerchief
5. 1 Razor
6. 1 Canteen
7. 1 10 cent Richmond Bill
8. 1 pocket Calendar

Harewood Hospital wounded, September 1862

Dread

Life without John Sullivan was worse than Mary ever imagined it might be. The war did not end quickly as had predicted, and without her husband's support and cooperation, she could not keep her job at the American Hotel. Her friend Mercy Abbott had been ill and was herself struggling, but even if she weren't, she couldn't expect Mercy to take her children six days a week. There was no one to look after baby John, so she had to take work locally wherever she could find it. The money John Sullivan sent home was meager and too sporadic to rely on. Mary took in laundry, sewed and mended garments, and provided day care for the two youngest Geary children downstairs so that Mrs. Geary could go to work. Mary baked bread to sell in the neighborhood, made soap and candles, and took on whatever task would pay her money without taking her away from her children. She followed her son's example and took the baby out at dawn to scour outside the saloons for dropped coins.

Young Jim was still a lamplighter boy, but she worried about him endlessly, always greatly relieved when he walked in the door safe and sound. He was doing well in school again, and what a relief that was, as he had begun looking for trouble at certain intervals when he was missing his father's presence most painfully.

Without his Pa's guiding hand he had begun to lose his way. James Stanton stepped in whenever he could, but he had remarried, and his new young wife was expecting her first baby. Baby John Sullivan was still a handful, colicky and unsettled, demanding Mary's full attention.

Mary waited in torment for any news about John. All she knew for sure was what was stated in the official letter that followed the newspaper notice by two weeks, declaring that John had been wounded at Bull Run.

Then, finally, horridly, two weeks after, without any understanding at all of the strange circumstances surrounding the nightmarish event, she received official notice that her beloved husband, father to her handsome growing boys, had died at Harewood Hospital in Washington DC on September 18th, 1862.

She contacted the authorities to ask, then plead, that his body be sent home. She was told, sorry, there's a war on ma'am. Private Sullivan had to be quickly buried where he died. But Mary protested, saying that weeks separated his wounding and the news of his death.

What happened during that interval?

Where was he during that month's time?

One day she encountered her neighbor Mrs. Harris on the street. Mrs. Harris had lost her own son in rural Virginia just a few days before. She told Mary that she had been informed by an official that the Union Army operated an embalming facility, administered by one Doctor Bunnell, in Virginia, and they were shipping soldiers' bodies home to grieving families for burial, including her own son's.

Mary was shocked.

They're embalming soldiers who fall on the battlefield in the middle of nowhere in Virginia, and sending these men home, but not her husband who died while under hospital care right in the nation's capitol? It made no sense. Mary Sullivan was beside herself when she learned this, and truly thought she could not survive the prospects of a life without John Sullivan—especially if she could not even bring him home to say their final goodbyes and provide a respectful burial.

Peter Halloran heard the news of John Sullivan's death and the strange circumstances surrounding it. He called on Mary and promised that he would use all his influence to find answers and if at all possible have John returned home. But truth be told, Peter Halloran had no influence, at least not any of the honorable kind.

Mary was again angry at herself for never having learned how to read and write. She did not know where to go or who to ask for particulars about where her husband's remains might be buried or if she might retrieve them. Her noble quest, primary in everyone's mind in the week following the announcement of John's death, was quickly forgotten with the advent of new deaths, new crises and fresh emergencies that distracted from hers. A war was raging. People were forced to move on to deal with more immediate matters.

Bureaucrats favored those who were more aggressive, knowledgeable and persistent in their search for answers. People who could read and write. Those who had money. Mary's thoughts were soon completely consumed with basic survival for herself and her boys. She was lost. Broke. She was overwhelmed with grief and anxiety, and abject uncertainty about the future. She needed money. What would she do? How would she feed and care for her children?

The anguish caused by Pvt. John Sullivan's death was amplified by Mary's desperate struggle to survive and to care for her babies. On October 20th, her and John's 12th wedding anniversary, she wanted to cry, but didn't have time. Staying alive took every ounce of energy and fight she had in her. Winter was coming on fast, cruel and tough.

John's friends, no wealthier nor better situated than he had been, could do little more than share what food and pennies they could spare with Mary and her boys.

On February 11, 1863, Mary, now in a state of desperation, was accompanied by her late husband's friends James Stanton and First Ward Alderman John Hanavan to the office of the Erie County Clerk. Five months after John's death she was still in the preliminary process of applying for her widow's pension, and her situation was dire. Her story had been brought to the attention of Samuel Lake, a Buffalo pension broker, who volunteered to act as her attorney to obtain her pension certificate. Mary was grateful for his help. She didn't know the first thing about such complicated matters.

James Stanton stopped at the house on Kentucky Street to pick up Mary and the children in a Buffalo Ice Co. wagon, lent by the sympathetic Mr. Clark for this occasion, to take them downtown. As Stanton drove up to Mary's house, Mrs. Geary, Mary's downstairs neighbor and landlady, came out and confided in him that Mary was far behind in her rent. Ellen Geary had many mouths to feed, and as awful as she felt for Mary Sullivan, she needed to have her rent money.

Stanton told Mrs. Geary that he would ask all their friends to contribute, and he would return on his rounds to give her further news. Immediately then,

Mary emerged from the house. She and Ellen Geary smiled and nodded politely to each other.

Jim Sullivan, less than a month away from his tenth birthday, hopped up into the wagon, very happy to see James Stanton. He was starved for adult male attention.

When his mother wasn't looking he would go to the drawer where his father's one and only letter written home was kept, and carefully take it out of its envelope. He would read it, and then inspect it. He was always vigilant for evidence of his father there. A fingerprint, or a hair. A faint smudge that might be his. He touched the Love, John signature, trying to absorb some essence from the place his father touched. He put the paper to his nose to see if he could smell his father's familiar comforting scent.

Mary strained to smile at Stanton as he reached for her hand to help her up onto the dray, while she supported baby John on her hip. Two-year-old John fussed continually. Stress and tension brought on by the family situation caused the baby great insecurity.

"Did Mrs. Geary say anything t' ye, Jim?" Mary asked.

"Aye, she said hello, good day, how are ye?" replied Stanton with a big smile. "We'll be stoppin' for John Hanavan up at the corner," he said as the wagon approached Elk Street. Hanavan was waiting there, and he climbed aboard and paid his respects. Mary had wished more than once that one or both of her husband's friends had not been married. She was in a mad fever just trying to eke out a living for herself and her boys. How convenient and blessed it would be if one of her dead husband's friends could step in to take his place.

"How soon do you think it will be then, until I receive my pension, Mr. Durkee?" she asked the clerk who took her application. "My boys are hungry, and they need clothes, and I'm behind on my rent. I didn't allow my husband to volunteer for the army so that me and my babies could end up starving in the dirt, or worse! Me husband sacrificed his life fer this country, but let me be saying' this: me and me children will not be doin' anything of the kind!"

"Mrs. Sullivan," said clerk Charles Durkee, "things are quite disorganized because of the war. I'm sorry to say that all of the country's resources and manpower seem to be aimed at trying to stay one step ahead of the enemy, rather than attending to important matters such as yours. It's a terrible situation, but we will do our best to get you and your boys your proper due as soon as possible."

Mary had been awarded her husband's pay for his final two months, but that was long gone. Mary's multitude of small jobs kept her head spinning, but combined together didn't bring in enough for rent, coal and food. She was desperate to return to her old job at the American Hotel, but there was no one who could watch the children for all those hours. Besides, she was still breast nursing two-year-old John because food was so scarce. She was determined her husband's namesake would survive.

"But please understand, Mrs. Sullivan, that it is surely in the government's best interest to hurry this along, since the promise to provide for a soldier's widow and children is a critical inducement for many men to enlist. After all, what kind of man would leave his family behind and go into battle without making certain they would be taken care should something happen to him?"

Mary knew the answer to that; her own husband was the kind.

The story of Amos Humiston had been published, a man who refused to enlist for the first fifteen months of the war, choosing his obligations to family over patriotic considerations. Only after Humiston had received assurance from responsible citizens of his town that his family would be cared for during his absence did he sign up. This story of conflicting duties illustrated the dilemma faced by the Union Army in attracting volunteers, and its formidable task of making the prospect of going off to war less unattractive to the prospective soldier.

"How much will I receive?" Mary Sullivan inquired.

Absentmindedly Durkee spouted the memorized answer as he went over her application.

"The amount of each pension depends upon the soldier's military rank and level of disability. Pensions given to widows, orphans, and other dependents of deceased soldiers are figured at the rate of total disability according to the military rank of their deceased husband or father."

The memorized speech didn't answer Mary's question, nor was it uncomplicated. But she decided to let it go. Durkee looked up and observed that the troubled woman's attention had drifted off.

"It will be half of your husband's monthly salary, so in your case, $9."

Mary's eyes lit up. It was not much, but she was now living on handouts and what she could eke out doing the dirty work refused by coloreds.

Gathering all the paperwork together was still an overwhelming prospect, for without irrefutable proofs she could not receive John's pension. Mary was required to produce documentation that she had been married to John Sullivan, and that her sons James and John were his blood children. Tracking down the priest who married them in Amsterdam N.Y. was proving to be a challenge, because for months she could not recall his name, or the name of the church. Mary felt entirely stupid when it finally came to her: St. Mary's Church. Other documentation had to be procured from the priests who had baptized young James at St. Joseph's Cathedral in Buffalo, and John, who was baptized in the neighborhood, at St. Bridget's.

Slowly the clock was running down, and for Mary Sullivan and her sons, it looked like it might soon stop ticking altogether.Mary returned home from the county clerk's office emotionally drained, but she had work to do, and inquiries to make around the neighborhood. As she walked with her boys, an already discarded idea again came to her. The difference being she did not push it out of her mind this time.

She returned home to prepare herself. Her first task was to take out her best frock from the clothespress and give it a good airing and a thorough shake.

The following day, Mary put on her freshened dress, worn at the seams as it was, and her bonnet, and paid a visit downstairs to Ellen Geary, tearfully apologizing for being so late with the rent. Mary told Ellen that her application for the pension certificate was nearly complete, and all that was needed was the proof of her marriage. She didn't reveal that she had no idea when she might receive her money. She was stalling for time.

Ellen apologized also, revealing to Mary that she also was in financial trouble, and needed to either have the rent, or regretfully and with much guilt, she would have to ask Mary to find someplace else to live. Rent and the price of food and fuel had skyrocketed since the start of the war, and Ellen, with a large family to support, needed to find a tenant she could depend on to pay the rent on time. Mary asked Ellen if she could watch her boys while she went out to see about a job in the neighborhood. She had a plan.

Encouraged by her optimism, Ellen agreed.

After Mary left Ellen, she walked down Kentucky Street toward the river and headed for Hamburgh Street and the saloon of Peter Halloran.

Mary was a proper woman. She knew the social risk she would be taking if she worked in a saloon, but she and her children were on the verge of no longer existing.

As she neared the intersection with Hamburgh Street, South Street drew very close to the edge of the Buffalo River. Two steam tugboats, belching black coal smoke, were struggling to pull a huge four-masted ship upriver to its destination. As Mary walked past this spot, a sudden herculean effort was expended by the tugs, and a great volume of dense black coal smoke burped into the air. The breeze carried it, with little dispersal, on a collision course with Mary Sullivan. Too late she saw it coming and was quickly enveloped in it, the particles of soot coating her face, hands, and her best dress.

Mary just froze in place. The event galvanized her, it holding the prospect of being a final straw in her miserable existence. A resident of South Street saw her, ran out with a brush and rushed up to her.

"Aye, I saw that comin'!" said the Good Samaritan.

She handed Mary her handkerchief. Mary buried her face in it, but instead of wiping, she bawled into its folds.

"There, there me darlin', come onto me veranda and have a seat and we'll clean you up. No permanent damage done, now, to be sure."

Her name was Mrs. McRainey, and she was a widow like Mary, except that her husband had left her in better stead than Mary's had. Even so, Mrs. McRainey's house was full of boarders.

"Now, where might ye be goin' on this fine afternoon?" asked the kind lady, making small talk.

"I'm ashamed to say that I am so without prospects for myself and my children, that I am on my way to ask Mr. Halloran if I might work in his saloon," blurted Mary.

Being Peter Halloran's neighbor, and familiar with his troubled history, Mrs. McRainey looked horrified.

"And how'd ye come about making the acquaintance of Mr. Halloran?" she asked timidly.

Mary did not want to tell Mrs. McRainey either the truth nor an outright lie, so she did neither.

"When my husband was living we would encounter Mr. Halloran on our Sunday walks, and that is how we became acquainted. "

Mary tried to completely forget about Halloran bailing her out of trouble at the police station when she was arrested.

Mrs. McRainey simply nodded. "And so, dear, do ye know the man well?"

"No, not really,' replied Mary.

"I see," said Mrs. McRainey.

"Why?" Mary asked in response to the kindly woman's concerned tone. "Is there something about Mr. Halloran that I should know, Mrs. McRainey?"

"Darlin', what I think I know I cannot swear to on the Bible, so I won't say. But I think it would be best if you would keep a good distance between yourself and that Mr. Halloran. "

She finished brushing Mary's dress.

"There, no one would ever know you were in a black cloud just a few minutes ago."

Not looking her new friend directly in the eye, Mary confessed, "Oh, but I still am, Mrs. McRainey, in a very black cloud."

Mary wanted to ask Mrs. McRainey more questions about Halloran, but stopped herself. She truly had no other prospects, so she decided it wouldn't hurt to just talk with Peter Halloran and draw her own conclusions. She thanked Mrs. McRainey profusely, and continued on her quest. At the intersection, she turned the corner. The saloon was the third structure down, a large house, with a full upstairs. She looked around to see who was watching. There were quite a few curious spectators. A women alone did not enter the front door of a saloon, but Mary entered regardless.

Peter Halloran spotted her instantly and practically leapt the bar to greet her. He quickly turned her right around to escort her out. He was concerned about her being seen.

"Mrs. Sullivan, how delightful to see you," he said in a sickeningly sweet manner.

"Let's have us a dander by the river, shall we? We'll talk there."

They crossed the street and slowly walked back along South Street in the direction Mary had come.

"Mr. Halloran. As you know I've lost me husband and I find meself in unfortunate circumstances. I was wondering if ye might be needin' someone as reliable and hard workin' as me t' help around the place. I worked previously at the American Hotel. I have references," she said.

'Why, Mrs. Sullivan, I meant my word when I offered my assistance. Why don't you allow me to make some inquiries first, since I wouldn't want you exposin' yourself to such a rowdy element as I've got in my establishment if it can be at all helped.

"Oh, would you please, Mr. Halloran? I would be most grateful."

"Certainly Mrs. Sullivan. I'll begin right away. Can I escort ye home, ma'am?"

"Thank ye, no, Mr. Halloran. I'll be on me way."

"I'll come by yer house tomorrow afternoon and tell ye of any opportunities I might find that might be to your liking, if that's all right."

"Yes, yes it is," smiled Mary with enormous relief.

Could this be it? Could this be what she had been waiting for, praying for?

"I'll see ye then. Tomorrow. Watch your step along the rail tracks on your way home, Mrs. Sullivan if you will."

"Yes, Mr. Halloran. Tomorrow. Thank ye."

For the first time since John had gone to war, Mary Sullivan felt the barest glow of hope. As she passed Mrs. McRainey's house, she saw her new friend in the window, waved, and smiled.

Mrs. McRainey smiled back, disguising her bad feelings concerning the future of Mary Sullivan. Tomorrow came and went. As did the next, and the next. Peter Halloran didn't show as he'd pledged, plummeting Mary further into hopelessness.

It was part of his plan.

When Halloran finally did show up a full week after he'd promised, he had no job to offer her, but he did have a proposal. He said, "Mary, I want you to be my wife."

October 1863
Samuel Lake

In October, more than a full year after her husband John's death, Mary Sullivan revisited the office of bounty agent Samuel Lake at the Hollister Block, again accompanied by John Sullivan's trusted friend James Stanton and First Ward Alderman John Hanavan. Mary was destitute.

Mr. Lake was still not in possession of all the documentation required by the government to allow Mary to collect her widow's and her sons' dependents pension. After a year of hunger and scraping by, arguing with the authorities, borrowing and begging, she was angry and exhausted.

When John Sullivan died, the Union Army, according to the documentation Mary was shown, seemed to be unaware that he was married, or had children. They didn't know what hometown he was from. They were not sure where his remains lay. They had four different dates of death spread across a dozen different official documents. Three different ages were listed for him.

Mary was not able to produce written proofs to verify that she and John were legally married. She lost her husband in a war that she didn't believe in. Her children lost their father. Their father lost his life. To add insult to injury, they had been left penniless and barely able to survive for an entire year already because the army could locate no records confirming that John Sullivan was a married father of two.

"Did John not tell them he was married with children? Why would he do such a thing? Might the army have lost his papers that contained this information?" She fretted and agonized.

Samuel Lake shrugged. He didn't know what to tell her. It was as big a mystery to him as it was to her. Mary's was a terrible case. Hell of a way for the army to treat the family of a man who died for his country, he thought to himself.

Mary's once-pretty face now betrayed its skeletal structure. John's friends and the Sullivans' neighbors helped out as best they could, but rents had increased 50% since the beginning of the war and most food prices had doubled as the conflict dragged on. Everyone was struggling to make ends meet.

Mary Sullivan's world flooded with fear and dread as the fabric of her very existence unraveled. She had signed a New York State Declaration for Widow's Pension back in October 1862, thinking that the family's long overdue benefits would soon be on their way. Yet here it was a full year later with the matter as unresolved as ever. No support at all was provided her or her children.

That first terrible winter, alone and grieving, hungry and ill, frightened for herself and her babies, was abominable. She feared she wouldn't survive it. Worse, she was afraid she might make the decision to no longer try. She wondered if perhaps they all might all be better off dead.

As she sat across the desk from Attorney Lake, he absentmindedly slid a letter along the waxed surface for her to read, forgetting she could neither read nor write. The letter was in the elegant hand of Thomas Mitchell, the surgeon who attended John Sullivan in his last days. In the letter were all the particulars, as well as answers to some of Mary's agonizing questions. Because she couldn't decipher it, and Samuel Lake was focused on getting the pension papers signed and the family's money flowing, Mary never absorbed the particulars. How John Sullivan died was far less important to her now than how his family would survive.

Sam placed the letter that told John Sullivan's story into Mary's file. Mary Sullivan and her children would live their entire lives without knowing the full story about John Sullivan's wounding and death because neither Mary nor John's friend James Stanton could read the letter Mr. Lake presented them that day.

> Harewood Hospital
> October 4, 1863
>
> Mr. Samuel Lake
> Dear Sir,
> Your letter of October 1st is at hand and the soldier of whom you inquire (John Sullivan, Co, E 49th Regt. NYSV) died at this hospital on the 19th of September 1862 of typhoid fever. He had a fracture of the arm between the elbow and the wrist caused by a musket ball. The wound was received at the battle of Bull Run August 28th and was not of itself a dangerous one but having a malignant attack of typhoid fever he sank rapidly from the time of his admission into the hospital. He was buried in the graveyard of the Soldiers Home three miles from Washington. Enclosed please find certificate of his death.
>
> Very respectfully
> Your Obedient Servant
> T.S. Mitchell
> surgeon in charge

A. SIMSON,   456 Main St.,   Buffalo, N. Y.

Mary Sullivan's pension agent Samuel Lake

November 1863
The Buffalo Asylum

A traumatized James Sullivan turned and looked disbelieving as his mother walked away. The matron, Superintendent Hopkins, dragged the ten-year-old from the vestibule toward the frightening stairway that led upwards into darkness. She carried three year old John in her arms. The baby screamed and cried and extended his pleading arms out as far as he was able, desperately attempting to grasp onto empty space with his tiny hands, imploring his mother to come back for him.

Mary only looked back once, horrified at what she was forced to do. She was extremely thin and persistently hungry. Placing her children in the orphan asylum was the only way she knew to save them.

Her visits to the office of Samuel Lake and his endless chain of letters to the government brought nothing but frustration and hopelessness to both Mary and her enduring advocate.

That John Sullivan had left his wife and two small children behind to join the Union Army as a volunteer at the very beginning of the war should count for something, Sam Lake said to himself as he buried his head in his wrinkled hands. Mary's papers were laid out in front of him. He felt responsible, even though he had never encountered a case as intransigent as hers. The process had been dragging on for almost a year, plummeting the family into desperation.

When Mary wed her husband it seems the priest had never gotten around to binding the documentation of their marriage into any kind of formal ledger as would be necessary to preserve such records. The loose pages that held years of histories of this priest's ceremonies—the baptisms, marriages and funerals he presided over— had been carelessly tucked away, or perhaps even thrown away. After the priest left St. Mary's Church in Amsterdam for his next assignment elsewhere, these records were nowhere to be found.

Mary could not recall the priest's name. She wrote to her brother James McGrady in Amsterdam for help in remembering, but learned from his wife Margaret that he was gone. He had been drafted into the Union Army. Margaret sent Mary her brother's mailing address, but more than a month went by before she received an answer from the embattled soldier.

Mary had to ask her dead husband's literate friend, First Ward Alderman John Hanavan, to write her letters for her. Her sister-in-law Margaret McGrady was in the same predicament as Mary, married to a man who was off fighting the war with small children of her own to be fed and cared for, despite their having precious little on which to subsist. Margaret was overwhelmed enough by her own situation. She didn't welcome being further terrified by the news that Mary Sullivan had been forced to place her babies in an orphan asylum as her only means to ensure their survival. She harbored deep fears that she herself might be compelled to do much the same.

Margaret put down Mary's disturbing letter and tried to distract herself with a days-old discarded copy of the Amsterdam Recorder. But its news was grim. The newspaper echoed everyone's suffering by publishing the fearful figures showing that the cost of living had risen past 100% from the beginning of the war in 1861 until the present autumn of 1863. Sugar went from 9 cents to 16 cents. Coffee from 22 to 40 cents. Butter, ham, pork, flour, coal, firewood, lamp oil and cloth had more than doubled. Potatoes and eggs were three times as expensive in 1863 than at the beginning of 1861.

James McGrady's response finally reached Mary, and he did indeed recall the name of the priest who officiated at his sister's wedding. It was Father William McCallion. He asked his sister why she had not thought to write directly to St. Mary's church to ask. Mary was crestfallen as Hanavan read aloud her brother's question. Of course! How could she have not thought of that weeks ago? She was so suffocated by her own struggles that even the most obvious solutions seemed to be hidden from her these days, obscured by her panic and depression.

Alderman Hanavan helped Mary compose a letter to send to St. Mary's church in Amsterdam, imploring the recipient to please and quickly provide proof of her marriage so that she might begin to receive her widow's pension.

Two weeks passed before a response arrived saying that no marriage register existed for the period 1844-1855. There were no records at all for the events of this period, neither for baptisms nor marriages. The priest wrote that he had notified Father McCallion, now assigned to a church in Camillus N.Y., and as soon as McCallion responded, he would write to Mary again.

Father McCallion responded to the priest at St. Mary's telling him that he had mislaid the pages from those early years before he could get around to having them bound into a book.

More critical time passed before Hanavan read this revelation from the priest's letter to Mary, and Mary, extremely upset, set out to visit Samuel Lake's office yet again. Samuel had now assumed legal guardianship over Mary Sullivan's children, for she confided in him that she feared she might not live through this endless ordeal. Samuel Lake wrote to the priest at St. Mary's admonishing him for not understanding the severity of the situation.

"Why didn't you simply get a notarized statement from Father McCallion that he had married John and Mary Sullivan? Don't you realize how dire her children's circumstances are?"

Lake proceeded to light a fire under the scatterbrained cleric to force a conclusion before any further tragedy could occur. He took advantage of his resources to track down the negligent McCallion on his own. He composed a directive in the harshest language compelling the priest to produce the documentation without any further delay under severe penalty of wartime law, despite there being no such law. He feared for Mary's sanity, so traumatized was she. Samuel Lake contacted the telegraph office and sent his urgent message to Camillus.

Within a week a sworn statement arrived from Father McCallion, notarized on November 20, 1863, by Onondaga County Justice of the Peace Sidney H. Cook. Fourteen difficult months had now passed since John Sullivan had died with no relief yet for his wife and children. Along with the latest documentation from the priests who had baptized her sons James and John, and a sworn statement from the boys' godparents, Samuel Lake was finally satisfied that a widow's pension payment was mere weeks away. He sent the documentation off to Washington.

He comforted Mary.

"You'll have your boys back soon, Mary. Before Christmas."

Orphaned

Jim Sullivan stood unfathoming as his baby brother was removed to the nursery wing of the imposing orphanage. He was told the two would not be allowed to be together. Children were segregated by age with no regard given to what emotional consequences might be caused by such familial estrangement. Separating siblings was routine, carried out in the name of institutional efficiency.

Every face he saw wore a frown, whether inmates or staff.

Jim was infuriated at their being referred to as orphans by the matrons, despite the women knowing full well that their situation was temporary. They had a mother, so how could he and John be orphans?

The matrons for their part had seen too many other cases like the Sullivans to extend them any hope. Few children, once left there by their families, were ever reclaimed.

As a hesitant Jim was led into the dormitory, he immediately took notice that there was a troubling differential in ages among the boys. Those assigned here ranged in age from eight to fourteen, with some of the older boys already challenging him with their ominous gazes. The matrons were not parents. They did not care about these misfits nor were they concerned about the sadistic bullying of the frightened younger boys by the older. Indeed, they looked upon most of their charges as impositions—castaways, ruffians, and trash, unworthy of basic tenderness, much less actual love. As if it were some failing of their own that caused their ending up here.

Strict discipline was demanded if only to make the lives of the overtaxed staff less arduous. The boys were not spoken to, they were yelled at. They weren't requested, they were ordered. No staff member ever uttered the words "please" or "thank you" in their dealings with the boys.

Jim was shown to his cot. It was a spare, narrow metal bedstead. Its linens were spotted with antique stains that refused to come out in the wash, linens that barely covered a mattress bearing years of witness to anguished boys' bed wetting. He had a tiny cupboard for his few possessions, with no lock to protect the contents. As he placed his marbles, handkerchief and his father's cap inside, the boy in the next bed warned, "That'll all be gone by mornin' if you leave it in there." So that night he slept with his treasures under the pillow, and his father's cap tucked snugly between his bony knees. He slept on his side. His knees ached at night when they touched, so thin was he. His father's cap provided a physical cushion and emotional consolation.

The orphans took meals in a large room furnished with long communal tables set with donated castoffs, chipped plates and cracked bowls and bent flatware on the bare wood. They were instructed to eat in silence. James could see his little brother John on the far side of the space, crying and frightened. He attempted to run to him, but was severely reprimanded and yanked roughly back. "You can visit your brother on Sunday when your mother comes to call," the matron snarled.

A much older orphaned boy sitting next to Jim at the table took great offense at overhearing the fact that Jim Sullivan had a mother. One who cared enough to visit him. This made him angry. As Jim reached for a piece of bread, the boy plunged his fork deep into the back of James' hand. A crimson flood poured forth to accompany Jim's useless scream. A matron rushed over to him in anger rather than concern. Surveying the scene, she wrapped his hand in a napkin and dragged him away brusquely by the arm, as if it were he who had done wrong.

His hand was bandaged. It was severely swollen and he was not able flex it. A bone was broken, but that detail was not of any particular consequence to anyone in charge. The matron who provided nursing care patched him up as she lectured the little newcomer on his manners. Then she sent him along with another matron to his little iron bed with the piss-stained mattress.

"I'm hungry," he implored.

"You'll be gettin' nothin' lad, not til ye learn to behave yerself!"

Later, as he lay in his bed, the other boys were filed into the dormitory by their escort to prepare for sleep. His attacker looked at him and laughed. He himself had suffered no punishment. Clearly he was sated with a full stomach.

It had been a terrible beginning.

Many weeks and too-few allowed visits later, Mary steeled herself at the orphanage doors for what was to come. She was still shaken by her discovery of Jim's injury, the details about which her son refused to elaborate. The matron dismissed his wound as the result of a simple squabble between boys.

It was Christmas Eve, and she had been offered an opportunity to work for a few pennies on Christmas Day. This meant she would not be able to see her sons at all on the holy day itself, only for an hour this afternoon. Samuel Lake had arranged with some difficulty for this special visiting privilege .

John Sullivan's old friend James Stanton accompanied the widow to the Hamburgh Street property out of concern for her safety, for it was increasingly a neighborhood of impoverished roughs. Mary had no money for Christmas presents, but Mr. Lake and his wife had prepared gift bags for the boys with candies. The rules of the orphanage were unchangeable, even for the esteemed Lakes, or so it was claimed. In order to avoid conflict and prevent discipline problems, it was policy that residents of the orphanages, whether they had families or not, were not allowed to accept any gifts besides those few items approved by the facility. Additionally, Mary was not allowed to take her children outdoors, or bring them home for a visit.

Until she was able to prove that she could care for them responsibly, her sons had to adhere to the rules like all the others.

As James Stanton waited patiently out front in the cold, Mary was escorted inside.

Superintendent Hopkins said, "I don't want you to be upset, Mrs. Sullivan, but young John fell out of bed recently and broke his collar bone. He's being attended to here in the asylum hospital."

Mary was shocked.

"When did this happen?!" she blurted.

"Oh, three or four days ago," Superintendent Hopkins smiled casually.

"Why wasn't I notified about this? Me boy broke a bone and ye don't bother to send someone to tell me? A patrolman, by chance?"

"Now, Mrs. Sullivan, what good would it have done for you to know?"

"What good?! I am his mother, and me boy must have been very frightened. I am angry that ye didn't think I had a right to know me own son was hurt!"

"Little Johnny is fine," placated the witch, "and he is in no danger. You would have worried for nothing. Here. I'll take you to see him."

Mary fumed as she was escorted into the hospital dormitory, a single room with ten beds. Little John was in the bed closest to the doorway, and as soon as she spotted her youngest she virtually flew to him. The boy appeared dazed, as if he didn't quite recognize his own mother. Mary sat on the bed and embraced him gently. His arm was in a sling.

"There's nothing wrong with his arm, Mrs. Sullivan, but in order for the collar bone to heal properly, the arm must remain secured in place. He's doing just fine."

Soon enough the three year old snapped out of his fog and began to cry, grasping at his mother's clothes as if trying to crawl inside them with her. Mary disintegrated at witnessing his primal desperation. She held her injured son as tightly as she thought safe to do so and tried to disguise her upset. She sat and rocked him until his sobs faded. Mary was thoroughly disconcerted by the unexpected revelation of his injury.

"Mama, can I go home with you now?" her child beseeched.

The experience tore at Mary Sullivan's heart. She suddenly suffered an acute flash of panic about Jim.

"Where's Jim? Where's my other boy?"

"He's waiting downstairs," stated the superintendent in her most calming official tone. "Children are not allowed in the hospital ward unless they are ill, to prevent the spread of illness. We're experiencing a plague of measles at the moment."

Mary hadn't even noticed the red spots on John's face, so thrown was she by the other circumstances.

"But my Jim has already had the measles. I want him here with us, so we can all be together!"

"I'm afraid that's against the rules Mrs. Sullivan. No children are allowed in the hospital wing unless admitted for an illness or injury."

Mary felt rage welling up from deep within. She had been holding this tidal wave back for what now seemed like forever, unable to allow herself to break down or fully acknowledge the torrent of misfortune and cruelty that life continued to heap upon her. She thought, What did I ever do to God, or anyone, to deserve such suffering? Why is He punishing me and my babies so?

"John, listen," she said to the whimpering boy. "I am going to go downstairs to see yer brother. He can't come up here because they don't want the other children to bring in any more illness than what's been already tormentin' ye."

John was protesting and clinging. "Mama, don't leave me!"

"John, look at me. I promise, I will come right back in a wee bit and see ye some more. I am just going downstairs to visit yer brother, and I will come right back. I promise."

John could not be placated, but Mary left his side regardless, anxious to scrutinize the welfare of her oldest. She would not be gone long. She had been given ninety minutes to visit with her children. Mary stood at the door and blew kisses at the inconsolable baby, promising to reappear in just a few minutes. Then she walked anxiously down the steps.

Mary was led to a small room where there were four straight-backed wooden chairs and a small table, to wait. A window looked out onto Hamburgh Street. In the front window of the house across the street a family was lighting the candles on their Christmas tree. Mary wanted to cry.

The door opened and her ten year old was brought in, the door then shut to provide them privacy. Mary was overjoyed and ran to him. Jim stood motionless just looking at her. He had counted the days and hours until this moment, but all he felt now was anger and betrayal.

"How could you put us here, Ma? How could you just get rid of us? We're not orphans! They won't even let me see my own brother! This is a prison! I hate you!" he shouted.

Then more quietly, "I hate you."

Mary sat and reached out and took hold of Jim's leg to gently pull him toward her.

He yelped.

"Jimmy, what's the matter with yer leg?"

"Nothin'. Nothin's wrong. Me and John just want to go home! Take us home!" he cried.

Mary quickly grabbed her chair by its back and lodged it under the doorknob to prevent any of the staff, especially Hopkins, who she knew were hovering just outside, from entering. A split second after she fixed the chair in place, there was an attempt to open the door.

"Mrs. Sullivan! What is going on in there?"

"Please. I am handlin' me children, Mrs. Hopkins. Go away and let me be!"

"Open the door Mrs. Sullivan, right now! We have rules of conduct here that must be obeyed."

Mary stooped down to her son's level as Superintendent Hopkins attempted to force the door.

"Mrs. Sullivan!"

Mary ignored her.

"Yer mother's goin' to have a look at yer leg, Jimmy." She took her son's face in her hands and forced him to look her in the eye.

"Look at me. Look. I love ye, Jimmy. Let me see."

"Mrs. Sullivan! Open this door right now!" insisted the angry voice on the other side of the portal.

Jim hung his head, as if ashamed. Mary undid his pants. They dropped to the floor.

The breath was knocked out of her.

She gasped and covered her mouth with her hand. Tears welled up. Jim's legs were covered in welts and bruises, including his bony kneecaps.

"Mrs. Hopkins, I'll be handlin' me own child if ye don't mind! Ye go away now and allow me to calm him down."

"Open this door right now, Mrs. Sullivan or I will get a patrolman in here!"

What appeared to be lash marks, both old and new, wrapped around both of Jim's sorrowfully thin legs, and as he was examined by his mother, he began to cry, then collapsed into her arms. Mary was devastated. She had placed her children here to provide them a safe haven, protection from those who might want to hurt or endanger them.

"Yes, Mrs. Hopkins!" Mary shouted. "Ye do that. Ye go and fetch yerself a patrolman, and while yer at it, get one fer me too!"

Mary comforted Jim as the shadow of Mrs. Hopkins ran by the window, right past the concerned James Stanton, who was suddenly alarmed that something might be wrong inside. Soon the superintendent returned with two patrolmen. They flew by James Stanton and into the institution.

There was a knock on the door, and Deputy Sheriffs Darcy and Sullivan asked Mary to be allowed in.

"No! They have beaten my child! He's covered in bruises! I am afraid of that woman."

Mary was not afraid. In truth she was plotting to strangle Hopkins. But she knew that given her diminished position in society, that the superintendent would have the upper hand. She needed to make it clear what her grievance was before she would open the door.

"Let us see the boy, ma'am."

"I will let ye see him, deputy, but that woman cannot come in here with ye."

Mrs. Hopkins was beside herself at hearing this challenge to her authority, and began shouting at Mary and the sheriffs. The patrolmen deduced from the superintendent's behavior that it would be best if the unruly Mrs. Hopkins were not allowed into the room.

"We're sending her away now, Missis."

The sheriffs lowered their voices and asked Hopkins to wait down the hall. She refused.

"I am in the official in charge at this institution!" challenged Hopkins.

"She has beaten me baby to a pulp!" Mary shouted. "Get her away from here!"

She was not about to allow this monster control over such a dire situation.

"Mrs. Hopkins, you will go to your office and wait for us there or else we will arrest you!" Deputy Darcy commanded.

Superintendent Hopkins huffed and marched noisily away.

"She's gone. It's just us here now," said Darcy. "Please open the door."

Mary held her son in front of her, just in case the police might rush toward her or were trying to trap her. But when she opened the door, they stood calmly in place, taking no action to seize her, nor to enter the little room.

"Look at me son's legs!" she cried. "Look what that woman done to him!"

Jim was embarrassed and frightened, his trousers still around his ankles. The sheriffs stooped down to have a look, one at the front and one at the back. The evidence was undeniable, and brought to Darcy's mind the endless beatings he had endured at the hands of his mother's common-law husband when he was a boy.

"I want that woman arrested and my children taken someplace safe!"

"What is your name, ma'am?" asked deputy sheriff Sullivan.

"Mary Sullivan."

"You're the Widow Sullivan, whose husband was killed in the war?"

"Yes."

"I don't believe we're related, yer husband and me, Mrs. Sullivan, but I am Deputy Sheriff Sullivan, and I'm very sorry to hear about yer husband."

Mary nodded acceptance of his condolences.

"We'll be takin' you and the boy down to the Police Court now, so ye can make yer complaint official.

"I need to see my other baby first! He's in the hospital ward. I promised him I'd come back."

"You can come back later, ma'am. But it's Christmas Eve and the Court will be closin' soon. We'll accompany you back here ourselves after you've made your statement to the Justice."

Deputy Sullivan was dispatched to check on Mary's youngest. Baby John was already fast asleep, hugging a rag doll puppy.

Darcy had Mary and Jim wait in the vestibule as he commanded the fuming Mrs. Hopkins to fetch Jim's coat, scarf and gloves. He helped bundle Jim up and escorted mother and son outside to the patrol wagon. James Stanton was unnerved to see Mary emerge with Jim and the two deputies so upset. She introduced him to the officers, and asked them if he could come to the Police Court with her as a witness. It was just 4 o'clock and already getting dark. The two wagons headed up Elk Street toward Lafayette Square.

At the Police Court, the usual newspapermen were present, as a good portion of the city's newspapers' popular salacious content was generated by the goings-on there. Mary showed her son's many bruises to the newsmen as she waited her turn to make her case. When called, she repeated the demonstration to Justice Marshall and two interested officers. All agreed that Jim Sullivan had been severely beaten about the legs, which were well marked and discolored from the effects of the blows.

Jim had told his mother the story on their drive to the Court.

"This crime was committed," Mary said, "by the Buffalo Orphan Asylum superintendent because me son refused to tell on another boy who stole a dollar from someone at the institute. Me young Jim had but two choices, yer Honor: get beaten by the thief if he snitched on 'im, or get beaten by the superintendent fer not snitchin' on 'im. That was really no choice at all fer a frightened child, now was it? It was the superintendent's job to protect my son from that boy who stole the money, but instead she used me son to try to get him to identify the thief. And now she wants to say that he is a conspirator in helping the thief evade punishment! Me son is only ten years old and that other boy is fourteen. He's twice Jim's size! Me boy was only trying to keep himself safe! I am requesting that you issue a warrant for the arrest of Superintendent Hopkins."

Mary Sullivan's word was followed and a warrant issued. It was turned over to Detective Mike Reilly. James Stanton vouched for Mary to the Court, and requested that she be allowed to bring her son to his own family's home to spend the night with them and have the boy attended by a physician. The Justice agreed. After all, it was Christmas Eve. Mary grieved and worried about baby John back at the Asylum. What would he think when he realized she'd broken her promise to come right back?

"We'll go back and look in on him, Mrs. Sullivan." said Darcy. "It's late and I'm sure being sick with the measles and all that he'll be sound asleep by now. Don't worry. You take your son Jim and do what you need to. We'll look in on Johnny and check his injury for any sign of mistreatment. I promise you, we'll look after him," said Darcy earnestly. "And if we find anything suspicious, we will come to Mr. Stanton's home to tell you immediately."

Inadvertently that night, Jim Sullivan found his fondest Christmas wish coming true; he was spending the holiday with his mother and with old and trusted friends. Jim was thrilled to see the welcoming face of Stanton's son Ed, and Mary was made to feel most welcome by James Stanton's second wife, Catherine, despite her knowing Mary's affections for her husband.

Stanton took Mary aside while the boys were preoccupied.

"Mary, your Jim came here to the house the other day. He ran away from the asylum."

Mary looked at her trusted friend in disbelief.

"He thought he was in trouble and that they were going to punish him, so he came here. We had a long talk with him, and told him he'd have to go back. So I took him. The superintendent made me believe she would not allow him to return unless he received punishment for running away. I never thought for a second that the punishment would be of such a severe nature, Mary. I swear. I am truly sorry."

Mary looked out the window, considering the layers of complications that were smothering her life.

"Why did he run away, James?" she asked quietly.

"Jim said that an older boy had been a bully to him and that the matron would not prevent it. He was afraid, and miserable. Mary, we'd take him if we could, but we are sufferin' ourselves. I can't even buy proper shoes for young Ed. I'm sorry."

Mary looked tenderly in James Stanton's eyes.

"James, yer a good man. A fine man. Catherine is lucky to have found ye."

The Stantons had little money, and no Christmas tree, but it didn't matter. Candles were placed in their window with a sprig of evergreen tied with a red bow decorating the candlestick, and carolers sung their way up and down the streets of the First Ward to provide sounds of Christmas cheer for the depressed neighborhood. With the cost of everything so dear because of the war, it was the poorest Christmas anyone could ever remember since leaving Ireland.

Catherine roasted a wonderful Christmas ham, gifted by Mr. David Clark to each of his ice company workers, and baked yams and apples with honey. She had made shortbread too, and there was sherry enough for the special occasion. Mary especially welcomed the drink. Because it was not in plentiful supply, the Stantons sipped theirs slowly so that Mary could partake sufficiently, for her nerves needed it. The sherry did its good work, and between its soothing effects and the joy at spending Christmas Eve with her oldest son, Mary allowed herself to appreciate what little she did have right then and there at that moment.

The adults clinked their glasses together, and all wished each other Merry Christmas in unison.

The following morning Mary visited the precinct house and Deputy Darcy drove her to the orphan asylum. No one interfered as Mary was led upstairs to visit her three year old. She damned the orphan asylum rules and brought him a ham sandwich, shortcake and candies. No one dared challenge her, especially with the deputy present. They played games with him and Mary soothed her boy with promises she wasn't sure she could keep.

"Missis, we have to be going now" said Darcy. And with great sadness and regret, Mary pulled away from her bawling toddler.

"I'll be havin' ye and your brother back home as soon as I can now, Johnny. I swear to ye!"

Deputy Darcy brought Mary back to the columned courthouse. She thanked him sincerely as she alighted from the patrol wagon. Surely a man that good must be married, she thought to herself.

"Merry Christmas, Mr. Darcy." she said sincerely.

Ironically, the Christmas Day job she had been offered was giving the courthouse a thorough scrubbing while its doors were closed for the holiday.

December 26, 1863
Boxing Day

Superintendent Hopkins appeared in the Police Court the morning after Christmas at the side of an attorney named Boswell who sat on the board of directors at the Buffalo Orphan Asylum. Mary was being outmaneuvered.

Mary spoke first, denouncing the harsh methods in vogue in the institution and demanding an investigation of the conditions there. This was followed by an impassioned plea from James Stanton for justice.

Mrs. Hopkins and her assistants maintained that Mary Sullivan and James Stanton's claims were exaggerated, that they were incensed that such charges were allowed to be lodged against their good names. Hopkins stated she had cared for thousands of orphans over the years, and she had never before been accused of cruelty. Immediately after this defense she freely admitted that she had whipped Jim Sullivan. She dismissed it as merely a matter of discipline, brought about by Jim's confession that he was complicit in the theft of the money.

Jim shouted, "Mama! I never confessed any such thing!"

Hopkins made clear her position that there was nothing at all cruel or abusive about her whipping a small child. Superintendent Hopkins made her statement to Justice Murray.

"A women who is employed in the asylum building came to me and said that a dollar had been stolen from her room. I suspected that her own boy who also lives here had taken the money, for the boy had been dishonest before. When the child was questioned the next morning, he admitted the theft and said that Jim Sullivan had stood guard for him outside the door. The children had spent a few cents of the dollar that morning, and Jim Sullivan, discovering that I had this knowledge, ran away to the home of Mr. Stanton. Mr. Stanton brought him back to the institution and wanted to know if we would take Jim back. I said we could not, unless he was punished, as all the other children knew of his connection with the theft and they could not be allowed to see such behavior go unheeded. Mr. Stanton agreed to leave Jim under those conditions."

Stanton interrupted. "I never dreamed for a second that her brand of punishment would be a severe beating in front of all the other children! That woman is a criminal!"

Justice Murray banged his gavel. "Here, here, now, Mr. Stanton, settle down."

Superintendent Hopkins continued.

"On the following evening, in front of all the other children, I whipped Jim and the little boy who had stolen the money. "

Mrs. Hopkins said that punishment in the asylum had always been a whipping with a small whip.

"I believe and always have believed this method to be the best in disciplining children," said she. "I have never allowed a child to be struck about the head or face by anyone. When they are chastised, it is about the legs, where no serious injury can possibly result."

James Stanton thereupon rolled up Jim's trousers and showed the Court that even Jim's little kneecaps were still swollen. The pain was causing him to walk precariously. Superintendent Hopkins claimed in mock indignation that such injuries could not possibly have been due to the whipping that she had administered. She insisted Jim had injured himself in some other way.

"I presume that the whip may have left black and blue marks on the little boy," said she, "for a child's skin is very sensitive. I understand that someone claims there has been discrimination against this child. Such a statement is utterly ridiculous. Jim has always been a favorite of mine! Why, we called him Little Blue Eyes, and treated him implicitly! His chastisement was simply a matter of commonplace discipline."

"Ye broke the little baby's arm as well!" screamed the enraged James Stanton. " He's in your hospital at this moment! What kind of animals are you anyway!?"

Hopkins was outraged at being called an animal in public court.

"That baby fell out of his bed while asleep a few nights back and fractured his collar bone. The night watchman heard him crying and upon entering the dormitory found him on the floor crying. He was taken to the asylum hospital, where he is receiving excellent care."

"Three year old boys have bones that bend, your Honor, not break! Ask any qualified physician!" shouted Stanton. "A three year old does not break a collar bone falling out of bed! That child was abused! He's just a three year old baby! I will see you and your fellow hoodlums in prison, Superintendent!"

Justice Marshall was approached by Superintendent Hopkins' attorney, and the two conferred in whispers for quite a while.

"Mrs. Sullivan, because through no fault of your own you are not able to provide even the most basic care for your children, that responsibility you have given over to those at the Buffalo Orphan Asylum. You are a Roman Catholic, are you not?" Marshall asked.

"Yes, sir."

"Why haven't you placed your children in a Catholic institution?"

"Because Mr. Samuel Lake is the guardian of my children, and his wife, Mrs. Lake, is on the board of directors of the Buffalo Orphan Asylum."

For a moment, a dropped pin could have been heard. All present were shocked, convinced until this second that they could sweep Mary Sullivan under the rug.

"Um. And where is Mr. Lake at this time?" asked Justice Marshall.

"I do not know, sir," replied Mary, cooly.

Mary suddenly realized she had more power than she'd realized, as the entire mood of the proceedings had now abruptly changed. Superintendent Hopkins and attorney Boswell looked concerned about this new complication.

"Did you ask Mr. or Mrs. Lake to appear here with you today?"

"No, sir. They know nothing of this."

"And why would the children's own legal guardian not be informed about, or be present in such a matter, might I ask, Mrs. Sullivan?"

Mary enjoyed no longer having to be on the defensive. She took her time, eyeing each of the main culprits before her. She thought for a moment, then stood and faced the Justice.

"Because 'tis Christmas, sir, and because I believe in God, and in the covenant of justice for citizens like me and my boys promised by yerself and by this court. I believed that I could find justice here in this room simply because it is the right thing fer ye to do, without draggin' those fine people down here and spoilin' their Christmas only to be confronted by the likes of a dirty child beater like Mary Louise Hopkins."

Hopkins and her attorney turned as white as the snow that blanketed Lafayette Park across the street. How could it be that neither was aware that these boys were under the guardianship of Samuel Lake? The asylum was the only one in Buffalo in which religion was of no issue, and Hopkins hadn't given enough thought as to why the Catholic boys had not been placed in a Catholic institution. Now it made sense.

Justice Murray, who up until a few seconds ago had been ready to dismiss the case, now seemed perplexed as to what to do.

Hopkins' Attorney Burrows shot up to his feet and said, "We board members of the Buffalo Orphan Asylum have perfect faith in Superintendent Hopkins' judgement and may I just point to her long and efficient service, Justice Murray. She has done no wrong here."

"Well, Mr. Burrows, the evidence and Mrs. Hopkins own admissions seem to support quite the opposite. Mrs. Hopkins, you will be released on your own recognizance until we take this matter up with Mr. and Mrs. Lake, who should certainly have been included in this hearing from the outset. Attorney Burrows, you will be notified when we are ready to proceed."

Mary Sullivan walked out of the courthouse with her son and James Stanton, feeling uplifted. They crossed the street and headed for the benches that ringed the frozen fountain at the center of the little wooded park that was Lafayette Square, piled with fresh snow. The coal soot had not yet sullied the snows' virgin beauty. Stanton brushed a powdery drift off a bench and the three sat for a few moments.

"Thank ye, James. You are a true friend. To me late husband. To me. To the children. If I had been alone here today I don't know what I would have done, or said."

"Mary, I'll always be yer friend, and do my best to look out fer ye and the boys. I wish I could do more. Ye did well in that room. Ye should be proud of yerself. I wish me Catherine possessed yer fightin' spirit," he smiled.

I wish I were yer wife, she thought to herself, silently.

January 1864
Desperate Times Call For Desperate Measures

Mary's demands for justice ultimately went unfulfilled. With much resignation she was forced to acknowledge precious little understanding of the social and political machinations of the world, where alliances among those who held power superseded basic precepts like truth and justice and fairness. Her dire circumstances had sown the seeds for her own defeat.

Samuel Lake made clear his acquiescing to Superintendent Hopkins' authority by not challenging her position at the asylum, only promising to speak to her about her brutish conduct. Mary Sullivan didn't know what to think about him. Perhaps he was just too old and tired to fight. He was in his 75th year and still going to his office every day to attend to his commitments.

As despondent as Mary was over meek Samuel Lake's refusal to stand up for her boys, despite his responsibilities to them as their legal guardian, Lake was also the one and only key to their future survival. Only he could surmount the cruel hurdles that the United States government had placed so mercilessly in her path. She had fearful dreams that old Samuel Lake might die before ever winning her case with the Pension Office. She felt powerless now, hopelessly at the unscrupulous mercy of the cruel fates. She had used up the last shred of hope from her depleted stores.

Mary Sullivan had placed her children in the orphan asylum mistakenly believing they would be safe there while she went about trying to gather her wits, improve her fortunes and provide a home for her children. But with both boys injured after only being installed there but a few months, and the authorities overlooking the gross nature of the circumstances, she knew she had no other choice but to pursue her plan of last resort.

She called on Peter Halloran.

"Yes," she told him, without emotion.

"Yes? Yes, what?" he asked.

"Yes, I will marry you." She managed to eke out a sickly smile from beneath her revulsion.

Peter Halloran said, "Well finally! That is just grand, Mary! Just grand! I promise to provide well for you and the boys Mary. I will."

Peter had found no position for Mary as he had offered. Indeed he never tried. Instead he had hatched a plan. He called on her every Sunday and proposed marriage each time, trying to wear her down. She was horrified. Mary spoke again with Halloran's neighbor Mrs. McRainey, who this time was more forthcoming than she'd been before. She convinced Mary that marrying this Halloran fellow was not an option. Not at all.

"Anybody but him!" cried Mrs. McRainey.

On Saturday afternoon they walked together up Louisiana Street to meet with Father Martin O'Connor and make the arrangements. Then, on Sunday, January 17, after the last mass at St. Bridget's was celebrated, Mary McGrady

Sullivan was wed to Peter Halloran, with the widow's husband's friend John Regan witnessing, along with Father O'Connor's elderly housekeeper, Winifred Wren.

Samuel Lake was crestfallen, sitting across his desk from the new couple, knowing full well the depth and breadth of Mary's impossible choices. With each new blow that life dealt her, she was forced to sink lower and lower into the muck in an effort to save herself and her children. The government still had not paid a penny in pensions to Mary or her children. This hopeless marriage was the end of the line for her, precipitated as it unquestionably was by the orphan asylum debacle.

She compelled herself to marry an individual who repulsed her as well as virtually all who knew him, solely to rescue her children.

Samuel Lake looked down at the papers on his desk. Although almost seventy-six years old, he did not require spectacles for close work. He was not happy about relinquishing his guardianship over the boys. But he was required to arrange for Mary's sons to be returned to her, now that she had a husband and a home.

He was not optimistic.

Peter Halloran boasted of his military service back in the 50s, trying to paint himself as best he could a brave hero in the Indian conflicts. It wasn't all a lie; Halloran's discharge had at least been honorable, but it seemed that his army days were the last honorable thing that the man had ever accomplished, and those days were long gone.

Samuel Lake would continue his fight to gain a pension for John Sullivan's sons, and for his widow, who was owed her benefits up until the date of her remarriage.

In a letter sent to the Pension Office describing the family's tragic circumstances, Samuel Lake wrote of Peter Halloran, "He was one of those, as Napoleon said, was good for nothing but to fill a ditch."

On Christmas Eve 1864, the first that the new family spent together, Mary Sullivan Halloran announced to her new and too often absent husband that she was expecting their baby. She had been working afternoons at the American Hotel again. Peter watched over little John in the saloon while she was at work. The Van Velsors sent a beautiful box of Christmas sweets from their bakery home with her for her family. Their kindness brought tears to her eyes. She wanted to make this holiday a true celebration. She longed to put the past behind her. She was anxious for the war to end. Mary hoped that the wonderful news about the new baby might redirect and refocus Peter's interest away from his saloon, from the lives of the unsavory denizens therein, and from his latest obsession, the Fenians.

After their first few weeks together upon leaving the orphanage, Peter Halloran had made no further attempts to win over Mary's boys. Four year old John, who had no memory of his father, quickly attached himself to his stepfather, but Peter found his infatuation annoying. Worse, Peter was butting heads with the independent Jim, now almost twelve. Jim attended school, had resumed his work as a lamplighter boy, and worked all day Saturday at the Bliss

Photography Gallery across from the American Hotel.

At one time Halloran thought he might like to have a child of his own, but Mary's boys made him realize that he simply didn't care for children.

Jim resented his mother's choice, even though it freed him and his brother from the horror of their months in the orphan asylum. What he wanted most, other than his father coming back to life, was to regain his stature as the man of the family. His common sense told him that this was not to be, but his instinct was to try and reclaim his power nevertheless.

Ruins of the American Hotel after the fire. Van Velsor's Bakery. left, is barricaded, with debris piled up out front.

🍀

April 1865
The Bliss Photographic Gallery

Jim Sullivan was sweeping up the floor of Mr. Bliss' Photographic Gallery & Studio when he heard the grievous news.

President Abraham Lincoln was dead.

He paused and looked out the second story window and down on the slow-walking crowds on Main Street. Many had stopped to gaze toward the spot where, until just three months previous, the balcony of the American Hotel had overlooked Main Street. It was on that very balcony that Abraham Lincoln stood in 1861 to address the citizens of Buffalo on his triumphal train journey to the Inauguration in Washington DC.

The American Hotel had incinerated in a spectacular conflagration on the freezing cold evening of January 25th, just three months prior, stealing his mother's employ along with it. That night the temperature was just eight degrees above zero, and a snowstorm was raging. Gale-force winds spread the flames from Peter Diehl's Eating House where it began to John Van Velsor's Bakery, Griffiths' Provisions, Richard Jenner's Drugs, Shryver's Shoe Store and ultimately to Paul Bouyon's Confectionary. From there it caught the American Hotel, forcing the area's entire population to flee for their lives.

The Michaels' two homes behind the American Hotel were destroyed, as well as all the ground floor businesses in the hotel building: three dry and fancy goods stores that served the moneyed hotel clientele and the elegant Charles Barthauer barber shop.

The fire then continued on its rampage to Horace Bliss' main competitor, Upson Photographic Galleries, then to Knight Liquors, Volger's Fancy Goods, Bullymore's Dining Saloon, Ransom Hatters, Gage Grocers, the Jewish Tabernacle and the Buffalo Savings Bank. The American Hall Building was also destroyed in its entirety.

Weather conditions made it almost impossible for the fire department to work their engines. The steamers barely operated because they had become encased in a thick shell of impenetrable ice. The firemen, after many hours of numbing battle and great loss of property, were forced to resort to blowing up the historic Eagle Hotel and the Old Eagle Tavern in order to stop the rampaging blaze's progress.

Courageous firefighters from all the houses in the city battled the conflagration, but none took it worse than the Taylor Hose Company. Three of their men were killed under the collapsing American Hotel's walls: George Harrison Tifft, age 25; James H. Sidway, age 25; and William Henry Gillett, age 21, all members of Buffalo's First Families. Horror and gloom slashed at the heart of the entire community as the news of their deaths flew through the city more swiftly than did the holocaust that the heroes died battling.

These men were deeply beloved.

Mary Halloran could not believe the news when she heard, and despite being very pregnant, she hurried her sons down to survey the awful damage. Gone was the hotel that had employed her and provided her with some cherished memories. Gone were the Michael family homes, and Mrs. Sherman's luxurious suite that had accommodated the nation's First Family. And Van Velsor's Bakery! All the lovely gifts of food they had given her when she was struggling to feed her children. A barricade had been hastily erected in front of Van Velsor's and the neighboring shops to keep away looters and errant pedestrians, while the burned and soaked debris from the mortally damaged bakery, the grocers and other businesses lay piled up on the sidewalk in front as waste.

John Van Velsor had awakened with a start hundreds of times during his career as a baker and volunteer fireman, dreaming each time that his house was on fire. Nightly he lit the oven that baked his breads and pies, and every day he worried a bit about an accident, or a lapse of attention that might lead to a blaze.

Once again, on the evening of January 25th, as he slept in preparation to arise at midnight to fire up the ovens and begin his workday, he awoke with a start. He thought little of it, until he smelled the smoke. He ran from the upstairs bedroom, calling for Barbara, his wife, but she did not respond. He then remembered she had gone out to the theater with her sister.

Smoke was thickening the air inside the Van Velsor's flat with each passing second. Van Velsor heard screams ricocheting up and down Main Street from all directions. There was a closed door at the top of the rear staircase, installed by Van Velsor to keep the oven's heat from rising into the family's living quarters during the sultry summer months, and as he touched the brass door knob to escape, his skin sizzled. He realized the flames were eating at the other side of the portal. He ran back down the hallway past the bedroom and into the parlor where the windows looked out over Main Street. There he witnessed bedlam.

Still in his night shirt, he grabbed his overcoat and brogues, put the shoes on, opened the window and began gagging. The bitter cold winds from the lake were driving the smoke toward the front of the building and curling it over the roof where the choking toxins found an expedient route into the house with his opening of the window.

John Van Velsor knew he had to either jump, or suffocate thinking about it. He climbed out onto the sill, his feet resting on the little ledge at the base of the Van Velsor Bakery sign, and without any further consideration, dropped to the sidewalk with a thud. It was a painful landing, and instantly he collapsed as his ankles buckled.

Onlookers rushed to him, and with a man propping him under each armpit, they lifted and dragged him to relative safety across Main Street.

Young Jim Sullivan snapped out of his daydream about the Great American Hotel fire and gazed down from Mr. Bliss' gallery windows onto the bustling pavers alive with the clopping of horse hooves. He discerned the exact spot where he had been excitedly hoisted upon his father's shoulders to get a once-in-a-lifetime view of America's Greatest President since George Washington himself.

He stood there stilled, remembering the day.

"Hurry, Jim," commanded boss Horace L. Bliss, the proprietor. Mr. Bliss was the foremost photographer in the city, making likenesses for people in almost every station in life, as well as photographs for many businesses, including ladies' fashion.

The wall of the stairwell ascending to the studio from the street level was adorned with wonderful enlarged albumen portraits and smaller cabinet cards of city dignitaries and local landmarks, as well as earlier daguerreotypes in lovely gilded cases picturing beautiful society ladies and scenes at Niagara Falls. He often stopped on his way up the stairs to gaze especially at a perfectly groomed and beautifully dressed woman in an oval frame, who bore a striking resemblance his mother. The enlarged photograph was a copy of an 1850 daguerreotype Bliss had taken back in his first days as a working photographer, his boss explained. The lady caressed what appeared to be a riding crop in her lap, but he couldn't be sure. Mr. Bliss had signed it in pencil. She looked like a kind person, Jim thought. Just like his mother.

The studio boasted a variety of painted backdrops in front of which the subject could be posed, seated upon one's choice of elegant chairs and settees, leaning on a lectern or column, or just standing for a full length portrait. Women in fine dresses with hoop skirts preferred the standing pose, as it exhibited their finery to its fullest effect, and since the camera had to be placed farther away to include their entire form, it also diminished the capture of facial wrinkles, and minimized disfigurements.

Mr. Bliss' seven-year-old son Frank was shooed away from the unwieldy tripod-mounted oak-encased camera by his father. Horace Bliss had every intention of mentoring his son when he became old enough to be trustworthy around the very expensive and heavy camera apparatus. But for now, little Frank occupied himself with a toy fire steamer. He proclaimed his intention of becoming a volunteer fireman one day, just like Mr. Van Velsor the baker, who after the fire was forced to relocate from his historic place across the street.

Jim Sullivan was grieved at the news of the President's death. His late father had joined the Union Army after being inspired by Mr. Lincoln's Buffalo visits to the city, and now the president too was dead. Jim felt a peculiar emptiness. He recalled the wild night he and his father ventured out to see Lincoln at The Terrace amid the thousands of burning torches held aloft by the long-ago disbanded Wide Awakes. Jim stopped sweeping and removed his calloused hand from the broom to ponder how that very same hand had once grasped Mr. Lincoln's.

"James, stop daydreaming, boy! There is work to be done! The alderman is on his way!"

"Yes, Mr. Bliss. Sorry, sir," replied Jim.

Alderman Fitzgerald, the newly elected representative of the First Ward, had an appointment to have his likeness made that afternoon. During his visit to the Studio the previous week, Jim had observed Mr. Bliss trying to talk Mr. Fitzgerald out of his plan to choose the painted backdrop of a forest glen, in favor of a plain background.

"Alderman Fitzgerald, we want people to focus on your face and your elegant suit, not the details in the backdrop. It is customary to have a plain background for portraits of dignitaries of your stature."

Fitzgerald's suit on that day was a little outre, as the French might say. It had broad vertical stripes, while his tie sported horizontal stripes. His stovepipe silk hat towered higher than any that Horace Bliss had ever seen. "It was thoroughly undignified," Mr. Bliss later told his wife in Jim's presence. He had suggested a plain dark suit and plain tie to Fitzgerald, "so as not to distract attention away from his classic features."

"Classic features, you say?" his wife laughed. "Is that what they're calling alcohol-inflamed noses these days?"

Up the stairs bounded Mr. Griffith. He had owned the grocers across Main Street. Very poorly insured, his business was ruined in the fire and he had not yet been able to rebuild.

"Did you hear the rumor, Horace?"

"What rumor Mr. Griffith?"

"The rumor that the President's body will pass through Buffalo on its way to his burial in Springfield!"

"And how in tarnation would you ever know such a thing? The man isn't even cold yet!"

"Alderman Fitzgerald was just telling people down on the street."

At that moment the heavy footfalls of the rotund Mr. Fitzgerald could be heard stomping upward from the bottom of the stairwell.

"I must get back to my errands," said Griffith, and with that he scurried down the steps past the wheezing Alderman.

Six months prior, Jim Sullivan's mother Mary had arranged for her oldest son to meet Mr. Bliss during the time she was still employed at the American Hotel. She had looked up and saw his placard from across the street as she exited Van Velsor's bakery just as he was placing it in the gallery window. She ran across the busy thoroughfare immediately to inquire, only to be nearly stampeded by a horse-drawn trolley. The sign read, Boy Wanted. Hard Worker. She climbed the stairs to the Bliss Gallery.

"Me son Jim is a very bright, dependable boy, Mr. Bliss." Mary enthused. "I am sure you will find him to be the kind of hard worker you had in mind. He has had to grow up quickly and become the man of the family ever since his father died in the war, and I can depend on him completely. He is quite mature for his age and he will not disappoint you."

Mr. Bliss agreed to meet Jim, and was in fact impressed with the boy's maturity and responsibility. Since then, Jim's small wage had been a great help to his mother, for it was revealed soon after their marriage that Peter Halloran had far less income than he'd boasted. It had also been revealed to Jim by his school friends that his mother's new husband had spent time in prison, but he was afraid to ask her about it, wondering if perhaps even she herself didn't know.

Mary Halloran certainly didn't love her new husband. But the union relieved the unrelenting exhaustion brought by the monumental struggles following John Sullivan's tragic death in the war. She had believed the marriage would be her family's salvation, never dreaming it might just as easily be the instrument of their doom.

Jim's position in the household had been usurped. His mother had taken him aside and explained it all to him. She told her son in the most tender way she could manage how much she loved him. How he had been her rock in the awful years after his father went off to war. But now the family had the chance for a new life and a new start, where finding enough money to eat and clothe themselves would no longer require their complete preoccupation.

The exchange was that Peter Halloran would now be the man of the family.

"Jimmy, I know ye might have a difficult time getting used to that."

Mary didn't know the half of it.

❧❦

April 1865
Lincoln's Funeral

A short few days after the news of Abraham Lincoln's death, plans were completed for his final visit to the city. There would be a great public funeral where the entire citizenry could gather to honor and view their beloved President as he lay in state.

"Mr. Bliss, might I have the morning off tomorrow to go to the station to witness the arrival of the President's funeral train?" Jim asked. It was to be an official day of mourning in the city, with most businesses closed.

"I think I have a better idea for you, James," he replied. "We have an exceptional view of the funeral procession route from up here in the gallery as it heads down Main Street. I plan to photograph the procession from the window. Why don't you come here instead, where you will be safe from the mob, and might actually be able to see something? I don't think that a small boy in such a crowd would be able to witness very much at the depot. And do you recall those frightening stories of what went on at the station, the last time Lincoln arrived there?"

Jim was quite excited about this invitation and thanked Mr. Bliss. He had always wanted to work the mammoth camera, and was only awaiting an opportunity to ask. But he had yet to be allowed to even touch it. He would observe Mr. Bliss at work tomorrow and learn how one might go about capturing a momentous event like the one about to occur.

"Let's go downstairs and talk to Mr. Woodward about taking down that awning of his, lad!"

As seen from their window perch, the awning directly below that shaded Mr. Woodward's shop from the afternoon sun fully blocked out a third of the view of the street. Mr. Bliss diplomatically approached the proprietor beneath his studio and asked if he could remove the canvas from the awning frame so as to have an unobstructed line of sight for his photographs of the funeral. Mr. Bliss had taken portraits of the entire Woodward clan at a reduced rate, so he did not expect the shopkeeper to object.

"Just as long as your boy puts it right back in place after the funeral, Mr. Bliss," smiled Mr. Woodward accommodatingly.

"Frank, don't you dare touch a thing up here while me and Jim are downstairs!" Bliss scolded his seven-year-old. And with that Jim helped the boss carry the stepladder down the stairwell and out the front door.

Mr. Bliss steadied the ladder as Jim climbed up and untied the stays that attached the canvas to the iron awning frame. Bliss made sure that passersby did not upset the ladder and startle Jim. Within twenty minutes Jim had the canvas unattached. Together they shook the grit and city grime off and neatly folded the awning pieces, then trudged their heavy burden upstairs to the studio for safekeeping. Mr. Bliss' obedient little Frank sat in a corner, content with his toy steamer.

The two planners peered out the window at the newly-unobstructed view. Mr. Bliss beamed with satisfaction. Now he enjoyed a wide-open vista within which to work. The iron frame that supported the awning would be visible in the photos, but that was a small matter, Mr. Bliss concluded.

The day's work done, Jim resisted returning home, a place he used to eagerly head toward like a shot. But that was before Peter Halloran let Jim see just what sort of creature he really was.

Most Saturdays nowadays Jim tarried after his work was done, having discovered the Young Men's Christian Union reading room, just a few doors down Main Street. The reading room had all the most recent newspapers from New York, Boston, Chicago and Baltimore, and the latest monthly periodicals. He escaped there after work whenever he was able for the remaining interval of his employ for Mr. Bliss.

As the martyred president's funeral train approached Buffalo through the countryside, every tree, ridge, spire, water tower, ledge, stairway, flagpole and rooftop offering a view of its progress was crowded with mourners. It appeared that the population had trebled from the previous day, and that its entirety had flocked to that portion of the city through which the train passed on its way to the station.

It was barely the break of dawn. The Exchange Street Depot was heavily draped in mourning. A scaffold had been built for the choir that now filled its four levels, nervously awaiting the arrival of the President's body. Thousands of citizens who had come from as far as 200 miles distant stood silent, waiting.

There would be no repeat of the chaos attending Lincoln's previous visit to Buffalo's Exchange Street Depot in 1861. No melee or disobedience or mild disturbance would be tolerated. Over three hundred uniformed police officers surrounded the depot and the train yard and intermingled with the crowd, instructing them as to how they will be expected to behave once that train pulls in.

The officers' primary goal was to maintain order.

The secondary goal was to arrest as many pickpockets as they possibly could. More than a hundred professional thieves were preceding the funeral route from Washington to Springfield to take criminal advantage of the preoccupied and densely packed mourners.

The pilot engine arrived first at the depot, draped in black, a flagstaff with a fluttering Old Glory decorating either side of the signal lamp. Ten minutes later it was followed by the locomotive Dean Richmond, pulling one baggage car, seven passenger cars, and President Lincoln's funeral car.

A large portrait of the slain President was mounted on front, beneath the locomotive's signal lamp, its frame heavily draped in black and white crepe. Beautiful bouquets of evergreens, ivy, and lily of-the-valley graced the flag sockets that adorned the Dean Richmond's signal lamp, each of which sprouted two American flags. Beautiful festoons were suspended from knots of white wherever they could be.

The crowd hushed as the train halted; heads were bared, and the scene was intensely solemn.

The city committee welcomed the officers and the escort accompanying the President's body. They were shown into Mr. Bloomer's Model Railroad

Lincoln's Funeral Train

*Lincoln's funeral car stops in front of St. James Hall at main and Eagle
streets. Photo taken from the Bliss Photography Gallery.*

Dining Saloon, on the depot premises, where a sumptuous breakfast had been prepared.

The walls of the depot were festooned in drapery of black and white, as were too the arched windows, including those of the dining saloon's, which in addition exhibited miniature American flags. The crowd stood outside and watched through the windows as the dignitaries ate their meal. Recently-promoted Police Chief Darcy had arrived on the grounds at the earliest hour with his full force, and kept the immense and almost irrepressible throng congregated there within their proper limits.

The dignitaries at Mr. Bloomer's Dining Saloon gulped the last of their meal as the soldiers inside President Lincoln's rail car prepared to move. The funeral car was the only black component in a train of yellow lacquered coaches. With twelve windows on each side, it was of the finest construction. At one end of the car's interior was the pedestal for securing the coffin, which was covered by a magnificent flag draped in black. A stateroom adjoined, with conveniences for the guard of honor accompanying the remains. The interior of the car was draped in black and finely decorated with the coat-of-arms of each state. It was furnished with sofas and settees, a wash table, and other appurtenances.

The remains were taken from the funeral car, borne upon the shoulders of ten of the immaculately outfitted soldiers, and conveyed to the hearse. The sergeants bearing the coffin were flanked by the remainder of the Guard of Honor with swords drawn.

The President's remains would be taken to St. James Hall at the corner of Main and Eagle Streets, just a few doors away from the Bliss Photographic Gallery. The latter street was closed off to all comers by a high wood fence, its entrances heavily guarded.

Main Street had never looked cleaner or more ordered. The weather was beautiful. All the stores and businesses along the route were draped, many in superb fashion. Private dwellings displayed the symbols of mourning in such manner as to speak volumes of their patriotism and the depth of their grief. A banner draped across Mr. S.O. Barnum's Store proclaimed He Still Lives In The Hearts Of His Countrymen.

Jim Sullivan had found it difficult to sleep in anticipation. He was up making tea before first light, and then started out on his route. He snuffed all the lamps in his district, even though it was still too early to darken them. He hoped that no one would complain. He ducked behind a shed to pee while a curious terrier watched. Then with pole in hand he headed toward Mr. Bliss' Gallery. Jim turned briefly to see the dog amble over to where he had relieved himself and add his own scent.

As the hour for the funeral procession approached, the sidewalks along Main Street, the buildings from ground floor to roof, and all the avenues converging on Niagara Square became thronged with people of all ages and classes until it seemed like the entire city had turned out onto the streets en masse. Buffalo was crawling with humanity and horses in such numbers that young Jim had never before witnessed. He made his way down Main Street to No. 293 and shot up the stairs. Mr. Bliss was cleaning a lens, a heavy brass configuration that looked like a small cannon, and must have weighed four pounds or more.

"James, my boy, we are going to very carefully lift the camera on its tripod and slowly...very slowly...walk it in small steps to the center window."

The large double-hung window was wide open. The camera itself consisted of a huge oak box, a foot wide and about as high, almost square-shaped. On its front was a hole encircled with a brass flange where the lens would be mounted. On the top, at the rear, was a wood and brass tray that pulled straight up vertically for the loading of the light sensitive glass plates into it.

Once loaded and secured, the tray is pushed back down snugly into the camera box, and a dark slide, which shields the sensitized glass plate from unintended exposure to light, is pulled out. This dark slide is placed on top of the camera so as not to become mislaid. Then the exposure is made. Afterward, the dark slide is reinserted, covering the exposed plate to protect it from errant light, and the tray holding the plate is pulled up. The exposed plate is removed and taken into the processing closet. A fresh plate is reinserted into the tray, and the tray slid snugly down into the camera box again.

"The rub," said Mr. Bliss, "is not becoming so wrapped up in making your photographs that you forget to first remove, then replace the dark slide, for then there would be no photograph."

It appeared very complicated, and Jim wasn't sure if he would ever be ready to operate something as technologically advanced as a camera.

After the device on the tripod was positioned in the open window so that it could be picked up and rotated in any direction to follow the progress of the cortege, Mr. Bliss attached the brass cannon lens snugly onto the front of the camera box, then gave it an extra turn just to make sure it was snugly seated.

There was a switch that opened and closed the aperture of the lens which would expose the plate to light for whatever length of time necessary to get a well exposed photo.

"How do you know how long to keep the switch open?" asked Jim.

"There is a formula to use, James. On a bright sunny day like today it would be opened for one second. For a bright cloudy day, two seconds. For a rainy day, four seconds. It's not an exact science, but the more photographs you make, the better you become at determining the length of exposure."

It was all Greek to him, and Jim was content just to observe. As they waited, Mr. Bliss made coffee and offered a cup to Jim. He had never tasted coffee before, only tea. He thought it awful, but kept his opinion to himself.

Promptly at eight o'clock, the first minute gun was fired. The bells were rung and the procession commenced to move on its sorry route, the military companies marching with arms reversed. This gloomy parade, two and a half miles in length, led by high ranking military, the 65th and 74th Regiments, and the Union Cornet Band and Miller's Band, began its way along the pre-planned route: Exchange to Main, Main to Niagara, Niagara to Delaware, Delaware to Tupper, down Tupper to Main, and finally down Main Street to the Young Men's Christian Association Buildings and St. James Hall.

One hundred thousand silent solemn people lined the route, grievers having journeyed from all reaches of Northern Pennsylvania, Western New York, and Southern Ontario. The movement of the procession was signalized by minute guns. Simultaneously, Buffalo's Canadian friends across the river in Fort Erie poured forth a volley of gun salutes as a tribute to the fallen hero, which echoed forlornly across the wide Niagara.

As the procession slowly passed them, the city's citizens in mourning attire began to move along with it, like a flow of creeping black lava. Only those in the windows of buildings and on rooftops maintained their stations. The military bore draped flags, and the decorations of the Fire Department's carriages, trucks, and engines were elegant and faultless.

President Lincoln's funeral car was fashioned of a superb canopy resting on four pillars trimmed with silver-fringed black velvet, the inside exquisitely draped in white and black crepe. In the center of the car, the coffin rested on a dais, and a black plume surmounted the canopy. It was drawn by six grey horses, each wearing on his head a black plume, and on his back a broadcloth trimmed with fringe. The horses were led by negro grooms.

"Here it comes!" exclaimed Mr. Bliss, as the first officers rode their horses slowly into view up Main Street. To follow the movement he and Jim had to lift the heavy apparatus and rotate it to a spot not yet reached by the cortege. Then Mr. Bliss had to quickly make the exchange of plates before losing his opportunity. He had never done this before but did not falter, partly because of Jim's facilitation.

As the procession neared its destination, the density of the crowd forced it to stop multiple times. This satisfied Mr. Bliss enormously, as moving objects might appear blurred in his photographs. He timed his exposures for those instances when the cortege was motionless. He dexterously went about exposing, shielding, removing and replacing glass plates, for a total of thirteen.

Jim Sullivan observed in silence as Bliss concentrated mightily, the boss knowing there would be no second chance. The procession slowly passed the vast gaping void on the opposite side of Main Street left by the great American Hotel fire, and as the cortege flowed along, so did the crowd after it, as all were intent on viewing Mr. Lincoln.

Jim had tried to get his mother and stepfather to attend. Neither wished to. His mother held President Lincoln personally responsible for her drastic losses and all the terrible sacrifices she had been forced to make. Peter Halloran simply didn't "give a hoot for that kind of malarkey," and knew very well that with most businesses and factories closed, his Halloran's Saloon would do a roaring good business. He was right.

Jim asked Mr. Bliss if he would come down the street with him to stand in line to view the President. Bliss said his wife and son were already there, waiting for him. He did not invite Jim to join them. Jim helped Mr. Bliss quickly return the studio to its approximate normal arrangement, for the boss was in a hurry to leave. Jim thanked his employer for the superb viewing spot, and departed to follow the throng.

After traversing its entire route, the funeral car stopped in front of the Main Street entrance of St. James Hall amid an enormous yet hushed and orderly crowd, where the Guard of Honor bore the remains of Mr. Lincoln inside. There they laid the remarkably beautiful casket on the prepared catafalque. The resting place consisted of a circular sable tent fifty feet in diameter by thirty feet in height, falling from the centerpiece in the ceiling from which the magnificent chandelier of St. James Hall was pendant. Two thousand yards of black undressed cambric were used in its construction. It was lighted solely by the large chandelier, its fifty gas jets creating a pleasing yet somber effect. Ten large mourning pillars were distributed around the sides of the canopy. Beautiful festoons of black and white serge, connected by black and silver cord, and bound up in white rosettes, swept around the circle.

The dais was on an inclined plane to make viewing the President's face easier for those being sped quickly along. The railings within the tent and along the ladies' walkway were handsomely draped, the total forming a stunningly beautiful structure in which to rest the President. Altogether the Temple of Mourning was as complete as it could well be made. To Monsieur St. Ody belonged the credit for the beautiful design, his reputation as Buffalo's foremost interior designer and gentleman of exquisite taste solidified.

The coffin having been placed on the dais, the lid was removed, and the Embalmer devoted some careful minutes to preparing the face of the great martyr for the eyes of the thousands who awaited, tearfully mourning his loss. The St. Cecilia Society occupied the gallery and sang the solemn dirge Rest, Spirit, Rest with an effect almost supernatural.

The delicate work of the embalmer completed, ladies from the Unitarian Church where Mr. Lincoln last took worship in Buffalo with President Fillmore, laid an anchor-shaped chaplet of white flowers at the President's feet. It bore an inscription commencing with Youth crushed to earth will rise again.

A few minutes after, a beautiful design in the form of a Harp, with one string broken asunder, was presented by the ladies of the St. Cecilia Society, and placed at the head of the casket. It was a delicate weaving of white roses, orange blossoms and daisies, seemingly of angelic fabrication.

The coffin was exquisitely constructed of mahogany lined with lead, with heavy silver handles and the richest white silk upholstery within. The upper third of the lid was thrown back so as to reveal Mr. Lincoln's head and bust. A silver plate on the coffin's center inscribed:

ABRAHAM LINCOLN
Sixteenth President of the United States
Born February 12, 1809
Died April 15, 1865

As Jim Sullivan quickly weaved his way though the massive gathering, running to secure a place to view Mr. Lincoln, he saw a familiar face.

"Ed!" he called.

He hadn't spoken much with thirteen-year-old Ed Stanton since the orphanage incident. The last time the two had done anything exceptionally fun together was when they were little boys, and their fathers took them to the Wide Awakes rally to see Abraham Lincoln for the first time. It was coincidental that they would meet again here, but not surprising. Both boys felt a closeness to the President due to their shared torch-light adventure back on that cold October night in 1860 at The Terrace. Ed had grown up a lot since then. He was just a year older than Jim, but appeared closer in countenance to a man than a boy.

Ed's father, James Stanton, had been Jim's late father's best friend. What Jim was not aware of was that his father's best friend had always carried a torch for his mother Mary, and still did, even though he had remarried. James Stanton would never dare admit it, but after John Sullivan's death, when he was helping Mary Sullivan, bringing food for her and the boys or accompanying her on business matters, he used to fantasize about his own new wife disappearing, leaving, or perhaps dying, resulting in him being free to wed Mary Sullivan.

Ed was with his friend Paddy Diggins, who was a likeable little roughneck.

"You headin' t' see Mr. Lincoln?" asked Ed, kindly.

Jim wasn't accustomed to other boys his age showing much cordiality to him. The First Ward was an adversarial colony, where even little boys had to fight to survive, dog-eat-dog.

"Yep. You two also?"

"Yep." said Ed.

"Yep," said Patrick Diggins. "But I'm standin' way up ahead with my Pa. He's savin' my place in line. I just came back to say hello to Ed. I better go. See you around Ed. See ya Jim."

"Yeah, see ya Pat," they chimed.

"Wanna wait together?" offered Jim. "I'd be pleased to have someone to pass the time with."

"Yeah, sure," smiled Ed.

Soldiers were all over the place, directing and corralling people into lines. Men into one, ladies in the other.

"I wonder why they're separatin' all the couples?" Ed asked, as he saw families go off in two directions according to gender, rather than being admitted together.

"Don't know," replied Jim. "Don't make no sense. When I met Mr. Lincoln at the American Hotel with my Pa, Ladies and Gentlemen were in the same receiving line together."

A soldier overheard the boys. "It's to keep the ladies' dresses clean of spittle from all the plug tobacco," the army private said. The boys nodded, understanding. Chaw was more popular than ever, and women clear hated it. Among the adult males they knew, unstained teeth were almost nonexistent. The boys themselves were getting spattered even as they stood and waited.

They were herded into a tightly organized line as they neared the door, and directed to stand four abreast. Soldiers patrolled constantly, walking the lines, keeping order, settling minor squabbles. But mostly, people were very peaceful. Very quiet. It was barely ten o'clock and the viewing would remain open until 8 o'clock in the evening. Jim and Ed saw that they were closer to the front of the line than to the rear, and were certain they would be admitted.

"I recall that at the American Hotel when Abe was here last, they had barrels at the door and made the men spit out their chewin' tobacco. Wish they'd do the same here," said Jim as he wiped an errant brown droplet from his face.

As the hours passed, the two became reacquainted. For years Jim had kept to himself mostly, not trusting anyone much, especially not boys his age and older. He was always on the lookout for trouble from them. He tried to shrink himself down so others would neither notice him nor aggravate him.

This along with his promise to his father to take care of his mother and baby brother John had turned him inward upon himself. He didn't really have a best friend. He hadn't really anyone to talk to, or laugh with. But there, in that gloomy queue that held so much promise for sadness and grief, Jim Sullivan renewed an old acquaintance, and by day's end, he would have a lifelong friend in Ed Stanton. Ironically the saddest day in the city's history opened a new chapter in Jim Sullivan's life. And for a very short of time at least, a happier chapter.

"I heard yer mother married that saloonkeep. Do you like 'im?"

No. I hate 'im. He's old, and he's coarse. He's mean to some people, the neighbors, and to me and Johnnie when Ma's not around. He don't like us.

"Yer Ma is havin' a new baby?"

"Yeah. A brother I'm hopin'. But my Ma wants a girl."

"Does he hit ye?"

"Who? Her new husband?" Jim broke eye contact with his friend. "No." he lied.

"They say he killed a man."

"What?!"

"Yep, that's what they say, that he killed a man and went to the state prison for it, in Auburn, for ten years!"

"Naw, ain't never heard that! He was in the army for ten years, that's what I was told."

"That's what my Pa said. I overheard him talkin' to John Hanavan about it. They both seemed to be well acquainted with all the details."

"What sorts of details?"

"Oh, the particulars. Yer stepfather stabbed him with a knife, they say. Over money, they say. But not just once. No. Twenty times or more. He was thoroughly drunk. They say."

Jim was stunned into silence.

"If he ever hits you, you just tell me, Jim Sullivan. I'll help you get back at 'im. My Pa says the same to John Hanavan, 'If that feller ever lays a hand on Mary Sullivan, we'll club the shit out of him!'"

"Why does your Pa think Peter would ever hit my Ma?" Jim replied, panicking a little.

"Guess it's 'cause he killed a man, that's why. But don't you be worryin', Jim. Everybody's watchin' out." Ed paused and studied Jim Sullivan's face. He continued. "Didn't mean t' put no scare in you, Jim. Thought you already knew."

"Ain't scared," Jim replied defensively. "I just didn't figger him for bein' such a nasty sort as you're tellin' me. Maybe now I have to keep my eyes open wider."

Ed tried to back peddle.

"Maybe he's changed. I wouldn't fret much, especially if he isn't mean to you and your brother, or your Ma. Maybe he learned his lesson. Anyway, your Ma's friends is lookin' out for her, so no need for worryin'."

And with that, the subject was dropped. Their conversation moved on to other things more pleasant and light. Ed was one grade ahead of Jim in school, and he didn't have to work.

"Anybody be botherin' you when yer lightin' the lamps, Jim?"

"Nope. Lots of fellas bid me hello, I'd say. A few look at me unpleasant like. But all in all, people know I have an important job. Everybody wants the streets lit. Especially the wives and kids of all the drunks tryin' to find their way home!"

Both boys laughed.

They passed the hours talking about mutual acquaintances, their lives at home, school. What they wanted to be when they grew up.

"I like writin', tellin' stories," offered Jim. "I don't tell them out loud or nothin'. They're mostly kept in my head, but I write them down sometimes. The periodicals are payin' a lot of money for a good story," said Jim. "Maybe sometime I can sell one of 'em."

"Meself, I wanna be a copper. So I can be the boss," said Ed definitively.

Jim thought to himself, that's odd. Ed Stanton was a big gentle lad with an agreeable nature. Why would he want to be the boss of people?

"I hate the coppers," said Jim. "They're always after the lamplighter boys.

And for no good reason. We just do our job and then go home."

Ed thought about it a few seconds.

"I think it's 'cause when you make your way around the Ward you see things. Things they might not like you seein', like them sleepin' on the job, or doin' wrong."

Jim laughed. "They do plenty of both, all right!"

At ten o'clock St. James Hall had been finally thrown open to the waiting public, and the rush was absolutely terrific. Several ladies fainted. The police and military were well rehearsed and kept the massive crowd in order, as per their carefully worked out plan. The soldiers had to be rough with some folks who didn't want to listen.

Jim and Ed stood amid a more subdued throng of men. Sniffling and sobbing were heard all around them for the entire four hours they waited. Men saved each others' places in line so they could go off to piss, or dash to buy a bread roll or a stick of dried beef from a vendor. At long last the boys were admitted, the soldiers making sure the mourners remained in formation, four abreast, marching them in a parade quickly up the stairs.

Jim was very surprised at how quickly the line was moving, wondering, when he and Ed finally reached Mr. Lincoln, if they would even be allowed time to sufficiently gaze upon his face.

The interior was kept very dim. The windows were covered and the only light was that emitted by gas lamps. As he passed the coffin Jim was excited at having been assigned the inside position closest to the bier, as they were ushered by very rapidly. There was not much opportunity to contemplate.

Jim again gazed upon the kind face he had seen twice before in life, now for the final time. He was startled by the sight, and it caused him to shudder.

President Abraham Lincoln. He really was dead.

Memories of Jim's father floated up from the deepest recesses of his remembrance. The evening the two met the new President at the American Hotel together. His father's smell. The Irish in his voice. His guarding, protective clutch. Memories of his Pa flooded over him, and enveloped him, and he felt all the gloomier for it. The boys were swept swiftly along by the guards, then marched speedily down the West stairway and out into the blinding sunlight of Main Street.

Outside, people shielded their eyes as they exited the door. The sexes mixed again as they reunited to reflect on what they had just seen. Thousands of handkerchiefs dabbed at teary eyes and runny noses as mourners recovered their composure.

It was four o'clock. The doors of the Hall would remain open until eight, but the line still stretched on as far as the eye could see. More than one hundred thousand souls would pass through the doors of St. James Hall by the end of the day.

Jim and Ed set out on their hike back to the First Ward together.

All the way to Hamburgh Street every house and shop, church and school was draped in mourning. One poor little house had a homemade sign in the window written in a child's scrawl, Goodbye, Abe.

As the boys approached the river, the mood changed drastically. The sound of music and laughter, chatter and brawling poured out of the saloons. The taverns were doing a rousing business. Uniontown's ironworks had shut down and its prisoners were freed to jump the fence and mingle with the rest of the ward. The boys parted ways at the Erie Railroad tracks, each going his own direction.

Jim walked into Halloran's Saloon to the melody of fiddle playing.

Blind Joe was serenading the crowd with a jig, his huge guide dog General Porter at his feet. Jim was greeted by the shouts of his stepfather's customers, unfamiliar faces to Jim but old acquaintances of Peter, hailing him. His stepfather was at the end of the bar, carousing with some customers, including the tart Talbot girls. Jim nodded a curt hello to the old man and darted up the stairs.

His mother sat, swollen and happy, knitting as she rocked the empty cradle that awaited the new baby with her foot, practicing, he supposed. Four-year-old John sat in the corner, playing with the brightly painted set of blocks his new step father had bought to welcome him. Suddenly, seeing his mother tranquil and at rest, Jim realized that he hadn't seen her this content and calm in... actually, ever.

If this is the effect that marrying that old sod has had on his sweet mother, finally allowing her some peace and happiness, then so be it. Jim made a pledge to himself at that moment to be a better son. To both of them.

July 14, 1865
A New Son And A Fenian Dream

Doc Greene rushed into the front door of Halloran's Saloon on Hamburgh Street, where Jim Sullivan directed him quickly up the stairs to where his mother struggled in labor. Five-year-old Chestnut snorted and waited curbside pawing at the planks, confident in his status as Doc Greene's most reliable and agreeable associate. The steed's beauty and bearing were remarked upon by all. Neighborhood boys stopped to stroke his glistening coat and scratch him and keep him company as he waited for Doc to return. There was no more popular or loved horse in the entire city, nor one whose owner took better care of him— or was more qualified to. Everyone in the First Ward adored Chestnut.

When Mary went into labor she asked for Doc Greene to be called. He had delivered baby John in 1860, and Mary wanted him to attend her again. His task proved more difficult this time, as little Daniel was not a remarkably quick or easy birth. But finally, Mary's young sons James E. and John P. Sullivan had a new pink little brother, Daniel J. Halloran, something JP was especially thrilled about. He would no longer have to suffer being the baby of the family.

And Peter... Peter Halloran was hesitantly, momentarily, enthralled with having a son to carry on the dishonored family name.

The Halloran Saloon at 16 Hamburgh Street was situated less than a stone's throw from the Buffalo River. From their living quarters above the saloon, Mary and her three boys had a panoramic view of the hustle of a thriving riverfront metropolis. Tugs, barges and ships of every sort, masted and steam-driven, sailed and chugged up and down the continually dredged course that was just two decades before a shallow creek, which along with the city's harbors, basins, canals and slips, formed the main artery of a dynamic waterfront community.

Like John Sullivan and his wife Mary McGrady, Peter Halloran had arrived in Buffalo from Ireland along with 10,000 other Irish ex-patriots. The Protestant city with the German majority was quite alarmed by this influx of Catholic garbage. Fortunately for the Protestants, the Irish rabble, almost to a man, settled in the dreary First Ward, by the dirty river, well removed from decent Protestant folk.

Though they came to settle happily in their new country, most Irish retained a fierce loyalty to Ireland, holding great contempt toward England, the oppressor of their homeland for close to 800 years. This disdain for the English was equally shared by the rest of Buffalo's citizens as well, given Britain's scheming betrayal of the United States during the Civil War, the wholesale breaching of the Neutrality Law of 1818, and the brutal murders of the city's women and children and its burning to the ground by the British terrorists in 1813.

In 1865 England slammed a tight clamp on Irish unrest back in the homeland after an unsuccessful attempt by Ireland to throw off England's shackles. Many of the sons and daughters of Eire in America wanted to do something about that, once and for all. Peter Halloran was one of these. Halloran's Saloon became a meeting place for a group that were "wantin' for a free Ireland."

They called themselves the Fenian Brotherhood. They gathered nightly in groups, these conspiring men with wives and children waiting at home for their return, unsuspecting as the subversives swilled beer and hatched their plans to free Ireland from the despicable grasp of the empire-grabbing Brits.

On Saturday, March 24,1866, in broad daylight, an 800-strong contingent of Fenian soldiers assembled in Buffalo fully armed for purposes of parade and drill in the square at The Terrace. The Terrace was the broad boulevard and open square opposite the city's finest hotel, The Mansion House. The Fenians' demonstrations and choice of venue could not have been more public, symbolic or conspicuous. The men, in Fenian uniforms and armed with rifles and bayonets, were formed into a line by their captains, then marched symbolically around the Liberty Pole.

Erected in 1838, the Liberty Pole was the towering symbol of Buffalo's fight against the British, for from this very site the Market House bell rang out in 1813 to warn the city's inhabitants of the British invaders landing at Black Rock.

The imposing mast stood taller than any city structure of its time and was easily visible from British territory, what with John Wheedon's gilded wooden eagle perched at its apex. The soaring American Eagle, four feet in height and six feet between wingtips, was positioned to face Toronto as if shrieking defiance against the British Lion. The menacing bird was a direct reply to a Toronto newspaper editor's call for extermination of the United States. Inside the eagle's breast was a copper box containing civic papers and an account of the Liberty Pole ceremony.

After duly honoring the historic landmark, the Fenian army marched through all the principal downtown avenues, followed by crowds of enthusiastic cheering citizen supporters. Every previous night during that same week, these squads of Fenians, or as they styled themselves for stealthy reasons, Independent Target Companies, drilled on the Terrace, armed and ready to enter battle.

Visiting Canadians from across the river witnessing the demonstrations were outraged at this, the foreign hypocrites claiming it a breach of the very same Neutrality Law of 1818 that they themselves had ceaselessly trod asunder from the moment the treaty was so long ago signed.

The Canadians had conveniently forgotten that they had most recently and shamefully harbored armed Confederate troops on their soil during the War Between the States, troops that were poised to attack the United States of America from the North.

Buffalo's visiting Canadian backstabbers were told to "get the fuck back to yer bloody homes."

On April 3rd, the Fenians held a mass meeting at St. James Hall, the venue of Abraham Lincoln's funeral, to listen to their proclaimed leader, General Tom Sweeny, U.S. Army. The Hall was filled to overflowing with wildly enthusiastic men and women. General Sweeny, along with Senator Morrison of Missouri and the other speakers had been escorted from their quarters at The Mansion House by two armed companies, led by the International Brass Band. The military took up position at the sides and ends of the hall, and an honor guard was stationed on the stage and on either side of the speaker's stand. Color bearers held in their hands both the American flag and the green banner of Eire.

Buffalo Fenian leader Paddy O'Day had been scheduled to call the meeting to order, but had fallen ill. General Tom Sweeny was received with terrific acclaim that continued for several minutes. His speech was repeatedly interrupted by deafening cheers. The General was followed by Senator Morrison, who eloquently exhorted the Brotherhood to "carry on the contest." The Senator said it seemed to him as if in Buffalo he was "near the scene of operations; and the nearer he got, the wilder was the enthusiasm of the Irish heart."

"The Irishmen of Buffalo know what to do, what they are about, and pretty nearly where they are going to strike. The reward of Irish patriotism," he remarked, "would be something which the entire wealth of the West Indies could not purchase" — and here the speaker grasped the green flag, and waving it amid tremendous cheers, shouted, "when this is flying over a big field of victory, only then is our reward, and not til then! Welcome wounds, welcome poverty, welcome sickness and privation, welcome death if necessary, til this flag shall triumph; we shall have neither wealth nor happiness nor pleasure til it floats free everywhere on Irish soil!"

Taking a musket from one of the guard standing in front of the stage, Senator Morrison cried, "I would rather have this than a million petitions to the British government; for the voice that resounds from its muzzle is far more potent for the liberation of Ireland! The bayonets you see which gleam around this Hall tonight with scintillating sparks of liberty, are not here for any holiday purpose!"

The audience went wild. Men stood on seats cheering and women shrieked with delight.

"I fervently hope never to be called to make another speech; for every speech is but putting the enemy on his guard. General Sweeny is preparing, and the blow must be soon struck or the contest abandoned, and there should be no more speech making! If Ireland herself were swept beneath the Atlantic's surge, Irishmen were not men if they did not still pant for revenge. Nations have no hereafter, and when they are the oppressors, they must be made to suffer here on this earth. England thought she had got rid of us when we came to this country, but we came here to learn liberty; and let us now send our voice across the Atlantic to tell our old Mother to keep quiet, to wait awhile and not to shed the blood of her sons in vain, to tell her that although we left for awhile, we come again to elevate her, with our blood, among the nations of the earth. She has not the money, but we have both men and money! And let us once just get our crowbar into the English government, and you will hear such a crash as the world never heard since Babylon fell!

The audience was then in the aisles, whooping and hollering. The troops rattled their bayonets.

"The roll of the English drum will soon be silent in at least one corner of the British possessions, and the Irish drum will be heard. Once give us a single road upon which we can plant our flag, and England will find us ready to strike her death blow!"

Peter Halloran sat there in St. James Hall stunned among his cheering compatriots. Could this be real? Can an American Senator be standing before us along with a General of the United States Army, sounding the battle cry for the Fenian army to invade Canada and take it hostage in the name of Ireland?

The answer was, without question, yes.

Senator Morrison was not finished.

He said that he himself, for twenty years, had looked anxiously forward to this time.

"Since I had learned to love God and hate the British government I have hoped for this hour, and now is the time when the lovers of Ireland's cause must show the world that their patriotism is not lip patriotism."

The Senator, evidently due to his proximity to the Canadian border, seemed disposed to believe that there were British spies in the Hall, that he did not pretend to know the military secrets of the planned invasion; for these were "treasured in a single brain and heart." He himself knew a few things which might be of advantage to the enemy, but he stated that it would be neither wise nor convenient for him to divulge them at this time.

The meeting raised $3500 for the cause, with Peter contributing $20. If Mary ever found out she would have wrung his neck. He headed home with his Fenian brothers in the highest of spirits, filled with the fire of Freedom for Eire.

The Fenians were being celebrated in Buffalo in lore, song, and even gourmet delicacies. Miss Lizzie Mitchell was appearing at Carr's Variety Theater singing Fenians' Delight. Martin & Meyer Confectioners, recently opened in the burned-out space formerly occupied by Van Velsor Bakery, was visited by Jim Sullivan one day after finishing his work at the Bliss Photography Gallery. Upon approaching the glass case that exhibited the tempting cakes, he saw a number of them had been newly named in honor of the Fenian Brotherhood.

As he headed home, eating his Stephens cake, Jim Sullivan had a hard decision to make. The system of lamp lighting it had been decided would be changed, and beginning May 1st the Committee on Public Lamps would begin taking bids from individuals who would be not only required to light and extinguish them, but to keep them in good repair. The bids were to include the area the bidder wished to service, and the cost per lamp. The contract would be for a year. There was already a lot of breakage in the First Ward due to idle boys with nothing better to do than throw rocks.

Thirteen-year-old Jim Sullivan was very good at arithmetic, but this new way of managing the city's lamps didn't add up in his favor at all. The new rules meant that others were now free to compete for his territory, and the lowest bidder would win. In order to compete he would have to learn how to repair the lamps, buy the supplies to do so, and carry the heavy ladder much more often. He had been a lamplighter boy since he was nine years old. That added up to over three years, with his stay in the orphan asylum the only interruption.

The lamplighter job had provided him the perfect schedule, allowing him to maintain good attendance at the Central School, get enough sleep, and earn money for books, supplies, and an occasional cake.

He wondered if he should talk about it with his stepfather.

❦

1866
The Fenian Invasion

In 1865 the Fenians held a convention of sorts in New York City. There they hatched a grand plan to invade British North America, as Canada was officially called, which would upon its conquering be held hostage until independence for Ireland was achieved. $50,000 had been raised from sympathetic Irish Americans.

With the war between the states ended, the Fenians were scooping up vast amounts of surplus arms being sold at a bargain rate by the pound by the government. In Boston a Fenian Cavalry was formed consisting of a thousand men committed for a minimum of one year. Well-trained, battle-hardened troops returning from the Civil War faced rampant unemployment; Fenian recruitment was greatly facilitated by these post-war conditions. Many in the US government were well aware of the planned invasion, but turned a blind eye. U.S. Treasurer Spinner, whose signature appeared on all US bank notes, was staying at The Mansion House on the day that the Fenian troops brazenly paraded their arms around the Liberty Pole at The Terrace. He watched the army's formations from his hotel balcony, unperturbed.

In the Civil War just ended, the Canadians had eagerly provided to the enemy a launching ground from which to attack the United States of America from British territory; territory they, by signing the Neutrality Laws Treaty of 1818 with the United States, had pledged would remain neutral soil.

Confederate troops trained on British soil to carry out the Philo Parsons affair on Lake Erie and the Saint Albans Raid into Vermont. Other planned acts of war against the United States hatched by sympathizers to the Confederate cause, such as Canadian industrialists George Wyatt and A.M. Smith, had made the prospect of an all-out war against Canada a real possibility.

When the Civil War hostilities ended, the United States demanded compensation from Great Britain for breaking the Neutrality Law of 1818, for unneutral acts which aided and abetted the Confederates during the War. The British were not only balking at any such reparations, but were openly laughing at the American ultimatum.

For their snarky duplicity, many Americans hungered to see the British enemy decimated and the lands to the North annexed by the United States. Not just a few citizens of Canada desired Canadian independence and a break with Britain. Most Americans were not at all bothered by what the Fenians had planned, nor were all that many Canadians.

Mary Halloran was angry about Peter's involvement in such a maniacal conspiracy, and resentful that one floor below the family flat, within earshot of her sons, a dangerous revolution was being hatched. She feared problems with the police. She feared losing yet another husband in some foolish war. But it wasn't just herself and John Sullivan's sons that Peter Halloran should have been concerned about. Mary had borne Peter his own blood son, Daniel, less than a year before. Baby Daniel's future was at stake as well. She confronted him.

"Me first husband left me alone in me adopted country with a baby in me arms and another clingin' to me apron, to fight in a war for altogether someone else's freedom. No one knows better than ye do, Peter Halloran, how we suffered, meself and the children. Me husband died! He died in a war he should have never been fightin' to begin with! And now ye want to do the same? We have a baby together, Peter! Daniel is still at my breast, and yer downstairs with yer drunken connivin' Fenian brothers hatchin' yer grand plans to free the home country?

"I will not lose another husband! Me children will not lose another father! We might be Irish to the very bone, but we all made a choice to leave Ireland and start a new life in a new country, and we can't be fightin' other people's wars for them. We are Americans now. Our children are born Americans, all three. Forget these fools' plans fer fightin' a war against the most powerful nation in the world, hatched from your little neighborhood saloon. Yer own family comes first!"

Peter was angry over being dusted off so righteously by his wife.

He loved Ireland. The Fenians—for the first time since he arrived in America—gave him genuine purpose. He finally had an accomplishment to strive for, something concrete, a reason to be here, something that would help make up for the failures of his past. He resented his new young wife for trying to take that away from him.

On the other hand, he had always wanted a family to call his own, and now he had one. He was getting old. He had finally sired a son to carry on the Halloran name. He agonized over Mary's demands and her sound reasoning, and finally, reluctantly acquiesced.

As much as he loved his native land, he decided his family must come first.

Mary Halloran took her boys back to Louisiana Street. She wanted to visit her old friend and former neighbor Mercy Abbott to talk about this Fenian nonsense, and get it off her chest. Young Jim Sullivan had avoided revisiting the environs of the old house he was born in, the home his family was happy in before his father went to war. His brother John didn't have any recollection of it, but listened raptly to Jim's stories of those early days when they'd had a real father.

"Don't you two go near the Basin!" Mary warned, sitting down on the step with Daniel in her arms as Mercy Abbott rocked on her porch. Mercy had not yet seen the baby.

"Oh, Mary, he is so precious! He looks exactly like you! The boys, they look like their late father, but Daniel, he's the spitting image of you!"

Mary was delighted. The last thing she wanted for her baby was the additional burden of his resembling Peter Halloran. Mary poured her anger out about her new husband, expecting Mercy's understanding and support.

"Mary Sullivan I am surprised at you! What true Irishman doesn't hate the British?" scolded Mercy. "What citizen of Buffalo — what American, for that matter, doesn't hate the British? Those scoundrels have been stabbing this nation in the back for over a hundred years now! Before the revolution the people of this country were no better off than those in Ireland. And that wasn't the end of it! No, I'll say not! Those scoundrels murdered half of Buffalo's town folk in 1813, and then burned the city to the ground. They conspired with the Indian savages, who murdered that sweet Mrs. Lovejoy and all the others, cutting off their scalps in the dirt as they tried to escape with their children! And now most recently they allowed those miserable Confederate devils to use British soil in Canada to launch attacks against the Union in the late war! This city could have been bombarded yet again! Invaded! How many times do the people of Buffalo have to suffer at the hands of the British? I say, death to Britain and all the dirty animals who live there! Let the invasion begin! Those Canadians to the North are not even human. They are not our friends as they pretend to be. They are highbinders and puppets, bootlickers of the British throne-squatters. The British have wrought more terror and torture and suffering on the world than Hannibal ever did! I hope the Fenians wreak the same kind of havoc on the British that the English have wrought upon us, and all the rest of the nations under their cruel tyranny!"

Mary was shocked, and deflated. She didn't know exactly who Hannibal was, but that didn't matter.

"I have me family t' keep, Mercy! Let Ireland and the United States destroy England if they so wish, I don't care! But I will not lose another husband in another war!"

Mary stormed off, offended that Mercy, as a woman, did not see that the issue wasn't retribution toward Britain, as well deserved as it might be. The issue was the very survival of her family.

She never spoke to Mercy Abbott again.

The Fenians battle the British at Ridgeway.

❧

Paddy O'Day

Among the Halloran Saloon's Fenian brotherhood was the lively Irishman named Paddy O'Day who ran his own saloon downtown. Paddy was the primary leader of the Buffalo Fenian Brotherhood, quite enthusiastic about the great cause and especially about his playing a historic role in it.

At what would turn out to be the final gathering of the Fenians at Halloran's Saloon, Peter convinced Paddy O'Day that Buffalo's Fenian headquarters should be relocated to Paddy's saloon on Pearl Street, providing a more direct route and straighter path to the Niagara River — the chosen launching site for the invasion — and a much more central location for receiving shipments of arms.

Although daunting, the Niagara River was not too formidable an obstacle in the Fenian quest to commence their invasion of Canada for the planned takeover of the British territory. The Fenian Army's first goal was to plant the beloved Irish flag on British soil and rechristen the country New Ireland.

Paddy O'Day was quite enthused over the prospect of his own business establishment playing such a significant role in the glorious events to come. Peter Halloran's proposal was indeed very good news for Paddy O'Day.

Wife Mary may have initially been victorious, but Peter Halloran could not quite fully give up his involvement in the Fenians. He secretly continued attending meetings at Paddy O'Day's Saloon, which was filling up fast with boxes of pistols, muskets and ammunition, secretly brought in on trains disguised in furniture crates. Drills were held in Paddy's basement with its windows blacked out.

As the planned spring invasion approached, Buffalo began seeing hundreds of new strangers in black felt hats and stovepipes arriving from Chicago, Columbus, St. Louis, Denver, Cleveland and Detroit. Buffalo police had been tipped off to new arrivals and were waiting at the Exchange Street Depot to arrest them. To circumvent this obstacle, sympathetic railroad engineers slowed their trains on the outskirts of the city allowing Fenian troops to safely disembark. These Irish soldiers were then whisked off into hiding by Buffalo Circle members to locations all over South Buffalo; at Indian Church, in Kelly's barn on Abbott Road, and even in plain sight at the popular Clark Hotel, where meetings were held in the lobby.

The last week of May, city officials grew evermore concerned with the vast increase in activity on the streets, knowing what was afoot. The Buffalo Courier reported that, "five wagonloads of ammunition had rolled into town." At Fort Porter, located at the foot of Niagara Street at the mouth of the river, Major Durr revealed he had at his command only 50 regulars and very little in the way of weapons or ammunition. Durr would be unable to confront the expected thousands of Fenians that would assemble nearby for the invasion. Many of the Fenians, in addition, were indeed much better trained than were his own troops, as they were elite veterans of the Civil War now unemployed, fed-up, fired-up, and itchin' for a fight.

Buffalo's Mayor Wells quickly telegraphed the mayors of Toronto and Hamilton across the border to warn them of the gathering forces. The warship USS Michigan was alerted for immediate service, and steamed into Buffalo harbor with her marine guard in formation on deck. The U.S. Marshal was notified, and Buffalo's police were ordered to remain on duty until told otherwise.

Come the dawn of May 31st, Mary Halloran was unaware the Fenian invasion had been planned for that very night. She had been on edge for weeks due to her husband's involvement, but was not especially concerned when Peter announced he would be out late that evening. Figuring his stepson was now past thirteen and no longer a child, Peter put young Jim Sullivan in charge of the saloon for the final two hours before closing that he planned to be gone. Jim didn't bother to ask questions. He was just happy to have his stepfather out of his hair.

Jim was observant of Peter Halloran's enthusiasm for the Fenians. Seeing the signs of the approaching invasion all around the city and noting the new intensity in Peter's surreptitious behavior, he suspected old pater was planning to participate. Halloran in recent weeks had become steadily more short tempered toward both Jim and his mother, and with Jim's friend Ed Stanton's forewarnings still ringing in his ears, he was newly fearful of this telling turn in Peter Halloran's behavior. Jim was not disturbed, neither by the invasion nor his stepfather's possible part in it, for he knew that it could well provide a welcome opportunity for Peter's demise.

Nervous, and looking for something to busy himself as he waited for the hour of departure, Peter Halloran went to the saloon's wash basin mirror and applied Dr. Knight's Oriental Hair Restorer, which promised to get rid of gray. Jim watched the ceremony askance and wondered, why does he even bother?

"Make sure ye lock 'er up good and tight at the end, lad," Peter said as he walked out the saloon door.

The Pratt Furnace lay along the Niagara River at the foot of Forest Avenue, shielded from view by Squaw Island from British observers across the Niagara River. Barges had been positioned at the Black Rock facility, rented for the invasion under the guise of taking Pratt employees on a company picnic to Squaw Island the following day. Tug steamers were to drag the barges loaded with soldiers and weapons across the river to Canada. Munitions had surreptitiously been moving across the river into Canada for days, and were being hidden at the mouth of Frenchman's Creek in Fort Erie.

At midnight, still feeling quite nervous, Peter joined the gathering forces at Paddy O'Day's, a thousand strong, along with a wagon train of arms and munitions for the march to Black Rock. At the same time, other Fenian groups and sympathizers were moving around Buffalo as a diversion to confuse military observers and the police. Thousands more Fenians were packed aboard trains chugging resolutely toward the city.

There was electricity in the air when Paddy O'Day's marchers arrived to find more than a thousand additional Fenians already gathered excitedly at Black Rock, waiting. Not one policeman was to be seen. None of Major Durr's forces from Fort Porter showed their faces. The city slept soundly. At about half past three, the assembled army of men and boys and their munitions began to board four canal boats which would ferry them across the Niagara River to Frenchman's Creek, where they would gather the arms secreted there and march south into the town of Fort Erie itself. The captain of the warship USS

Michigan had received orders from the US Attorney General to stop any and all movement across the Niagara River, but the orders were relayed too late.

Peter looked around. Most of the men were in their early 20s, green and eager and blessed with the young man's lack of fear of consequence. He grew uneasy as some of the other gathered men, themselves having second thoughts, began drifting away. He thought of his own son Daniel, and his two stepsons whom he had come to begin to care for, especially John Patrick, who although a Sullivan, had never known any other father but him.

Surrounded by two thousand eager armed troops salivating for a fight, Peter Halloran shifted his weight nervously from one foot to another as the men began filing onto the barges. He looked at the faint lights across the river in unsuspecting Fort Erie. He began to be haunted by Mary's stories of John Sullivan's leaving and the endless months of fear, hunger and uncertainty that followed, culminating in the horror of the news of his death. As he watched the faces of those around him, he saw a baby-faced red haired boy of no more than fifteen years turn and run in the direction of home, the act slapping Peter Halloran with the reality of what he was about to do. He had seen in his two older boys' forlorn faces the terrible result of losing a father. He decided he could not abandon his family for this political cause or any other, no matter how noble, the way John Sullivan had.

He turned and walked away, joining the deserters. He did not look back.

Peter Halloran climbed into bed alongside his infuriated wife, just as the first light of June began to color the sky. She could smell no liquor on him, and that frightened her. She didn't ask any questions, nor did he offer any explanations.

The following day both husband and wife, along with the entire city, closely studied the reports of the Fenian's progress in the newspapers.

The warship USS Michigan was ordered to steam down the Niagara River, taking position opposite the Clinton Mills at six o'clock on June 1st, hours after all the Fenians had already safely crossed. Peter Halloran doubted the ship's tardiness was mere coincidence, and later, the Hamilton Sentinel newspaper in Ontario would claim that the ship's Commander and the Chief Engineer were large contributors to the Fenian funds. Word of the crossing spread like wildfire around the Niagara Frontier, and that day thousands of citizens set out for the riverbank and lake shore to see what evidence of battles across the water they might witness.

After taking Fort Erie without violence, and winning the admiration of the town's citizens for their polite treatment of them, the invaders led by General O'Neil headed west to Ridgeway, where they met a force of 1500 British troops on June 2nd. There they were defeated. Of the 2,000 men assembled at Black Rock, it was reported that just 1,500 followed through to the landing across the river. Like Peter, upon being faced with the hard reality, others had changed their minds and walked away.

As the days passed, thousands more Fenians continued to flood into the city, too late to participate in the invasion. They numbered 10,000 total, and had they arrived in time, history would have written a different tale.

On June 2nd, General Ulysses S. Grant arrived in Buffalo to take control of the situation, placing General William F. Barry in command of the frontier with authority to call out the national guard if necessary. Since thousands of frustrated Fenians were now roaming Buffalo's streets, stymied by their having arrived too late to cross into Canada for the fight, the guard was put on alert for expected outbursts.

There were none.

A U.S. Army detachment was ordered to Fort Porter to help prevent further hostile movements from the American side.

Mary was relieved when the Fenians were forced to turn and withdraw after their first and only victory against the British at Fort Erie, and hoped that their retreat back across the border would finally put an end both to the revolutionary group, as well as her husband's reckless interest in war.

"Ye ran like a coward, ye did, Peter Halloran!" boomed Paddy O'Day. "Ye betrayed us when we needed you most. We lost good men we didn't have to lose because of yellow bellies like you. But worse, you were a leader! We met in your saloon and made our plans together as brothers. You yourself persuaded sweet Michael O'Shea to join the Fenians, and now the beautiful lad's dead at Ridgeway, and yer sorry ugly arse is still walkin' the earth! Shame on ye! And to crown it off, at Black Rock, ye turned and ran like a little girl. Ain't that just grand now!"

The customers at Halloran's saloon had fallen dead silent after Fenian invader Paddy O'Day, newly released from jail, stomped into the establishment and began his tirade. He timed his visit for Saturday night, when the place was packed, and still early enough so that people wouldn't be too drunk to understand what he had to say. Peter Halloran had bragged for a week to all his friends that he had personally shot two Redcoats up at Ridgeway, and they treated him like a hero. He had become drunk on their praise and the glory and admiration they heaped on him, all for his fabricated valiant deed.

But then, Paddy O'Day had to come stalking in, determined to put the liar Peter Halloran in his place, secure in the fact that an account of his confrontation at Peter Halloran's Saloon that night would be spread all over the Ward by the next afternoon.

It was.

The saloon lost 75% of its customers the first week and 90% the second. Irish crossed the street to avoid having to offend their noses with the scent of the traitorous skunk. Peter Halloran was shunned and berated, ridiculed and loathed.

Mary Halloran was stunned into prayerlessness. God had not just forsaken her, he most assuredly hated her with a vengeance, and was determined to torture her continually until the day she died.

When business abruptly stopped at the saloon she had not yet heard a reason. She was preoccupied at home caring for the baby. Had she ventured out she would have been shunned just like Peter, but it was three days before Jim came to her with the truth after witnessing Peter's belligerence at home increase. He was now worried for his mother and brothers.

Jim had been set upon by a gang of lads while walking down South Street with Ed Stanton, but stopped them cold by telling them he wanted no part of Peter Halloran, that the scoundrel had tricked his mother into marrying him, and that already having spent time in prison, he was surely destined to return there. "Go ahead and give me a whippin' if you will, but I hate the man now far more than you ever will, and I sure wish you boys would do me the favor of saving your energy for when you come upon the sight of him. As you can see, me, my mother, and my baby brothers are already being punished enough."

His speech in the face of such an overwhelming threat made a mark on his would-be attackers, and recognizing that the deep suffering in his eyes only reflected their own, they backed away.

Fenian Troops drill in preparation for invading Canada at Malone NY.

1866
Unconstitutional

"It appears that yer poor late husband died fer nothin, afterall," said Mrs. Malone in a mournful tone.

Mary and Peter Halloran had taken baby Daniel and young JP up to Elk Street to shop at the hardware store and the grocers. No one had spoken to them in over an hour. Neighbors and former friends crossed the street or averted their eyes. Peter Halloran was being shunned.

Peter had charge of the boys while Mary picked vegetables from the wooden bins in front of the grocer's. Mrs. Malone had approached cautiously.

"What ever do you mean?" responded Mary, her feelings wounded.

Mrs. Malone was well over seventy years old and still straight of spine and sharp as a tack. Her late husband had been the founder of the upstate town of Malone, N.Y., presently shut down and occupied by U.S. Army troops.

"No, no, Mrs. Sullivan, um, I mean, Mrs. Halloran. No offense meant whatsoever! It's just this terrible situation we're in, now that they've placed us practically under martial law!"

Mary had avoided the newspapers, and even contact with her neighbors, just wanting the whole Fenian affair and everything connected to it to go away. Not that anyone was coming into the saloon anymore, ever since Paddy O'Day publicly shamed Peter. She assumed the whole matter was finally over. All she had to do now was to wait for the dust to settle.

"Yer late husband gave his life so that the Union could remain together, but I ask ye, fer what purpose? The war's over and the men have come home, but we're all practically prisoners in our own country now!"

"Forgive me Mrs. Malone, but I don't know what yer talkin' about," said Mary, her patience giving out.

"Why, darlin' girl, I'm talkin' about the military men that those rats in Washington have sent to Buffalo to enforce civilian laws! That's illegal! Our rights have gone! How could you possibly not realize?"

Mary didn't realize, that's for certain. But no one had ever suggested that her sweet John had died in the war for nothing. The thought of such a thing set her blood to boiling against old Mrs. Malone. Surely the old girl must be getting batty to say such an awful thing.

"What rights have they taken from us, might I ask?" demanded an exasperated Mary.

"Why, they have forbidden the transportation of any Fenians—or any Fenian supporters—which amounts to the entire population of our city! What American does not want revenge upon the English for what they have done to our nation? We're not allowed now to board our own trains or boats! We've been prohibited from using the telegraph! We can't travel outside our own city and we cannot even notify anyone outside our city what is going on hereabouts!

"The American government in Washington completely overlooked England's breaking of the Neutrality Law of 1818 for a half century when it was trampled upon, over and over again by the British and the Canadians, especially during the late Civil War! But now suddenly the dictators are enforcing it so that our sons and brothers cannot aid our own people in Ireland in their fight for freedom from under the English boot heel!

"They are allowing those British hoodlums to the North and on the other side of the Atlantic to execute our Fenian sons for doing exactly what they themselves did against us during our late war!! I never would have believed that our own government would hand over our boys to the enemy!"

Peter glanced over, and recognizing that Mary was becoming upset, approached with the boys in time to hear Mrs. Malone's speech.

"No, ma'am. It is only the Fenian troops that are temporarily under these orders," said Peter.

"I beg to differ sir. Read your newspaper!"

Mrs. Malone pulled that morning's issue of the Buffalo Courier out of her bag, and began to read the editorial aloud. A curious crowd had gathered, attracted by her loud voice and unbridled agitation.

"The order of Gen. Barry, issued in pursuance of instructions from Gen. Meade, prohibiting the transportation of Fenians by rail or water in any direction, and forbidding them the use of telegraph wires for any purpose, strikes us as an extraordinary stretch of military authority in time of peace. The military authorities have no right to issue an order of this character, any more than they had a right to try civilians by courts martial in time of war, or to close newspaper offices."

Mrs. Malone was now enraged.

"The military," she lectured, "have determined that a Fenian, by their definition, is anyone who believes in the cause! And that, Mr. Halloran, is every one of us!"

Mary was rattled by Mrs. Malone's fervor. Her children were becoming distressed.

"You're upsetting my children, can't you see?"

"No, Mrs. Halloran, the question at hand is, can't you see?" scoffed the now-imperious Mrs. Malone.

"Good day, Mrs. Malone!" Mary huffed, and stormed off with her husband in tow.

Peter stopped a newsboy and paid his penny for the morning Courier.

He was having a brain storm. It came to him that he might rally a public outcry demanding the repeal of the Neutrality Law of 1818, and he could headquarter it from his surely-to-be bustling-again saloon.

Mary couldn't get Mrs. Malone's words out of her head. They angered her so much precisely because they echoed her own beliefs, beliefs she had been too fragile and frightened to give a voice to. She went about her chores and attending to the children with her mind completely removed from each task, so festering was her brain with long-buried thoughts. She had been living on knife's edge since the moment John Sullivan's train steamed away from the depot on that hot August day five years previous, always fearing that the least little new irritation might be the final thing to drive her over the brink of sanity and reason. Her strategy was to simply not think about it. That is, until she ran into Mrs. Malone.

Mary asked Peter to read to her from the newspaper as she worked. The saloon downstairs was devoid of customers. They would hear a bell ring if anyone came in the door. It had been silent for days.

He began reading aloud.

"The neutrality law is a civil one, and the penalties it prescribes are to be inflicted by civilian tribunals, not the military. The military and naval forces may be employed in its execution, but it is certainly nowhere provided that such extraordinary interference with private rights may be exercised. There remain at this time four thousand Fenians in this city. How can they, if this order is strictly enforced, return peaceably to their several abodes?

"Why should American citizens connected with the Fenian organization who themselves cannot be called 'belligerents' be arbitrarily deprived of the right to employ the telegraph? We fail to see the necessity or propriety of so sweeping an order as this."

Peter paused and looked at his wife.

"Mary, I want your boys to know that their father didn't die so that darkeys can run free among us whilst at the same time we Irish are deprived of our most basic rights. And it isn't just Irish that those Washington bastards have turned against. It's everybody who hates the British—which includes every last Union soldier and their families, and yes, every nigger even! Your John would be turnin' in his grave to know what was happenin' to us here! God damn that Andrew Johnson! I wouldn't be surprised if he placed the pistol in Booth's hand at the Ford's Theater himself!"

Peter Halloran was getting more worked up the more he put the puzzle together. He was devising a plan that could well save his reputation while at the same time demonstrating his fury at the American government.

"Mary, I'm going to call a meeting at the saloon for all citizens who are fed up! Everyone who is furious about the British betrayal during the late war! If it wasn't for that scum interferin' in our affairs, that war would have been over in months instead of years! All those dead boys would be here with us today — alive. Those English snakes have vexed us Irish almost to extinction. Our people were forced to either starve to death or leave our homeland to escape them, only to come here and be conscripted to fight in a war that wasn't just against the Confederacy, but against the South's bloody interfering British allies too! The world is fed up fighting off the British at every turn!"

"What can you possibly do about it, Peter?" moaned the exasperated Mary.

"I'll get the people together to demand we dump that neutrality law into the drink just like the revolutionists dumped the tea into Boston Harbor!" he gushed animatedly. "That beer downstairs is just goin' to sour anyway with nobody buyin' it. I'll have a rally, offering free beer, and show that bastard Paddy O'Day what I'm really made of! It's time for the free Irish of this country to show their indignation directly to those Royalists in Washington!"

Peter Halloran ran out of the saloon to the printers. He ordered 500 pasters and spent the entire next day with his pot of glue pasting the notices to fences and fixtures. The pasters cried:

RALLY!
To Abolish The Neutrality Law of 1818!
Down With The British Traitors!
FREE BEER!
Halloran's Saloon

The First Ward I

No. 16 Hamburgh Street
Saturday Night June 9th!
(Bring your own drinking vessel)

The neighboring saloonkeeps were none too happy to learn that free beer would be provided on what would ordinarily be their most profitable night of the week, and they weren't shy about letting that Halloran scum know about it. "Then join with me, lads! Show the Irish in ye! I'm donating my beer, so why not join in? The goodwill that this will create will benefit us all. I expect some 500 men will attend, from all over the city. Maybe more. Let's show 'em a grand time and gain some new customers for ourselves! Let's show 'em that we Irish river rats can throw a party they'll never forget!"

The other saloonkeeps were suspicious.

Halloran's reputation was in the gutter for a multitude of well-deserved reasons.

They decided to just wait and watch.

Peter Halloran was right. More than five hundred men came down South Street and plied Hamburgh Street's planks on Saturday night for free beer and a rousing rally condemning the American government for its defending British interests. Peter found he more than had his hands full. Jim Sullivan worked the kegs, dispensing brew to enthusiastic lines of men, assisted by his friend Ed Stanton. Peter had promised the fourteen-year-old free beer to work for the evening. Ed's father James Stanton reacted angrily to the plan, so Halloran paid him twenty-five cents instead.

Peter had asked Mary to remain upstairs, fearing trouble from rowdies, but despite the free beer, the crowd was admirably well mannered. He took a moment to go up and visit with her and ask if she might be willing to bring the children downstairs and say a few words about John Sullivan.

"No!"

Mary was dumbfounded. Peter had never wanted to hear anything more than necessary about her late first husband.

"Are you serious, Peter? Why would I speak? And why about John? What ever would I say about him?"

"Mary, your John's a hero. He died for his new country, to the greatest of sacrifices of you and your boys. I would like to honor John by your sayin' a few words about him to the other men, and if you're up to it, about how you feel, you know, about this awful situation of none of us Irish being allowed on a boat or a railcar. You must feel some insult about that? After all, you were made a widow, and your sons given to an orphanage, all in the name of freedom. And now those same government people who sent John into battle and kept your rightful pensions from you have taken away your freedom and that of your children? That's unforgivable! Right now, you and John Sullivan's sons are prisoners in your own city."

Peter kissed her on the cheek and descended the stairs. Mary was left confused and not just a little apprehensive.

One of the crowd of saloon attendees was Charles W. Murphy, attorney at law, who knew nothing of Peter Halloran's reputation, but had seen the pasters, and had a great interest in the cause. As an attorney and a constitutionalist he was incensed over the illegality of the current government policy. The two men talked at length and found common ground. Attorney Murphy wanted to make an announcement to the gathering. It took quite some time to quiet the group down. Murphy stood on the stoop, so that those both inside and out might hear him, for the street was full of men lined up for their free beer.

"Gentlemen, my name is Charles W. Murphy. I am an attorney at law, and I would like to encourage you and invite you all to attend a mass meeting this Tuesday at St. James Hall concerning Fenian matters and the reprehensible Neutrality Law of 1818.

"Senator Fitzgerald and Senator Hines will speak, along with other high-ranking officials. They will provide authoritative information and irrefutable arguments. Their analysis of the situation will prove most valuable to you in understanding the circumstances. Now, allow me to introduce to you your generous host and provider of fine brew, Mr. Peter Halloran."

Much applause and cheering followed, to the great pleasure of Halloran, who had in his life experienced no such accolade previously. Peter stepped up to say a few words.

"Thank you gentlemen. I am very much heartened by your attendance at my humble little tavern and I hope you will come back and see us again soon. My desire tonight was to provide a place for you to gather with your friends and relax where we all might learn a little more about our terrible state of affairs here in Buffalo, and in other nearby towns like Malone."

Peter spotted Mary with the baby in her arms and Jim and John by her side. She had come down to join her husband. She smiled and nodded her approval.

"Gentlemen, as some of you might know, my beloved wife Mary here is the widow of the war hero John Patrick Sullivan, who was shot at the battle of Bull Run and died thereafter. John Sullivan's tragic death left my Mary alone and penniless, and their sons without a father. The family suffered greatly for quite some time, but I am proud to say that this same brave lady is now my wife. I would like you to meet her."

Peter beckoned Mary and the boys to the front where all could see, and a cheer rose up the likes of which had never before been heard in the First Ward. Mary was brought to tears as men gently touched her and the boys as she made her way to where Peter stood. Peter kissed her and for the first time since they had met, he displayed a true measure of pride and admiration in her and for her. Mary found herself unexpectedly moved.

The men quieted, and Mary struggled to compose herself. Jim had his arm around his mother, and from out of nowhere, she would later recall, the words just flowed.

"Me name is Mary Halloran, and I am the widow of John Patrick Sullivan, who many of ye knew as a good man and a fine father to his children. And these two handsome boys here are his sons, Jim and John." A wave of emotion flowed from the crowd toward the family that was in part alcohol-inspired, and part gratitude for the sacrifice she and the boys had made for their country.

"As ye know, we have thousands of Irish Fenian sons and brothers here in our city at this moment who have nowhere to go and nothing to eat. These men have been told they cannot enjoy the most basic freedoms that they themselves fought to preserve in the late war, and at a terrible cost to us all. This is not only unfair, it is an insult. To ask us to risk everything we hold dear in the name of freedom, and then to... to take that freedom away from us after we have done our duty, is...well... I don't quite know words strong enough that can describe such a betrayal of our citizens by our own American government.

"Most of us in Buffalo are especially acquainted with the scurrilousness of the English, for they lay lurkin' just a mile across those waters over there." Mary pointed down the river toward Fort Erie. A great murmur went up from the gathering.

"We have seen these British face to face at their most cunning and vindictive, both at home in Ireland and now here again in our new country, in our adopted city. It pains me terribly to know that throughout the time that me own husband John was tryin' to keep himself alive for me and his two boys, that the English, both those on the opposite side of the Atlantic and those right there across that river in Canada, were schemin' and plottin' to defeat us by aidin' our enemies in the South. If not for those two-faced scum, perhaps me boys' father would still be here with his sons today!"

She paused to think. The crowd was now completely silent. Jim was bursting with pride for his mother, who he had never seen speak to more than one or two people at one time before. Mary paused nervously, not quite knowing what to say next. But then it came to her. She stammered a little.

"We all... we all have to attend this meetin' at St. James Hall on Tuesday evening so that something like this is not allowed to ever happen again. And the only way to do that, and to punish the English, is to rip that double-dealin' neutrality law right out of the books and begin treatin' those scum the same way they've been treatin' us in this country—and in Ireland— for the past two hundred years and more!"

A roar went up from the admiring throng, and befuddled by her own unprecedented pluck, Mary longed to run back inside. But the enclosing crowd made that impossible. Mary for her part had no idea at any point what she was about to say, and was as surprised as anyone at the words that tumbled from her lips. Especially the part about everyone gathering at St. James Hall. With the passage of just a few minutes' time, she had become an activist.

Men wanted to meet her, and thank her, and Peter was suddenly filled with delight and optimism, for he could never have predicted just three days before that their dire situation in the First Ward would turn around so fast, and become so well appraised. He knew at this moment that he had his saloon back, and that Mary needn't worry about poverty and misery coming to stalk her again.

Attorney Murphy stood up and asked that the men who were able, to contribute whatever they could to the Fenian cause, and that Peter Halloran would bring the funds to St. James Hall on Tuesday in their name. Hats were passed, and the breathtaking sum of $112 was collected.

It was in Peter Halloran's basic nature to formulate other less noble plans for such a large windfall, but he was clever enough realize that the greater good for all, especially himself, would be accomplished by following through and delivering the entire sum to the Fenian officials.

Faux Pas

On Tuesday Peter begged Mary to come to the meeting, but she claimed she was not feeling well, and she did not feel safe leaving the baby with anyone. On the previous Saturday night Peter had seen with his own eyes that he had a heretofore undiscovered asset in his wife—the use of her, her family, and her troubled history to fuel his plan to regain respectability and bring business back to his saloon. It wasn't as if the Fenian cause did not take some precedence, but surely putting bread on the table came before all else.

He had $112 to present at the meeting, and attorney Murphy had arranged for a public announcement congratulating him to be made from the stage. Buffalo's Fenian leader Paddy O'Day would have to eat his hat when confronted with Peter Halloran's new powerful friend Murphy, and the accolades sure to come from his fund-raising efforts.

Peter Halloran couldn't wait.

As early as half-past seven o'clock the body of the St. James Hall and the galleries were densely packed, till nary sitting nor standing room was left unoccupied. The press was well represented, including a spy from the Hamilton Sentinel in Ontario.

Peter Halloran arrived early, and saw a single empty seat down front. As he made his way along the irritated seated citizens in that row, he noticed that to the seat was affixed a brass plaque, impeccably polished. He quickly read the inscription.

> Here sat President Abraham Lincoln
> on the evening of February 17, 1861,
> while he attended a lecture at St. James Hall.

Out of deference, no one ever occupied the seat, but Peter Halloran, sorely lacking in both the common sense and the sensitivity that most others possessed, took no notice. Before his descending hind-end could make contact with the seat's surface, he was hoisted up rudely by the surrounding crowd.

"Sir! That's the late President's seat! No one ever sits there but him!"

Peter Halloran hadn't ever blushed in his entire life that he could recall, but his face grew burning hot as a thousand sets of eyes locked upon him, witnessing his blunder. He apologized profusely and backed his way down the row again, bowing and scraping to the entire crowd. He finally located a single unoccupied seat toward the back.

A document was being circulated among the audience on which those attending were asked to affix their signature:

> To the Representatives in Congress, Assembled—
> The undersigned citizens of Buffalo would respectfully represent
> that certain persons, officers of the United States, have lately, here

in our city, through the exercise of (as we believe) usurpation and entirely without shadow of legal authority—

1st. Virtually closed this port.

2d. Suspended ferriage on the Niagara River.

3d. Prevented free trade traffic and travel.

4th. Prohibited "suspected" persons from utilizing public conveniences.

5th. Interdicted the use of public lines of telegraph to "suspected" persons.

This is invading the interest rights of free citizens, and as we believe without shadow of law. To the end that our liberties may be asserted and vindicated, and that parties offending in this flagrant manner may be brought to condign punishment, we respectfully ask that a Committee of Congress may be directed to come here and investigate the facts and report to Congress the result of such investigation.

People eagerly signed the document, and for the next two hours it flew around the Hall like a canary suddenly liberated from its cage.

The meeting was called to order by Albert Sherwood, Esq., at half past eight. Mr. Sherwood thanked the meeting for the compliment implied by calling upon him to preside over the deliberations of so vast an assemblage. His sympathies were with all with the boys in green; and as an American citizen, he would say that his warmest feelings were fully in accord with the action of the government, so far as that was necessary to maintain its dignity and honor.

But himself and many others felt that the United States government had gone much farther in observing the Neutrality Law of 1818 than the English and Canadian governments did during the late war. He understood the object of this gathering was to endorse the action of Congress which would give to England and Canada the same brand of neutrality which they gave us from 1861 to 1865. Which in point of fact, was none at all.

Mr. Sherwood concluded his brief remarks amid a storm of applause, after which Buffalo City Clerk, C.S. Macomber Esq. was called upon, and made a speech which was characterized by genuine and impassioned eloquence throughout. Divested of glowing rhetoric, the following captures the substance of Mr. Macomber addressing his fellow citizens from all over the country:

"It is the darkest hour that precedes daylight. The utmost despondency precedes the brightest prospects and the most brilliant success.

"These are old and trite sayings, and exemplified a thousand times in every man's life, and they are particularly exemplified in the revolutions that have occurred in this as in every other nation of the habitable globe. I understand from a notice which appeared in one of the daily journals of the city that this meeting was called to give expression to the sentiments of our citizens to the resolutions introduced into Congress for the repeal of the Neutrality Law of 1818."

Mr. Macomber continued by saying that he was in favor of strict neutrality, but there appeared to be two kinds of neutrality at work here. One of these he was in favor of and the other he wasn't.

"Individuals constitute the component parts of a government, and the government should be responsible for the fulfillment of the stipulations and conditions of its contracts as rigidly as in the case of individuals. The Neutrality

Law has existed for over forty-eight years, and in every instance where the liberties or interests of Great Britain were at stake, this country has enforced it to its very letter. On the other hand. England, in every case, and especially during the late war, proved false and faithless to every condition which has been recognized and enforced by the American government.

"I cannot forget that during the late rebellion they did, not as individuals but as a people; not as a single community, but as a nation; not as an isolated newspaper, but the English press as an entirety, derided our brave army and navy, scoffed at the ability of our Generals, traduced and maligned our motives as a nation; jubilant when our army was in its adversity, and sorrowful when in its triumph; conspiring and combining, aiding and abetting our enemy.

"I personally would feel that I was forgetting my manhood and unworthy to be protected by the laws of my country if I myself withheld, aye, if I did not express my strongest sympathies in favor of the cause of a people, as a class, who have stood by us as a nation in every struggle for national existence, power and greatness; whose acts of valor and heroism have long been historic and will occupy the brightest pages in the history of our country.

"If England shall insist upon her pound of flesh after proving herself faithless and false to the obligations of her treaties with this government in every respect, there will be a voice go up from the people in whose hands the power rests, demanding and insisting that our government shall exact from the British government full indemnity and satisfaction for property destroyed, and for lives of the brave sailors that have been sacrificed by reason of the armed vessels that have been fitted out in her own ports, under the eyes of her own government officials, and within reach of her own guns.

"If England shall refuse to pay this in pounds, shillings, pence and farthings, and war must come to enforce this demand, then let it come! For every thrust of the sword and every cannon shot will bring nearer the era so wished for by so many who are here tonight; the era when a million American soldiers as brave as ever trodding the battlefields of the world will stamp beneath their feet British pride, British aristocracy and British buffoonery!"

He had great praise for the thousands of Fenians who were still assembled along hundreds of miles of international border.

"The men who have come here from their homes to strike a blow for Irish liberty, who have come from Kansas and Nebraska, from Louisiana and California, from all the states of the Union, who have been stretched 50,000 strong along a frontier of nearly four hundred miles, have conducted themselves in every community where they have been in such a manner as to win confidence, esteem and admiration of all classes of our citizens, and eliciting the most cordial sympathies in behalf of their cause.

"Be patient. Be not carried away by your passions. Be not hasty in your judgement of the acts of your rulers. Wait. Bide your time. You have stood by your government, and so far as lies in their power they will stand by you. The time may not be far in the future when you can plant the green flag upon the soil of your Fatherland, where God's green sward lies over the graves of your country's patriots."

Mr. Macomber was frequently interrupted by the most enthusiastic applause and his address was most warmly endorsed on every point. At its close, which was signalized by the wildest cheering, Lyman B. Smith, Esq. was called to the stage.

Mr. Smith said that he had no idea a half hour before this meeting commenced of his even attending, much less being called upon to address so large a number of his fellow citizens and sons of the Green Isle. But in the cause of human freedom he was ever ready to respond. He stated that he understood the meeting's purpose was to endorse the recent action in Congress, looking towards the repeal of the law between the United States and Great Britain. That was a step in the right direction, he believed.

Mr. Smith recollected being down south during the late Civil War, and had quite a correct idea of neutrality as viewed through English spectacles. He recollected at the capture of Norfolk, that the finest guns found in the possession of the rebels were of English manufacture and furnished by English speculators. He recollected well, a shell picked up on the battlefield of Seven Pines, covered with the blood of his countrymen, that bore the impress of English manufacturing. He had at this very instant at his house just a short walk from this very Hall, bullets of English manufacture which had been collected from many battlefields of the South that carried desolation and mourning to the homes of his friends who held them. Such was the kind of neutrality that perfidious England dealt out with unilateral hand to this country during the struggle for the preservation of the United States of America.

He could not forget that the cruiser Alabama, fitted out in English waters, cleared from an English port, furnished with an English armament and supplied with English gold, had destroyed our ships, killed our boys and preyed upon our commerce. He could not forget that England, to cripple her rival for trade in the world, had furnished the sinews of war that had caused the deaths of hundreds of thousands of brave American men. Had it not been for England, her perfidy, her sedition, her treacherousness, the rebellion would have been put down in half the time. In spite of the profanation, outrage and lawlessness of English interference however, our flag was sustained and the Union preserved.

"It is the intention of the people of this country to perpetuate the principles of our free institutions," he said, "and sustain the hands of the oppressed in every land. If necessary, we will give substantial aid. We who have Irish blood in our veins have a lively recollection of the martyrs who have suffered in the cause of Irish freedom; of those who have been transported to Van Dieman's Land for revolting against the iron heel that was endeavoring to crush out their manhood. We cannot but sympathize with the poverty-stricken people of the fairest Island on the Globe, whose very substance is seized to pay for the luxuries of a pampered British aristocracy.

"With such scenes of oppression and outrage perpetrated upon a brave people before them, Americans cannot withhold their sympathy or fall to aid Ireland in shaking off the yoke of the oppressor!

"We wish it understood however, as a people and as a government, we will sustain the laws of the land so long as they are in existence; but we intend there shall be no obstacle to human freedom, and if our laws are in the way of granting aid to the oppressed, especially to those who have fought so nobly to preserve freedom and free institutions in this country, they must be repealed. This country is the champion of human liberty, and we must aid all people who are striving for their freedom."

Mr. Smith paid a just tribute to the soldiers of the Irish Army, now in Buffalo, for the good order they had maintained, and their quiet deportment under the most trying circumstances. He said he believed that it was hardly possible that so large a crowd of men to have behaved more discreetly; that their praise was sounded by every mouth. This remarkable behavior and respect for the laws and quiet of the city had won them an additional sympathy, and he hoped nothing would occur to forfeit such a bright record of unparalleled conduct. He had frequently heard it asked, "How is it possible for so large a body of soldiers, eagerly waiting for the opportunity to meet the foe, act so discreetly and preserve such order?" He conjured them not to act indiscreetly. Time would make all things even. Smith quoted some appropriate lines from Byron:

> But time at length makes all things even,
> And if we do but bide the hour,
> There never yet was human power
> That could evade, if unforgiven,
> The patient search and vigil long,
> Of him who treasures up a wrong.

"Now, if the Irish people have not treasured up wrongs, if they have not suffered all and been ground under the heel of the oppressor, in the name of God, who has? Their time, I hope, has come. They stood on the rock of liberty. They stood among the people who had more regard for human freedom than any other people on the globe. Let Irishmen be not discouraged. If they could not act just then, the day was not far distant when they would successfully accomplish the object so near their heart's desire."

Great waves of applause and wild cheering were the response in grace to Mr. Smith's inspired statements. The uproar had to be repeatedly quieted in order to allow the presentation of Senator Hines.

Hines detailed in glowing colors the scenes he witnessed at Malone, N.Y., and other points of the frontier; the eagerness with which the soldiers of the Irish Army had pressed to the front, and the difficulty they had to undergo in obtaining transportation, on account of the severe measures taken by the United States authorities to prevent them reaching the Canadian line.

"Some of the men—American citizens who had fought the battles for the Union—after having purchased tickets and paid for their own passage, and who were without arms in their possession, were, for no other cause than that they bore unmistakable evidence of being Irishmen, were physically hurled from the railcars by order of the government officials. Even under such adverse circumstances, hundreds of these men had walked a distance of seventy-three miles to their destination. Such men could not be crushed by paper proclamations."

He was furiously critical of General Meade for the extreme measures he had enacted, even forbidding the citizens of Malone from furnishing the famished soldiers of the Fenian Army with food.

His remarks caused a wave of resentment to flow through the Hall.

Paddy O'Day followed next on the dais, incensed that General Barry had seized Fenian armaments under orders from General Meade. He said he had demanded their return, claiming them as his private property, legally acquired as an Auction and Commission Merchant. He fumed at General Barry's reply claiming that he had seized the property by command of his own superior officer; and that he would remain as custodian until he received further orders.

Next to speak was Senator Fitzgerald. His was an effective address; rather denunciatory of the President and expressive of a confidence in Congress in regard to the repeal of the Neutrality Law as a foregone conclusion, as a fact to be. A sure thing. He reminded the audience of the great sympathy shown by the United States government toward the struggles in Greece and South America for civil liberty, and the duplicity evident in these as opposed to the government's policy toward Ireland.

"Is not Ireland entitled to such sympathy and aid as were extended to the Greeks? It seems that if a nation is weak and the risk small, America rushes forward, proclaiming its authority to compel liberty upon downtrodden peoples. But when the consequences might prove more dire, when trade might suffer or the possibility of war with a mighty foe may be a result, the American government shrinks from its professed superior moral authority and turns its back on those who suffer most, such as those under the iron mallet of the British Empire."

Before concluding his speech, Fitzgerald made an appeal on behalf of the welfare of the Fenian soldiers now within the city. This appeal was responded to most satisfactorily once he had called for Peter Halloran to come forward before the eyes of the entire city to present his contribution. The Senator and other officials gratefully accepted the amount, and Peter asked if he might say a few words to encourage the assembled to contribute as well.

He nervously took the stage.

Paddy O'Day, who had defamed Halloran at his place of business just ten days before, attempted to give him the evil eye, but Halloran resisted looking in his direction.

"Ladies and gentlemen, these funds do not come solely from my own pocket, but from children's candy jars and from under the mattresses of the laboring Irish poor in the First Ward who struggle just to feed their own. Our benefit held at Halloran's Saloon on Hamburgh Street last week accomplished this contribution of $112, and I encourage all here who are able to give, as well as those who might be in a position to raise funds from your own customers and neighbors, to please help our boys."

Then he shouted, "Three cheers for the Irish Army!"

In unison the sardine-packed Hall erupted in thundering Hip-Hip-Hooray cheers for the Fenian soldiers.

Paddy O'Day, who rested in an honored place on the flanks of the stage, sat in rigid festering consternation, fuming that his public denunciation of Peter Halloran just days beforehand had provided the very vehicle for his reinvention as a respected leader in the Irish cause.

O'Day knew full well the true construct of the fabric that made up the whole of Peter Halloran, and he vowed to himself that the entire city would know it too, no matter what that might require.

On June 7th, eighteen Fenian officers who had been arrested posted bail before Judge Clinton and were released. All other prisoners were set free on their own recognizances. Although fresh Fenian troops continued to arrive in the city, on June 12th orders were issued commanding the entire Fenian force to return to their homes, General Barry providing transportation.

Grateful Fenians had a bulletin of thanks printed in the city newspapers on June 14:

On behalf of that portion of the Fenian Army who rendezvoused in this city but a few days, the undersigned beg to return their most profound gratitude to the citizens of Buffalo. Coming among you as strangers and stigmatized by those in British interests, the courtesy and aid you have so generously extended is therefore the more appreciated, and is characteristic of the indomitable love of liberty which is a prominent feature of the American people. Those who have thus shared your hospitality are now compelled to return to their homes without accomplishing the object dearest to their hearts, for which they were ready to offer up their lives. In conclusion, it affords us much pleasure that the conduct of the men has been such as not to disgrace the cause and to meet your general approval.
J.W. Fitzgerald
Michael Scanlan

1869
The Assault

Peter Halloran's dream of achieving respectability and accolades was not to be, due to his irascible and erratic behavior. Halloran was less than a patient man. His attention when applied to any new endeavor or idea faded quickly, diminished by self-doubt as to his ability to accomplish what he'd set out to. He tried to resurrect his past glory by joining an anti-British Fenian demonstration in New York City in March 1868 that attracted 100,000 supporters. Public opinion had turned against the Fenians as internal feuding between factions increased and the splintered group was increasingly seen as a threat to the country's stability.

In 1869, with the Fenian movement dead, Peter Halloran faded back into his familiar state of invisibility, and with that his anger and violent tendencies resurfaced. He was arrested on a number of occasions and became a familiar face in Justice King's Court.

Mary Halloran no longer looked hopefully toward the future but rather concentrated on just making it through another day with her family unscathed.

On August 2nd, heat and humidity hovered over Buffalo like a wool blanket, imprisoning the smoke and noxious gases incessantly spewed by industry and thickening the air to an intolerable degree. After an angry incident with a customer, Peter Halloran ordered the man out. Doc Greene, who tried mediating the spat, and who was quite inebriated himself, made a woozy attempt at attending to Peter Halloran's bruise and stopping his infuriated friend from leaving his company.

"Get off me, Doc!" screamed Halloran. "Too late now!"

Upstairs, Mary toiled in the kitchen, wiping sweat away from her eyes with her apron. Little Daniel played quietly on a cot while Jim and JP did piecework at the kitchen table, assembling artificial violets.

Peter Halloran clambered clumsily up the stairs, enraged. He entered the kitchen and immediately pounced on Jim, slapping him in the face.

"What did I tell ye about moppin' out the saloon, ye worthless bastard!

"But I did!", defended the boy. "I did mop it, just an hour ago! Look! The pail of dirty water's still sittin' yet, right over there in the corner, sir!

Halloran grabbed Jim's hair. Jim howled at the lunatic's attack.

"Don't sass yer Pa, ye hobbledehoy! Ye think yer board 'n' room 'round here is free fer the havin'? Ye think youse..."

Mary placed herself between her husband and son as the violence escalated.

"Stop this, Peter! You're drunk! Jim did mop it out! I inspected it when he got done! It's all clean!"

"Inspected it, did ye? Maybe best ye shoulda inspected yer dead husband's dirty little cock before ye let him plant these two useless good-for-nothin's inside yer old saggin' cunny!

Scuffling with Peter, Mary tried to reason with the corybantic fool.

"Don't talk that way in front of our children, Peter! Please!"

"Our children? Our children? I can't even be sayin' fer sure that little simpleton sittin' over there's mine, ye whore! He's slower'n molasses 'n' don't look nuttin' like me!

Halloran grabbed a butcher knife off the table, sending a glass pitcher earthward to shatter. Using his body as a battering ram, he backed Mary into the hot stove and plunged the knife blade into her neck. Screaming, Mary's dress caught fire.

The boys shrieked at the sight of their beloved mother enveloped in blood and flame. Jim picked up the scrub pail and doused his mother and Halloran with the dirty water, then walloped Halloran over the head with the heavy copper vessel full force, sending him sprawling across the floor. Jim pulled his mother away from the stove, checking to make sure the flames had been fully extinguished.

Mary sat on the floor leaning against the table, hyperventilating, her hand pressed against her neck wound instinctively. Blood mingled with dirty mop water trickled over and between her fiercely trembling fingers. Jim grabbed a flour sack and secured it against the laceration.

"Ma, sit! Hold this tight against yer neck! Doc Green is drinkin' right downstairs! I'll run down 'n' git him!"

Jim raced down the steps and screamed at the drunk doctor dozing at the table.

"Doc! Hurry! Peter shanked Ma straight in the neck!"

Doc Green abruptly snapped out of his stupor and tripped up the stairs right on Jim's tail. Customers ran into the street in search of a patrolman.

Mary shuddered violently. Baby Daniel howled. JP cowered in a corner traumatized. Halloran lay passed cold on the wet floor. As Doc tended to Mary, Jim took charge. He comforted his mother and picked up the baby, consoling him. With his free hand he pulled terrified JP gently from the corner.

"C'mon, JP. It'll be all right now."

Doc Green inspected Mary's wound, then told her a white lie.

"Now, now, Mary, darlin'. There's barely goin' to be a scar. It's not bad at all."

Then Doc directed his attention to Mary's sons.

"I need one of you boys to run downstairs to fetch my satchel off the table for me."

"I'll get it!" volunteered JP.

JP flew down the stairs and grabbed the doctor's bag. Just then the customers returned with patrolman Steven Whelan.

"Where are they now, son?" asked Whelan of JP.

"Upstairs, sir!" the terrified boy responded.

The officers quickly mounted the steps by twos and entered the room to witness the sadly common scene; alcohol, bleeding wife, crying baby, and the debris of rage borne out of a failure's lifetime of disappointments.

Doc Green accepted his satchel from JP. He removed stitching needles and cat gut to close Mary's wound. She slumped in shock, incapable of response. She hadn't yet reached out to her four year old, still whimpering in Jim's arms. Even though Mary had seen Peter's behavior becoming more erratic and angry in recent months, she chose to ignore it and just hope for the best.

She never dreamed he'd take a knife to her.

Whelan bent down to assess Peter Halloran, unconscious and bleeding.

"John Sullivan would be climbin' out of his Civil War grave right about now with bloody murder fillin' up his eyes," said the Doc, "if he only knew what this old bastard just done to his sweet family!"

Jim Sullivan looked down at Halloran splayed on the floor, snoring, as Doc Greene finished stitching his mother. Jim set about imagining killing Peter Halloran in various ways over and over in his mind; kicking his forehead in, taking a broken bottle to his groin, slowly, pleasurably choking the life out of him.

Patrolman Whelan said not a word. He sensed what Jim was thinking, for he'd thought similar thoughts himself, many times over. He imagined how Mary must feel. He saw the terror in the eyes of the smaller children. Whelan just waited silently, patiently for the Doc to get around to sewing Halloran up so that he could drag the old bastard off to jail. Again.

Doc finished dressing Mary's wound, squeezed her hand reassuringly, then gave his attention to Peter, while Jim got a broom to sweep up broken glass so the Doc could kneel on the floor.

"I can't bend over him and do this by myself! Just help me get him up in a chair, Jim."

Jim stood there, unmoved and unmoving, enjoying Halloran's open wound, planning others larger, bloodier and more impressive.

Momentarily Mary dreamed of the comparative peace and harmony of their lives previous to Peter Halloran's invading it, before recalling all too well her altogether different misery back then. There was no winning, she concluded. She had only jumped from a burning-hot skillet into the fire itself.

They may have been desperately poor, she and John Sullivan, but they loved each other, and they loved their children. She sorely missed the easy comfort so freely provided by her first love, father of her two older boys, her John. He may not have been perfect, but he was certainly nothing like Peter Halloran. John Sullivan had rarely offended her even with an abrupt word, and yet here she was now with a man who'd sunk a knife into her neck while her children watched.

Mary called for his arrest, and the patrolmen readied themselves.

Peter Halloran slowly roused and became more alert, opened his eyes, and groaned as he saw the familiar face of patrolman Whelan. Whelan hoisted the belligerent assaulter off the floor with Doc's help.

"You've gotten yourself into yet another grand fix now, haven't ye, Peter?" said Whelan. "C'mon, ye narky aul' git. I'm runnin' ye in! Shame on ye! Shame!"

As he watched Halloran brought unsteadily to his feet, ten year old JP was conflicted. Halloran was the only father JP had ever known. The older Jim had vivid memories of their real father branded indelibly into his mind, but JP remembered not a thing about him. Jim experienced no such disaccord as did his younger brother, and wished for Peter Halloran a ghastly demise.

Peter hung his head while being led out. Jim and JP set about cleaning up blood and glass, Jim refusing to acknowledge the departing scoundrel. Doc Greene, finished with his stitch work, said his goodbyes to Mary. She rocked little Daniel in her arms on the bed, as much to comfort herself as her child.

On the stifling hot morning of August 3rd, The Buffalo Courier let the entire city know of Mary's shame, right on the front page, with this notice:

Danny Halloran

> ASSAULT WITH A KNIFE. —Peter Halloran, a man who has served a term in the state prison, yesterday assaulted his wife Mary Halloran, with a butcher knife. Mary caused his arrest, and he was arraigned this morning at the police court, charged with an assault with intent to do bodily harm. He was fully committed for trial on the charge.

Mary and the children luxuriated briefly in the peace that Peter Halloran's absence brought them. But within two days' time Mary grew unsettled over the likely outcome of this criminal affair, both for them as a family, and financially.

Mary had only wed Peter in the first place out the bleakness of desperation, and at the time was grateful to find a man to provide and care for her and her two children. She was happy to give him a son of his own to solidify the union.

It was looking poverty and despair directly in the face that prompted her to marry Peter initially, and now with the serious charges against him, a repeat offender, they discussed the prospect of his going back to prison for a long time, and what that might mean.

Jim Sullivan had had his fill of saloons and drunks and the troubles they caused. He'd been surrounded by them from birth. Like most boys his age, he had big dreams of his own. He wanted to become a somebody. He had no desire to keep a saloon, but a saloonkeep he would become if it meant keeping his family together.

On August 5th the family reopened Halloran's Saloon, but the newspaper's revelation of the events of the night of August 2nd kept the regulars away. Indeed, their customers had many alternate choices, for there were 11 saloons right in that same corner block. Mary's old fears of destitution returned. She didn't know if she would be able to operate the saloon without Peter, just she and her Jim. She had never paid any attention to the business end of it. Her biggest fear was that she might lose her boys again.

She began to have second thoughts concerning Peter.

Mary collared patrolman Whelan on his rounds the next day and asked him into the empty saloon for some advice.

Whelan was acquainted with far too many widows whose husbands had died in industrial accidents, on the railroad tracks, in the river or canals or in the war, who were now existing at the very edges of misery. One widow had slashed the throats of her babies, and then her own. Her beautiful babies died. But she recovered, and now resides in the state lunatic asylum where she will remain until old age or disease claims her.

"Mrs. Halloran, I have seen the worst of the worst on me daily rounds, and I know ye don't want to hear this, but maybe there is some hope for Peter." Whelan said. "I have me doubts about how well the business might do without him, with so many other saloons located just a few steps away. I believe that only yerself, and yerself alone, can decide what is bearable to ye and what is not."

Patrolman Whelan said he would talk to Peter, find out what was going on in his head, and report back to her. The patrolman promised Mary that he'd put the fear of God Almighty into him.

Whelan visited Peter Halloran later that day and came upon a man in a blind panic, scared to death at the dire prospects that certainly lay ahead. Although Halloran tried to plead the tired chestnut that it wasn't him, rather "twas the drink," the patrolman stopped him cold.

"You are a bitter old Irishman, Peter Halloran, and yer not deservin' that beautiful family of yers. Whatever devils ye have in yerself, they'd better be driven out, or I see this as bein' the end of the road for yr. Ye know better than I do what the inside of that prison is like, and if that is the life ye choose instead of the warmth and comfort of yer own family, then I can't help you. Nobody can. But only a bleedin' depraved pervert would ever choose prison over such a lovely family."

Peter pleaded with Whelan to help him, to please petition Mary on his behalf, to ask her for forgiveness, to give him a second chance. "Me own father was a bastard who beat me bloody, and there isn't a night that goes by that I don't dream about murderin' him," he confessed.

"Yer father's been dead now goin' on thirty years," replied Whelan, "and there's not a damn thing ye can do about him. So, need I take it that ye think the solution for yer own problems, Peter Halloran, is to become the same kind of worthless drunken bastard to yer own children as yer father was to ye? Is that how we're gettin' revenge on our dead ancestors now, is it? By hurtin' our own children the same way our elders hurt us?

"I should think that if yer own mother and father put ye in the dirt, and ye know what that feels like, that doin' the same to yer own little ones would be unthinkable. But ye have chosen to do exactly that. Well, then, ye'd better think of a way to change, because if Mary agrees to drop the charges against ye and take ye back, there will be no more chances for ye in the future. Ye can either smother that anger ye have toward yer father, one way or another, or it will destroy both ye and yer family. Is that what ye want?"

"I do not!" cried Peter Halloran. "I didn't cross the bloody Atlantic to end up in a prison, or to ruin me life. I promise ye I will find a way past me problems, and stop me drinkin', and that Mary and the boys will never feel the wrath of me anger ag'in. Please tell her that. Tell her that I love her and the boys and that I am beggin' her to drop the charges ag'in me, and give me another chance!"

Uniontown

The Buffalo River snakes through the First Ward like a huge black python, deadly and still and lying in wait. The serpent's course sinuously follows the curve of Lake Erie's shore, able and willing to crush and swallow any of the Great Lakes steamers momentarily not minding where they might be going. In some places its coil slithers within an arrow's shot of the lake's shoreline, coming very close to but not quite joining it, until finally vomiting its filthy effluents into Erie's clean blue waters at the harbor's lighthouse.

This monstrous viper has consumed many a small sweet-faced Irish child playing too inattentively along its flanks. Decade after decade it has also swallowed confused or set-upon drunks who stumbled out of the dozens of saloons crowding South Street and Hamburgh Street side-by-each, as the polacks say, the men tragically under some delusion that they might soon arrive home to their beds, safe and warm.

The serpent lies almost motionless; deep, languid, its body convoluted by a series of hairpin turns inside of which, improbably, a convoy of behemoth ocean-going ships navigate skillfully and unceasingly throughout the day. These hairpin turns in the river's course have required the construction of slips that the passing giants can retreat into with the help of a small navy of stout tugboats, for such times when surrendering the right of way becomes a matter of survival.

The river wasn't always this menacing. Fifty years prior it was but a wooded creek with a bright sandy bottom and pure clear flowing waters only waist deep, where residents fished, took their drinking water, cooled off in the summer, and did their wash. The subsequent construction of a great seawall in the harbor successfully blocked the insistent intrusion of lake sand, and continual dredging excavated and widened the bucolic creek into a deep shipping channel, now filthy with waste and stinking to the heavens.

The houses, schools and stores of the local inhabitants lay mere meters from the river's banks. When the monstrous steam vessels wind and turn their way upriver to upload iron or unload coal, or spit out their bounty of crops from America's heartland into huge grain elevators, newcomers to the neighborhood gasp right out loud, so imminent seems the prospect for collision and disaster.

One such extreme turn in the river's course lies mere yards from the L-shaped intersection of South Street and Hamburgh Street.

Jake Triepil's Saloon occupies the corner property at No. 10 Hamburgh Street, a structure with a small barber shop attached at the rear that serves as family business as well as home to the eight Triepils. Next door to Triepil's, at No. 12, the Rapps reside, but at the rear of their home is found Mrs. Maloney's Hole In The Wall Saloon. At No. 16 Hamburgh, the two story clapboard up-and-down Halloran-Sullivan home-and-saloon provides a front-row seat from the upstairs to all the frightening riverfront prospects and more: the constant din of river tugs nudging giant tankers round the bend, choking thick black smoke belching from every kind of land and river engine all roaring in unison; the shouts of sailors, fireboat crews, deckhands and grain scoopers, the jarring clanking of metal from all directions, and the acrid effluences of the Union Ironworks into both air and water. Uniontown's dark enclosed presence looms right across the street known locally as "The Plank" — Hamburgh Street.

A wooden fence surrounds the vast Union Ironworks property, circumscribing a slum of fragile shanties known as Uniontown. These hovels are passed off as company housing, providing scant shelter to the daily sufferings and frustrations of the unfortunate Irish and German immigrant families who have stumbled into the lethal grasp of The Company. The shanty town was forever flooding, exacerbating the inhabitants' already dismal existence. The Company had the bright idea of dumping slag, the by-product of its iron manufacture, right there on the grounds of Uniontown amid the shabby structures, in order to raise the ground level.

The wood fence that surrounded the Ironworks community was as much there to keep residents in as intruders out. Within its confines were dirt streets bordered by wooden sidewalks having names like Monitor, Excelsior, Mill and Pioneer. Along these primitive sooty avenues the inhabitants would find most of what they required: housing, saloons, stores, and Dennison's Hotel, a boarding house for single male mill laborers at the end of Excelsior Street.

On Saturday evenings, after supper was served, Mrs. Dennison would clear the hotel's capacious dining hall of furniture. With a week's pay newly in their pockets, the rough mill men would brush their Sunday coats and hats free of acquired mill grit and grime, and renew their boots with a fresh coating of The Rising Sun stove polish, whose label claims "A Thing Of Beauty Is A Joy Forever."

Then they'd tap the kegs brought in for the occasion.

Uniontown females who had prettied themselves up took fresh-scrubbed children in tow and joined the men for a shindy. Tickets cost an astronomical twenty-five cents, but nobody complained because the profits went to the wives and children of the many men killed or injured at the Union Ironworks who had been left destitute by the loss of the breadwinner.

The well-known fiddler from Michigan Street, Blind Joe, a friend and good customer of Peter Halloran, was the favored entertainer at the Dennison's shindies. Joe's big dog, Porter, named after the celebrated General, went everywhere that Joe did, leading him, protecting him from the dangers unseen by Joe's dead eyes. Porter lay at his master's feet as Blind Joe, despite not enjoying the gift of sight nevertheless was able to identify others by their scent or the sound of their voice. He would begin calling out to everyone attending by their names, non-stop, once he'd tuned his fiddle and waxed his bow.

"Eight hands circle to the left, back again.—Arragh, what the devils ailin' ye, Patsy Carrey? First four forward, forward again, swing the girl with the hole in her stocking! Sides four forward—wake up there Jimmy Cassidy. One couple in the center, six hands 'round—oh my, ain't we bashful? Kiss her, man. What the devil's the matter with ye?"

Hamburgh Street bordered the Union Ironworks on its westerly side, and although located outside its fence, Hamburgh Street businesses served those who lived within, and was considered part of, Uniontown. The huge iron mill across the street from Halloran's saloon and household never ceased activity, and especially for those living in houses on Hamburgh Street, the clamor and stink never abated. It took five years for Jim Sullivan to get used to the midnight screeches and blasts of the steam whistle that signaled the change in shifts. Resigned, he ultimately learned to sleep through it.

Despite the ugliness and miserable lives being lived within and around Uniontown, the gangs of children meandering home from school paid no mind. They giggled and pushed, bullied and cajoled, celebrating their few minutes of responsibility-free play before they arrived at their own front steps to begin their chores.

The Erie Railroad tracks complete the longest side of the right triangle formed by the rails' diagonal bisecting of Hamburgh and South streets. Trains bulldoze right across both of these busy thoroughfares, demanding eminent domain. The railroad companies ignore the outcries and furious protestations of the nervous citizenry and laugh in the face of the local governments.

Blind Joe and his dog General Porter

Drunken Treasure

In the First Ward, virtually every family house harbored a saloon of some description — on the ground floor, street side, at the rear, or in a shack in the yard. There were also numerous grocer-saloons, barbershop-saloons, cobbler-saloons, laundry-saloons and every other imaginable combination.

As his old clock bonged midnight one Tuesday, James Manahar began tidying up at his saloon at 24 Hamburgh Street. He woke the only remaining customer, a drunk sleeping at the table, and told him it was time to go home. As the drunk walked out the door he tripped, plummeting full force nose-first into the planks. He was too hammered to feel his beak break. Out of his pockets rolled some small coins which quickly sought the nearest dark places between the rough-hewn boards.

The drunk collected himself, then struggled to rise. Once on his feet and having steadied his balance he realized he had to take a piss. He staggered the seventy yards to the end of Hamburgh and stood at the edge of the river. He unbuttoned his trousers, pulled out his penis, relaxed and threw his head back. He sighed as his bladder fully emptied. Teetering, he smiled at his success in remaining upright until fully drained. As he attempted to rebutton he lost his balance, fell into the river, and sunk into the inky murk like a stone where he drowned silently.

A few hours later, just before six o'clock, JP Sullivan emerged from the family flat to search between Halloran's planks in the gray gloom of first light.

"Ouch! Damn ye!" he complained unquietly. A sizable sliver from the roughly sawn boards punctured and sunk itself deep into the heel of his hand. He gnawed it out with his teeth, grimacing at the pain, spitting blood. Then he proceeded onward up Hamburgh street stopping at each saloon, finding nothing until he reached Manahar's.

Jackpot.

His practiced eye caught the slightest hint of a glint which upon silent examination in the obscure illumination revealed a nickle and two pennies.

"Aye, me pretties. Come to yer new keeper," he sang a bit too loudly.

The tromping of a fat man's flat feet was heard descending the stairs as JP furtively mined the coins out from their stubborn hiding place, then ran.

Manahar emerged limping in his nightshirt, waving a club, rewarded at last with the opportunity to catch the constant thief red-handed.

"Hey, youse! Boyo! Hey! Is that youse ag'in, Sullivan? Whaddya t'ink yer doin' there? What'd I tell youse? Getcher buggerin' fingers out from between me planks! What gets left on me premises belongs t' me! Come back here!"

JP took off like a bat out of hell toward the river.

A huge smile lit up his face as he outdistanced his pursuer. He slowed when he reached home, then turned to make sure Manahar wasn't in pursuit. It was getting too light to safely continue without risking the chance of getting caught. He pulled the loot from his pocket. As he calculated his eye caught something familiar-looking bobbing at water's edge. The drunk's body was so common a sight that it didn't warrant his second look.

JP was always awake and out by dawn's first glimmer these days. Seven mornings a week he scoured the perimeter of the family's saloon — Halloran's — first. Then he moved in one direction or another, depending on a whim. He visited Triepil's Saloon at the corner, the Hole In The Wall at No. 12, Halloran's at No. 16, Smith's Saloon at No. 20, Zeller's saloon at No. 22, Manahar's saloon at No. 24, Short's saloon at No. 28, Heilback's at No. 48, and then paused for good measure at Louis Zittel Grocers—also a saloon—at No. 50, to examine between the boards closely for any shiny possibility.

If it wasn't too light yet at that point he went back to South Street and went around the corner to examine Dalton's grocers-saloon, and next to that, Sullivan's saloon, no relations of his dead father or so he'd been told.

The best thing about drunks, he believed, was that they were always losing things out of their pockets—coins, hopefully—and once, a glorious green wadded ball of six one-dollar bills. Now, that was an amazing day of great fortune that JP Sullivan would not soon forget.

He returned home when it was too risky to continue his thievery and climbed the stairs up to the family's flat above the saloon. The kitchen always smelled of stale beer and soggy cigars no matter what his mother was cooking for breakfast.

"How'd we do this mornin' on yer hunt fer drunken treasure, JP?"

"Just grand, Ma! A nickel and three pennies!"

"Now that's me boy! Ye go wash up fer school now while I get yer porridge fixed."

"All right, Ma," JP responded, and headed for his wash basin. Four-year-old Daniel happily gnawed a heel of rye bread as his mother hummed a tune of old Eire.

After breakfast JP headed back up Hamburgh street to PS 34, his text books cinched in a strap. When he reached Jimmy Conners' house, JP threw a pebble upward at the bully's bedroom window to rouse him.

JP rued the day he slipped and inadvertently told Jimmy Conners that he'd found some pennies between the planks. He tried to take it back, but it was too late. Jimmy Conners smelled money with a primitive instinct like that of a starving dog smelling meat. Jimmy correctly concluded that this find of JP's was not an isolated event. Jimmy was an unpredictable, pugnacious and conniving little tough, with a temper easily ignited, who also happened to cry quite easily, a combination JP found both puzzling and amusing.

Jimmy wanted in on JP's action, and would not take no for an answer.

Conners emerged from his house to the racket of his parents' loud arguing. Hair uncombed, he carried no schoolbooks. His greeting consisted of a hard punch to JP's shoulder. Then he laughed and tucked his shirt in half-assed as they began their daily walk together to school.

"Say, JP, how much youse t'ink youse take in, scourin' the planks?"

JP may have been three years Conners' junior, but he was nobody's fool.

"Oh, I only just found a coin once or twice, when I remembered to set my eyes to lookin'."

The boys paused to study the Erie Railroad train parked on the tracks bisecting Hamburg St. It was going nowhere, completely blocking all street and sidewalk traffic. As was often required by this common obstacle they would be forced

JP Sullivan

to climb between the cars in order to pass. A number of reluctant kids paused there alongside them until the bravest decided to lead the way. Smaller children marched ahead of them, but Conners bulldozed right through, knocking one little girl to the ground. He hopped up and over the coupling and when safe on the opposite side he turned to see JP helping the little girl up off the tracks. Suddenly, when they were squarely between the cars, there was a deafening slam as the freight cars heaved murderously forward with an unexpected lurch. JP and the little girl barely escaped amputation.

"Golly, there Sully!" laughed Jimmy Conners, "T'ought fer a minute we was gonna lose youse 'n' yer little girlfriend!"

JP was badly rattled. That was his closest call yet. The little girl ran away in a panic once they were safe on the other side. Those children yet behind them just stood where they were, terrified to proceed.

"Gimme a figure. How much youse t'ink yer takin' in a week?"

"Can't say."

"Can't say is won't say. How much?"

"Ye think people are droppin' good money helter skelter around here every day, Jimmy Conners, just throwin' it on the ground? That the streets of the ward are littered with silver and gold? If indeed they were, yerself would be the first t' be findin' it."

"Youse'll give me half of what ye take, JP Sullivan..."

With that, JPs rear end slammed hard into the dirt with a thud.

"...or else."

JP considered for a moment telling brother Jim what Conners did, but decided first he would try to handle it his own way.

Words first, fists last.

JP never did reveal to Jimmy Conners that he was always up well before dawn on his daily treasure hunt. That on most days he always found a penny or two. He took to telling Conners fibs such as his mother was keeping him from scouring the planks by making him do chores before school, or he was sick, or he overslept, or there was just nothing out there to scour. Still smarting from his friend's bullying and closed fist, he kept to himself what ciphers remained, and learned an early lesson about trust and divulging secrets that could never be taken back.

JP never mentioned scouring the planks again, not to Conners or anyone else, disclaiming the lucrative endeavor, announcing that any effort applied to it was a fool's errand.

As they walked the last block to school together, JP called no attention to the environs he'd already scoured for himself earlier, keeping Conners distracted with his jokes. But as they proceeded, JP noticed Conners' squinty eyes darting down, studying the cracks and crannies where errant coins might well be hiding.

JP's clever wit and humorous jousting kept him barely a half step ahead of the obtuse, dominating Conners. People who didn't know him well might say admiringly that Jimmy Conners never ran away from a fight. But those who did have his acquaintance were well aware that it was usually Jimmy Conners who initiated the ruckus in the first place. Conners tackled obstacles in his way like some earth-moving contraption, whereas JP tackled his with the finesse of a diplomat.

After school the two reengaged out front and dawdled back home between the Erie Railroad tracks.

JP pulled out two pennies and said to Conners, "Me Pa gave me two cents for scrubbin' the saloon floor. C'mon. I'll buy us sumpin at Dalton's."

"Okay!" whooped Conners.

The little bell tinkled in contact with the opening door of Mrs. Dalton's store-saloon. She was busy behind the counter.

"Me Pa makes me drain and scrub clean all the fouled spittoons at his saloon," Conners offered, "and all I get fer me trouble is a swift kick in the arse if'n it ain't done to his likin'. Them t'ings stink somethin' awful, JP! Can't hardly eat me supper afterward."

Jimmy Conners didn't quite know what to make of people who were kind to him. That big chip on his shoulder, JP knew, came from a terrible family incident that Jimmy never talked about in any detail, but inadvertently referred to sometimes without meaning to. JP was too smart and too cautious to dig any deeper whenever the affair presented itself.

During the 10 years of his young life that he had known JP, going all the way back to when JP's father was still alive and the Sullivans and Conners lived just a block from each other on Louisiana St., Jimmy Conners had never known JP to scorn him. But regardless, he was unable to trust him either. Jimmy Conners could never trust anyone, not after what had happened to him. Not family. Not friends. Not even the younger and wholly unthreatening JP, who could always make him laugh just as effortlessly as he was able to extricate himself from just about any sticky fix by calling upon his gift for humor.

Jimmy Conners' earliest lesson in life was that the very people who should be protecting you the most fiercely from damage are, in his experience at least, the ones doing the fiercest damage. He had been wounded in a grievous way, one that would pain him and drive him throughout his entire life.

Jimmy led the way inside the store to the pleasant squeak of hinges and floorboards, where the odor of bread and candy was barely discernible above the stench of the Union Ironworks fumes, thick with sulphur and coal soot.

"Mrs. Dalton, can I have two pennies worth o' licorice?"

Mrs. Dalton was a sweet but tough soul, a necessary combination if one were to survive in a neighborhood business that catered to all varieties of local citizenry, both friend and foe. Everyone in the neighborhood walked through her door at one time or another.

She raised the lid and reached barehanded into the glass licorice jar and fished out ten big chunks of black, sticky nirvana. She dropped the nuggets into JPs cupped hands after accepting his pennies. She smiled at JP but cast a wary eye in the direction of Jimmy Conners, who was clearly casing the joint. She gave him the stink eye as their gaze met. He smirked, knowing what she was thinking.

The sound of the tinkling bell followed them out onto the front stoop. They took a seat on the top step of the South Street store. JP divvied up the candies. The boys studied the clamorous river traffic as they chewed. Steam engines roared. Coal smoke belched from every boat and factory stack. Ships' conveyers squealed as they elevated cereal to the tops of the towering grain elevators.

"Bet I kin git me teeth blacker 'n' yers," Jimmy challenged, and smiled a gruesome grin wide with stubby blackened licorice-coated teeth, which made JP howl with amusement.

Jimmy Conners beamed from his success at making the neighborhood comedian laugh. He looked at JP's flushed pink cheeks and brilliant blue eyes, sparkling with the tears produced by his robust giggling mixed with the acidic fumes from the ironworks, and it occurred to him that he hardly ever made anybody else laugh. That was one more thing to like about JP. That, and the protection the friendship afforded from the wrath of Jim Sullivan, JP's older brother. Jim had whipped Conners real good a couple times after he'd mouthed off when he shouldn't have.

JP had placed himself between the two rivals just a few weeks earlier when seventeen year old James had seen almost-thirteen year old Jimmy push ten year old JP while they argued over some now-forgotten incident. But he sure didn't intend any harm to JP. They were friends. To hear Conners say it, it didn't mean much of anything at all. He'd just found himself more riled up than he should've been over some unimportant nothing.

As they neared the corner of Hamburgh and South streets, a mighty horn blast from two struggling tugboats made them both jump. A huge burp from the tugboats' stacks enveloped them in thick smoke. They choked. They tried to outrun the black cloud, but to no avail. Angry cursings ricochetted across the river between rival boat crews. Whistles screamed. Ships competed for right-of-way. Mothers called loudly for errant children late from school from the upper story windows of riverfront houses, the air so heavy with gray soot the sun barely shined through.

Bedlam reigned.

Up ahead the sight of JP's mongrel brother Jim lurking on the saloon stoop caused Jimmy Conners to shrink just a bit.

"Git inside JP! Yer late again. Ma's waitin'! I ain't doin' yer chores for ye, just so's ye know it," scolded Jim.

"The railcars was blockin' the street. Tweren't my fault," lied JP to his older sibling.

Jim Sullivan's rough tone was borne more out of frustration than from any annoyance JP caused. Jim's teenaged sullenness materialized from his lack of stature in the family and the subsequent drama and continual suffering that interloper Peter Halloran visited upon all their lives.

As he passed JP dropped two big blocky pieces of licorice into his brother's hand, and with that loving token Jim was reminded yet again that he was taking his anger out on the wrong person.

As he entered the saloon, JP encountered his mother and father hollering at one another. The Hollerin' Hallorans, he had christened them. A destitute drunk named Hannity pushed past JP to enter the saloon as his mother ran upstairs in tears, leaving Peter to resume his attentions to the tavern.

Spotting the drunk, Peter Halloran played out one of his favorite games.

"If yer expectin' to suck it, Hannity, you'll have to give up a penny."

The drunk, wobbly on his feet, watched as Peter took the filthy rag he had wiped the bar with and held it over the tub, teasingly poised to wring it out.

"I don't have all day!" warned Halloran as the first drops plummeted toward the receptacle.

"Alright, then!" slurred Hannity.

Hannity produced his precious penny. Peter handed over the repulsive rag. Hannity pressed it greedily to his mouth, sucking out alcohol mixed with equal parts grime and tobacco spittle.

Peter Halloran laughed cruelly, shaking his head derisively in judgement as though he himself wasn't personally familiar with the desperate practice from his own dark days past.

The ringing in of the new year found the troubled family still together and Peter Halloran once again renewing his pledge to become a changed man. He stopped drinking spirits altogether for a while as promised both to his wife and to justice King. It was a difficult challenge for a man spending 14 hours a day in a saloon. In his less bestial intervals, he had even encouraged Jim to make a good life for himself, better than the one Peter Halloran had made for himself.

Jim Sullivan was no longer in school. He'd worked for some time on the docks but foresaw no future for himself in a laborer's occupation. He was looking into getting some formal training in writing or law.

Peter told Jim he could live and work at the saloon as long as he wished, "to make followin' yer spirit that much easier." But in all practicality Jim Sullivan never once entertained any intentions of leaving. He couldn't. There was no way he would not remain in the home to protect his mother and brothers. And if push ever came to shove, there was always the convenient river a few steps away to sink Halloran in. Drunks were always toppling into it anyway. No one would ever suspect nor care.

The Thayer Brothers

At No. 16 Hamburgh Street, in addition to the Bain family boarding with the Hallorans, Patrick Sweeny's family resided there as well in rooms behind the saloon. Patrick referred to himself at seventy years of age, without so much as a twinkle in his eye, as a "crusty old codger"; his wife Ellen was eleven years his junior. Together they had two young sons, aged 16 and 21.

Ever since Peter Halloran had been arrested for stabbing wife Mary the previous year, the boarders were on alert for any change in demeanor that might indicate a repeat of Halloran's heinous act. Peter was well aware that he was being monitored by everyone in the house, as well as the neighbors all surrounding. One might say that he was on his best behavior, but truth be told, he was so being closely scrutinized that he had to think twice before even turning his head the wrong way.

Despite Halloran's reputation, all the Sweenys seemed to tolerate him well enough anyway, and more than a few times Mary Halloran and Ellen Sweeny would collaborate on an especially fine Sunday meal for the joined families. The Halloran saloon had not yet been permitted for opening on Sundays.

Patrick Sweeny, who was born a native in the region providentially on January 1, 1800 of Irish parents, had lived through the burning of the city by the British in 1813. After each Sunday meal, Sweeny reveled in the Irish passion for telling a fine story, relating mesmerizing tales of his personal history. Mary was surprised to learn Sweeny's stories agreed in facts with those of her former friend Mercy Abbott. She had thought that Mercy Abbott might have been exaggerating her past.

The young boys sat around the table with the Sweeny family, awestruck, soaking up old Patrick's wild-yet-true tales from the frontier days, wishing themselves having been born in those feral times of savage Indians and equally barbaric Redcoats. Most Sundays Peter Halloran would haul a bucket of beer upstairs from the saloon whereupon everyone gathered round, settling in for a good long listen.

Sweeny had been just a week shy of his 26th birthday when the notorious Thayer Brothers murder was committed on Christmas Eve 1825. It was legend in the city, and few others besides Patrick Sweeny were still alive and lucid enough to tell the tale.

"John Love was a Scotsman, a sailor by profession," he began in the dramatic voice of a stage actor, "who peddled small wares during the winter months. Love boarded with a family in North Boston N.Y., that of Israel Thayer and his three sons and their wives, the boys all in their twenties. The Thayers were part-time farmers, but they worked in the saw mill mostly, and John Love had lent the family money from time to time. The Thayer wives were sent away by the men under the guise that they were going to do the butchering that day, and poor Mr. Love was swiftly set upon and done in with a pistol and an axe. The Thayers believed the man's blood wouldn't be noticed amidst that of the hogs.

"They buried poor Mr. Love in a grave only 19 feet from the house in a hole so shallow that the toes of his shoes stuck up out of the ground! The earth was frozen over and they could dig no deeper. They piled thickets on top to disguise the dead man's presence, and prayed for a good snowfall.

"The Thayers were known throughout the neighboring townships as being just one step ahead of pennilessness, so the following day when they began spending money like never before, the neighbors grew suspicious. The Thayers claimed that Love had gone away on his peddling route; yet there they were riding Love's horse around town, which surely Mr. Love would have required if he had, as they alleged, left the area.

"They also insisted that Love had authorized them to collect money due him. They produced a letter of power of attorney that was so rank a forgery that everyone to whom is was presented immediately suspected that nefariousness had been perpetrated on the unfortunate Mr. Love!"

Interrupting to enjoy a few slow gulps of his beer provided Sweeny the perfect dramatic pause, and the boys as well as the adults were on the very edge of their seats.

"Well, what happened then, Mr. Sweeny?!" enthused Jim.

"Yes! Tell us if they got them killers!" shouted little JP.

"Now, ye just let the speaker whet his whistle a bit, laddies, won't ye?" Sweeny scolded with a teasing smile.

He resumed his recollections.

"In February, two of the brothers were arrested, and the magistrate of the town offered a reward of ten dollars for the recovery of John Love's body. After a long search throughout the countryside it came as a shock to all that the body was found just feet from the Thayer house itself, and upon its discovery, the third Thayer brother—and their father—were also arrested.

"The three brothers were tried at the end of April in the court of Over and Terminer, and on their own confession, found guilty. The evidence was of such character that it could not be rebutted.

"On the morning of the execution, Judge Walden—they named Walden Avenue after him—was riding his horse into town from his home in Hamburgh when he encountered old Chief Red Jacket at his little log cabin near the Seneca Mission Church. Red Jacket was wearing his large heavy Peace Medal, as he always did, a gift from President George Washington.

"Judge Walden halted to greet the respected old Indian and said, 'Why, how is this? Why don't you go to see the execution like all the rest?'

"The Chief pushed back the long grey hair that the breeze had blown into his eyes.

"'Ugh,' grunted Red Jacket, 'fools enough there now.'

"The hanging gallows were constructed by my old friend Henry Fails, and erected on the west side of Niagara Square. On the opposite side of the square there was a hill that acted as a natural amphitheater. 25,000 people from hundreds of miles around and from across the river in Canada flocked to the site, as if in anticipation of some great celebration. The new Wilkeson Mansion on the Square was not quite finished, and Sam Wilkeson had to hire guards to keep the crowds away from his grand estate, lest they walk off with everything. No one present had ever seen a gathering of that size in these parts, since Buffalo itself only had a little over 2,000 citizens at that time."

The group was spellbound, and no one made a sound. Sweeny took another two gulps, then recommenced.

"As you might imagine, it was only just barely spring, and the town's streets and lanes were soft and muddy. The feet, hooves and wagon wheels of the 25,000 witnesses visited upon our city's roads such onerous damage that for years afterward, we were still roundly cursing them! And the stench from their offal perfumed the air for more than a full week, causing our womenfolk to walk with a handkerchief practically glued to their noses!"

A round of laughter rose up from around the table.

"The Thayers were brought out from the stone jail a little before one o'clock, to be hanged at two. They were marched down Court Street, which was known back then as Cazenovia Trail, with hands tied and the ropes already around their necks, to Niagara Square. The crowd became quite agitated upon their arrival, parting like Moses' sea, with hundreds loudly condemning and damning the murderers. The victim's friends, all of whom were also neighbors of the Thayers, were the most vocal of all. The Thayers didn't even flinch, nor did they take a single hesitant step. They all marched up onto the scaffold, and the ropes around their neck were hooked to it.

"The senior Thayer had been exonerated right before the march to the gallows, but he was made to watch his sons die. The funeral sermon was preached by the clergymen Glezon Fillmore. Go back to the Dark Ages and inhumanity was considerably tolerated in those days. I thought it was early in 1826 as well, when I witnessed with my own eyes these men hanged.

"The Sheriff said, 'Stand up.' They stood up. Then he said, 'Thayers, you have five minutes to live!' Next, 'Thayers, you have three minutes to live!' Next, 'Thayers, you have one minute to live!'—and then he cut the rope holding up the gallows floor. All three dropped at once and the enormous crowd gasped at that instant. Even the murdered John Love's most ardent mourners were speechless upon witnessing the violent sight. The ropes they were hung by were made of shoe thread!

"Men bellowed and women cried out, seeing that the thread had almost decapitated the brothers, as they kicked and spasmed, wallowing in mid-air as the life went out from their bodies and blood dripped from their necks. They hung there for about 15 minutes.

"Many onlookers left immediately, sickened by the sight, but thousands remained to gaze upon the conclusion of the Thayers' terrible deed. A dray was pulled up and positioned under each brother, who was then cut down, his body dropping with a thud onto the wagon. When all three had been detached, the crowd surged forward to claim souvenirs, and that's when the inhumanity became most apparent.

"Women pulled bunches of hair right out of the Thayers' scalps, the brothers' clothes were ripped to pieces, their shoes stolen...and there were precious few peacekeepers to prevent any of it. The Thayers' father looked upon this scene with a dropped jaw, then he buried his head in his hands, weeping, and ran away back down the Cazenovia Trail.

"Mr. Fails charged the town magistrate $60 for his construction of the apparatus, and just two years ago his son told me that in looking over his late father's books, he found that Erie County had repudiated the debt!"

The table cheered Patrick Sweeny all around, and newly enervated, they demanded more.

"Tell us about the Redcoats!" JP cried.

"The Redcoats, lad! Those damnable murderers! I witnessed them struck down with my own eyes, at the very end of Ferry Street, where it meets the Niagara River!"

"So, tell us!", everyone beseeched excitedly.

Sweeny relit his cigar and took another slow turn at his beer glass.

"All right, laddies."

He thought for a moment, conjuring up the scene from the memory of his early years.

"When the war was first declared, we well knew that Buffalo was on the front line. That any British invasion would come right through here. And so we prepared as best we could. Volunteers drilled for many hours each Sunday in preparation. We knew that if the British moved upon us, with the regular army being so far away, perhaps as far away as Washington, that we would have to hold off the Redcoats by ourselves with just the few military who were present on the Niagara Frontier, until such time troops could reach us. It was a notably unsettled time for everyone in the region. On one side of the river we had to keep our eye on the Indians, never knowing which was friend and which was aiding the Redcoats. And then there was the ever-present threat of invasion by the Redcoats from across the river that might occur at any moment. The times required constant vigilance, with no opportunity to relax, nor for untroubled sleep."

Shivers of excitement ran up and down Jim Sullivan's spine, so enthralled was the teen by the authentic legend. It was a rare opportunity to experience history related by someone who had actually been present. The young man sipped his beer and drifted within its languorous effect.

"On July 10th in my 14th year, word came to us that the British had joined with a savage band of Canadian Indians at Niagara Falls and were coming upriver to destroy Buffalo. It was only my father and me that summer, my mother and sister having died of fever the previous year. My Pa tried to make me go with the neighbors who were fleeing, but I wanted to remain with him. I had been practicing with a musket for some time, ever since the British let it be known that they were going to invade our country. It had not been even 40 years since our Independence, and yet there awaited on our doorstep those very same despised hooligans, determined to take back the land that so many Americans had already given their lives for. What a fools' errand that proved for the Redcoats!

"The united tribes of savages of skin both red and white reached Black Rock and captured the stores and arms located there. The call went out from General Porter, and the volunteers, including my father and me, rushed in from all over—Cold Spring, Buffalo Plains and all the surrounding hamlets—until there were several hundred men assembled, poised to attack the red-coated raiders. When General Porter gave the direction, the volunteers attacked the British on three sides and drove them from their position, sending them scurrying down Ferry Street to where they commandeered some small boats tied up there. Most of the Indians scuttled into the underbrush like the rats they were.

"We were right on the Redcoats' tails. They retreated from us right past General Porter's own fine home on Niagara Street, which overlooked the river. We caught up with them just as the last boat was shoving off with about sixty men and most of the officers crowded into it. The first boats had already begun to round Squaw Island and were effectively shielded from our fire. A mad rush was on for the Redcoats to get across the river. We were enraged, and poured a merciless fire upon the last boats with a consummate ferocity!

"Some of the men carried the Pennsylvania rifle, which is not a smooth bore like my ancient Brown Bess, but rather a rifled barrel that lent accuracy and range. In a panic to kill the invaders before they could get away, I kept reloading my musket and firing as best I could under the circumstances, knowing the further from me the escape boats got, the less range my Bess would have. I poured about 120 grains of black powder into the mouth of the barrel, packed it down tight with a wood rod, then packed in a wad of cotton rag on top of that to create the pressure for the projectiles. Then I poured in my ammunition: rusty nails, broken glass and pointed pieces of flint. I wanted those blasted invaders to feel sorry they'd ever set foot in Black Rock! My Bess had a spread of about fifteen feet, but even at that you had to be pretty close to the target to inflict any real damage. I was just hoping and praying I could hit just one of them Redcoats. But the men behind the sights of their Pennsylvania rifles delivered a telling fatality! Calmly they stood or knelt, centered the target in their sights, and their true-hearted volley efficiently prevented the last boat's escape!

"British Colonel Cecil Bisshopp, who had set fire to every schooner, storehouse and barracks at the Black Rock during his attack, was hit more than once, and he died before his craft could reach the opposite shore. They buried the scoundrel over at Lundy's Lane.

"The total loss to the British in killed, wounded and prisoners taken was close to a hundred. The volunteers crowded into a small boat that remained tied up there, and rowed out to retrieve the last boat after most of its occupants had been shot. A few survivors were waving white handkerchiefs, the murderers now pleading for their lives. The volunteers brought them back to shore and took their prisoners.

"A few days later hearts were gladdened by the news of Harrison's victory over Proctor, and the death of that venomous old reptile Tecumseh, the Indian who gave the Americans more trouble than all of the rest of the Indians put together!"

Sweeny gave a self-satisfied belch, glowing in the rapt attention afforded him. The families were bewitched and enthralled, but the hour was late.

"Tell us about when the Indians scalped Mrs. Lovejoy!" JP pleaded.

"No more, John Sullivan," his mother interrupted, "ye'll be havin' a hard time goin' off t' sleep as it is with images like these in yer head. Now, go on with ye, wash up and get ready for bed."

JP whined in protest.

"Another time, lad. I promise," said Sweeny. "There are plenty more stories inside old Paddy Sweeny, I assure you. Now, off t' bed like your mother says."

JP whooped like an Indian as he charged out of the kitchen.

"Shhh! Ye'll be wakin' yer brother Daniel!", scolded his mother.

"Those are some fine remembrances, Mr. Sweeny," enthused Jim Sullivan. "You should be writin' them down, because they're history that's been all but forgotten!"

"Sorry to say lad, but I can't write much more than my name and some simple things."

Sweeny considered a thought, then spoke it out loud.

"Say, Jim, why don't you write them down for me?", the old man proposed.

The light went on in Jim's eyes upon stumbling over this new opportunity. He had been creating stories straight out of his imagination for some time already, but with Mr. Sweeny's mentorship, he might be able to write something of authentic importance, something people might love to read. Exciting facts. True facts. Before they disappeared from history.

And so, in bed by lamp light, he set to recording what he could remember from that evening's story-telling, page after page, before sleep claimed him unwillingly, mid-sentence.

1870
Mr. Sam Clemens

One muggy August Saturday morning in Buffalo's sooty First Ward, after cleaning up Friday night's revelry from the saloon and receiving delivery on a couple of barrels, seventeen year old Jim asked to be excused for a few hours. He'd been anticipating riding the trolly downtown to the big stationers' store to purchase a proper bound writing journal. Jim had taken to inscribing his stories and ideas helter skelter on scraps of paper which he came to discover were easily lost or misplaced.

Peter agreed, handing Jim 25c to purchase a new ledger for the saloon business while there.

Jim changed out of his work clothes, combed his hair, placed his cap on his head, and walked up to Elk Street to hop on a streetcar headed for city center.

In Jim's estimation, Young Lockwood & Johnson Stationers on Main Street came about as close to being a wonderland as might be conjured by any civilized being. The venerable establishment flaunted shelves of blank books in every style and size, ponderous folios and black-letter quartos, tidy twelvemos, all variety of loose writing papers and envelopes from exotic Japan, French pens, colored pencils in a rainbow of tinctures from Germany, and the blackest India inks. After careful deliberation Jim chose a plain parchment-covered duodecimo for his initial foray into the world of authorship, the book shading off at seven and a half inches by five.

His penmanship was awkward, so he preferred writing in pencil, as he usually made quite a few mistakes. He could never easily settle on a sentence construction as it initially emerged from his head, preferring to disassemble and reconstruct it in various ways until it read perfect. When writing in ink, his pages tended to turn into a scramble of ink puddles, crossings-out and untidy corrections. He was reassured and emboldened by the impermanence of pencil.

Jim lusted after the larger leather-bound blank books in steer and buffalo hide disported there before his covetous eyes, pigmented in every hue from camel to ebony. He silently vowed to return with the remuneration from his very first written piece sold to purchase a deluxe journal the likes of these.

As he exited the stationers', bundle in hand, a gust carried grit and dirt into his face. He grimaced and pulled his cap brim down closer to his eyes to shield them. Not hearing the rich-man's rig because it was traveling so slowly, he stepped off the curb.

The inattentive coachman was engaged in a lively discourse with his sole passenger. The carriage's wheel grazed a couple of Jim's toes, causing him to yelp, and both coachman and passenger jumped out in alarm to inquire after his condition. Initially startled and perturbed, the genuine concern and apologetic nature of the men soothed young Jim Sullivan's irritation.

"I don't think any bones are broken…" said Jim.

"Can I offer you a ride somewhere?" the older of the two men asked.

Jim had been raised to shun the help of others for no reason other than foolish pride, something that would never hold him in good stead. His initial reaction was to say no, but before he could demur he was quickly hustled into the carriage by the two.

"The name's Samuel Clemens," the wild-haired man boomed as he grasped Jim in a firm handshake, "and my fine coachman here is Mr. McFey." A lit cigar was clenched tightly between his teeth, his eyes squinting from the irritation of the smoke. He smiled just as expansively as his face would allow.

Before Mr. McFey giddy-upped the horse, the young driver turned round and said, "Patrick. Me name's Patrick." He had an Irish accent and wasn't much older than Jim.

"Jim. Jim Sullivan," Jim echoed. Patrick nodded in acquaintance. The coachman following behind their rig cursed loudly for them to hurry it up or get the hell out of the way.

"Where do you live?" asked Mr. Clemens, ignoring the driver behind them.

"Down in the First Ward, by the river, Sir. But I don't want to inconvenience…"

"Nonsense!" interrupted Mr. Clemens, before Jim could finish his sentence. Mr. Clemens smiled and said, "I grew up by a river myself, once upon a time. To the First Ward, Mr. McFey!" and off they went, clip-clopping down Main Street like lifelong friends who'd only now just finally met.

They spoke easily as the carriage made the lengthy trip in the opposite direction from where Mr. Clemens initially intended, and as they went, they discovered a shared affinity. Mr. Clemens revealed that he was a newspaper man "with the Buffalo Express." Jim was not only impressed, but excited as blazes, for somehow the aspiring young writer had managed to acquaint himself with a real honest-to-goodness newspaper man.

Jim had wild stories creating themselves in his head all the time to the point of distraction and confessed as much to Mr. Clemens.

"It's an infernal disease, my boy. Incurable. Unrelenting! Be very cautious." They both laughed at the diagnosis, as Jim was already intimate with the symptoms.

Jim showed Mr. Clemens his bundle, and told him he had made the trip downtown expressly for the purpose of officially commencing his own writing career, by purchasing the necessary tools.

"But I'm not sure quite how to go about this, Mr. Clemens. When I get an idea, I write it down, but they're mostly small ideas, not book ideas."

"Don't fret, James my man, because small ideas fit perfectly between newspaper columns. And people get to read those the very same day you write them. That's the rub. Book ideas, on the other hand, are much more grand, take a lot longer, and can fill entire journals. You don't have to worry about choosing your stories, son. They'll choose you."

Jim became self-conscious of his own broad First Ward accent and grammatical idiosyncrasies once more as he spoke with the worldly Mr. Clemens. He had noticed a marked difference in the way those living outside the ward spoke compared to his own diction when he was first old enough to venture out. A sales lady at one of the dry goods stores downtown had mocked his speech. She wasn't trying to be mean, but he was embarrassed nonetheless. He had been making an effort ever since to enunciate, to speak more correctly, so that he might attain a higher station upon venturing out in the world.

Although he caught himself reverting now and again, he made a concentrated effort not to use "ye" instead of "you," and to not drop the -g at the end of words. He never had made much use of the word "youse," the localized form of you. Mostly dock workmen and roughs like Jimmy Conners employed that primitive idiom.

"I bought a bound journal because I'm always losing the pages I write on." Jim said, referring to the package. "Do you write in journals, Mr. Clemens?"

"Not so often nowadays, Jim. I like to shuffle my pages, so I write on loose papers and keep them clipped together in a folder. It's less of an expense that way, incidentally. And I like the impermanent nature of unbound leaves. I can rearrange their order or shuffle the sequence of scenes...try out new and different ideas."

Reading a look of disappointment on Jim's face, as if the boy suddenly thought he had made an errant purchase, Sam extended himself.

"Especially for newspaper work, I need to be fast and loose. But for those writings that hold the most value for me, Jim, I do fill my bound journals. A writer really needs both."

Jim rebrightened at hearing this. And for the rest of the ride he found the words spilling out of his mouth in as effortless a fashion as almost never happened around anyone else.

He told Mr. Clemens how he had lost his father in the late war, that it had been rough going for a time, with a baby brother and widowed mother to look after. Practically before he could finish the part where his mother had remarried, Mr. Clemens exclaimed, "Now there's your story, by golly! Making things up is great good fun, but writing about the things we know, the experiences of our own lives, well...that just rings solid and true. Start there Jim. Begin with what you know. Your own history."

Sam stole a few sideways looks at Jim's handsome young appreciative face, his brilliant blue eyes reflecting a capacity for unbounded optimism, and a lump grew in his throat for the similarities Jim held to his own beloved brother, Henry Clemens.

"How old are you, Jim?"

"Seventeen, sir."

"Seventeen? Yup. That's a real fine age."

Twelve summers previous, Sam Clemens had become a cub pilot on the sidewheeler Pennsylvania on the Mississippi River and convinced his younger brother Henry, just nineteen, to join the Pennsylvania's crew. Sam knew how much his brother would love getting out of their tiny Missouri town and onto the open waters and exuberant freedom of traveling the endless length of America's greatest river.

Henry Clemens, motivated by his older brother's colorful anecdotes, signed on. But in New Orleans, Sam found himself in a heated quarrel with the Pennsylvania's pilot, and was transferred off to another vessel, one which left New Orleans two days after the Pennsylvania. Sam arranged with his brother that they would meet upriver at their sister's house in St. Louis.

Near Memphis, the Pennsylvania's boiler blew, and many onboard were killed. Reaching Arkansas, Sam read Henry Clemens' name in the local newspaper listed as safe. But the corpses he continued to see floating down the Mississippi from that disaster haunted him, and when he finally arrived in Memphis, he found his Henry lying in a makeshift hospital, horribly injured.

This once beautiful boy lay shredded and burned, yet uncomplaining. Over the next two days, suffocating fluids pooled slowly in his brother's lungs until young Henry cruelly drowned in them.

Sam Clemens was made distraught almost beyond the edge of sanity by this loss, as it was he who coaxed his reluctant brother to try the river life, and had he not, Henry would still be alive, still bringing joy to his heart. Sam blamed himself for the death of his brother. In a grief-filled letter to a friend written the evening of Henry's death, he wrote, "the light of my life has gone out in utter darkness."

Sam wiped a tear from his eye.

"Damn blasted Buffalo dust!", he sniffled.

Jim glowed in the attention of the newspaper man, and was preparing the courage to ask him if he might be willing to look at some things he had written, when unexpectedly, Mr. Clemens asked if Jim might be available to do some work at the Clemens home, one or two days a week.

"The yard needs tending, we've got more loose chores than we can keep up with, and fancy Mr. McFey here is just about useless for anything more bedeviling than just pulling my carcass about town."

"Sir! I am deeply wounded!" cried McFey.

McFey had quickly wheeled around in his seat toward Mr. Clemens and feigned mortal injury to his honor, before both men burst out laughing, for this was a scene between the two obviously well-rehearsed.

"If you're dexterous, you can try your hand at fixin' a few things." Mr. Clemens offered a lofty twenty-five cents an hour, so in consideration of the fine wages, and the fact his employer was a newspaper man who well might provide guidance for him, Jim whooped at the prospect. It was agreed that Jim Sullivan would report to the Clemens home on Delaware Ave. at eight o'clock the following Saturday.

Delaware Avenue was Buffalo's version of New York's grand Fifth Avenue, and Jim was fired up to have met one of the city's aristocracy, especially one who didn't put on airs, and a writer having the whole city for his audience to boot. Finally, he would get to see the inside of one of those fancy mansions that lined the grand Avenue.

As the Clemens carriage headed down Seneca Street from Main Street all the occupants swooned as they inhaled the heavenly yeast-tinged scents wafting from the famous Jacob Roskopf Bakery, Confectionary, and Eating Saloon.

Just as they were passing, four men were cautiously exiting the building carrying a giant, elegant, astonishingly festooned wedding cake of at least six layers, borne on something resembling a stretcher for transporting the battle-wounded.

Mr. Roskopf was in a panic, trying to shield the cake with his coat from the rising dust caused by an American Express stagecoach galloping past just at that instant. They'd chosen the worst possible moment to transfer the cake onto the livery, but they somehow succeeded. Jim's stomach growled as he thought of how wonderful a strawberry ice cream from Roskopf's would taste right about now.

The carriage soon reached Louisiana Street, and after turning right, the trio passed along the repulsively scented, barge-crowded Ohio Basin with all its maritime pandemonium.

"My father was one of those who dug this basin in the '50s..." Jim noted proudly as they made their way along the quay.

They passed the Conners' Maritime Home, where Jimmy Conners, brother JP's hoodlum friend, stood out front looking for trouble. His bruised face gaped in disbelief at the sight of his older nemesis riding high in a carriage so elegant that it caused all other First Ward street traffic to slow in admiration.

Patrick McFey chuckled at the wide array of Irish-monikered drinking establishments the locals had to choose from here. The carriage passed right by the Sullivans' first home, "...and there's the little house we all used to live in, when my father was still alive."

Sam sensed the longing in Jim's voice. Jim recalled Sunday strolls along the quay and the river when he was a young boy with his mother, baby brother JP, and his achingly-missed father.

Mr. McFey turned left onto South Street. The coach followed the river six blocks to Hamburgh Street, then swung round the corner and stopped in front of No. 16. Sam Clemens took note that Jim lived in a saloon, on a street lined with saloons, around the corner from a street lined with saloons.

After Jim hopped out, they waved goodbye.

"See you next Saturday morning, Mr. Clemens!"

Jim Sullivan ran up the steps and inside, where a few stray micks were arguing local politics over tepid beer. Peter Halloran was behind the bar.

"Who's fine carriage was that ye just stepped out of?" his wary stepfather queried as Jim entered the saloon.

"Mr. Sam Clemens, of the Buffalo Express. He's hired me to do some work for him next Saturday." James didn't ask for permission, as a reminder to Peter Halloran that he was not his father.

"Sam Clemens, ye say? Do ye mean the Mr. Sam Clemens?"

Jim paused a few beats to consider.

"I suppose as much. Is there another?"

"Mark Twain?"

Jim looked puzzled. "I don't..."

Peter reached under the bar and pulled out the subscription book he had been chuckling through whenever business got slow. A salesman had paid a visit to the saloon a few months back, peddling all manner of published works. It was titled Innocents Abroad, by Mark Twain. Its subject matter scratched Peter Halloran's unrequited itch for wanderlust.

"This Mark Twain?"

Jim was shocked, feeling stupid all of a sudden for not making the connection. And thrilled.

"He liked me, Peter! He's paying twenty five cents an hour for me to work around his big house up Delaware Avenue."

Peter just whistled and rolled his eyes, awed and puzzled.

"Delaware Avenue! Twenty five cents an hour! And how did ye happen to meet up with the famous and wealthy Mister Clemens?"

"He ran over my foot with his carriage after I left the stationers."

"Ran over your foot?"

"Yup."

Peter Halloran glanced down at Jim's empty hands.

"Where's my ledger?"

Jim startled, groaned, then flushed. "I must have left the package in the carriage!"

At that very instant, Mr. Sam Clemens bounded through the door of Halloran's Saloon and laughed, "You skedaddled before you could grab your package, Mr. Sullivan!"

Peter was still holding his copy of Innocents Abroad. Sam Clemens glanced quickly at the blue and gold cover, recognizing the man's choice of the deluxe edition approvingly, and said, "You must be the young man's father? I'm Samuel Clemens."

"Stepfather, yes. Halloran, Peter Halloran. Very pleased to meet ye, sir."

"You've got yourself a fine young man there, Mr. Halloran. Very fine."

"That I do indeed, Mr. Clemens," said Peter, uncharacteristically proud.

Jim glowed in the adults' assessment of him. For once the usually blunt and demeaning Peter Halloran was not at a loss for kind words, and managed to blurt out an additional thank you before Mr. Clemens turned to leave.

"And thank you immensely for purchasing my book, Mr. Halloran!" Sam called over his shoulder, and was gone.

Jim and Peter just looked at each other, smiling as the few patrons attendant looked on dumbly, not comprehending the scene they had just witnessed.

"Blast it that I didn't ask him to sign it!" Peter exclaimed as he opened the blank frontispiece.

Jim seized the opportunity. "I'll take it with me Saturday if you'd like."

"Yes, I would like that, very much, Jim. I've never laughed so heartily reading a book in me entire life."

Peter beamed at Jim.

"Imagine. Me own son. Working for Mr. Mark Twain."

It was the first time in the almost six years since he had married Jim's widowed mother that Halloran had called Jim his son.

Samuel Clemens

Home Again

"I'm worried for you, Mister Clemens," said Patrick McFey, as he tried to hurry.

It was a long way back to the Clemens house, and the streets were crowded with Saturday shoppers. Not being familiar with the First Ward, Patrick, instead of remaining on Hamburgh Street until it intersected Seneca Street, decided to make an early left turn onto Elk where he and his charge were soon embroiled in the swirl of humanity that was the Saturday Elk Street Market.

Carriages, livery wagons, mothers holding tightly to their children while balancing baskets and satchels bursting with vegetables, salt pork, butter and other purchases all together caused the Clemens carriage to come to a dead halt. The two men looked down the rows of sellers, toward the centerpiece structure, a vaguely Greek-style wooden edifice completely skirted on all four sides by covered breezeways, supported by handsome two-story high columns numbering more than a hundred. The peaked roof was crowned by a three-story cupola with a rounded cap roof of copper, bringing the highest portion of the building to over five storys. Sellers completely filled the interior of the building as well as the shaded porch breezeways, and twice as many more set up around the building's perimeter with rows of tables and stalls, parked wagons, drays and liveries from which to sell their cornucopia of wares.

Shoppers and vendors stared at the immaculately polished carriage, and especially the finely turned-out and elegant Mr. McFey. Patrick basked in the crowd's admiration momentarily, until seized with the urge to gallop right out of there. But there was no moving the rig, not just yet.

Sam was exhausted, and looked every part the physically drained man he was. He and his very pregnant Livy had just returned from Elmira, New York, and the endless days and nights nursing Jervis Langdon, Livy's father, through the ups and downs of his final illness. Sam had taken on the rigors of the midnight-to-four o'clock watch and did not fare well.

It was Jervis Langdon who had purchased the beautiful home for them at 472 Delaware Ave. as a wedding present, and had it beautifully furnished. It was Jervis who purchased the interest in the Buffalo Express so that Sam could have a strong career foothold in which to begin married life with his beloved daughter.

Sam had met Langdon onboard ship during the great Quaker City Holy Land Excursion — the first excursion of its kind ever planned — which sailed to Europe and the Holy Land. Sam had convinced a number of newspapers to purchase passage for him, to the tune of $1200, a princely sum, for which he was to write copious articles for serial publication to post back to his benefactors from stops along his exotic route. These travel reports were what first brought Mark Twain to the wide attention of the reading public. These travelogues collected together became his first best-selling book, Innocents Abroad.

Sam's humor and good nature warmed Jervis Langdon to him during the long journey, where they spent many hours in conversation, shuffleboard, and attending shipboard lectures. Jervis liked Sam Clemens so much in fact that he invited him to pay a visit to the Langdon home in Elmira N.Y. after returning to America.

Jervis Langdon had never considered Sam Clemens as a possible suitor for the hand of his daughter Olivia. Not for a second. But that's exactly the way things turned out.

After heartening everyone for a time with the deceiving illusion of his recovery, Jervis Langdon had finally succumbed just the week before, on August 6th.

Sam was bereft now, as Jervis had become a strong compass for him. He had counted on Jervis Langdon's stability and kindly presence in their lives to help guide him and provide the kind of family life stolen from him by the deaths of his own father and siblings. It was the warmth and the solid underpinnings of family life that he had missed most, and just when Sam believed he'd become established in a new lineage, the head of that family was taken from them.

The irony of this troubling coincidence did not escape Sam Clemens, and he wondered once again if there might just be something about him that was not healthy for those unlucky enough to receive his love.

Sam announced, "Might as well take advantage of a disadvantageous situation, Mr. McFey," and stepped out of his rig. He bought apples, pears and yams.

Within three minutes the roadblock had dispersed and McFey hollered, "We have clear passage now, Mr. Clemens!"

Sam climbed wearily into his seat, and McFey sped him homeward. McFey pulled into the driveway and stopped the carriage at the front porch, allowing Sam to climb out with his market purchases. Livy loved pears, and these were beauties.

McFey continued onward to the arched entrance of the brick carriage house where he occupied the second floor, to attend to the horse and rig and wash off the grime accumulated on the day's outing.

Sam climbed the five porch steps wearily and walked up to the double front door. Through the glass he saw Livy's tiny form slouched, sick and depleted, dozing in an easy chair in the parlor. Sam sighed deeply, noting he felt today much older than his 34 years.

He opened the door quietly. It squeaked. He made a mental note to have Jim Sullivan oil the hinges next Saturday. Livy stirred.

"Darling, let me take you upstairs to bed."

Livy had made herself sick caring for her father, and she was now five months pregnant. Sam had worried that she might even lose the baby. But Livy was far stronger than her petite frame indicated. Sam picked her up and carried his bride-with-child upstairs to the front bedroom, to their beautiful massive bed.

The carriage of Miss Coatsworth, one of the most elegant on the Avenue, glided past the house on the street below just then. Sam glanced out the window as he eased Livy under the coverlet. The Coatsworth woman sat straight and proud as a plank, looking quite blank and bored, as her carriage headed downtown toward Niagara Square. Sam chuckled a little as he noted that her coachman was not attired nearly as elegantly as his own Mr. McFey. The Coatsworths were not exactly noted for their ability to retain loyal servants.

Livy slept soundly throughout the afternoon, and then all night long, beginning from the exact moment her lovely head touched the freshly ironed linen cover of the goose down pillow.

The Colored Girls

Jim Sullivan admired his finish work on the sparkling clean double hung windows before setting out to bundle the pulled weeds and trimmed hedge trimmings gathered from the Clemens' front, back and side yards with twine. He lopped a few stray low hanging branches from the tall elm that stood to the right of the front porch. He strengthened the wobbly porch railing with shims, oiled the entry door hinges, carefully cleaned the front door's ornately framed plate glass right to the edges, where the beveled glass met solid oak, and picked up papers strewn by careless passers-by who should know better.

"This ain't the ward, you people. It's Delaware Avenue," he muttered out loud to himself.

He ran after a fine carriage that passed when he noticed that a beautiful French lace handkerchief had floated off it. The elderly rich lady occupant barely sniffed a curt thank you upon its return.

"Yer welcome, you old bag. I shoulda kept it for my mother," he murmured as the carriage pulled away, not caring if she heard. But at her age she was most likely deaf anyway.

The Clemens might be living in high cotton, but Buffalo's genuine swells lived a little further north, where large baronial estates, their porte-cocheres shielded from the seething masses behind twelve foot stone walls and Versailles-worthy iron gates, lined Delaware Avenue. Maybe Delaware Avenue was not quite up to New York's Fifth Avenue standards, but it was impressive nonetheless.

The Clemens house was comparatively modest by their neighbors' robber-baron standards, yet was still so fine that Jim stood for long minutes out front before he left, admiring his handiwork and taking in the beautifully carved oak front doors inset with six-foot plate glass lights, the lovely curve of the wrap-around porch, and the fact the home sheltered three full floors, plus a basement. He fancied himself occupying the attic with its large gabled windows and all the hidden treasures such a space most assuredly would conceal. He sat down on the middle of the five porch steps and took off his shoes to empty them of debris, then climbed the top two and knocked on the glass door.

Sam Clemens amused himself by referring to his two Caucasian Irish servants as his "Colored Girls" since their family names were Brown and White. Margaret Brown answered. She was pretty in a friendly looking kind of way, and not too much older than Jim. She was polite but business-like. Jim decided she didn't much care for him.

"Can ye ask Mrs. Clemens if there's anything more she'd like me done before I leave, Miss Brown?" said Jim.

"Mrs. Clemens is asleep, so I think maybe you should just go."

"Surely. Fine. I'll be back next Saturday. Good day, Miss Brown."

As he turned to walk southward toward Niagara Square, Jim realized he may have been making a racket while Mrs. Clemens was trying to sleep. He looked back up at the second floor street-facing windows, knowing that behind them lay the Clemens' bedroom, and cursed himself for not remembering that as he worked. He would have tread more lightly, had he realized.

As he walked down Delaware to catch a streetcar home, he thought about Mr. Clemens, slaving at his office today. As his trolley passed the Buffalo Express offices on Washington Street, he looked up and imagined himself inside, writing something important for the Sunday Illustrated edition, Sam Clemens nodding his approval. He daydreamed for the next fifteen minutes until he reached his stop at the corner of Elk and Hamburgh Streets.

As Jim got off the trolley, he spotted his brother JP walking quickly toward him, looking grim.

"Pa's drunk again."

"Jesus. Where's Ma?"

"She's still at confession with Danny."

"We'd better get home quick then, to see if we can avoid the two of 'em meetin' up," fretted Jim. The brothers strided briskly toward the river.

Too late.

From a distance the boys saw their mother, holding little Daniel's hand, approaching the house while they were still far down the block.

Mary Halloran came upon her husband in the saloon at 4 o'clock in the afternoon already passed out at the same table where Doc Greene and old Pat Sweeny, their boarder, sat bantering in a drunken state.

Last year, Peter Halloran had promised that if Mary dropped the charges stemming from his shanking her that he would quit drinking. She did, and he did. He also promised to turn over a new leaf. He tried.

Most of Halloran's promises had been broken by now, along with the troubled couple's newly forged and fragile bond of trust. It had been almost a year that he'd managed to hold himself to sobriety. Mary looked at his sorry figure with contempt and a good measure of apprehension.

She turned to see her sons coming through the door, out of breath from running. Before she commenced her climb up the stairs, Mary shot a look at Doc, who, more than anyone else alive, should know better. Then Mary said, "Jimmy, ye'll have to keep the saloon for the time bein' or these good-fer-nothin's here will drink us into the poorhouse. I'm going upstairs to start supper."

Doc Greene visibly sank into his chair as her eyes assaulted his.

Fingy

Jim had been out with his friends Mike Regan and Ed Stanton, fully intending to be home by dark, but good times turned into better times, and it was now 10 p.m. He hurried toward home, hoping to avoid any toughs looking for trouble. Up ahead on Louisiana Street he saw a flash of red. As he drew closer, Jimmy Conners flew past him as if being pursued, but no one was on his tail. Jim could now see the flames leaping from the roof of Conners' Mariners Home saloon and hotel. Probably Jimmy was running for the fire box, Jim thought, until he realized the box was located in the direction opposite Jimmy's flight. He stopped to watch as confused neighbors shouted and pails and pots were brought out and filled with water. A sailor jumped from an upper story window. Jim could not yet hear the clanging of the firemen's wagons.

He continued on his way.

At midnight Jim and JP were awakened from a sound sleep by firefighters' bells. As they stood at their bedroom window they watched as a steamer pulled up, its water hoses quickly unraveled. It was immediately followed by a ladder truck. Standing on the planked sidewalk below, Jimmy Conners lurked, watching, fascinated by another act of arson.

The roof of the Union Ironworks office was ablaze.

"What's that little rough plannin' on doin', JP? Burnin' down half the city?"

After JP finished up his dawn search for drunken treasure and ate breakfast, he made his daily stop at Jimmy Conners' house so they might walk to school together. Mrs. Conners had been feeling sickly and was short-tempered. She had hollered at JP to stop his practice of bouncing pebbles against the window in order to rouse Jimmy, lest he crack the glass, so he just knocked on the door. He was never invited in. He waited on the stoop until Jimmy finally appeared.

Jimmy, shapeless and pale as a cadaver, face and torso bruised, walked out into the cool morning without shirt or shoes.

"Git along wit'out me, JP, I'll be quittin' the school. Me Pa's sendin' me off t' sea t' work on a lake steamer."

Jimmy then turned around and went back into the house without saying goodbye. His back bore wide red welts from a belt beating.

JP saw Jimmy's father looming in the window, scowling at him.

JP walked on alone to school, recalling the fires of the previous night.

With his announcement young Jimmy Conners had exchanged book learning for the kind of post-graduate studies that only Real Life can offer, and his mind made up for him, he was quickly sent steamboating.

He was his mother and father's only child, the son of an Irish Canadian stonecutter, saloon keeper, boarding house manager, and sailor. One might think that when a boy so young is dispatched to a new life aboard Great Lakes ships that there might be some concern on the parents' part, being his father's sole heir and all. But there had been more than just a few suspicious fires of late in the ward, commonly believed set by the belligerent boy, and his father was anxious to be rid of him after being told of his son's boasting of such exploits around the ward. He feared lawsuits, reprisal, or worse. The previous year there had been a similar blaze at the Mariners' Home that made Peter Conners suspect foul play. The previous night's second fire at his Mainers Home was the last straw.

Jimmy had been going through a phase of experimenting with bottle bombs filled with kerosene, and on the night of May 9th after fleeing the fire at his father's saloon he had walked down Mill Street and thrown a bomb atop the roof of the Union Ironworks, then fled to the Hamburgh street entrance to watch the excitement unfold from afar. The two fires lit up the First Ward sky and kept the volunteers busy.

The Ironworks fire was the much larger of the two and raged for a time across Hamburgh Street from where JP and Jim Sullivan watched transfixed from their bedroom window. Everyone in the neighborhood awoke to the clamor to watch as the blaze got doused. The following day in the Buffalo Courier it was stated that both fires caused $1000 damage each, mentioning that, as always, Peter Conners was very well insured and "this will go far toward covering the loss."

Jimmy's father had learned from experience to suspect the worst when it came to matters pertaining to his son. With Jimmy around, insurance was indeed the wisest investment, the elder Conners concluded. The newspaper said it was thought sparks from the furnace at the Ironworks was the cause of the fire there, but took no guesses for a cause for the blaze at Conners' Mariners Home.

Jimmy Conners approached the steamship William M. Babcock, his half-empty sack slung over his shoulder, surprised to see a familiar face.

"Kennedy! What're youse doin' here?"

Kennedy laughed, not as surprised to see Conners as Conners was to see him.

"Same as you, I'll bet!" he answered. "Me Ma kicked me out. Said it's either work the lakes and make somethin' of meself or she'll have me locked up in the workhouse! Did yer Pa want t' rid himself o' youse, too?"

"Nah! They tried t' stop me! But me Pa and Ma need me help. Business is in the shitter and they got lots o' bills. They cried like babies when I was leavin'! "

Kennedy scrutinized Conners' bruises, doubting his story.

The leery Captain, John Kirby, spotted the boys on the gangplank and dispatched his flamboyant steward to intercept them.

"Hey, youse two!" The steward grabbed them by their shirt backs like a bitch hoisting her puppies. "Come wit' me!"

Steward rudely dragged the lads into the galley and tossed their sacks into a corner. He pushed Conners toward a mountain of potatoes, handing him a knife. Next to it was a half barrel of water.

"Make 'em naked as little white boys in a swimmin' hole! An' don't ye be wastin' none o' the flesh!"

Steward sized up Kennedy approvingly.

"And you there, lad, what's your name?"

"Kennedy, sir."

"Kennedy, looks t' me like a big strappin' laddie like yerself would know exactly what to do with a nice firm arse the likes o' the one I got. Ye come wit' me," said the steward with a wink.

Kennedy suddenly experienced a sick, panicky sensation.

The steward slipped into the dark ice closet, regarding Kennedy solicitously. He beckoned the hesitant boy. Fearfully, Kennedy followed. Once inside the cramped cold space he saw Steward grappling with the front end of a lamb slaughtered fresh just a few hours previous.

"Whaddya waitin fer? Take hold o' that rear end like ye own it!"

Relieved, Kennedy giggled.

Awkwardly he maneuvered his end, hoisting the heavy carcass onto the chopping block with a grunt.

"There! Now you get over there and start peelin' and choppin' them beetroots and turnips, Kennedy, and don't let me catch either o' youse tuggin' at yer dicks! There's plenty that needs doin' 'round here before we all go beddy-bye together tonight."

Steward laughed teasingly.

The boys proceeded uncomfortably.

The day lengthened toward afternoon. The steward ran the boys ragged. The frantic boys scrambled, tripping over one another to perform chores best they could to his satisfaction.

The smiling Captain, smoking a pipe, steered the ship through Erie's calm blue waters toward a lowering sun. Passengers dressed for dinner gathered at the rail with drinks to enjoy the sunset.

After dark, the exhausted friends curled up on crude wood bunks in the dank smelly ship's hold. Conners extinguished an oil lamp. Under his blanket he quietly masturbated before falling asleep to the ship's loud groaning.

The Sturgeon

Conners and Kennedy quickly settled into Steward's routine, displaying enough proficiency in their duties to make them confident about the near-certainty of continued employment. They bustled about the galley prepping for dinner. Steward wiped his hands on his apron, then took it off and hung it on a coat hook on the ice closet door.

"I'm leavin' now t' go ask me lovely Captain what his majesty's pleasure might be fer his supper. You two wankers know what not to do. No dabbin' each other whilst I'm away, ye hear? Wet or dry, I'll be returnin' in five minutes."

The boys nodded affirmatively. Steward left on his errand.

Kennedy stood stationed at the chopping block disassembling a pile of chickens with a meat cleaver. He playfully somersaulted the cleaver into the air, expertly catching it by the handle every time. He eyed Conners devilishly.

"Say, Conners. Betcha ain't got the noive t' have me chop yer finger."

Jimmy Conners responded with bravado.

"Bet youse ain't got the dash-fire t' chop it, Kennedy!"

"All right, laddie, c'mere. Let's see what yer really made o'. Lay 'er right down here."

Kennedy pushed aside the pile of chicken parts. Undaunted, Conners offered his left hand, palm up.

Kennedy appeared to have second thoughts.

Confidently, Conners scoffed, then taunted his challenger mockingly.

"Ha! T'ought so, Kennedy! Knew ye didn't have the balls!"

As Conners began to reclaim his hand from the chopping block, Kennedy pounced, pinning Conners' wrist with his free hand. In a flash he slammed the cleaver downward with the abruptness of a guillotine. Kennedy detached Conners' left thumb with a sickening wallop. For a brief moment the tough little bully stood motionless, stunned speechless before suddenly set to wailing. He clamped his wound closed with his intact hand, then flew out of the galley, dripping blood as he screamed.

"Me fingy! Me fingy! He chopped me fingy!"

Conners shot around the ship from deck to deck howling the phrase over and over, immortalizing the nickname destined to follow him from that day forward throughout the rest of his life: Fingy.

With Conners' tortured cries echoing out in the background, Kennedy chuckled, damned PROUD of himself. He bent over closely inspecting the detached digit. He picked it up to get a better look, turning it every which-way, examining it closely in a shaft of sunlight.

Kennedy chuckled mockingly.

"Tsk, tsk. Jimmy Conners! Ye have got t' stop bitin' yer nails, son!"

Kennedy laughed at his own joke as he walked out on deck. He took one last look before tossing the amputated appendage into Lake Huron. He waited a few moments to see whether it would float or sink. As the ship steamed away it left Fingy Conners' thumb bobbing in its wake.

Suddenly a sturgeon shot up from below the surface and swallowed it.

The Mishap

Four days after his amputation, Fingy toiled in the ship's galley as best he could, feverish from the throbbing pain.

"Hey you there! Fingy! Take this soup up to my Captain. And this time don't youse be spillin' none on any o' those pretty petticoats o' yers!"

Fingy, his hand haphazardly bandaged, winced as he awkwardly accepted the tray from Steward. He balanced it precariously as he made his way along the deck. The ship rolled in heavy seas as passengers gripped hard to the arms of their deck chairs. Stepping up onto a stair, Fingy lost his balance. Soup spilled out onto the tray and his clothes. He looked horrified as he began to bawl. The passengers took pity on him.

"There, there, laddie. It's all right!" soothed a male traveler.

"No it ain't, Mister! The Captain is gonna whip me hide! It's gotten all over me trousers now! He'll put me off in Duluth fer sure, wit' me havin' nowheres t' go an' no money t' get there!"

"No, no. He won't. Listen to me. How's this? I'll go tell the Captain that I caused the upset. That it was all my fault."

The inconsolable boy couldn't stop crying.

The passenger dug deep into his pocket.

"Tell you what, lad. Here. I'll give you a dime for the remains. It's clean, and it looks quite good, actually. Run along now, leave the tray with my wife. I'll go speak to the Captain while you go and get him another bowl of soup. How's that sound?"

Fingy, sobbing with great heaves of his barrel chest, rubbed his eyes and nodded affirmatively. He accepted the dime weakly with his blood-stained bandaged hand.

He retuned to the galley, not realizing that Steward was yet there. Fingy buffed the silver coin on his bandage and chuckled to himself.

"Heh, heh, heh."

Steward poked his head out of the ice closet.

"Again? How long do ye think ye can keep gettin' away with yer little scheme there, Fingy?"

Facing himself away from Steward in a feigned display of shame, Fingy smiled broadly.

Miss Emma Nye

Jim had done a lot of thinking on the trolley. He had hoped that his commendable work habits at the Clemens house might make Mr. Clemens amenable to reading some of his articles and stories. Oftentimes Jim didn't even see Mr. Clemens on Saturdays, as that was his preferred day to work long hours at the Buffalo Express. Sunday was the biggest day for the paper, when that day's number was rechristened the Buffalo Illustrated Express, with wood engravings of photographs and illustrations to accompany the special Sunday features.

When he did have the luck to see Mr. Clemens he was often in a doleful mood, or preoccupied. Sam had just moved his mother and widowed sister to nearby Fredonia, New York, and was trying to find a good journalistic position for his brother Orian. These things took up what free time he had, Jim supposed. But Jim was puzzled when he learned that the position Sam was searching for his brother was with some small newspaper away from Buffalo. He wondered why Sam didn't just provide his own brother a position at the big city newspaper he was co-owner of. Considering that, Jim's high hopes for Mr. Clemens' help began to fade a little.

Peter Halloran was drinking again and Jim's mother and stepfather were arguing too often about it, but mostly they were trying to just avoid each other. It was hard on Jim and JP, but more so on little Danny, who couldn't understand what all the strife was about between his mother and father. His father had grown detached from him once more, after making a half-hearted effort for a while to become a better parent and spend more time with his only natural child.

It was early September, and as Jim raked up clippings and debris, Mr. Clemens arrived home in his carriage. He got out in a jolly mood and approached Jim. He began kidding him about Jim's new female interest, Mary Ann Bain, the daughter of another of the Hallorans' boarders. Sam questioned the wisdom, and propriety, of his interest in this shy young girl who happened to be a boarder in the same house that Jim's family owned, thus putting her in a compromised position.

Jim assured Mr. Clemens that Mary Ann Bain was not at all shy.

"You realize, Mr. Sullivan," said Sam, "that I say these things only to try and influence you to a higher moral altitude. I did not gather these things from personal practice, mind you, but from observation. To be good is noble; but to show others how to be good is even nobler, and no trouble at all."

Jim laughed for almost a half-minute straight. Sam in fact didn't have a hypocritical bone in his entire body. He had never met a man funnier or more forthright than Mr. Sam Clemens. The front door opened and the exceedingly pregnant Olivia Clemens emerged onto the porch, weakly, looking quite troubled.

"Sam, I need to speak with you."

Sam smiled at Jim and went up on the porch where he and Livy spoke in hushed tones. Jim raked up stray leaves.

Livy had been ill through most of her pregnancy. Complicating this delicate state was the physical and emotional exhaustion she suffered while trying to nurse her dying father back to health in Elmira the month before. She was of recent very sick and quite weak, and in a letter had revealed as much to her old friend and schoolmate, Miss Emma Nye.

Emma insisted on traveling from Elmira to stay with Livy to help and care for her friend for the remaining weeks of her pregnancy. Livy was due in mid-December.

Sam welcomed her visit, as he was guilty for his long hours spent at the Express. Emma Nye had arrived at the beginning of the month, but almost immediately she herself took sick.

Olivia momentarily raised her voice louder than intended, and Jim heard her tell Sam, "The doctor said that Emma has typhoid fever."

Typhoid was what had ultimately claimed Jim's battle-wounded father. Jim shuddered.

Sam was shocked and greatly disturbed by this news. He immediately worried about their baby. He rushed into the house.

Jim shook his head at all their bad luck, and began to wonder, will the Clemens ever find any peace and comfort? He took no satisfaction from the fact that rich people seemed just as vulnerable to misery and tragedy as the poor, for he was growing to love Sam Clemens, and wished him and his family nothing but happiness.

Jim carried on with his chores.

Livy was in an exhausted state from caring for the very ill Miss Nye. Ellen White, the older of the two servant girls, was terrified, for her husband and baby had both died from typhoid. She did not wish to go anywhere near Sam and Olivia's bedroom, where Olivia had now installed her best friend, putting her friend's comfort and well being above her own.

Ellen White and Margaret Brown both knew how precarious Mrs. Clemens' health was, and her time for giving birth was approaching. They were extremely worried about her, and pleaded with Sam to hire a qualified medical nurse to care for Miss Nye, both for Livy's sake and their baby's—as well as Miss Nye's.

They unashamedly admitted they would feel great relief knowing that they would not have to be exposed to this deadly disease—one that had touched almost every family in America—any more than need be.

Sam told Livy he was going to hire a nurse, but Livy would not hear of it.

"Emma is my closest friend, and she would never have become ill had she not come here to see me through my troubles. I will attend to her."

Sam silently questioned his wife's state of mind. Surely she must care about their unborn? Exhausting herself, and putting herself and their child at such risk was not something he felt Livy would do if she were in her correct mind. He had always admired her caring nature—indeed that was what first drew him to her—but not at the expense of her own health, and their baby's.

Sam told her that he was worried about the baby, which already had been put under tremendous stress during its early gestation by the excruciating, weeks-long, round-the-clock nursing of Jervis Langdon. "You must take care of yourself, Liv. At least allow a nurse to help you."

Livy turned a deaf ear, but Sam overruled her and hired a nurse regardless, who when Sam was not at home, was allowed to do very little. Only when Sam was present did Livy let the nurse perform the tasks for which she was hired.

The following Saturday, September 17, Jim boarded the streetcar with his copy of the Buffalo Express to read, and scanned it for the byline of Mark Twain. There it was.

In his piece, Mr. Twain responded to a couple of practical jokers who had sent the Express a marriage notice for two people not even contemplating matrimony. Twain wrote:

"This deceit has been practiced maliciously by a couple of men whose small souls will escape through their pores some day if they do not varnish their hides."

James chuckled out loud, then read the line again, trying to figure out how Sam came up with it.

He arrived at the Clemens house and as quietly as possible performed his duties. But Miss Nye was in such a terrible state, with a deadly migraine and severe nausea, that even the slightest noise caused her great suffering and anxiety. So Jim was asked to leave much earlier than usual by the servant Ellen White. He never laid eyes on Sam that day.

The following Saturday, September 24th, he read on the trolly a tirade by Mr. Twain titled A Curious Dream, in which vivid prose and clever observations riveted readers' attention to the neglect of Buffalo's old North Street graveyard. Twain painted frightening visions of ancestors deserting the decrepit cemetery en masse, carrying their own coffins on their backs, and created such a picture, more humiliating than amusing, that reform was sure follow, for that was the power of the pen he wielded.

Jim arrived at the Clemens house to learn that now Mrs. Clemens was very ill in bed, and that Sam was at the Express. Ellen White told Jim that she had been instructed to tell Jim to set to work in the carriage house, replacing mortar that had crumbled from between the bricks, and giving the structure a thorough cleaning. But by no means was he to venture outside, or make any noise that might disturb the sleep of Mrs. Clemens.

Jim performed his duties as instructed, worried about Mrs. Clemens, about Miss Nye, about Sam, about the baby. Worrying, perhaps selfishly, if Mr. Clemens would ever have things settle down in his life enough to read some of Jim's stories. Jim decided he needed to be more patient. His meeting Mr. Clemens was a wonderful stroke of luck, an opportunity he would not put in jeopardy by making poorly timed demands.

After he had thoroughly cleaned the carriage house, and placed the horse droppings in the refuse pile in the back corner of the garden along with the green clippings and leaves, and wetting it all down to speed composting, he walked up the driveway toward the avenue.

Ellen White came out of the house from the side door and thanked him for being so silent.

"I had forgotten you were even here," the servant girl said, kindly, handing Jim his pay.

"How is Miss Nye?" Jim asked.

"The poor soul died last Tuesday, Jim. Pray for her. And for Mrs. Clemens too." Then she closed the door.

Jim was alarmed. What was wrong now with Mrs. Clemens? Did she have typhoid? He hadn't prayed in ages, but decided for the sake of his new friends, he would take up the practice again right away.

After the death of Miss Nye, Olivia Clemens, pregnant and weak almost beyond comprehension, should have immediately taken to her bed. But another friend from Elmira came to call, believing he was offering comfort and companionship, when what Livy desperately required was complete bed rest. But again she could not help herself, and attempted to be a genteel hostess.

Worse, after the visit, she insisted on accompanying the visitor back to the train station in the Clemens carriage. Because they left the house late, Mr. McFey was ordered to drive as fast as he could so as not to miss the train, over rough bumps and deep ruts, bouncing and jarring poor pregnant Livy, who was now feeling every bone in her body as each one absorbed the volley of shocks.

After her goodbyes to her guest, she was driven home along a more gentle route, and reaching her bed finally, was prostrated in it for an entire week thereafter.

Peter Halloran's relapse into drink did not last long. Mary stopped speaking to him or even looking at him. She made him invisible, which caused him to cease drinking again and to renew his promises.

Once more he took extra time to be with his son. Danny wanted to go rowing with his father on the river, but Peter was terrified of the water, and even more frightened of the idea of his helpless young son being on the river at all. Peter had bad dreams of Danny falling in, himself being unable to rescue him.

The Buffalo River had recently swallowed another of Halloran's favorite customers, continuing its reliable late night habit of claiming the ward's most inveterate drinkers after staggering out to find their way home.

Peter and Jim began to talk more as they worked together in the family saloon, and Peter was beginning to treat his stepson more like a man than a boy. Jim's friendship with the illustrious Sam Clemens made Peter realize that he had been overlooking much of what was of value in Jim.

Jim had read Innocents Abroad whenever he could wrestle it away from his stepfather, enjoying it immensely, but now that he was friends with the famous author himself, the volume became even more meaningful to him — more alive and intimate. Peter also reread it once more. They enjoyed discussing it. Peter asked questions about it that he hoped Jim would take to Mr. Clemens.

"How often does a man get the chance to ask an author questions about his favorite book?" They both awaited Mark Twain's next volume expectantly.

Sam Clemens had been taking stabs at writing his next masterpiece. Small essays embracing its planned subjects appeared periodically in the Express. He told Jim he wanted to call his new book Roughing It. But finding the time, the peace, and the inclination to make any actual headway was a real problem for Sam these days. Writing anything humorous was increasingly challenging, considering his troubled personal circumstances.

Buffalo had not been at all kind to them. The Clemens had experienced nothing but stress, illness and heartbreaking loss during their first year in the city, and Sam's written output was at a near standstill. He had only written something like thirty essays for his own newspaper thus far, over the span of the entire year, that's how empty he was.

Jim rarely saw Mr. Clemens most Saturdays, and when he did, Sam was so preoccupied and frazzled that he felt he shouldn't bother him, except to be as kind as possible. He missed his friend.

Jim knew his day would come. He knew that Sam really cared about him, and the household was very happy with his work. Even Mr. McFey praised the job he had done on the carriage house, and not just because it meant McFey didn't have to do it himself. Jim was appreciated by all.

Jim wanted to be a better friend to Sam, but seeing so little of him, did not quite know how. He wondered if he perhaps should just write him a letter.

The Clemens home on Delaware Ave. in Buffalo NY.
photo: Buffalo & Erie Cty. Historical Society

It's A Boy

Jim made another Saturday morning journey from Hamburgh Street to the Delaware Avenue mansion of Sam and Livy Clemens in high spirits.

Sam had told Jim that he would be at home all that day, and Jim Sullivan was trying to figure out a diplomatic way to get Sam to read one of his short essays, which he had tucked into his jacket pocket.

Jim had been reading the Express every day since he met Mr. Clemens, looking for his by-line. When he did find it, which curiously for one who owned his very own newspaper was not very often, he read and studied it, laughing, dissecting, trying to figure out precisely what made Sam Clemens Mark Twain. Today was a good day, for his by-line was there.

He studied the construction of the sentences, the ease and informality of the language and the liberties he took with it. But most of all, Jim admired that even if Mark Twain was writing about a subject that might not be of much personal interest to the reader, he made it so, regardless, through his gift for relating facts—or the facts as he interpreted them—along with a generous dash of jolly good story-telling.

Jim smiled broadly as he began reading the story in that day's paper—about Sam Clemens, by Sam Clemens—and the very home that was now Jim's cherished place of weekly employment:

> I arrived after dark on a February evening this year, with my wife and a large company of friends, when I had been a husband for 24 hours, and they put us two in a covered sleigh and drove us up and down and every which way through all the back streets of the city until at last I got ashamed. I had asked Mr. Slee to get me a cheap boarding house, but I didn't mean he could stretch economy so far as to go outside of the state to find one.
>
> The fact was, there was a practical joke to the fore. My father-in-law had been clandestinely spending a fair-sized fortune upon a house and furniture in Delaware Avenue for us, and had kept his secret so well that I was the only person east of Niagara Falls who hadn't found out.
>
> We reached the house at last, about 10 o'clock, and were introduced to a Mrs. Johnson, the ostensible landlady. I took a glance around, and then my opinion of Mr. Slee's judgement as a provider of cheap boarding houses for a man who had to work for a living dropped to zero. I told Mrs. Johnson there had been an unfortunate mistake. Mr. Slee had evidently supposed I had money, whereas I only had talent; and so, by her leave, we would abide with her a week, and then she could keep my small trunk and we would hunt another place.
>
> Then the battalion of ambushed friends and relatives burst in on us, out of closets, and from behind curtains; the property was delivered

over to us and the joke revealed, accompanied with much hilarity. Such jokes as these are all too scarce in a person's life. That house was completely equipped in every detail—even to house-servants and a coachman—that there was nothing to do but just sit down and live in it.

Sam's words to Jim that first day in his carriage as he drove Jim home came back to him: write what you know.

Sam was writing in this instance, and almost always, from his own life and his own personal experiences, and that seemed far more interesting to Jim than any fiction one could conjure up out of the blue.

Jim took his own essay out of his pocket, and reread it yet again, wondering if Sam Clemens would like it. He had taken Sam's advice and his example to heart. It was the story of the day he, baby brother JP and their mother all bid goodbye to his father at the train station as he left for war. It contained no humor. He had even cried while writing it.

There was snow on the ground now that November was hard upon the city. Great gusts blew unfettered across Lake Erie for almost 200 miles west to east, slamming into Buffalo after picking up unfathomable amounts of moisture along the way, and immediately dumping vast deposits of snow the moment the mass reached dry land, which happened to be this city.

As he walked down the driveway to the carriage house to fetch the snow shovel to clear the walks, Jim heard the cry of a little baby. He looked up with delight to see Sam waving and beaming like a lunatic down at him through the window, and hurried over to the side entrance.

Sam opened the door a bit.

"It's a boy, my friend! Here. Have a cigar!"

Sam presented a lovely Havana to Jim, who didn't smoke, but knew right off he might trade it if he wanted. Or maybe, he should just keep it as a souvenir of this wonderful day.

Jim was thrilled for him. For the Clemens Family.

"Congratulations Mr Clemens! Boy! You've got a son. You must be over the moon!"

"Over the moon doesn't even begin to describe it, Jim," he waxed enthusiastically.

After so many troubles in the lives of the Clemens, Jim was heartened that finally something wonderful had happened, and was greatly relieved at the robust sound the little one's cry made.

"And how is Mrs. Clemens doing, Mr. Clemens?"

"Just grand, my boy. Just splendid. The baby hasn't smiled yet, but Mrs. Clemens is all smiles, despite being confined mostly to bed. We are all heartened that she is eating like a horse. And I do hold the baby myself, and do it pretty handily too, although with occasional apprehensions that his loose head will fall off."

Jim laughed as Sam mimed the scenario.

"There's a draught, so I'll need to close the door over now. Ellen told you what we'd like you to do today?"

"Yes, sir, she did," Jim smiled, trying to prolong the encounter.

"Fine, fine," said Sam, the door now only open just a crack. "Call for Ellen if you need anything."

"I will Sir. Please give my very best to Mrs. Clemens."

And with that, Sam disappeared into the warmth of his beautiful house to enjoy, with great relief and happiness, his new family.

Jim finished the day without meeting Sam again. He rode home on the trolley a little sad and not knowing precisely why. He took his essay out of his pocket, and read it once more.

He timed it. It took three minutes and fourteen seconds to read. That's all the time he wanted from Mr. Clemens, but today it was not to be. Next Saturday, maybe. He'd take it with him again next Saturday.

Winter passed slowly, and spring tried its best to arrive despite the reluctance of the snow to melt, but still Jim had barely seen Mr. Clemens.

The baby, named Langdon after Mr. Clemens' beloved father-in-law, had been born five weeks premature, weighing four and a half pounds.

The first week of Langdon's life was touch and go, allowing neither his mother or father to get much sleep. Depleted by the ceaseless colicky crying of their new son, Sam wondered if the strain of Livy's nursing both her father and her best friend within weeks of each other might be responsible for the premature arrival and the fragile health of the young one.

The unsettled circumstances of Langdon's first week gave way to steady weight gain and improving health thereafter, but colic continued to plague him. Livy had, in a fit of absolute frustration, happily discovered that if she bundled Langdon up and had Mr. McFey take them both for a drive in the carriage, that the baby would quiet right down. She wasn't sure if it was the fresh air or the motion of the carriage that was responsible, but it didn't matter. Daily carriage rides became a Clemens household ritual, and in part, she felt, necessary for maintaining her own sanity.

The Misses Brown and White enjoyed this ritual as well. With Livy and the baby out of the house the servants could set about doing the noisier and more odiferous chores without fear of reproach or waking the baby.

Jim Sullivan stood proudly outside the residence with Sam. He noticed that the roof of the fine house directly across Delaware Avenue had burned, yet its occupants were calmly enjoying rocking themselves out on the front porch in their overcoats, watching him and Sam and the traffic.

Jim meant to ask what happened, but was distracted by Sam's stories.

The coaches and carriages of the neighborhood's wealthy glided by the Clemens home all day long, and when Sam laughed heartily at Jim's jokes, or put his arm around his shoulder as he often did easily, Jim was proud that others witnessed this. He felt almost like a son to this man sometimes, he was treated so kindly by him. Sam did not regard him, or Mr. McFey, or his "colored girls" much like servants at all.

While driving Mr. Clemens about town, Patrick McFey was oftentimes so turned right around in his seat, cutting up with Mr. Clemens and laughing, that the buggy was put in a precarious predicament more than once. Jim worked outside all day. He saw scores of carriages go by. Not once, in any other rich man's carriage, did he see the coachman having as much fun as Patrick McFey. Nor any passenger as playful as Sam Clemens. Samuel L. Clemens was indeed an unusual man.

"Well, I just cannot bring myself to climb up on your roof, Mr Clemens. Me mother would whip me hide, first off," Jim said mimicking her accent, "that is, if I indeed survived it, which I do fear I would not. Second, I am right afraid of heights." Jim winked at the coachman. "Perhaps Mr. McFey might be akin to doin' it?"

Jim observed the wild dark curly hair and even wilder mustache that Mr. Clemens sported.

"Mr. McFey will have people believe he knows all manner of things, and even if he does not, he will let on in such a natural way as to deceive even the most critical. So I am apt to not even ask."

McFey, in the rig at the ready, laughed uproariously.

"Mr. Clemens, I'll ask around the ward, because I'm certain there is someone capable, if not extraordinary, who can repair the roof leak in fine fashion."

Sam Clemens, if cornered, would have to admit that he had more or less run out of jobs for Jim to do, and was now trying to create some. The roof had sprung a leak, not too serious yet, and knowing that Jim had some experience unloading freight at the docks, and working some at heights, he didn't think it would hurt to ask. But he was relieved when Jim declined. There had already been enough tragedy and illness in this house without young Sullivan tumbling off the roof.

Jim did not fully realize what was occurring right around him right at that moment.

Livy's health was terrible. The baby was continually sick and miserable. Sam, weary and dejected, beaten up and taken down by life since arriving in this city, unable to even make any headway on his new book, was now gazing eastward to Hartford, home of his book publisher, and, he decided, a beautiful place in which to raise a family.

Having a child changes a man.

Sam finally concluded that he was not a newspaper man at all, as borne out by his paucity of contributions during his year-and-a-half ownership of the Buffalo Express. He was an author. A book author. And that's what he wanted, and needed, to be.

Buffalo was a progressive city — a beautiful city, as American cities go. But this house in Buffalo was under a dark cloud, and as lovely and exciting as its urban situation might be, Sam Clemens felt stagnant and imprisoned here. His creativity was at a standstill. He had already wandered the world, from the rim of Halemaumau's molten crater on Hawaii's volcanic island, to the desert campfires of ancient Syria, and as young as he still was, there was yet so much more to see.

Mark Twain's days in Buffalo were over.

He had quietly been trying to sell his share in the Express, and had met with an agent about putting the house up for sale. He had not yet let on to Jim Sullivan about any of this, for he knew that it would be a great disappointment to him.

Sam would tell the boy when the time was right.

Sam's plans moved almost too quickly, once he'd had made up his mind. He disposed of his interest in the Express in April at a loss of $10,000, and as soon as Livy and the baby were well enough to travel on a mattress in the carriage, Sam Clemens wanted to get them all out of there. He would take his family out to Elmira, to Livy's sisters' home at beautiful Quarry Farm, to plan the next phase in his family's future.

Sam Clemens and Jim Sullivan stood out front of the grand house on Delaware Avenue, having finished assessing the steeply sloping roof. Mr. McFey sat in the carriage, the horse hitched and eager to move, ready to drive Mr. Clemens off to work at the newspaper.

Mr. Clemens was dressed in his collar, coat, vest and tie, and the shiny lace up shoes he'd brought all the way from San Francisco. His cigar had gone out and the stub looked to be permanently lodged in his clenched teeth as he spoke. Jim pulled a match from his pocket and offered it to Mr. Clemens, who raised his hand in reluctant protest. "Thanks, son. But I promised Livy I'd try and stop."

Jim wanted to dress like Sam Clemens, own a grand house like Sam Clemens, and if possible, be as funny as Sam Clemens, even knowing that it was his younger brother who was the family comedian. Like Sam, JP Sullivan just had a way of putting things that made people laugh, whereas if anyone else said the identical thing, people wouldn't crack so much as a smile.

"Mr. McFey," bellowed Sam to his elegantly costumed driver, as he climbed into the carriage, "How is it that I have managed to outfit you better than I do myself?" Sam studied with pride his young coachman, whose style and dignity, he thought, were outstanding.

Mrs. Clemens came out on the porch, looking stronger and healthier than the last time Jim had seen her, with their crying baby in her arms.

"Mr. McFey, I'll expect you back promptly so we can take Langdon for his drive."

"Yes, ma'am, right away," replied Patrick McFey.

Langdon was not yet six months old, and still cried most of the time. Mr. Clemens said, "I'm not entirely sure if it's because Langdon is sickly that he cries so much, or if his misery comes from knowing that of all the other towns he could have been born in, his parents chose Buffalo."

Jim roared at the truth in that.

Sam waved goodbye to his wife. "I won't be late this afternoon, Livy. Have supper waiting for me?"

Olivia winced from the pounding headache caused by the baby's continual crying and the stress of his ongoing upset. Sam had made the same promise the day before, yet had not returned home until almost eleven o'clock. Because Livy had two servants, Sam didn't feel the pressing need to be home, neither to offer help, pleasant company, or comfort.

"Mr. Clemens?" ventured Jim Sullivan. "I wonder if I might trouble you to read this very short essay I've written? I know you're very busy, but I timed it, and it only takes three minutes and fourteen seconds. Your opinion would be entirely valuable to me, Mr. Clemens, good or bad. I need to know if I'm any good. I'm hoping you might tell me."

Sam reluctantly took the papers from Jim. Jim saw this hesitation and at once felt that he had overstepped, and a mild panic came over him. But in fact, Sam was thinking about the difficult conversation with Jim that lie ahead.

Sam tucked the essay into his pocket, and said with a huge smile and twinkling eyes, "Of course, son. I will make the time to read it. I promise."

Jim was absolutely elated. The rest of the day would be just a blur, so beside himself with joy was he.

Jim watched as Mrs. Clemens entered the house, then he waved goodbye to Sam and Patrick as the carbuncle-colored carriage drove off, and set about with the ladder and pail and a brush to wash the first floor windows. He had only stepped inside the house on a couple of occasions, and was awe-struck by its grandeur. He was very eager to have the opportunity to climb the staircase and see the second floor.

His ruse was his claimed fear of heights that prevented him from climbing a ladder to reach the windows on the upper storeys, which was half-most true. He offered that he could wash the upper story double hung windows from inside the house by sitting on the sill, thinking that would be his ticket in. But draughts were always on Livy's mind, and as much as she seemed to be fine with Jim being around, outside the house at least, she was not especially warm to him. Jim attributed this to all her heartaches, her fragile health, and since his birth, to doing what was best for baby Langdon.

Patrick returned with the carriage and let Mrs. Clemens know he was ready when she was.

"We're goin' t' miss ye, Jimmy," said the young coachman, as Livy came out of the house with her baby bundle.

Patrick McFey had no idea that Sam had not told Jim Sullivan about their leaving Buffalo, and Jim thought Patrick was just saying goodbye for now. It didn't hit him until after he found out the news that, "We're goin' t' miss ye, Jimmy" was not something Patrick might ordinarily say before leaving on his usual afternoon carriage ride to The Front.

Jim Sullivan was too elated by Sam Clemens' accepting his essay to notice this at the time.

Goodbye Mister Clemens

Jim Sullivan's world came crashing down.

He showed up for work to an almost empty Clemens house. Ellen White was there finishing things, and for the first time, opened the Clemens home's front door wide to him. "Come right in Jim, there's quite a bit left to do. I'm glad for your help."

Jim looked around at the empty house, then felt his breakfast rise in his throat.

"What happened? Where...where is all the furniture?"

The windows were bare of drapes, and only boxes and crates remained, opened, ready for Jim and Ellen to fill with what little was left to pack.

Ellen was momentarily horrified. The look on Jim's face told the story.

"No one told you?" she exclaimed.

Jim just stood frozen, staring.

"They've left, Jim. We're movin' to Elmira. Didn't Mr. Clemens tell you?"

Jim had just recently turned seventeen, and for the first time in years, he cried.

Ellen was shaken, for she could not believe that Mr. Clemens hadn't told Jim, of all people. Had he not even said goodbye to his young friend? She had seen them happily together so often, laughing and joking. She knew that Mr. Clemens was very fond of Jim, speaking about him often between his visits to the house, bragging to Livy about him. She could not for the life of her understand how or why he could leave without telling his young protégé goodbye.

Sam Clemens was nervous his last week in Buffalo, elated to be leaving, but dreading having to face Jim Sullivan.

So he didn't.

Every time Sam looked squarely at Jim Sullivan, his late brother Henry's face appeared. Jim was so much like Henry that sometimes it physically hurt. Sam could not shake the horror of Henry's agonizing prolonged suffering and death. As hard as he tried, there was no excuse that Sam could conjure that did not make the loss of his innocent brother entirely his own fault. The prospect of looking Jim Sullivan in the eye and saying goodbye was akin to saying goodbye to Henry all over again. He couldn't explain it properly to himself, but his friendship with young Jim had come to mean more to him than he had allowed himself to concede.

Sam had toyed with the idea of offering Jim a job as his assistant, of taking him to Hartford. But he realized one day that the reason he never made the effort to help Jim by hiring him at the Buffalo Express, or even inquire about his ongoing writings, was because it was too difficult to be around him for very long. Jim Sullivan possessed Henry's smile, Henry's kind heart And sometimes, it seemed, Henry's soul.

Sam could not exorcise himself of the terrible fear that, if Jim were allowed into his life, that he too would suffer the same tragic end that had befallen so many of Sam Clemens' other loved ones.

And so he just packed up his family and left. Without saying goodbye.

Jim was embarrassed that Ellen saw him break, and quickly regained his composure. They finished up after four hours, and as he departed, Ellen handed him his generous severance, five dollars, and a large envelope.

"Mr. Clemens left this for you."

Jim was so heartbroken he couldn't remember a thing about the walk down Delaware Avenue to catch the trolley home. His dreams had disappeared as assuredly as the sun sinking below the horizon. All his happy imaginings about working at the newspaper, of having his first article published — perhaps becoming a celebrity something like Mark Twain — all these wonderful fantasies that had made his unhappy and unsettled life newly joyful and hopeful, instantly evaporated.

As he sat on the trolley, feeling walked-out on and depleted of optimism, he opened the large envelope. Inside was the following morning's Sunday Express and a smaller envelope on which Sam had written "James E. Sullivan, author." Inside was a check for fifty dollars.

Jim was puzzled. He opened the newspaper, and at the top left of the page, a headline with a phrase familiar to him caught his eye: The Last Goodbye. Beneath that, in smaller print: A Fine New Author Remembers His Beloved Father, Killed in the Late War. And beneath that: by James E. Sullivan. Jim began to read:

As we stood on the platform of the Exchange Street station, I looked at my father, rucksack at the ready, mother crying and baby John just about ready to, and I felt but two things: love and dread.

A boy of seven is endowed with more understanding than older people might wish to recognize, needing perhaps to protect themselves from the pain of realizing that children might feel as deeply, might ache as longingly, might cry as remorsefully as do they.

My father and mother both were born in Ireland and crossed the open ocean to the United States for a chance at a new life, and that is what they found. They found a new beginning, they found each other, and they found that they deeply loved their new country.

I looked around the railway platform and saw other boys and girls as confused as I was. I saw crying wives and mothers, grey-haired fathers with foreboding looks on their serious faces for their beloved young sons, and brand-new soldiers trying to put on a brave and optimistic front, as we all awaited the train that would separate us from the ones we loved most.

Just six months before, at this very station, a different throng and a different emotion had prevailed, as president-elect Lincoln's train was due to pull in on his way to his inauguration in Washington. Crowds of citizens wished to see him while he was here, to shake his hand, to speak to him.

My father and I were two of those citizens. He and I stood beneath the balcony at the American Hotel to hear Mr. Lincoln speak movingly and convincingly despite the winter cold about his selection to lead the country through the troubles that lay ahead. We stood for hours in the receiving line shivering, my father and I, fearful that before we reached our hero that they might shut down the queue, for the new president looked weary.

But they didn't.

My father almost became tongue-tied when at long last we were in the presence of that great man. Lincoln politely nodded a greeting to him as we approached, but to me he reached out and took my hand in his.

That day standing by my soldier-father's side at the station I yet again became one of those people, wanting to see, to shake his hand, to respectfully ask, Mr. Lincoln, can you please protect my father? Can you see to it that neither musket ball nor point of bayonet harm the man who gave me life? Can you provide him duty somewhere well behind the lines of battle, so that he might come back to us? For we love him so.

But Mr. Lincoln was not at the depot that day. He was consumed with trying to keep our nation together and repel those who seemed determined to trod asunder what George Washington had so courageously stolen away from Britain a little less than one hundred years ago, this glorious collection of states, united.

The train arrived, and I felt my throat close up and the tears begin to flow. My father crouched to my level and took my face between both his hands, and said softly, "I will always love you most, son, because you were my first."

As our mother held baby John, my father stood and buried his face in their new infant's chest, and the grown man began to bawl, and for the first time, I felt his fear, and that terrified me.

I had never seen my father cry. He was a dock worker. He dug the canals. He was strong and steadfast and tough.

But on that day, at that moment, he cried.

And seeing this big man cry caused us all to cry, for the façade had fallen. The brave front he carefully created to shield us, that of a soldier marching off fearlessly to defend the freedoms that Mr. Lincoln proclaimed, had crumbled.

As we saw his rarefied tears catch the glint of the early morning sun, for the first—and what would prove to be the last—time, I realized that my mother and I were not the only ones fearful that our loved one might never return.

The baby screamed, disconcerted by all the emotion, and I wrapped my arms tightly around my father's waist, for I was too small to reach any higher, and I pleaded with him, "Papa, don't leave us here!"

Patiently, and without embarrassment, he stood and allowed me to cling to him, until I was ready to let go. And as my arms loosened and dropped, I backed away a bit, and looked up into his face. The train whistle blew and the men were being herded aboard, torn from the loving lips and arms of their families. He embraced his fragile wife as she cradled their baby snugly between them, and suddenly, he was whisked off.

I do not remember the train pulling away, or watching it disappear from sight. I don't know if I simply don't remember, or if the scene was a too painful for me to watch, but I do recall burying my face in the folds of my mother's skirt, my tears lost among the threads.

As we three left the station, I was consumed for the first time in my young life by the terrible emotion of loss.

To this day, we don't know where my father is. An official letter claimed that he had died, but unlike some of our neighbors who lost sons and husbands, our family received no sorrowful coffin to bury, nor any map or description to reveal where we might find him. I have dreams at night that he didn't really die at all, that he simply became lost, or that is suffering with amnesia and is still living somewhere, waiting patiently and hopefully for his eldest son to come find him.

John Sullivan, Company E, 49th Regiment, New York Vols., disappeared beneath a cloud of heavy black Rogers locomotive smoke one hot August day at Buffalo's Exchange Street station. And still today, even though ten years later, I find myself going back there every few weeks, wandering beneath the ached glass roof, looking, searching the crowd for his smile, still believing he will return.

1873
Breathe

Mary Halloran's news that she was expecting the second of Peter Halloran's children was not met with a family-wide celebration, except for the whooping of eight-year-old Danny, who was fired up at the prospect of having a little brother or sister. Preferably, a brother. Danny had been the baby of the family for far too long and in his estimation was still treated as such. Maybe now, no longer being the youngest, his older brothers and parents might just allow him to grow up.

Being the most junior had its advantages, but Danny Halloran's mother still kept an eagle eye on him, fretting whenever she saw him disappear along the river. He would be down by the water exploring, when above the din of the tugboats and steamers, of horns hollering, work whistles screeching and the clanging clamor at the Union Ironworks, he would hear "Daaaannyyy! Danny!" coming from the river-facing top floor windows of No. 16 Hamburgh Street. His friends teased him, calling him a Mama's boy, because he always responded.

"Don't pay no attention to her," scolded his playmate and neighbor Freddy Triepel. Freddy was three years older and unceasing in his endeavors to keep Danny under his thumb. But Danny was suspicious of him. Being the youngest and most closely watched Halloran, Danny didn't have much freedom as it was, so he wasn't about to let some neighborhood misfit add to his woes. The whole Triepel family was a little odd. They made Danny uneasy. But Freddy's father John Triepel cut Danny's hair for free in the little barbershop in a wing off of his saloon, so he always kept his opinions to himself.

"I got to," replied Danny, and off he'd run to report to the Boss.

"What were you doin' down by the river, Danny?" scolded Mary Halloran. "You know I told you to keep away from it. Remember what happened to little Henry Zeller!"

The Zellers ran a grocery just up Hamburgh Street, a few doors away at No. 50. The previous year, four-year-old Henry Zeller got out of the house, toddled down the street past the Halloran and Triepel houses, and fell into the river.

Jacob and Wilhemina Rapp, who lived at No. 12 Hamburgh, the house between Halloran's and Triepel's on the corner, were just going out when they saw the baby fall in. Jacob ran and jumped in after him. The fireboat was just across the way at Farmer's Point and saw the scene, but Jacob got to Henry pretty fast. Sadly though, when Jacob pulled Henry from the water, he was as lifeless as a rag doll. Neighbors all heard the screaming and the ruckus and rushed out.

Horrified, they saw the dead body of sweet little blonde Henry Zeller being retrieved from the filthy river.

And then something extraordinary happened.

Wilhemina Rapp snatched little Henry away from her gasping husband, placed him on the ground on his back, and bent over him. She opened his mouth and began blowing air forcefully into his lungs. The more primitive of the Catholic Irish witnessing this bizarre ritual were convinced the Protestant Germans were performing some sort of heathen ceremony on the corpse, when all of a sudden a powerful geyser of water shot up noisily from Henry's mouth. After a few more forced breaths from Wilhemina, Henry began to choke mightily and cry. He then slowly wrapped his little arms around her neck and hung on for dear life, terrified.

At that very moment, a hysterical Barbara Zeller plowed through the crowd that had gathered, and found her soaking wet oil-coated little son crying the robust cry of life. She fell to her knees and began frantically thanking Wilhemina Rapp in staccato German.

Observers were astonished and thrilled.

They had never seen nor even heard of such a thing. A few of the more backward specimens looked upon Wilhemina Rapp suspiciously as if she were some form of Teutonic witch or devil sorceress. But when it was done, Wilhemina and Jacob Rapp reigned as the heroes of Hamburgh Street from that moment forward.

The fireboat pulled to shore, and firemen jumped out, not believing their eyes at the sight of little Henry Zeller back from the dead. They surrounded Wilhemina, asking about how she had accomplished this, and she explained that it was a well-known technique practiced in her village ever since she was a child. She was surprised that nobody here seemed to know about it, and demonstrated for the firemen how to perform it.

"With an adult you seal your mouth firmly over his, pinch his nose closed, and blow strongly, to force the water out of his lungs. Then you continue doing it until they can breathe on their own. But a small child, you must blow into his mouth and nose at the same time, more gently, but still strong."

Everyone oohed and aahed, dumbfounded.

By that evening just about everyone who witnessed this astonishing miracle had recalled someone they'd known and loved, a child or an adult, who had drowned, just like little Henry Zeller had. None of them knew about this breath-exchange method at the time. Could they have saved their loved one if they had?

To the last individual, they each drifted off into a troubled sleep, wondering, what if?

Mary hoped that the news of her being again with child would nudge Peter Halloran back on the right track. He was only drinking temperately these days, just having himself a beer or two. He was spending more time with Danny. Jim and JP were growing older, stronger, less tolerant of Peter's angry outbursts and clueless experiments in parenting. The brothers had long ago set to looking elsewhere for guidance, because they were getting none at home. Peter knew he had lost them.

Jim had exhausted his tolerance for working under Peter's oversee. He went back to the docks, loading freight and occasionally grain-scooping. He also worked for old David Clark the iceman the winter before, and was enraptured hearing Mr. Clark's recollections of his father, back when he too had cut ice for him. He was tickled by Mr. Clark's story of the company excursion to see Blondin's wire-walk cross the Niagara Gorge back in '59. Jim barely remembered it. Mr. Clark's account was so colorfully detailed that it made Jim feel like he hadn't even been there. He returned home that evening and asked his mother about it. She happily recalled that long-ago day for her son as being one of the most delightful of her life.

JP was 13 now, enrolled in the high school and determined to get an education. JP Sullivan promised himself he would not be a grain scooper, dock worker, puddler or any other kind of common laborer. He had bigger fish to fry.

Peter Halloran did not want another baby, but resigned himself to the inevitable. He was fifty-four years old. Tired. He was feeling relief about Danny's finally growing up and becoming more independent, because he knew he was not equipped to be a parent. Fortunately for Peter, Danny's brother Jim had stepped into that role.

When he was only just starting to walk, Danny would follow his father everywhere. When Peter left the flat and descended the stairs to set to work in the saloon every morning, Danny would stand at the top of the stairs, behind the gate that kept him from tumbling down, crying for his Papa. Peter would climb back up the stairs and try to calm him, but as soon as he started down again, Danny would howl.

Then Peter began bringing Danny down into the saloon, but he was too busy to properly supervise him, and Danny would fall, or get out the door, or get tripped over. Danny loved his mother, but without a doubt, he was his father's boy.

Jim Sullivan on the other hand felt like nobody's boy, and had turned quietly inward since Sam Clemens moved away.

For Christmas, Peter had purchased Mark Twain's newest book Roughing It for Jim as a present, thinking he'd be elated. But it was weeks before Jim could bring himself to pick it up. Peter was so out of touch that he just assumed Jim had lost interest in the works of Mark Twain. Jim was still reeling from the treachery of Sam Clemens' unannounced departure. He had virtually ceased his own writing. Except for occasional spurts of creativity, he focused his energies on the strenuous labor required of freight handlers on the docks.

The family fortunes had improved a good deal. The saloon was booming. Jim brought much of his salary home to his mother even though Peter had plenty of money, more than what the saloon's books said he should. Nobody asked the ex-convict where it was coming from. The house was empty of boarders now. They had it all to themselves, except for the new servant, Eliza Beatty.

Just three years previous the house at No. 16 Hamburgh was full of boarders. Besides the Halloran family of five, they boarded the Bain family of four, the Sweeney family of four, and the Collins family of four. Mary was happy to be free of all the noise and lack of privacy, but the income produced from the paying guests was necessary at the time.

They were all gone now. Old Patrick Sweeny had died right there at the dinner table while the families celebrated the New Year together. It was his seventy-first birthday. January 1, 1871. He died before having fully tapped the rich stores of wild tales and remembrances that so enthralled the boys.

Jim was thinking about his future, about getting out on his own, of becoming somebody. He planned to resume his writing at some point, recalling Mr. Clemens telling him how just one book, Innocents Abroad, had made him a rich man. If Jim could only come up with an idea for a book that everybody would want to read. He poured over his written accounts of Patrick Sweeny's exciting stories to see if he could make them into a book, or at least a feature that a monthly periodical might wish to buy.

Peter continued expanding upon his reputation as unstable and unreliable. Ever since Peter had stuck that butcher knife in his mother's neck almost four years back Jim had resigned himself to the necessity of remaining close to home. Besides, it wasn't as if the First Ward belles were beating a path to his door. All he wanted to do when he got home from work was wash, eat, and sleep. On Saturday afternoons and for a few hours on Sunday he still helped out in the saloon, but the place repulsed him. He saw how many lives were wasting away to nothingness there, and he was determined he wasn't going to become one of them.

Jim did wonder though where Peter's money was coming from now that the boarders were all gone. He had asked Peter if he might be allowed to contribute a little less at home so he could save up some for his future. Peter's response was, "How do you think we'll pay for the girl to help your poor mother?"

Eliza Beatty was far from being a girl. She was more Peter's age. She began working for the family last year, after everyone except for the Bains had moved out. She was a tremendous help to his mother, as well as working in the saloon, and would be even more so now that Mary Halloran was expecting again.

Eliza Beatty was grateful for the work and for a pillow upon which to lay her old tired head at night, safely. She had come from Ireland, hoping for a new life, and a husband. She found the new life, managing to find continuous employment as a servant and housekeeper. She had a fine reputation as a hard worker. But the husband had yet eluded her.

She worked as much as she could down in the saloon, surmising that with all the men there, she might meet a good match, or finagle an introduction from someone. Jim found this humorous, since most of the men in the saloon were married drunks. To balance things out, Eliza went to mass at St. Bridget's and volunteered to help out at church events, like the annual lawn fete, where she believed she might snag a lonely, financially comfortable widower.

But all in all, Eliza Beatty was a hard worker, without complaint, and didn't talk much. They all liked her.

One morning Jim was feeling terrible, but needed to go to work if he expected to retain his place in the dock gang. When a man didn't show up for work, there were always others, hungrier and more desperate, lurking, waiting to be chosen to take his place. And the new man might just be a better worker, or offer the boss a kickback for hiring him. So Jim dragged himself out of bed, spent quite a while in the crapper, and then stumbled off to work amid the distractions of nausea and aching muscles.

He labored for more than an hour, vomiting twice, with nothing coming up but bile. As foreman Kelly shot him disagreeable looks, Jim tried to get back to it. But he was dragging, and work needed to get done. Tom Kelly had been his foreman for six months, and although there was no love lost between them, he knew well that Jim was among a mere handful of his best workers. With a pat on his shoulder Kelly said, "Sully, getchyer ass home, now, will ya? I'll save yer place, not for worryin'. Go, get getch yerself feelin' better."

Relieved, but sicker than a dog, Jim Sullivan slowly made his way home along Ohio Street to South Street, then along the river to Hamburgh, and home. He barely made it up the porch steps, weakly opened the door, and stumbled into the saloon to catch Peter humping Eliza Beatty, skirts up, in the corner, under the stairs.

"You fooker!" nineteen-year-old Jim shouted, and lunged for Peter.

Eliza pulled her dress back down and fled out the door.

Peter fought back, and taking advantage of Jim's weakened sick condition, punched him deep in the gut, causing Jim to buckle and collapse. Halloran left to run after Eliza, who was now standing across South Street, looking out over the river, wondering if this might just be the end of her.

Jim could barely get up. He pulled himself to his feet by grabbing the coat hooks on the wall. He vomited again, heaving dryly in convulsions that produced nothing but pain. Then he climbed the stairs. He needed to lie down. The room was spinning. He did not see his mother. Danny and JP were both at school. He made it to his bed and collapsed.

Mary walked in the saloon door a half hour later with bundles of vegetables and a loin of pork.

"Hello, Husband," she smiled, as Peter wiped down the tables in the saloon.

"Hello, me love," he replied, smiling back. "Happy t' have you home."

Mary was heartened by Peter's attitude lately. She was afraid he would be angry about the new baby, but he seemed hopeful, calmer, happier, especially since Eliza had arrived.

She had taken a big burden off Mary's back, and Mary attributed her own improved mood to the improvement in Peter's as well, and in their relationship, not fully realizing at first that it was Eliza alone who was engendering this effect in her husband.

As Mary lay her packages on the kitchen table in preparation for setting to work on the contents, she discerned movement in the darkened room that Jim and JP shared.

She walked over cautiously, and saw the figure of her son in his bed.

"Jim, is that ye there? Are ye okay?"

"No, Ma. I'm really sick. Kelly sent me home, I was so useless."

"Aw, me poor baby. How does a bowl of broth sound now? Can I fix ye some?"

"No, Ma. Just the thought of eating makes me want to retch, even though there's nothing more in there for to come out. I just want to sleep."

"All right, darlin'. I'll close over the door."

Mary set about preparing food for the midday and evening meals as quietly as she could, and as he drifted off to sleep, Jim could hear the faint chop-chop of carrots on Mary's cutting board. He pictured himself holding Peter's head under the waters of the dirty river, smiling contentedly as he watched life drain from his stepfather's eyes.

Tom Kelly

Peter Halloran avoided his stepson.

They had never come to real blows before. Peter was oddly unconcerned considering the severity of his offense, even though Jim was now a strong, tough nineteen year old man, and a dockworker at that. Peter was secure in the idea that as Jim's stepfather he was the boss, that his stepson would ultimately yield to his authority. A strong enforcer of "my house, my rules," Peter felt he could, and should, do as he wished.

Mary was on her way to the Elk Street market with her wheeled pull-cart. Eliza wanted desperately to go with her, not just because Mary was pregnant and was concerned about her, but because she loved to ogle the varied selection of men at the market. The rows of vendors and the wares they offered expanded in number with each passing year, and at the height of the business day Eliza Beatty found the pandemonium there exhilarating.

She loved the variety of goods offered from the backs of wagons, carts and rows of tables. Live chickens, puppies, geese and rabbits, cabbages, cantaloupes and pears, ripe fragrant softball-sized peaches with their stems dripping thick sticky sap in season, fresh butter and cream, breads and biscuits, tea from China and coffee from Guatemala, Italian olive oil and some odd German foods that looked like something no decent human should have to eat.

Mary had made a good friend in her next-door neighbor Wilhemina Rapp, the woman who had revived little Henry Zeller. Wilhemina was lively company and still quite young. Mary liked being around her. They shopped at the Elk Street market together, hopping on a trolley, but sometimes on especially lovely days, walking the entire way. They asked Eliza along for her extra pair of hands to help carry their bounty home.

They had a grand time, complaining and laughing. Wilhemina was angry that the new Buffalo Directory listed her and Jacob as "Krupp," instead of "Rapp" after she went and spent $3.50 to buy the damned thing. Mary drew laughs complaining about how difficult it was getting just to move her big carcass around, sure that this new baby would outweigh Daniel, who at his birth was a full eight pounds. The contented Eliza Beatty had no complaints at all.

The women had been gone for some time when unexpectedly, Jim Sullivan, who had arranged to leave work for this special errand—but upon hearing what the task entailed, Tom Kelly insisted on helping—crashed into the saloon and jumped on top of Peter Halloran.

Brawls were a part of life in the First Ward's Uniontown, and the most common form of entertainment. The three unrepentant drinkers who were present in the saloon welcomed the break in the day's monotony.

Tom Kelly stood at the ready, but wanted the pleasure to be all Jim's if he could manage it, and Jim did manage nicely. He had considered using brass knuckles, for fear of hurting himself to the extent he might not be able to work, but decided that this might be interpreted as a weakness by Peter Halloran, or some unfair advantage. Jim wanted and needed an untainted, unchallengeable victory.

And so he bare-knuckled it, aiming for Peter's tender parts, avoiding bones or teeth that could injure his hands. Taken by surprise, Peter was totally unexpectant of Jim's strength and rage.

With Peter down and almost out, Jim would not stop pummeling. The foreman, being concerned about one of his best workers, bent over and slid his burley arm around Jim's waist and gently but efficiently pulled him away from Peter.

"No need to actually kill the fucking bastard, Jimmy" said Tom.

Jim, out of breath, pulled himself together while Tom good-naturedly brushed the sawdust bits and floor debris from his friend's shirt and black hair, as Peter writhed on the floor.

"You'll be comin' back to work soon, won't ye?" asked Tom. "Be certain to grab yerself somethin' t' eat for the walk back, Jim, because I can't give ye no more time off for lunch," he laughed as he walked out the door.

Mary, Wilhemina and Eliza walked by just then, glancing appreciatively at foreman Tom Kelly exiting the saloon, their arms and carts loaded with goods from the market. Mary handed off her cart to Eliza. She wanted to continue on and stop next door at Wilhemina's to see her new frock, and sent Eliza inside with the goods. Arms full, Eliza struggled to open the saloon door.

Peter was still on the floor behind the bar, out of her view. The drinkers were carrying on as if nothing unusual had happened, because in fact, nothing unusual had happened. Jim brushed by her, not looking the devil herself in the face, and exited the saloon, as Eliza made her way up the stairs.

Jim saw the back of his mother as she entered the Rapp's house, and seizing the opportunity afforded by her absence, wheeled right round, reentered the saloon, and ascended the stairs.

"You old whore!" he growled, as he grabbed her by her greying hair and pulled her backwards.

"Yer fookin' the old man while my lovely mother carries his baby, right here under our family's very noses, you disrespectful ungrateful bitch?" Before Eliza could react, his fist slammed down on top of her head, and she collapsed, more to get out of his reach than from the blow itself.

No man had ever assaulted her with a closed fist, and she was trembling with fear for her life.

"Ye go near 'im again, you bitch, and I'll drag you into the river that very same night, by God!"

Jim grabbed a couple of biscuits and an apple and descended the stairs to see a battered Peter standing woozily at the bottom. Still craving blood, Peter read Jim's menacing face accurately, and quickly jumped backwards to get out of his way. Jim whacked him hard with his shoulder in passing, then left for the walk back to work.

Jim took his position back on the dock. He caught Tom's eye, who gave him a wink. They were now friends for life.

After just over an hour, Jim, heaving for breath in the heat of the sun, exhausted from unloading crates from the barge, turned around when he heard his name.

"Jim?" Patrolman Steven Whelan and Patrolman Paddy Mahoney stood at the ready. "We've received a complaint."

Whelan remembered well the night that ex-convict Peter Halloran went berserk and put a knife into the neck of Jim's beloved mother. Patrolman Whelan despised Halloran. He would never forget the look of helplessness and terror on the innocent faces of the three children that night, all horrified at what they had just witnessed the head of the family do. A beholder to similar scenes such as this almost daily, Whelan was tired of stupid people and their stupid shit.

But a complaint had been made, and they were bound by duty and by law to follow through, so they removed Jim Sullivan and took him in.

Instead of arresting him and putting him in a cell, they sat him on a bench as they handled the paperwork. They did not question him at all. They did not insult him with Peter Halloran's tainted version of the incident. They quietly whispered a few details that they knew would influence the judge. Jim was written up, and let go, without having to post any bond.

It was too late to go back to work, so Jim went home. He walked into the saloon defiantly. Peter could not conceal his shock and anger that Jim was not in jail, for Halloran's face was badly bruised and swollen.

Jim climbed the stairs and kissed his mother on the cheek as she prepared supper. Mary smiled at her oldest son, looking so much like his father now. Eliza Beatty sat unbruised, except for a lump, unseen beneath her hair. She slunk down in her chair as she shucked peas into a pot, avoiding looking at Jim.

Mary Halloran did not ask Jim any questions. She never acknowledged or questioned the bruises covering Peter's face. She made an especially nice supper, and all sat quietly eating, except for Danny, who asked. "What happened to your face, Pa?"

His father answered, "I may've interfered in a brawl down in the saloon I shoulda stayed out of, son."

Jim was tired, and wanted to turn in early, but JP asked him for help with his essay for school. Jim stayed up for an extra hour to help him write it. Then he slept the sleep of the angels, with the door latch engaged and a butcher knife tucked under his pillow, just in case.

The next day, down at the docks, right before noon, Jim turned around again after hearing his name. It was déjà vu, as the figures of Patrolman Whelan and Patrolman Mahoney stood before him once more. "There's been a complaint filed, Jim. You'll need to come with us again."

Infuriated at the police for allowing Jim Sullivan to get away with the assault on his person, "this outrage," as the veteran resident of the New York State Penitentiary had dramatically framed it, Peter demanded that Eliza Beatty file assault and battery charges against Jim.

Eliza was terrified to do it, for she had taken Jim at his word. And Mary would hate her, as too would the boys.

Eliza had dreamed a nightmare in her most recent sleep in which Jim had attempted exactly what he'd promised he would. In the dream he grabbed her out of bed by her ankle, dragged her down the stairs, out the door, across the street and into the river. She had awoken in a pool of terror sweat, unable to breathe.

She was torn between the fear of inciting Jim to keep his promise and incurring Peter's psychotic wrath, and took her chances that Jim would not hurt her because the police had already arrested him once. So she acquiesced to Peter's demand, and Eliza Beatty filed charges against Mary's boy Jim. Mary was furious.

The police were not able to shuffle the affair aside this time around, and Jim Sullivan was compelled to appear before the police court of Justice King.

The arresting officers testified that the alleged victim of this crime was being compelled against her wishes to bring charges against Jim Sullivan by an abusive drunken ex convict who had previously served a long term in state prison, a miscreant with a history of serious assault charges against him, including a more recent charge of first degree assault with intent to do bodily harm, brought after sticking a butcher knife into the neck of his wife as her three little children watched. As the officers recited Halloran's substantial criminal history, they stared a hole through Peter Halloran's skull, who up until that moment seemed to be under some bizarre delusion that he was to have his day, and his revenge, in court.

Jim testified that his stepfather was engaging in sexual relations with Eliza Beatty directly under the nose of his mother, the victim of a previous stabbing by her adulterous husband. That even though an adult, Jim could not leave the house for fear of what Halloran might do to his mother and brothers.

Eliza had never been so humiliated in her entire life. Every man in the court looked at her as if she were some wanton vengeful whore. In truth, Peter Halloran had wasted Eliza Beatty just as willfully as any other victim, but no one present saw it that way. She wanted to be anywhere but there. Jim called attention to the fact that his mother was presently carrying Peter Halloran's own child, and added that Mary was terrified of Peter, for proven historical reasons well understood by all.

He related the butcher knife crime with great detail and emotion, the original record of which had in fact been placed right there before Justice King, courtesy of patrolmen Whelan and Mahoney.

Justice King leered at Peter Halloran with such contempt that Peter had to concede that he had now suffered a complete defeat. That whatever complaint he may have in the future, whatever it might be, that if this particular judge or these officers were involved, Peter's goose was already cooked. He had burned his last bridge. He had become a non-person no longer regarded as equal to his contemporaries under the law, at least not here in the First Ward.

Eliza was degraded openly in the courtroom, her reputation soiled and her word discredited. Mary refused to acknowledge her existence for weeks thereafter even as they worked side by side.

Justice King shared in Patrolman Whelan's weariness concerning stupid people and their stupid shit, and punished Jim Sullivan with the minimum allowed under the law. Jim was fined five dollars for each offense. Jim had the cash, but his mother made it a point to step forward with a flourish and pay the fine herself, just to make her point clear to Halloran and Eliza.

Unlike four years previous when the Buffalo Courier's published account of Mary Halloran's assault by a butcher knife by her husband had caused her great shame, the next day's public notice didn't faze her a bit:

LATEST LOCAL
Police Court
James Sullivan was fined five dollars for assaulting and
battering Peter Halloran, and later the same amount for
like treatment of Eliza Beatty.

Mary Halloran believed that this time around, the neighbors would understand.

1875
Dennis Halloran

The family stood together in the rain at Holy Cross.

The Catholic cemetery had been established because the waves of Catholics who flooded the once-Protestant city — Irish, Italian and Poles — had struck terror into the residents' Calvinist hearts. They banned Catholics from their sacred Protestant graveyards, so the Irish established Holy Cross Cemetery, well south of the city at Limestone Hill. The Italians established their Catholic cemetery in the north part of Buffalo. The Poles put theirs to the east.

Some Irish mourners had retrieved the buried remains of their loved ones from their original, less sacred resting places to rebury them here, with honor and proper Catholic ceremony once Holy Cross was established.

This is where they had brought little Dennis Halloran today, only one year and two months after his life had begun.

Mary Halloran was devastated. Her husband Peter would never dare admit such a thing, but he was relieved. He was too old for children.

Jim Sullivan was only six years old when three-year-old sister Elizabeth Sullivan died, and he could just barely recall her. Jim struggled at times for memories of his mother's first daughter, not knowing if the hazy recollections he had were genuinely his own, or hers. But the sadness of her loss had never abandoned his mother for a moment, not even after all these years.

Baby Bridget Sullivan had lived for eleven months, born the year after Jim. He had no recollection of her at all, yet they had lain side by side together for almost a full year of bright days until death took her suddenly as she slept, with no forewarning. Surely he must have engaged in long curious looks at this newcomer, cooed at her, and she too must have looked into his eyes. She died lying right next to him, perhaps as they touched.

He wished he could remember.

Each time Mary Halloran became pregnant, she was fearfully elated. Dennis was the third living child she had lost now, and as she stood by the tiny coffin, her sons ready to lower the baby into the ground, she decided she could not bear to ever go through this again. She longed for the change of life to find her doorstep.

One might think that the solace of having her three living children present would be an affirmation, but in seeing three, Mary pictured six.

Instead of a trio of grieving sons, Mary envisioned her four sons and two daughters and herself, celebrating, at a picnic, laughing, teasing, arguing; them being children, Mary smiling with pride and contentment.

Somehow, Peter Halloran was absent from that fantasy.

But the dripping rain soon brought Mary Halloran out of her dream and back to the sorrowful task at hand, to the droning priest and the few neighbors who were able to take time off work to make the long trek out here from the First Ward.

The lads said they wanted to bury their brother with their own hands as a family should, and Peter did not protest. The boys, twenty-one year old Jim, fifteen year old JP, and ten year old Danny lowered the casket into the hole with ropes, and as Mary sobbed with deep mournful retchings, they heaped on flowers, then earth, then the maple sapling.

Dennis' stone would not be ready from McDonnell & Sons for a week yet. The city's premier monument makers were backed up.

The previous night, unable to sleep, Jim picked up the Daily Courier for something to take his mind off his grief. His eyes were drawn to a headline.

$500 REWARD.

He began reading.

Five Hundred Dollars reward will be paid by the undersigned to any person who will restore the body of my wife which was removed from Limestone Hill Cemetery on Tuesday night, and secure the conviction of the criminals. Said amount to be paid as follows: $250 for the recovery and restoration of the body, and $250 for the conviction of the person or persons who robbed the grave.

Signed, Richard J. Carey.

A news story in the next column accompanied the advertisement. It told that a cemetery attendant had noticed the fresh grave of Mrs. Richard Carey had been disturbed, so the staff excavated it. Within the grave they discovered an empty coffin containing only Mrs. Carey's clothes. Following a hunch, a police officer got a search warrant for the Medical College. Accompanied by the dead woman's husband, her sister, and the undertaker Mr. Dan Crowley, the group proceeded to the corner of Main and Virginia streets. College officials tried to keep them from entering, but the police prevailed. They discovered the corpse of Mrs. Carey on a slab in the school's dissection room, surrounded by eager students with the tools of their trade in hand.

All thirty-eight students were arrested.

The undertaker, Dan Crowley, was one of Jim Sullivan's close friends. Crowley swore, along with the widower and the sister of the deceased, that the body was that of Mrs. Catherine Crowley.

However, her attending physicians, Dr. Loomis, Dr. Buswell and Doctor Green, all of whom had attended the deceased during her illness, had made an examination of the body at Crowley's morgue, and officiously testified that the body taken from the College was not that of Mrs. Carey.

Bizarrely, the court accepted the doctors' conclusions over those of Mrs. Carey's own husband, Mrs. Carey's own sister, and her undertaker, and dropped the charges against the students.

"The College paid the fucking doctors off!", murmured Jim angrily as he shook his head in disgust. Holy Cross and Limestone Hill were the same cemetery. All three doctors were closely affiliated with the Medical College. The city was riveted by the scandal.

Greatly disturbed by this worrisome story, Jim retired to his bed and experienced a nightmare. In the dream, after burying sweet little Dennis, Jim returned to Holy Cross by himself to visit and grieve, but could not find Dennis' grave. He searched everywhere. He found himself overcome by blind panic, running around the cemetery for hours, desperately searching for the place. But Dennis was not there. The ground where Jim thought the baby had be buried had never been disturbed. Dennis was lost forever.

Jim awoke in a sweat. It was already light out. He quickly got out of bed, dressed, then crept into the parlor where his mother had sat the entire night by the opened casket, her hand gently holding Dennis', keeping watch, unsure whether, when the hour came, she would be able to let her baby go.

"I'll be ready to begin dressing to go to the cemetery in a little while, Jim," she whispered, almost apologetically.

"All right, Ma. Take your time. I just need to get something and I'll be right back."

Mary Halloran didn't hear what he said, or much care. She was lost in a haze.

Jim walked up the street a few doors to Zeller's grocers, where bundles containing maple, elm and apple seedlings, three feet tall, their root balls neatly wrapped in burlap, were sold out front for fifty cents. Jim selected a golden maple.

After lowering the baby into his final resting place, the boys shoveled earth to fill the hole. Before they completely finished replacing all the soil, they planted the maple tree squarely atop Baby Dennis, to assuage Jim's fears, so that Dennis would never be lost, stolen or misplaced. So that the roots would grow down, and around, embracing him, protecting him, keeping him from being disturbed. So that his body would nourish and become part of the tree itself, allowing some essence of him to live on, perhaps even past the time when all here present had themselves long joined him in this very plot.

For the next forty-five years, whenever Jim Sullivan returned to Holy Cross Cemetery to visit and to cry, he would pluck a shiny green leaf from his stalwart tree, kiss it and say, "Hello, baby brother. I missed you."

1878
Katie Hanson Returns

Jim Sullivan was troubled by his unsettled place in life.

He was midway through his twenties. He had imagined himself being successful by now. Established. A famous writer, or at least one who made some money at it. Sundays were the best day to try and figure out a plan to better his situation, when he'd rested a bit and his head wasn't filled with the voices and clanging that bombarded him at the ironworks. He always scoured the Sunday Express for clues about opportunities.

He drank his tea and was alone in the family's Hamburgh Street house. JP slept. Peter Halloran was downstairs diddling about in the saloon. Mary was attending Mass at St. Bridget's with Danny.

An interesting heading in the paper caught his eye:

KATIE HANSON'S FORTUNE.

He assumed it would be a story about someone striking it rich, and from it he might gain some inspiration for himself. He began to read.

> Twenty-two years ago Katie Hanson disappeared from her home in Tioga County, Penn. She was only 17 years of age and had grown up among the lumber woods of Northern Pennsylvania. She had a predilection for masculine ways. She was expert with the rifle and fishing rod, and spent much of her time in the woods. Unlike other Tioga County girls her age, she wore her hair very short, but her most unique and striking feature were her large brilliant violet-colored eyes.

Jim choked on his toast. His mind went back... was that a dream, or...?

He recalled a day, a sunny Sunday like today, walking with his father and mother along the Basin, when they encountered a person with striking violet eyes, the likes of which he had never seen before or since. He remembered asking them innocently if this person was a boy or a girl, and making his parents laugh.

A short while later he heard a rustle as his mother climbed the stairs. She was carrying her missal and rosary beads. She wore a scapular. Jim was in awe of her ability to still believe.

"Your father just took Danny to Dalton's for some candy and I am starved." She had fasted so that she could take holy communion.

"Mama?"

"Yes, darlin' boy."

"I might have imagined this, but do you recall a day when Papa and you and me, we were all walkin' by the Ohio Basin and we met an odd person who asked you some questions, who had very strange eyes, violet colored?"

The phrase violet eyes triggered her memory, and Mary began to think. After a few moments she said, "I believe I do remember that. Ye asked us if that was a girl or a boy because…"

"Yes! I thought maybe I was makin' that up!"

"Although carryin' a rifle on a strap, and acting like a boy," she recollected, "I thought that he looked more like a girl. What made ye think of that?"

Jim showed her the paper.

"This is a story about that very same person, I could swear, Ma. Listen: 'Unlike other girls her age, she wore her hair very short, but her most unique and striking feature were her brilliant violet-colored eyes.'"

"Why do you think this is that same person? That was a long time ago, Jim."

"Listen to the story and then you tell me, Ma. I was only about six then, or thereabouts."

Jim began to read aloud as his mother busied herself preparing her post-communion breakfast.

> Twenty-two years ago Katie Hanson disappeared from her home in Tioga County, Penn. She was only 17 years of age and had grown up among the lumber woods of Northern Pennsylvania. She had a predilection for masculine ways. She was expert with the rifle and fishing rod, and spent much of her time in the woods. Unlike other girls her age, she wore her hair cut very short, but her most unique and striking feature were her brilliant large violet-colored eyes.

"Hmmm," said Mary.

> Her family was highly respectable, and she was more than usually intelligent. In spite of her dislike for the pursuits of her own sex, she bore an unsullied reputation. She left home one day with her rifle, which her father had given her. She never came back. Nothing was ever heard of her. Her father advertised throughout the country for traces of her and visited all the large cities in the state seeking for tidings of her, asking everyone he met 'have you seen a young girl with the appearance of a boy, with bright violet-colored eyes?'.
>
> It being known in the neighborhood where the Hansons lived that Katie had formed an attachment for a worthless young man named Johnson, and that her parents had positively forbidden her having anything to do with him, many people believed she had run away from home for that reason, to lead a life of shame. Others held that she had accidentally shot herself in the woods, or had become lost or died in some out-of-the-way part of the forest. Her parents, after searching a year or two, gave her up for dead.

Mary was making noise, putting away dishes she'd washed before going to church.

"Are ye listening, Ma?"

"Yes, Jim, I'm listening, go ahead."

Jim continued.

Col. Grant Wilson of Philadelphia was spending the winter of 1876 in Cuba. During his stay there he met Major James Hopkins, formerly of Ohio, who served in Gen. Thomas's division during the late war. Major Hopkins owned a fine plantation in the interior of the island, and Col. Wilson accepted his invitation to become his guest during his stay in Cuba.

"The Major's family consisted of a handsome and dignified wife and two interesting children. When Col. Wilson left Cuba he was entrusted with an errand in this country by Mrs. Hopkins. On arriving in New York he started at once for Tioga County, Penn., and found the family of Elija Hanson. He caused great rejoicing by the announcement that he knew their long-lost daughter, Katie; that she was alive and well and preparing to pay the old homestead a visit in the summer of the present year. Katie Hanson and Mrs. Major Hopkins were one and the same, and the following was the strange story she told to the friend she found in Col. Wilson:

"The young man Johnson, referred to above, was in the habit of accompanying Katie Hanson on her hunting exhibitions, and being an excellent woodsman and hunter, was a most congenial companion to her. His family was dissolute and ignorant. When her father ordered her to cease associating with Johnson, Katie rebelled against the order for a time. The last day she left her house with her rifle she concluded that the association was not a proper one for her, but she could see no way for its dissolution but by leaving home.

'She passed that night in the woods and the next day went to the cabin of some hunters in the vicinity. The hunters were not in the cabin but she appropriated a suit of their clothes and disguised herself in them. Her features and short hair favored the deception. She reached Buffalo, N.Y. in her wanderings. She secured the position of cook in a lake boat running between Detroit and Buffalo. This position and life were entirely to her liking.

'While in Buffalo she read in one of the papers an advertisement offering a reward for any information of where she was, making special note of her unusual violet-colored eyes. This alarmed her for she feared she would be apprehended and returned home.

'On returning to Detroit she gave up her position and went to Cincinnati. She found employment on an Ohio River steamer. She continued on the steamer until the breaking out of the war. No one had ever suspected her sex. She determined to enlist and joined an Ohio regiment and was in all of the engagements of General Thomas's division. In 1863 she was promoted to Sergeant of her company. In 1864 her captain met her one day as she was returning from stationing a guard. He said to her that he had long suspected that she was a woman and demanded to know if such was the case. The charge was so sudden and unexpected that she lost her self possession, and convicted herself by her reply. She begged the captain not to reveal her secret, but he took her before General Thomas and made the strange fact known to him.

'Katie was at once sent back to the rear, and ordered to resume her proper attire. She became a nurse in the hospital and soon had in her care her captain, he having been wounded in a skirmish. Between the Captain and the nurse whom he had detected in the ranks of his company, a strong affection formed. At the close of the war they were married, the Captain, meantime, having been promoted to the rank of Major. Major Hopkins' family was one of the best in Ohio, and it refused to recognize his wife.

'She had $900 which she had saved from her earnings on the steamers. This was in a Cincinnati bank. She drew it out, and with her husband, went to Cuba. There they prospered and were found by Col. Wilson in 1876. Word has been received from Mrs. Hopkins that she and her husband and children will sail for New York in August, and visit the home she so mysteriously left nearly a quarter century ago.

Jim laughed.
"Isn't that incredible, Ma? We met this girl! This is the very same girl!"
Tears streamed down Mary's cheeks.
"What's wrong, Ma?"
"I miss your father so very much," she sobbed.

1880
Sometimes, Out of Tragedy Springs Opportunity

Twenty-year-old Fingy Conners and his boys began the evening with beers at his father's Mariners Home saloon hotel at 193 Louisiana Street. It was located on the quay overlooking the wide and very busy Ohio Basin.

The Basin covered an area of ten acres. It was joined to the deep, lazy Buffalo River by a narrow slip, allowing even some of the larger lake vessels to unload their richly varied shipments right within the heart of the First Ward. Louisiana Street along its east quay was especially blessed with an extraordinary collection of saloons, all competing for the pennies of thirsty toiling dockers and the sailors who gazed longingly toward the tempting array of gin mills from their craft as they passed in and out of the Basin.

At the Basin's inland boundary, the narrow Ohio Slip burrowed even deeper into the city, allowing barges to traverse still further. The slip eventually connected the Basin with the 100 foot-wide east-west Main-Hamburgh canal, the largest of Buffalo's intracity canals, which at its terminus connected to the Erie Canal. The city was a maze of waterways.

Saloon-hopping along Louisiana Street made for a rollicking good time for those working men who had money enough to engage in such entertainments. On this particular Sunday night in late September 1880, Fingy Conners' roughs, having earlier successfully completed a profitable shakedown, were in a celebratory mood.

Fingy's father, Peter Conners, a no-nonsense Irish-Canadian, worked behind the bar at his Mariners Home saloon this night, freely serving his son's gang, which included Fingy's step-brother and best friend, Dennis Hurley, and their mates Slattery, Donnelly, and the boy who provided Conners his nickname by chopping his thumb, Kennedy.

They drank and cursed and relived the afternoon's events. They boasted how they'd procured their new bounty with none of them having received so much as a bloody nose. Conners' Saloon was half full with a joyless group of exhausted dock men drinking away their troubles, as well as solitary sailors and sad-faced barge handlers winding down from the week's toiling. The boys' happy revelry stood out in a singular fashion, attracting curious glances.

They soon decided to head up the street two blocks to John Rochford's saloon at the north terminus of the Basin, just across from the mouth of the Ohio Slip and the little Mackinaw Street bridge that traversed it. There, the revelry and drunken boasting continued, until the saloon's door opened and thereupon entered the three victims of the earlier shakedown, along with a few invited friends.

Before anyone could react, the eight newcomers set upon the five Conners' Boys with a ferocity unprecedented in the First Ward.

Saloon brawls and callings-out were part and parcel of the scores of drinking establishments that lined Louisiana Street, South Street and Hamburgh Street, where saloons outnumbered every other kind of small business.

There existed unwavering and universally adhered-to ground rules that governed this seemingly free-for-all brawling. These criteria called upon the better instincts and manners of the men to use only their fists, to not hit below the belt, to not hit a man when he was down, and to keep the fighting fair, one-on-one. And when it was all over, it was more rule than exception to see the two combatants sitting with each other over a few beers as if nothing unpleasant had taken place between them.

This Sunday night at John Rochford's all of these working class gentlemen's rules, for the first time in any First Warder's memory, would be shattered.

The eight newcomers pounced on the five with a savagery heretofore unknown in these parts, so shocking Mr. Rochford and the other patrons that they immediately fled the building. Chairs and glasses not only flew, but were used as weapons. The First Ward's gentlemen's agreement of fists-only was abandoned, as was very other precept. Broken beer glasses slashed at tender flesh, heavy boots landed in the stomachs and faces of those who had been knocked to the floor, gonads were assaulted mercilessly, and the hateful threats and epithets of the gladiators ricocheted all around the basin. Someone at long last shouted "The police are on their way!" and the eight attackers vacated the little shambled saloon in a flash.

The Conners gang picked each other up, bleeding and battered, and quickly got themselves out the door. Fingy's stepbrother Dennis Hurley had endured the worst of it with many cruel kicks delivered to his face, groin, head and neck. He was passing out.

"Where should we take him," shouted Kennedy as he and Donnelly, barely able to walk themselves, propped up the limp form of Dennis Hurley, "to the hospital?"

"No. To my Pa's house!" ordered Fingy Conners, and they headed at once one block down and two over, to the little one-and-a-half story frame house at the corner of Tennessee and Sandusky streets.

It was one o'clock and there were no lights. The door was locked, so Conners banged on it as he looked around anxiously for signs of any pursuant peace-keepers. The sleepy form of widow Julia Hayes, Hurley's sister and Fingy's step-sister, cautiously opened the door and rubbed her eyes as they pushed past her.

"Good God, what happened to Dennis!" she cried, seeing blood dripping from his mouth, ears and scalp, his face battered.

"We met with a little brawlin' on our rounds, Mrs. Hayes. Nothing serious, but Dennis requires some attention," said Kennedy.

Hurley's face by this time had swollen alarmingly, and he tried to speak, but his teeth were clenched and could not seem to open his mouth. His jaw appeared broken.

Julia ran to the little ice box in the kitchen and took out what remained of the chunk of ice from the last delivery. The Buffalo Ice Co. wagon wouldn't be by again until morning, so she worried a bit that the food in the icebox might spoil.

She dropped the ice chunk into the canvas sack that the company provided its customers for this very purpose and whacked it with a Compliments Of Buffalo Ice Co. mallet to break it into pieces. She transferred the ice pieces into a clean flour sack.

Fingy unfolded the blanket that decorated the back of the sofa, his step-sister's pride and joy, and carelessly covered her treasured acquisition in a half-hearted attempt to keep Hurley's blood from staining the new piece. Julia looked guilty, wondering if it were right that she was equally concerned about her brother as she was her new sofa. Dennis was laid upon the blanket. Julia sat down on the edge of the davenport and tried to conform the cold compress to the contours of his lower face. Fingy retrieved some bandages to dress his step-brother's other wounds. The others left, limping home to their own beds and to tend to their own injuries.

"Where's Ma?" asked Fingy.

"She went to Fredonia to look after Aunt Jessie," Julia reminded him.

"Remember?"

"Oh, yeah."

"Jimmy, I think we should try to take Dennis to the hospital," said Julia to Fingy.

Conners wasn't so sure, as the cops would then surely find out about this brawl. There would be questions and arrests. He decided to wait and see if Dennis got worse. He kept Doc Greene, who lived just a few blocks away, in mind.

Fingy tried to send Julia to bed, but she insisted on remaining by her brother's side. She tended to Dennis throughout the night, rearranging the flour sack as the ice melted, sopping up the melt with another, and snoozing on and off by his side until the sky began to lighten. She threw on a shawl and quickly half-strode, half-ran the few blocks to Doc Greene's house. She knocked soundly on his door to rouse him. As she waited for a response she looked upward. The sun's earliest rays were just beginning to color the cirrus clouds suspended high above the city.

She was relieved when Doc Greene answered the door himself, fully dressed.

"Mrs. Hayes, hello, what is it?"

"Doctor Greene, there's been a brawl, and my brother Dennis is hurt, badly I'm afraid. Could you please have a look at him?" Julia could smell liquor on him.

"Of course... of course I can. If you wait a few minutes for me to get my carriage ready we can go there together. Please come in a moment and wait."

"Thank you, no, I'm fine here," sighed Julia, relieved.

Doc Greene's Irish servant girl Bridget, plain of face and hard-working, accompanied him to the small barn to help ready his trusted steed Chestnut and the carriage. That accomplished, the doctor and Julia sped immediately on their way. Chestnut, being a physician's stallion, was accustomed to galloping wherever his master needed to go, since the doc was usually in quite a hurry. The dust that Chestnut's hooves stirred up arose in a cloud behind the carriage. The rig pulled up to the Conners house. Quickly alighting, a soft breeze deposited errant particles of dirt upon horse and human. They rushed inside.

Fingy was awake, tending to Dennis. Doc Greene could see immediately that Dennis' jaw was broken. Things did not look promising for Dennis Hurley. He was in great pain, and extremely thirsty.

"What I am most fearful of is lockjaw," said the doc. "If he can't open his teeth, he can't eat. We might have to knock out a couple teeth if that happens."

Doc Greene asked Julia for a sheet of writing paper which he rolled tightly around a lead pencil to form a drinking straw. They sat Dennis upright and supported him awkwardly so that he could draw water from a glass through the straw. He did so with enormous difficulty, as the experience was a new one for him, and the pain caused by the slightest movement in his lower face excruciating. But the need to sate his thirst overcame his agony, and within a couple of minutes he had drunk the entire glass. They then helped him off the sofa and outside into the yard and into the chilly air.

Julia turned her back as Dennis fumbled to open his pants to piss. Doc Greene, experienced in such matters, helped him with his buttons, and afterward closed him up. When finished, Fingy and Doc Greene supported Dennis on either side to lead him back indoors to the sofa.

Julia meanwhile had retrieved another blanket to further protect her prized upholstered piece, and Dennis' own bed pillow as well, which she quickly covered in two layers of flour sacks, knowing that preventing the pillow's staining might be a futile effort.

Over the next few days, Dennis' condition did not improve. The kindly Buffalo Ice wagon driver was informed of Dennis' plight by Julia, and while she was away at her job at the City Hall, he entered the house and fashioned ice packs every morning after checking the block of ice in the icebox. Fingy went off to his work on the docks, one eye always open for any sign of an approaching member of the assaulting eight who might still be looking for further revenge, worried for Dennis and hurrying home to check on him in the evening.

Two nights a week Fingy replaced his father in the saloon, Thursdays and Sundays, allowing his father to keep the books, run errands, or just come home early for a rest.

On the Thursday night following the saloon brawl, alone with Dennis in the house, Julia went to bed about half past nine after making Dennis as comfortable as she could. Peter Conners stayed at his saloon to catch up on paperwork while Fingy tended bar.

Dennis had barely eaten since Sunday night's beating. Julia had made broths and thin soups, but despite mashing carrots and meats into a paste with mortar and pestle, then creating a watery mixture thin enough to be drawn through a straw, Dennis was in so much pain that the effort wasn't worth it to him. As hungry as he was he could not produce enough suction to get anything much thicker than water through the straw. And so he lived on water, milk, whisky and broth.

Dennis had been able to move into his own room upstairs on Tuesday, his bed certainly more comfortable than the sofa, which heartened Julia for two reasons. She could look in on him during the night more easily, since he slept in the room next to hers, and she could renew her prized davenport.

The upholstery fabric was of a deep burgundy color, mohair, with a carved wood frame, and she was rewarded when her mixture of equal parts ammonia and hydrogen peroxide removed all trace of her brother's blood and fluids. She was grateful for the first time that her original fabric color choice, green, was not available at the time of purchase, and she reluctantly settled for her second choice, the burgundy. No stain showed at all. When she was finished cleaning, it looked like new.

Her late husband, God rest his blighted soul, had taken a life insurance, and upon his untimely end, she for the first time was able to partake in three extravagances she had longed for all her life. One of these was the sofa.

Wishing to put most of the insurance money into savings for her future, she had been obliged after her husband's passing to take the only job offered her, at least for the time being, that of a janitress in the City Hall. After cleaning up after other people all day, and enduring their looking down on her station in life, she was gladdened to return home to her beautiful sofa and her second indulgent purchase, a beautiful Flint & Kent silk frock.

She had yet to have a fancy enough occasion to wear the dress. She entertained a persistent fantasy that one day some handsome attorney or politician at the city hall might ask her to dinner at one of the fine hotels. Julia was, if nothing, a hopeful and optimistic sort. For the first time in her life she had been able to purchase a ready-made garment of high fashion, but for splurging on this beautiful grey silk dress from Flint & Kent, her step-father Peter Conners had soundly berated her. "When will a plain girl like you ever have occasion to wear a costume like that?"

The widow Julia was becoming an accomplished seamstress, and her visits to Buffalo's largest dry goods stores always included a close inspection of the garments representing the latest style. She focused on the methods of construction, turning garments inside out to study the seams, much to the chagrin of the sales girls, who knew she was not there to buy. Afterward Julia would return home to Sandusky Street where on her prized Howe sewing machine she would try her hand at duplicating the handiwork she'd inspected, creating garments that were the envy of her less-proficient friends and neighbors. She created frocks for herself that she hoped would stand out beneath her utilitarian janitress apron. These she wore to work on those special days when an attorney or alderman she was smitten with was scheduled to appear, hoping to be noticed by him.

Her dream was that one day soon the mayor's wife or mistress or other society ladies might recognize her talents and commission one of her creations, so that she might finally leave her exhausting menial custodial position at the City Hall behind forever.

On Thursday evening Fingy came home at nine o'clock on a short break from the saloon. He took Dennis into the yard to relieve himself, then helped him up the stairs and into his bed. Fingy removed Dennis' chamber pot, emptied it, then replaced it beneath his cot. Dennis was sleeping more and more, which concerned Doc Greene, but Julia was grateful. She believed it allowed him an escape from his pain.

Fingy left to return to work at the saloon. As he entered he was glad to see the place was almost half full, busier than usual. He quickly scoured all the faces present, just as he had on his walk back along Louisiana Street's cobblestones from the house. Walking the Ohio Basin quay concerned him. People were always falling in, or being pitched in involuntarily, especially drunks. Aware he could easily be bricked and tossed in by his enemies and have it appear to be an accident, he had walked warily with eyes in the back of his head, tripping here and there on a raised cobble. He was certain that he had not seen the last of the infamous gang of eight.

At closing, Peter Conners was still working on the books. Fingy told his father that he was going upstairs to his cot above the saloon to sleep, instead of going back to the house, as it was closer to the next morning's work site. The cot was a poor substitute for his own bed, but he could get an extra half hour's sleep sleeping there.

On the opposite corner of Sandusky and Tennessee Streets from the Conners' house, Mrs. Susan McNamara was awakened in her upstairs bedroom around half past three by the smell of smoke. Six years previous, her home had burned in the night, stealing the lives of two of her precious children. She never recovered from the horror and had ever since slept with her nostrils wide open.

She bolted from her bed not pausing to put on her slippers. The floor was icy, a good sign. She ran to her daughters' room and sniffed, but smelled nothing. She went to the head of the stairs leading down to her parlor, and sniffed. Nothing. Back in her room the smell of burning wood was even stronger than before, and through curtains that covered the cracked-open double hung window she saw an alarming flickering coming from the first floor windows of the Conners house.

Mrs. McNamara's seventeen year old son Jeremiah ran into her room, himself awakened by the smell, and saw the same sight as his mother. He hurriedly put a long coat over his nightclothes.

"I'm running for the fire box, Ma! Go across the street and holler for the Conners! But don't go too close!"

As he exited his house Jeremiah screamed "Fire!" at the top of his lungs over and over, stirring the neighborhood from its slumber. A fire in one house could quickly become a conflagration that could consume the entire block in no time.

Jeremiah ran at top speed two blocks west to Louisiana, then north two blocks to the alarm box on the corner of Elk, in front of Schenck's Grocery. Shaking and out of breath, he pulled the alarm, and waited anxiously so he could direct the bombardiers to the exact location. On second thought he wasn't quite sure if he should wait there or just bolt for home. His mother would surely be all right, he imagined. At least, he hoped as much.

Within seconds he heard the clamoring bell and the thud of galloping hooves slamming into the ground as the Babcock ladder truck drawn by four powerful workhorses, along with a Babcock Hose Carriage and a Cole Bros. Engine flew from the station house just a block away. Jerry began jumping up and down, waving wildly so they would see him waiting there in the dark.

"Sandusky and Tennessee!" he screamed at the ladder truck, and as the hose carriage rounded the corner, he jumped on it. "The house at Sandusky and Tennessee!" he told the second wagon's lifesavers. "Please hurry!" he implored.

Mrs. McNamara ran out of her house and stood in the street. She looked back to make sure her daughters had not ventured outside. "You two stay there!" she bellowed at them menacingly.

"Mrs. Hayes!" she shouted as loud as she could at the house on the opposite corner. "Fire! Fire! Mrs. Hayes!"

The blaze at 51 Sandusky Street was spreading shockingly fast.

Julia failed to arouse. Mrs. McNamara screamed louder with each attempt. Over and over she bellowed. Other voices joined with hers.

"Mrs. Hayes! For God's sake, wake up! Why can't you hear me?"

She turned to see that everyone else in the neighborhood was up and running frantically about, everyone except the occupants of the house that was on fire. Mrs. McNamara picked up a rock and aimed it at Julia's window. It missed, hitting the siding instead, but the sound was enough to startle Julia from her sleep. A shot of adrenalin caused her to overcome her grogginess and quickly jump out of bed. She dashed out into the hallway. Smoke and heat rushed up the narrow stairway from below. She shut her door behind her and ran into her brother's room.

"Dennis! Dennis! Wake up! We're on fire!"

Dennis was more unconscious than asleep. She grabbed his foot and literally dragged him out of bed. He yelped in exquisite pain as he hit the warm floorboards.

"Dennis! We have to get out! The house is on fire! It's right now flyin' up the stairs like a hellish tornado! We have to go out the window!"

Mrs. McNamara fretted as Julia tried to raise the window. It was stuck. Julia reached for Dennis' brogue, smashed out the glass and knocked aside the muntins. Dennis, dazed, confused and disabled, struggled toward her. Smoke had filled the room with the opening of the window. She slammed his bedroom door closed against the fire's progress.

Dennis stuck his head out into the cold air and looked down. It wasn't such a high drop, ordinarily, but in his condition he knew the landing would be excruciating. He could see flames beginning to seep outside the parlor window located directly below. He knew they had only seconds to escape. Julia pushed against his back, hurrying him, pain be damned. He climbed out as Julia tried to hold tight to his elbow to steady him. Dennis felt broken glass enter his flesh. He tried holding onto the sill with both hands to lower himself, but being so weak, lost his grip and dropped in an agonized heap to the cold, shard-strewn earth. The heat from the shattered first floor window just a few feet away was immediately scorching. Neighbors ran in to help. With their aided locomotion he was able to scamper painfully on all fours along the ground, away from the house a safe distance to the curb. There he passed out in the gutter.

Having practically pushed Dennis out the window, such was Julia's haste that those who witnessed this act of unselfish heroism might certainly expect her to immediately follow.

But she did not.

The heat of the planks beneath her bare feet and the choking smoke commanded her to get out, but her new silk dress from Flint & Kent and all her customers' half-finished frocks she had lovingly sewn were just steps away. The doorknob was made of faceted glass and thus touching it gave her no sense as to the intensity of the temperature on the other side of the door.

Impetuously Julia flung it open and dashed out of Dennis' room into the narrow hallway's searing heat. Flames crawled along the ceiling immediately over her head. She could smell her hair singe. Into her room she flew, slamming the door tightly behind her, then feverishly gathering up items to save.

"Mrs. Hayes!" Mrs. McNamara shrieked, recalling her own tragedy. "Leave your things behind! Come out! Mrs. Hayes! Jump! Jump now!"

Mrs. McNamara was beside herself, suffering a level of terror that only personal experience could inflict. All the neighbors were now removed from their beds and out in the cold. Men filled buckets and any opportune vessel with water, dousing the meager contents futilely upon the Conners' flaming structure. Soon enough though they realized it best not to waste their scant resource on a lost cause, but rather put it to use wetting down their own homes instead.

Mrs. McNamara wanted to run to Dennis, but he was out of immediate peril from the fire, whereas Julia was right in the thick of it. The recollection of her own disaster and the loss of her babies inflamed her senses with the horror of

A TERRIBLE FATE.

Mrs. Julia Hayes Burned to Death While Trying to Save Her Property from Destruction.

At half-past three o'clock yesterday morning the alarm from box 23 called the Fire Department to the corner of Sandusky and Tennessee streets, where the house of Peter Conners, a story-and-a-half frame building, was discovered in flames. The fire was too far advanced for any successful resistance, and the building was entirely consumed. Soon afterwards, while the firemen were wetting down the ruins, Dennis Hurley, who had been occupying the house, was noticed searching in an anxious way for his sister, Mrs. Julia Hayes, a step-daughter of Conners', whom he declared to be missing. He said she had discovered the fire and awakened him and then busied herself in saving property and that was the last which had been seen of her. He had been obliged to drop from an upper story himself, but had supposed that she would be able to save herself. A general inquiry elicited the fact that she had thrown a trunk and some clothing from an upper window, and had then been observed working over a sewing-machine, when she suddenly disappeared. Surmising that the woman had been burned to death, Assistant Engineer Hornung, who was in charge of the firemen, instituted a search and the woman's body was found burned to a crisp. Mrs. Hayes was a widow, thirty-two years of age, and was employed as a janitress in the City and County Hall. Coroner Fowler will hold an inquest. The loss on house and furniture is estimated at $2,000, with an insurance of $1,000 in the Ætna Company.

her own history as she witnessed the entire first floor of the Conners house now completely engulfed in a roaring conflagration. She feared that Mrs. Hayes was already doomed. With great anxiety she watched as Julia tried to open her bedroom window. It too seemed stuck, a coincidence that did not go unnoticed. In the light of the flames coming through the glass Julia was horrified to see that a nail had been hammered into the window track, preventing its opening. She swooped down to pick up a small trunk and used it to bust out the glass, then tossed the container out. It burst upon hitting the ground, scattering papers, mementos, jewelry, ribbons, and a framed memorial portrait of Abraham Lincoln, its protective glass now shattered into a thousand pieces. It lay forlornly on the walkway, the dead president's likeness dancing in the glow of the roaring pyre which animated his expression as if bemused by the dramatic goings-on.

Julia grabbed her dresses, poked her head out the window and screamed, "Please Mrs. McNamara, save my dresses!" She threw them down, then dashed away from salvation again. Mrs. McNamara dared not approach to retrieve the garments, for they had landed too close to the flaming inferno and were beginning to smoke.

"It's getting too late now, Mrs. Hayes! I can't go near! Jump for your life! I'm imploring you!"

The neighbors watched in horrified puzzlement as the woman continued to frantically toss out unsalvageable objects in preference to saving herself.

The flames shooting out from the parlor window on the first floor were licking at the window sills of the second, making Julia's escape more and more doubtful with every second that passed.

"Mrs. Hayes! Save yourself! Damn the clothes, you crazy woman! Jump!"

Like some apocalyptic apparition, Julia once more appeared at her bedroom window, silhouetted against the bright red flames now glowing behind her, this time heaving her heavy, unwieldy, precious Howe sewing machine. At the exact moment that she hoisted it up with an explosive grunt onto the sill, flames having eaten through the supporting beams below, the floor collapsed beneath the combined weight of Julia Hayes and her cumbersome Howe. She fell backwards, disappearing into the demonic glowing hole, the heavy machine toppling with her, landing heavily upon and crushing her dainty chest.

She ended on her back amidst the blazing conflagration.

Julia was conscious enough to realize her plight, and as she tried to draw in the breath that had been knocked out of her so that she might scream her last scream, the burning heat that she pulled in through her mouth fried her throat tissue and mortally consumed her lungs. No sound except that of her crackling skin was to be heard from her ever again. Julia Hayes writhed there in agony for more than two full minutes before she expired, her hair and face afire, wanting desperately but unable to scream, convinced in her final conscious seconds that surely this was some horrific nightmare from which she would soon awake. Now blind, ultimately, quietly, she submitted to her fate.

Mrs. McNamara, sickened and distraught at having seen Julia Hayes and her Howe sucked into the abyss with her own eyes, ran to Dennis and helped him up. He was delirious.

"Julia? Where's my sister?"

"She's all right, Mr. Hurley. Come, let's back you away from the danger," and with the aid of the neighbors O'Neil and Snyder she led Dennis back across the street to the stoop of her own house.

The fire brigade then roared up, their horses snorting in unison. These surest-footed and bravest of equines, unyielding in their dedication to their calling, were barely fettered by the smoke or flame. Firemen unhitched the steeds and led them away to safety while others unreeled the hoses and began to douse the house next door to Julia's with the Cole Engine's 700 gallons-per-minute pump. The firemen could easily see there was no saving anything or anybody at No. 51 Sandusky Street.

Peter Conners had fallen asleep over his ledger at his desk. He was awakened by a heavy banging on the saloon door. He rushed to deal with the upstart.

"Your house is on fire, Conners! Come quickly!"

Peter spotted the glow in the sky two blocks south. "Jimmy!" he shouted. "Wake up!"

Peter rushed upstairs to get his shoes and coat and shouted again to Fingy, who had only been asleep a few hours, and understandably might well be dead to the world.

"Get up, boy, now! There's a fire!" The elder Conners headed toward Fingy's cubicle.

"Damn you, Jim, hurry!" shouted Peter as he entered. Fingy's bed had been slept in, but he was not there.

Peter ran out the door, and unaccustomed to sprinting, immediately felt a sharp pain in his chest. He stopped to catch his breath and looked up. The glow in the sky had lessened. He interpreted this as a good sign.

There was much confusion and fear as the neighbors gathered in a group to watch the heroics of firemen saving the adjacent structures from annihilation, although one house did suffer serious damage. The Conners house had mostly collapsed in a charred heap. As firemen stood over the pile, wetting down the remaining flames, Dennis Hurley struggled up from his secure place on Mrs. McNamara's stoop wearing a borrowed pair of Jeremiah McNamara's slippers and limped over to Fireman Michael Danahy.

"Have you seen my sister?" he mumbled almost unintelligibly through his pain and clenched teeth. "Has anyone seen Julia?"

He was bewildered and confused from his physical agony and the harrowing nightmare that immediately preceded this moment, but lucid enough to surmise his sister was missing. No one had seen her, they told him.

Dennis insisted on climbing through the soaked ruins, clumsily overturning debris, losing his balance, falling repeatedly.

Mrs. McNamara, her son Jeremiah and two daughters huddled on their stoop watching Dennis Hurley. He had spent the last two hours there with them, wrapped in a blanket, uncomprehending. Mrs. McNamara had told her son what she had witnessed with her own eyes.

"We gotta tell him, Ma. We can't let 'im be the one to find her."

Knowing all too well what such a sickening discovery could do to a person, she crossed the street and slowly approached Dennis. He had begun searching most frantically at the perimeter of the ruins. She put her arm around him. He stopped. Fireman Danahy glanced over.

"Dennis. I saw Mrs. Hayes trying to save her sewing machine...she was trying to get it out the window, when suddenly the house just collapsed, and she disappeared."

It took him a minute to process such horrific news.

"You couldn't be mistaken now, could ye, Missis?" she thought he said through the agonized look on his face.

"No, Dennis. I'm afraid that I could not be. I'm sorry."

Fireman Danahy had overheard her revelation and upon exchanging looks with Mrs. McNamara, went to tell assistant engineer Hornung that there was most likely a victim in the ruins. He grouped his men together and searched, soon finding the wasted form of Julia Hayes burnt to a crisp, flat on her back. Her scorched Howe was lying atop her, her blackened arms raised over her head in a gesture of capitulation .

Mrs. McNamara approached Danahy and told him what she had seen, Julia struggling, unable to open either window.

"They was both open just this afternoon. I don't understand why she couldn't open either of the two tonight. Something is wrong."

Danahy waded through the debris and found a charcoaled window frame. A close inspection revealed a substantial nail pounded into its track. He called Hornung over to have a look at the anomaly for himself.

Dennis Hurley was devastated. The sister who looked after him as a boy, who cared for him in his current infirmity, who pushed him out the window to safety, preserving his life, died trying to save her goddamned sewing machine.

"We could always replace a sewing machine, my darling, but now I have no sister!" he shouted through locked jaws, sobbing.

Peter Conners came upon the tragic scene gasping for air. He saw Dennis wrapped in a blanket standing near the rubble intently watching a group of firemen who were bent over inspecting something. He ran up to Dennis.

"What happened Dennis?!"

Dennis just looked at the incinerated pile and sobbed.

Peter Conners dashed through the smoking rubble, a nail going right through his shoe and into the bottom of his foot. He didn't even feel it. But before he could get a good view, the firemen rose up to block him.

"You don't want to see this Mr. Conners," instructed fireman Danahy.

Peter peered through the space between the men. Emerging from a charred human-like form he saw a mound of pink organs. Intestines. He was sickened and horrified. His lovely wife's lovely daughter, dead, and looking like that.

Peter Conners turned back and hugged his stepson, and as he did, Dennis Hurley collapsed in his arms. The days following the tragedy were most abysmal, especially so for Dennis. With trauma freshly heaped atop tribulation, his condition worsened. Fingy had arrived to the hellish scene after sunrise with liquor on his breath, hands smelling of kerosene, and only the sparest of explanations as to where he had been. Doc Greene arrived, concerned about the family, but especially so Dennis. He offered to take them in his carriage wherever the family wished. They decided to take Dennis back to the Conners' Saloon, for it was all they had left. Fingy scooped Dennis Hurley up and gently placed him on the carriage seat as Chestnut snorted and turned to look at them with tender concern on his beautiful face.

The next day Doc Greene called in a trusted colleague to examine Dennis Hurley, as he himself could do no more for him. As the days passed Dennis' condition grew more critical. He could now hardly swallow at all, neither water nor milk. He was a thin man to begin with, but he had lost twenty five pounds.

Doctor Cunningham said to Doc Greene, "I believe Dennis Hurley is going to die."

In view of this, Police Captain Shanahan concluded it was proper to arrest the men who made the assault on Dennis Hurley and his friends. He arrested Patrick and James McNierney, Samuel McComb, Daniel Moran, Michael Haug, Joseph Gavin, A.C. Eldridge and one other unnamed. The first five were taken into custody, while the last three fled for parts unknown. Those who apprehended were committed to jail by Police Justice King to await a hearing, which could not be scheduled until Dennis Hurley was well enough to appear against them, or until he died.

Fingy made careful notation of the attackers' names for later reference.

The loss at 51 Sandusky Street, house and furniture, was estimated at $2,000 with an insurance of $1,000 in the Aetna Company of Hartford.

Mrs. Peter Conners hurriedly returned from her dying sister's bedside in Fredonia upon hearing the awful news. It was said that the shock of her daughter's hideous death and the critical condition of her son, along with the imminent demise of her favorite sister were too much for Mrs. Conners to bear. "No heart could support that amount of grief," friends were told, as an explanation for why she unexpectedly succumbed.

It was also said that a nail that pierced Peter Conners foot as he searched the wreckage for his dead daughter initiated blood poisoning followed by a cascade of other serious illnesses that brought about his death as well.

During his father's incapacitation, Fingy Conners gladly abandoned his longshoreman's labors at the docks and took over the running of the Conners saloon. For months Peter Conners remained ill, until, just shy of a year after Julia's tragic death, he expired as well.

To everyone's astonishment, Fingy's stepbrother Dennis Hurley, on the contrary, after shaking hands with the grim reaper repeatedly in the weeks following his near-fatal beating and escape from the fire, began to heal, and within a few months was well enough to join Fingy in helping operate the Conners saloon.

The mysterious fire at No. 51 Sandusky set in motion a fascinating cascade of events that set the stage for the reincarnation of Fingy Conners, the proceeds from which would finance the birth of his vast empire.

1881
The Mutual Rowing Club

"Don't you think it's just a wee bit coincidental," asked Jim of his brother JP, right before they drifted off to sleep, "that Fingy Conners' brother-in-law, sister, mother and father all up and died within months of each other and now, quite improbably, our formerly beggared friend is now, curiously, a rich man?"

"What are you getting at Jim?" asked his half-asleep brother.

Jim sat bolt upright in bed, invigorated by the impact of what he had just deduced.

"Think about it, JP. Julia Hayes' husband dies, with nobody clear on the cause, and he leaves his insurance and belongings to his wife. Then Julia dies in a terrible fire that no one knows the cause of and her life insurance and her husband's estate all go to her mother. Peter Conners collects the insurance money on the burned house, then shortly thereafter Julia's mother dies and leaves her insurance, her estate and all that she inherited from her daughter and son-in-law to Peter Conners. Then Peter dies soon after that and leaves his insurance on the house, his life insurance, all the property and insurance money he inherited from the other three, the lot that the burned house sat on and his saloon business and the lot that sits on—all of it—to his only natural son, Fingy.

"After Fingy inherited the saloon, the decedents' estates, and the life insurances on all four, he immediately goes out and buys himself another saloon, as if he's celebrating. As if the emotion of grief doesn't exist for him. I ask you, JP. Does Fingy act like someone who just lost his father, mother and sister? I've never seen him so invigorated!"

"Are you saying... that Fingy killed his parents and sister, Jim?" laughed JP.

"I'm not saying anything for certain, JP, except, what an interesting and profitable sequence of coincidental events to have occur in such a brief period of time."

Jim fell silent for a minute, thinking. Then he continued.

"The witnesses say Julia might have made it out of that house in time, JP., had she been able to open the windows. The girl died trying to save her damn sewing machine! Her neighbor said the only reason Julia woke up at all is because she stood beneath her window throwing rocks and shouting to her over and over again. Why was Julia sleeping so soundly? And acting so strangely? How did the fire start to begin with? And on the one unusual night when neither of Fingy's parents were home, nor Fingy neither? And with Dennis unconscious in his bed from his injuries and unlikely to be able to awaken and escape on his own?"

"Fingy dotes on Dennis, Jim. There's no way he'd want to see Dennis hurt!"

"Well then, JP, are you in effect saying that he might not mind seeing Julia, his step mother and his father hurt?"

JP didn't answer. Jim continued.

"Dennis' mother took out a $5000 insurance on Dennis' life too. It's only a miracle that in the shape he was in that he was able to make it out of there. And he never would have made it out if Julia hadn't finally woken to the neighbors screams and pushed him out the window. Why did all the neighbors wake up, but not the people in the burning house? By all rights Dennis should be dead too, with his insurance in Fingy's pockets as well. Mrs. MacNamara said she had to shout over and over before Julia woke up and came to the window. That house was fully gone in five minutes more or less. Mrs. McNamara said she never saw a fire spread so fast, and since her own house burned a few years back, she should have a good idea about such things. She said it wasn't much more than five minutes from the time she first discovered the fire until Julia was killed. Five minutes!"

"Jim, you know I have no particular affection for Fingy Conners. But are you really thinking he could do something like that? Is that what you're saying?"

"I'm not saying anything for certain yet, JP. I'm just thinking about what happened and how freakish it all was that it happened exactly the way it did. That they died in the order that was required of them for Fingy to inherit everything. It's left Fingy thriving rather than devastated, which he clearly is not considering the way he's acting, that's all. I'm just thinking about this situation like a copper would. Like a policeman who doesn't know any of the people involved. If someone came to you with that same incredible story, what would you think, if you were a policeman?"

JP remained quiet.

"Would a cop think, 'Golly, what an unlucky but innocent set of coincidences,' or would a cop think, 'Golly, that whole thing sure sounds awfully suspicious to me'? Think about it, JP," encouraged Jim.

"Aw, go to sleep now, will you Jim? I'm bone tired," JP whined.

Concurrent with the period in which Fingy Conners' relatives died there had been much labor unrest on Buffalo's docks, resulting in a series of prolonged and nasty strikes in which shipping came to a near-complete halt. The strikes' devastating economic effects echoed along the shores of all five Great Lakes. Dock workers refused to load and unload. The dock workers held the upper hand, for if the vessel owners wanted their ships serviced and the money to keep rolling in, they would have to buckle under to the dock workers' demands.

Fingy Conners, having spent his younger years working first on the lake vessels, then on the docks, listening to the men beef and complain all the while, knew only too well their deepest vulnerabilities and weaknesses. One day in 1880 the gang boss of the crew Fingy worked on took him aside.

"Conners. I see'd how youse hold yer own wit' dis gang, least yer not exactly the biggest man amongst 'em. So's I decided t' try youse out an' make youse the new boss of dis here crew."

Fingy was thrilled.

"I won't disappoint youse, Mr. Riley! T'anks!"

Riley led Fingy back to the gang, his hand approvingly on Fingy's shoulder.

"Lissen up all o' youse. Conners here is yer new boss. Show 'im the same regard as me or else!"

Riley sneered at the gang menacingly, then walked away.

The novice gang boss turned and faced his first band of brawny underlings.

The unconvinced little detachment awaited the turn-to from their new leader that would start them off on their day's labors. Fingy assumed a walloper's posture and announced, "If'n there's a mother's son in dis gang what t'inks he kin lick me, let him came and do it right now."

It wasn't an unusual challenge on the docks. This is how a man became a foreman, and held on to his superior position—mostly through his ability with and readiness to use his fists.

One huge Irishman, six-foot-two, with powerful forearms that looked ready to could snap Fingy in half, stepped out. As he rolled up his shirtsleeves to reveal raw sinew, he answered the challenge.

"So, ye t'ink youse are as good a man as meself, eh, Pat?" smirked Fingy.

"Tis within an inch of yer life I'll be baitin' youse, Fingy Conners, as soon as ye take yer coat off." provoked the freight-man. The other men formed a circle around the combatants, egging them on.

Conners' arms remained at his side as the giant raised his fists.

"Well, then, youse is fired! I won't have no man in this gang what t'inks he kin lick me."

Contained in this confrontation was a seed, an example of the brazen and primitive character that would propel the rise of Fingy Conners. In order to rule in the primeval world of the docks, a boss longshoreman had to be a boss scrapper as well. A boss had to win his spurs by walloping every member of his gang and step out the second he was no longer up to the challenge. One thing could be said about Fingy: he never backed down from a confrontation. He loved a good fight and his reputation was that of a first-class scrapper. Fingy Conners was known for his doggedness in a brawl. He always held his own. Every scuffle only made him more self-assured, pumping up his swagger.

In his own mind he was the boss, a leader of men. Whether by use of his fists or his gifts of intimidation and manipulation, he was hell-bent on ruling.

It had begun in earnest not long after the tragic deaths of his family. No longer having anyone remaining who formerly kept him in check, the antediluvian moral down spiraling of Fingy Conners accelerated unsupressed. From career street thug, idle tormentor and inveterate thief he morphed into a fearsome slave master and primordial afflicter; the unrelenting wedge that drove the tortured families of the First Ward apart.

While working behind the bar one day in his bawdy inherited saloon mere weeks after the death of his father, Fingy's brain began to glow warm with a new scheme. His customers wore armbands emblazoned with the word STRIKE. Although business was very good, it still was not to his liking. Fingy formulated a plan. He confided as much to his stepbrother Dennis Hurley.

"Don't be tellin' me now that yer waxin' sentimental fer yer old days on the docks, Fingy! Not with all these strikers sittin' around here drinkin' away their kids' dinner, all to yer benefit! These tomfools lose more money strikin' than they ever earn workin'! Ye got it made here, brother. Ye've got the easy life fer yerself."

"Ye know, Dinny, I do. But I find I'm missin' all the old hubbub I used t' love. Just look around ye here. See these men sittin' here doin' nuttin? They're all proud lads. When the gang boss don't treat 'em right, or the shippers don't treat 'em right, they get up and jus' walk out. They lose money. The shippers lose money. I don't know -- it's just so interestin' t' me how willin' everybody on both sides is t' be throwin' good money into the wind. Somebody ought t' be out there wit' a net catchin' it as it flies by!"

One September night in 1881 Dennis Hurley went out back of the saloon to empty the spittoons onto the ground. He watched curiously from the shadows as the solitary figure of Fingy Conners disappeared up the darkened street, making not a sound, save for that of the sloshing heard in the half-full can of oil he lugged.

Less than fifteen minutes later as Dennis poured for the customers, a man ran into the saloon and screamed, "There's a fire on the docks! It's the Union Steamship warehouse!"

Men shot out from the saloon toward the firey scene, joined by hundreds of others streaming frantically out of neighboring taverns, homes, and businesses. A fire on the docks meant just one thing: potential financial disaster for everyone. As the fire steamers raced toward the conflagration, the First Ward's citizens amassed to help control its spread.

The following day, Union Steamship president Washington Bullard stood amid the still-smoking ruins of his great warehouse assessing the damage, careful not to dirty his fine attire. He was approached there by a crude individual having an unsettling sneer.

"Say dere, Mister. Youse wit' the shippin' company wot once owned this here blue ruin?"

Bullard leered at Fingy Conners as if he were some hydrophobia-infected mongrel.

"Did you have anything to do with this, boy?" he demanded, contemptuously.

"No. But I can have everything to do wit' makin' sure it never happens t' youse ag'in, mister. In fact, I can even guarantee ye'll never ag'in have a labor strike waged ag'inst youse."

Bullard looked Fingy up and down.

"And how might a man of your limited standing bring about such a miracle?" sniffed the gentleman.

"Well, all youse gotta do, mister... uh, wot's yer family's name, there?"

"Bullard. I am Mr. Washington Bullard."

"Yeah. All youse gotta do, Mr. Bullard, is sign a contract wit' me t' exclusively provide yer company with me own hand-picked professional-trained labor. Me own lads will never strike. Me own lads will never destroy property. In fact they'll protect yer property like a pack o' wild guard dogs. They will get the job done quick, and they will cost ye less in wages than yer present workers is costin' ye now."

Fingy sniggered, his arms sweeping over the disastrous cataclysm.

"Tsk-tsk! Just have yerself a look around at all this calamity! Ye don't never ag'in wanna be caught standing out here bollixed, in broad daylight amongst such a dead relic! Holdin' yer cock in yer hand wit' everyone watchin' ye, mockin' ye, shakin' their heads in derision atcha! Now do youse, Mister?"

Bullard flinched in repulsion at this vulgar little gnome, yet he was intrigued. He resurveyed the monumental destruction smoking all around him.

"What's your name, lad?"

"Conners. William J. Conners."

"How old are you Mr. Conners?"

"Twenty-four."

"Hmm. Twenty-four. Well, Mr. Conners, just how would you plan to bring about this domestication of the common wharf rat? This marvel of tamed labor?"

"Dat's fer me t' know and fer youse t' find out, Mr. Bullard. As far as I can see, standin' here appraisin' dis mess and all yer ruined shipments, youse got nuttin at all t' be losin' by takin' a chance wit' me. Do youse really t'ink it can get much worse than this? These strikers is gonna put youse outa business entirely!"

Bullard thought for a few moments, ruminating.

"Come over to my office this afternoon at four o'clock, Mr. Conners. We'll discuss it then."

Fingy thrust out a meaty fist. Bullard gripped it with a bit of hesitation, after which he turned and walked off.

Fingy immediately set out to pay a visit to his attorney's office to have a labor contractor's agreement with Bullard's Union Steamship Company drawn up.

Upon completion of the agreement, Fingy returned to his saloon, changed his shirt, combed his hair and set out for Bullard's office, contract in hand.

"And so, Mr. Conners. How much are these laborers of yours going to cost me?"

"How much youse payin' fer men now?"

"Between $17 and $19 a week."

"Mine'll be costin' youse just $15 a week, Mr. Bullard."

"Fifteen? How are you going to convince your men making $19 a week to suddenly accept $15?"

Fingy chuckled and threw out his chest. "I'll be usin' all me considerable charms o' persuasion, Mr. Bullard. Ye'll see," he boasted.

Fingy emerged into the sooty sunlight smiling. He stopped a moment to admire Bullard's signature on the one-year contract, then tucked it into his breast pocket and headed back to his saloon.

There, Kennedy, Fingy's brother Dennis, and Fingy's young muse, David Nugent, just fifteen years old, greeted him.

"Kennedy, me boy, I'm in! An' I'm promotin' youse. Yer now me official right-hand man. Let's you 'n' me go 'round 'n' have a talkin' to wit' dese strikin' lads here. Let's see who wants to feed their little babies next week, and who don't."

Feeling left out, young David asked, "What about me, boss?"

"Yer time's comin' Davey. Yer still young yet. Just watch fer now an' go about doin' yer chores. Look 'n' learn."

Nugent was disappointed but observed attentively.

Brother Dennis felt completely overlooked, because he was. Wounded, he angrily washed mugs and glasses as Fingy and Kennedy interviewed the strikers. Objections and shouts rose up from the men immediately.

Ye can't be serious, Fingy!" shouted a well-weathered laborer named O'Brien. "I'm makin' $19 a week, and yer offerin' me $12! Go sink yer ass on a rail spike and spin like a top!"

WASHINGTON BULLARD, DIED OCT. 30, 1896.

Washington Bullard, Union Steamship Co,

Fingy sneered.

"Have it yer way, O'Brien, but let me correct youse a bit beforehand. Youse was makin' $19 ye mean, durin' them few times when there was such jobs to be had, but now there ain't none. There ain't no work fer most o' youse -- not after that fire on the docks. What are yer kids gonna be eatin' next week? Cattails dug up from Dalton's Pond? Oh! No, wait! I fergot. Them wops come down from Dago-town and stole those all away weeks ago! See here, O'Brien. Workin' fer me will mean steady work. Steady. No idle intervals. A wage paid every week. Steady work ye can depend on. Yer kids'll be eatin' regular. That's a promise, unlike in the past when youse'd never knew if ye'd be workin' from one day t' the next."

O'Brien thought it over for a minute.

"All right dere, Fingy. I'll give it a try, damn it."

"T'morrow, then, seven o'clock. Be there on the dot. The Union Steamboat dock."

Fingy and Kennedy then proceeded from man to man. The desperate laborers were unhappy about lowered wages, but reassured that the recompense would be reliable employment.

A week later, a hundred men lined up outside Fingy's saloon awaiting pay for their first week's toilings. Howls arose when the men received $10 in cash and $2 in brass tokens — slugs that could be redeemed for only one thing — alcohol at Fingy's saloon.

Laborer O'Brien was infuriated.

"Wot de hell, Fingy! Wot is dis? I got t' buy food fer me kids! We have t' pay de doctor! I don't want yer fuckin' brasses!"

O'Brien fired his tokens across the room in anger.

"Well, ye got 'em anyways, O'Brien! Throw 'em away if ye want. Go ahead. Be a fool. But that's how it works. If youse're expectin' t' be workin' fer me steady every week, that's the way we do it around here. Ye scratch me back, I scratch yers."

"Well, ye kin scratch me balls, rather, Fingy Conners, ye dúnmhartóir! I can't be feedin' no six kids and breakin' me back for no ten dollars a week!"

Pleased with the opportunity to set an example early on, Fingy jumped on O'Brien, punching him non-stop in the face and stomach alternately so lightning-fast that O'Brien never had a chance to respond. Fingy threw him out the door and into the street while all the men in line watched. O'Brien lay deposited in the mud, groaning.

Fingy proceeded to put on a vivid show for his captive audience.

"Watch who yer talkin' to with that dirty lyin' mouth o' yers, O'Brien! I'll knock out the rest o' those rotted teeth next time if you ever talk to me like that ag'in. Now git out, and don't youse ever come crawlin' back to me fer work! If yer kids starve, it'll be yer own doin' now! I feel sorry fer the tykes, havin' a damn fool like youse fer their father!"

Those in line were taught a lesson. They proceeded to collect their wage, silently for the most part. An occasional howl rose up. But with few exceptions, desperate men with nowhere to turn swallowed hard and accepted what was handed them.

Fingy barked at the assembled.

"Any man wot walks out on strike ag'in me will be shut out — forever! Are youse all hearin' me? Don't none o' youse git no ideas! Youse'll never work again! The First Ward is full o' lads wot'll step right up and fill yer place. This is the way this is gonna be! Like it or lump it. If youse t'ink youse kin do better elsewheres, then go. But don't youse even t' ink about comin' crawlin' back t' me once ye do. I got a memory like a elephant, and youse'll never work fer me ag'in!"

The men's expressions confirmed the realization that they had been hopelessly entrapped.

Fingy resumed doling out the paltry wages. On the sly, Dennis pulled Kennedy aside.

"Jesus, Kennedy! Fingy's gettin' $15 from the shippers fer each man but he's only paying the man $10. That's $5 a week he's puttin' in his back pocket fer every man wot works fer him! That's...that's..."

Kennedy and Dennis racked their brains attempting the math.

Kennedy exclaimed, "Almost $500 a week fer hisself! Whew! And I'm only gettin' paid $20!"

Dennis is shocked.

"$20? You get paid five dollars more than me? But...but I'm his own brother!"

Damn! Dinny, I shouldn't o' said nuttin'!" bawled the embarrassed Kennedy. "Don't tell Fingy wot I told ye — or he'll skin me alive!"

As the calendar pages were turned and his fortune piled up, Conners honed and polished his predatory prowess. He approached the owners of other vessels with the proofs of his success and won their contracts one by one. His empire was growing briskly. The average wage of a longshoreman before Fingy Conners came into the picture was between $16 and $20 a week. Conners negotiated with the delighted vessel owners to accept from them just $15 a week per man. He then paid each worker $10 a week. Fingy banked the difference.

The vessel owners rejoiced. Word spread. Before long Fingy Conners had most of the independent small vessel owners under his wing, but all the while he had his eagle eye set high on the biggest prizes of all, the big Great Lakes Lines.

His schemed monopoly on its way to fruition, Fingy had effected a revolution in the methods that freight was handled in the region. He had introduced a system that transformed the industry, bringing order from chaos and profit from loss. Quite enthusiastically, upon witnessing the spectacular overnight results of his prowess at corraling Buffalo's untamed dock workers, the remaining managers of other lakes lines beat a path to his door, including shippers from Chicago, Detroit and Duluth.

As Fingy Conners roped in Buffalo's longshoremen and decimated their wages, so too was the local economy ensnared. The grocer, the shoemaker, the dry goods store, the dressmaker, the housekeeper, the candy-seller. They all felt the devastating effects of customers disappearing altogether, or at best, greatly reducing the amount of business transacted with them.

The churches felt it too — in the collection basket.

Fingy Conners, having hit the Church where it hurt the most, was roundly demonized from the pulpit. And whenever he heard about an especially vehement public verbal flailing, Fingy would dispatch one of his thugs under the cover of night in earnest effort of rehabilitating the errant priest.

The ears of clerics in the First Ward and beyond were raw from the burning sobs and wails of wives of laboring men exorcising their pain and frustration in the confessional. But fear is a most potent weapon, and for a while, even as the women continued to wail — and worse — the priests maintained their silence.

Although they were still friendly with Fingy, both JP and Jim Sullivan felt the ferocious greed of Fingy Conners nipping at their own heels. They too were laborers, and the First Ward was a compact neighborhood community.

Jim Sullivan had made a promise to himself that he would never set foot inside the wood fence that surrounded Uniontown's ironworks on Hamburgh Street across from his home. That he would never work in such a dangerous, filthy, cruel environment. But faced with the style of servitude that Conners established on the docks, and unwilling to accept Fingy's offer that he sign on as a walloper in the saloon boss' gang of thugs, Jim Sullivan chose to take work as a puddler at the Union Ironworks. At least, he told himself, he could sleep right up until it was time to walk across the street and report to work. He hated the dangerous toil, but his plan was to take the police exam and become one of Buffalo's men in blue at the first opportunity. He would tough it out until his time came. He wasn't married yet. He still lived at home. With no family fully counting on him, he still had choices.

Jim's brother JP had been a dock laborer since the age of sixteen. He endured an especially sharp vantage point from which to view Fingy Conners' ensnaring trap.

"It's like what Ma described she witnessed from the ship when she came over from Ireland; a huge school of thousands of blue-fins encircled by just a half-dozen of sharks, who easily managed to corral them and send them into a blind panic."

At twenty years old JP had already begun laying the groundwork to eventually establish his own business. But for the time being he found himself toiling among desperate, infuriated, hungry men, watching them take their anger and frustration out on each other for want of anywhere else to turn.

Young and single, JP Sullivan stood out from the pack of hope-depleted family men. He had more ambitious plans for his future than did the others. Being a dock worker, he told himself, was just a stepping stone on his way to where he intended to go. With his easy-going nature and effortless sarcastic humor he was able to lighten the dreariness around him a wee bit, and quickly made friends. In the deeply exhausted eyes of those other men he saw a vision of himself as someone who might be able to help them, who could possibly change things. It was those men who anticipated no other life for themselves who became the most easily-entagled victims of Fingy Conners' saloon-boss system. Concluding that gaining status and power though politics would be the best path for him, he made it a point to shake everyone's hand and tell them his name.

Working conditions on the docks deteriorated as atmosphere of anger, despotism, hunger and fear worsened. Once working men had been successfully pressured into executing their tasks with less attention to safety in the name of speed and efficiency, tragedies began to occur.

A crane hoisting a load of ill-fastened crates towering over young JP crashed down on him as he guided the block and tackle to deposit the load on the dock. His leg snapped and an exposed nail ripped a six inch gash in the quadricep.

Blood flowed from the wound and dripped into the Buffalo River. JP silently cried for his mother. The men lifted him in his great agony onto a freight cart, which was little more than a wheelbarrow, and rushed him along the pier toward a summoned ambulance. The freight cart jolted hard with each uneven plank in the pier its wheels collided, causing JP to scream out with each kick.

The fracture was severe. JP had only woozy memories of arriving at the hospital — the anesthesia, the stitching up of his thigh, the complicated-looking apparatus that surrounded and immobilized and protected the injury. JP had never set foot in a hospital before, but now here he was. How would he ever pay for this?

Riveted by the news, his mother rushed to her youngest's school, grabbed Danny out of class, and dashed to the General Hospital. The doctor told Mary that JP would need to remain there immobilized in traction for four or five weeks, then stay quiet and immobile at home for a month or more after that.

The hospital ward was noisy, upsetting, and lonely as darkness fell. JP tried his best to doze, but the morphine had worn off and the throbbing in his leg was keeping him wakeful.

"Pssst! Hey, JP! Youse awake?"

JP opened his eyes in the dim light to see the figure of Fingy Conners standing there.

"I wuz bothered t' hear what happened t' ye, so I came to see fer meself if youse wuz all right."

"It hurts like hell, Fingy," JP groaned, "but the doctor said if I follow orders and take care of myself that I should be able to walk just fine."

"Okay. Yeah. That's good. Youse just go t' sleep. Rest. I gotta git. I'll be keepin' me eye on ye."

Fingy pressed paper into JP's hand, then squeezed it closed.

"Off t' sleep now," he whispered.

He patted JP gently on the head. Then he walked out.

Groggily, JP held the paper up to catch the light coming into the ward from the corridor so he could read what it said. It was four fifty-dollar bills. He had never see a fifty dollar bill before. He couldn't make out which President's likeness was on it.

JP was determined to be a compliant patient once assured by his doctors that his adherence to their directives, as difficult as that might be, would determine the quality of his life from that day forward. Because of his dedication his shattered leg, which doctors feared might have to be amputated, mended faster than expected, albeit four inches shorter than it had originally been. For the rest of his life John P. Sullivan would have to wear a prodigious orthopedic shoe causing him to walk with a characteristic gate.

His nickname from then on was "Hop."

Three months passed before JP could get around again without help, more or less. As he healed he had lots of time to simmer and think. He worried terribly about his future. How ever might he make a living now? He regretted not going further in school, not setting his sights higher. He'd never run bases again, and football and handball were a thing of the past. As he wasted away in the house he saw his circumstance shrinking both physically and materially. He'd never been a brawny lad, but now he saw his reflection in the mirror growing thinner and more wan with each passing week. He needed to exercise, but the doctors' words came back to him; he had to lie low until the leg had completely healed.

He looked out from the second-story windows a lot, across the river toward the lake, out over the ironworks property, up and down South Street. The city was installing new street signs and he passed the time monitoring the workers' progress. On the new signs they'd spelled Hamburgh Street, Hamburg, leaving off the h.

He was frustrated with new ideas he couldn't do anything about. He couldn't leave the house to go execute any of them. He was restless. He had cabin fever.

JP counted the hours until Jim came home from work. They'd had many talks in the evenings as Jim unwound from his hot, dangerous toil at the ironworks. JP told him about the gangs of their lads he'd observed from the windows, gathering, carousing out on the street.

These accounts only motivated Jim more than ever about his need to pass the police exam, not only to get away from the ironworks, but also to help keep the neighborhood together and maintain order. No one wanted to live amid chaos. He feared for their friends' prospects.

Jim had but one thing in mind these days; to acquire a stable, respected job with a future, and having grown up without any security at all, peace of mind too. He wanted to ask Hannah Nugent to marry him, but not before he had secured a respectable position for himself. Hannah was not thrilled about his wanting to become a patrolman, especially with all the crime in the ward these days. But it was the best of the limited choices he had. The puddling burns on his arms convinced him against a position in the city fire department.

As JP sat at his perch one day itching for some physical way to blow off steam and get back in shape, he witnessed some of his neighborhood friends surround and attack two men who were only minding themselves and toss them into the river. The lads had nothing to do, and the result was beginning to be felt throughout the neighborhood in the form of increased rowdyism.

Two men in a rowboat quickly made for the victims in hopes of rescuing them. As JP watched the paddlers, one of whom had his shirt off, his attention was drawn to how the man's muscles stretched and strained and flexed in his race to reach the victims. He also noticed that the men, as furiously as they rowed, didn't need to engage their legs or feet primarily in order to accomplish their work. The rowers reached the victims and successfully pulled them into their scow. That motion too required relatively little strength below the waist.

His brother Jim had become a fan of sculling in the mid-70s or thereabouts, absorbing news items from wherever he could glean them. The previous year he had been obsessed with Edward Hanlan of Toronto after he defeated Ned Trickett of Australia at the 1880 World Championship match in London, England, right down to memorizing the competitors' strokes and times. The Championship had been held in November in the London cold and pouring rain, and yet thousands turned out to watch. Hundreds of thousands of dollars were wagered, and an individual bet of $42,000 was ventured from Toronto. Jim had wondered at the time if there could ever be that kind of passion for the sport stirred up in Buffalo.

JP had never particularly shared his brother's enthusiasm for the sport.

Jim had even taken the train up to Toronto the previous year with Ed Stanton to watch their hero Hanlan in action. Jim was a little put off by his clownish antics — such as when Hanlan, far ahead of his competitor, paused mid-race to wash his face — but still idolized him anyway. And not just because the handsome sculler had hordes of girls chasing him wherever he went.

JP grew excited. He hunted around the house for the Harper's Weekly issues that Jim had saved which featured accounts of the sculling teams of the universities Harvard, Yale and Syracuse. He was getting worked up. He could do this, even with his bum leg. He found an article about the Henley, and read every word. It was the perfect sport, an ideal way to let off steam and stay healthy. They could get their rowdy friends involved. The river was right outside their door, wide and flat and free for the taking. JP could hardly contain himself.

When Jim walked in the door, hot and dirty and itching to go in the yard to wash off, JP pounced on him.

JP said, "Jim, our lads need something to do, to keep them off the streets and out of trouble and away from the saloons. They need some way to blow off steam that won't land them in jail. They need somethin' that'll wear 'em out, like athletics."

"What's gotten into you?"

"I'm going a little crazy being cooped up here all day. And I saw Donovan and his gang toss two men into the river today just for fun. Those lads need something to do. I need something to do."

"Like what?" asked Jim.

"What do you think about sculling? I've been thinkin' about it! We've got a big wide lazy river right across the street. You were already thinking about joining the Celtics down at The Beaches. Why not just start a club of our own, right here?"

Seeing JP getting so excited switched the light on in Jim's eyes.

"That is one capital idea, JP! I was wonderin' about the possibility of doin' something like that, but I wasn't sure if anybody else from the ward would be interested."

There were already a number of rowing clubs in Buffalo. The Celtics and the North Buffalos. The West Ends were located way over on the west side of the city. They used the Erie Canal or rowed on the lake inside the break wall.

The Sullivans' neighborhood pals the Sheehan brothers had founded the Celtic Rowing Club a few years back, and even though Jim thought it wise to keep his distance from the Sheehans, he and Ed Stanton tried out for the team anyway. He had thought seriously of joining, but the barrier was Billy Sheehan himself. Of the two brothers Billy was especially controlling, exhibiting an insane need to be in charge. When they were boys, he owned footballs, baseballs, bats and other sports equipment that nobody else had. When Billy called together a game, and things weren't going his way, or the other lads balked at having to play by his own unique made-up rules slanted to his advantage, he'd take his ball and bat and storm home in a huff.

Blue-eyed Billy Sheehan was not one who Jim Sullivan wanted to be involved with, especially not in a competitive sport. Billy had somehow procured the Celtic club's one and only scull, and when Jim went out in the boat with him and the other Celtics, the frustration of being trapped out on the water with such a domineering personality made him realize that joining the Celtics would be a poor idea.

JP said, "Ed Stanton would want to join. And Tom Nunan for sure."

"Those sculls, JP... those things are expensive. I'd have to figure a way to get our hands on one."

"Maybe we could get Fingy involved. Separate him from some of the money he keeps stealin' from our mates," JP enthused. "He's helped put many a lad out on the streets, so maybe now he can help bring a few back in."

"Well, you know Fingy. He'd want to be in charge of everything."

"I'll talk to him and see how he feels about it," replied JP.

JP had obviously been giving this matter quite a bit of thought, mused Jim.

"Tom Nunan is no corner boy, JP. He's moving up. He isn't exactly hanging out with roughs," said Jim.

Tom Nunan was JP's closest friend and a self-motivated go-getter.

"Yeah, I know that. But if we want a club that'll get the troubled lads off the street," figured JP, "it'll have to be a mixed organization. There will have to be members who will be a good influence on the roughs. If we only get the corner boys and wayward lads it will be rowdy and hard to keep order. We need to get them motivated. We need to get all our friends involved... the leaders, not just the ones headed for trouble. So they can help one another out. But best of all, I can row too. I don't need my legs or my feet for anything more than balance and stabilizing myself. I was watching some lads rowing on the river today, paying real close attention, and it hit me: that's something that I can do too. I'm ready to burst just sitting around here. I need to get out and move!"

"I see you've been reading my magazines."

"Right. And you're exactly the person who can get this started, Jim. I don't know the first thing about it. Will you think about it at least?"

"Cripes! The only thing I really have left to think about, JP, is how do we get our hands on a scull?

The next day Jim came running in from work all stirred up. He had been informed by one of the other ironworkers, a man whose brother had been a member, that the Black Rock Rowing Club had disbanded the year before. They were storing their scull in the shed behind his family's house and they wanted to sell it. Jim washed up as fast as he could and hopped a streetcar to Black Rock to have a look.

Jim called a meeting on July 24th at Triepil's barber shop, at the corner of Hamburgh and South, and all interested parties who the Sullivan brothers had spoken to about their idea gathered together. Fifty-five young men crowded into the tiny space with their enthusiasm spilling out the windows. Jim Sullivan tore around like an unstoppable whirlwind and quickly had things in order for an August 1st incorporation date.

"But where will we get the money?", Thomas Kelleher inquired.

"I've been thinking about a few events we could organize that would help raise the money we'll need. Like a picnic. How does August 27th sound?" offered Jim.

"But...that's less than four weeks from now, Jim."

"Yep. Best we get busy." And busy they got.

The Buffalo Express called the event "the largest picnic ever held by any Buffalo club." The fifty-five charter members among their numbers were acquainted with virtually every citizen in the entire teeming First Ward, and the turnout was tremendous. Revelers enjoyed athletic events, games of skill, barbecued chicken and kielbasa, rivers of lemonade brimming with crushed ice, spirited band music and drawings for prizes donated both by local merchants and the larger downtown businesses.

Jim Sullivan tapped into the members' great reservoir of social connections like some wizard of old and accomplished an event unlike any previous private fund raising effort. The police precinct was duly notified and involved, and most of its members who were not on duty brought their families. Jim took advantage of the police department's presence to make some new friends on the force. His undeniable organizational skills were noticed by precinct Captain Hanlan both for their ambition and swiftness of execution.

Fingy Conners too recognized an opportunity when he saw one. The turnout convinced him without a doubt. He would buy himself the position of club vice president. It would be one of the last times in his life that Fingy would ever be content with accepting second position.

On September 10, 1881, the club's constitution was adopted and Jim Sullivan—the organization's founder, mover, and shaker—was unanimously elected president. Fingy Conners, whose Midas touch was forged of cunning, unceasing ambition and steely focus, was elected vice president upon his promise to purchase the club's first two custom built shells. Old Doc Greene was asked to join the Mutuals as official team physician.

Ambitiously, four four-oared shells and five single sculls were purchased by the club in all; the first was christened the *Jim Sullivan* in honor of the club's founder. Immediately the Mutuals demonstrated that although they were the newest rowing club in the area, they would have no betters on the local waters. They organized a chain of social events that raised money and quickly made the Mutuals the most highly visible and envied club in the region. There soon was a lengthy waiting list for membership. Their events attracted legions of spectators, who in turn spread the word to all their friends. The local newspapers were squarely in their corner, publicizing every new upcoming event and afterward reporting in great detail all the particulars.

In 1882 the Mutuals rented out St. James Hall, the venue of President Abraham Lincoln's funeral, for their first annual ball. The Adelphi Band furnished the music, which included their performance of the Mutual Rowing Club Waltz. "The Hall was tastefully trimmed," reported the Buffalo Courier. "On the floor in the center of the Hall was painted a full-sized four-oared shell with the crew in it in the club colors." Later and more economically, the close-by parish hall at Our Lady of Perpetual Help Church was chosen for the club's dances and masquerades. The Mutuals organized smokers and banquets, socials and benefits, boxing matches and foot races, and staged colorful noisy parades both on the water and through the ward's streets. Compared to all the other local clubs, the Mutuals were a well-oiled machine and a public relations dynamo with the most visible presence on the city scene.

The bottled-up energy and workaday frustrations of its members poured out in the form of formidable industriousness and drive. Wishing to measure their skill against the best four-oared crews in the country, for their first official national race the Mutuals entered a crew in the national regatta held at Pittsburgh. Ed Stanton, Tom Nunan, James Short, and Dennis J. Daly were selected to represent the Mutual Rowing Club. The crew had never rowed outside its native waters previous to this time, but was imbued with the Mutual spirit. They surprised

231

even the club's most ardent admirers by capturing third prize, which was valued at $154. A Mutual crew was also quickly entered in a regatta held at Rochester, and in this race the Mutuals won second place. They were on their way.

The Sullivan brothers discovered that their efforts to drive the Mutual Rowing Club to the top of the heap had the welcome effect of greatly expanding their social alliances. Jim made new friends among the police department after they solicited his advice on some of their own events. His new uniformed friends suggested it was time he wrote the police exam, knowing his skills would be an asset to their organization.

Nobody knew it until Doc Greene brought him in to meet everybody, but the physician had mysteriously become fast friends with Alderman Jack White, who was excited about what was newly happening in his First Ward domain. Nobody actually liked Jack White, save for the Doc and possibly Fingy Conners. Fingy's attraction was obvious: ruthless birds of a feather. But the kindly, generous, always reliable Doc Greene? Nobody could understand their connection. JP's political interests were aroused. He decided to make the most of their meeting and introduce himself to Jack White as one of the club's two founders. JP had heard the Jack White stories for years, and was fascinated to know if they were true. The two men hit it off immediately.

While JP was cornering Jack White, Doc Greene took Jim Sullivan aside to ask him if Jack White might join the Mutuals.

Jim was taken by surprise. "No," he said, dumbfounded. What an odd thing for the Doc to ask.

"He's too fat and too old." Jim said. "We're an athletic organization, Doc, and every member has pull his own weight, literally. And clearly Jack White has enough of a challenge maneuvering his big arse around on dry land as it is. Every member has to be able to pitch in, do his part and put in his time just as well as the next. Train, row, repair, clean. Jack White would do nothing more than sink the boat. And besides, he's a Republican."

He thought it went without saying that he hated the alderman, so he didn't say it.

"I myself don't row, Jim, yet you asked me to join," implored the Doc.

"Doc, you're a physician! We need you more than just about any other member. You're not expected to row, because you take care of all the rowers. What can Jack White possibly contribute except to sit around and talk dirt behind everyone's back — and fart? And then claim he done neither?"

Doc was disappointed. Jim was surprised by just how much. White clearly had no interest in athletics, and as much a social club the M.R.C. was, every member trained, pitched in with the work and put in his time. Jim also was certain that Jack White's nature would lead him to try and take over, the inclination being simply in his blood.

"I brought you and your brothers into this world, Jim Sullivan. And half the members of this club," said the Doc, pouting. "You just remember that."

%

1881
Grover Cleveland For Mayor

Like millions of other American parents, Grover Cleveland's mother had told her male child when he was just a wee one, "Son, someday you could be President of the United States."

When he had stood in the crowd out front of the American Hotel twenty years previous in 1861, basking in an address by his idol Abraham Lincoln, the young attorney Cleveland pictured himself up there on that balcony in Lincoln's position. He wondered then what Lincoln must be feeling, having won the leadership of the entire nation, looking out at the sea of worshipful supporters joyously welcoming him to Buffalo. He knew right then that he wanted to find out.

In 1881, Grover Cleveland ran for the office of Mayor of Buffalo. One of his chief adversaries in politics was veteran alderman Jack White of the First Ward. Not that the alderman had any desire to be mayor, for he had feathered a comfortable nest for himself in the city's political hierarchy that allowed him both power and freedom, where public opinion concerning his personal life counted for little. He lived life exactly as he wished, warts and peccadillos notwithstanding. He was his own man.

Grover Cleveland's principal issue in his campaign for mayor was Jack White's corruption. Cleveland called his opponents "Jack White Republicans," to differentiate them from real Republicans. He inferred not too subtly that White was responsible for chicanery and duplicity at the City Hall. One of Grover Cleveland's campaign strategies was to visit the saloons in Jack White's First Ward to court the city's toughest balloters.

On the evening of November 5th, a Saturday, he visited Halloran's Saloon at No. 16 Hamburgh Street, arriving with a number of men who appeared to be policemen outfitted in gentlemen's garb. All wore wool derby hats. Jim Sullivan and his brothers JP and Danny were managing the saloon that evening because Peter Halloran had been incarcerated in Oswego Prison for three months, only his most recent reunion with old penitentiary cohorts. Mary didn't care enough anymore to feel any shame over this. She was happy to have him out of her hair for a while.

Daniel Halloran, heir to his father's saloon empire, was feeling his oats this night, and made his standing known to Mr. Cleveland. He was curious about politics and the candidate who would be mayor. His brothers were amused at witnessing this surprising new cocky side to their sixteen-year-old sibling.

Jim recognized one of the gentlemen accompanying Cleveland as a copper he'd met at the Mutual Rowing Club picnic at the end of August. An hour earlier the man had entered the saloon to pre-arrange permission for the candidate to speak. Jim was puzzled that Halloran's had been chosen, wondering if the committee had any idea about Peter's deplorable reputation. Moreover, Grover

Cleveland was out to get rid of their neighborhood friend and Celtic Rowing Club co-founder John C. Sheehan, brother of Billy Sheehan. Harboring first-hand knowledge of Sheehan's criminal activities in the city comptroller's office involving embezzling, Cleveland refused to run for mayor unless Sheehan's name was struck from the ballot. It was, and the Sheehan brothers were livid about it.

John C. Sheehan was more a useful friend than a close one, but still the Sullivans had to think twice about possibly alienating him. Uncomfortable with having to make a definitive decision so quickly, they ultimately erred on the side of Cleveland. After all, if Cleveland were elected mayor, Sheehan's career, due to his criminal mischief, might well be over and they would need someone new to ask favors of. Jim was told that Cleveland would be visiting four or five other neighborhood saloons on his campaign stops that night, including Fingy Conners" saloon on Louisiana Street. When the brothers heard that, they all looked at each other, thinking, we'd sure like to see for ourselves what happens when he shows up over there! Sure, Fingy might be a "Republican" only for the convenience of it, but in any case, the Democrat Cleveland was not at all his style of candidate. He was far too upright and honest. Cleveland's invasion of Halloran's Saloon lasted just twenty minutes. He railed against the opposing Republican leader and rallied the people of the First Ward's support to clean up city government. He politely refused a free beer.

"It'll put out my fire!" the candidate exclaimed, to overall laughter.

The group left, and visited two other saloons before arriving at Fingy Conners'. Fingy stood out front, arms crossed, waiting with a club in his hand, surrounded by his gang. Grover Cleveland would never step foot in a Conners establishment, not if Fingy had anything to say about it.

Patrolman Jim Sullivan

In early 1883 Jim Sullivan wrote his police exam and passed. On May 14 he was appointed to the police force. When Captain Hanlan pinned his badge on, Jim smiled contentedly. No more Union Ironworks for me, he declared silently. He stood there remembering the past, as if once collected and firmly bundled with twine he might put it all behind him. He thought about the terrible years during the War Between The States, the orphanage, the fear and uncertainty of his fate as a boy having been placed in the hands of a elderly legal guardian, his long-suffering mother's pension agent Samuel Lake. He would now have the comfort and security of the badge and the gun and a police pension at the end of his days. The only celebration he had planned was the one he'd been waiting months for: a romantic dinner for two after which he would propose marriage to Hannah Nugent.

Sam Lake was 93 years old, having been born shortly after George Washington first took office in 1789. Every day Sam still reliably arrived at his office at nine o'clock in the morning and put in a full day. His personal recollections of Mary Sullivan and her sons' predicament were now a trifle hazy, not so much from age, for he was still sharp as a tack, but because it was all so long ago, and so many others with pressing problems had required his dedication since.

His final day began typically. He welcomed his office clock chiming noon and, stomach growling, donned his coat and hat against the fierce lake winds. He stepped out onto Franklin Street to walk a few doors down to his favorite lunchroom. As he crossed the street a speeding carriage neglected to slow or stop, the horse trampling old Sam Lake asunder. He died an hour later.

Election time in the First Ward was predictably tumultuous, akin to gladiatorial combat in fact, where most any weapon might be used that would do the most damage. Jack White ruled supreme in the Common Council as Alderman of the First Ward. Jack White was widely recognized in both public opinion as well as newsprint as the most corrupt and most powerful politician in the city. His Democratic opponent in the 1883 election to retain his aldermanic seat was the equally odious John C. Sheehan, former city comptroller, demonized by Mayor Grover Cleveland himself. It would be difficult to determine which of the two men, White or Sheehan, Mayor Cleveland deplored more.

John P. Sullivan had been incisive in observing his friend Fingy Conners' rise to First Ward dominance. JP knew he did not possess the heartlessness or the stomach for cruelty that Fingy did, nor the enthusiasm for fist fights and violent verbal encounters. Nor did he have an army of thugs in waiting. But he had seen how Fingy was able to sway the elections his way, or in one particular candidate's case, Jack White's way, by installing his friends as inspectors of elections.

An Inspector of Elections was, in the official definition of the job, charged with being on premises at the polling place to make sure only legitimate voters voted, to keep order, to assure that voting was carried out according to the established rules, and perhaps most crucially, to hand-deliver the ballots to election headquarters after the polls closed.

It would seem Officer of Elections might be an unrewarding position, perhaps carried out by those who felt some responsibility as citizens to pitch in and do their part. But in fact, many of the votes being hand-delivered to headquarters by Inspectors of Elections were themselves pitched in—to the canals.

Opponents running against the Inspector of Elections' favored candidate sometimes found that votes cast in their favor went missing, were blown away in a sudden gust off Lake Erie, or dropped by accident into a canal or slip.

The story went that when Republican Jack White was an elections inspector, he accidentally tripped and stubbed his toe on the loose boards of the Hamburgh Turnpike Bridge, which caused him to lose his grip on a bundle of ballots that he was personally conveying to the county hall in order to be certain of their safe delivery, causing all the Democratic votes to fall into the river.

Another time the lights in the polling places were mysteriously extinguished and no one knew when they came on again whether the same ballot boxes lay on the table or if new ones had replaced them in the dark. One also might wonder if the ballots that started out from the polling place were the same ones that arrived at the county hall.

Votes for the favored candidates, on the other hand, had the magical power of multiplying like rabbits, in far greater numbers even than there were voters eligible to cast ballots. More often than not in Buffalo's First Ward, the outcome of the elections was more in the hands of the Inspectors, rather than the hands of the voting citizens. To be an election officer meant possessing true power. May the craftiest elections inspector win.

John P. Sullivan had made many friends on the docks as a longshoreman, among them longshoreman's union treasurer Joseph McCarthy. McCarthy was a twenty-eight year old hard working First Ward son who all other workers respected and looked up to — unlike the effete alderman Jack White, who was a native of Boston.

McCarthy told JP of his plan to run against Jack White for alderman of the First Ward and recalled that JP had once mentioned that he would be interested in becoming an Elections Officer.

"Joe, I'm only twenty-two," said JP "John Rochford owns his own saloon, he's over forty, and he really wants the job."

"It's required that an inspector need only be over the age of twenty-one," McMahon replied with a wink. "Anyway, Rochford is up for Ward Committee, which he will get. The Officer of Elections job is yours if you want it."

On October 23, the Democrats of the First Ward, united and determined to win that year, placed a strong ticket in the field for ward officers. They held their caucus at the home of Simon McMahon on Elk Street. The nominations were without opposition. For alderman, they chose Joseph McCarthy. For Inspectors of Election in the sixth district, the picked Mutual Rowing Club allies Peter P. Dalton and John P. Sullivan.

Come election day, there was such extreme corruption at the polls that the outcome of the election took weeks to sort out. Despite McCarthy's overwhelming popularity and John P. Sullivan's enthusiastic efforts in favor of the Democratic party in executing his role as Officer of Elections, in the end the wily Jack White somehow got himself reelected alderman once again. Fingy Conners had declared himself a Jack White man. But with Conners' unstoppable rise to power Alderman Jack White found himself, especially after this particular election, a Fingy Conners man.

The Buffalo Times wrote, "Just as Paul Bunyan's Blue Ox left lakes where his hoofs had fallen, so Jack White has pulled ballots—and even ballot boxes fully stuffed—out of thin air."

After witnessing for himself what transpired during the election of 1883, JP realized his future right then and there. He had a lot to learn if he was going to play with the Big Boys. And he certainly did want to play.

Hannah Nugent Sullivan moved in to No. 16 Hamburgh Street with her new husband Jim, her in-laws Mary and Peter Halloran and their sons JP and Daniel, and servants Eliza Beatty and Mary Dorning. With the saloon business booming and the incomes of her three sons, Mary was delighted to find herself handing over most of her work to the help. For the first time in her life, she could finally sit down and put her feet up.

Mary thought Hannah was a treasure. Hannah Nugent had placed first in her class at the Central High School three years in a row, and graduated with top honors. She was awarded the city's top scholastic honor, the Jesse Ketchum Prize. Her teachers and classmates were sure she was destined to go on to become famous, perhaps as the city's first female surgeon, or maybe an outstanding lady attorney.

Jim had been telling everyone who'd listen that Hannah was the smartest girl he ever met. They all roared one day when brothers JP and Daniel—independently but in perfect unison—replied, "So why does she want to marry you?"

Hannah knew that she and her Jim would eventually have a place of their own, but she was told circumstances called for Jim to remain in the home for the time being. What she didn't find out until later was that these circumstances involved Jim protecting his mother from the unpredictable pile of felonious shit known as Peter Halloran.

Soon after their marriage the lovely twenty-one year old Hannah found joyously that she was pregnant. The family celebrated with a special dinner, which Hannah and her mother-in-law prepared together. Neither woman was feeling well. Hannah suffered morning sickness all day long at times, and Mary Halloran didn't really know what was wrong, but she just didn't feel very good these days.

"Now that I've fixed it so don't have to work anymore, Mary, you have nothing but time on your hands to sit around and think about little more than what ails you, that's all that's wrong with you." diagnosed Peter Halloran.

Mary'd had a few heart-to-heart talks with her daughter-in-law, telling her about the birth of her sons and the loss of her three babies, Elizabeth, Bridget and Dennis. Hannah listened politely, but Mary's stories were beginning to frighten her. Her joy at giving birth slowly turned to fear of losing her child. In her second trimester, a difficult time both physically and emotionally, Hannah began to obsess in distressing ways.

She found herself being drawn to the awful and sensational stories that the dailies delighted in printing in an attempt to boost sales of their newspapers.

She couldn't help herself, even though some of these were appalling in nature. In the Courier, a bizarre story appeared about a monomaniacal all-female sect in Russia which operated under an oath of secrecy. These female fanatics had become infamous under the denomination of "Angel-Makers."

The women secretly executed babies who were committed to their charge, generally infants at the breast. Acting either as nurses or as care-takers of illegitimate children, they did away with their charges in any manner which promised the best means against detection. They professed that their mission was to murder for the eternal salvation of the souls of their innocent victims and at the same time to earn for themselves eternal glory. One who was brought to trial was a twenty-eight year old woman who had strangled her own child. The newspaper said that the woman appeared entirely unaffected, and when condemned by the judge, replied simply and with the utmost composure, "Do with me what you will, I am in your hands."

Finishing the news article, Hannah ran to the back porch and threw up in the scrub bucket.

To add to Mary Halloran's burden of illness, Peter Halloran was now old and sick himself, and at times demented. Whatever happened in Oswego Prison three years previous had since changed him for the worse, if such an adversity could be at all possible. Halloran's outbursts put Jim on high alert. Jim not only had to worry about his mother, but his pregnant wife as well. He was a Police Special, and enjoying the work for the most part, except when he walked into a domestic disturbance reminiscent of those of his own past.

Together, the three brothers, Jim, JP, and Daniel were holding up the Halloran's Saloon business, what with Peter out of commission so often, either sick or getting himself in trouble. Only Daniel had any actual enthusiasm for the vocation.

Mary asked her sons one day when the boys had gathered together if they might include Peter in the doings of the Mutuals. Having lost interest in the saloon, he was upstairs in their flat with Mary and Hannah more and more, underfoot, critical, controlling, his nose in their business, making ill-tempered demands.

"Mother, you know that Peter is old and sick. Everybody hates him. He has alienated himself from everyone by his own doings. A third of all the oarsmen are patrolmen or men working for the police department. Geary, Coughlin, Short, Stanton—especially Ed Stanton—all the coppers hate him for attacking you, and because even as a feeble old man he still can't manage to keep himself out of prison. He has a nasty disposition and nobody wants to be around him any more than you do." He looked at his brothers for their approval. "I say, how about if we just kill him?"

The boys all laughed. Their mother didn't.

"Why don't you just pawn him off on Eliza Beatty?" said Jim, suggesting the obvious. "You're her employer. She wanted him at one time. Let her have him. Let her be the one to take care of him now."

Mary just stared in disbelief at her clueless son.

"I think it was you, Jim Sullivan, who effectively put an end to that possibility when you hit her, if you might recall."

It dawned on him then, finally.

Jim had never even considered it before, so wrapped up was he in his own emotions and his loyalty to his mother. Mary Halloran was telling her son that she had not been unhappy in the least about Peter's affair with Eliza Beatty. In truth, she had welcomed it.

Jim Sullivan was feeling exhausted, overwhelmed with the explosive growth of the Mutuals, his new marriage, the new baby on the way, his new police career, keeping an eye on his stepfather, facilitating for his brother, and turning thirty years old. He gave notice to the members that he could no longer be president of the Mutual Rowing Club.

The Mutuals, now numbering one hundred, were shocked. He had led them through their first years like a tornado. The Mutuals dominated both the athletic and social calendars of the First Ward, summer and winter too.

The members had just wrapped up constructing a stunning jewel of a boathouse right behind the Halloran's Saloon facing the river, brought to completion by the formidable dedication and enviable construction skills of three of the constituents: Peter P. Dalton, and police patrolmen John Coughlin and Jim Geary. The Mutual Rowing Club was famed throughout the Northeast U.S. and Canada, and with their new Eastlake-style boathouse they had quickly become the envy of every rowing club in Western New York and Southern Ontario.

The members responded to this crisis in leadership logically by electing Jim's brother, twenty-four year old JP, as the new president. His dedication was almost equal to that of his brother's, and since they lived in the same house together it would be almost like Jim was still president anyway. The club had gotten its feet wet by hosting its first regatta in 1883, but for 1884 they planned to pull out all the stops. They were determined to make the '84 Mutuals Regatta the finest the city had ever seen.

JP resolved to prove his mettle as the new president. He always did love to throw a party.

The family was excited by the club's expansive plans for the gala event, and Mary wrote to her brother James McGrady in Amsterdam to please come visit with his family so they could see for themselves what her sons had accomplished.

The 1884 Mutual Rowing Club Regatta

The Mutual Rowing Club's 1884 Regatta Day was held Sunday, July 13. The dizzying schedule of preparations and meetings that preceded the event were rewarded with one of the grandest affairs of its kind afforded by the season, unprecedented in the city.

Hordes of citizens in their summer Sunday finest flowed down Hamburgh Street past the now-abandoned Union Ironworks Mill like a white tidal wave toward the river. When the Union Ironworks closed down, it left the river and the air far cleaner, and the neighborhood more peaceful, much to the relief of the families who lived tooth and jowl with the furnaces' toxic effects. Most gratifying to Mary Halloran was the silencing of the shrieking Union Ironworks work whistle, a jolting cacophony she had lived with for two decades. It is doubtful had the iron works remained in production that the Mutuals would have ever been established in this location, the environment had been so thoroughly dirtied.

Such a crowd as had not been seen at any aquatic event in many a day gathered at the foot of Hamburgh Street in the bright sun and afternoon heat eagerly anticipating the celebration and contests. All along the banks of the river, on the piers, in the street, in every open window of the boathouse and the neighboring domiciles — even woven tightly into the riggings of the sloops and schooners — people crowded and jostled each other for a place. Scores of boats filled with observers constantly moved about in the water, to the great annoyance and obstruction of the oarsman.

The sophisticated manner in which the entertainment had been advertised attracted a crowd which numbered somewhere in the three thousands. The river bank along the line of the course was packed almost to the last inch of space. The little peninsula on the opposite bank of the slip, called Farmer's Point, was likewise crowded, and spectators who had come down the harbor from the upper part of the city lined either bank.

A score of sailors perched up in the rigging of the majestic Edward B. Harris watching the sport like so many birds on the telegraph wires, while the captain — happily puffing his pipe — took it all in with his first officer from the deck below. A huge old laker was tied up opposite the starting point, and the sailors viewed the scene from her rigging as well, with evident satisfaction.

The river in the vicinity was filled with boats of all sizes and characters. Two large fishing boats attracted much attention from the fact that one of them contained a colored man who discoursed popular negro ballads accompanied by his violin, while his partner shook the bones. The other boat made just as much noise, but of a different character, as the sounds were actuated by fondness for beer rather than music.

The Mutuals' newly painted boathouse at the head of South Street, topped by its sturdy little domed tower, was decorated in flying colors, the flagstaff being topped by the stars and stripes. A line of flags of all nations, donated by the

Altman Bros. Store on Main Street, was strung gaily from the boathouse across the river. In the midst of all these fluttering colors the Adelphi Band, having been engaged to furnish music from the tower surmounting the clubhouse, discoursed popular airs including Sailing, Sailing, Blow The Man Down, and many Gilbert & Sullivan tunes.

The course was laid out from a point in the river a little below the boathouse to a buoy anchored three quarters of a mile to the north, and included the return. The visiting crews who participated in the regatta were the Queen Citys, West Ends, Buffalos, Celtics, and North Buffalos. Not a word of contention or dissatisfaction marred the enjoyment of the day. The water was quite rough, but everyone considered that it was as good for the one as for the other, and so there was no complaint. Those attending were furnished with programmes in which the color of the caps worn by the various crews were given so the teams could easily be picked out by anyone. To raise funds, Jim had the idea of printing tiny paper pennants in the colors of the competing clubs to sell. The members had spent hours at the last meeting gluing them to toothpicks, and now hundreds of people were sporting them in their lapels, hat bands and tucked behind their ears.

The first competition was the four-oared race between the two crews of the Mutuals. The first crew included the Sullivan brothers: John P. Sullivan, bow; Ed Stanton, No. 2; Patrick Nunan, No. 3; and Jim Sullivan, stroke. Not incidentally, their scull, named the Jim Sullivan in honor of the club's founder, had the moniker painted boldly on its bow.

The second crew pitted the Sullivans against their younger brother Daniel Halloran, bow; and Louis Zimmerman, No. 2 ; Dan Crowley. No. 3, and Michael Kelleher; stroke. This scull had been christened with the name Gus.

Mary Halloran had been feeling ill earlier in the day and planned to watch all the hubbub ensuing on the river below from her perch high in the upper-story windows at No. 16 Hamburgh. But as the crowds gathered and gaiety filled the air and the music echoed over the waters from the famous Adelphi Band playing atop the boathouse tower, Mary became infected with the enthusiasm and festivity of the occasion.

Her brother James McGrady had arrived from Amsterdam by rail the day before with his wife Margaret, their five daughters, and their only son, John. The Halloran-Sullivan house was delightfully noisy and full. Mary decided to put on her prettiest summer frock and her giant straw bonnet in the latest style featuring a very generous front brim. She tied the ribbon under her chin to secure it against the stiff breeze and descended the stairs to join Hannah and her brother and his family in the crowds.

Mary took Hannah's arm and the two made their way carefully through the throng to the boathouse, where the McGrady clan stood and watched with great interest, especially son John McGrady. Daniel Halloran stood at the ready in his rowing tights and singlet, commiserating with a beaming Doc Greene. When the two spotted her, Daniel ran and hugged his mother. "You look beautiful, Ma!", he gushed, happy to see her up and about with eyes sparkling.

Jim and JP had already set out in their scull for their starting place on the water when they spotted Mary, and the entire crew hollered and whooped a big hello to their most ardent admirer. Mary excitedly waved and shouted back, bouncing on her toes. She flushed with pride seeing the scull emblazoned with the name of her eldest son.

"If only his father were here to see this!" she bubbled to Doc Greene.

The doc looked at her acting so happy. He remembered the knife in her neck and sewing her up. He could detect the scar, but the minor mark hardly betrayed the brutality of its origination. He recalled driving Mary and her late husband and the children in his carriage to the depot back in '61 to see Pvt. John Sullivan off to war. He remembered saying his goodbyes to the soldier. So much sadness in her past to at last see her so happy at this moment.

A lovely constant Lake Erie breeze was buffeting and cooling a grateful crowd but roughening the water's surface and creating a problematic headwind for the oarsmen. Jim cursed it. Altman's line of flags of all nations, stretched across the river, snapped like a hundred firecrackers, their dancing colors frantic in the bright sun.

Daniel Halloran eased into his scull as Mike Kelleher beckoned and Dan Crowley shouted in his best mock-Irish accent, "Hallo, Mrs. Halloran! Tis grand t' see ye on this beautiful day!" They took their place for the start. Peter Halloran, having a good day himself, stayed behind to man the bar at the family saloon. As he predicted, business was very brisk, much to his pocketbook's delight.

Doc Greene gave Mary a big smile and took her hand. Hannah and James and Margaret McGrady and their son and five girls joined them. They all stood together to watch the race, trading comments and appraisals. As Mary concentrated on the preparations, Doc Greene stole looks at her, troubled by what he had now concluded about her condition. Hannah noticed him studying her mother-in-law and detected the concern on Doc's face. The gun signaled the start of the heat, and they were off. Mary Halloran smiled broadly at seeing all her sons together, competing wildly with one another as thousands of admirers cheered them on. She was in heaven.

The Sullivan crew pulled out ahead and was almost two full lengths ahead at the turn. Daniel Halloran exerted himself to his limits, so wanting to beat his brothers at their own game, especially with their mother watching. The Sullivan scull was far ahead at the finish, and made the course in 9:30 to the Halloran crew's time of 9:50, but the race was given to the Halloran crew on account of an improper turn made by the Sullivan crew at the stake boat. This race had been a match to settle which was the better of the two crews, and $40 a side was put up by the club.

Nineteen-year-old Daniel had grown up in the shadow of his two older bothers, and while he gloried in the upset, he knew that his brothers rowed the faster race. Next time he'd be sure to prove his resolve and take his just victory without the aid of a penalty.

The next event was a double-clinker race between Michael Kelleher and James Egan of the Mutuals, and Dan Crowley and Louis Zimmerman of the same club. Crowley and Zimmerman won the race in 13 minutes. Prizes—$3 and $2.

The single-scull race between Thomas Dray of the Celtics and Dan Crowley of the Mutuals proved to be one of the most exciting in the regatta. Dray had for some years back enjoyed the reputation of champion single-sculler of Buffalo, and Crowley was by no means an easy man to pass. The start was a good one but the cheers seemed to be principally on Dray's side. When the sculls returned in sight, however, Crowley, much to the surprise of the crowd, was ahead, making the race in twelve minutes, while Dray was eight seconds behind.

When Dray came up near the judge's raft a disappointed admirer asked him what was the matter. With exasperation in his voice and perspiration rolling down his face like Niagara, be held up a small bottle and yawped, "That's what lost the race for me! I thought that was oil in the bottle and took it to grease the slides of the seat, and I'll be hanged if it isn't varnish!"

Dan Crowley looked at his Mutual club mates and winked.

The crowds were in a highly festive mood and much socializing was taking place between events. Ladies in full skirts, half-sleeves and wide-brimmed hats piled high with artificial flowers and fruits carefully shielded their white skin under parasols and brollys so as not to acquire the hue of farmhands. Gentlemen had shirtsleeves of white or sky blue rolled up and their colorful suspenders displayed. They tipped forward the brims of their caps and sennit straw boaters to cut the sun's glare, many sporting the tiny pennants tucked into their headbands to indicate their favored club. A few sported the newly fashionable Ayscough dark eyeglasses to cut the glare of the sun; since their eyes could not be read, these individuals were watched suspiciously by the police officers in attendance. People jostled carefully for a good position, no one wishing to end up in the dirty river smelling of oil, iron and dead fish.

Next, the water was cleared as far as possible and the roaring, screaming, side-splitting highlight of the day took place. Seven half-nude boys with as many wash tubs and paddles were brought forth and their race began. There was a panic at the starting gun and in their rush to shove off, many of the little fellows upset and were obliged to empty their tubs and begin again. Sometimes the boys were the ones on top and at other times their tubs were. At one point both tubs and boys were lost to view for so long a time that the shouts of laughter from the crowd were turned to cries of alarm. Soon enough though they came back in sight. Out of the seven, three little fellows made the voyage across the river and back with very few disasters. The winner, William O'Dell, was given a dollar prize, and Daniel Driscoll, second best, received a ticket to the Mutuals' upcoming picnic.

A tug-of-war in boats, something exceedingly novel in the line of boating, called forth as much interest as any other attraction presented. There were two double-clinker boats to a side. At the very outset the coupling rope of the first boat was snapped asunder and the second crew began taking their opponents, or rather half of them, downstream. The break repaired, the crews went to work again, the first crew winning at the end of five minutes' time by steady pulling.

At the close of the races a Hirayama Day Shell, a previously unknown style of pyrotechnical manufacture, especially intended for use during daylight, was sent aloft. Exploding at an attitude of about 300 feet the shell scattered forth a number of designs cut in bright colored paper. These figures proved to be quite artistic in design, and when each became inflated with air, representations were seen of fish, turtles, elephants, Japanese women, men and children. The toy-like bits of paper danced in the sky in most grotesque fashion. Big and little elephants, turtles and alligators floated away into space to the delight and wonder of the awe-struck crowd.

Quite a number of spectators, including members of the opposing clubs, took a look-see inside the Mutual's handsome boathouse. The parlor had been newly finished and decorated. The walls were ornamented with professional oil paintings and easy chairs and other furniture arranged about the room. The floor was covered with rugs of varied patterns purchased from the city's Syrians. The center of attention in the room was a color lithograph by George Rees beautifully framed in oak and entitled Edward "Ned" Hanlan of Toronto—

Champion Sculler of the World. Hannah gazed at the pictured figure of Hanlan admiringly. Mary and the pregnant Hannah, fatigued by the sun and the excitement, occupied two upholstered chairs. They commented in quiet tones about the rubberneckers milling around.

As the brothers held court and shook hands with admirers, someone caught Jim's eye. He looked up. He couldn't quite believe who was approaching him. In a smashing white linen London summer suit, fashionably rumpled, with his lovely wife on his arm and two small children in tow, was Ned Hanlan, the champion himself, in the flesh.

"We took the train across the International Bridge to come have a look for ourselves, Jim," he said casually. Ned shook Jim's hand just as if they were old friends. "Everybody's talking about the Mutuals," enthused Hanlan.

Jim stammered and Hannah swooned, for she didn't know such a handsome man actually existed outside of the fashion illustrations in the weeklies.

"We're hoping we'll get to see your club up in Toronto soon. We'll be excited to have you at the Point."

"You bet!" replied Jim, for once at a loss for words. Ned yet looked wan from a recent bout with typhoid that almost claimed his life. Jim wanted to mention something about it in support, but decided against doing so for fear it might come out sounding wrong.

"You drew quite a turnout today. Not nearly like the 25,000 that come to see us in Toronto, but..." Hanlan ribbed good-naturedly.

"Well, Ned. I'm proud to tell you that I was one of your 25,000 this year," Jim responded with a big smile. "And I'll be there among them again, just to see you row."

"Oh no you won't. I want you out on the water with me, Sullivan, not sipping lemonade on the veranda of the Toronto Rowing Club!" He put out his hand again, and they shook. "Hope to see you again soon."

And with that Ned and his family said their goodbyes and melted into the crowd.

If Jim was on Cloud Nine, then Jim's cousin John McGrady's jaw was on the floor. His cousins had founded this club, organized this fantastic event, and are in a friendly way with the World's Champion. McGrady thought to himself, we live just steps away from the Mohawk River ourselves. We can do this in Amsterdam too.

Mary Halloran gauged the curious crowd's oohing and ahhing. She felt a lovely warmth fill her heart which obscured the memories of bad times past. She wondered to herself, after everything her boys had been put through while growing up, how they managed to turn out so admiringly. As modest a person as she was, it didn't occur to Mary that it was she who was responsible for that.

An ostentatiously-attired Fingy Conners suddenly approached the Sullivan brothers, Hannah, and JP's fiancé Annie Saulter. He firmly gripped the shoulder of his young protégé, David Nugent, Hannah's eighteen year old brother. Fingy's increasingly disenfranchised stepbrother Dennis Hurley lagged unhappily behind.

Estranged siblings Hannah and David exchanged chilly nods.

"Hey, JP! Ain't yer big cousin gotten here yet?" bellowed Fingy.

JP jabbed his brother Jim playfully and winked. "Just watch," he muttered softly.

"Uh, you mean big cousin John? Yep, of course, Fing! He's right over there," responded JP, brightly.

JP called out, "Hey Cousin John! Come on over here a minute. I want you to meet somebody special!"

Not hiding his excitement, Fingy preened himself nervously as he gawked about, searching the crowd.

"I don't see him, JP."

Cousin John approached and thrust out his hand.

"How do you do? I'm John P. McGrady. And you are...?"

JP, smiling gleefully, introduced the men.

"Cousin, this here is Jim Conners, who I've told you so much about. Fingy, this is cousin John."

Fingy wasn't amused. McGrady nodded hello, then continued on his way.

JP and Jim could not stop laughing.

"Yeah, funny one, JP! I was askin' fer the other one, yer famous fightin' cousin, John L."

"Oh! You mean John L. Sullivan, the World Champ! Oh. Nope, sorry Fingy. John L. couldn't make it today. He's in training for his next bout as we speak. But he's due for a visit next month sometime, I believe. I'll let you know just as soon as I find out when he plans to be in town."

Fingy didn't hide his chagrin at being the butt of JP's joke.

As the men continued talking, Hannah gave her young brother David a critical once-over. She took him aside.

"You been behavin' yourself, Davey, I hope?"

David took umbrage at his sister's patronizing.

"Tend t' yer own knittin', sis! Y'ain't me mother!"

Hannah's temper flared.

"And Fingy Conners isn't our father -- nor are you his son! You're barely even his fart-catcher! You just remember that! You just remember where you come from, David!"

Teenaged David seethed at his sister's meddling.

Fingy continued his conversation with the brothers.

"Yeah, you do that, Jim. Say, JP, what's this I hear 'bout youse buyin' the house right next door to yer old man? No!"

"Yes. It's for me and Annie, for when we get married. We can't be livin' in the same house with Halloran, that's for sure! Jim's poor Hannah is already at the end of her rope puttin' up with that old pile o' shite! Livin' with Halloran would tax the bonds of anybody's marriage."

Jim and Hannah shot JP a dirty look. Fingy looked puzzled.

"Then why'd ye buy the house right next door to the old bastard?"

'Oh, Fingy -- you know me and Jim have to keep a close eye on Halloran. You recall his history with our mother!"

JP comically stabbed his finger into his neck, to Jim's displeasure.

"Oh yeah. Forgot. Listen, JP, I can't be stickin' round fer long. I'm buyin' a brewery and I gotta go sign some papers. Jus' wanted t' come by t' tell ye I'm proud o' youse. You 'n' yer brother. Look at all these people here! The rowin' club is thrivin' jus' like youse said it would! It's just grand! And it's all because o' youse two. So's I want me 'n' youse t' sit down 'n' have us a little talk together later on, JP. Just youse and me. About yer future."

Fingy began to walk off.

JP, puzzled, called after him.

"Wait! What do you mean? What about my future, Fing?"

Fingy stopped and turned.

"Well... fer one t'ing, JP, t' me eye -- jus' lookin' 'round at alls ye got goin' on here — yer future's lookin' just as sunny as this very fine day. Youse recall when I tried me damndest t' get rid o' old Jack White last year when I tried t' put meself ag'inst 'im fer Alderman? He trounced me. We all know that bastard's got more friends than I meself got. But I don't t'ink White's got more friends than youse. Especially seein' all these happy people here t'day. I been t'inkin' -- maybe I should try runnin' youse fer public office next time instead o' meself! Now youse — youse could beat Jack White!

Fingy winked. JP looked excited. Jim appeared concerned. Fingy nodded in the direction of the massive crowd.

"Git yerself out there 'n' shake some new hands t'day, JP. Build yerself some bridges."

Fingy and David Nugent departed. Dennis Hurley waited to be invited along but the invitation wasn't forthcoming. Embarrassed, he trailed like a neglected puppy.

Hannah called after her brother.

"G'bye, Davey. You be good now."

David Nugent's sole response was a dismissive grunt.

Bless Me Father, For I Have Sinned

Fingy Conners had spent only about forty minutes at the Regatta, making aware his presence to those who might best benefit from knowing it.

He reminded those he spoke to that they might wish to come by one of his saloons, for he now had three. Sunday was an important business day. His saloons would be jammed with men desperate to work the following week, spending money they didn't have on beer and whisky they didn't want to curry favor with a man they didn't like, all for the slim chance they might be chosen for a little work that would barely feed their families.

The agonized wives and hollow-stomached children of these men, expecting the breadwinner to win bread, worried every day as to his whereabouts long after his work day was finished. Children fretted about their father coming home so late night after night, so very drunk.

Domestic battles ensued.

The men, caught at odds between a tyrannical unyielding taskmaster and their own anguished families, most of the time took their frustrations out on whichever family member was unlucky enough to be within arm's reach, as if that poor soul's existence wasn't already wretched enough. Police were called to the home. The women sobbed to their priests in the confessional in church on Saturday afternoons. Some good Catholic women had even been driven to selling themselves in order to provide food for their babies.

By 1884, any man seeking employment on the Buffalo docks would have to visit Fingy Conners' saloon to apply, for by this time he controlled virtually the entire workforce. While waiting to see if they would be hired, applicants would take notice that those men who bought drinks, food and cigars at Fingy's saloon were given a job straightaway. Those who didn't, weren't.

It was not long before all realized that unless they spent money with Fingy they would not be employed.

Moreover, they were required to report to Fingy's saloons to receive their pay, which under Conners' predatory contracting had been slashed by forty percent, providing him a hefty take as middleman.

Fingy Conners had clamped a stranglehold on his own people, in his own First Ward, and refused to let go.

In the days before Fingy's system had been applied the methods of employing workers were disorganized, random and uneven. Previously, laborers unhappy working for one shipper could simply switch to another. By this ploy they were able to keep wages high, since shippers with a pressing need would pay more to have their ships serviced. That all began to end the day Fingy Conners entered the picture.

The contractor's consolidation provided an unchallenged position from which he alone made all the decisions. The First Ward's workers soon found themselves yoked under Fingy Conners' mercilessness. Not only did he have the only say in who would receive work, but he held back a 20% portion of every worker's pay until the end of the season as leverage against any hint of uprising or conflict. He referred to it as the men's "strike insurance premium."

Not content with this heinous system, Fingy Conners felt his workers were not spending nearly enough of their pauper's salaries in his saloons. The laborers, under the belief that their babies needed food and such, only spent what cash they could with Fingy, which he quickly deemed insufficient.

So Fingy invented the brass check.

Fingy conceived the idea of issuing credit in the form of brass checks so the men who'd already spent all their money could better compete with their opponents to buy more drink, and secure their getting hired again the following week. The amount of checks spent was deducted from their next pay. When the day came to hire again for the next week, Conners would count the brass checks. The men with the most checks were the men who had spent the most money at Fingy's saloons, and the first chosen to work. Pity their starving families.

One of the outcomes of boys left virtually fatherless due to Conners' system of holding men hostage at his saloons during their off-hours, was the rise of youth gangs. Life in the First Ward began to take a more troubling turn in 1881, and things had not been at all good before that.

Hoodlums began hitting men, women and even children over the head for the smallest prize. Their favorite haunts were the streets surrounding Conners' saloons, since his establishments were always awash with desperate men competing to get themselves chosen for work. Drunken workingmen, obliged to spend what little money they earned on beer and liquor rather than milk for their children, staggered out into the night, never to be the same again once the gangs got hold of them. Thugs cruelly beat and broke them for mere pennies, or just as often, for nothing at all, for usually there was nothing left in the pockets of these downtrodden souls except lint.

The residents in the First Ward began to fear leaving their houses, not only at night, but in the bright light of day as well. Children were gathered together in groups and escorted en masse to and from school by organized armies of mothers and grandparents armed with clubs and walking staffs, who then returned home again as a unit for mutual protection.

Buffalo's penny sheets were filled with gory accounts of fruitless assaults, attacks that left men unable to work, or dead, their families defenseless in the face of the most dire of circumstances. The daily journals never ran short of gruesome accounts of suicides both successful and failed, of mothers killing their babies and themselves out of despair, of entire families drowning themselves together in the canals, of cruel crimes of the most violent and animalistic nature perpetrated upon the weakest, poorest, and hungriest members of society.

Fingy Conners was remorselessly manipulating entire communities into serfdom. A full quarter century after many of these very same men had marched off to war in the name of freedom and emancipation of the negro slaves, they themselves were locked down in virtual servitude. This wasn't the all-too-familiar scenario of one race claiming superiority over another in a contest of domination. It was Irish enslaving Irish, a people who'd recently escaped a 700-year history of enslavement by the British in their own homeland, finding themselves caught up yet again, as anthropophagous a catastrophe as could be imagined.

The railroads and shipping lines rapidly took notice of Conners' virtuoso corralling of a once-volatile work force. The docks began to hum like a finely oiled machine, profiting everyone involved except the workers themselves. Fingy was on his way to his ultimate goal of controlling virtually all shipping on both land and water, not just in Buffalo, but in Duluth, Minneapolis, Chicago, and Detroit. His saloon boss system quickly made him a millionaire. None of those corporations who profited by his methods much cared how he went about it; they were just pleased as could be with the favorable and harmonious transformation that Fingy's stewardship had brought about for their businesses.

Fingy Conners hadn't been to confession since he had made his First Communion at age seven. But as his own city ward rose up to rant and rail against him for his crushing subjugation of them, as rocks flew at him from out of the shadows at night, as decaying vegetables and rotten eggs were hurled by furious women spitting vile invectives at him in broad daylight as he raced down the street to escape them, as human waste was dumped stinking onto his waiting carriage seat, he began to experience vivid nightmares of burning in hell, forever and ever, and ever and ever, endlessly.

In these dreams he felt his skin splitting open and his eyeballs vaporizing just as must have his stepsister Julia Hayes, the memory of whose terrible death his riches had not quite wholly deleted from his mind. She had never done anything to hurt him. She had dedicated herself to caring for their brother Dennis in the days following his near-fatal beating, a fight instigated by Fingy himself. And then, heroically, in her final minutes of existence on this earth, she saved their brother's life. Increasingly Fingy Conners' dreams were being kidnapped by her tragedy as he tried to achieve restful sleep. He had been successful at giving the entire affair little thought until quite recently.

But these days even a quick catnap was no longer tranquil.

To distract his turbulent mind from unthinkable thoughts, Fingy went looking for some fun in his saloon on payday. He approached a skinny young man named Pat McMahon who was twenty years old and wore a distinctive eye patch.

"Say laddie, youse got yerself some little ones t' home, aintcha?"

"Yes sir, Mr. Conners," said Skinny Pat. "I do. Two girls."

"Well, youse see, it's this way: I only got one place wot's remainin' on next week's work gang, and it's now between youse and that big fella over there."

Fingy pointed out a much larger man opposite.

"Youse gotta know that I favor me best customers like youse wit' work, but that big fella's already two drinks ahead o' youse now."

"Mr. Conners, sir, I used up all me brass tokens. I'm flat busted. Me littlest one's sick. I ain't got no more money."

Fingy reached in his pocket and produced five brass checks.

Tell ye what, laddie boy," began Fingy Conners in his most fatherly tone. "Uh -- what's yer name ag'in?"

"McMahon, sir."

"Yeah. Here's some brass checks, McMahon. These'll get youse drinks on credit, so's youse'll be able t' overtake that big fella and win the job. I kin take the cost outa yer pay next week. Here. Take 'em."

"But Mr. Conners, I can't afford to feed me family on what little yer payin' me now. I can't go into debt even more!"

Without warning Fingy brutally smacked the frail boy in the face. Skinny Pat toppled over backwards in his chair.

"Well, it's up t' youse, laddie!" bellowed the bully. "Some money comin' in's better'n no money at all comin' in! Up yer dick, caffler!"

Fingy slammed the five brass checks violently down onto the table and walked off. Skinny Pat, flat on his back, cradled his bloody nose.

Fingy headed in the direction of the big fella.

Fingy's stepbrother Dennis stepped from behind the bar to help Skinny Pat McMahon off the floor.

Dennis whispered something in McMahon's ear on the QT as he raised him up.

Fingy grabbed the big fella's shoulder.

"Say, big fella. Youse see that skinny laddie over there by the stove wit' me brother, bleedin' a bit? Well, he's two drinks ahead o' youse at this point, an' I only got one open spot remainin' on the gang next week that's unloadin' the Pride o' Minnesota. I'd like fer youse t' claim that spot because o' yer impressive size 'n all, but sorry t' say, looks like that skinny boyo might just steal the work from ye."

"Me, I just traded off me last token, and me wife's no longer speakin' t' me as it is, Mr. Conners. Ain't got but a penny."

"That's no worry, big fella. I got a generous heart. I can give youse credit usin' these here brass checks. You kin trade 'em fer drinks t'day, an' next week I'll take the cost outa yer wages." Fingy patted the big fella's shoulder forcefully.

"I wanna help ye out, big fella. Ye can do twice the liftin' compared to that skinny laddie, but he's runnin' ahead o' youse right now."

With an anguished foreboding, the big fella accepted the checks.

Skinny Pat McMahon brooded head down inside his home, a barely-floating one-room canal boat listing precariously in the fetid Commercial slip, shared by three families. Miserable children cried. Hanging tattered blankets divided the dank claustrophobic space. Pat's wife lingered close by, deeply troubled and drained of all hope. Skinny Pat sat alone at a small lopsided table illuminated by a dim solitary flickering oil lamp.

Pistol in hand, he pondered.

Drops of blood from his squashed nose plopped heavily down onto the gun grip, propelling minute red splatter onto his shirt..

An hour later, Fingy and six lackeys exited the saloon, carousing. Fingy called back over his shoulder to Dennis mockingly.

"Stepbrother? T'ink youse kin manage t' keep customers from walkin' off wit' half the furniture and most the liquor whilst I'm gone?"

The group laughed derisively.

It was difficult for Dennis to pinpoint exactly when or why he had become the object of so much of Fingy's scorn, but he traced the onset of the change to a short time after the fire that killed their sister Julia. Fingy made it abundantly clear he never liked Julia; even so, Dennis had it in his head that somehow Fingy blamed him for her death.

If I wasn't injured in that brawl, both me and Julia might have gotten out alive, he oft-times thought to himself. It hadn't yet occurred to him that it was Fingy who had instigated the brawl that left Dennis with permanent incapacities in the first place. Nor did he entertain any notion that Fingy resented being deprived of the $5,000 insurance payout had Dennis conveniently perished in the fire as well.

As the group headed up the street raising Cain, shots were fired. The men scattered.

"Oy! Kennedy! Davey!" Fingy screamed. "Git them sons o' bitches! Git their whole damned family! Git 'im all an' bring 'em t' me!

The bullet came so close to his skull that Fingy grabbed his ear fully expecting to find blood. His henchmen drew their pistols and ran in pursuit of the phantom gunman obscured in the blackness.

As they scrambled in the dark, shouting threats and oaths to flush out the culprit and leaving Fingy unattended, another shot rang out from under a parked dray very close by, hitting his shoulder. Fingy screamed in anger and fear.

Skinny Pat McMahon anonymously evaporated into the night.

Fingy's men brought their boss back into the saloon and removed his coat, only to find a raw groove carved on the surface of his deltoid where the bullet had grazed the flesh. It hardly even bled, so they poured some whisky on it, placed a bandage over the wound, toasted Fingy's good fortune, and put him to bed. Then they went out, remaining up all night beating the bushes, rousing the sleeping, shouting vows of vengeance, intent on finding their man. But as thoroughly as Fingy's human mastiffs scoured under planked walkways and atop sleeping First Warders' roofs, the shooter was nowhere to be found.

Throughout that night Fingy awakened continually in a pool of his own sweat, gasping for breath, a crushing sensation compressing his chest. He felt as though he might be having a heart attack. He got up and poured himself a whiskey. Then another.

Fingy Conners had always controlled his drink, something his father had drilled into his head as the son of a saloon proprietor.

"Yer own drinkin' will destroy yer business, Jimmy. Have yerself one, and then stop. Otherwise they'll steal ye blind and ye'll be ruined. We didn't build this business all our lives just to have it wrecked for us because our son can't control his drink."

For once he broke with his father's counsel. He needed a few drinks to loosen the steel cables that were squeezing his heart so cruelly that he could hardly suck in a full breath.

Fingy continued to be agitated and disquieted throughout the entire next day. He drank continuously, attempting to ease his torment. His men, never having seen him drunk, were watchful. Finally in the early afternoon, Conners told his henchmen that he was taking his carriage home to crawl into bed. All present thought that a good idea. Only a half-hearted attempt was made to stop him from driving himself. Fingy stumbled intoxicated into his rig, alone, and passing his own house on Elk street, set out for downtown and St. Joseph's Cathedral.

No one knew him there, he believed. He crept into the magnificent church and waited in the dim light for the first available opening at the unfamiliar confessional. A recently installed priest was hearing the guilty outpourings of his newly acquired flock, sins both venial and mortal.

The priest, an eager adventurer in his youth, had come to believe it was his destiny to live an audacious life. To the enormous pride of the men in his family, he had won a competitive examination for entrance into West Point Military Academy. Some time thereafter, having been blessed with the miracle of a heavenly apparition one portentous afternoon, he forsook his military ambition to instead study for the priesthood.

He matriculated at the University of Innsbruck in Austria and the College of Propaganda in Rome. On his European journey along his priestly path, he encountered street urchins, pederasts, opium addicts, violent sadists, and prostitutes of both sexes; he had heard and witnessed it all.

Nothing shocked him.

The priest could smell the whiskey through the screen that obscured the face of the confessor on the opposite side.

"Sir? Are you drunk?"

"Uh, um, a bit, Father. Y' see, I took a bullet last night, and the pain is somethin' terrible, 'n' , uh, I needed t' partake of a little somethin' t' ease me by."

The priest weighed the situation for a moment, then said, "Proceed, my son."

Fingy began his confession clumsily and in a loud voice. It had been a long time. The priest gently counseled him to lower his tone so that others would not overhear.

In a rambling, drunken and psychotic rant lasting a full half hour, Fingy Conners spilled the secrets of years past, the most dramatic of which, involving his family tragedies, so shook the priest that he lost his composure. The depth and breadth of the man's confessions were so vile and so astonishing that it caused the cleric to involuntarily gasp. He found himself shaken to the core by the primitive nature of the man's staggering revelations.

At long last the confessor concluded his venting.

Unsettled, the priest reluctantly absolved the man of his sins, unsure exactly what kind of contrition such heinous acts could possibly require. Trying to disguise his alarm, the priest urged the man to pay a visit to the police headquarters a few steps away to confess his story to them as well. Upon hearing this completely unexpected directive, Fingy Conners exploded angrily from the confessional and stumbled still shit-faced out of the booth in the direction of the altar.

Wasn't the confessional a guaranteed sanctuary, free from the intrusions of any other but the confessor and his priest? Wasn't this priest bound by Church law to keep what was told him strictly, privately, completely to himself?

It seemed as if the priest was implying that what Fingy Conners always believed to be true about what was divulged in the confessional might not be. Fingy was completely unprepared for his confessor's horrified reaction. He fully expected to be forgiven, imposed a penance, and quickly sent on his way.

The priest had come from a privileged urbane background. Unlike most clerics who had seen far less of the world's underbelly than he, this man of God possessed the intelligence, faith, and arrogance in his own experience and judgement to factor into church policies his own standards of morality. In the distant past he'd found himself deeply torn between church policy and social responsibility. This was no longer the case in this regard.

Fingy panicked and bolted, immediately tripping and colliding into a group of timid women awaiting their turn to confess how many impure thoughts they had allowed to linger that week. Seeing that he was headed in the wrong direction, Conners turned on his heels, and hightailing it toward the exit, tripped and took a hard fall.

The priest peeked from behind his curtained portal at the commotion outside to view for himself exactly what kind of creature was capable of such horrific deeds just as Fingy raised himself up from the cold marble onto which he had just been splayed. The priest would never forget that antediluvian face, nor the man's coarse linguistics.

The following day, Conners suffered a mortal hangover and ineradicable humiliation over perhaps making the greatest blunder of his life. Angered into a state of near-conniption, Fingy sent his amputator Kennedy to St. Joseph's Cathedral to learn the identities of the priests established there.

A towering uniformed patrolman with Aryan features, six foot three or thereabouts, collared Kennedy out front and threw him brutally into the street, ripping his trousers and tearing the skin from his knees.

"Get your sorry Irish buggered ass back to that First Ward gutter yer mother-whore crawled out of! If I ever see you in my precinct again, I'll be draggin' you by yer balls directly to the workhouse, that is if you survive me clubbin' you senseless along the route!"

September 24, 1884
A Night At The Theater

Mary Halloran sighed loudly as she deciphered with some difficulty a letter from her brother James McGrady in Amsterdam N.Y. She became quite upset at its contents, which included a news clipping from the Amsterdam Daily Democrat, along with a dash of guilt.

Mary's brother was asking her if she might impose upon her patrolman son Jim to intervene in this latest drama involving his cousin John P. McGrady. Mary felt trapped by her brother's request. He made it a point to remind Mary that she, although understandably due to illness, had not attended his only son's wedding in May, but that he and his family had recently traveled all the way to Buffalo for the Mutuals Regatta. Mary simply had not been well enough to make the long rail journey to the Johnstown nuptials, and neither Jim nor JP had any desire to accept the wedding invitation, so disheartened were they by their cousin's ongoing disasters.

Jim had already told his mother what he thought of the hoodlum and of his reckless shenanigans of the past few years.

"He keeps bad company, Ma, because he likes keeping bad company. You just have to accept that nobody is making cousin John do anything he doesn't want to do. He likes trouble and if there isn't any to be found in the immediate vicinity, he'll go looking for it until he's satisfied. Poor Kittie! You'd think that having a new wife at home now would have instilled some responsibility and settled him down. It seems to have had no such effect."

"Jimmy, please. Johnny's me brother's only boy. Ye should try and do something."

"Ma, what can I do? I have only been a policeman for a year, and I have no influence on matters in Buffalo, let alone Amsterdam. Anyway, what is it he's done this time?"

Mary scanned her brother's version of the incident, which did not seem to differ too much from the newspaper account. Then she looked back at her son.

"Me brother says that Johnny and his friend Parm and their friends all got drunk and decided to attend the theater. John apparently wasn't happy with the quality of the performance and began criticizing the actors loudly from his seat in the audience. This led to a policeman tryin' to arrest 'im, which caused all his friends—the news article says there were thirty of 'em—to pile on the policeman. The members of the audience were none too pleased with havin' the boys spoil their theater night, and soon half the men in the audience were throwin' punches at Johnny's lads. Things got out of hand and the entire theater erupted into a brawl. A lot of faces were bruised and a lot of gentlemen's fine theater clothing got torn."

Jim couldn't keep his disapproving countenance any longer and burst out laughing, imagining the insane scene.

"That's our Johnny!" he said.

"Here, Jim. As the newsies like to say, 'read all about it,'" said Mary, handing him the clipping. Jim pulled up a chair and began reading out loud just as JP walked into the room. The newspaper had placed the story dead center at the top of the page where not even a blind man could miss it.

ROWDIES ON A RAMPAGE.
Baker & Farron Performance Interrupted by a Fight In The Gallery.

John P. McGrady went to the theater in the company with Frank Parmentier, more commonly known as "Parm" last night. It is to be hoped he will in the future be more careful in the selection of his company or refrain from accepting his freely-given advice to kick up a row. As it chanced both had imbibed rather too often in the early part of the evening and there was just liquor enough inside them to create a desire to criticize the performance out loud. It is not known exactly to what canon of dramatic art Mr. McGrady holds, in forming his opinion of a performance, but it is certain that his expression of his views were frank. Talking in the gallery so loudly as to disturb players or the audience is expressly forbidden by Manager Neff, and Special Policeman Woodruff, who is stationed in the gallery to prevent disorders from occurring there, has strict orders not to allow it.

Observing McGrady's proneness to talk out loud, Neff went up to him and cautioned him against it. Shortly after, about ten o'clock, during the third act, Farron's character asked Baker's who was going to be elected. This put McGrady on his political nerve and remembering the enthusiasm he had seen exhibited at the depot in the afternoon, he shouted, "Blaine!"

This was too much, and Woodruff came down and asked McGrady to come up one side as he wanted to talk to him, thinking in this way to get him away from Parmentier and keep him quiet.

McGrady went in spite of Parmentier's advice not to, but on getting out to the aisle, repented and said "What in —— do you want of me?" and tore the left lapel from Woodruff's coat. Woodruff saw that it was necessary to put him out, but Parmentier and about thirty others of their comrades present thought differently. Springing out of their seats they made a dive toward Woodruff and his prisoner. They were now on the right side of the gallery and a free fight from here all the way downstairs into the lobby took place amid much excitement, the people all rising from their seats and the play being stopped entirely. Woodruff faced the crowd and dragged McGrady to the head of the stairs where he got a firmer hold on him and hurried him down. Once on the ground floor the cowardly roughs "gave it to him" from all sides. Woodruff was struck behind the ears and kicked twice, once in the ribs and once in the leg. "Bite him, McGrady!" yelled Parmentier, and the dramatic critic fastened his teeth to the policeman's forehead. The latter raised his locust to club the man who was chewing him, when the leather strap was broken by a violent wrench from behind and the club torn from his grasp. Finally someone separated the two men and McGrady was taken by sympathizing friends to the Globe Hotel.

Woodruff, it is said on good authority has an old grudge against McGrady and so was a little too fast in ordering him about. "fresh" and a "crank" are epithets applied to him by McGrady's friends. Manager Nell is criticized for not making more effort to quell the disturbance.

Officer Firth this morning arrested McGrady. Application has been made to Judge Westbrook to take the matter before the grand jury.

Jim's amusement turned to disgust when he read the part about John McGrady biting the police officer.

JP was none too entertained by his cousin's latest brush with the law either.

"What is it with that lad biting everyone?" exclaimed JP. "Remember when I was about twelve and they came to visit and he bit me on the back and I ended up in bed with a fever for a week? Only little girls bite!"

Mary did remember that, well enough. The bite became seriously infected and she asked her brother to take his "untamed spawn" and go back to Amsterdam. They didn't speak for two years following.

"No Ma. I do love you, and Uncle James too, but this rough needs to learn his lesson the hard way. Let him sit in jail and take his punishment. That Woodruff fellow is now going to have to walk around with my cousin's teeth marks permanently displayed in the middle of his forehead for the rest of his days. Let Johnny McGrady rot in his cell for what he's done."

Mary was disappointed, but she knew her son was right. She'd done her best.

She immediately began drafting a reply to her brother, telling him that his boy's misbehaving had gone on too long, and he should must ready to pay the price.

"You can't rescue him, Brother James," she wrote in her childish scrawl. "You and I might well be gone tomorrow. Our grown children have to learn to stand on their own, without us.

"He's a married man with responsibilities now."

1885
Mary McGrady Sullivan Halloran

Jim Sullivan awoke with a lurch. He was having a nightmare.

The magnanimous iceman Mr. David Clark had passed away just the week before, saddening both brothers, both having enjoyed the advantages of his employ, as well as their mother, who retained joyful memories of his kindness. Mary fondly recalled once again the magical excursion he had provided the family at the end of the '50s to witness Blondin walk the wire at Niagara Falls.

In his dream, Jim had been trying to save Mr. Clark who had fallen through the ice. They reached for each other but couldn't quite touch. Jim woke and tried to shake off its effects. He propped himself up in his bed, and reached for the cup of water on his night table to quench a fierce throat. He must have been sleeping with his mouth open.

Then he remembered. His head resumed throbbing.

He hoisted himself laboriously out of bed, went into the bathroom and doused his face with cupped hands filled from the faucet over and over again. He tried but couldn't wash away the dread. He looked in on Daniel who was still sound asleep. Good. Let him slumber as long as he was able. The door to their parents' room was shut. Normally he'd tip-toe by it, but not today. Not any more.

He tottered into the kitchen and looked out the window to witness the clouds over Lake Erie to the west tinting pink with the reflected light of the rising sun opposite. He made tea. He'd try and be quiet, on second thought, because he didn't want to awaken anybody, least of all the new baby.

He'd rather be alone for a while, and silent.

As he watched the tea steep in the glass and its dye slowly spread through the hot water, he answered the irresistible call to enter the parlor where his mother lay in her coffin. Jim took his glass of tea and sat by the casket, opened to reveal an uncharacteristic serenity of expression that Mary Halloran had rarely exhibited in real life. The Crowleys had done an admirable job.

He was completely cried out. He just sat and stared and shook his head slowly, perplexed by the unfairness of life. He seethed at the idea that Peter Halloran still lived and breathed, and yet the woman that he had abused and hurt and tormented for 22 years now lay dead, taken away from her adoring sons, leaving the monster they hated slumbering peacefully in her bed. The very same bed she had once shared with their late father. Jim's hand tightened around the glass as he thought about it, then he stopped himself, lest he break it.

Jim recalled the dark years that had dragged endlessly on, intensifying in their agony year by year. The loss of his father and the cruel, disconcerting, hungry months that followed. The orphan asylum and the long lonely separation from their mother. His mother's rash choice to take a husband in a desperate move to save her children's lives. Peter Halloran's violence, his crimes, his follies, his prison sentences, followed by another round of hunger, new uncertainties, and fresh anguish.

Mary McGrady Sullivan Halloran

He marveled about his unsettled youth. How he went from being the man of the family at such a young age, holding two jobs, to ending up in an orphanage with his innocent little brother, to being degraded and abused by a felonious, violent drunkard newcomer. Why couldn't he have saved his family from all that?

Mary McGrady Sullivan Halloran had taken her final breath in the earliest hours of the previous morning, at four o'clock. Her sons, all three, had been up all night, and then longer still after Doc Greene had left. "There's nothing more I can do, lads. I've given your mother morphine, so she is not suffering any longer. But I'll need to come back in a few hours with more. Your sweet blessed mother has endured enough pain during her short life."

Doc Greene didn't need to come back. Mary died less than an hour after he left. Her three sons all sat on her bed, holding their mother and each other, and crying. Daniel was just shy of twenty, but at that moment, in that light, he looked like a crestfallen fledgling schoolboy. As anguished as Jim Sullivan himself felt, his heart went out most to his youngest brother.

Peter Halloran had put in a brief appearance at the bedside of his dying wife after Doc Greene left, but quickly excused himself to go downstairs to the saloon to resume getting drunk.

Jim's recollections of his mother's final night now seemed as intangible as the steam rising from his tea glass. The others in the house began to stir and wake. They rose and got dressed. The McGradys arrived from Amsterdam. Mourners arrived, and the priest. The hearse, with one black and one white horse, driven by Dan Crowley. Jim's brothers-in-blue from Precinct Seven, paying their last respects. Food was brought, And whiskey. The weather was beautiful, a brilliant spring day. How appropriate. Jim's mind wandered. His Hannah was sick and Jim forbade her to come to the cemetery. But he hadn't needed to be so forceful. She readily agreed, and told him in confidence that she'd rather not go. Hannah had had a difficult birth, and Jim was more protective of her than ever. At least Mary Halloran had lived long enough—just barely—to delightfully mollycoddle and hold her first grandchild in her arms, sick as she was. Thank God for that. She was gone only 31 days after James Jr. had entered into the world. Had she lived, James Jr. would surely have become the most spoiled child on earth.

The three brothers assembled in that same sorrowful place again, where ten years before they had lowered their fourth sibling into his tiny grave. Now their mother would finally be reunited with her youngest. Jim counted silently on his fingers. Had Dennis lived to be standing with his brothers here today, he'd be almost thirteen. The roots from the golden maple had spread, making it difficult to excavate the pit for Mary. Jim worried now with the roots having been chopped into, that the tree with baby Dennis's essence contained in every leaf might die.

When the shoveling was done, the brothers accepted condolences beneath the bursting spring buds of the maple, and the mourners drifted away one by one. Daniel Halloran departed to take his sick hung over old father back home. Across Ridge Road from the entrance to Holy Cross Cemetery, the premises of McDonnell & Sons beckoned. The notion of preserving the names of loved ones in eternal granite seemed consoling somehow. All the mourners had departed now except the Sullivan brothers.

Jim and JP crossed the road and paid a visit to the monument-makers' establishment. They'd decided to erect a dignified magnum opus for their mother and baby brother. They'd observed that the marker indicating baby Dennis's resting place, set flat into the ground, was already disappearing under grass, roots, fallen leaves, and snow. They wanted an upright, distinct memorial befitting their love and respect. A monument to mark the site so that no matter what the season or weather conditions, they could come to Holy Cross and walk directly to the spot where their family lay at rest.

They agreed on a design; a tapering granite column, set on a heavy base, with an ornament at the crest resembling a church roof, topped with a large heavy cross, all together about six feet tall.

Carved on one facet:

Dennis Halloran
d: July 28, 1874
Aged 1 year and 2 mos.
born: circa May 28, 1873

Carved on the next facet:

Mary Halloran
born in Ireland
November 30, 1830
DIED
April 27, 1885
Aged 54 years and 5 mo.
May her soul rest in peace

Erected by her sons
James,
John, and Daniel

The Halloran monument swallowed by the Golden Maple

October 15, 1885
Return To Holy Cross

JP Sullivan came upon Peter Halloran cold and dead and smelling of shit in the saloon when he went down to answer a knock on the door at 7 o'clock. It was patrolman Steven Whelan pounding. Whelan had looked in the window and saw Peter lying there on the floor in a puddle. He wasn't surprised, or troubled. JP looked down at the dead body on the floor, immediately dreading the cleanup.

They sent for Doc Greene.

Whelan had been making his morning rounds. It was barely light. On South Street he peered out into the gray gloom of a cold dawn to see Jim Sullivan in his scull, training hard out on the river. Whelan waved, but Jim didn't see. *I gotta get myself back in shape*, he said to himself. When he turned the corner onto Hamburgh Street and peered into Halloran's window, he spotted Peter sprawled out there.

In the weeks following his mother's death, Jim had increasingly been at odds with his nasty, cantankerous, abusive, sixty-five year old stepfather. Halloran had commanded him to move out of his house.

"Yer mother's dead and I don't want nothin' more to do with you two bastards!" he had blurted out. Jim wasn't sure whether the other bastard he was referring to was JP or his wife Hannah. Either way, he was incensed.

Jim had punched him in the face the previous week after walking in on him shouting abuse at his sweet Hannah while she fearfully cradled their new infant in her arms. It had required every fiber of his being to remain in control, and not throw the fucker out the second story window. Through clenched teeth and fists Jim strongly advised the increasingly senile old dirt bag that he might just want to do everyone involved a favor and go drown himself in the river across the street.

"We're not goin' anyplace, me and my family, you stinkin' pile o' shit! We're stayin' put!" Jim bellowed at the old man.

Peter Halloran's very existence had always seemed as pointless as it was unavoidable. But with their mother now gone, the sheer excess of his presence on earth was amplified, a hideous and continual reminder to all involved of the very worst events that had occurred in their lives. Even Peter's own blood son Daniel was ready to throw his hands up and be done with the brutal degenerate.

Jim commiserated with Patrolman Whelan and Doc Greene, and together they provided a scenario that negated the need for the coroner to bother coming by.

Doc Greene looked down at the crumpled mess formed by his old drinking partner on the saloon floor. He'd seen the heartless savage grow progressively worse as the years passed. How does a man well acquainted with the inside of the Penitentiary not rejoice in getting a second chance with a new family, with children of his very own? There was no answer to that, for only Peter Halloran knew what demons possessed him and compelled him to loathe himself and to torture those closest to him. There was nothing left for the doctor to do but wonder what kind of God would allow such a shitty old bastard to outlive his lovely long-suffering wife, denying her the well-earned reward of widowhood. She had fully merited it.

Peter's body was given over to Crowley Brother's Funeral Parlor. Ben and Dan Crowley were good friends of the family and members of the Mutual Rowing Club. They had handled Mary's arrangements. The Crowleys were soundly familiar with Peter's history of violence toward Mary, his children, friends, enemies and strangers. The undertakers could plainly see that his body had a number fresh bruises. Under his hair near the base of the skull was a narrow elongated nasty purple contusion, which could have been caused by a fall, perhaps down the stairs. Or someone whacking him with a lead pipe. Didn't matter. Ben and Dan Crowley had more important matters to concern themselves with than what finally did in as despicable a character as Peter Halloran. His demise was long overdue.

There was no funeral at the house. Daniel seemed hurt at first that his father was denied the ritual, despite his being so universally reviled.

"Who the hell do you think would even come, Daniel?" asked JP. "We'd be sittin' here alone, reminded with every passing minute how hated he was by the complete absence of any mourners."

Daniel realized his brother had a point, imagining himself the sole bereaved in attendance.

Jim declared he wanted Peter buried anywhere except Holy Cross. Certainly not lying eternally next to their precious mother who Halloran had almost murdered more than once. Not lying alongside the precious baby son he had completely ignored.

Jim still held out hope that they might one day soon locate the grave of their father from his Civil War resting place, so they could finally lay him beside their mother.

Daniel had always been united with his brothers in everything, but not this time. A serious rift threatened to tear them apart when Daniel insisted his father be buried with Dennis and Mary. The brothers argued heatedly for more than a day, late into the night. Barely twenty, Daniel battled his brothers fiercely for the first time in his entire life, and he would not back down.

"He's my father. She's my mother. And Dennis is my brother. He gets buried with them. Final word!"

When he was alone with JP, Jim, frustrated and angry, spat out, "We protected Daniel much too well. We should have let that old fucker have at him a time or two just to teach him a lesson."

JP laughed out loud at the absurdity of such a thing.

"You idiot! Who the hell do you think you're fooling? If Peter had ever laid a heavy hand on Daniel you would have clubbed the old fucker into raw pulp. Danny's more like your own son than he is your brother. You are his true father, and always have been. Not that old drunken wreck!"

JP's personal feelings were somewhere between those of his two brothers. He was not Halloran's blood son, but Peter Halloran was the only father that JP had ever known.

"Daniel's our brother, and we love him dearly, and this is what Daniel wants. And as much as I hate to say this Jim, I'm bettin' Ma would want the same thing.

We have to allow him this. I say we have to give this to Daniel. And to Ma."

"Ma should be buried next to Pa!" Jim shouted, his voice breaking.

"Yeah, but we have no idea where Pa is," reminded JP quietly.

Jim was chastened, knowing JP was correct on all counts, and regretted his tantrum.

"Yeah. You're right, JP. I am an idiot," he snickered.

JP laughed and roughed up his brother's hair. "Settled?"

"Yep."

With the matter dealt with, Jim took a deep breath, then left to go find Daniel.

Silently he approached him and wrapped his arms around his youngest brother.

"I'm sorry."

Daniel sniffed, "Me too. I'm an orphan now!"

There was a pause, then they both broke out laughing.

This time, they were the only ones standing beneath the golden maple at Holy Cross.

Considering the thousands of drinks served in that goddamned saloon, one might think more than three people would show up for the burial, at least for Daniel's sake, thought Jim. Didn't matter what kind of bastard Peter Halloran was, because he's dead. You show up for the ones he left behind, or in this case, the one.

As reprehensible a parent as he had been to Daniel, the nineteen-year-old was nonetheless grieving.

Carved on the third facet:

Peter Halloran
born in Ireland
DIED
October 15, 1885
Aged 65 years
May his soul rest in peace
Amen

Jim Sullivan had been given the day off work to attend his stepfather's funeral, but he didn't feel like going back to the family house. He didn't want to see anybody. Now that it was finally all over, he felt quite ashamed for strong-arming Daniel. He really loved the kid.

He made his way down to the docks instead, and asked Tom Kelly if he might just sit there with him for a while. Tom pulled a flask from his pocket, and as Kelly's charges handled freight, Jim and his very good friend, the man who stood watch that day in the family saloon while Jim laid waste to his mother's abuser, shared the comforting container with nary a word said between them.

"To yer lovely mother Mary; God bless 'er and keep 'er," said Tom Kelly, raising the flask.

October 22, 1885
Old Doc Greene

Doc Greene never regretted calling on a sick friend, and in such case was as generous with his money as his time.

A few evenings after Peter Halloran's burial, Blind Joe the fiddle player was returning from a visit made to a fellow musician, and the evening being somewhat snowy, he slipped and fell while crossing the culvert of the Lake Shore & Michigan Southern Railway at Mackinaw Street. He was so painfully injured and disoriented that he could not remove himself from between the ties. Some friends happened along, heard Joe's old dog Porter hoarsely yelping, and rescued Joe from his potentially deadly position between the ties. Since he was unable to see or walk, they retrieved his cane and fiddle from the snowbank and with Porter leading the way and barking, carried Joe back to his apartment at the hub, where Doc Greene was summoned to dress his injuries. The Doc had been out drinking with alderman Jack White, who decided to accompany his friend as he attended to Blind Joe.

Alderman Jack White was known as a staunch and committed teetotaler. Old acquaintances swore that the alderman's devotion to the cause of temperance was sincere; however, neither Doc Greene nor Jack White were feeling any pain when they arrived teetering to Blind Joe's place.

Several minor bruises were found on various portions of Blind Joe's anatomy. The principal damage was to some ligaments in his right leg, which his friends feared was broken. Doc Greene reassured them on this point, and upon his positive prognosis their spirits rose to such a height that one of their number was dispatched to the saloon downstairs. There they fetched a bottle of whiskey to rub on the injured limb, and a pail of beer.

Blind Joe's group of attendants seated themselves on the chair, the windowsill, and the bed, and drank the beer as Joe played a tune on his fiddle and Porter lay in the corner contented and Doc Greene applied the whisky to the blind musician's leg. Running out of beer, and too lazy to walk downstairs to the saloon, they decided to drink the remainder of the whisky as well. Three sheets to the wind, they continued to drunkenly rub the empty whiskey bottle in a therapeutically useless manner against Joe's injured leg. Tapped out of drink, one of the group who was best able to still walk was dispatched to the downstairs. Blind Joe's landlady was the saloonkeep as well, and being quite fond of Joe, and as much relieved by the good news as anyone, she happily furnished the liquid refreshment.

The visits downstairs were made so frequently thereafter that finally the little party, in a very hilarious condition, was unable to even leave the room, and all finally tumbled into bed with Joe and the Doc, dead to the world. As daybreak came, the awakening revelers saw that Doc Greene and Alderman Jack White had left, most likely to tend to an emergency more urgent than the one at hand.

Patrolman Steven Whelan had been a policeman since before there was even a Buffalo police department, when he was a Niagara Frontier copper. He was weary. His brother-in-law was a supervisor with a firm that built lake ships and wanted Whelan to come work with him as a manager. The copper was torn. On one hand he was fed up with the despicable wife-and-child beaters and the violent thugs who'd brick someone's skull just to steal a few pennies. On the other hand, he knew every soul in the neighborhood, and everyone knew him. Steven Whelan held the peace in this district of the First Ward, and had done so for more than twenty-five years. His methods were mostly not much more heavy-handed than a stern expression and a determined stance.

Sunrise was still about two hours away, but there was a nice moon reflecting light off the snow. Whelan peeked into the Dalton Store on South Street, where Mrs. Dalton was busy by kerosene lamp, trying to decipher her own handwriting in a ledger. He tapped on the glass. She looked up and waved hello, and he walked on, past the Mutual Rowing Club boathouse, then around the corner onto Hamburgh Street.

Up a ways he could see an Erie Railroad train through some lightly falling flurries parked on the tracks, blocking the street. Kids would be starting out for school in a little while and Whelan wanted that train out of their way and gone by then. He peered in the various saloon windows as he headed up Hamburgh, checking to see if everything was as it should be inside. He passed Halloran's saloon, the remembrance of Peter Halloran dead on the floor on just such a morning as this one fresh in his mind. He peeked between the houses to make sure there were no passed-out drunks who may have frozen to death in the snow during the night. He looked into Zittel's grocery. It was 6 o'clock. The Zittels were inside, the gas jets lit, stocking the shelves, doing inventory. They'd be opening up the store at 7:30. They looked up and saw him at their window, and smiled and waved. Mrs. Zittel came to the door and opened it. The delicious smell preceded her offer.

"Steven, can we offer you some coffee?"

Whelan savored the thought, but demurred.

"Thank you, Missis. But I have to be finishin' my rounds. I might be stoppin' by later, though, if the offer's still good?" asked the patrolman.

"It surely will be. Until later then, Steven!" she smiled.

As Patrolman Whelan made his way further up Hamburgh Street, he saw that the train did not extend fully across the street. It wasn't completely blocking passage, but it was still offering a hazard in any case. The odiferous remains of frozen Dalton Pond, bordering the tracks on his left side, its volume contained by the rise of the rail bed, presented a slippery obstacle to his progress. Its frozen surface just the night before had hosted a hundred neighborhood ice skaters or more. It served as the local equivalent, at least in winter, to Frederick Law Olmsted's Delaware Park Lake and was a magnet to First Ward children and adults alike seeking winter recreation. In summer, however, it was a stagnant stinking petri dish for the cultivation of the cholera germ. Whelan walked to the right and around the back of the last railcar, then up the opposite side of the train toward the engine to see if he could rouse someone to move the damn thing.

Just up the tracks at Vandalia Street he saw what looked like a bundle of clothes piled by the tracks, but as he grew closer, he realized it was a person.

How many dead bodies will this make now? He wondered. Five hundred? He was weary of discovering people whose lives had just ended, him being the very first to know about it usually, and then having the awful duty of telling their families. His brother-in-law's job offer flickered in his mind once again.

The deceased was lying on his back perpendicular to the tracks. Steven cautiously approached, and saw that the legs had been severed above the knees and were lying side by side between the tracks, neat as can be. His torso lay serene in a large pool of blood which had mostly soaked into the snow. He bent over and looked closely at the man's ashen face, and was startled to see that it was Doc Green.

Doc's stovepipe hat, removed some six feet away, lay on its side in the snow, spattered with mud. His Prince Albert coat, white vest, and immaculate shirt were stained crimson with his life's blood. The look on his color-drained face was benign. Steven scrutinized the surroundings but saw no sign of Doc's carriage or his ancient horse, Chestnut.

How did he end up here? Where was he going? Whelan could smell whisky on him. A large bruise colored the left side of the doc's face, and a small quantity of blood had been expelled from his mouth. His watch and sterling fob were still in his vest pocket. He fervently hoped that Doc wasn't conscious when he got run over.

Then it hit him.

What in the world will the First Ward do now, without dependable old Doc Green?

1885
Manslaughter

Alderman Jack White awoke to a heavy pounding on his front door. At first he didn't even know where he was, and registered surprise when he recognized that the room he was in was his own. The pounding was incessant.

"All right!" he tried to holler, but his voice was choked and dry.

He hefted his substantial girth up from the too-soft mattress and stumbled to the front door. He unlocked it clumsily, then opened it. Before him stood patrolmen Jim Sullivan and his partner John Geary. The morning light was brilliant and the massively hung over alderman was blinded. He didn't see the look of shock on the detectives' faces as they stared at the blood spattered all over his shirt. Jack White had slept in his clothes.

"Jack, you'll need to be comin' with us."

At the precinct house, Jack White was sequestered out of sight of prying eyes as the Captain tried to decide what to do. He concluded there was no way to disguise this, for two witnesses had reported what they'd seen with their own eyes, and the many witnesses at Blind Joe's also testified that they had been with Doc and the alderman until just a couple of hours or so before Steven Whelan found Doc's body.

"What happened, Jack?" asked the Captain.

"I have no idea!" shouted Jack White. "The last I remember we were all drinking at Blind Joe's. Next thing I know, Sullivan's pounding on my door, waken' me up. I don't even remember ever leaving Blind Joe's!"

Hours passed. Witnesses said there was a scuffle at the Vandalia Street tracks and that the two had fought. There was snow on the ground, and a brilliant moon. There was sufficient light so that there was no mistaking who and what. The much larger alderman slugged the slightly built old Doc in the face, who then crumpled to the ground. The alderman then drunkenly stumbled away.

Before they could react, the witnesses stated, a train pulled in. They ran up to where the doc was and saw all the blood. They got scared. They knew how powerful Alderman Jack White was. They feared for their lives. But then they thought about poor Doc Greene. Everybody loved Doc Greene. They knew they had to come in to the precinct house and tell their story.

Jim Sullivan and John Geary had interviewed their share of liars in their time, and although Jim intensely disliked Jack White, both patrolmen believed he was telling the truth. Jim had never once known the cocksure career alderman to be flustered or distraught, but now Jack White was both.

It was decided that no good would come of the story being made public. The details were kept within the department so successfully that even neighboring precinct captains didn't know much about it.

Justice King charged alderman Jack White with manslaughter in the fourth degree in closed chambers. He was allowed his freedom on his own recognizance until a final determination could be made. Eight weeks after Doc Greene's tragic

Alderman Jack White

death, a judgement was arrived at.

Justice King fined the alderman $250, and the new interim Governor of New York State, David B. Hill, after discussing the matter in confidence with his immediate predecessor and current President of the United States, Grover Cleveland, pardoned him.

President Cleveland, White's most powerful nemesis and harshest critic, finally having the perfect chance to dispose of Jack White once and for all, instead evidenced his great capacity for benevolence, or perhaps some political advantage. The matter was dropped.

Jack White was deeply ashamed.

He'd killed his one and only true friend, and now he missed him terribly. The entire First Ward was in mourning, and it was all his doing. Doc Greene's name would be spoken of with gratitude and reverence for decades henceforth. White didn't remember anything about that night.

He never again touched another drop of alcohol. He never again had a genuine friend to call his own. But what Jack White did have was a quarter-century's accumulation of enemies waiting in line for their chance to do him in.

In the final years of Peter Halloran's life, his often-bustling saloon saw several declines as the disinterested and distracted barkeep alienated customers and friends alike in ways too numerous to ledger.

When Daniel was fifteen and had two more years of school still ahead of him, his father tried to manipulate him into quitting his education to take over the running of the saloon. Although Daniel did have an interest in the saloon, he did not see in it an opportune future for himself, mostly due to his mother's influence.

"What saloon owner can you name who has become prosperous in this terrible business, Daniel?" Mary Halloran quizzed her youngest back then.

"That's easy, Ma. Fingy Conners."

"Fingy Conners," Mary Halloran hissed, "has not prospered from the saloon business. He has prospered from the saloon-boss business, if ye want to give validation to white slavin' by callin' it a business. Is that what ye want Daniel, to be an oppressor of men? To see the people of this ward walkin' the streets in rags, scourin' the empty fields fer somethin' t' eat?"

"No, Ma. Of course not. I was just pulling your leg."

"I'll not have my brightest son wasting his future chasing after drunks and interferin' in brawls just to sell a few drinks. There ye have it!"

Jim and JP just looked at each other open-mouthed and dumbfounded. "Did she just call him her brightest son?" gasped JP in mock indignation.

"You can see Daniel, by our own empty saloon, how quickly things can go to pot. If yer father wants to keep his saloon, then it's up to him to keep it, not his son. Yer life is all ahead of ye, Daniel. Yer father's is all behind 'im. Make yer own plans fer yerself, whatever they might be."

Daniel graduated from the Central High School with high marks, and through his brother JP's connections, won an apprenticeship with an attorney at Grover Cleveland's former law office. He was fired up when he was accepted, certain he was on his way to success. But swiftly he found himself floundering and overwhelmed, running breathlessly from one task to another. He was slower to catch on than his patron had expected, and always felt challenged to complete his tasks in the length of time allotted. Simultaneously organizing legal documents, doing research in the law library, and fetching materials from all over town proved to be more than he was capable of handling. His workday often stretched past fourteen hours with no extra pay. His dreams of becoming a lawyer someday were fast dwindling, until that morning when he was told, with regret, that his services would no longer be required.

Daniel searched elsewhere on JP's counsel for another situation, but found nothing.

His father's saloon began to look more and more like a promising opportunity, despite his mother's warnings. He had lots of saloon business experience, and people liked him. But Daniel finally had to acknowledge that no matter how much effort he put into bringing in business, the dozen other saloons within a one minute stroll of Halloran's were themselves not thriving. Most of them were obliged to provide additional services like shoe repair, barber shop or grocers just to keep their doors open.

It was with a very heavy heart that Daniel stood in line at Mixer and Company that depressing day, hoping to be chosen for day work unloading lumber from barges coming up the Ohio Slip. Brother JP and his partner Tom Nunan's new ice company was only just hanging on, unable to hire Daniel. They had already taken on Tom's brother the previous year, and were now finding it difficult enough to keep him in light of the previous two warm winters producing so little ice.

If the coming winter were cold, they might be able to hire him beginning in January or February, but that was still many months away. Daniel became downhearted, thinking his once-bright future may have already dimmed.

🍀

1885
Fingy's Outrage

"The majestic form of the Hon. Thomas B. O'Brien, the Demosthenes of the First Ward, appeared to be in temporary danger on Tuesday when the Hon. Finggy Conners, also of the First, sought him out in the recesses of the city treasurer's department. The Hon. Thomas recently had occasion to address the longshoremen, who were thinking about reorganizing their union, and it appears that in the course of his remarks, he stamped upon the toes of the Hon. Finggy, who, it is reported, contracts for the work of the dock laborers, and pays them off at his saloon on Ohio Street. Mr. O'Brien sternly criticized the new system by which the men who formerly earned $16-$20 a week are said now to earn but $10 to $12, and have a portion of their wages kept back until the end of the season. Mr. Conners visited him with the avowed intention of compelling him to retract publicly his utterances. As both are Republican politicians and both are pillars of the G.O.P. in their ward, there was naturally much interest exhibited in their meeting. There was a great flow of language on both sides, resulting it is claimed, in an oratorical triumph for the Hon. Thomas, who put his antagonist to ignominious rout, and left him capable of nothing beyond vowing the direst personal and political vengeance in the near future."

—The Buffalo Courier

Hannah Sullivan looked up after reading the news article out loud, and said to JP's wife Annie, "The nerve of that deranged little bulldog! To berate a pillar of the community who is clearly his superior in every way, for only speaking a truth about him that everyone already knows. And vowing personal vengeance against him, besides? He's a violent animal!"

Baby Jim Jr. fussed happily on her lap.

Hannah and Annie regularly got together a couple of afternoons a week to have tea and discuss their husbands. Annie had only recently married Jim Sullivan's brother, whereupon JP bought the house next door at No. 12 Hamburgh, and sold his interest in the house at No. 16 to his older brother for a dollar. The two women soon found they had more in common than just being married to brothers.

Jim had always told Hannah something she found to be as true as it was brilliant:

"Nothing makes people angrier than hearing the truth."

Hannah quoted him as also saying, "Far more people have killed another human being over the truth than over a lie."

But to confront a highly regarded gentleman like Mr. O'Brien, and threaten him with violence, in a public place, because he stated the truth about Fingy, to

Fingy? That was psychotic.

But, on second thought she decided, interesting as well.

"We have a Lunatic Asylum on Forest Avenue overflowing with a lot of people who shouldn't even be in there," she said to Annie, "but the most dangerous lunatics of all are free to go about their ambition of ruling over this entire city."

"You said it, Hannah!", smiled her brother-in-law Daniel, who had just gotten home from work, covered in oat dust.

"Daniel, what did I tell you? Get out into the yard and brush yourself off before coming into the house!"

Most recently Daniel had found work as a grain scooper. The household had experienced a problem in the water closet pipes due to the buildup of the dust he was rinsing off every day, which over just a few weeks had turned to paste within the works. It cost a small fortune to remedy. For now, because it was warm, washing off out back was fine. But come fall they'd need to find a more permanent solution.

Jim Sullivan walked in the door two minutes after Daniel, tired and worn, shedding his wool uniform. It was a hot summer and he had already had more than his share of difficult arrests, both the heartbreaking variety, and the infuriating. He was compelled to arrest an eleven-year-old boy for burglary and larceny for stealing merchandise from a railcar. Taking the boy to his home, Jim found a widow with four more children, all younger than the boy, all very thin and much too lethargic. It brought back memories of his own nightmare at that age. The boy had been only trying to find some way to feed his family.

Next he had to pull a fifteen-year-old off the train at the Central Depot headed for Denver after the boy stole $250 from his employer. His boss had given the money to him to deposit at the bank. Upon searching him at the station they found that his slight physique was covered with bruises both recent and historical.. When visiting his home to notify his family Jim discovered the horrific existence the boy had been so desperate to escape that he ended up robbing his employer. He found it hard to resist the urge to bring the boy home with him to live.

Jim rarely came home and talked about such things, so Hannah knew that when he did share these distressing stories with her, it was because he had come through an especially bad day. His worst laments always involved someone whose circumstances were similar to those of his own past in some way. Jim looked down and noticed what Hannah and Annie had been reading in the newspaper. "That Fingy is an imbecile," he criticized, uncharacteristically, shaking his head. His guard had been knocked flat by the terrible day he'd had. "That caffler never did have a brain in his big knobby head. Not when he was a lad, and not now neither."

"You know something Jim?" asked a suddenly enlightened Hannah. "I don't believe I can completely agree, come to think of it. Actually, I think he's brilliant in the diabolical sense. He's a master at manipulating people."

"Are you defending Fingy Conners now, Hannah?" mocked Jim, feigning shock. "You hate that man. Look what he's turned your own brother into! And confronting Tom O'Brien within earshot of a news reporter? That's not what I'd call very smart."

"My brother turned himself into whatever he happens to be of late, thank you, James! David Nugent is responsible for his own decisions, and no one else. But it dawned on me just this second that maybe this confrontation of Fingy's was contrived. A public tantrum in front of a reporter who just happened to be there writing it all down? What news ever occurs at the treasurers office that a reporter would just happen to be down there? If you think about it, no matter what odious thing Fingy ever does, in the end he always gets his way. I think that maybe Fingy planned that scene beforehand. That man's up to something."

Hannah looked at her newspaper again. She considered how skillfully Fingy was able to use her husband and his brother—and her own brother—to do his bidding.

"Fingy Conners knows better than anyone how to manage any given situation to get the result he's after. That's a fact."

With His Drinks He Mixed Sundry Brands
of Politics

Illustration of Fingy Conners tending his saloon from a magazine of the day.

August 1, 1886
McGrady's Best Man

Jim Sullivan dragged two reluctant very well-dressed ladies into the precinct house kicking and screaming. He'd caught them red handed shoplifting at Flint & Kent. They had padded their bosoms and their nether regions with the store's most expensive silk ladies' undergarments. Now he had to recruit two more officers to witness them undress and fully reveal the extent of their cache.

When the deed was accomplished, Jim Short, who was on desk duty, corralled his M.R.C. colleague.

"Say Jim, isn't that cousin of yours in Amsterdam named McGrady?"

"Um. Yeah, why?" replied Jim Sullivan, reluctantly.

"John McGrady?"

"Yeah."

"You'd best read this." said Detective Short, handing him a copy of the Amsterdam Daily Democrat that his sister in Montgomery County had sent him.

A DISGRACEFUL AFFAIR

John McGrady Bites John Bulger's Ear Off at the Windsor.

At the Spinners' picnic on Saturday, some trouble arose between John McGrady and John Bulger, two well-known young men of this city. Bulger claims that McGrady tried to bring out a quarrel between him and John Kehoe, but that he refused to enter into any wrangle, saying that was not the place for it. Saturday evening, about 9 o'clock, while McGrady was in the bar-room of the Windsor restaurant, Bulger came downstairs and entered the apartment. McGrady seized him by the

BACK OF THE NECK

and struck at him. Bulger is a light fellow, weighing little more than half as much as McGrady, who tips the beam at considerably over 200 pounds. He possesses plenty of pluck, however, and was not at all dismayed at the attack, but struck his bulky assailant a powerful blow, knocking him down. McGrady rose to his feet and clinched with Bulger, who put him on his back twice more in succession. The friends of the combatants then

PARTED THEM

and a seeming reconciliation was effected. As Bulger was standing by the bar, McGrady put one arm about his neck saying "you're a better man than I am, and we'll be good friends", suddenly seized the latter by the right ear with his teeth and bit it badly, so that the blood gushed freely and a piece of the ear hung down. The wound was dressed and the ear will heal in a short time. There had been ill feeling between McGrady and Bulger for some time. The two were formerly

INTIMATE FRIENDS

and Bulger acted as best man at McGrady's wedding a little over two years ago. McGrady is naturally kind hearted, and the disgraceful performance of Saturday night was due to too excessive indulgence in liquor. Both young men are prominent politicians, Bulger having an active influence in the local Democratic ranks, and McGrady possessing equal power among the Republicans.

M'GRADY'S STATEMENT

To a Democrat reporter to-day, McGrady said that he greatly regretted the occurrence and that it would not have taken place if he had been himself. He claimed, however, that he had been much persecuted and abused by Bulger and his friends, who he thought were actuated by jealousy, and their treatment of him had aroused his temper. He also said that just before he encountered Bulger, he had been run into roughly by John Kehoe, which had much

IRRITATED HIM

He claimed that to the best of his recollection, the injury to Bulger's ear was caused not by his teeth, but by a swinging blow from his fist. He had always been a warm friend of Bulger and regretted that the intimacy between them had ceased. It was not his fault that it had done so.

"Can I borrow this to show my brother?" asked Jim.

"Be my guest. You might want to preserve that in the family Bible!" smiled Jim Short.

"Ma would've just loved this!" Jim moaned.

1888 Mutuals Regatta

MUTUALS REGATTA

The Mutuals' regatta will be given the latter part of July. The Mutuals have two good crews in training. The first crew (subject to substitution) is composed of Sam Shaver, bow; James Manahar, 2; John P. Sullivan. 3; James Sullivan, stroke. The second crew includes Ben Crowley, bow; Lon Zimmerman, 2; James Eagan, 3; Daniel Halloran, stroke.

The chances are that there will be no rowing regatta here on July 4th. There may possibly be a single-scull race, but the four-oared crews are unwilling to row for a mere pittance.

—Buffalo Express, June 17, 1888

The 1888 Mutual Regatta was finally scheduled for August 26th. Daniel had been improving his stroke steadily now, inching toward his ultimate goal of besting his brothers' unbeatable team. He'd been getting stronger with every practice and every heat until one day in early July when he started to feel discomfort in his lungs when winded. He found himself coughing after practice and was more tired than usual after training.

He was working all day scooping oats at the Elevator and hated it. He concluded that breathing all that grain dust in the elevator was lunacy, and now he was paying the price. Between working in a cloud of grain powder and all the deafening clanging and shouting, he needed to try something different if he could.

As he and Ben Crowley enjoyed a beer in the boathouse with their scull mates one evening after practice, Ben mentioned that an intern at the funeral home had been caught stealing a gold ring off a cadaver, and he had to fire him. He said needed to begin looking for a replacement and he dreaded the chore.

Daniel Halloran said, "How about me?"

Crowley was surprised. "I thought you once told us that you would never be up for doing our kind of work, Danny," Ben replied.

"Well..." Daniel paused a second. "I've been thinking, Ben. I hate my job. It's making me deaf and sick and I need a change. I hear its plenty quiet over there at your place."

The men all laughed.

"All of us are friends Danny, and if things didn't work out, if me and my brother took you on, I mean, the last thing I want is any hard feelings between us. We're all brothers here."

"If you'll give me the chance I promise I will do my best." Daniel replied.

Daniel thought for a couple of seconds and proposed, "Say, how does this sit with you, Ben? I'll work for you for two weeks as a sort of trial period, and we'll both agree that after the first week if either one of us wants to end it for any reason at all, we can do so with no hard feelings to anybody? You said you need someone right away. This way you can keep looking for someone during my trial."

Crowley seemed to like the idea.

"Then how's about we shake on it?" Daniel said.

Ben thought it was a fine plan. "But I do have to ask my brother."

The Crowleys agreed that Daniel Halloran might be the ideal solution to an ongoing problem. The men all clicked their schupers together the next evening in the boathouse to toast the new union. The following morning Daniel Halloran showed up at the Crowley Bros. Funeral Parlor for work.

Ben and Dan Crowley had known Daniel since he was a little kid, and feeling protective, their plan was to ease him into the macabre work slowly. His introduction was a visit to the embalming room where luckily, an elderly man awaited the brothers' skills. Ben Crowley thought to himself, how lucky we didn't have a child right now, or the victim of a grisly rail accident.

Daniel was curious. He surprised even himself at how at ease he was. His initial duties were to clean up and do janitorial tasks, and accompany the brothers to pick up the recently deceased. When it was agreeable, Daniel would take over the bathing and preparing of the corpse prior to embalming. The brothers would not allow him to witness an actual embalming until they were sure he was comfortable with his other duties first.

Into his third week Daniel was thriving in his new job. He did not dream bad dreams as he had expected, and although bathing dead people, especially those who were victims of terrible accidents, was not pleasant, he found it to be an honorable and respectful endeavor.

He was often alone as he bathed a cadaver. One day he found himself becoming emotional when his charge was a young man his own age, appearing healthy and uninjured, looking as if asleep. Usually he set right to work and didn't think too much about the task, occupying his mind with thoughts of an upcoming race or drinking with mates at the next M.R.C. function. But this young man was different. He was nice looking, healthy and athletic. What happened to him? Daniel stopped to take a long look at his charge from head to toe, imagining that just twenty-four hours ago he too may have been thinking ahead to this coming weekend and having a beer with his mates. He thought to himself, someday I might be lying here myself on this table. Who'll be washing my naked body?

He hoped it would not be some disrespectful brute.

And then, like a bolt, it hit him.

"My own mother was laid on this very table," he whispered aloud.

The Crowleys had long been troubled by their inability to find and retain a trustworthy and dependable employee. Success had eluded them for some time, but with Daniel's arrival, they were finally able to breathe a sigh of relief. They had found the best employee they'd ever had when, as the saying goes, they were all in the same boat the entire time, literally. For Daniel's part, the negative aspects of the job were not nearly as repugnant as the hard labor, conflicts with fellow workers, unbearable noise, and the choking dust of the grain elevators. It was peaceful work, and he felt strangely solaced at the end of his workday.

Daniel's training sessions in the sculls measurably improved once he had removed himself from the grain elevators, but his cough persisted. Dr. Buswell told him it might take a few months for his body to completely rid itself of all the foreign material.

On the day of the 1888 Mutual Rowing Club Regatta thousands swarmed into the First Ward on foot, by streetcar and carriage and aboard boats large and small. The Club's annual contest had become such an anticipated event that some Great Lakes captains even rearranged their schedules to arrive earlier or remain in port later in order to join in the festivities. The fire tug J. M. Hutchinson chugged back and forth around the bend in the river thrilling the crowd with a play-out, shooting formidable geysers of water through her five water monitors in a celebratory display to the rousing cheers of those along the shores. The boathouse sparkled in the sun with its new coat of forest green paint.

One of the windows had been switched out for a beautiful and colorful depiction of the Henley Regatta in leaded stained glass that Jim Sullivan had commissioned in Toronto. Everyone wanted to see it up close.

Hannah and Annie, both pregnant, conveyed their children down to the riverbank in anticipation of the contest between brothers. Jim Jr., Nellie, John and Thomas were all rooting for Uncle Daniel to best their own fathers. Baby Thomas wore a miniature M.R.C.-emblazoned singlet over his shirt that JP had made especially for him.

Uncle James McGrady arrived from Amsterdam with Aunt Margaret and their daughters, but son John P. McGrady couldn't get time off. He had passed the police exam the previous year and was now an officer on the Amsterdam Police department. This mystified the Sullivan brothers, especially Jim, considering their cousin's shameful behavior of the past.

"They sure must be desperate for coppers in Amsterdam," laughed JP when Jim told him the news.

The first race was getting ready to start. But at the last moment, burning with fever and coughing heavily, Daniel Halloran was forced to drop out of his scheduled heat. His scull-mates and his employers Ben and Dan Crowley were all disappointed, but foremost in their mind was their friend's health. Daniel Halloran had proven himself an indispensable employee, and the grateful Crowley brothers' days especially were made all the easier for it.

The Mutual Rowing Club

1889
April 6th

Dan and Ben Crowley arrived on Hamburgh Street in tears to claim their rowing-mate's body as both Sullivan families stood out front and bawled openly at the curb. Other members of the club hung back painfully on the perimeter of the scene, not knowing quite what to think of the tragedy. No amount of strangers' deaths could numb the Crowleys to the pain of losing a loved one of their own.

Twenty-three. He was just twenty-three. How could someone as lovely as Daniel Halloran already be gone?

Jim felt ashamed of himself for standing there and thinking, thank God Ma went before him, because this would surely have killed her.

Daniel never did get better.

Dr. Buswell had been summoned on September 3rd, when Daniel was burning up. He'd been sick for a month, and with each passing day he only grew worse.

"It's consumption," Dr. Buswell said. "You'll have to send him to the sanitarium. He can't be in the same house as the children."

JP's ice business with Tom Nunan was doing well enough. He and Jim decided to send Daniel to Saratoga, to the sanitarium there. The mountain air would be far more conducive to Daniel's recovery than the coal soot and sulphur of the First Ward.

Daniel didn't want to go. He had never been separated from his family before. But when Dr. Buswell explained the circumstance of contagion to him, and the danger to the others, Daniel resigned himself.

The final months of his life were the loneliest he'd ever known. He had always had his brothers to talk to, to rely on, to be comforted and surrounded by. And these days he felt additionally blessed to have his brothers' wives and children for family as well. He missed his new job and all his team mates, He missed kissing his nephews and niece. Both Hannah and Annie were pregnant again, promising to make him a new uncle twice more. He wanted to see them, but knew he could not.

Jim and JP took turns boarding the train to Saratoga to visit him just as often as they could manage to get away. Together they traveled to Saratoga to bring Daniel's body home on the train. He looked terrible; gaunt and colorless. Shrunken. They treasured the memory of the tanned lithe smiling eager young sculler, grinning broadly, muscles straining as he skimmed across the still waters of the Buffalo River, training harder than almost anyone else in the club. So, to see him so wasted, looking like this...

It was heartbreaking.

Ben and Dan Crowley gazed down upon the diminished naked body of their much-loved friend, laying on the same table where Daniel himself had bathed and prepared so many others before him. The morticians had only twice before taken in someone who was as close to their hearts as Daniel. A task that had become an everyday process now landed like a kick in the stomach as they prepared to ready Daniel Halloran for his wake. Dan Crowley stood on one side of Daniel, and Ben on the other. Together they tenderly bathed and anointed their friend, as onerous as that proved to be through the distortion of their tears and the weight of their shared grief.

The entire one-hundred member body of the Mutuals gathered together at Holy Cross Cemetery. The first and only brother they had ever lost through death turned out to be the one most loved. The green, white, and black colors of the Mutual Rowing Club flag were lain across the casket, and no one was ashamed to cry. Daniel's trophy was removed from the Mutual boathouse display case and placed in the coffin with him, along with the rosary his mother had given him for his first communion.

The Sullivan brothers stood in the exact place they had stood three times before. Memories of their mother and baby brother Dennis filled their heads and hearts. Jim again wrestled with the decision to bury Peter Halloran there, among all the sweet and good people and mused about how complicated it might be to have Peter dug up and burned and his name chipped off the monument.

With prayers said and tears running free the men walked away at the ceremony's conclusion, arms securely around each other's shoulders, comrades all. For the next few weeks, neither Jim nor JP could bring himself to visit the boathouse, even though it was just a few steps away from their homes. They needed time.

On the fourth facet of the Halloran monument was carved:

Daniel Halloran
d: April 6, 1889
Aged 23 years 9 mos. and 20 days
Born: circa July 13, 1865

A few months passed. The Sullivan brothers were alone, their closest blood family all gone. JP was successful in distracting himself by readying his entry into politics. He met with Fingy Conners almost nightly to plan strategy. They met at Fingy's boarding house-saloon at 444 Ohio Street, the hotel providing an atmosphere more conducive to sleuthing than the Mutuals' boathouse.

Hannah Sullivan went into labor on September 14th. Doctor Buswell was called, and he brought a capable and experienced midwife with him as well, Mamie Edson. Mrs. Edson's daughter, also named Mamie, had been Daniel Halloran's girlfriend when they were sixteen, and spoke lovingly at his funeral, so Mamie senior's presence was welcomed by all.

A beautiful pink little girl popped out after just an hour, and the women all congratulated Hannah and themselves on such an easy and speedy delivery. Patrolman Jim Sullivan had been fetched by Doctor Buswell as he passed by the precinct house. Buswell came running in shouting for the father to hurry. His fellow officers slapped Jim on the back as he rushed out.

As Jim held his new daughter up to the light of the bedroom window to get a good look at her, he smiled and said, "Hello Hannah. We're naming you after your beautiful and brave mother."

The gloom that had permeated both Sullivan houses since Daniel's death in April suddenly began to dissipate with little Hannah's birth, allowing some golden light of hope to at long last shine in. Doctor Buswell, after having attended Daniel from when he first took sick, was heartened to now be a party to a joyous Sullivan family occasion.

Despite his joy, Jim couldn't easily shake the loss of his brother Daniel. In a moment of weakness he decided to write a letter to his cousin John McGrady, so they might reconnect. He wrote that he wished they might try to become friends again.

Mysteriously, in return he received an envelope postmarked Amsterdam N.Y. with no return address, and no message inside. But there was a newspaper clipping.

> At one o'clock Tuesday morning officers Soles and McGrady engaged in a brutal fight on Market Street, Amsterdam, in which McGrady was knocked down with a club and badly beaten over the head, receiving a number of severe cuts. During the fight a pistol in the hands of McGrady was discharged. Soles claimed that he pounded McGrady because he thought the latter was going to shoot him, and that throughout the battle he acted in self defense. McGrady says that while Soles was striking him with the club, he fired the pistol in order to scare him away. Charges have been preferred against both men, and they have been suspended from the force pending an investigation. It is reported that Soles has resigned. He told a friend that he intended doing so. Soles has been on the force for three years and McGrady for two. While Soles was not as popular as McGrady, there has never been any complaint made against him, while charges have been preferred against McGrady on two or three previous occasions. It is alleged that the officers were intoxicated that night.
>
> —the Fulton County Republican

October 1889
Vote Sullivan for Alderman

It rained that October night in the First Ward. The citizens' desire for change hung heavy in the coal-smoke scented air. Large, clammy drops fell softly through the slowly rising putrid vapors of the stagnant abandoned Hamburgh Canal. Pools of water glistened here and there in the Elk Street Market Square, and the yellow electric light procured through the political influence of First Ward Alderman Jack White sputtered and flickered dismally. The citizens of the First Ward had their choice of political meetings that night.

The members of the Jack White Club came out in full force and proclaimed their allegiance to their great Boss.

Alternately, the voters who were against White, the petty despot who had for so long tyrannized over them, held another and altogether rousing meeting under the shed of the Elk Street Market. They had learned nothing yet of the great secret that could destroy the object of their hostility.

The rain-soaked wind whistled drearily through the rafters of the old market building. A stench rivaling that of the fetid Hamburgh Canal rose from the smoky torches of the hucksters. Hundreds, who in earlier and more naive days had voted for wily Jack White, came out to bask in his condemnation and to shout their determination to do all in their power to defeat the old-time political master.

The Democratic meeting was presided over by John C. Sheehan, who had been city comptroller until dumped in 1881, when Grover Cleveland refused to have him on his mayoral ticket. Sheehan had embezzled $5900 from the city's orphans fund. Sheehan's slippery younger brother, William F. Sheehan, was a clerk in his brother's comptroller's office and was known to be part of the scheme. John C. Sheehan himself had previously been a candidate for alderman from the First Ward, running unsuccessfully against the insurmountable rampart that was Jack White: entrenched, corrupt, shielded and protected, and very powerful.

Jack White was without question the most powerful politician in the city's Common Council, and it was often accused that regardless who was mayor, it was the First Ward Boss who was running the entire city of Buffalo.

John C. Sheehan, along with his brother William F. Sheehan, currently the New York State Assemblyman campaigning to retain his seat in that body—who was also present at the meeting—was a voracious politician. John C.'s employ was as contractor for coal handling, and his chief rival was contractor Fingy Conners. Contractor Fingy Conners was backing Jack White for reelection. Ergo, contractor John C. Sheehan was backing a young successful ambitious man in the ice business named John P. Sullivan.

Chairman John C. Sheehan spoke long and loudly. He told several truths and made several predictions. He was applauded and interrupted as often as an excuse could be found for doing so, and even on one or two occasions when excuses were quite thin.

JNO. P. SULLIVAN, Buffalo.

John P. Sullivan in 1889

A Republican named Carmichael was running for mayor, against Democratic candidate Charles F. Bishop. In referring to the Carmichael Deal, by which the City of Buffalo had paid an exorbitant sum for the property acquired for the Elk Street Market extension, Sheehan said that no citizen of the First Ward had ever been able to profit so handsomely as had Carmichael and his partner from that land deal.

Republican mayoral candidate Carmichael had in fact told the citizens of Buffalo that it was none of their damned business what share of the $50,000 profit was now sitting in his bank account.

John C. Sheehan ranted and railed. "It has now devolved upon the people of the city," he exhorted "to say whether they would choose for Mayor the man who had dealt in City warrants, and who had been making money hand over fist out of the very city he professed to humbly serve, or whether they would vote for a clear-headed, conscientious businessman, who believed in conducting the affairs of the city in accordance with correct business principles, Mr. Charles F. Bishop."

The gathering of working men jumped to their feet, clapping and shouting for Charles F. Bishop for mayor. Mr. Bishop, standing off to the side, smiled and nodded in warm appreciation.

The crowd was incensed by the growing corruption in their city. It was bad enough that their own First Ward was ruled over by a monster, but the entire city had to now fight off a mayoral candidate who was equally as corrupt and rapacious, if not more so.

The subject then turned to the office of First Ward alderman. Speaker Sheehan continued. "The young man who represents the Democracy of the First Ward is one who has carved out his own political future, one who has not dominated political office for the last 20 years as his opponent has done. He is a young and energetic man named John P. Sullivan who would ably and fully represent the people of the ward. Are the people of the First Ward so deeply indebted to the man named Jack White that they could not possibly vote against him?"

Cries of "No, no!" swelled up from the gathered.

"Was it not time that the citizens who had heretofore supported him now determine that Jack White should no longer dominate them?"

Cries of "Yes! That's true!" resounded through the rafters.

"The people of the First Ward," Sheehan continued "should try the experiment of having another representative! Mr. John P. Sullivan is the man to be substituted for White!"

The men applauded vigorously.

"If Sullivan does not make a better alderman than Jack White," lied John C. Sheehan, "if he does not prove to be a member of the Council who would look first and foremost after the interest of his supporters, I pledge that I will personally come down to the First Ward two years from now and work for the re-election of Jack White myself!"

Sheehan was enthusiastically acclaimed by grinning men with tobacco-stained teeth, brown-spattered blue work shirts, and soiled canvas jackets. The kind of men who regarded John P. Sullivan, former longshoreman, as one of their own.

During one of the countless dock strikes that paralyzed shipping on the Buffalo waterfront, John P. Sullivan decided that he had endured enough uncertainty and determined to free himself from the tyranny of the fates. For three months during the winter of 1882-83, JP, along with his brother Jim and best friend Tom

Nunan, cut ice on Lake Erie together for David Clark. Following David Clark's death in 1885, and inspired by Mr. Clark's stories of their father John Sullivan's cutting ice for him in the late 1850s, JP and his friend Thomas Nunan established the Sullivan & Nunan Ice Co.

Sullivan & Nunan culled their winter workforce from friendships forged on the docks, choosing the most rough and tumble of the lot. In those early days, after the ice had formed and was ready to be cut, competing companies would duke it out for the prime spots. Fist fights out on the frozen lake at the foot of Michigan Avenue would often determine which company got the choicest area, and Sullivan & Nunan grew to prominence in large part due to their discerning staffing choices.

The next speaker at the Elk Street Market meeting was John C. Sheehan's brother, New York State Assemblyman William F. Sheehan. The local hero received a wild reception, and kept his remarks short and to the point. He confined himself mainly to the ward issues, and protested against the election of Jack White:

"It is time that the honest men of the ward banded themselves together for the sake of throwing off the bondage of Jack White! For the past 14 years this man has ruled the people of the ward with a hand of iron, and it is time that his power was broken. Now is the time to do it. Now is the time to defeat him!

"The election of the iceman John P. Sullivan means the emancipation of the voter from ignoble political bondage. I am determined to fight Jack White to the bitter end. It is now war between me and Mr. White to the knife, and the knife to the hilt!" Sheehan bellowed.

William F. Sheehan then brought all the candidates up onto the boards so that the audience could get a good look at them. The suffrage seekers included Democratic mayoral candidate Charles F. Bishop; city comptroller candidate Michael Nellany, founder of the Buffalo Shirt Co.; State Senate candidate Matthias Rohr, editor of the Volksfreund German newspaper; and John P. Sullivan, ice company president and candidate for alderman.

All the candidates spoke in turn, echoing similar concerns and exhortations. William F. Sheehan was especially gracious to Nellany, for he would be marrying the comptroller candidate's daughter in just a few weeks.

That very same night, a few blocks further down Elk Street, Charles W. Barker's wagon shop was being used as a wigwam by the supporters of First Ward Alderman Jack White. The shop was crowded, and his backers were both loud in their hurrahs for Alderman White and in their expressions of appreciation of the numerous good things said of him by men, it was asserted, he had assisted to good positions.

The First Ward Band had set the tone for the evening by parading up and down the ward's streets picking up willing stragglers who plodded through the mud with them to the music of Marching Through Georgia, and whooped it up for the First Ward magnate.

It was not until after eight o'clock when, a Buffalo News reporter having arrived, the word was given to "get this business started."

Alderman White looked a bit tired and did not lecture with his customary bluster or flow of wit, although his abusive powers were as finely tuned as ever.

He began by thanking the crowd for "attending this meetin'." He said he wanted to say something about a few insulting assertions which had been made "ag'in me in the Courier and the Crimes." The Crimes he alluded to sarcastically was the Buffalo Times newspaper. The moniker referred to that organ's preference for publishing the more sensational news stories of the day.

"Now," said he, "what has Jack White ever done to offend the voters of the First Ward? To hear these fellers talk and read some of these things in the newspapers you'd think I was some big bad wolf going 'round and bitin' all the people in the ward!"

The crowd laughed at the idea of Jack's ever being anything like a wolf.

"The Democrats had a meeting the other night an' of course old Jack White got it all around. Who were the men that spoke at that meeting'? They were men under Sheehan on the canals, who've got to be ag'in me, or else lose their jobs!

"They charged me in Wednesday's Courier," continued Alderman Jack, wiping his brow, "with breaking up the Scoopers' Union! I brand that as a downright lie! Any man or set of men who say I interfered with any union's affairs, lies! And they know it.

"I believe in a fair fight," continued Jack, managing to keep his face straight, "and I think men should be fair in politics as well as anything else. A man that never made an enemy never made a friend. I've made a few of both. I'll give any man my house and the lot it sits on that'll show I had anything to do with breaking up the Grain Scoopers' Union. I came here with my union card from the old country and I've always been a union man, and I've been in many a hard strike in this town."

Faced with all the muddy shoes and pant cuffs that stood before him, the Alderman felt he needed to explain why, in a city renowned for having more miles of paved streets than any other city in the world, the streets of his own ward were not yet asphalted.

He drew a nice picture in which there were poor men with homes unpaid for who could not afford asphalt on one hand, and himself on the other, posing as a model alderman refusing to order asphalt until the majority of the property owners asked for it.

As to criticisms that he ran the fire and police departments, he said that if he didn't get men positions in the Police or Fire departments he would be blamed for "doing nothing to help you boys," so why should he be abused for doing the best he could?

Jack White accused Assemblyman Billy Sheehan of importing teachers all the way from Batavia, and asked the crowd, had he himself not always got positions for nice First Ward girls whenever he could? Then the Alderman made one of his whining exhortations for which he'd become famous, and said that the voters "must decide who will best represent their interests, John P. Sullivan, or me."

"I'm willing," he said, in his sweetest manner, "to abide by the will of the majority. If the majority think I am the best man... I hope, I hope," he emphasized earnestly, "they'll vote for me.

"But if they think Sullivan's the best man, then I hope..." he said not so earnestly, "that they'll vote for him."

"Who is this man, Sullivan, anyway? What does he know about governing? What experience has he ever had other than cutting ice off the lake? I'm willing to compare notes, and if I haven't served more young men and young women than the whole caboodle of 'em put together, then I'm ready to get out of this fight."

The Alderman took a long breath, glanced toward the reporters, and then let loose a volume of abuse of newspapers, which doubtless pleased him and certainly pleased those who had gathered.

"I've had a good deal to contend with in this fight," said he. "The Courier has been upon my back, the Crimes has been upon my back, and the Irish-hating Express has been upon my back. The Courier has abused me and it has lied about me. I suppose they're against me, perhaps, because I don't wear a stand-up collar," he scowled, flashing an ugly look toward the Express reporter that was present and garbed in the latest style, size fourteen and a half.

"And all I ask of the Express, and there's one of its reporters here tonight, is that they'll hammer me like hell, and for every hammer I'll make a vote. The Express has been after me a great many years, but she's never caught up to me yet. It is all right to beat a man on paper, but I tell you the only paper that'll hurt me will be the little bit of four-inch paper that'll be put into the box next Tuesday!"

In response the crowd nearly yelled itself hoarse and Jack stopped to allow The First Ward Band to enter the wagon-shop, remarking in his childlike innocent manner, "What band is that?" The crowd appreciated the joke and laughed at the question. The band tooted a few toots and Alderman Jack concluded, "In view of the abuse and vilification that's been heaped on me I ask all my friends to vote for me that I may be vindicated."

Alderman Jack sat down. The crowd cheered and the band tooted.

Alderman Jack White didn't campaign much, besides shaking the hands of a few drunken constituents in his favorite saloons between chugging down schupers and sending The Band out to play and parade through the ward streets.

He didn't have to.

JP Sullivan, on the other hand, well known only in his own 6th district, had to hit the streets hard in the more unfamiliar divisions of the First Ward. Used to being the man in charge at the Sullivan & Nunan Ice Co., he had an uncomfortable time at first allowing others to step in for him at the icehouse. But step in they were obliged to, for campaigning had to be done and won, even at night in the dark when the voting men would be home from work and almost asleep.

JP affixed SULLIVAN FOR ALDERMAN banners to three sides of his carriage, and hung four lamps, one over each wheel, so as to stand out and be conspicuous. Street lighting was dim, if a street even had any at all, and what with holes, hounds and hooligans, he needed to be seen as much as he needed to see. Even though nary a flake had fallen, he retrieved the sleigh bells from the ice company barn and attached them to his horse Billy's reins. He'd named his horse after Blue-eyed Billy Sheehan.

Most of the time he interrupted a family's supper. The ward's men were depleted and drained from working twelve hours and longed for their easy chair or their bed. Often JP was unwelcome. Known for having an affable manner and the ability to tell a good tale, he tried to be his most charming and persuasive, even as his pregnant wife and baby yearned to have him at home. He tried to keep each visit under two minutes in length, that is, when they'd even open the door to him.

Right before election day, the faces he passed on the street that had been only vaguely familiar a few weeks ago now had names and homes and families attached to them. He'd call out as he passed, crying, "Michael, it's John P., sayin' hallo!". Blessed with a sharp memory for names and numbers, this talent of recollection won him many supporters, with neighbor remarking to neighbor that John P. called out to them on the street, by name. They knew him now as one of their own.

After he'd finished his rounds, JP engaged in late night conferences with his brother at home, or if Annie was asleep, over beers at the Mutuals' boathouse. The brothers planned strategy and talked out new ideas. JP confessed that unseating the deeply entrenched Jack White might be close to impossible, not so much because of the man's popularity, but more for his ballot-stealing and his full array of underhanded ways. Jim read the exhaustion in his brother's face. He wanted this election win for his brother perhaps even more than JP did himself.

Jim's demeanor turned dead serious. "I've been keepin' a secret from you Johnny, and you and me don't keep no secrets from each other," said Jim after he retrieved a third beer. "But this one is a police department secret that could get me fired if it's found out I told."

JP recognized resoluteness in his brother's expression, but said nothing to encourage him to do what he seemed to be saying he shouldn't.

"So, I need to tell you this, JP, and I know you will keep it to yourself, because that's what we do. I didn't tell you before because I didn't have good reason to, but now I do. So don't be mad at me. I had to keep it to myself for my family's sake."

JP sat with his left ankle resting atop his right knee, slouched in his chair. He was becoming nervous, realizing something momentous was coming. He set his beer down on the table next to his chair.

Jim Sullivan leaned forward and grasped his brother's shoe with one hand.

"It was Jack White who killed Doc Greene."

The Endorsement

The First Ward has been disgraced and hampered these
dozen years by Jack White. Under the guise of advancing its
interests, he has used the ward's influence as an instrument
with which to open the corporation oyster for his own benefit.
The First Ward can do itself and the other twelve wards an
inestimable service by sending the iceman John P. Sullivan to
the Common Council in place of the spoilsman John White.
—Buffalo Express
October 30, 1889

That same evening, respectable voters eager to be rid of Jack White, citizens
of the First Ward who believed that their rights and privileges had been
systematically bartered away during the preceding 14 years, convened at
Chambers' Hall on Elk Street near Louisiana. They declared that the reign
of their tyrant must come to an end. Never more, they said, shall Jack White
misrepresent the people of the First Ward. Never again shall he enter the City
Hall to take the oath of office. There were hundreds who concurred in this
determination, and their enthusiasm rose to fever heat.

The hall was a large one, but it was crowded to its utmost capacity. Not just
with Democrats, but betrayed Republicans were present as well, both sides
itching to get rid of the scoundrel Jack White.

Many a sturdy Republican voter who in the old time had worked for the
election of White said that the time had come for returning their boss to private
life. There were lots of good speeches, plenty of hilarity and enthusiasm, and
everyone seemed to think that the prospect of downing the notorious alderman
should cause everyone to burst out in thanksgiving. The language of wit, of
eloquence and of satire, of denunciation and ridicule and scorn was employed
in heaping opprobrium upon the head of the devoted Jack. And the audience
enjoyed the meeting immensely.

Mr. Jeremiah O'Shea stood up and told how Alderman Jack White had asked
him for his support.

"I met him on the street," said Mr. O'Shea. "I heard his voice long before I saw
his form, though the latter was big enough, God knows!"

The audience howled.

"He says to me, 'Come now, Jerry, I don't want you to say anything ag'in me
I haven't done!'

"I told him I had never attacked him morally and that many things I knew
about his past life had never been mentioned by me. He is not the kind of man
we can support. He is made up of bluff. Come on now," O'Shea shouted to the
crowd, "where shall we cast him?"

Voices cried out, "Into the Hamburgh Canal!" "Into the soup!" "He can go to
hell!"

William O'Laughlin took a turn swinging, and told in a humorous manner of the attempt Jack White had made to secure the support of him and his fellow workmen.

"White bought us drinks and explained several little local happenings in a way favorable to himself. I says, 'Mr. White, you are quite a politician, ain't you?'

" 'Yes,' he says."

"'Well,' I says, 'you have such a double-faced way of doing business down here in the Ward, and such a confiscating way of doing business up there at the City Hall, that I think you are not the kind of a politician we want'. Oh, but he's a dandy, this Jack White. There was Jacky McMann who was promised a job for voting' for him last fall. Well, Jacky hung around all winter not known' whether he'd go to work today, or tomorrow or the next day. Well, Jacky didn't go to work at all. It came spring and one day White beckoned Jacky across the street. 'Oh, here's my job!' thought Jacky.

"'An' what are youse doin'?' says Jack to Jacky.

"'Nuttin' sir,' says Jacky.

"'Well, there's a manhole down at the corner of Louisiana and Miami streets, go down there and you may get a day's work at ten shillin's.'

"That's what he gave poor Jacky fer 'is votin' fer 'im! A ten-shillin' job!"

The men were riled, and shouted angrily, as it became apparent that Jacky McMann's experience was not at all unique.

All the big ward Democrats spoke, but there was nary a mention of the name of Jack White's opponent. The meeting was far more a "Get Rid Of Jack White" convention than an "Elect John P. Sullivan" rally.

Jim Sullivan, in uniform, sat at the right hand of his brother the candidate, shouting louder than almost anyone. This was his little brother's big chance. Both their entire lives had been spent rising from pennilessness to power. Finally, it came JP's turn. John P. Sullivan, candidate for alderman, stood and addressed the throng:

"If I am elected, a fact which now seems beyond a doubt, I will be a Democrat; I will remain true to the interests of the people of this ward. I think we can easily put a clincher on what remains for us to do, to keep what we have gained. The fight is won. Stand by the guns and the victory will be ours."

A voice called out, "You bet we will."

"What we want to do, gentlemen," Sullivan continued, "is to get to the polls early in the morning of election day. Jack White, at his meeting last night, advised his men to be on hand early. This shows that he is afraid of us and that he knows we are in better shape than ever before to beat him. All we need to do is to work early and late and we will win! It seems like an old story to be rehearsing the peculiarities of Jack White, does it not?"

The crowd agreed loudly.

"He is not even a consistent Republican. He is not so well regarded in the Republican wards of the city. There might be many men in the ward who had received positions at $1.25 a day through the influence of Jack White, but it was equally certain that in every such case the alderman had pocketed the extra 50 cents which belonged to the workingman by right."

Meanwhile, Fingy Conners was steamrolling ahead in a dizzying acquisition of power and money ceaseless in its drive and awe-inspiring in its scope.

Conners bought the controlling interest in the Buffalo Vulcanite Company, despite the fact the company had yet to win any significant contract to asphalt the city streets. Buffalo at this point correctly boasted that it had more miles of paved streets than New York, London or Paris, or for that matter any other metropolis in the world. The city was exploding with growth, and its appetite for asphalt was voracious.

Fingy saw dollar signs, thinking of his friends in the city's Common Council who owed him tribute.

One of the Vulcanite stockholders, W.H. Albro, sold all his stock to Conners, at par, explaining he was "interested in other matters and did not care to hold his stock any longer." This exact quote was echoed by a second officer of the company when asked why he sold his stock to Fingy Conners as well, again at par.

Conners was also embroiled in controversy over a number of vacant lots he was trying to sell to the city, one specifically for the construction of a new public school. The price he wanted for the lot was exorbitant.

The Buffalo Express, along with every other newspaper in the state that hated Conners, insisted on referring to the Hon. W.J. Conners as "Fingy," or "Finggy" Conners, much to the upwardly mobile Conners' outrage. Fingy himself insisted upon the prefix of "Honorable," even though he had never held office, served as a judge, nor earned the title in any of the customarily honorable ways.

The Express asked in reference to the school lot affair, "Why do not some of Finggy Conners' friends do something to break the awful monotony of this silence? If Mr. Conners' friends are only suffering from a lack of means to reach the public, The Express freely throws open its columns to them. Come, now, what have you to say for yourselves?"

The response was a letter from Conners himself, going to great lengths to justify the cost of his lot, the gist of which was he had to charge so much because "the fact of a schoolhouse being built on this lot will materially depreciate the value of all of my other adjoining property for residential purposes."

Fingy's justifications ended with a terse request: "In the future please quote me, if you have occasion to use my name, as W.J. Conners."

On the Saturday night before election day, JP eased his weary bones into a hot bath. His wife brought him two fresh towels and tried to keep the baby out so her husband could gather his thoughts. But JP wanted his boy with him as he mused. Annie brought the year-old in, and tried standing baby Thomas upright on the little octagonal white tiles. She supported him as he tested the cool flat floor with his strengthening legs, anticipating his first unaided walk across it.

"What trouble did you cause your poor mother today, Thomas?" asked his proud father. The baby immediately spit up as if to provide an example.

Annie was fatigued, and had been feeling poorly as the date for the birth of their second child approached. She'd found she was pregnant again just as baby Thomas celebrated his fourth month. She felt inundated. It was difficult enough having one infant. She didn't quite know what to think of her being with child again so soon. What if the new one isn't as healthy, or doesn't sleep as well as Thomas?, she asked herself. JP had been boasting to one and all that he was going to have a new career and a new son within a month of each other.

There was a knock at the door. It was JP's brother Jim.

"Go on in, Jim. He's in the tub," said Annie, picking up Thomas from the tiled floor.

Jim walked in the bathroom and had a seat on the commode, then reached out and shut the door over.

"Aren't you going to do anything with the information I gave you about Jack White?" Jim asked.

"What can I do with it?" replied JP "You told me in confidence. I can't just go and announce it to the world. I have to consider you and your family first. I think I can win this thing fair and square without it."

"JP, this is politics. There ain't no fair nor square. Jack White will play any dirty trick he can to beat you. If he had any such information on you, he'd be spilling his guts to all the newspapers the day before the election. There must be some way you can make use of it."

JP seemed unusually unconcerned, almost as if he didn't care if he won or not.

"What's goin' on JP? What have you got goin' on inside your head you're not tellin' me?"

"Nothing, Jim. What's your suggestion? If I tell people, then the department will know exactly where I got my information, and that might mean the end of your job. And then what? You'll go back to the furnace and to puddlin' molten iron? There's no way I will ever allow that to happen. You just trust me. Trust me to know what I'm doing."

"You're sayin' you don't have some plan that you're not telling me about JP?", asked the doubtful Jim.

"Absolutely not," lied his brother.

On election night a few voters ventured out into the freezing night air in order to glean a few inconsequential facts from the bulletin boards. It was the general impression even before the polls shut down that the widely despised land-stealing Republican mayoral candidate Carmichael was in the soup. Democratic candidate Bishop claimed an early victory as mayor.

Inside the headquarters of the Democratic County Committee, a dense crowd filled the rooms and extended back to the head of the stairway which was in darkness, accounting for the constant stumbling upstairs and the tripping downstairs of anxious men. The crowd was a quiet one though. Occasionally a crumb of information would be doled out and the boys would whisper the fact, nodding with the air of men who had foreseen that everything would go just as they had predicted. The smoke of thick, heavily built cigars made an atmosphere which no one who had lungs of any material more delicate than leather would be justified in breathing.

Several bonfires on the streets were provided through the zeal of festive small boys who had been hoarding boxes, barrels, and other combustibles for the previous few months for this occasion. Down at Police Headquarters, a number of candidates and their friends were milling about the offices and the corridors. William F. Sheehan came in to find how he stood. That he was expecting a big majority in his reelection to the State Assembly was not denied him.

Fingy Connors was on hand, swaggering about with the boastful statement that Jack White had defeated John P. Sullivan by 15 votes.

"Fifteen votes?" cried Sheehan. "Listen here Conners. You send your men out to make sure those remaining votes don't arrive here. Fifteen is far too close."

An hour later three thugs accosted a Democratic election inspector on the Turnpike Bridge. Yellow arc lights illuminated a shower of ballots as they fluttered down into the waters of the canal.

Some people who knew them since childhood wondered what could have ever happened between Fingy Conners and John P. Sullivan to drive such a wedge between them that Conners would work so incessantly to have White installed in office over his childhood friend.

Surely, John P. must be infuriated.

But others, such as those who would see them together at one of the many Mutual Rowing Club functions—laughing, joking and trading stories with each other—knew something about them quite different altogether.

Christmas 1889

Jim was highly suspicious of his brother's fine mood following his defeat, and confronted him.

"You'll see tonight," promised JP.

That evening JP Sullivan hosted a powwow at the Mutual Rowing Club's boathouse involving saloon boss Fingy Conners, Alderman Jack White, the Sheehan brothers, and his own brother Jim.

A tinseled Christmas tree sparkled in the corner of the boathouse parlor, a handsome new oil painting depicting the Royal Canadian Henley Regatta had just been hung, and wreaths were suspended in every window in preparation for the M.R.C. Christmas Dance & Gala scheduled for the following evening. JP's Annie and Jim's Hannah were in their most festive holiday spirits in anticipation of this, their favorite club event. But Annie was expecting the baby at any moment, and she feared she might miss it.

There in the club's parlor, between cold beers and beneath the mistletoe, the plan was finalized on an agreement which would give every player present, except Jim, exactly what he wanted.

The closely coordinated maneuvering between Fingy Conners and Jack White, both Republicans, and their comrades the Democrat Sheehan brothers, immediately following the 1889 election, had been focused on the redrawing of the ward lines. The final details of the plan were revealed on that snowy evening to John P. Sullivan, much to brother Jim's surprise.

The First Ward was being split in two, giving JP his own ward.

Alderman Jack White, who had mysteriously defeated overwhelming favorite John P. Sullivan in the recent election, would find his home still located in the old First Ward. But John P. Sullivan's home, formerly in the First Ward, would now be located in the newly-reconfigured Second Ward.

JP Sullivan and his allies on this evening began planning his 1890 campaign for alderman in the Second Ward despite it having been already awarded to him by those present. The Democrats in the coming months agreed to slowly but surely lose interest in the current Democratic Alderman of the Second Ward, James Bradley. Alderman Bradley had on this night been summarily retired without his knowledge.

Jack White was compensating JP for his silence, and the Sheehans for manipulating the district lines in a favorable way that might just allow White to own his seat in the Common Council until the day he dies.

JP would owe much to the Sheehans in the future.

As beer glasses clinked and the men celebrated the success of their newest scheme, Hannah Sullivan ran in shouting for her brother-in-law.

"JP! The baby's coming!"

The Caucus

All was right with JP's world. The new baby, Daniel J. Halloran Sullivan, named in honor of their late brother Daniel, was thriving, as was JP's ice business. His oldest, Thomas, was fascinated by his baby brother and Annie was on top of the world. JP had also recently signed a contract to supply ice to the railroads, and was gearing up the business to be ready to fill up two thousand of their refrigerator cars come January, weather cooperating.

Despite the redrawing of district lines on paper, the First Ward's original boundaries in every other respect—especially its fierce sense of place and neighborhood—remained solidly intact.

Just as the citizens of Brooklyn would continue to be Brooklynites even if Tammany politicians schemed to move the Queens boundary a few miles west and rename that section of Brooklyn "New Queens", Buffalo's "New Second Ward" existed in name only. It was an imaginary place. The First Ward was in reality being represented by two Aldermen in the Buffalo Common Council, the only city ward for which this was true, or even possible, so powerful were its politicians.

The First Ward retained its singular identity despite the redistricting. First Warders would have it no other way. The candidates in the 1890 election for offices in the New Second Ward made precious little use of that moniker and continued to refer to their home turf as the First Ward. Much confusion ensued because of this, as candidates running in the New Second Ward almost always referred to themselves—as did too all the newspapers—as First Ward candidates.

On October 14th a monumental battle was waged in this confusing New Second Ward over the nomination of ward officers on the Democratic ticket: Iceman Sullivan vs. current Democratic Alderman Bradley.

Not for many years had there been any such scrimmage in the Ward as had occurred at Simon McMahon's saloon on Elk Street. The morning caucus had been called for eleven o'clock and for some time the saloon had been jammed with a crowd both outside and in. But when it came time to start getting organized, the fun began.

One corner of the room had been partitioned off with pine boards, forming a little box about six feet square for a polling booth. This little box was the key to the situation. The goal of the supporters of each candidate was to get their men nominated for the caucus offices and declared elected, and then to get them in possession of their places in the polling-booth. This done, the battle would be half over.

When it came time to call the caucus it was discovered, so the Sullivan men said, that a lot of the Bradley men had already gotten inside the booth. The door had been locked but they had gained entry by knocking a board out over the door. Both sides were eager enough to organize, but could not legally do so until eleven o'clock. The Sullivan men claimed that the Bradley men jumped the gun by ten minutes.

What took place in the confusion is not very well known. John Finn, a Bradley follower, stepped up to call the caucus to order, or rather tried to. But Democratic rules require that the chairman of the ward committee should call the caucus to order. This was not John Finn, but rather Mr. Charles McDonough, section superintendent of the Erie Canal, and a Sullivan man.

At eleven o'clock by his watch, McDonough made an attempt to call the caucus to order and put before the meeting the names of John J. Coughlin for chairman, John J. Lynch for secretary, and William Ross and John Morrissey for inspectors. These names were quickly shouted out, shouted for, and the men were duly declared elected. Walter Dubie and John Finn, Bradley men, were also declared election inspectors.

The saloon was now the scene of the wildest kind of confusion. Men were shouting and swearing, pushing and tearing. Part of the bar gave way and whisky kettles went on the floor and were trod underfoot. The men who had been declared elected officers of the caucus were seized by their supporters in the crowd and whether they were willing or not, over they all went in some fashion or other into the coop in the corner. The door could not be unlocked in the crush, but that didn't matter.

One big Bradley man, weighing nearly 300 pounds, was boosted into the booth from the street through a narrow transom about a foot high. How he could have possibly fit through was a mystery, but he did.

Chairman Coughlin, in being boosted over, had his coat slit up the back, his collar torn off, his hat smashed, and was generally mutilated when he got into the polling box.

Secretary John Lynch exclaimed "I had to come over the shoulders of the crowd in order to get into the booth!" His clothes were badly torn, too. Hardly any of the men who went into the box in such a sudden manner escaped without being bruised and torn, but John Miniter, a ship carpenter, got used the worst.

When he was fired through the hole above the door, Miniter's ear caught on something and was half torn off. It was afterward bandaged and sewed up, but he had lasting cause to remember the Democratic ward caucus of 1890. Another man lost a watch, and still another a watch chain, while a police officer lost his badge, though it was afterwards recovered. In the meantime the police officers— nearly a dozen of them—had been trying to clear the saloon of the crowd. When after long-continued and hard work they succeeded, the coppers' helmets were battered and their faces streaming with perspiration. When the smoke of battle cleared away the Sullivan men were in possession of the booth. In there with them were Messrs. Dubie and Finn, as inspectors for Alderman Bradley.

The voting went on for some two hours.

When Alderman Bradley and his supporters saw the day was going against them, they became greatly agitated. At about one o'clock, Alderman Bradley went to the window of the booth and called to his two inspectors inside, asking them to leave.

"What for? We're getting a fair shake," said one of them.

Bradley would not accept that he might be taking a licking fair and square. Even his own inspectors had just indicated as much. On Bradley's repeating the request, the Bradley inspectors vacated the booth. Alderman Bradley then mounted a wagon in a huff, and advised those of his friends who were nearby to let the caucus go to hell, as it was a fraud.

"Billy Sheehan," he shouted for all to hear, "has the police on his side, and it's no use fighting any more. Talk about coercion in Ireland! That was nothing compared to Billy Sheehan's methods of beating me out of this nomination!"

No matter who the caucus might nominate, Bradley declared that he would run as a candidate of the people. He called a meeting of his sympathizers at Walsh's Hall for that night. Upon Alderman Bradley's withdrawal from the caucus, few votes were cast for him thereafter. Shortly after four o'clock it was declared that 540 votes had been cast for John P. Sullivan as the nominee for alderman, as against 97 for Bradley.

The fight caused quite a split in the Democratic forces in the ward. Alderman Bradley and a party of his friends called at the office of the Buffalo Express that night to tell their side of the story. They were particularly bitter against the police, who they said, did Sheehan's bidding without question, and in so doing, broke up a legitimately organized caucus.

"The First Ward just now," said Alderman Bradley, "is flooded with letters offering work at from $1.50 to $2.50 a day on the State job on the Bird Island Pier. Of course this work was nowhere to be found earlier in the season, but now that election time is approaching jobs are flowing like Niagara. Well, a boat called the City of Buffalo took about 150 of these men, some of whom do not even live in this city, from Bird Island Pier yesterday morning. They were landed at the Ohio Basin slip and from there were transported to the caucus. Oh yes, sure it was a Sullivan crowd, paid by the State to do what Sheehan told them to do. I wanted no bloodshed at this caucus. I realized I could never get a fair shake there, and so I asked my friends to withdraw. But I am in this fight until the polls close on election day."

After the imbroglio, Alderman Bradley filed a certificate of nomination, as under the new law he had the right to do upon procuring a sufficient number of backers. But his papers revealed that the wily Bradley had anticipated this exact outcome all along.

The Sullivanites had been greatly depressed in the weeks before elections by the reports concerning the health of their candidate. John P. Sullivan had been very close to death's door, and it was stated that his condition was so poor that he might not survive more than a few days.

JP laid in his bed and gasped for air in a feverish delirium, cursing the additional blast furnace newly built across Hamburgh Street. The Buffalo Furnace Company had bought the abandoned Union Ironworks property and was engaging in the manufacture of charcoal pig iron, and thus bringing to an end more than a decade of bluer skies and breathable air. JP blamed the fouled atmosphere for allowing his pneumonia to take hold.

Two days after that first statement was issued, the new reports were more cheerful. His physicians, it was reliably confirmed, announced that JP Sullivan would most likely recover. His illness was the result of a cold, which developed into pneumonia. He had rashly ventured out while ill in order to attend the Democratic County Convention, and suffered a relapse.

For the next ten days none of the would-be alderman's adherents were permitted to see him. Annie stood guard with Hannah's help to keep all visitors away.

Alderman Bradley's forces had been completely routed at the caucus by the iceman John P. Sullivan's followers, who were reinforced by Blue-Eyed Billy Sheehan and friends. Angered at being bested, the independent Bradleyites held a separate caucus and nominated the gas-man Bradley as their Independent Candidate. Curiously enough, when the ousted Mr. Bradley filed his Certificate of Nomination to run as an Independent, it was found to be dated several days prior to the regular caucus, showing conclusively that he anticipated his defeat there. Bradley was forced to make a public statement justifying his filing of a Certificate of Nomination before the caucus ever took place.

"The cause of the revolt in the First Ward," Bradley explained, "is owing to Billy Sheehan's interference in ward politics. He and his men ran the caucuses in our ward to the exclusion of all others. I was told that Sheehan boasted that I would not get the nomination even if I got 10,000 votes at the caucus. I knew that I would not receive fair treatment, and so I got up my certificate ahead of the caucus.

"I feel sorry for Mr. Sullivan, for I don't think he will live, according to the report I heard today."

John P. Sullivan issued a bulletin less than a week before election day.

To the Electors of the First Ward:

After weeks of serious illness, I have now recovered sufficient strength to be informed of some of the malicious falsehoods which have been circulated against me by my opponents in the struggle for Alderman. Weeks ago, when in good health, I declared over my own signature that I would submit to the judgment of the ward caucus, but learned, to my surprise and disappointment that Alderman Bradley would run on election day, whether renominated or not.

I am the regular Democratic nominee for alderman, and therefore I assert that all loyal Democrats should support me on election day. I have been attacked in this campaign most maliciously while lying at times near the door of death, when my opponents knew I was unable to reply or defend myself against baseless and unfounded statements. These misstatements I will not now attempt to specify, for they are already familiar to the voters of the ward; but I do appeal to the manly instincts of our citizens to defend their neighbor from brutal attacks when too weak to defend himself.

I am no more the creature or candidate of a "ring" or "clique" now than I was last year when I made the best fight ever waged in this ward against Alderman White. This is my first opportunity in many weeks to appeal directly to the voters of my ward for their support, and while I refuse to make extravagant promises, too easily broken, I do agree, if elected, to be an honest, hard-working and attentive public servant.

John P. Sullivan
November 1, 1890

A Promise Kept

"By hook or by crook Johnny, Billy Sheehan and me is gonna get that office for ye." so promised Republican Alderman Jack White to Democratic aldermanic candidate John P. Sullivan. They kept their oath. At a wild Common Council meeting immediately following his resounding defeat in the election, Sullivan's rival for the office, Alderman Bradley, shouted his indignation to the rooftops.

He was ignored.

The City Clerk submitted the official vote of the election to the Common Council. In many of the election districts he reported that clerical errors and discrepancies had been found which, however, in no instance affected the result. The votes were duly canvassed by the aldermen. A motion was then made to approve the figures as compiled by the City Clerk.

Alderman Bradley panicked.

They weren't going to even listen to what he had to say.

A stormy scene erupted in the Council between Aldermen Bradley and White. Alderman Bradley gained the floor just barely before the returns were officially approved. He launched a vigorous attack on First Ward election methods.

"I want to enter a protest, as a citizen of the United States and of the city of Buffalo," Alderman Bradley exclaimed, "against the way the election was conducted in the First Ward! I want to protest against the manner in which the election was conducted in my ward, in the interest of an outraged people and in the interest of ballot reform."

Continuing, Alderman Bradley said he had filed his certificate of nomination in due time, properly signed by over 50 citizens of the First Ward. The Deputy County Clerk, Mr. Avery, had informed him that his papers were indeed in order, but subsequently County Clerk Orr had seen fit to reject them, alleging that they were irregular.

"I can't imagine what influence was brought to bear upon Mr. Orr," he said, implying quite the opposite, "to have him do this."

Bradley next referred to the unusual doings in the fourth district of the First Ward on election day, which in fact were historically speaking quite usual, albeit corrupt. He charged that the inspectors of election were not sworn in according to law and were not qualified.

"In the First Ward's Eighth District I received, according to the inspector, just 10 votes, and Mr. Shaver, the candidate for Assembly, received 15 votes. I thoroughly canvassed this district and can produce over 50 citizens living in the district who will swear that they voted for me. You can talk about election frauds, but the First Ward election was more rotten than a South Carolina election!

"I see that Mr. Sheehan and others advocate an amendment to the law so as to permit inspectors of election to be appointed rather than elected, but the press should cry down any such amendment with a fury, for if it is passed the bosses will do the appointing and counting, and the people who do the voting might just as well just stay at home and not vote at all!

"I hope the press will take up this matter and help place the guilty offenders where they belong. In the State Prison!"

Then the cat fighting began.

Ald. White: "Oh, Bradley was beaten and feels a little sore."

Ald. Bradley: "I don't."

Ald. White: "To believe him, there are no honest men in the First Ward. Why, I couldn't secure any of the inspectors. Alderman Bradley wanted all of them for himself, and got them, too."

Ald. Bradley: "Yes, but weren't they tampered with?"

Ald. White: "Here he is, accusing his own friends—men appointed by himself! He has accused the election boards of being frauds. Everybody knows that I asked for the appointment of some of my friends as inspectors, but Alderman Bradley wanted them, and got three of his friends appointed in each district of the ward. Now, because he was beaten, he charges these very same friends of his with swindling! He says the votes were not honestly counted, but I believe that they were correct, as there is a God in Heaven."

Ald. Bradley: "Fifty men in one district will swear that they voted for me, but only 16 were counted!"

Ald. White: "Oh, pshaw!"

Ald. Bradley: "I am proud of the fact that I got more votes in your district than you did!"

Alderman Jack White whined that he would not play the baby act, like Alderman Bradley was doing.

"I won't act underhanded either," Jack White continued. "I'll say, and I'm not afraid to say it either, that I worked and voted for Mr. Sullivan, Alderman Bradley's Democratic rival, and I'm glad of it. I went for Sheehan too, and worked for him and I'm not ashamed to say so, even though I am a Republican and those two men are Democrats. The votes that were cast for you, Alderman Bradley, were in fact votes cast against Mr. Sheehan, on account of some ill-feeling caused by his leadership in the First Ward.

"If a block of wood had stood in your place on election day it would have received as many votes as you did! I am satisfied that the election in the First Ward was as honest as in any ward in the city. You have no right to accuse honest men of being frauds and perjurers."

Alderman Bradley reiterated that an inspector in the fifth district was at the ready to swear that the election board in that district did not organize as required by law. He said he did not accuse the people of the First Ward of being dishonest. He intimated, and not incorrectly so, that Alderman White had made a deal with Billy Sheehan.

"Whoever says I made a deal with Mr. Sheehan states an untruth!" bellowed Alderman Jack White, indignantly and with a straight face. "Of the two evils I chose the least of the two and voted for Sullivan, as I believe Sullivan will be better here than Bradley."

Alderman Bradley looked around the Council Chamber. His eyes met no others except those of Alderman Jack White. He realized at that moment that he didn't have a single friend in that room, that none of his glaring evidence would be admitted or considered.

This ended the wordy row. Alderman Bradley's protests were completely ignored.

The returns were then approved, all the aldermen except Bradley certifying to the correctness thereof.

Alderman-elect John P. Sullivan meanwhile celebrated his victory with a long rest to try and regain the strength lost to his illness. He planned his future in the interim.

Inspired by his brother Jim's enthusiasm, a meeting was called in the parlors of the Mutual Rowing Club on December 30th for the purpose of expanding the Mutuals into a full-scale athletic organization for the Southside's many athletes. Already the rowing club headquarters had hosted handball matches and boxing bouts.

Jim and JP spearheaded the movement, but Jim made it clear he was stretched pretty thin, and after his initial push to get things going, others would have to take over. Having compiled an unchallengeable record organizing and promoting the M.R.C., Jim immediately proposed that the new Southside Athletic Club enter some members in the approaching athletic games, a mere six weeks away. No one was going to argue with the founding father. If anyone could hit the ground running with a grand new idea, and make a go of it, it would be Jim Sullivan. With the successes of the Mutual Rowing Club approaching its tenth anniversary, they set about formulating ambitious new plans to expand opportunities allowing the athletic sons of the ward to prove themselves.

With JP's aldermanic election win, the brothers' options were expanded immeasurably. Across the river, on The Island, lay an enormous tract of unused land that they had been eyeing for the M.R.C.'s athletic field.

One of JP's first goals as alderman would be to create Mutuals Park there for the future athletes of the First Ward.

With the installation of the new members of the Common Council in January 1890, a major change was made in the awarding of spoils. No longer could the Council members divvy up the choice posts to reward their friends. The Civil Service Commission would now have charge of that task.

The line between Democrat and Republican so finite everywhere else in American politics was indistinguishable in Buffalo's First Ward. Republican Alderman Jack White held himself above party lines, being out for no one but himself. His loyalties shifted with the breeze, depending on what was in it for him, but more often than not those loyalties were bestowed on the Democratic side, despite his official designation as a member of the Republican party. There was great frustration and righteous anger among Buffalo Republicans that the money sent into the First Ward to elect their candidates was being used to put Democrats in office instead.

In 1889, When John P. Sullivan (D) ran against Jack White (R) for alderman, the Democrat received 1,825 votes, and the Republican received 1,871.

In 1890, just a year later, when John P. Sullivan (D) ran against Bradley (Independent) and Byrnes (R), the Democratic candidate received 1,161 votes and the Republican received just 138 votes.

The incredible disappearing Republican vote was the mystery.

Republican campaign funds sent into the First Ward—and that one ward had often monopolized the entire Republican city fund—were in actuality being used against Republican candidates. The party at large was heartily tired of this state of affairs. It was deduced that the Republican party would be better off if all of Jack White's Hessians were kicked out of the Republican party and into the Democratic party.

The Republicans found they were powerless to change this situation, for Jack White ruled. The Republican Chairman was elected by First Ward votes. White's lieutenant, John Devine, had just been retained as a member of the Republican Executive Committee. No one had the power to challenge Jack White.

The very Charter bill which the Reformers drew up in the winter of 1890 redistricted the wards in such a manner as to make it virtually impossible ever to oust Jack White from the Common Council. Jack White was shut off by himself in a snug vest pocket of a ward, which at election time, he could easily carry every time. The Honorable Jack White was very bullish about this feature of Charter Reform.

The First Ward and its politicians dominated the city.

But a few of these First Ward wharf rats had their eyes on something much bigger: ruling the entire state and beyond.

1891
The Southside Athletic Club

The January 12th parley of the lovers of sport in the First Ward, held at the Mutual Rowing Club, was called to order by Alderman John P. Sullivan. He delivered a few words of advice to the club before it proceeded to the election of officers. The result of the voting put Buffalo City Comptroller Joseph E. Gavin in as president, and William J. "Fingy" Conners as vice president.

The constitution and by-laws were adopted and the initiation fee set at $3. Permission had been granted by the venerable Buffalo Athletic Club, owing to the influence of Conners, for the Mutual Athletic Club members competing in the fast-approaching joint games to use its gymnasium for training. The enterprising Fingy then used his leverage to submit a membership application to the A.A.U. for the as-yet homeless and unproven new club.

The Mutual A.C. took off like a flash, with members competing in the games held February 1st at the 74th Regiment Armory on Connecticut Street. No ribbons were won, but William Aman and James Connolly established names for themselves in the one mile run. Two weeks later at a joint U.S.-Canada games at the same venue, Mutual A.C. member Ed Sarre placed first in both the 220 yard run and the 220 yard hurdles.

The search was on for a permanent home for the Mutuals' new south side athletic club, but it was soon realized that an existing building would not be suitable for the ambitious organization. The deed for a large property located on Louisiana Street below Elk, owned by Fingy Conners, was transferred over into the possession of the now officially renamed Southside Athletic Club. Work instantly began on erecting a stunning new clubhouse. It was completed in less than two months. Other clubs in the city looked on in astonishment, as only four months had passed from the date of the founding the Southside Athletic Club to the completion of a beautiful clubhouse and gymnasium.

"There's even a skating rink on the roof, for God's sake. Where in Christ's name did they ever get the money?" the other clubs wondered. Even the venerable Iroquois Athletic Club didn't yet own its own clubhouse.

Observers were amazed at the wonders that could be brought about by an association with Fingy Conners.

On the afternoon of April 30th, the Southside Athletic Club opened its new home with a gala athletic and social event attended by all the brawn and muscle in the First Ward, in addition to large crowds from the Buffalo Athletic Club, the Queen City A. C., the Iroquois A. C. and others.

Over 900 excited people packed the new structure, well-lighted and handsomely decorated with American flags and arrangements of bunting in the club's official colors, black and cardinal. For the time being they adopted the Union Jack as their official club flag, for reasons little understood by the Irish population. At one side of the exhibition hall sat the officers of the entertainment, Fingy Conners, President Gavin, and the Sullivan Brothers, while opposite them a string band was stationed, providing delightful musical selections between events.

The first exhibition of the afternoon was a comedic set-to between Fitzdempsey and Killsimmons, a pair of midget boxers who sparred with blackened gloves designed to leave behind an imprint. The fun was seeing how fully covered in black smears the little men could become before the scrapping ended.

Southside Athletic Club members William Aman and John L. Sullivan—no relation to the world renowned boxer of the same name— followed, providing a lively three-round boxing match with six-ounce gloves. Neither was stingy in his attentions to the other, and compliments were showered thick and fast. Aman had slightly the better of it owing to his quickness.

The next exhibition was a heavyweight wrestling bout for blood, between Green of the Buffalo A. C. and Bauerman of the Southside A. C. This was followed by a number of other less feverish matches. In between bouts the string band played and children ran around in defiance of their parents, whom, having a wonderful time themselves, failed to be very strict. The crowd could smell the chickens roasting on spits outside at the back, and stomachs growled in anticipation. The Riverside Bicycle Club pitted two of its members against each other in a wrestling match. Then, a boxing bout between lightweights Jack Smith and Billy Purdy, the clever little mulatto, ended when Purdy was delivered a ferocious uppercut and the contest had to be stopped. Everything was conducted in the most becoming manner. There was no rowdyism or roughness at any stage in the proceedings. The Sullivan wives and children delighted in the boisterous of the affair, although Hannah and Annie, both pregnant again, found themselves at wit's end trying to keep control of their children in the huge crowd as their husbands freely socialized.

Cousin and disgraced police officer John P. McGrady accepted JP's invitation and took the train from Amsterdam with his wife Kittie. He was trying his best to patch things up with his cousins over his past behavior. He'd been reduced to working in his father's Wall Street grocery store, and feeling less than successful. He spent most of his time with the more forgiving of the two Sullivan brothers. He sought JP's advice on a number of topics, including political office and a similar athletics organization for Montgomery County. He told Jim that he regretted his conduct as a police officer, and wanted very much to return to the department.

"The nerve of that guy," snickered Jim to JP when their McGrady cousin was out of earshot. "He stages a Wild West shootout with another officer in the middle of Main Street, and he thinks he can just rejoin the department when it suits him? Amsterdam would have to be off their rockers to allow him to ever pin on a badge again!"

"Don't let him hear you Jim," cautioned JP. "I've read somewhere he bites!"

The two laughed so loudly that everyone around them turned to see what might be so amusing. The music proved a popular ingredient in the day's entertainments and a few souls chose a partner for an impromptu jig. But owing most to the triumph of the Southside Athletic Club's christening was the logistical feat of serving lunch to 900 hungry guests.

Later, as they surveyed the crowd, Fingy Conners stood on the other side his old friend the Alderman.

"D'youse believe dis, JP? We done it ag'in. Everyt'ing we set out to do together turns t' gold."

1891
A Boat House Conflagration

On July 26, Patrolman Jim Sullivan came home early due to baby Hannah being sick. She had just turned two.

Hannah Sr. had given birth to their fifth child, Daniel, the previous month and had her hands full. Annie too was pregnant and due in October and was feeling ill much of the time, and with a two year old and a three year old of her own couldn't help Hannah as much as she would have liked.

Jim cleaned up the house, supervised the three older kids and took turns with his exhausted wife attending to the sick baby and newborn Daniel. It was very hot and humid, and they were using iced cloths to keep baby Hannah cool. The stifling air was so thick with industrial smoke that there wasn't even a clear view to be had across the river.

At a little past 6 o'clock, Jim was washing supper dishes when he heard a woman outside scream "Fire!" He peered out the back window to see black smoke shooting upward from the rear portion of his cherished Mutual Rowing Club boathouse.

The boathouse fronted South Street just around the corner. The backs of both Jim and JP's houses on Hamburgh Street nearly butted up against its east wall. Jim ran down the stairs and outside toward the fire alarm box shouting "JP! Fire! Fire!" as he passed No. 12 Hamburgh. Annie immediately poked her head out the window. "The boathouse is on fire, Annie! Tell JP!"

Jim then ran back to his house and up the stairs to evacuate his family.

"Hannah! We'll have to get out... I'll start gathering things!"

She couldn't believe it.

"What next?" she thought as she raced about.

Jim ran around gathering up both babies' needs: wicker bassinets, medicines and clothing, the enamel bowl filled with ice, baby bottles and purified water. Hannah was aghast, and exhausted from caring for the babies. She hollered at the three older children to gather a few things and get ready to leave.

"What should we take?" asked Jim Jr.

His mother, discombobulated, had no idea what to tell him.

"Forget it. Let's just go!"

Hannah waited with the children at the head of the stairs.

The stench of smoke invaded the house and Jim flew around slamming windows shut against it. When he was done he took newborn Daniel in his arms while Hannah carried sick baby Hannah and the other three held on to their parents' clothing. The family virtually flew out the front door.

The boathouse was located behind their home to the West, and luckily the smoke and embers were blowing North. For the time being the shaded front porch would be the safest and most comfortable spot for the family. Crowds were flashing past the house to witness the exciting drama, some on velocipedes. The ladder truck and engines would soon be racing in.

"We don't need you kids getting run over by a steamer!" their father yelled at them as he placed the newborn in the bassinet. "You all stay on the porch in the shade and don't you dare move unless your mother tells you to! Hannah, stay here unless the smoke gets too bad. I'll just be gone for two minutes," he instructed. "I'll keep checking up on you."

"I want to go with you to see the fire!" shouted Jim Jr.

"You stay safe right where you are young man, or else! All of nature is going to be headin' down this way any minute now!"

Jim Jr. was familiar with that threatening tone and the consequences of disobedience, so as anxious as he was to follow his father and the excited crowd, he remained on the porch.

Jim ran around the corner onto South Street intending to enter the boathouse building to save the sculls and perhaps rescue the trophies from the upstairs parlor. But as he approached he saw Ben Crowley, Ed Stanton, James Short and a couple of other members out front, choking and gasping. They had tried to reenter the building after first fleeing in order to save the boats, but blinding, choking black smoke was billowing at a furious volume from the open front door. Without their realizing it, the open portal was now feeding oxygen to the insatiable blaze, helping to doom the structure.

"The sculls!" shouted Jim. "We're gonna lose them!"

The roll-up door behind which the sculls awaited their rescue was double-locked from the inside, and no one had the keys with them. But it was too late anyway. The only portal for getting back inside the clubhouse was now belching out a suffocating intensity of opaque black smoke. Even if they had the keys, they'd be foolish to risk their lives attempting to go back in. There'd be neither seeing nor breathing inside.

The call had gone out to Hook & Ladder No. 8 on Chicago Street, located just doors away from the Sullivan & Nunan Ice Company. Almost immediately the firemen pulled up like all creation in a glorious steamer, bell clanging at a piercing pitch, the brass boiler and all the fittings beautifully polished and gleaming, the boiler belching thick smoke in the rear.

The engine's wheels were huge, for speed. Those in the rear measured five feet in diameter; the front, four feet. In a beautiful demonstration of choreography under duress, the horses were instantly detached and led to safety as the water hoses were hooked up and readied and the ladders removed from the ladder wagon and raised. Brave firemen clambered skyward to bust in the windows to poke a hose through.

The fire was engulfing most of the upper story by the time the first water was poured on, and Jim was grateful for the river being just yards away. The firemen labored furiously, awaiting a second company, Hook & Ladder No. 10, which had to come all the way from Southside Parkway. A stiff warm breeze was blowing steadily off the lake and the flames were spreading with lightning speed.

Jim saw that the blaze was growing so large that flames were sure to catch the family's houses. They were already licking at Dalton's Store on the boathouse's western side. He ran around to the front of his house to remove his family from the porch just in case. He found them shade across the street in the shadow of the tall elm at the corner of the L-shaped intersection right at river's edge where a crowd watched the drama in fear and wonder. Neighbors volunteered to help watch the children and keep them safe. Hannah tried to keep ice on the sick one. Annie joined her there with her two, and took charge of Hannah's newborn. Soon, a thousand people or more had gathered nearby from around the neighborhood and from the Union Ironworks across Hamburgh Street. It was absolute bedlam.

Hook & Ladder No. 10 roared up just in time. The Alderman ran up to the newly arrived firefighters and exclaimed, "I'm Alderman Sullivan, and that's my house, and my family's inside! You have to keep the flames from spreading there!"

JP's Annie was safely outside with her babies, in fact standing next to the river with Hannah and her kids watching the drama unfold. The alderman was trying his best to get the firemen to do his bidding.

"Well, then, you'd better run and get your family the hell out of there, you idiot! What in God's name are you waiting for? Christmas?"

The fireman was appalled that the Alderman would not have already evacuated his family.

JP, embarrassed, made a big show of running toward the front of his house to pretend to evacuate his family in order to save face with the firemen, but the firefighters had their eyes averted to a more immediate concern. They clearly concluded the boathouse was a lost cause, so their priority became saving the surrounding homes. The two fire companies labored together for over two hours, successfully preserving the adjoining structures.

The Mutual Rowing Club boathouse, a two story structure constructed entirely of wood, was totally destroyed.

The boathouse faced the hot descending sun with nothing to shade it, so to cool the interior, the door leading out to the rooftop cupola had been left wide open to vent the late afternoon buildup of heat. The result was a chimney effect that allowed the fire, once started, to spread very rapidly.

A loud cry arose from the entranced crowd as the beautiful cupola, where the Adelphi Band had sat on so many occasions playing for the throngs attending the Mutual's regattas, collapsed into the structure as the roof gave way. A pillar of sparks and red hot embers blasted vertically high into the sky. The firemen followed their ascending path with their hoses to douse them before they could set flame to neighboring structures.

The backs of both Sullivan homes were damaged, but minimally so.

As for the Mutual Rowing Club, it was all gone: the expensive sculls and the fruits of ten years of rowing, the gleaming silver trophies.

The next morning, Jim and JP combed through the wreckage, hoping to find something undamaged. As JP moved away some charred roof, underneath he discovered the barely readable script on the blackened blistered scull named in honor of the founder, the Jim Sullivan.

Misshapen blobs of metal lay scorched where proud trophies once displayed. As he surveyed the sorry collection, Jim recalled overhearing someone at Daniel Halloran's funeral quietly lamenting Daniel being buried with his trophy, and what a waste he thought that was.

Now that same "wasted" trophy was the only one left surviving, albeit, six feet under.

At least we know where it is in case we ever need it, Jim thought, with a smile.

The Mutuals are now Homeless. The Mutual Rowing Club's boat

house on South Street, near Hamburgh, was entirely destroyed by fire last night entailing a loss of $8,000. The flames were discovered in the rear portion of the building at 6:05 by a woman, and officer James Sullivan immediately sounded an alarm from box 129. When the firemen arrived the destructive flames were eating up the rear and upper sections of the building and it required two hours of hard work to extinguish the flames. There was a brisk wind blowing and at times the surrounding property was in danger. The adjoining residences belonging to Peter P. Dalton, James E. Sullivan and Alderman John P. Sullivan were slightly damaged.

The boat house was erected in 1881 and was 70 x 20 feet in dimension. An addition 60 x 20 feet in size was built in 1883. The structure was two stories with a dome, totaling 45 feet in height. The rooms were handsomely furnished and the gymnasium was complete with many valuable boats. Among the property destroyed were eleven four-oared shells, nine single sculls, two clinkers and two private boats, some of which were new. The many valuable prizes won by the members at different times were consumed. The origin of the fire is a mystery but it is thought it was caused by a lighted cigar carelessly thrown among some inflammable material. A meeting of the Club was held in the afternoon, but at the time of the fire no persons were in the rooms. The loss is estimated at $8,000 and the insurance at $4,000. Notwithstanding the severe loss, President Daniel Nunan says the club will rebuild a house immediately. The burnt building was considered the finest boathouse in this section of the United States.

—The Buffalo Commercial

1892
Baby Hannah

Baby Hannah continued to be ill. She got better for a while, then relapsed. The doctor prescribed various potions and pharmaceutical preparations to try and arrest her vomiting and diarrhea. Unbeknownst to the physicians, these methods were interfering with the baby's own body's attempt to ward off her intestinal invaders, making her worse, and ultimately, fatally shutting down her ability to digest food.

On September 19th, two-year-old Hannah Sullivan died of cholera infantum. With the arrival of each new summer's heat the dreaded condition had become every parent's worst nightmare. Hannah Sr. struggled to carry on for her four surviving children. Jim turned inside himself. The double loss of the daughter who had quickly become his favorite, and the rowing club he had founded and built with his own hands, both within weeks of each other, compelled him to attack his work with more intensity and anger than ever before.

Among other innocents, he took his rage out on the tramps, 800 of which were already crowding Erie County Penitentiary. A major economic depression held the nation in its grip, and Buffalo, being a railroad hub, saw hundreds of tramps and hoboes and entire homeless families stealing rides on the railcars passing through the city.

No matter child or adult, spry or lame or halt, the police branded them all irreclaimable bums.

> *Every workingman is a tramp in embryo.*
> —*Alarm, October 11, 1884*

> *The policemen swung their long nightsticks right and left, left and right, and every time they hit a man he fell bleeding like a stuck pig, and whining and moaning like a kicked dog...The horses were pulled up on their hind legs and mowed down the hoboes like grass, tearing their scalps open and bruising and wounding them.*
> —*Buffalo Evening News*

The Buffalo Police Department waged a vicious and prolonged campaign against these transients, whose only crime was losing their jobs, their dignity and everything they owned. The Tramp Acts, widely adopted around the nation in the 1870s and 1880s, made it a crime to be homeless, and the penalty was six months in prison at hard labor. As many as 140 tramps were pulled from the Buffalo rail yards and vagged in a single day. In a disciplinary action, Police Special Jim Sullivan was reduced in rank and transferred out of Precinct 7 into Precinct 1. As Alderman John P. Sullivan's fortunes and family grew, his brother Jim's diminished. The silent partner who had facilitated and paved the way for his young brother to rise so rapidly in the world of politics and business was himself drowning.

1892
"Defeat John P. Sullivan"

A Buffalo Express editorial on election day eve, November 1892, called for the defeat of Alderman John P. Sullivan. The very same paper three years before had called for his victory.

> John P. Sullivan, who is Republican candidate Mr. Donovan's opponent for Alderman, has earned an unenviable reputation for himself in the Board of Aldermen, where he was placed two years ago as the result of a surprising vote. The Republicans were not alone in their surprise back then when it was announced that Sullivan had carried the Second Ward election by 500 votes. There were many Democrats who looked askance at the returns, and even yet it is freely declared that fellow Democrat Bradley, who was forced to run as an Independent, "was counted out." Mr. Bradley's friends are looking for their revenge this year.
>
> Mr. Sullivan is in the ice business, and lives on Hamburgh Street near South Street. Sheehanism is a dominant feature in the Alderman's character, and in no place has this been more strongly displayed than in the legislation over the election inspectors. True to the principles of his leader in this case, Mr. Sullivan took the grab-all-leave-nothing side of the question, and it was not his fault that both parties secured recognition on the boards of inspectors.
>
> Among other things against Mr. Sullivan, it is said that when the resolution was offered in the Council abolishing street-car transfer charges, giving our citizens a continuous ride all over the city for five cents, Sullivan voted against it.

An afternoon paper editorialized:

> The 2d Ward has hundreds of people who barely get by as it is, who must travel to work on the West Side. Their own alderman, John P. Sullivan, was the only man in the entire Council of twenty-five aldermen who voted in favor of a continuation of the street-car transfer charges."

Hannah put her paper down on the kitchen table and sipped her tea while feeding baby Daniel at the same time. She still expected to see little Hannah toddle in and laugh her mischievous cackle. She would have turned out to be a little devil for sure, that one.

Hannah wondered about what she'd just read.

What or who could possibly influence JP to vote against something that every citizen in the city was loudly demanding, and every other alderman in the Council voted in favor of,? The question set her mind to churning. It proved a welcome diversion from her sadness.

Despite his very poor public record, John P. Sullivan was awarded the election by his friends. Wholesale election fraud was subsequently screamed from the ward's many rooftops and as a result twelve duly elected Inspectors of Elections were arrested. The group was indicted on December 22 and arraigned before a judge. Attorney Moses Shire was hired to defend all twelve, with various local shining lights stepping up to post bond for each and every one of the accused.

Alderman John P. Sullivan made sure that elections inspector James Duggan Jr. was bailed out in time to spend Christmas with his family, to the tune of $3,000.

The question of prime interest at the City Hall was, had Alderman Sullivan perjured himself by putting up the bond? He had sworn to the unencumbered possession of certain property which County Clerk's records clearly showed as encumbered.

The Buffalo Express stated:
> This is a clear case of perjury, that is if no mistake has been made (in the records), and may result seriously for persons concerned if it is not explained satisfactorily.

That same night, two local boys broke into the ice company barn and stole a sleigh and a horse to take for a joy ride. They returned it before midnight, but JP wasn't feeling any too charitable this holiday season.

He had them arrested.

She Coughs Up Teeth

Reinstated Special Jim Sullivan received the hearty congratulations of all those present at Precinct Seven as Captain Ryan announced his promotion to the rank of Detective and presented Jim his new badge. Jim inspected it, and smiled. He'd worked hard for it. It should have happened long ago.

His first task along with Detective Jerry Lynch was to call at the home of a negress by the name of Vetrell Russ. They were to investigate the attempted kidnapping of her person by Medical College students.

Three years previous the woman's fascinating condition attracted widespread attention and notoriety throughout the entire northeast for the reason that, at intervals, she coughed up teeth.

These teeth did not originate from her mouth and gums, but instead were choked up and expelled by the woman from the deepest recesses of her corpus. They were fully formed teeth, root and all, bathed in blood, indicating they had previously been rooted in her throat or lungs before being dislodged.

The medical world had been so intrigued by her sensational case to the extent of their engaging in criminal behavior.

Since the first discovery of the disease the woman had been a subject for every kind of experiment. She had undergone, she said, every examination known to the medical profession. It had almost come to pass that a young man contemplating the study of medicine did not enter college until he had visited the woman's home, questioned her interminably and induced her to undergo a thorough medical examination.

Vetrell Russ' brother Jonas Russ had read a story in the newspaper about a certain police officer who lived on Hamburgh Street who had gone to extraordinary lengths to rescue a dog. The animal had been suffering severe abuse at the hand of its owner, a worthless and hopeless case who had taken to alcohol. Jonas Russ, heartened by the story of the rescue of the forlorn beast, appeared on the stoop of Jim Sullivan's home on Hamburgh Street to appeal to him with the support of a dozen relatives and neighbors. The delegation of negroes crowded onto the front stoop as Jonas rang the bell.

Hannah, with baby Daniel in her arms, went to answer the bell, but seeing a dozen dark faces at the window she became frightened and called up to her husband. She was reluctant to open the door.

Jim came down the stairs from the kitchen, pushed the curtain aside, surveyed the crowd quickly, and determined that they had come in peace. He opened the door.

"Officer Sullivan, sir?"

"Detective Sullivan. Yes, that's me. What can I do for you?"

Jonas Russ cried out, "Somethin' must be done, Detective, sir. They ain't no livin' down at Vetrell Russ' house for de gang of students dat pour in from mawnin' till night. They's be keepin' dat business up now for nigh on to two years, and she and me and everybody else am tired of it. We didn't make no kick till they tried to poison her and take her away."

"Poison her? Some students tried to poison your sister?" Jim wasn't sure he had heard right.

"Yessir, dat they did!"

The complainant went on to describe how one night not long ago a crowd of students boldly opened their front door without warning and entered their house. Suddenly one of them took a big bottle from his pocket and forced it under the screaming Vetrell Russ' nose. She fell asleep, and according to her brother's story, the students then tried to pick her up and cart her away like she were some captured animal.

Jonas Russ stopped the students in the act of kidnapping his sister, threatening to take his axe to them if they did not leave. He declared that the students told him that they were going to carry her to the Medical College to see if they couldn't discover the secret of her peculiar malady. The students were persuaded to leave under the threat of his raised axe, but they returned again the following Friday night in even greater numbers with weapons of their own.

Jonas Russ claimed that the young mob then tried to break into the house through the door and windows and steal his sister again. Neighbors rushed to their aid and the attack was turned back. His sister was now so terrified that she would not even leave her room, and Jonas was quite fearful that she would be killed unless she was protected from the students.

Jim recalled the time Mrs. Cleary's body was dug up and stolen by medical students at Holy Cross Cemetery. Jim Sullivan had heard a lot of strange stories in his time, but this latest one earned a spot at the very top of the heap. Hannah and the children had joined Jim on the stoop and listened wide-eyed and open-mouthed as Mr. Russ and the group of his neighbors related their bizarre tale.

"I promise you, Mr. Russ," emphasized Jim, "that in the morning I will visit your home with Detective Lynch and we will see what we can do to put a stop to these shenanigans."

The group bowed and nodded in gratitude, and seemed genuinely relieved that their complaint had finally found a sympathetic ear.

Early the next morning Detectives Sullivan and Lynch set out for the Russ' home in a patrol wagon with Ed Stanton, police department driver and Jim's lifelong friend. Miss Russ became very much frightened when she saw the officers approach and ran screaming hysterically into her backyard. She believed that the police were yet more medical students coming to try and take her away in an ambulance, and it was some time before she could be made to accept otherwise.

The detectives were at last able to talk with her. Miss Russ begged them for protection from the medical students, and pledged she would get it even if she had to swear out warrants against each and every last one of them.

Just as the policemen conferred with Miss Russ, a group of well dressed young men thoroughly convinced of their own eminence pulled up in an elegant carriage and alighted in front of the Russ house. They carried black medical satchels. Miss Russ ran inside, shouting for them to go away. Jim locked eyes on one of the young men who seemed to be the leader and strode toward him with determination.

The haughty group reacted with annoyance.

The detectives flashed their badges.

"We have it on good authority that you thugs here have been breaking into this home and that you attempted to kidnap Miss Russ." said Jerry Lynch.

"Oh, that was not the case at all," the leader disdained, clearly insulted at being called a thug. "We were just trying to induce that negress to come with us for an examination. You see," he announced imperiously, "as medical students we are preordained to determine her condition."

"And we police officers are preordained to run you arrogant little pricks in to the precinct house and charge you with breaking and entering, assault and attempted kidnapping, intent to do bodily harm, and if I can manage it, attempted murder," Jim replied with a big smile.

The students looked at each other and laughed scornfully at first, as if they thought the officers must be joking, until the handcuffs clicked snugly around their wrists and they were rudely loaded onto the patrol wagon.

As the wagon departed for the station house, Vetrell Russ stood in her front window with her brother's hand on her shoulder, feeling relief for the first time in more than two years.

"Now, we might jes be gettin' us some peace," her brother sighed.

The medical students were aghast that they were being treated as common criminals, and with a grandiose display of entitlement made that quite clear to Sullivan and Lynch on the way to the station house.

"Are you aware, sir, who my father is?" sniffed the leader.

"Are you aware, you arrogant louts, that there is a minimum sentence of twenty years in federal prison for attempted kidnapping?" growled Jerry Lynch. "The President of the United States himself couldn't get you fools out of this hole you've dug for yourselves. Looks like your medical professions have finished before they even started."

Jim whispered to Jerry, "Are you sure there's a twenty year minimum?"

Jerry smiled and replied, "Who knows? Remind me to look it up at some point."

The shocked students, suddenly awakened to the legal gravity of the charges against them, wailed and bawled. The moment the tears began to flow, Sullivan and Lynch knew they were well on their way to ending the two year nightmare suffered by Vetrell Russ.

Within a week of picking up the outlandish story, word of the students' arrest had spread among newspapers and medical colleges all over the East. No longer did fancy carriages filled with entitled eager white boys toting black leather grips venture out into the negro neighborhoods in search of a ready medical experiment. No longer did mollycoddled medical students claim that they were preordained to invade the intimacies of Vetrell Russ or anyone else for that matter, although she did become comfortable enough with all the attention to welcome a newspaper reporter or two.

At the dinner table that evening the family gaped out the kitchen window at the sight of two coal-smoke-vomiting tug boats easing an enormous grain ship around the river bend so close to the pavement that South Street pedestrians could have poked the behemoth with a stick. Jim told Hannah all about his day.

The kids ate noisily as Hannah held baby Daniel at her breast.

"Did those boys really just bust through that poor woman's front door during the night to try and cart her away? Jimmy, eat you peas or ye'll get no pie."

Jim Jr. was pushing peas around with his fork, trying to figure out how to get rid of them without actually consuming them.

"Not only did they, but me and Jerry were standing right there talkin' to her in front of her house when these students come driving up again with their little medical bags, brazen and pompous as can be, paying no attention to us at all, like we were there to clean out the sewers or something. They were expecting to just stroll into her house and absquatulate with her. I have to tell ye, Hannah, I've encountered some big-headed people while carrying out my duties before, but these boys were so full of themselves they were like a whole new species to me."

Hannah was visibly troubled by the story.

"I can't imagine being in my own home feeling safe and sound some quiet evening," worried Hannah "and suddenly have people just burst through my door to grab and skedaddle me off like some circus curiosity! It's absolutely terrifying."

Surrounded by her vulnerable offspring, Hannah shuddered and grew all-overish at the mere thought of such a prospect.

"Once we told them they were being charged with attempted kidnapping and would spend the next twenty years in jail, they seemed to develop entirely different opinions about the propriety of their errand," he smiled.

"I should expect so!", Hannah said indignantly, imagining all too vividly Vetrell Russ' distressing predicament.

"What does piety mean?" asked Jimmy.

"Propriety, Jimmy," Hannah corrected. "Well, it means... proper. What's proper and what isn't. Some people these days seem to be confused about what is, and what isn't!", her voice cracked.

"Oh," replied Jim Jr. quietly, not at all sure about the reason for his mother's upset.

August 18, 1892
Fly Street

The next morning a more calmed Hannah was busy in her kitchen just after sunrise, preparing a pan of H-O Oats and stewing dried prunes. The baby lay in his cradle next to the breakfast table, cooing. The window over her kitchen sink allowed Hannah to survey the always-fascinating activity on the river below. Right at the foot of Hamburgh Street there was built a small dock, and on it in the brightening light she saw a man's coat and hat neatly folded and placed there. No owner could be seen.

Jim came into the kitchen in his uniform. He was scheduled that day to make an inspection of the dreadful slums in the Canal District with Jerry Lynch, as the city was newly in a fervor about the possibility of a cholera outbreak.

He couldn't wear plain clothes today. In dangerous neighborhoods police needed to be as visible as possible and conduct themselves with authority.

Quite a few persons suffering from cholera had landed in Manhattan on immigrant ships the previous month and New York City was in a panic, especially the teeming Five Points. In Buffalo, conditions along the Erie Canal and the intersecting Hamburgh Canal had degenerated in recent years, what with the canals no longer being the bustling thoroughfares of commerce that they once were. What not too long ago were thriving hotels, offices and warehouses lining the ditch were nowadays slum hovels sheltering hordes of mostly Italian immigrants. Jim, Detective Jerry Lynch, and a reporter from the Buffalo Express were going to assess the conditions and report back.

"What are you lookin' at so intently, Hannah?" asked Jim.

"There's a nice coat and a hat sitting out there on the pier, but there's nobody around to claim them, at least no one that I can see." She looked over her shoulder at her husband, appreciating how attractive he looked in his uniform.

"You look very handsome this morning, Jim. Yes you do. Here, your oats will be ready in a minute, darlin'. Take your seat."

Jim didn't hear her. He was fixated on the clothing on the pier. He turned and trundled down the stairs, through the front room that Hannah had converted from the Halloran's Saloon of his boyhood into a stylish parlor, and out the door.

He crossed South Street and walked over to the little dock, bent down, and inspected the coat. It was in very good condition, as was the hat. Not something that anyone in this neighborhood would forget or leave behind on purpose. He looked around, up the river toward the bridge, out along the river straightaway toward the grain elevators on The Island, then to the left into the little slip that had been carved into the Buffalo Furnace property.

He saw nothing.

Jim then traced the riverbank along South Street, and within a few seconds spotted the body of a man floating face down in the murk.

Jim raised his eyes toward his kitchen window and saw Hannah framed there holding his baby son in her arms, watching him. He pointed to where the man floated. She raised up on her tippy-toes and peered toward where he indicated, trying to see what he was seeing, but from her vantage point all Hannah could make out through the bushes obscuring the riverbank was something that might possibly be a person's foot.

Martin Lauder was 70, and lived at the Old Folks Home on Pine Street. Lauder had left the home and spent the night with the Vetters, who lived next door to Jim and Hannah at No. 18 Hamburgh. Louis Vetter had once been the deceased man's son-in-law, and now was the only family the old man had left. Mr. Vetter stated that the old man had been of weak mind recently and had threatened suicide many times before. Thus little attention was paid to his most recent bluster.

Shortly before six o'clock that morning Mr. Lauder had left the Vetter home, walked a few doors down to the foot of Hamburgh Street, removed his coat and hat, folded them neatly and placed them on the pier, then slipped silently beneath the sulphur-infused waters.

After Coroner Durney finished his assessment at the river bank, Jim's friend, undertaker Dan Crowley, removed the old man to the morgue.

Jim climbed the stairs and gulped down his cold oatmeal. He was late.He arrived at the precinct house still hungry and busied himself with paper work until Jerry Lynch arrived. They were scheduled to meet the Buffalo Express reporter at 11 o'clock and then proceed together to the Canal Street district, where any comparison of evils is almost lost sight of in the general depravity and filth.

There the Schoellkopf Block stood out head and shoulders from all the rest, just a gunshot away from the City Hall itself. Schoellkopf Block was their first destination.

The Express reporter was a young man named Ronald Gworek, timid but unflappable, happy to have the company and protection of the officers as he steeled himself to enter the lion's lair with his camera and heavy tripod. Gworek's own parents had been immigrants, from Poland. So had both police officers' parents, they from Ireland. But what these hardened sons of immigrants saw along the old Erie Canal shocked them.

They stood on Canal Street and looked down at the canal. Babies of Italian immigrants played on the towpath amid piles of human excrement covered with swarms of black flies. Garbage, floating planks, newspapers, and a dead dog, bloated and ghastly, choked the canal's black and deadly motionless waters. No guardian's eyes watched over the imperiled toddlers who waddled much too close to the canal's edge. It seemed a miracle that the cholera bacillus had not yet visited here.

The men's first objective lay directly ahead. They decided against knocking on the front door that faced the street. Instead they stabilized themselves on a rickety wooden fence alongside the wood frame building as they descended the embankment to the towpath. The stench was nauseating. They approached around the back of the old structure and poked their heads into a low doorway.

"Hello?", Jim shouted.

A little old woman having no teeth, swollen with bloat, half-blind, and foul to any degree one might imagine, met them. She acknowledged that she was the proprietor. Her failing eyes initially did not discern their police uniforms and she at once began the tricks of her trade, but quickly recovered and realized the men's true purpose.

Divided between fear of the law and a compulsion to appease, she lead Detectives Sullivan and Lynch and reporter Gworek through her "apartments" as she called them. There were perhaps a dozen little rooms, all stuffy and close and reeking with the filth of years of uncleanliness. A ruined negro wench, the knots of her hair tied in a rainbow of unraveling rags alive with crawling lice, was her sole companion.

Sanitary arrangements were nowhere to be found. An ancient bucket sat out in the open in one corner of the front room. This was the only toilet. An identical state of affairs would be found throughout the entire district. The canal itself would be the final receptacle for the buckets of filth when the tow-path itself was not used instead.

In one corner of this same front room where the stench was the most terrible, the fetid drippings from an overflowing bucket-toilet on the floor above were plopping down from the ceiling and streaming down the wall, collecting in a festering pool on the floor.

"It is only logical to say that nowhere shall we find a worse case of filth than this," exclaimed Gworek. The detectives suspected from their experience, however, that the green newspaper reporter was most likely in for a surprise.

Already physically nauseated as well as sick at heart, the three proceeded up the dark, unstable stairway to even worse quarters, where any opportunistic cholera germ would happily flourish in luxuriance. Filth was found there, poverty was found there, abject wretchedness was found there — but the people, strangely enough, seemed happy.

Jim had recently read Thomas de Quincy's Confessions of An English Opium Eater. The horrific pictures that the book had painted in his imagination instantly popped into his consciousness. He was observing people apparently immune to the filth and horror engulfing them, drowning them, living happily in some parallel carefree world only they alone recognized.

Recalling De Quincy's book reminded Jim of yet another volume, Salvation Army founder William Booth's gruesome In The Darkest England, with its nightmarish expose of London's slum dwellers and homeless human sewer-rats. Jim shivered in repulsion, for right here in front of his burning eyes was almost exactly the scene that Booth had written of.

The Canal District swelled with Italians that had mostly journeyed from Sicily. They cooped up in dank, stinking dens adjacent to irretrievably fouled waters when they might just as well have remained beneath sunny skies in their own far-off land, the transparent Mediterranean at their doorstep. Instead, they migrated here, seemingly merry and content.

Little Josephine was eleven years old. She had seen strangers visit before and knew at once what the men wanted. She alone of all the occupants of this tenement could or would speak more than a few words of English. She'd memorized every inch of the tenement's crowded floors and gladly showed Sullivan, Lynch and Gworek around, and seemed thankful for a kind look and a few pennies.

Each floor was like all the rest, though as one climbed nearer the roof, the picture grew darker and the blight grew more sickening. Through the center of each floor ran a long, broad wall, once neatly plastered. But now only enough of the original coat remained to give a hint of its former glory, when the Erie Canal was a great roiling, streaming highway of endless traffic, and this house was a prosperous hotel that sheltered a decidedly more refined clientele. The floors were cut and broken by decades of continual chopping, and in places boards had been torn up to burn during the cold winter nights for fuel. Through these holes the officers could see clearly the most intimate details of the lives of those who dwelled on the floor below. An old woman sat on a pail grunting loudly, evacuating her bowels while peering upward at the visitors as she went about her business, oblivious to their revulsion.

As Josephine lead the trio from room to room she pointed to where three families were living in one little cubicle, and where two women and six or seven men, to say nothing of their countless children, made their home in another.

She told the three something of her own life; how she is happy here and does not regret leaving Sicily. Her voice was plaintive as she told of the sufferings of a poor woman who lies on a death bed they have to squeeze past, the patient wheezing and gasping her last. The men cover their faces with their handkerchiefs to assuage the smell and provide some protection from germs.

Josephine's face suddenly lights up as she tells them how she is going to a "far-away countra next-a week-a." Some very kind woman in North Collins was coming to fetch her away and care for her, she claimed. "Only next-a week-a, now," she says, and her little swarthy face beamed and her great black eyes shone with a new light—the light of hope. It was the same horror story from room to room: babies, babies, babies; all the way from the two-day-old lying on a bed beside its haggard mother to youngsters of 12 years.

Josephine's family was more prosperous than the others, for they owned a machine for making macaroni. They sold the staple to their neighbors for five cents a pound. Whenever they made a good deal of it they sold it on Seneca Street, she said. Despite the presence of the little machine, in most cases the noodle was all made by hand.

Each afternoon the women of each family gather around a low table and roll out the dough between their unwashed fingers and leave it to dry on dirty string looped round the decaying fence posts in the sun, where myriads of flies attack it and glutton themselves until sated. Children play beneath it, knocking it into the dirt, where it is picked up, brushed off and re-hung. The fumes from the feces and garbage bathe it in their vapors, and birds steal any piece they can, defecating on those that remain.

"Best we try and forget how this is made," Jim said to Jerry Lynch, "or we'll never again be able to stomach it."

Tomatoes, too, were plentiful. Nearly every stove had its boiler filled with stewing fruit, which, when done, is plastered on shingles and left to dry in the sun. Jim's pleasant memories of neighbor Wilhemina Rapp, his mother's German friend who introduced her to Italian foods at the Chippewa market, feeding him chewy sweet sun-dried tomatoes, would never be the same again after this.

Jerry Lynch was sickened. He stuck his head out the window to vomit. He wiped his mouth with his kerchief and continued on.

"This is all well enough, and no better than what these people surely deserve," he bleated as he looked out onto the disgusting state of the tow-path.

As a fact though, this was the only way their landlord provided them of getting rid of their filth. Could they be most to blame if cholera knocked at their doors and found a ready welcome? A man named Haley sublets this building,

Inside a tenement on Fly St.

and collects the rent. Just now he was in terror of a general condemnation of his house, and should have been, for the Health Commissioner was hotly after him. He had promised to whitewash his walls and improve the sanitation of the building, and if cholera never reaches Buffalo at all, it will have been a marvel not of Haley's hand.

Across Canal Street, opposite the Schoellkopf Block, lay the ironically christened domicile, The Palace, inhabited also by Italians to a great extent. The premises were measurably cleaner and better kept up, but still not fit for humanity.

The Bailey Block on State Street, leased by Hume & Sanford, was another Italian rendezvous. About 18 families lived in it, each family having from 4 to 20 members. Next to the sights in the Schoellkopf Block, the most dangerous result of uncleanliness could be seen here at Bailey Block.

Beneath the building sat a shallow cellar, accessible from the rear by small windows. From the building's windows above, all the filth and refuse was calmly dumped into Davenport Alley, the lane running between appropriately named Fly Street, and Canal Street. As it collects in great scandalous piles in Davenport Alley, it is shoveled, literally shoveled, into the dwelling's cellar. The offal lay there rotting and reeking, crawling with maggots, fermenting and bubbling, sending up its fumes of death through the entire building and impregnating all with its lethal, nauseating, fetid stench, while babies in the rooms above struggle against all the odds to survive yet another day.

Another house paradoxically is called Roma d'Italia, for a lovingly scripted sign installed above the entrance assigns it as such. It is quite a romantic name for such a hovel of wretchedness. In three rooms on the first floor, and just above the point in the cellar where putrid layers of refuse lie rotting, live about 20 Italians; men, women and children. The dwelling's centerpiece is a magnificent clock. Commanding in its contrast to the general surroundings, it ticks bravely away on a mantelpiece.

From the roof hang multiple bunches of green bay leaves to dry in the summer heat. Several cases of lemons were being unpacked and a swarthy fellow stood sharpening a sinister-looking knife on a stone which he proudly showed off as a relic of his distant home. This same fruit will be sold on the street to innocents unaware of its being brought to ripen in the fumes of rotting detritus. Above stairs the dense population lives in stolid indifference to its surroundings. What must their lives have been like in Italy that they so contentedly pass their lives here in festering tenement houses like these? the men wondered.

Other nearby buildings are much the same; the Urban Block on the corner of Fly Street and Maiden Lane, leased by Hume and Sanford. The Ottenot Block on Maiden Lane, opposite Fly Street, leased by Kingsley, and others just like them that shelter the same wretchedness. Well enough, some might say, if the people know no better life and are happy in it. But in all of them, the same lack of proper sanitation is seen; the same use of buckets, the same dumping of sewage and garbage onto the towpath or into alleys.

Of the three most serious infractions of sanitary laws, the third is in the block in which the Alhambra Theater offers its attractions to foolish youth and corrupted manhood. Kittie O'Neil, the once-and-forever famous jig dancer, is the mistress of this particular establishment. She collects the rents. Kittie O'Neil is outspoken despite appearing to be in ill health and appearing much older than her 37 years. As she limps her stout frame about the premises, leading the three men, she

Kittie O'Neil in her prime.

claims she is ready to do all in her power to remedy the evils here.

"Did you know that as a girl I was discovered by Tony Pastor while jig dancing at Wild's? That he brought me to New York for a four week performance? They loved me so much I played Pastor's Theater for two seasons! I was a big star in New York!"

The men were all aware of who Kittie was, aware of her fame. The irony of this sick, fat, once-famous woman climbing over trash, feces and discards to show them the house she was now managing was not lost on any of them.

"Can I snap a photograph of you, Miss O'Neil?" asked Gworek, playing the innocent fan. She smiled at first, then quickly corrected herself, remembering where she was. There was no way that Kittie O'Neil should ever be photographed in a dump like this, and she said as much to him in reply.

They all mounted the stairs running up the outside of her building and walked around the balcony to the rear of the edifice. Looking over into the alley far below, they took it in. There, covered by a scant layer of sawdust, lay the accumulation of years of human filth. Despite the fact a water-closet had been installed in the building six months previous, residents apparently preferred the older methods, or perhaps were just too tired to walk downstairs to use the installed bathroom. Filth remained where it always had and continues to be, dumped casually from festering pails from the upper story windows.

Detectives Sullivan and Lynch and reporter Gworek, dejected by what they witnessed and exhausted from holding their breath for three long hours in the late August heat, wore their despondency in their expressions. But they had one final stop yet. A grocery store that fronts on The Terrace, on the corner of Evans Street, and owned by H. Barrett. In the rear it is bounded by the Hamburgh Canal. A narrow railing projects from it, below which lies a rotting mass of vegetable refuse and discards, handily disposed of by Mr. Barrett himself; a fitting habitation of the cholera germ. Starving dogs and rats were not the only species digging through the maggot-swirling pile; a negro family was searching for anything at all edible.

Health Commissioner Wende was conversant with every detail seen by the trio. In several instances he had given the landlords 24 hours notice to abate the nuisances. Two inspectors were at work. So far as possible the landlords were being lead while those who were unresponsive were being driven. In a few days Jim Sullivan and Jerry Lynch were scheduled to pay a return visit to see what had been done about the conditions, and what hadn't. All three men felt wretchedly filthy. The officers returned as quickly as they could to their precinct to clean themselves up before going homejjj.

"Don't ye know that Kittie O'Neil's been married twice and is livin' in sin these days with that Al Pettie, right above his saloon on Clinton Street?" sang Jerry. A shower had been installed at the precinct house, gravity-fed by the water tower on the roof. All summer, rain had been plentiful and the sun hot, and Jim Sullivan looked forward to the warm rinsing of the filth from himself, lest he track it home to his family. He couldn't get himself cleaned and out of there fast enough; he was aching to get back to his spotless home and the embrace of his freshly washed wife and children.

"No, I didn't know that," replied Jim. "Good for them."

Autumn, 1893
Uncle Tom

The end of 1893 found John P. Sullivan mired in debt, due in part to his falling out with his business partner and closest friend Thomas Nunan, half of the Sullivan & Nunan Ice Company.

Nunan had decided to run for public office in the Assembly as a Home Rule candidate, opposing the Sheehan Machine candidate. Thomas Nunan's hatred of the Sheehans and their voracious ambitions was in direct opposition to the feelings of his business partner John P. Sullivan, a staunch Sheehan ally.

Complicating politics in the First Ward was the reality that most of the players on opposing sides were all friends since childhood. Tom Nunan, in addition to being a lifelong friend, was one of the founding members of the Mutual Rowing Club, and continued to play a vital role there. Uncle Tom was a fixture in both Sullivan households on Hamburgh Street, and the children were upset noticing his abrupt absence. JP's boys Thomas and Daniel were especially attached, as their father and Uncle Tom usually worked at the house two or three nights a week over company books after eating supper with the family. Uncle Tom was always around.

Recently-pregnant Annie Sullivan was distressed by this latest tantrum thrown by her husband, who once again was magnifying a common difference of opinion with a friend into some kind of personal betrayal. JP had an interesting definition of betrayal that involved its running in only one direction, self-righteously claiming himself incapable of it despite contrary evidence. JP had been quoted in a Buffalo Times article as having said, when it came to his own political ambitions that he "could play for any team."

Hannah admired Tom for taking a stand against the reprehensible Sheehans, something neither her husband or brother-in-law had the guts to do. When newly promoted Detective Jim Sullivan came home and told Hannah about the rift, declaring they would now have to curtail their social interactions with the children's Uncle Tom, Hannah put an instant stop to the nonsense.

"JP is your brother, not mine. If you want to continue doing all of JP's bidding for him, that's your choice. But Tom Nunan is family, and he will be as welcome here as ever. No... in fact, probably now even more so. Your brother will not be telling me or my children how to live our lives! You raised that brother of yours, and yet now you've become his lackey? Since when does he tell you what to do? Develop some backbone, Jim!"

Jim Sullivan did not at all like the assertive changes in his Hannah's personality. He was hesitant to acknowledge that most of these differences in Hannah had been prompted by the negative turns he himself had made. He was no longer the same man she'd married.

JP was being stretched in all directions—political scandal, pressure from Conners and the Sheehans, damaged friendships, pregnant wife, hostile sister-in-law, mounting money problems. Things were spinning out of control like a kite diving headlong for the ground. The effect was being felt by both families. He searched for ways to overcome his most recent financial setbacks. Breaking with Tom Nunan was turning out to be a very expensive undertaking. Now the entire operation of the new Sullivan Ice Co. was squarely on his shoulders. His public image, that of the successful businessman and savvy politician, was being damaged by the notices that were popping up in the newspapers' legal pages attesting to his financial troubles. Successfully arranging for a suit against him by James Adams to be held over to March 8th in Superior Court, JP then proceeded to sign promissory notes to Henry Scaeger for goods needed for the ice company that he could not pay for. Scaeger delivered goods worth $113.00 on a promise in early March, then accepted his promise again on May 4th for goods worth $650.00. Scaeger ultimately was compelled to sue JP Sullivan in Superior Court in order to collect his money.

1893
The Sheehan Political Machine

As if the stench of scandal were not already a historical given in Buffalo's elections, 1893's electoral contests established a new nadir.

Alderman John P. Sullivan had been reelected the previous year, but 1893 found the Sheehan brothers strategically turning against Alderman Jack White. The Sheehans decided that Jack White would be retired and their cousin John Sheehan would take his place in the Common Council.

Cousin Sheehan was sent to make the rounds of the district's saloons in order to manipulate saloonkeepers and their customers into providing voters for him. He was routinely accompanied by Police Captain Michael Regan, whose imposing presence helped drive home the wisdom of backing his favored candidate. The cousin was a weapon in the Sheehan brothers' multi-pronged full-scale attack on democracy in New York State. William F. Sheehan was currently the Lieutenant Governor of the State of New York. His brother John C. Sheehan, embezzler of Buffalo's Orphans' Fund and disgraced city official, was now District-Leader Police Commissioner of New York City, as well as a thriving city sewer contractor, as was appropriate, considering.

> It is no surprise to the people of Buffalo to learn that John C. Sheehan is able to combine the responsibilities of the offices of Police Commissioner of the City of New York, Tammany Leader of the Thirteenth Assembly District, and President of the Pequod Club. It would not surprise them to know that he had charge of, and was responsible for, almost any other department of the City Government. His younger brother, William F. Sheehan, the Lieutenant Governor of the State, his student, has demonstrated that his schooling was proficient, but, unfortunately, he has shown such rashness in methods as brings little credit upon his preceptor.
> —The New York Times, December 25, 1893

In early October The New York Times began shouting from its pages stories about the colonization of voters in Buffalo. Men were being temporarily relocated into the First Ward in great numbers for the sole purpose of voting the Sheehan ticket.

Co-conspirator Fingy Conners' willing puppet James Kennedy temporarily moved into a room at the swanky Mansion House hotel so he might qualify to vote in the First Ward. James Kennedy, brother of Alderman John Kennedy of the 19th, who as a boy had dared to chop off his friend Fingy Conners' thumb, and himself the Democratic Leader of Buffalo's 19th ward, did so that he could vote for Sheehan in the upcoming election. Kennedy's actual residence was out of the district, on Water Street. His plan was to remain at the hotel for the required time period, vote in the election, then check out and go back home.

With election day a little more than two weeks away, the registration of new voters proceeded at a steady pace in the city, but nowhere as briskly as in the First Ward.

In the previous year's presidential election, a total of 1309 votes were cast in the First Ward. By October 23rd of 1893, more than two weeks before election day, the registration count was already up to 2200, with hundreds more voters anticipated. The colonization of voters into the First Ward by the Sheehan-Conners-Kennedy combination accounted for the astonishing increase.

During the last week in October, Buffalo newspapers along with the New York Times and the New York Herald revealed that over 500 men who had taken the civil service exam for places in the Buffalo Police Department had been provided typewritten copies of the correct answers beforehand in exchange for their Democratic Sheehan ticket vote.

The foremost name connected to the police exam scandal was that of Alderman John P. Sullivan.

The New York Times wrote:

> BUFFALO, Oct. 24.—A sensation which puts certain Democratic Aldermen and members of the police department under the gravest kind of charges came to light last evening when the Civil Service Commission met in the Mayor's office. Previous to the meeting, evidence of the most indisputable character had been placed before the commission proving that copies of the questions prepared for the Police Department had been secured by unlawful means, that the questions and answers to them had been typewritten and distributed among certain of the applicants. The undoubted purpose was to help certain Democratic candidates by winning to their support applicants favored by advance copies of the questions.
>
> Among the persons mentioned in the affidavits as being engaged in this business of cheating the commission are Aldermen John P. Sullivan, who is a working member of the machine and bondsman for several indicted election inspectors; Alderman Carey, another Sheehan henchman; John Sheehan, a relative of the boss and candidate for alderman from the First Ward...

Alderman Sullivan's wife Annie rocketed next door and shouted up to Hannah. Annie was in a panic, not knowing what this new development meant for her husband. The New York Times was now trumpeting their local scandal on its pages and naming the father of her children as primary ringleader.

Hannah had already read the opening salvo of the scandal in the Buffalo Courier the previous day, but was horrified when Annie produced a copy of the New York Times.

"If they are putting this on the front page of the New York Times, then this is an even bigger nightmare than I thought it was!" cried Annie. "Why would New Yorkers even care about what happens in Buffalo, unless it's really, truly scandalous!?"

Hannah's eight-year-old son Jim Jr. was at school. He had come home the day before with a black eye and a bloody nose. His schoolmates had slandered his father the detective and his uncle the alderman, denouncing them both as crooks. Jim Jr. jumped on the accusers. He had no real idea what the defamation even meant, but put himself in harm's way to defend his kin. For this, Hannah was infuriated. That their own children should suffer for the political aspersions of their father and uncle was the final stroke.

"Where would JP ever get the answers to a police department exam?" cried Annie. "Do you think Jim somehow got his hands on them?"

Hannah didn't want to even think that her Jim would go so far as to break the law and endanger his career and family only to aid his idiot brother and those bastard Sheehans in their nefarious schemes.

But she was now forced to.

Hannah had reached her point of tolerance. From that day forward, Hannah Nugent Sullivan would regard her husband's brother John P. Sullivan as a dangerous pariah, a looming threat to the very well being of her family. He was the enemy.

JP had established himself over and again to be a wantonly reckless and narcissistic creature willing to put in harm's way his entire family, and hers, just to achieve his own slimy political ends. Annie was beside herself, following Hannah around the kitchen, reading from the New York paper.

"Listen to this, Hannah!" Annie read aloud: "Commission Chairman Wheeler said, 'We have conclusive evidence that Alderman Sullivan helped to distribute the questions. One of our informants used the expression 'Alderman Sullivan had his list full of them.'

"Hannah, doesn't this mean that JP might end up going to prison?"

In Hannah's assessment Annie had always seemed too naive and much too accepting concerning her husband's endless string of shady dealings. Hannah had once told Annie that her chronically absent husband JP was "obviously someone who thrives on chaos." Annie didn't seem to quite understand what that meant.

"JP sets his own hours, Annie, don't you understand that? He's an alderman for God's sake. There's nobody he has to answer to except Fingy Conners and those Sheehans. He's never here at home because he doesn't want to be home. He prefers to be out there commiserating with those hooligans rather than be here with his own wife and children."

Annie had been stung by Hannah's assessment. She had been just as preoccupied having babies as Hannah, but unlike Hannah she found it easier to bury her head in the sand so as not to be troubled by her husband's lengthy absences and relentless wrongdoings. Annie's fears and disappointments were counterbalanced by her ascending star in the city's social hierarchy. She loved accompanying her husband to banquets and political functions in Albany, New York City and Toronto. She loved having live-in help, and lovely clothes.

JP's income — both on the books and off — was much higher than brother Jim's; consequently Hannah enjoyed no such perks as did Annie to help mitigate her apprehensions. All Hannah ever received for her husband's endangering of himself and his persistent rescuing of his younger brother was the snowballing of isolation and grief. Both women had begun to find comfort in food.

The evening before, at supper, when her husband had asked his son how he got the black eye, the detective only briefly exhibited any flash of concern upon hearing the reason, before quickly erasing all traces of emotion from his expression and changing the subject. Hannah watched as it happened. Jim said nothing. He didn't talk to his son about it. He didn't express regret to his son or his wife that he was the reason for his son's injury and torment. Hannah waited for it, but it never came. Was he somehow proud of Jim Jr. fighting in the street in his defense?

As she washed the dishes at the sink after supper, Hannah looked out the window and down on the smaller house of her brother-in-law next door. She could see her nephews Thomas, age 5, and Daniel, age 4, playing in their brightly lit parlor. She thought of her own little Daniel, just two, dead now barely three months, the loss of him still achingly raw.

As JP and his pregnant Annie continued adding to their family next door, Hannah and Jim subtracted.

It was all becoming too heavy a burden anymore. Hannah resented Jim's baby sitting his younger brother, cleaning up his messes, endangering himself, forsaking his own family almost daily to attend to JP and his. And all of this going on concurrent with her suffering such deep loss and bereavement along the way, with no partner there to provide her comfort or support. It was all too much.

"And what does this mean when the New York Times says that JP is 'bondsman for several indicted election inspectors'?" asked the freshly unglued and reeling Annie.

Hannah was losing her patience. She cleared her throat and paused a second, trying to maintain her composure.

"It means, Annie, that your husband, with pockets full of cash, runs down to the police court to post bail for his criminal friends every time one of them gets arrested, so that they don't have to sit in jail. Like that elections inspector last Christmas he posted $3,000 of your children's education fund money for."

"How would you know about such things, Hannah?"

"Jim told me," she calmly stated.

Annie looked blank. A few seconds passed.

"Annie." Hannah looked her straight in the eye. "Ignorance is not knowing something. Stupidity is not wanting to know."

Annie, with a startled look on her face, stared at Hannah in silence as the cold, targeted, methodical delivery of her statement was absorbed.

Annie sensed it was time to go.

Hannah was glad to be rid of her. She felt she had accomplished the task quite diplomatically, considering her simmering rage. Hannah had no one to consult with or confide in about this mess—certainly not Annie, who was clearly not facing the truth of the matter. She had no answers with which to comfort her, nor herself either, for their husbands were in now deep trouble of their own making.

Jim's immediate superior, Police Commissioner Ryan, the Buffalo papers said, was up to his eyeballs in the scandal. Ryan was an eager lackey of the Sheehan brothers. He owed his post to them. And thus, Hannah reasoned, it would follow that Jim, a police officer under the direct command of Ryan, as well as being friends since childhood with both Sheehan Brothers, must be entangled in this scandal as well.

She trembled as her mind churned. Was Jim responsible for procuring the answers to the police exam? Did he distribute the answers to people right along with his brother? Will he lose his job? Will he go to prison?

Worst-case scenarios swirled round in Hannah Sullivan's head. Tears filled her eyes. She gazed upon the two black ribboned framed cabinet photos on the wall taken at the Bliss Bros. Gallery, one of baby Daniel, the other, baby Hannah. She was already so badly heartbroken. Hannah didn't see how she could possibly sustain any more tragedy.

More troubling questions filled her head. How could our husbands' loyalties to politicians and politics be stronger than those to their own flesh and blood? What was it about these Sheehan fools that made them "leaders" to all these other men—even to the police? Why did these other men, powerful in their own right, need leaders anyway, especially those of such a perverted variety?

Hannah didn't understand men. Not her father, not her husband. Not her stupid brother. Why must all the burdens be on the women?, she wondered.

Hannah once loved her Jim without question. He was older than she by eight years, and for the first few years of their marriage she just assumed he was more mature and stable than she.

Not any longer.

Hannah had once admired how Jim was always poised to jump into the fray on his brother's behalf. She concluded that a man like that would do the same for his wife. For his family. But Jim had been proven time and time again throughout their decade-long marriage that it was JP who was Jim's priority. Not his own children. Not his own wife.

When Jim came home that evening from the station house, she didn't turn to greet him as she normally would. He entered the kitchen and picked up on her dark mood with just one glance. He walked over behind her at the sink, and slipped his arms around her, bumping her behind suggestively.

Hannah said, "Annie was here at noon in a complete hysteria, with that New York Times headline in her hand," she said, pointing to the newspaper on the table. "I had nothing whatsoever to say that could possibly reassure her."

Hannah still hadn't taken her eyes from the view of the river.

"There are just no words, Jim," she sighed.

Jim withdrew his arms and pulled out a chair from the kitchen table. He sat quiet and still, looking at the back of her head.

He knew he was in trouble.

First Ward Colonizers:
The Buffalo Express

The Sheehans may have been more efficient at packing the First Ward with colonized voters for the upcoming battle, but Jack White was responsible for his own modest share of colonizers too. Health Commissioner Dr. Wende was a Jack White man, favoring his official duties be directed mostly toward those tenements that were being filled by the Sheehans rather than Jack White. The newspaper cried the alarm.

RICH IN CITIZENS

The 1st Ward Is Apparently
Boiling Over With Men.
NEW JOBS FOR DR. WENDE
A Macedonian Cry To Inspect Dinny Doyle's and Lovely Charley
Flinn's Caravansaries, Among Others - Kilcourse's Beverage

From the accents of gentlemen who should know the condition of affairs thoroughly, like Alderman Jack White, Hank Kilcourse and Jim Kennedy, election day in the First Ward is going to be like Resurrection Day on a small scale.

With the first peep of day over the Ohio Basin Slip, longshoremen and scoopers are going to burst forth from the pavements, descend from the trees, crawl forth from the sewers, climb out of the chimneys and swarm from the houses and barns where they are now living perdue, and flock to the polls to cast their freemen's ballots for Jack White or Johnny Sheehan.

Perhaps the most surprised man in town is Dr. Wende, the Health Commissioner. But a short time ago and the city was to him like an open book, and he could lay out a campaign against tenement bosses at his leisure. But now lodging houses are springing out of the ground in the 1st ward like mushrooms. They rise before the Health Commissioner like Roderick Dhu's men before King James. At every breath he hears of a new one, each with its 40, 50, 60 men packed away snugly, like sardines, waiting for the trump to blow on election day.

The result is that the Health Commissioner is very busy these days, looking after the public weal in the 1st ward. First he had to inspect those popular Caravansaries maintained by Mr. Kilcourse and Mr. William J. Conners; and now these worthy gentlemen, filled with the

anger of injured innocents, have gone to fighting the devil with fire,
and have cut out a new and large job for Mr. Wende.

By the hand of a 1st ward citizen, the Health Department has received
intelligence of several more crowded lodging houses. This in the way
of tidings reached the Health Department:

Ernest Wende, Health Commissioner, City:
I notice in this morning's Express that you have been investigating
a few of the many lodging houses in the 1st ward. Now, why
should you choose No. 133 Main St., No. 444 Ohio Street, and No.
33 Exchange Street and leave out such eyesores as Fagin's on Ohio
Street, Buller Mahoney's on Ganson Street, Dinny Doyle's on Ganson
Street, Lovely Charley Flinn's on Ohio Street, and Johnie Mack's on
Elk Street?
If you will serve the people who are instrumental in placing you
where you are, instead of serving Jack White, you will investigate
those places. You must be silly to think that you can pull the wool
over our eyes as easily as that.
I respectfully request that you investigate those places and cause the
report to be published, as you did the others; if not, I will find a way
to accomplish it.
Respectfully, James Collins
First Ward Democrat, Taxpayer.

In his reply, Mr. Wende called the comments of taxpayer James Collins
"impertinent and uncalled for," and insisted his department only was required
to inspect buildings upon receiving a specific complaint, rather than to canvass
Buffalo's problem neighborhoods and search out violations on their own.

The Commissioner was apparently more angry than alarmed about Mr.
Collins's not-too-subtle reference to the people who were "Instrumental" —as
Mr. Collins rightly claims—"in placing him where he is."

On the following night after Collins' letter was printed, Detective Jim Sullivan
marched into Hanrahan's Saloon on Michigan Ave. There he confronted the
man named James Collins, who enjoyed writing letters to local newspapers,
and who himself had strongly resisted becoming a colonizer on behalf of the
Sheehan Machine. Collins didn't favor any side: he was angry at the entire
corrupt system.

A colonizer's politics didn't matter. If he had been awarded a job, or hoped
to be awarded one in the future, or was easily intimidated, he would comply
with the directive given. Many colonizers were literally bums and itinerants
off the street, rounded up by the police, recruited by saloon-keepers afraid of
losing their liquor licenses if they didn't supply their required quota of voters.
Vagrants and drifters were happy to move indoors out of the cold for a month at
no charge. But men who'd worked hard to make a nice home for their families
were a different matter. They didn't cotton to being kidnapped.

A colonizer's actual home address was irrelevant. If he kept his eyes open and knew the correct response to questions asked, he didn't even have to actually live full time at his assigned new address in the First Ward, just perjure himself by swearing in court that he did. A colonizer didn't even have to be an American citizen: Canadians were being brought in from Ridgeway and Hamilton and Port Colburn.

Detective Sullivan stood inches from Collins' face.

"You didn't do what I told you to, Collins, and now you'll have to pay the consequences," Sullivan remarked, threateningly. "You'll have to register next Saturday in the 2nd district in the First Ward or you'll get into trouble."

Collins replied, "I can't do that. I live outside the district."

Sullivan replied, "That cuts no figure. You will register there and vote against White. If you don't do what I tell you and vote for John Sheehan, I'll vag you."

Collins stood up to the bully.

"That's contrary to law and I won't do it," he said.

"You've got to. You've got to do just as we tell you or you'll go to jail." The detective instructed Collins to claim his residence as the Hanrahan Saloon, or else. And then he walked out.

The following day Patrolman Jordan visited the saloon and took Collins away, claiming Collins was drunk and making a disturbance behind the bar, neither of which was true. Collins was thrown in jail. A few hours later, Hanrahan the saloonkeeper appeared at the jail with the bail for his friend in hand, but was turned away.

"That man has a right to bail!" declared the saloonkeep, angrily. "It's guaranteed by the Constitution!"

Patrolman Jordan laughed, shaking his head back and forth to mock to naivete of the saloonkeeper.

"The Constitution cuts no figure in the First Ward," he scoffed.

Jordan returned Hanrahan to his saloon with a serious warning to keep quiet about what had occurred.

All the slums and alleys and under-bridges of the decrepit Canal Street and Commercial Street districts had been thoroughly relieved of their human vermin. The docks had been raked over and under and every vagrant, tramp and bum who happened to wander into the infected 19th ward within the previous few months who could be persuaded, threatened or bullied into doing so had been relocated into and registered to vote in the First Ward.

A large number of affidavits were secured against these newly registered voters, outlining the disqualifications of those named therein. These affidavits were served on the Boards of Inspectors for the First Ward's 2nd and 4th districts, and the demand was made to strike the illegal names from the voter registries.

The Chairman in the 2nd district read the affidavits that were served him out loud, but his board declined to take any action. Over at the 4th district, Chairman John O'Connell did not even read the affidavits before contemptuously throwing them on the floor.

Police Captain Michael Regan continued to trek from saloon to dive to hell-hole—sometimes with candidate cousin John Sheehan and sometimes alone—

rummaging for every last possible man to relocate. He strongly urged the saloon proprietors to send any errant derelict or vagabond they encountered over to Fingy Conners' in the First Ward to be registered, or else.

Sunday night October 29 was a mighty cold one, a portent to winter. Liquor was rumored to be an effective remedy for such discomfort, and so the liquor in Fingy Conners' saloon and boarding house at 444 Ohio Street was dispensed like water to the frosty hooligan colonizers imported there to vote against Jack White. The colonizers were growing restless. They were bored, aimless, and rowdy awaiting the big day, so as a considerate gesture, Buffalo Police Captain James Walsh and candidate Johnny Sheehan arrived on the scene to do their part in keeping the troublemakers' spirits up.

The good Police Captain stepped out front and led the parade of thugs in song: And We'll Hang Jack White To A Sour Apple Tree.

They departed the saloon and marched through the dead-quiet streets where First Ward laborers were sleeping away whatever exhaustion they were able before having to trudge off again to their twelve hour workday. The gang's hoots and hollers and drunken chanting awakened sick babies who had finally been coaxed off to slumber by depleted mothers now blessedly unconscious after scrubbing their babies' dirty diapers and family's threadbare clothes against a washboard all day.

It was past midnight.

The rudely awaked souls of the First Ward cringed and awaited the imminent arrival of the police to put a stop to the alcohol-fueled parade, for the police were certainly in the vicinity. But only one was in full view: the drunken Police Captain James Walsh, leading the law-breakers in a march with his keepers' cousin, candidate cousin John Sheehan at his right hand, and Fingy Conners' marionette James Kennedy of the 19th on his left.

Surely someone as powerful and important as a Police Captain could not be so disgraced as to lead a gang of rowdy drunk homeless degenerates at the behest of a candidate in order to retain his position?

Every little while a new saloon would be entered and the three head men would treat the entire gang. Then someone would get up on a table and make a lovely speech. Speeches were recited that could make even the dour Sheehan cousin smile a sickly smile as the drunken wharf rats covered him with glory.

The morning of November 2nd, Hannah Sullivan, reading the newspaper, was appalled at the deposition published therein, sworn by Mr. James Collins, describing her husband's threats to his person at Hanrahan's Saloon and Mr. Collins' subsequent arrest for standing up to him.

She began to cry.

A related article in the abutting column told of the invasion of a particular saloon owned by a registered Republican, its patrons held hostage by Police Captain Michael Regan, his police officers, and the Mayor's own license clerk. The police physically assaulted and threatened the detained customers and bar owner, and commanded them to vote for Sheehan. The saloon owner was told that his liquor license fees would be increased by $500 and his saloon's Sunday permit rescinded if he and his customers did not comply.

Hannah just stared at the crazy words. This was not the America she had learned about in school. This was not what Jim's father had died for in the Civil War. This was the exact opposite, and John Sullivan's own two sons were neck-deep in it.

The city's newspapers continued to be filled with similar stories daily, revealing the most blatant abuses of constitutional rights and freedoms by the puppet-police and their politician-owners. The newspapers did not mince words — they named names and called a spade a spade. Even the New York Times was shouting the names of those responsible for Buffalo's scandals to the heavens.

So why are they all still being allowed to run amok, to trample over the people? Hannah wondered. Why are none of them in jail?

"Who's in charge, after all?"

William F. Sheehan, Lieutenant Governor of New York

Justice King's Night Out

Justice King was plain worn out. His wife had been reminding him for weeks that this was one social obligation he would not be getting out of — even if it meant her coming down to the Police Court and physically dragging him off the bench. And so he got dressed up went, but dreamed of his bed during the entire tedious affair.

Justice and Mrs. King had just snuggled in under the warm covers. It was past midnight.

Someone pulled the doorbell.

"Who on God's earth could that be?" he grumbled, throwing off the covers. Mrs. King was used to it, after thirty years of marriage. She went back to sleep.

Justice King flung open his front door to confront the rude intruder only to find a lawyer he greatly respected standing there, looking quite humble. An innocent man had been arrested for standing up to the Sheehans. The Justice was asked to come downtown and release the blameless man on bail.

The prisoner was William Morris, a man who had been hired by Canal Street saloonkeeper and cock-fighter Henry Kilcourse to watch over one of his flophouses. With the influx of colonizers, Kilcourse had been expanding his business, filling the human rat holes on lower Main Street and Washington Street with tramps and bums right up to the ceiling.

William Morris had been given a lengthy and very strict list of orders by Kilcourse. But the work of keeping track of all the imported colonizer scum and putting up with their drunken bullying and thieving and assaults upon his person had worn him down. On October 22 he was set upon by three of them and badly beaten up for just a few cents in beer money. So he fled.

Kilcourse the cock-fighter was infuriated by William Morris' irresponsible neglect of his duties, and sicced a crooked policeman by the name of Pike on him. Within a couple of days, Morris was located and Pike arrested him quietly. Morris' name was not entered on the police blotter, and his friends and family were never notified of his arrest. He was made to disappear, for a while.

An honest cop, observing the actions of the despicable Patrolman Pike, notified the Attorney John Hazel as to what had happened, and Hazel, despite the late hour, pulled the doorbell at the King residence.

The next day Morris appeared in Justice King's court, along with Patrolman Pike. Pike attempted to charge Morris with carrying a concealed weapon without a permit, but spoke so softly that no one in the room could hear him.

Attorney Hazel requested that Pike speak up so that his lies could be heard by all. That made Pike somewhat surly, and he blurted "If you want to hear me, then you get closer!"

Justice King nearly flew right over the bench at the patrolman.

"Now you see here! You're a disgrace to this already-rotten police force! I'll not let you come into this courtroom and practice your Sheehan tactics. I never saw such damnable work in the Police Department before. I was out pretty late last night, and when I went home I was tired out. Somebody pulled my doorbell some time near midnight and when I opened it I found that lawyer there fixing to get me to come downtown with him and release an innocent man on bail! That innocent man was Mr. Morris here, who was arrested because Billy Sheehan knew he couldn't use him to carry on his dirty work. Now Pike, or Perch, or whatever your name is, you keep a decent tongue in your head, or I'll send you to jail. Do you hear? You answer these questions as a gentleman would."

The now flustered Pike lied that he was told that Morris had been threatening to kill people, and was compelled to arrest him. Judge King scoffed, and looked down upon the self-shamed officer with contempt.

"I have been a Democrat all my life," said the Justice, "but I cannot vote for a man like Billy Sheehan who has corrupted the police force! I have never heard of such desperate work. Here our policemen are arresting decent citizens when they refuse to carry out Sheehan's orders!"

Without explaining his reasons for coming to such an odd decision, Justice King then adjudged the defendant guilty as charged, but suspended the sentence.

Morris walked out of the room a free man, but angered at King's judgement. He wondered if this would be the end of it or if he were being set up for some future calamity.

On November 1st, Detective Jim Sullivan's duties included serving warrants on those involved in the police exam scandal. On his way to perform his obligation Jim looked through the warrants a second time, suspecting he was being set up. How would it look if he had to serve a warrant on his own brother? There were warrants for cousin John Sheehan and his coconspirators Shiels and Duffy for complicity in the fraud. He was relieved to confirm there was no warrant calling for the arrest of Alderman John P. Sullivan, the scheme's ringleader. Perhaps they gave that job to someone else, just to make sure it got done.

Shiels could not be found, but Duffy and Sheehan were.

"Sorry, John," said the detective as he handed Sheehan the papers.

Detective Sullivan was instructed not to arrest any of the men, only to notify them that they needed to appear before Justice King "sometime on November 2nd or 3rd". Commissioner Wheeler had made the trip into the Police Court on the 1st fully expecting the defendants to have been taken into custody and be arraigned right then and there. They were not. Unrequited, Wheeler was forced to leave and return again at the defendants' convenience. He was furious.

On the afternoon of November 2nd, candidate John Sheehan finally appeared before Justice King, along with a circus troupe of Sheehan heelers and colonized voters who assembled to see how the defendants would fare. The ringmaster was none other than Fingy Conners, with his friend James Kennedy and Assemblyman John Claban at his heel. Like a bee hopping from flower to flower, Conners was the most animated person in the courtroom, busily engineering the moves of his co-mates.

Sheehan and Duffy decided not to risk an open examination in the Police Court. Each pleaded not guilty and waived examination, and each was held for the grand jury. Neither was obliged to go to jail to await the grand jury's action. Their friends Messrs. Kennedy and Claban were at the ready to demonstrate their brotherly interest by coming forward to post bail. Each man was released on a $500 bond.

The following day Fingy Conners appeared before Judge Hatch, arguing against the striking of more than twenty of his hotel's "guests'" names from the voting registers. Evidently a very curious lot of people lived in the First Ward; their families lived in one place while they lived in another—"because," as one man claimed, "board is cheaper at Conners' hotel than it is at home."

"Mr. Conners, take the stand," Attorney Adalbert Moot said to William J. Conners at 5 o'clock in the afternoon in the court proceedings before Judge Hatch.

Fingy was engrossed in trimming his finger nails and did not respond.

"Mr. Conners, please take the stand," repeated Mr. Moot.

Conners appeared not to hear Mr. Moot's repeated request. The hour was late, and Fingy and his Attorney William Armstrong were each creating their own commotions and diversions in the room trying to kill time and delay Conners' examination until it was time for court to adjourn.

Finally Mr. Moot repeated his request to Mr. Conners for the third time. It was not until 5:30 o'clock that the recalcitrant Fingy Conners finally shuffled up to the stand, slowly.

"You own No. 444 Ohio Street, do you not Mr. Conners?" asked Mr. Moot.

"Yes." replied Fingy.

"How long have you owned it?"

"For nine or ten years."

"Is it a hotel, or what is it?"

"Yes, I guess."

"You guess what?"

"It's kind of a boarding house."

"Been such all these years?"

"Yep."

"Been shut up at any time recently?"

"Last December."

"How long was it closed then?"

"Fer two or t'ree months."

"That would mean, then, that it was closed until March? April? But some of the witnesses have said it wasn't opened until about October 2nd."

"Didn't keep no boarders until then on account o' so much other business."

"What other business?"

"Saloon business."

"Mr. Conners, do you know anything about the men who came to your hotel about October 1st?"

"Not that I know of."

"You do know something about them?"

"I know there are some men there."

"Some of them work for you?"

"And some of 'em don't."

"Answer my question."

Fingy sighed loudly and looked away, to convey his boredom with the whole business.

"Oh, some of 'em work for me, I suppose."

"Tell me the names of some of the men who are working for you who went to live at your hotel before October 1st."

"Well, I know there are some."

"That isn't my question."

Fingy Conners was not enjoying himself on the stand. He fell silent. For the second time the question was asked.

"Oh, he understands the question all right," said Fingy's Attorney, Mr. Armstrong.

"You're right. I think he does," said Mr. Moot.

"Mr. Moot is tryin' t' tangle me up, o' course," objected Mr. Conners, in wounded little-boy tones. Fingy continued his tactics of distraction by conversing rudely with the Judge, but Judge Hatch silenced him with "Now stop, we'll have none of that."

Fingy claimed there were men living at his hotel who went there in September, but he couldn't provide a single name, or give a physical description, or much of anything else.

"Are you a party to this proceeding?" asked Attorney Moot.

"No."

"You are interested in the case?"

"No."

Mr. Moot was having considerable difficulty in getting Conners to answer his questions. Moot asked whether any men had come to his hotel to live after October 8th, which would have been too late to be legally registered as a voter. Conners answered that he thought they got filled up between the 2nd and 4th of October. Conners couldn't remember but one man who hadn't registered on the first day.

Fingy then tried to counter-examine Attorney Moot.

"You keep quiet! Restrain yourself!" Judge Hatch commanded Fingy.

"Did you talk with any of these men present here today about going to your hotel?" asked Moot.

"I refuse t' answer."

"On grounds that it will incriminate you?"

"No. I'm just not goin' t' answer."

A loud argument ensued between the two, but the Judge compelled Conners to answer.

"I don't know whether I did or not," replied Fingy finally.

"Did you talk to any of these men about registering?"

"Talk about what?"

"About moving in to your peculiar rooming house, about registering and voting."

"Do you want me to answer five questions at once?"

"No, you can answer them in pieces."

"Well, I don't know whether I did or not. I told the boys t' see that all the boys was registered."

Fingy admitted that he was in the registry booth on the first and second days of the registration "because I was just a little interested...things are done a bit different in our districts from yours, you know."

Fingy Conners had successfully stalled the proceedings. Court was adjourned at 6 o'clock.

The following day, attorneys appeared in Judge Hatch's court again to argue the proceedings to have 14 names stricken from the voting registry of the 2nd district of the First Ward.

David J. Nugent, brother of Detective Jim Sullivan's wife Hannah, and member of the Mutual Rowing Club, was called to the stand.

Nugent was one of the colonizers at Fingy Conners hotel at 444 Ohio Street.

Nugent owned a comfortable home at No. 86 Kentucky Street but moved into a tiny closet shared with four other men at Conners hotel on October 2nd.

When asked if moving from the privacy and comfort of his own home was not a disadvantageous thing for him to do, he claimed that since he kept the books for Conners hotel, it would be much more convenient for him to live there as well. He said that he then leased his Kentucky Street home to Peter P. Dalton, another Mutual Rowing Club member, who "intended" to occupy it.

Judge Hatch reserved decision on the matter.

Matthew Patten, a florid-faced man of 28, followed next. He said he had lived with his father at No. 81 Hamburgh Street until October 2nd, at which time he moved into one of the cubicles at 444 Ohio Street "to save a walk."

"For whom are you working?" asked Attorney Moot.

"Mr. Conners."

"Fingy Conners?"

"William J. Conners."

"Whom do you pay board to?"

"Peter P. Dalton."

"How long have you made your arrangements for?"

"That depends."

"Depends on what?"

"Things."

"Things?"

"That's right."

"What kinds of things?"

"All sorts of things."

Exchanges continued to escalate angrily between the men until they culminated in the witness lunging for the attorney and grabbing him by the lapels. A violent tussle ensued. Because the two ignored the Judge pounding his gavel, Hatch had to finally instruct the police to step in and separate them.

Patten had slipped up in his testimony and said that his board at Conners' hotel was "taken out," as in, "taken out of his pay before he ever saw it."

The attorney was trying to snare him.

Fingy sat not ten feet away in the courtroom, staring daggers at Patten for departing from the script they'd rehearsed.

"Taken out of what?" the attorney wanted to know.

"Uh, taken out?" backtracked the witness.

"I asked you, who takes it out?"

"Out of what?"

And on and on it went in circles, the witness trying to avoid admitting that Conners was holding back $2 a week for his board from his pay.

Fingy Conners had become wealthy by cornering the market on the hiring of longshoremen and assigning draconian conditions to their employ. Come election time, an additional caveat had been appended: if a Conners man who did not reside in a Conners-required district of the First Ward wished to remain in the running for employment, he had to move into a rooming house designated by Conners so that Fingy might sufficiently colonize each of the First Ward's districts with enough voters to ensure victory for his Sheehanite candidates. If questioned by the law, the man was expected to testify that he left his family, claiming strife or some such as the reason, in order to fulfill the residency requirement in whatever district of the First Ward he'd been assigned to, and thus retain his job. Not all family men who were required to move were actually willing to occupy their assigned place full time. Regardless of whether an employee actually lived in his new temporary home at a Conners hotel, Conners had the audacity to charge him for compulsory room and board anyway.

Matthew Patten's brother William Patten followed him on the stand. He too worked for saloon boss Fingy Conners. He testified that he moved to 444 Ohio Street because it was cheaper, and he didn't have so far to walk.

"What did you bring with you when you moved down to 444 Ohio Street?" asked Moot.

"What I have on my back."

"What did you leave at home?"

"Nothing. I had nothing to leave."

"You don't own anything?"

"No."

"Property records show that you own a very nice house located at No. 81 Hamburgh Street, where you moved from in order to make a new home for yourself in a tiny cubicle at Mr. Conners' extremely crowded and noisy saloon. The same house on Hamburgh where your brother lived before he too moved to Conners' hotel. And where your father still lives. And where your wife and children live, and your brother's wife lives."

Patten, flustered and red-faced, then changed his story and admitted that he did own the house, but since the end of September he had been thinking about moving to Conners' hotel "ever since so much sickness was around."

William Shaw followed Patten on the stand to rebut Patten's testimony.

Shaw had sworn out the affidavit in the Patten brothers case, and said he received his information from William Patten's own wife who answered the door at No. 81 Hamburgh St. when he came to call and identified herself as such. Mrs. Patten told him that her husband would be staying at Conners' hotel "until after the election was over."

William Patten was then put on the stand again, and swore once more that he was not married, nor was his brother Matthew. He called Shaw's testimony "a packet of lies."

Judge Hatch reserved decision on the matter.

Next on the stand appeared James Dee, a 28 year old man with a wife and three children. He too worked for Fingy Conners. His wife and family lived at 252 Katherine Street, but he claimed he hadn't lived with them for a year and a half and didn't know how they were or how they were being supported.

"A real man supports his family, Mr. Dee. Your little children, aren't they starving?"

"No."

"How would you know if you haven't seen them for a year and a half?"

"My friends check up on them."

"You do not support your family, even though you have a job working for Mr. Conners?"

"That's right."

"Why?"

"I don't make enough money."

"So you're saying that Mr. Conners doesn't pay a man enough money to even support his family?"

"I moved to the hotel because board was cheaper."

"Cheaper than living in your own home with your own family?"

"Yes."

"Why then didn't you move to Conners hotel before October 2nd, or after October 2nd? Why exactly on October 2nd?"

"They only opened the hotel for boarders on October 2nd, I believe."

"And where did you live before the hotel opened?"

"That's none of your business."

"You answer the question, Mr. Dee," said the Judge.

"No, Judge. I don't have to answer that question. This hearing or whatever you're making it out to be can only investigate the immediate concern, which is those who now live at the hotel. Where any of us lived before that is not any of your affair, legally speaking. Only in a trial before a jury would I be required to answer that. This hearing is a joke. I see no jury in this room."

The Judge and the attorney were none too happy about being one-upped.

"So...tell me about the hotel, Mr. Dee?"

"I don't know much about it."

"How many rooms, how big are they, how many floors?"

"I don't know for sure."

"You have lived there for a month now and you can't tell me a thing about it?"

"Not much to tell."

The attorney knew he'd be getting no further with the self-assured Mr. Dee.

John Milligan was called to the witness stand next. He had lived at 178 Mackinaw Street with his mother and father up until October 2nd. Also in the courtroom were two of Milligan's friends, Norton and Watts, who lived at Conners' hotel as well, and had been questioned earlier.

"The board at Conners' hotel is cheaper than at your own mother's. Mr. Milligan? I find that hard to believe," mocked Attorney Moot.

"Yes."

"How much does your mother charge you?"

"Four dollars a week."

"And Fingy Conners, how much does he charge you?"

"Three dollars."

"When you lived at home with your mother, did she do your laundry?"

"Yes."

"Does Fingy Conners do your laundry for you?"

"No."

"Your mother bakes pies every week, doesn't she?"

"Just about."

"Has Fingy Conners baked any pies for you yet?"

"No."

The courtroom erupted in laughter.

"Did your mother ever take care of you when you got sick? Let you stay at her house even when you were broke? Cook your meals for you?"

"I guess. Sometimes."

"Does Fingy Conners do any of those things for you?"

"I never asked him to."

"So, if you no longer pay board at your mother's, then you no longer eat there, correct?"

"No, I don't."

"Isn't it true you ate dinner there today? I mean, just two hours ago?"

"No sir — and Mr. Watts and Mr. Norton are telling a fib if they say I did."

"Mr. Watts and Mr. Norton saw you having dinner at your mother's, because they were there having dinner with you ...at your mother's."

"They daren't go on the stand and swear to that!" he shouted, shooting them nasty looks.

Subsequently, despite their flimsy explanations rationalizing why they all suddenly moved to Conners' boarding house at the beginning of October, the testimonies given by those called to the stand proved for naught.

Mr. Dee was correct. Legally there was a singular unanimity of opinion that Judge Hatch had no power to pass upon any case in which the election inspectors had not the same power. The judge was not legally empowered to determine whether or not a man came into the district for the sole purpose of voting there. That was a question of fact that only a jury could rule on after examining all the evidence.

The majority of Fingy Conners' employees already resided in their proper voting districts, so his nets had to be cast far and wide for new bodies to fill the ratholes on the waterfront. Wherever men could be found in circumstances worse than those of the rooming houses of lower Main Street, they were persuaded to change residence. The great gangs of loafers now familiarly known to the public as the new colonizers of the First Ward grew ever bolder in their criminal daring on the city's streets as the date of the election drew nearer.

Hannah Sullivan felt powerless in her brother-in-law's ever-expanding shadow. The Alderman's hubris was out of control. She smelled doom. She could no longer sleep at night. She wondered what she had gotten herself into by marrying Jim, once so kind and dutiful, and to what tragic end his blind devotion to his brother would lead her family.

A frightened, grieving, distrustful and increasingly isolated Hannah Sullivan waited on Elk Street for the streetcar to come. With Jim Jr. and Nellie at school, Hannah had taken five-year-old Johnny in hand, and not wanting anyone to know what she was up to, was making her way to Attorney Cornelius Brown's office. She was determined to find out what legal repercussions might be in store for her husband and his brother. Even more importantly, what might befall her and their innocent children if worse came to worst.

The trolley was full, with some people standing up toward the rear of the car. Yet lucky for her, there was an empty seat right in front. She grabbed it. All the windows were open but still the car smelled bad. All too soon she learned the reason. One or both of the horses had terrible gas that wafted into the car after much ghastly sputtering, causing the passengers to gasp. All of them had something—a proper fan, a magazine, a folded newspaper—to ventilate themselves with and get the foul air moving.

"Mama, look, the horse is pooping," said Johnny with a look of disgust on his cherubic face, and indeed the animal was. The poor thing was in distress, expelling great volumes of diarrhea horizontally. Passengers pulled the bell cord in a panic and more than a dozen disembarked before the car had even come to a full stop.

"Hold your nose Johnny. It'll only be five more minutes," she fibbed.

Hannah occupied her mind with swarms of thought.

Mary Halloran's heart-wrenching stories about her destitution and suffering had greatly troubled her daughter-in-law from the moment she first heard them. But in recent days Hannah couldn't get them out of her head. The specter of being left alone to fend for herself and her children haunted her.

She had often questioned what could ever compel her dead father-in-law to up and volunteer for the army at an age close to forty years, abandoning his wife and children to their fates. That would be an advanced age to embark on a military career any way you sliced it. And no matter how patriotic, what kind of man chooses war over his own babies? Volunteering at the very beginning of the war was something for single eighteen-year-olds to consider, not established family men more than twice that age. It didn't make any sense.

Most men at that time refused to volunteer precisely for the reason that there was no way of ensuring that their families would be provided for if anything should happen to them. There was no procedure in place early in the war to guarantee that widows and children of volunteers disabled or killed in battle would be taken care of.

Adding to the matter, the First Ward was a dangerous and frightening place back in 1861, especially down near the Ohio Basin where the family lived. Drunks, itinerant sailors, aimless barge-dwellers, violent thugs, predators. Who leaves his wife and babies to fend for themselves amidst the likes of that?

Even if John Sullivan's friends had pledged to keep close watch on Mary and her sons, those friends would still have to be at work twelve hours a day. They'd have families of their own to look after once they got home, first and foremost. There was always the possibility they themselves would be drafted, along with all the usual troubles and worries of daily life to consider as well.

Hannah began to suspect that John Sullivan may have joined the army to in fact run away from Mary and his children. Her mother-in-law had never let on that her marriage was unhappy, but on the other hand she didn't exactly rhapsodize about it either. Considering the dire straits they'd been left in, Hannah wouldn't expect Mary to canonize the man.

Then there's the mystery of the army not knowing after his death that John Sullivan was even married and had children. Did he purposely not disclose this? Wasn't he sending his pay home to the family, and wouldn't the army know this? Any man going off to the uncertainties of war would at least want his children to be taken care of, wouldn't he? Or, perhaps the army did lose John Sullivan's records in the chaos of war, as old Sam Lake had theorized. It was a mystery.

Mary was the only one who could answer Hannah's questions, and Mary was gone. Having suffered the unfathomable loss of two of her own children, Hannah couldn't imagine anyone intentionally going off and leaving theirs behind. It was unreckonable. Despite her husband's hero worship of his late father, Hannah was having a difficult time of it convincing herself that John Sullivan was entirely a good man. And the more she considered these riddles about him, the more Hannah concluded that her Jim must have been tortured himself by these exact same questions over the decades. Maybe that explains both brothers' ease at detaching from their families and their extraordinary closeness to each other. Maybe Jim and JP were too damaged by their past to expect them to be rational, logical, or even routinely cautious.

Hannah couldn't stand the stink any longer. She pulled the cord, grabbed Johnny and got off the trolley one stop before their destination. They crossed to the shady side of Main Street and headed north. Abruptly, Hannah found herself violently jerked backwards by two colonizers grabbing at her coat. They demanded money for beer. One of the men's hands went into her pockets and touched her private area. She screamed and yelled for help from a patrolman who stood not more than fifty feet from her. He looked at her impassively, then turned and looked the other way.

Hannah was horrified, and realizing she and her young son would receive no rescue from the officer, stuck the point of her brolley squarely into the right eye of one of her molesters, then darted into the attorney's building, dragging her son so roughly that he began to cry.

"Those vagrants will grab you and kill you just to steal money for beer, yet the police merely look on with complacency!" she screamed at Attorney Brown. "These bold beggars are infesting Main Street! They carry on unimpeded by the police. Everything goes these days!"

Cornelius Brown apologized profusely, and realized that things in the heart of the business district had gotten so out of hand that not only were his clients in danger, but his very livelihood was in jeopardy too, now that people couldn't safely visit his office.

The attorney ran out onto Main Street and spotted the offending officer. It was the regular patrolman, Bill O'Reilly. He confronted him with a volley of insults, endured by the surly patrolman only due to the legal problems he knew the advocate was capable of causing him if he reacted as his natural instincts indicated.

"This is my place of business young man! Your job is to protect the citizenry, yet you'll stand by and let the wife and baby of a fellow police officer suffer molestation by thugs? I will have you brought up on charges of dereliction of duty and whatever else I can dream up!"

Patrolman O'Reilly looked at Mr. Brown with contempt, then calmly walked over to the vagrants, engaging them in a mild discussion punctuated with smiles and friendly touches on their arms. The bums laughed and shook their heads and walked away, the vag with the handkerchief held over his eye turning to cast a menacing look at Attorney Brown. O'Reilly then just stood there, staring at him, daring the attorney to take it further. Brown, disgusted and wondering what had become of the wonderful city he once knew, returned to his office and the waiting Hannah Sullivan.

With great emotion, Hannah poured out her fears and the circumstances of her situation to the advocate. She cried about her dead babies and her absent husband and his involvement with the crooks and scandals of the day.

"What shall I do about this situation? What will become of us?" she wailed.

"Mrs. Sullivan," Brown said, pausing to carefully assemble his words, "your husband, as you tell the story, grew up with, and went to school with, and caroused with the Sheehan brothers, as well as the infamous Fingy Conners. And your husband is also the brother of nigh on just about the most powerful alderman in this city. If you've noticed, in the newspaper accounts, Alderman Sullivan isn't even mentioned in connection with the police exam scandal any longer. Two weeks ago his name was at the very forefront. Now, it's nowhere. Such is the man's power and influence and that of his friends.

"Truthfully, if you had the money to be independent, and you could run off to France or somewhere and start a new life, I might be inclined to advise you to take your children and do that. But you have no money. You don't know anyone who would take you in and care for you. You admittedly have no skills that could support yourself and your children.

"I am a man and an attorney, Mrs. Sullivan, yet I myself am frustrated and angered beyond my capacity at what is happening in this city, because there is so little that I can do about it. The Sheehans have Buffalo in an iron vise because they've bought the police department. Frankly, I am grateful I am not in your shoes.

"I'll walk you to the trolley and make sure you get safely aboard without any further interference from those roughs."

With that, Attorney Brown grabbed the baseball bat he had brought from home two weeks before when the troubles first began outside his door, and summarily escorted Hannah and little John across Main Street to the trolley stop. There he waited with them until the car arrived, keeping an eye on the bums outside cock-fighter Henry Kilcourse's rooming house for any sign of trouble. Once mother and son were safely aboard, he cautiously walked back to his office, shooting a nasty look at the crowd of toughs gathered in front of Kilcourse's house, they and their friend O'Reilly still scowling at him.

The colonized criminals were brazenly confident that the Sheehan Machine could not afford to lose them at this late date, and took full advantage of the situation to lay waste to the city. They also knew that the Sheehanized police force dared not arrest them for anything short of murder lest they take affront and vote for Jack White for revenge.

Following this strategy, the gang of toughs living at cock-fighter Kilcourse's tenements on lower Main Street boldly accosted people in broad daylight for money. The tenement at No. 133 had been written up by the inspector, Dr. Constantine, on October 17th for among other things, lodging 125 men in only 17 rooms on a total of 17 beds, 3 cots and a sofa.

The colonizers' agreement with the Sheehan Machine may have provided them board and lodgings, but the beer stipend evidently was not generous enough to quench the insatiable thirst of an army of idle punks.

The Skillet

Hannah was preparing dinner when her husband walked in the door, slammed it, and then stomped loudly up the stairs. He sent the children to their rooms, entered the kitchen threateningly, and closed the door.

"What were you doing at Attorney Cornelius Brown's office today with my son?"

The surly patrolman on Main Street had taken revenge on Attorney Brown by informing Detective Sullivan that he saw his wife and child meeting with a lawyer.

Jim was livid.

In the ten years of their marriage, Jim Sullivan had never once spoken to his wife in a threatening manner. But now, he grabbed her arm and shouted, "I will ask you for the last time, Hannah. What were you doing meeting with that lawyer?"

She realized that she no longer knew who this angry man was anymore.

Hannah's late father Jeremiah Nugent had left her property in his will, and anticipating the possibility of being asked this question by someone, planned to use the real estate matter as a cover. But Jim was hurting her. He had no right. She looked down at his hand squeezing her arm so tightly that his fingers were white, then looked up again to see the menace in his eyes.

"Who told you I was seeing a lawyer?" she angrily demanded.

"Patrolman O'Reilly told me! He saw you with Cornelius Brown!"

Hannah determined right then and there that she had had enough. She was finished. She'd had her fill — to capacity — of ten years of covering up her own hurts, loneliness and anger, and buckling under for the sake of the Sullivan brothers.

"I'm divorcing you!" she screamed, surprising even herself, and pushed her husband away so forcefully he lost balance.

"That's why I went to see a lawyer!" She picked up her cast iron skillet and took a stance.

Enraged, she screamed "Did your dirty copper friend O'Reilly forget to tell you, Jim Sullivan, that on my way to see the attorney with your youngest son, two vagrants grabbed your wife and tried to rape her while your patrolman friend just stood there and watched it happen? Is that the kind of brotherhood you boys have forged down there at the Precinct, Jim? Your fellow police officers allowing your wife's private parts to be grabbed right on the street in broad daylight, vagrants' hands clawing in my pockets trying to rob me while your baby son screams in terror? And your corrupt friend O'Reilly just standing there and allowing it to happen? Did that bastard tell you that?!"

She took a swing at him with the skillet. He ducked.

Jim was shocked. Never had his Hannah showed him overt anger before, much less rage. He had never heard her curse, except once. He'd handled his share of drunks and crazy people and recognized the deranged look in her eyes.

He put his hands up defensively, surrendering gently, and said, "All right." He stood slowly upright and backed away.

Nellie and Jim Jr. were drawn by the ruckus and sneaked up to the closed swinging door between the kitchen and dining room and listened intently.

"What do you mean, divorce?", he said calmly. "We're Catholic."

"Divorce? I just told you that your son and I were assaulted and I was almost raped — and your response is to ask me about divorce? What do you intend to do about that patrolman? How dare he! How dare you! You don't defend me against your fool of a brother, and now you don't defend me from that despicable O'Reilly character?"

"I'll take care of it, Hannah! Tomorrow. I'll hunt the bastard down, I promise you. He's a criminal and an idiot. If he's stupid enough to indict himself to me like he did, he has no business even being a police officer. I will teach him a lesson, I promise you, for Christ's sake."

"You have betrayed me and your children over and over again in favor of your sniveling coward of a brother! You put those Sheehan criminals and that subhuman Fingy Conners before your very own flesh and blood, and your brother's children, and all the suffering people of the First Ward! My own brother had to leave his house to go live in that stinking Conners hotel for a month because that bastard ordered him to! How dare youse! What is wrong with the men of this ward?"

She was escalating, he recognized. She held the skillet higher and widened her stance, as if ready to attack again.

"Your brother left of his own accord, Hannah! Why won't you accept that? He's in partnership with Conners, open your eyes! He's planning on marrying Fingy's niece, for Christ's sake! I can't talk to you if you're ready to clobber me, Hannah!"

Momentarily she was distracted by the shocking revelation of David's marriage plans.

"Get out of here! You do not come back into this house until you are prepared to apologize to me and to your oldest son who came home the other day to his mother bloody and beaten from defending a father who deserves no defense whatsoever!"

Jim abruptly sprung for the skillet, but Hannah was faster, bringing its lip down hard on his shoulder, slamming him to the floor. "I will put you in that river! I'll collect my widow's pension!" she promised, spitting out the words.

Terrified, Jim Jr. and Nellie quickly retreated to their rooms and quietly shut the doors, where they sat trembling. Johnny awoke from his nap, startled by the commotion, and began to cry in fright.

Jim writhed in pain, crumpled on the floor. The shoulder surely must have broken.

"Get out of this house!" she screamed raising the iron skillet over her head. "Get out! Now! Now, I said!"

Ten years of anger and frustration — of grief and babies' funerals, bereavement and utter loss; of disrespect and disregard, of fear, scandal, and coming in dead last on her husband's long list — all melded into an exquisite outpouring of rage that so shook Detective Jim Sullivan that he took off down the stairs like a flash and straight into his brother's front door at No. 12.

As he left, Hannah reeled from Jim's revelation.

"My brother is planning on marrying that Fingy Conners' trollop of a niece?

My God! I will kill him!"

The Alderman had only just walked in the door himself, pausing for a moment first outside at the unprecedented sound of shouting coming from his brother's house next door. He could hardly believe his eyes at the expression of pain on Jim Sullivan's face as he burst in cradling his injured shoulder.

"What happened?" exclaimed the Alderman incredulously, thinking a burglar may have gotten the best of his brother.

"Hannah hit me with a skillet!" he said. "I think it's broken." Alerted by the commotion, Annie ran into the front parlor to investigate the scene, and immediately realized what had transpired.

"I'll call Detective Lynch!" said JP, to which his wife seethed, "You will do no such thing! You take your brother to the Fitch Hospital! I will go see Hannah. Go! Go!"

Startled, JP was so thoroughly unaccustomed to his Annie barking orders at him that he simply complied.

The doctor told Detective Sullivan that the shoulder had been wrenched from its socket. He gave the officer what looked like a rubber horse-bit to bite down on, then distracting him, snapped the shoulder neatly back into place with a violent pain that caused Jim to scream out loud. Then suddenly, except for a dull ache and throbbing, the pain stopped.

"I suspect your collar bone may be cracked," said the physician, "so you will have to have your arm in a sling for a week or so, until the bruising fades. Then we can have a second look."

Annie hugged Hannah, who was trembling, but completely unrepentant. There was no regret in her voice or in her demeanor.

"His name was in the newspaper for threatening a man with jail if he didn't vote for John Sheehan! What will Junior have to endure out on the streets now?! If I could shoot those damn Sheehan bastards, I would do it in an instant!"

Annie suddenly feared for Hannah. The twin towers of the lunatic asylum on Forest Avenue were a convenient place for controlling husbands to imprison willful wives.

"Hannah, you have to consider the children!"

"I am considering the children, you ninny! Have you considered your children? What they have to endure at the hands of their moron father, always gone, always away someplace else? Is that man's money so important to you, Annie Saulter, that you sell your children's future away for pretty dresses and fancy socials? Our husbands will either end up in prison or be found floating dead in the canals! And then where will you wear your pretty dresses? What will I and my children be left with—and you and yours—when their father is found dead?" She virtually spat out the words.

"You and I will still be around long after our husbands are gone, Annie Saulter, unless they kill us first! So you had better straighten out your spine and begin thinking about that—and what will become of you and your children when the inevitable catches up with the criminal shenanigans of your husband!"

Annie was shaken by the ferocity of Hannah's words and the absolute certainty of her conviction.

Annie calmly asked her, "Where are the children?"

"They're all right. They're in their rooms," replied Hannah.

"You'd better go to them. They must be very frightened."

And with that Annie descended the stairs to go home.

Hannah Sullivan ran the carpet sweeper in the parlor as a way to alleviate some of her pent-up anger. As Jim Jr. walked in from school, he was concerned to see his mother embroiled in the activity to the point of perspiring heavily. He still wore remnants of his black eye, the fading bruises now taking on a greenish hue.

"Ma, why isn't Nellie doin' that?" Carpet-sweeping was usually his sister's chore. "Or Johnny?"

Poor little John had been sitting silently on the wingback chair, watching his mother's fervor with apprehension.

Hannah's attention had momentarily been diverted by the discovery of a dried-up rosebud, brown and fragile, under the sofa. It was a remnant of baby Daniel's funeral, held in this spot only a hundred days earlier. She had to stop herself from picturing the tiny white coffin that had occupied the space, and instead diverted her emotion toward her oldest.

"Why aren't you doing this, Junior?" she shouted. "Perhaps that's the real question!"

Her unprecedented explosion knocked Jim Jr. squarely off kilter. Then she regained her composure and said, "Junior, Johnny's too small to be doing this, you know that. And Nellie, she's got an arithmetic test tomorrow. I told her to go upstairs and study."

"It's all right, Ma, I'm sorry. I'll do it," said Junior apologetically as he reached for the handle of the sweeper to take it from her.

"No!" she snapped with finality. "I'll finish this. You go upstairs and peel the potatoes for supper."

Hannah had sent Nellie to her room to do her homework, and Nellie, seeing her mother still so unsettled after the frightening argument she and her brother had heard through the kitchen door, did so without complaint.

Jim Jr. climbed the stairs, placed his books on the kitchen table where his mother had repeatedly told him they didn't belong, and began his chore.

Some of Nellie's friends had tumultuous home lives, but she had never seen her own parents argue violently before. This was something extraordinary. She had always known her mother and father to pull together in the bad times, especially during the last few years after the babies died.

But now, her parents weren't even speaking to each other.

Annie next door was busying herself, trying her best to keep her distance from Hannah. The Alderman continued to display outrage over Hannah's assault on his brother, coming as it did right after Hannah announced her decision to attend persona-non-grata Tom Nunan's campaign parade. JP was limping angrily around the house, his heavy orthopedic shoe landing heavily with each step, spewing expletives denigrating to his sister-in-law. Annie didn't like the sound of that one bit. She pictured him in jail, and herself alone with her children living in uncertainty and fear.

By her unprecedented outpouring of rage, Hannah had forced Annie to finally begin confronting who she herself was, and perhaps more importantly, what kind of man her husband had become. Hannah's hurtful accusation about how pretty dresses were an acceptable payoff for the Alderman's neglect of her and the children struck at her heart, for its containing some substance of truth.

The provocative headlines associated with the police exam scandal, and the election fiasco as a whole, had unbalanced Annie and nudged her right off her pedestal. The city was close to anarchy and her husband was at the head of the list of those fueling it. Police were beating and arresting hard-working family men who refused to move into a Conners hotel or Sheehan rooming house. America's Constitution wasn't only being stepped on, it was being trampled to shreds. Gangs of imported vagrants, drunk and perverted and vile, with nothing to do, were roaming the streets literally right outside their door, a threat to every woman and child in the ward. Her own husband and his friends put those derelicts there on the street, kept them there and protected them, and Hannah's husband and his friends were safeguarding those animals, rather than their own families. It was diabolical. Annie, finally assembling all these pieces together, was for the first time truly frightened for herself and her children.

Hannah's fears concerning her kids caused Annie to wake up to how distanced she had allowed herself to become from her own children, and she felt ashamed. Annie had the luxury of live-in help, and that freed her to live an expanded existence outside the immediate family. It also meant she did not have to be present every minute of the day to attend to the children, like Hannah. She didn't have to be home when they came in from school, nor did she have to cook supper every night, like Hannah. She no longer needed to keep to a schedule like that demanded of most other wives and mothers. Her relationship with her sons was less close than Hannah's was with her children, because Hannah required of herself to be present for hers, always.

What if somebody shot JP, or he was set upon by his enemies? Killed, or incapacitated? Sent to prison? What, as Hannah asked, would she do? How had she breezed along so carefree while JP increasingly complicated their lives during the previous four years with his political ladder-climbing, criminal manipulations and unholy alliances?

The night of Hannah's attack, Jim Sullivan ended up sleeping on his brother's sofa. The next morning, he returned to his own house to prepare for work, expecting to find Hannah cooled down and contrite.

She was neither.

Hannah banged around the kitchen as she cooked breakfast for the children and got their lunch pails prepared. He tried to speak to her but she kept her back turned and increased the volume of her activity the closer he got.

The children were afraid to enter the kitchen. Their father had his arm in a sling. Their mother was acting like someone about ready to blow up.

Jim took what he needed, walked to the top of the stairs and announced, "I'll be home at 4:30. I'll expect you to be in a better humor by that time."

"And I've already told you about what I expect," she replied with venom.

Soon after, the children left for school.

Next door, the Alderman watched out his parlor window at his brother's departure. Annie caught him disguising himself behind the curtain and scolded, "Whatever are you looking at JP?"

"I was waiting for Jim and the children to leave so I can go next door and have words with Hannah." The Alderman had become quite comfortable with his growing sense of entitlement, both inside the Common Council Chambers, and out.

"No. I don't think you ought to do that. Hannah needs time to sort things through. This is none of our business."

"You're half-right, my dear. It is none of your business, for sure! But that is my brother's family living right next door, and I'm responsible for them. So it certainly is my business."

"You dare not come between a man and his wife, John Sullivan!"

Annie was insulted and hurt. JP had a pompous way of dismissing her that he had been increasingly employing as of late, even in front of the children. For the first time in her marriage, she demonstrated her anger.

"JP! You come right back here now!" she shouted.

JP turned and stared right through her.

"Don't you ever tell me what to do, woman! And you keep away from Hannah and her bad influence from this moment on!" he barked back.

All it took was just that one statement, spat out in exactly that tone, to change Annie Saulter Sullivan's entire life direction.

The Alderman limped next door attired in his aldermanic suit and his aldermanic derby, looking just as official as he could be, to make one of the biggest mistakes of his life.

The Alderman Meets His Match

Hannah glanced out her kitchen window in time to see the little tomfool headed for her house, rocking back and forth with his characteristic hobble that, when angry, she thought made him look comical.

The nerve of him, she thought to herself.

JP didn't knock.

He entered the former saloon of his youth, now the family's parlor, and headed laboriously up the stairs as if he still lived there and had every right. The arrogant meddler entered the very same kitchen where his mother had been bent backward impaled on the blade of Peter Halloran's knife while his juvenile self cowered in the corner terrified.

Hannah stood facing the intruder, tall and proud, a slight smile on her face, relaxed, hands casually behind her back. She had heard the famous butcher knife story a dozen times or more.

"Hannah Nugent, I wish to speak with you about your lunatic behavior," proclaimed His Honor, angrily.

"Yes?" she answered.

"How dare you assault my brother! Do you have any idea how close you are to being placed in the lunatic asylum?"

"No." she said, pulling her hands from behind her back, revealing a huge wooden-handled butcher knife. She slammed it soundly down on the kitchen table with a wallop. "Why don't you tell me how close I am, JP?"

She locked her eyes on him with a primitive ferocity he had only ever witnessed previously in Fingy Conners. He stole a glance down at the knife, and swallowed hard. He was standing in the exact spot where his mother had been skewered.

Hannah's eyes never once detached from his.

"You have meddled in my family's life long enough, you lily-livered little cripple."

The acidic words vomited from her lips.

"You are a filthy, corrupt, spineless little Napoleon who has made a pact with Satan himself, and you will soon be looking out from behind the bars of Sing Sing, if I have anything to say about it."

The Alderman was struck totally speechless for a few seconds, for he had never before seen even so much as a hint of this side of the compliant, pensive Hannah Nugent.

"You'd be making the mistake of your life, Hannah, you had better come to your senses!"

"I came to my senses the morning I read your dishonored name on the front page of the New York Times shaming your entire family, you craven ball of horse shit!"

JP was shocked at her language—language even stevedores wouldn't use. Surely, this woman was crazy.

"How dare you spit in the face of your late father and his memory!" she smeared, loudly. "And that of your own brother who without, you would never have survived! I know full well what was done to you at that orphan asylum, JP."

The Alderman was sickened. Jim promised that no one would ever, ever find out about that. They had agreed that their orphanage years were sacrosanct, to be forgotten. Locked away forever in the past.

"You have defiled and betrayed the father who gave you life, the father who gave his own life so that the tortured wretches of this country could be set free. Then you and all your dirty Irish gutter-scum grew up and grabbed every opportunity you could to grind the fine Sullivan name into the dirt with your shit-covered fancy brogues!

"You are an alderman in the government of this city! You are supposed to be representing the miserable thousands of suffering Irish in this ward who your blood brother Fingy Conners is flagrantly starving to death. But you remain blind and silent all the while! I hear the sobs of the mothers crying out from behind the confessional curtains every single Saturday, their lives hopeless and dark and filled with fear and suffering, their children sick and hungry, because of Fingy Conners and his gutless boot-licker, John P. Sullivan!"

JP had been stupefied into complete silence by this point, so unfamiliar was he with hearing merciless truth.

"You, Alderman Sullivan," she seethed, "have prostituted yourself to a megalomaniacal hyena! A dictator and murderer! And you have the gall to talk to me about the lunatic asylum? I have more respect for the whores who sell themselves for half a dollar down on Canal Street than I do you and yours!

"Your brother full well remembers his father even if you have no memory of the man, Alderman. Maybe that's why you're so comfortable and at ease fouling your father's sacrifice! Your brother devoted himself from the day of your sorry birth to protecting you and defending and rescuing you, year after wretched year, right up to the present day.

"Then, to dishonor what your father and your brother provided you, you sold your puny soul to Satan himself for a few gold coins and your little throne of power down there at the City Hall. And whenever your evil doings begin to catch up with you, you drag my husband away from his children and his wife and place him in harm's way just to do your immoral and illegal bidding for you. You have manipulated your brother into betraying his own beloved father's memory by making yourself into the exact opposite of what John Sullivan himself was!"

JP was reeling under the unrelenting ferocity of her attack. Bang! Bang! Bang! She hammered and pounded without pause. Ten years' worth of bottled-up fury exploded. Yes, JP Sullivan was well aware that Hannah Nugent had been awarded for her scholastic excellence, that she had been voted valedictorian of her class. He had happily bragged about her academic achievements in his campaign speeches to boost his own status. But he had never before witnessed any such explicit manifestation of what had earned her those honors, until now.

"Now you go back to your home and set to packing what you think you'll be needing at Sing Sing—or maybe better still, Auburn Penitentiary! Perhaps you can use your political influence to get yourself situated in the very same cell there that Peter Halloran occupied between his attempts to murder your poor mother! Wouldn't that be a fitting and proper legacy for you, now!"

Hannah lowered her eyes to the knife placed on the table, then slowly raised them back up to meet JP's.

JP glowered at her. There would be no besting this woman, not today, nor ever again. She had collected and hoarded his sins and his secrets, and was about to set them free.

"Leave!" she commanded, as she took a half step toward where the knife lay. He quickly scuttled.

Imported Police

During the morning of November 4th at the Police Court, Justice King called to the stand a total of five men who had all taken the civil service police exam. All five men had answered the same questions with the exact same wording as each other, and with the exact same wording printed on the cheat sheet widely distributed by Alderman John P. Sullivan and his friends in exchange for their vote.

George Schintins was questioned as precisely as the four other witnesses who came before him. All five swore they had not received the answers in advance. When asked how it happened that he answered the questions exactly as many of the others had done, and exactly as they had been formulated in the list, Schintins said: "I didn't see no answers. I got the answers that way because of my perfect knowledge out of my own head."

The witness had even placed "etc.," after the answer to the third question, exactly as it had been formulated on the illegally distributed answer sheet, and testified that he did so because he considered the "etc.," to be a "very important" part of his answer.

Justice King also presided over the hearing for two of the first three of more than a hundred Sheehan men charged with false registration of the imported colonizers. The attorney for the men, the corrupt former city clerk William E. Delaney, screamed loudly for a postponement of a hearing for the accused until after the election, so as to try and minimize any damage to the Sheehan campaign.

Confoundingly, Justice King, despite his own personal hatred of the Sheehans and the obviousness of Delaney's blatant calculations, granted his demand, just as he had the day before for Delaney client Henry Kilcourse, the Main Street cock-fighter who had 125 colonizers illegally registered at his 17-bed rooming house.

Justice King, who threw starving twelve-year-olds into the workhouse for ninety days for stealing food just to keep themselves alive, while at the same time forging a questionable reputation for himself by pardoning unrepentant gamblers, was nothing if not completely unfathomable.

The revelations of how far the Sheehans would go to steal the Buffalo elections were trumpeted from the pages of the city's newspapers.

The Buffalo Express published the following:

FOR USE ON ELECTION DAY!
IMPORTED POLICE!
What the New York Sluggers May Do in Buffalo.

INTIMIDATING TACTICS
They Will be Expected to Assist Sheehan Police to Get the Machine Vote Into the Ballot Boxes.

The indications of a terrible struggle in the 1st and some of the other wards on election day are already evident. The stories of large gangs of the scum of the tough tenements of New York City being brought to this city are supported by circumstantial evidence from various sources, and yesterday it was asserted that a number of them had arrived and were in the custody of Sheehan's henchmen. In an interview yesterday Mr. Sheehan asserted he had not brought any of the New York element spoken of to this city, but forgot to state that it is not necessary for him to actually travel to Buffalo on the trains in their company in order to ensure their presence here before election day.

Yesterday there was a great commotion at the Law Exchange in the office of Devoe P. Hudson, one of the Sheehan attorneys. About 50 of as rough-looking men as ever visited the city were at his office for a long time. They went away with the cock-fighter Henry Kilcourse, head of the colonization center at 133 Main Street. The men were said to be so tough that the elevator boy got away from them as soon as he could, and generously allowed them to walk up the two flights of stairs to Mr. Hudson's office.

It is asserted that these men are an installment of the New York thugs, but Mr. Hudson as well as others state that they were men employed on the docks who had been called to his office for the purpose of furnishing affidavits in the legal registration cases. Assertions are positive, however, that these men came from New York City, and two reputable citizens say the men themselves made no secret of it.

That a lot of the scum of New York will be brought to this city ere the dawn of election morning there is little doubt. The Sheehan machine needs them in the lower portion of the city. This they have shown by their every action since the opening of the campaign. Some of them will probably be required to vote, but the real purpose of bringing such a crowd to the city is plain to be seen. They will be, with the assistance of the Sheehan police force, lined up at the booths in the districts where they are expected to prevent the casting of ballots for Jack White and other Republicans.

That the police and particularly the Commissioners and Superintendent fear trouble on election day they themselves confess. Yesterday notice was given that they would appoint a number of special patrolmen to serve on election day and that those who desired to serve as such should make application to the Commissioners or the Superintendent.

One report last night had it that some of the heaviest of the New York bruisers would be sworn in as special policemen and thus, under cloud of the law, they could work their will and the orders of the Machine upon the legitimate residents of the ward.

The reason for such a selection is evident.

Denizens from New York City's Bowery were imported into Buffalo to crack heads, wreck saloons that hosted union meetings, and terrorize Republican voters.

The police expect there will be slugging and they are confident that their force will be wholly insufficient to cope with the immense amount of slugging for which the Sheehan Machine will be responsible. These very same imported New York thugs will be sworn in as special patrolmen for that day because of their peculiar and special fitness for such drastic work, and will be assigned to the districts where there is likely to be the most trouble.

The Commissioners in their announcement have failed to state the number of specials to be sworn in for duty on election day. That troubling omission is suggestive in itself. They plan to have enough of their singular kind of people in the city by that time to fill all the vacancies that may occur in the list.

The call for extra patrolmen is also evidence that the police force of regulars, patrolmen, specials, captains and other officers is insufficient for carrying out all the intimidation of voters that is deemed necessary to divert the election their way. The imported element can be used largely for stifling any protests against the unscrupulous Sheehan Machine methods, which will be practiced in every section of the city.

Sluggers and other hooligans of that kind may not be the only methods used to embezzle the ballots of the honest voters. In Onondaga County last year, "misplaced" ballots played an important part in the election and caused the loss of a Senator to the Republicans. Republican voters should look carefully at their ballots and see that their ballots are properly marked for the district in which they vote. Be sure that you have the ballots for your own district. In the Onondaga case, the court held that transposed ballots of this sort constituted marked ballots and should not be counted.

The Home-Rulers are after the Sheehan thugs with a vengeance. They assert they will have them all in the Penitentiary if they can be found and they will not be allowed to do any of their dirty work in this city. Franklin D. Locke last night said that he would make it his business to have them arrested as vagrants as soon as they could be found, as they come under a class under the law if unable to show some visible means of support. The Home Rulers stated that no effort would be spared to make it very warm for the imported beings who may be brought here by the Sheehan Machine, whether they are sworn in as special patrolmen, or are stationed at the voting booths as simple sluggers and repeaters.

A Vicious Assault

The very same morning that the Buffalo Express sounded the alarm on its front page about the Sheehans' importation of violent gangs of New York thugs and goons into the city, former Buffalo Alderman Edward Byrnes, an old enemy of William F. Sheehan, was making a purchase from a stall at the Elk Street Market.

From out of nowhere in broad daylight six burly New York pugilist Bowery scum imported by the Sheehans jumped and viciously assaulted him. As a business owner in that neighborhood, Byrnes was well known to all, and his neighbors instantly reacted and set upon Byrnes' attackers with bricks, bats and fists.

One neighbor reached the harrowing scene just in time to plow his bunch o' fives into the kidney of a man ready to pitch a seven-pound rock at the now-prone former alderman's head. Helpless on the ground, the missile would surely have killed him. Others arrived almost simultaneously and routed the toughs, who took off in all directions, one hopping a passing freight train.

No one had ever seen any of the hooligans before.

The thugs had arrived in Buffalo on a Sheehan train for the express purpose of terrorizing First Ward voters at the polls on election day. But Billy Sheehan had an old score to settle with his enemy first, a man who, during his reign on the Common Council, was not afraid to challenge the Sheehans and call them any name that fit—and most of the worst did.

One of the assailants was apprehended by Ed Byrnes' defenders.

Alderman Ed Byrnes as a young man had once been propositioned by a man for sex, a man by the name of Chandler Wells. Wells' advances had made Byrnes very uneasy, and Byrnes walked the other way whenever he spotted Wells along the streets of the First Ward thereafter. One day some years after, an older Byrnes spotted Chandler Wells with twelve-year-old Johnny Sheehan, the current candidate for alderman, who seemed to be with him willingly. Johnny Sheehan's parents were dead. He had been living with his aunt and uncle and two cousins. The family was destitute, and Ed Byrnes had never seen Johnny Sheehan wear any clothing that had not been previously well-worn by another. For once he was not dressed in someone else's patched hand-me-downs, but wearing a new jacket and pants. Ed Byrnes was suspicious.

A week afterward, Ed Byrnes ran into Johnny Sheehan at the Elk Street Market and asked him how his job was going aboard the Buffalo River ferry.

"Oh, I ain't workin' there no more. Mr. Wells adopted me."

"Adopted ye? But ye still have yer aunt and uncle," said Byrnes.

"I dunno. He asked the folks if he could adopt me, and they said yes," beamed Johnny Sheehan. "So now I live in a nice house, eat good food, and wear new clothes to school!"

Byrnes was startled. "I have to warn ye about something, Johnny," confided Ed Byrnes cautiously. "When I was younger Mr. Wells offered me some money if I would drop me inexpressibles an' let him suck me cock. Has he ever laid a hand on ye?"

Johnny Sheehan turned a glowing bright red. "Fuck, naw," he stammered. "Mr. W-Wells wouldn't do nothin' like that. Ye got it wrong, Ed. He ain't no cocksucker!"

Ed Byrnes could tell by Johnny Sheehan's ill-concealed humiliation that he'd gotten it right.

Most boys and young men have their story of sexual experience with other males, and Ed Byrnes was no exception. But this was different, he thought. Wells was not just another boy exchanging curiosities. He was an old man. And Johnny Sheehan was living with him in his house.

As they grew up to manhood in the same neighborhood, Ed Byrnes wondered a few times what went on in Johnny Sheehan's new home, why Sheehan's aunt and uncle would allow some man who was not even a relative to adopt their nephew and go live with him. The story on the street was that Wells paid the Sheehans and helped the struggling family out in the following years.

Wells also saw to it also that both of Johnny Sheehan's cousins, John C. and William F., completed courses of study at St. Joseph's College. The previously unhappy John C. Sheehan, thrown upon his own resources at a very early age by his father's misfortunes, working as a ferry boy on the Buffalo River to help support the family, recognized an opportunity to bring himself up in the world and remain in school. The Sheehan parents never gave a hint that they had any concerns about their sons, their nephew, or Wells.

Cousin Johnny Sheehan was never known to have a serious belle, nor did he show interest in anything other than his work and building himself a future that might blot out the poverty of his childhood. As both his cousins' tarnished stars began to rise in politics, he rode along with them, the brothers Sheehan tutoring their cousin Johnny in most everything they knew.

Opposing political views, usually involving ethics, put the adult Ed Byrnes at odds with the adult William F. Sheehan on more than a few occasions. Billy Sheehan, as he ascended to power, became more and more prone to belligerent tactics like intimidation, overt threats of violence, and the recruiting of henchmen willing to do his dirty work for him.

One day, after a heated confrontation, the slimy Billy Sheehan made an untrue and unforgivable remark about Ed Byrne's beloved wife. Ed Byrnes responded with a humiliating yet truthful fact about Billy's cousin Johnny, something Billy Sheehan had up until that moment believed was a well-buried secret.

Billy Sheehan froze in absolute stupefaction. His special brand of deluded self-entitlement allowed for his concocting a nasty lie to slander Byrnes' wife, but Byrne's embarrassing truth in response to that spiteful lie instigated an insane plan for retribution.

"You had better keep that lyin' mouth of yours shut, Ed Byrnes, or I'll perform the shuttin'!" seethed Billy Sheehan. Billy swore comeuppance, and walked away.

Blue-eyed Billy Sheehan waited quite a few years to get his revenge. But get it he did, on November 4th 1893, at the Elk Street Market, while the city found itself totally distracted by the fearsome complications of other events. Ed Byrnes and the secret he kept were a threat and a liability to the Sheehan cousin's election. Byrnes hovered near death for days.

THE FIRST WARD I

The evening of the attack on Ed Byrnes, Alderman Jack White, running scared for the first time in his marathon career, called a meeting of his constituents.

His opponent, John Sheehan, was the most formidable foe Jack White had ever encountered, not because cousin Sheehan had any real power of his own, but because of his family connections, for whom he was a dutiful manikin. Jack White was not about to give up his long-held empire. Walsh Hall was jammed, and the crowds spilled down the stairs and out onto the street.

Family men were infuriated by the Sheehans' colonization of their First Ward with criminal scum who were allowed to run wild in the streets while the laborers toiled at their jobs, unable to protect their wives and children.

"Gentlemen and fellow citizens of the First Ward." Jack White began. "I address you thus because I do not see before me any of the scum of the 2nd and 19th wards, but rather, only resident citizens of my own ward."

The pot calling the kettle black, the "scum" that Jack White was referring to were the Sheehans, John P. Sullivan, and Fingy Conners.

The Second Ward had only recently been carved out of the original First Ward, that once-clever but now-backfiring scheme having been originated by Jack White himself with the Sheehans' cooperation. Soon afterward Jack White experienced a curious falling-out with Billy Sheehan. Now all his former allies had turned against him: Fingy Conners, John P. Sullivan and the Sheehans.

White never realized this had been the plan all along.

After the district lines were redrawn, Alderman John P. Sullivan became the powerful head of the new Second Ward. Sullivan had previously at different times been both ally of and opponent to Jack White. But now, as an unrepentant Sheehanite, Sullivan was set squarely against him. Jack White's once indestructible political alliances had crumbled almost overnight.

"This is not just the fight of those of us who are gathered here tonight," shouted Jack White to his supporters, "it is the fight of all the citizens of the First Ward against the saloon boss Fingy Conners and his imported voters! I ask you, who ought to decide the election in this ward, the people of the ward, or men who are outsiders and have nothing to do with the ward's affairs?"

"The people of the ward!" came the thundering response from hundreds of throats.

"Well, I don't believe they are going to let us do it," said the speaker in deliberate tones. "The Sheehanites have proposed to go to the polls early on election day and form a line which, with the full cooperation of the Buffalo Police Department, they intended to maintain all day long, in order to prevent any citizen who is not with the Machine from casting a ballot."

"They can't do it!" shouted the crowd.

"Well, we can't afford to get into a row with the police," counseled the Alderman, "for it is not the fault of the men of the police force, but of their bosses who have to obey the mandates of the Big Boss who awarded them their places."

Jack White dwelt on the fact that there were just as many good men on the force now as ever, but they had to obey orders, as their job meant bread and butter to their wives and children, "But if any row takes place on election day," he declared, "the Police Commissioners will be directly chargeable with whatever damage is done to human life or to property on that day."

He said he didn't blame the Police Commissioners in trying to assist Sheehan, for he was their benefactor, but there was a line they should not cross.

"They swore an oath before Almighty God when they took office that they would do their duty," said he, "but are they doing it? I wouldn't like to charge anyone with perjury, but I swear I would like to have a pair of suspenders made out of the consciences of these same Commissioners!"

Jack White went on to say that every man had a day of reckoning, and perhaps the Police Commissioners would meet theirs earlier than they expected. He took up the boast bellowed by his opponent's cousin, now-Lieutenant Governor of New York State William F. Sheehan, at Music Hall just a few days before, that the present police force was incomparably better than that of a year ago.

Jack White asked the voters, "Do you consider it a sign of improvement when an intoxicated Captain of Police, Captain James Walsh, leads a drunken gang of toughs through the ward at midnight, shouting and singing and cursing crude epithets, waking up every child and hard-working parent in the neighborhood and making the night hideous with their primitive cries?

"Do you think it a sign of improvement when yet another Captain of Police, Captain Michael Regan, went to the saloons in the 19th and ordered the saloon-keepers to send every bum, whether citizen or alien, into the First Ward for colonization purposes, or else find themselves in real trouble?

"We are fighting for principle," White continued, "for home rule in the First Ward. Are they willing to give it to us?"

The citizens of the ward, Jack White exhorted, were indignant at the actions of the Democratic boss, and would vote against him not from love of their present Alderman, for he was merely a cipher in the fight, but because they objected to having the scum of Canal Street shoved in the faces of their wives and children.

He asked the voters what the visitors to our city, and foreigners passing through from the 1893 Chicago World's Fair, think of the Irish and their famous First Ward when they are being violently molested for beer money by the bums on lower Main Street?

"Allow me, gentlemen," Jack White went on, "to draw a contrast between myself and saloon boss Fingy Conners, and his stooge alderman John Kennedy of the 19th ward. I am not a wealthy man by any stretch of the imagination, but what money I did make was not wrung out of the sweat and blood of the laboring man on the docks!

"I would be deeply ashamed of myself if I ever caused a single woman to cry on my account. Yet we have a man ruling over a thousand families in our ward who drives hundreds of despairing, hopeless wives and mothers to tears every single night of their darkening lives! Our careworn parish priests carry on their shoulders the ponderous burdens of the confessions of our desperate brothers and sisters having nowhere left to turn!

"Jack White has never taken a man's wages in over a bar and changed money into drink that should have been sent home to feed crying babies weak from hunger and sickness!

"That is the crying shame committed in our ward by Fingy Conners!"

Jack White neglected to mention that in previous years, Fingy Conners' exact same crimes against humanity seemed to cause him no pangs at all, back when

Conners was for him rather than against him.

"My countrymen left Ireland because it was under a one-woman British Royalist rule. Other voters here may have left their native land because it was in the hands of one-man power, and we all came here for liberty. But are we getting it? Do we want to build up a king here?

"I say to you that the Czar of Russia has not got a deadlier grip on his subjects tonight than the Lieutenant Governor of New York State Billy Sheehan will have on the citizens of Buffalo unless they vote against Fingy Conners' dummies on election day!"

On Monday afternoon election eve, November 6, former Alderman Ed Byrnes died of the injuries he suffered at the hands of the gang who attacked him at the Elk Street Market.

A man by the name of Charles Murphy was arrested for the assault on Byrnes, coincidentally so by Police Captain James Walsh, the same leader of his precinct's peacekeepers who had headed the infamous midnight drunken parade of thugs through the slumbering First Ward with a Sheehan on one side of him and a Kennedy on the other.

As Ed Byrnes languished in agony from mortal injuries inflicted by a dozen or more murderous kicks to his abdomen and head, Captain Walsh took the former alderman's accused assailant before Justice King. Walsh withheld the details from King. He did not tell Justice King that it was Ed Byrnes who Murphy attacked, nor did he have Murphy appropriately charged. Police Captain Walsh had Murphy arraigned on the petty charge of assault in the second degree, meaning the Captain was claiming the assault was spontaneous rather than planned, allowing Murphy to be immediately released on $500 bail.

Who exactly stepped up, having both the financial resources as well as the urgency to put up such a large amount of cash to bond a common vagrant—and come forward with it so very quickly too—was not revealed.

Murphy jumped bail and fled across the river to Canada.

When Justice King learned later that Murphy was one of the assailants who laid waste to Ed Byrnes, a small detail that Police Captain Walsh had neglected to reveal to him, the judge was incensed at being duped by the Captain.

Then, when Justice King learned that Alderman Ed Byrnes had died, he was enraged beyond tolerance.

Justice King was quoted in the newspapers, "Captain James Walsh ought to be dismissed from the police force! Any man who will do as he did is not a safe man to have as a police captain."

That same night, a gang of Sheehan roughs, headed by Fingy Conners' stepbrother Dennis Hurley, who longed to reclaim favor in his brother's eyes, dutifully terrorized the neighborhoods of the First Ward. Hurley had about a dozen men with him, most of them policy writers, all shouting the glories of John Sheehan as they stormed from saloon to saloon, awakening sleeping citizens along the way. They raised quite a ruckus, their goal to intimidate and put fear into the quiet voters of the ward who might venture out the next morning and dare cast a vote against John Sheehan.

At William Stafford's Saloon, located at the corner of Louisiana and Perry

Streets, one of Alderman Jack White's friends was set upon by Hurley. Dennis Hurley, apparently short of memory concerning a particular saloon brawl from his earlier days and the hideous consequences that held for him personally, treated Richard Burrill quite roughly.

A neighborhood legend apparently unfamiliar to the dense Mr. Hurley, small of stature yet possessing imposing strength, interceded on behalf of his friend Burrill. One powerful blow from Dan Moran's fist to Dennis Hurley's glass jaw suddenly caused him to vividly recollect that night in 1880 when he was so badly beaten at John Rochford's Saloon that he nearly died—first from his injuries, and then again a few days later from the fire that mysteriously erupted in the home of his sister Julia who was tenderly nursing his wounds, killing her horribly.

Witnessing Dan Moran knock out Hurley with just a single punch, the dozen tough guys scattered to the winds, dragging Hurley with them. Their destination was 444 Ohio Street, Fingy Conners' Saloon and his rat's nest of colonizers.

There they told their tale.

The toughs returned to Stafford's Saloon with three dozen of their friends, including candidate John Sheehan, Fingy Conners, "Bully" McDonald, "Sloak" Slattery, and other colorfully named hooligans wielding an assortment of pistols and clubs. The gang, bent on avenging their humiliation at being run off by what amounted to one solitary diminutive individual, broke down the front door of Stafford's Saloon and began firing pistol shots. A man named Meaghan took a bullet in the temple, and the neighborhood was thoroughly terrorized.

The police were summoned by infuriated citizens, but the patrol wagon, leisurely rattling down the cobblestones, was intercepted by some of Sheehan's friends and sent away.

The melee was out of control. Saloon owner William Stafford, a small harmless cripple, had a heavy coupling pin thrown at him, which had it not just missed his head by an inch, would have killed him. Stafford ended up out front in the street, firing several rounds into the air to scare the Conners gang away from his establishment. Within minutes, the police returned and arrested Stafford and dragged the disabled saloonkeep roughly away to Precinct 7, charging him with the "illegal discharge" of his weapon.

No other arrests were made.

From Stafford's Saloon, the gang rampaged onward to Diebold's Saloon on Ohio Street, where they nearly killed a man named Toomey, then jumped a Jack White man in front of Simon McMahon's saloon at Chicago and Elk Streets, severely injuring him.

No arrests were made during the hours-long ruckus, for the police didn't happen to be detaining any Sheehan men as of late.

That same evening, 129 arrest warrants were taken to Police headquarters. The warrants had been sworn for individuals who it was believed were illegally registered to vote. The warrants were turned over by Superintendent of Police Chambers to Captain Michael Regan of the First Precinct to be served. Captain Regan did something unusual: he gave the entire batch of 129 warrants to one single individual, a patrolman named O'Donnell.

Patrolman O'Donnell was in no hurry to find those men named in the warrants, because he had been so instructed. O'Donnell walked the warrants on foot to 133 Main Street, the location of cockfighter Henry Kilcourse's nest of colonizers, at about 9 o'clock. O'Donnell methodically read off each of the 129 names to the negro clerk who was manning the desk of the rooming house, asking 129 times if the man named was "stopping there."

The clerk answered "No" 129 times, after which time Patrolman O'Donnell departed, unconcerned.

On that same Monday evening, election eve, a parade was planned in the Fourth Ward by the Workingmen's Independent Club for Home Rule for Assembly candidate Thomas J. Nunan, former ice business partner of Alderman John P. Sullivan and currently director of the Union Ice Co. The membership consisted of a coalition of both Democrats and Republicans seeking an end to the Sheehan Machine. Hannah Sullivan was bullish about having the Sheehans rousted, preferably right into the Penitentiary.

Jim's shoulder was throbbing.

All through that day at work he had been haunted by the things that Hannah had said about his brother the alderman, mostly because of their verisimilitude. Her unprecedented rage had set him to thinking.

He wondered why JP had kept the secret, even to this day, of Jack White's killing of Doc Greene when he might have effectively used it against him. There had to be a reason. And why it had never been confided in him that the 1889 election that JP had lost to Jack White had been engineered for that exact outcome? Jim felt like a fool then, campaigning as hard as he did for his brother, taking it so personally when JP lost, when it had all been planned from the outset to play out exactly that way without his knowledge. He'd been left the odd man out, a fool.

Jim had risked his own career by telling JP about Jack White's crime, but JP conversely did not trust his brother enough to tell him beforehand about his arrangement with White, Fingy Conners and the Sheehan Brothers to throw the 1889 election. It was not until seven weeks afterward, at that Christmas meeting held in the Mutuals boathouse, that it was first revealed to him what the real plan had been all along. JP didn't even prepare his brother for what was about to happen that evening. Jim felt humiliated upon the plan's revelation. JP had shut him out.

And Hannah was right; whenever JP needed him, or was in trouble, or required Jim's badge to help him intimidate someone, there JP stood at Jim's door, expectant of his full cooperation, even right in the middle of eating supper with his family. Despite the obvious advantages that came along with holding aldermanic office, Jim rarely asked JP for favors in return. More telling, JP didn't offer.

Jim looked around the precinct house, watching the men's faces. With his arm in a sling he would be on desk duty for a few weeks most probably.

He missed Hannah.

He watched what was transpiring around him. Nearby stood Captain Walsh joking with Michael Regan. How is it that Idiot Walsh had ever made Captain in the first place? Walsh was a classic dunderhead. He'd only gotten as far as the sixth grade, Jim recalled, and even at that he was failing nearly all his subjects. Although Regan was far better educated than Walsh, he didn't seem to display a whole lot more common sense than Walsh. Jim Sullivan liked and admired

Mike Regan a lot better back when they were kids, he hated to admit. Mike was a real swell fellow back then. Mike's father had stood up as witness for Jim's mother Mary when she married Peter Halloran. That's how close the families were. And after all the favors Jim had done for the Sheehans, and Fingy, how is it that the Alderman's own brother wasn't rewarded with a Captain's badge and the salary that went with it? His family could certainly use the money. Why hadn't JP ever approached him about it, or made any such deal with his partners in crime?

JP liked to parade around like a man who has power, but did he really have power? Jim always just assumed he had, but now that he was thinking about it, the more JP seemed like no more than a lackey for all the others. Jim had to fight tooth and nail for ten years just to finally make Detective, while the other Sheehan stooges like Regan and Walsh and others seemed to just breeze their way up the ladder lickety-split. Jim had already been performing exceptional detective work for years unacknowledged before the department finally considered him for that promotion. He should have made detective back in '89 just for keeping his mouth shut, if not Captain.

Jim wasn't even sure whether he'd accept a Captain's badge if offered. At times he felt he was already in far too deep as it was. If he were Captain then the pressure might be on to do something really risky, or humiliating, like Walsh's midnight parade at the head of the army of drunken goons.

Walsh walked by just at that moment. What an ass. Jim tried to discern in his face some clue. I'd die before I'd do something as degrading as that, thought Jim. He had become so myopic looking out for his little brother—literally, from the day their father left for the army—that it never occurred to him that JP might not be looking out for him too. This was a jolting realization.

JP had grown up being taken care of, and still to this day fully expected that, not only from his brother, but from everybody around him. He chose Annie to marry primarily because she was enthusiastic to do whatever he needed done, to the point she never complained that she was really quite on her own most of the time. Maybe that's why he had her pumping out babies so regularly, to keep her distracted. JP was a self-important man, deluded, who saw himself not only as a leader, but as the boss. The boss of everyone, apparently, including even his older brother.

Jim could now more clearly see why Hannah had begun to view him as JP's supplicant.

Another of Hannah's truisms came back to him: "What sets humans apart from all the rest of God's creatures is our singular capacity for denying the truth."

He'd been going about his life denying that he chose to do the things he did. For his brother. For the department. For crooked politicians. Things that adversely affected his wife, his children, even his own best interests.

Jim's head was reeling with new realizations, as if he had just awoken from a long drunk.

He noticed himself distracted throughout the entire rest of the day, impatiently eyeing the clock for his first opportunity to go home. Suddenly, at three o'clock the precinct door opened and in slithered Patrolman Bill O'Reilly, there to commiserate with Captain Regan. Before O'Reilly could so much as blink, Jim tightened his fist and recalled the useful advice his old friend Tom Kelly had given him: "When you punch a man in the face, aim for your fist to go right through his face straight into the back of his skull, rather than just aiming for his

367

nose. That way, you'll pack far more power, and there'll be less chance of your injuring yourself."

So, with his one good hand he demolished O'Reilly with just a single slug.

"You stood there while my wife and my boy got molested by vagrants, and you did nothing about it, you bitch?" he screamed. Every man stopped what he was doing.

"You had better stay the hell out of my path from this moment forward, O'Reilly, if you expect to go on breathing!"

Complete silence fell over Precinct Seven's house as all were awed by Jim Sullivan's unexpected detonation. The Captain tried to dress his detective down.

Without taking his eyes off his bleeding victim on the floor, Jim cut the Captain's protest off by shouting to any and all, "This sorry piece of shit stood by on Main Street like a coward and allowed two vags to grab my wife's privates —and then went off smiling about it. He's done!"

The Captain simply shrugged and walked away. Nobody could much argue with that.

Jim shuffled into the house and climbed the stairs. He was tired. Hannah waited for him, still seething. The children busied themselves around the kitchen table setting it for supper, apprehensively awaiting their father's arrival.

Hannah looked at him when he appeared in the kitchen doorway and recognized the gentleness in his gaze as being identical to that which she had once known quite intimately, but believed was lost forever. Jim wrapped his good arm around his wife and held her close.

"I'm sorry. I love you with all my heart," he said distinctly so all the children could clearly hear.

"I love you too," she replied as she melted into him. She wiped her face on his good shoulder before the kids could see her tears.

The three children witnessed their parents' embrace and heard their words. They audibly exhaled. Great relief filled their hearts, so worried had they been about the terrible things they'd heard through the door.

At the supper table, the detective said to his oldest, "Son, I don't want you to ever again get into a fight on my account. You just walk away, hear? Let people say what they will, because they will. It's just human nature. You can't stop 'em. I'm sorry it happened. The last thing I ever want is for you to get hurt on my account. Understand?"

Jim Jr. nodded, relieved of his burden, and continued eating.

After supper they hurried to prepare themselves.

"Dress warm, you hear?" Jim hollered to his children as they readied in their rooms.

Hannah decked herself out in her Sunday best, rushing to finish so as not to make her children late for the parade in support of their honorary Uncle, Tom Nunan.

She'd made a point to tell Annie she was going to go, and hoping to rile the Alderman really good, invited her to come along right in front of him.

"JP would scalp me!" Annie giggled, later. "But tell Tom that me and the children send our love," she instructed.

The Alderman had distinctly heard Detective Jim Sullivan forbid Hannah to attend the rally for Tom Nunan, and was made uneasy both by her determination to attend and his brother's apparent unwillingness to stop her.

Jim made sure his children were dressed snugly enough against the November cold and that their coat pockets secured the graham crackers that he had wrapped in waxed paper for them in case they got hungry. He kissed Hannah and caressed her face with his good hand, and accepted hugs from his kids. His youngest, Johnny, whispered in his ear, "I love ye, Pa."

As he stood in the window watching his family board the Hamburgh streetcar headed toward the 4th ward, he smiled once more and waved goodbye to them. Then he settled in with a whisky glass to continue rereading an old favorite by Mark Twain, The Adventures Of Tom Sawyer.

The Alderman concealed himself next door in his darkened window. He saw the family leave and, gratingly, witnessed his own brother waving goodbye to them.

The Alderman fumed next door as his sister-in-law defied him and boarded the streetcar out front with her children. Once she was out of sight, JP marched over to his brother's house in a huff and banged angrily on the locked door to confront him. Jim heard the pounding downstairs, but was too amused by Tom Sawyer's whitewashing scheme to be bothered getting up.

The turnout for the parade was huge. The club assembled at its headquarters at 628 South Division Street and from there, preceded by the Chapin Post Drum Corps, marched through the principal streets of the 1st Assembly District. A vanguard of club officers led the parade carrying the banner for Thomas J. Nunan to whose candidacy the club had devoted itself enthusiastically. Illuminated transparencies were hoisted aloft by marchers, bearing such inscriptions as Friend Of The Workingman and Tom Nunan Fights For Democracy.

Election Day 1893
In The 4th District

Sheehan's thugs had sneaked up upon the First Ward's 4th district polling place at 3 o'clock in the morning on election day, led by Fingy Conners.

Conners ordered that the booth itself be physically picked up, moved and rotated, so that an approach to it could only be accessed from one direction. The idea being that the prizefighters that Fingy had hired to hijack the entrance be shielded from any counter-challenge from the flank.

The booth was finely situated for the work of the pugs and thugs, halfway between Perry and Elk streets on Illinois Street. It had a high fence on one side and a row of boilers bordering the other; with no pavement. Just in front of the door of the booth there was a big mud puddle where the victims could be landed, as if on a feather-bed, and it was not only just a few who were destined to be put to sleep there. The bulldogs would be ejecting all variety of Jack White men, tossing them bodily into the mass of sticky muck.

Even before dawn broke, Alderman Jack White had arranged that his supporters, mostly Italians, rush to the polls to claim their place in line. White's men beat the Sheehan men to the polls by over an hour, but they didn't beat them to the punch.

Fingy Conners claimed ownership of the 2nd district polling place in the 1st Ward, despite the fact he now lived in the 5th ward.

James Kennedy, Democratic leader and brother of Alderman John Kennedy kidnapped the 1st Ward's 4th district polling place even though he lived in the 19th ward.

The Sheehan forces in the city now controlled the Buffalo Police Department, the Buffalo Sheriff's Department, and the employees of the Assessor's and Controller's offices. New York State Lieutenant Governor Billy Sheehan on this day schemed to graphically demonstrate to the citizens of Buffalo what he could accomplish by his ownership of their police and sheriffs on election day. Afterward he planned to additionally demonstrate what he could get away with by his controlling of the Assessor's office, which would be the body that oversaw jury selection in the trials of the Sheehan men certain to take place after the debacle was over.

At dawn a line of 72 Jack White voters stood in queue in an orderly manner at the 4th district polling place tent.

As they watched the opposing Sheehan gang approach, the White men saw that the Sheehans had put four local brawlers out front of their ranks: Reddy Strauss, who was a bouncer at an especially infamous Canal Street dive; Bill Baker, who had already served two terms in the penitentiary for prize fighting; Charley Marks, another bouncer at an even worse dive; and a massively built crusher who drove a truck for Kennedy named Charley Farrell. All wore the badge identifying each as a newly-sworn Special Patrolman

There were others, including the star boxer of the Sullivan brothers' offshoot of the Mutual Rowing Club, the South Side Athletic Club, a pug named Marty McDonough. A score of policemen were present on the scene, including Detective Jim Sullivan, who was told to do away with his arm sling and station himself out of harm's way as best he could. There was great fear in the city about what might transpire in the First Ward on election day, especially in the 4th district, and police manpower was overwhelmingly focused there. The coppers needed every uniform they could get, including the wife-injured Jim's. He took a good hard look at the volatile mix at hand and decided he would stay as far away from the front of the line as he was able. He claimed a distant spot back at the street entrance.

The fun, as the pugs later put it, began very early in the morning.

The imposing form of local hero Bartley Hines was passing down the street after returning home from a previous evening's dance and providential copulation opportunity when the 72 Italians who were lined up waiting for the polls to open asked his assistance.

Bartley Hines was a physical culturist sculpted in the same mold as the currently famous bodybuilder Eugen Sandow. Every young man growing up in the First Ward and beyond looked up to Hines with awe and respect. Hines, a Jack White man, told the Italians he would help them out and took his place at the front of the line next the voting booth door. The 72 Italians were lined up on the Perry Street side of the booth, while 21 Sheehan men were forming a different line on the Elk Street side. The cops paid no attention when the longer line of Jack White men was shattered and tossed around by the battering ram of Sheehan's penitentiary graduates.

When the dust settled, Captain Michael Regan of the 1st Precinct arrived and ordered the Italians to either get into line or move on. Bartley Hines insisted that his men were in line; they were on the ground first and had the right of way. But Regan would have none of it. "There's more men in that other line," the Pharisee stated, pointing toward the 21 Sheehan men lounging opposite. Mathematics be damned, that settled it. "Ye'll git in the other line or git out," commanded Regan. Hines knew there was no going against the police, so he lined his 72 men up in back of the 21 Sheehanites.

Jim Sullivan, positioned at the perimeter of the carnival as distant from potential trouble as allowed, engaged in numerous conferences throughout the day with Captain Regan. Jim spent most of his time doing what was expected: posturing; shooting dirty looks at the dagos and staring daggers at the Republican watchers who were pacing around infuriated at being barred from their rightful legal duties.

Democratic Leader James Kennedy produced a packet of freshly minted white ribbon patches with the phrase Special Deputy Sheriff printed on them, and pinned them on the lapels of fifty or more of his bullies. He then stationed the four principal pugilists at the entrance of the voting booth to await the opening of the polls.

The polls were opened and the 21 Sheehan men cast their votes first.

Then came strongman Hines' turn.

Just as he reached the door, the four bulldogs jumped on the awe-inspiring Hines all at once. He later described his shedding of the four as being "like branches falling off trees" once they attempted to pound him.

They had struck the wrong man. Bartley Hines gave them all they wanted and then some. He sent the intimidating Charley Farrell crashing through the fence, and shed the other three branches off just as handily. They all tried pounding him, but within seconds he quickly laid each one on the ground, throwing the two-time ex-con Baker especially hard into the large mud puddle at the center of the spellbound crowd with a painful "Oof!", much to collective awe and delight.

Witnessing the mountainous Bartley Hines lambasting the four professional fighters all by himself, the rest of the Sheehan subservients thought twice about entering the fray, then thought about it once more for good measure.

Hines flashed one last intimidating scowl at his victim wallowing in the puddle, and Regan and his police giving him wide berth, he departed. The laughable report was given wide circulation by the humiliated Sheehanites that Bartley Hines had been almost killed in the fray, but the only injury to Bart Hines was the loss of his hat.

Hines made his way to the home of candidate Alderman Jack White to tell him the situation. Jack White was deathly ill with a burning fever.

"You need to come down to the 4th, Jack!", the strongman told Alderman White.

There was nothing more that Jack White wanted in the world than to be on the scene to try and stop the Sheehanite shenanigans. "Bart, I can't. The doctor told me if I venture out, they'll be pickin' out a wooden suit for me come tomorrow mornin'."

The determined Bart Hines marched away from Jack White's house and returned to the polling-place. He got in line again, right at the front.

When he came up to vote the pugilists somehow got busy turning their attentions elsewhere, and Hines wrote his ballot unmolested. His good work completed, the White men were sorry to see the civilian peacekeeper depart. The hero hadn't yet slept, and longed for his bed.

No one else who was unacceptable to the four pugilists was allowed entry to the voting booths that day. When a man came up to vote, one of the special deputy thugs would approach him, and if he were on the correct team, he was escorted to the booth. No man was allowed to vote after 10 o'clock unless he entered the booth under escort of a "special deputy." Jack White voters were pulled or dragged out of the line before they even got to the front. From that time forward there was no question how the 4th district was to be carried. All pretense of upholding the law and enforcing Constitutional rights were cast aside. Anarchy ruled. All except the Democratic watchers were either denied admittance to the booths or were thrown out bodily.

Men were stationed at the various compartments who generously provided pre-folded ballots for the convenience of the voter. Only the straight Democratic ballot was to be voted, and any opposing ballots were thrown on the floor. By this time-saving means many more ballots were cast than would otherwise have been possible. All a voter had to do was to accept a pre-folded bundle of five ballots and put them in the box.

Morris Smith of No. 42 Perry Street went into the booth early in the morning. He was given his five ballots and started for a compartment.

"I'll fold yer ballots fer ye," stated a thug.

"No ye won't," replied Mr. Smith.

"Then ye don't vote here," countered the goon.

"That's what you think!" said Smith a split second before he was sent bleeding into the mud puddle.

"I said, then ye don't vote here," repeated the assailant.

And he didn't. Voters were punched and assaulted in a wholesale manner throughout the day by the pugilists as the police looked askance.

Wallace Thayer, a Republican election watcher assigned to oversee the polling place, confronted Democratic Leader James Kennedy, who had taken over control of the voting booth, about the underhanded tactics. With the police lined up along one fence, watching, and the lines of voters alongside the opposite boilers, Kennedy picked up Thayer and tossed him into the mud puddle at the center, broadcasting his control over the turf.

At 9 o'clock, Judge Hatch called Sheriff August Beck into the Superior Court and handed him a warrant, instructing him to go to the polling place immediately and arrest James Kennedy for assaulting Wallace Thayer. Thayer had made a complaint, and Judge Hatch issued a peace warrant, which was all he was able to do because it was election day and the court was not legally in session.

Ex-Streets Commissioner John Martin was appointed a Republican election watcher at the polling place as well, but when he showed up for his duties, two-time felon pugilist Baker refused to admit him. Martin approached Police Captain Michael Regan, standing a few feet away, to challenge the affront, but Regan just turned his back to him.

The infuriated Martin took a carriage to see Superintendent of Police Bull, but it wasn't until a heated argument took place between the two that Martin secured an order from him for Regan, compelling him to allow Martin into the booth. When Martin returned to the polling place and presented the written order to Regan, the Captain mocked, "Oh, all right. If yer goin' t' cry like some little girl then I suppose I'll have t' put ye in."

But not so for any of the others. When voters in line finally reached the front, having waited for hours, they found themselves thrown out by the prize-fighters on one dismissive pretext or another. Any who protested were dumped hard into the puddle for all to see.

Cock-fighter Henry Kilcourse acted as the polling-place's banker, hurrying excitedly back and forth with vote-sellers in tow between the voting booths and a room located back of a Perry Street saloon. All day long, voters offering to sell their ballots were escorted to the saloon, and the transaction completed, hustled back to the booth and rushed to the head of the line to carry out their civic duty. One of these was Paddy McGee, who exclaimed to a friend as he exited the booth, "I got t'ree dollars fer mine!"

As the day dragged on and the roughs remained in control to the extent that they met little resistance, Captain Regan's police officers relaxed. At first, flasks were passed among the boys in blue, and then, as all present began to experience the effect of diminishing judgement, whisky bottles were produced and traded openly. Jim Sullivan, in pain and with nothing much to do but make sure nobody bumped into his injury, welcomed the diversion when Detective Flynn passed him the bottle.

Captain Regan participated, unconcerned with the neighborhood onlookers observing from the requisite 150 yards away; the citizens, mothers with children witnessing this enormous farce, all worrying about what kind of future they had to look forward to in a place like Buffalo when its peace keepers saw fit to share whisky bottles with a criminal New York gang they were protecting while physically barring American citizens from their right to vote. Few police officers were able to even remain standing by the time the polls closed.

At the end of the day the four prizefighters, who had been promised $25 by the Democratic General Committee for their unique skills, were paid but $20. They didn't seem to mind. As pug Charley Marks expressed it, by any previous standard it was a big payday for the pugilists.

The 4th District polling place crowd surrounds the infamous mud puddle.

Meanwhile, Over
In The 2nd District

Over at the First Ward's 2nd district polling place, Dennis McCarthy from East Market Street had arrived precisely at 6 o'clock. Before the polls opened he was one of a line which formed reaching up to the door of the booth. Abruptly, a little before 7 o'clock, the sergeant of police in charge ordered all the men in the line to back well away from the booth.

Just then, Fingy Conners marched in with a large gang of his New York and Canal district accomplices, each thug displaying a deputy sheriff's badge or ribbon. McCarthy was very troubled to see some of the worst effluence of Canal Street wearing these special sheriff's badges. He knew there was sure to be trouble.

Conners, when he saw the line already formed in front of the booth, marched his men around to the other side of the booth and formed a second line. Then Fingy snapped his fingers and ordered that there should be but one line.

McCarthy was outraged at the affront. He held out for a half hour, but it was no use: the 7th Precinct police broke up the first line and scattered the men every which way by force. A sympathetic copper saw the look of dismay on McCarthy's face, and on the faces of those with him.

"You'll have to fight for it," the policeman told him, "if you'll want to vote to this line."

Some of the men then went away disgusted and disheartened. Others formed behind the second line. McCarthy finally decided to fall into the second line as well.

There was plenty of time to kill. The line was moving imperceptibly. McCarthy watched the goings-on with fascination and contempt. He saw that there were fifty or sixty low-lifes with Conners, newly pinned as deputy sheriffs, but he thought it revealing that the showboating Fingy himself did not deem it necessary to wear a sheriffs badge. Conners was quite secure in his own authority and knew that others were just as certain of it as he.

Finally, about noon, after six hours in line, Dennis McCarthy got to vote. As he entered the booth, he saw Fingy Conners talk to a man inside the booth who had a bundle of paster ballots in his hand. Conners entered into a compartment with this man to fold his ballots for him. Only if someone were disabled, and specifically requested assistance in the booth, was that kind of "help" legal. McCarthy recognized the strapping young man was not disabled in any way.

He then witnessed Conners pinning a badge on yet another reprehensible and depraved local sewer-dweller nicknamed Tiger, known all around the ward for having molested little girls. He wore a patch over his missing eye, the result of one of the little girls' mothers sticking a knife into it. Her prescription seemed to have cured him lately of his obsession. That, and her swearing she would cut out the remaining one as well if she so much as even heard a rumor that he had not reformed.

John Coughlin was another watcher on election day in the 2nd district. Coughlin watched as Conners lieutenant Peter P. Dalton, one of the poll-clerks, creased the straight Democratic ballots and commanded when he handed them out, "this is the one to vote." Dalton creased a bundle at a time and pushed them into willing hands all day long. Coughlin recognized that it was the men who voted from Conners' hotel at No. 444 Ohio Street who got most of these, the men having been instructed beforehand to vote the creased ballots.

Sheriff August Beck, with the warrant for the arrest of Democratic election watcher James Kennedy in hand for his tossing Mr. Thayer into the mud puddle, had taken the entire day to reach his destination. He wandered the city circuitously on foot in the general direction of the 4th district polling place, stopping in a saloon here and there to quench his thirst, pausing to chat with friends, appropriating a sausage sandwich from an obliged street vendor or two. Slowly he made his way toward the scene of the assault against Thayer where everyone in town knew Kennedy could be found. Shortly before Sheriff Beck arrived, seven hours after he started out on his journey, a precinct detective was seen to whisper into Kennedy's ear, whereupon Kennedy left the booth. One of the Democratic election-watchers that afternoon in the booth was Detective Jim Sullivan's in-law David Nugent, brother of his wife Hannah.

Nugent told Kennedy to go hide, and he would signal him once Sheriff Beck departed.

Sheriff Beck came swaggering down Illinois Street from Perry Street followed by two deputies. Stepping into the 4th district's polling booth, looking none the worse for wear after his seven hour stroll, Beck smiled—and looked about him as if to say, How are you, boys? How's it going?

He went inside the booth briefly, and may or may not have asked whether Kennedy was present. After a minute he came out again and stood among the gathered, leisurely gazing around. It appeared he thought it likely that he might find Kennedy lounging atop some of the boilers that lined one side of the property. A fledgling reporter named Bukowski had seen Kennedy in the booth just a few minutes before Beck walked up and witnessed him scuttling behind the tent. In the interests of justice the reporter told the Sheriff where Kennedy could be found hiding.

Beck stood there and just smirked at the insolent reporter, taking his time to formulate a response.

Beck thought it would be an amusing idea to invite Bukowski to come and inspect the booth for himself, offering to personally accompany him on his quest. The other officers chortled at the entertainment certain to ensue.

Bukowski may have been green, but he wasn't stupid. He wisely declined to place himself in Beck's company away from witnessing eyes due to the Sheriff's violent reputation. The offer was then repeated to a second reporter, well known in the city, who accepted, confident that the peacekeeper would be foolish not to honor his title, if only because of the newsman's status. The newsman followed Beck into the booth and successfully returned intact. He reported to his colleagues, "The Sheriff opened each compartment, and in three of these I observed two men: a voter, and a helpful 'assistant' folding his ballots for him."

Meanwhile a diabolical plot was being formed among the sheriffs to teach a lesson to reporter Bukowski for having the audacity to try and hold Sheriff Beck to his sworn duty. Overhearing the cops' conspiracy plans, four of the veteran reporters approached Police Captain Regan, demanding protection for their inexperienced colleague.

Regan laughed in their faces.

"Oh, yer just suffering from paranoia," he scoffed.

"You may be able steal the election from these voting men, Captain," said the lead reporter, "but you had better think twice before trying to steal freedom of the press. You will be held directly responsible if there is a single hand raised against Bukowski. We all have pistols here and we will use them."

He engaged the Captain in a threatening stare before stalking off.

Nothing more than ugly looks and threats came of it finally, the police taking the intentions of the reporters seriously. All involved preferred going back home to their families minus any bullet holes.

"When did you receive this warrant for James Kennedy, Sheriff?" a reporter asked Beck as he was leaving the grounds, the paper still in his hands.

"Oh, about 1 o'clock I'd say," lied Beck, arrogantly, and four hours off.

"Why haven't you served it before now?" quizzed the reporter.

"Well, you see, the complainant, Mr. Thayer, didn't want to come down here without any protection, and it took me a long time to find those two deputies that I have with me. I got here as soon as I could."

"How about all these deputies who are already here? There seems to be plenty of them, and in addition, there are 20 Buffalo police here on this spot," the reporter countered.

"Oh, but I wanted men I could depend upon. This situation could have turned out like the polack lumber strike back in June, when I couldn't depend upon my men. Down at Tonawanda then I had men I could trust, you know, and there I saved the city thousands of dollars."

"So then, you're saying you couldn't depend upon any of these policemen already here to protect Mr. Thayer?"

"I didn't say that! Don't you put words in my mouth!"

"Well, that's exactly what you just said. It took you hours before you could track down two deputies whom you could trust before you would risk coming here!"

Beck denied it vehemently.

"Sheriff, did you swear in these temporary deputies wearing ribbons? Surely you didn't swear in the jail birds Baker, Strause and Marks?"

"I don't know anything about it. I didn't swear any of them in. The Under Sheriff did that."

"You mean Mr. Steele?"

"Yes."

"And your warrant. What about James Kennedy? Will you arrest him?"

"We'll have him before the night is over. He won't try to get away."

After Beck left the polling place he headed uptown to the Democratic General Committee rooms. At about 9 o'clock Kennedy showed up on the street outside, and unable to concoct any additional excuses, Sheriff Beck served the warrant. But instead of taking Kennedy back before Judge Hatch at the Superior Court at the City Hall—where the Justice had been patiently waiting more than 12 hours to arraign Kennedy — Beck took him before Judge Titus, who accepted bail and set him free.

The following day an indictment was issued against Sheriff Beck and sent to the debauched Tammany Governor of New York State, Roswell P. Flower. It demanded Beck's firing for his actions concerning Kennedy and for his allowing the wholesale appointment of hundreds of special deputy sheriffs without any investigation pertaining to their qualifications or characters. The indictment stated that among those deputized were well-known thugs and pugilists with criminal records, sworn in not at the City Hall, but at the canal offices conducted by Sheehan appointees. In fact, many of those wearing badges that day had never been sworn in at all.

Anyone who expected the nefarious Governor Flower to do anything more punitive than congratulate Sheriff Beck for his fine work and shake the man's hand would be dreaming.

Warrants were also issued for the prison alumni Marks and Strause, but after the polls closed the two got out of town efficiently. Not that the police were in any hurry to arrest them.

Slugged

Hannah massaged Jim's shoulder with liniment right before they went to sleep.

"Was there trouble down at the polls?" she asked, as much curious as sarcastic.

"Pee-yew! That stuff stinks. And go easy on me, will ye? You've already done enough damage as it is. No, thank God. It looked bad for a while, but I stayed in the back, right at the street entrance."

"The children were afraid for you," she revealed. "Their friends told them that the newspapers were screaming about a potential riot. They worry. More than you think."

"You believe I'm more unaware than I actually am, Hannah. I have a job. And orders. I have to do what I am told or I will lose it. There are hundreds of men waiting to take my place. Do you want me to go back to being a laborer? Well, I'm too old, and the pay is shit."

"You don't need ever be a laborer again, Jim. After all you've done for your brother? He owes it to you to find you a place, a safe place, with good pay. A position that is secure. And honorable. He can do that. Don't ask him to... tell him. He owes you that much."

The day after the elections the newspapers celebrated voters' unanimous rejection the Sheehan Machine, whose demented agenda was defeated everywhere except the First Ward. The dailies screamed about voting abuses, especially those in the First; the thugs, the assaults, the complicit police. They called for indictments and arrests and long prison sentences. But as the dust settled, the pattern was repeated of matters such as this having their own way of just slowly evaporating away with scant attention paid.

In the end no one was punished except for the chosen sacrificial scapegoat: Captain Michael Regan. The formal charge against him had to do with dereliction of duty in passing on the 129 warrants assigned to him to patrolman O'Donnell rather than serving them personally as ordered. But it was clear that the newspapers sought retaliation for Regan's treatment of the newsmen on the scene at the First Ward's 4th district polling place. Regan was stripped of his rank and the pay that went with it. He was sent back onto the streets, walking the beat in the sleazy Canal District.

Jack White sued his opponent for stealing the election, but after months of wrangling, cousin John Sheehan ended up retaining his seat in the Common Council after all, and Jack White, the longest-serving Buffalo alderman in history, disappeared unceremoniously from the political scene. John Sheehan may have stolen his alderman seat, but the election of 1893, with it's brazen maneuverings and usurping of rights and power, marked the beginning of the end for the Sheehan brothers and their gross perversion of Democracy.

From here on, Fingy Conners would step out from the shadows into broad daylight and claim political power for himself on his own.

He no longer needed these puppets to enforce his agenda.

A number of JP's friends dragged him home at three o'clock in the morning. His face was badly smashed up, with an especially serious gash on his forehead. His Honor had been strolling down Main Street at half past twelve in the dead of night, just minding his own business, not doing much of anything while his children slept and his pregnant wife worried herself sick at home over his whereabouts.

As he passed the office of the Buffalo Morning Courier, a couple of thugs out front piled on and began beating the tar out of him.

"Jack White sends his best," they informed JP as they pummeled away with brass knuckles.

JP freed himself somehow and ran into the Courier building and down a hallway in an effort to escape and seek help. The newspaper office was wide awake and buzzing at that hour as the morning paper was rolling off the presses. The thugs pursued him into the building and jumped on him again, inflicting more damage. The Courier's night watchman went to find a policeman and another employee telephoned for a patrol wagon, but by the time help arrived the goons had accomplished their purpose and fled neatly down the street and disappeared.

Annie stood in the parlor in her robe, questioning his escorts.

"Is this retaliation for the police exam? Did the Sheehans do this? Did Fingy Conners' enemies do this? What in blazes were you doing walking down Main Street by yourself in the middle of the night, JP?!"

The men were all silent, shrugging their shoulders, patching up their charge.

"They were just some ordinary bums looking for alms, Annie, and I said no, so they got angry and pulled out brass knuckles, that's all," JP lied. "The night watchman ran and got the police. That's the truth."

"Brass knuckles? What kind of 'ordinary bums' have those?" she scorned. "And what do you mean, the night watchman ran and got the police? Isn't policing the night watchman's duty? He surely must have had at least a club with him. That's his job, for God's sake! Jesus, Mary and Joseph, JP! What is going on with you?"

"Annie I just want to go to bed."

"JP, you need to see a doctor."

"What I need is sleep. I'll see the doctor first thing tomorrow."

"You were walloped in the skull, JP! If you go to sleep now, you might never wake up!"

"I'll be all right. I need to sleep."

Annie tried to get him to tell her who did this and why. She was frightened, and rightfully so. The Alderman had been out until all hours yet again, leaving his pregnant wife and small children all alone at home to fend for themselves whilst he slithered amongst those inhabiting the city's underbelly, involving himself in God-knows-what manner of chicanery.

"You have to stop these shenanigans, JP! Right now! You have babies at home! Stop all this nonsense! Your enemies might just decide to come to the house next time around and go after your defenseless family!"

"Oh, damn it Annie, stop! Now you're being ridiculous! I'm going to bed!"

As Annie lay there unable to sleep while JP snored away, Hannah's words again came back to haunt her: "They will either end up in prison or be found floating dead in the canals! And then where will you wear your pretty dresses,

Annie? What will I and my children be left with—and you and yours—when their father is found dead? You and I will still be around long after our husbands are gone, Annie Saulter, unless they manage to kill us first! So you had better straighten out your spine and begin thinking about that—and what will become of you and your children when the inevitable catches up with the criminal shenanigans of your husband!"

The following morning Annie forced JP to go see Dr. Buswell first thing. Then she marched next door in a fury to have it out with the protective Detective.

"Jim! Who beat up my husband last night?" she demanded after stalking into his house. "What was he doing out at that time of night on Main Street, for God's sake? He's got babies at home!"

"Annie, he's a grown man. I'm not his baby sitter," replied the detective in a weary voice.

"Oh, you're not, are ye?" she shouted. "Well, you sure could have fooled me!"

Hannah smiled, impressed by Annie's new-found indignation and pluck.

The Buffalo Express reported the story with a wink and a smirk:

ALD. SULLIVAN SLUGGED
THE ANCIENT MYSTERY OF WHO STRUCK BILLY PATTERSON
NOW HAS A MODERN COUNTERPART.

They editorialized about JP's beating in their usual coy manner with a telling comment:

"Who they were no one knows, unless it is Alderman Sullivan, and he has not disclosed their identity."

Buffalo Police parade

June 1894
The Annual Police Parade

Jim Jr., Nellie and Johnny Sullivan were outfitted in their best Sunday finery for the annual Parade of Buffalo Policemen. Hannah had bought a new hat using her squirreled-away pin money. Her husband assured her that she looked lovely. She wanted to look her best, what with Jim leading his unit as Commander of the Tenth Company under Captain Ryan, and she and the children slated to be formally presented to the captains and the Chief after the event. Hannah had her reservations about commiserating with the very same scoundrels who had helped defile the previous November's elections, but was determined to be gracious for her husband's sake.

At nine years of age Jim Jr. was old enough to have exciting memories of three or four previous police parades, but seven year old brother Johnny had been sick for last year's spectacle and couldn't attend. The year before that he was only five and had little memory of it. So this year he was gripped with an excitement that could not be quelled anticipating his dad leading his unit.

Jim had been preparing his dress uniform for a week, brushing the wool fabric and polishing the buttons meticulously. Hannah took care of a dropped seam and a few loose threads. Ever since his promotion to detective he wasn't required to wear the uniform much anymore. Most days he worked undercover in his street clothes as a fly cop.

Jim Jr. and Johnny had taken to practicing drill in the kitchen under their father's careful direction every morning after breakfast. He was nearly the highest ranking copper among all their friends whose fathers were coppers, and there were dozens those in the immediate neighborhood.

Johnny was the youngest of his father's children. For this he carried a heavy sadness in his heart, knowing by all rights this was never meant to be the case.

His baby sister Hannah Jr.'s death when he was four years old was a terrible loss for him. She was his principal playmate, friend, and student. Hannah Jr. latched onto her older bother, literally, before she was able to toddle. They had been inseparable. Johnny could not understand back then where she went so suddenly and why everything changed that day. He was too young to comprehend exactly what died meant. All he knew was what he'd been told — that she was gone and he would never again hold her hand, not as they both rejoiced in her new freedom at learning to walk, not as they played together in the yard, not as they watched the world go by while sitting out front on the stoop with the rest of the family on warm summer evenings.

His mother was so tortured and grieved at the loss of her baby daughter that for a while she wasn't cognizant of how the baby's death had affected all the other children. When she finally came out of her black fog and recognized this fact, she was ashamed. She quickly went about trying to set things right.

Her grieving eyes were opened widest to her middle son. Johnny didn't laugh anymore, as much a loss for mother as it was for child. Nellie and Jim Jr. were tippy-toeing around the house as if in church. Hannah was determined that Johnny would laugh again and the older kids would be freed from the shackles of her personal loss.

She bought tickets for all of them on the excursion steamer Gazelle at the booth at the foot of Main Street. She had gathered her three oldest, swaddled two-month-old Danny against the sun and the lake breezes, grabbed Annie and her kids and the servant girl, and they all steamed off to Crystal Beach to ride the rides and swim in Lake Erie. They ate hot dogs, gobbled fish and chips from greasy newspaper cones, and licked peanut suckers purchased from stores and vendors all of whom, the children pointed out, exhibited a large framed visage of a scowling Queen Victoria. Hannah made sure they all could feel like children again. On the return she danced with each of her children one by one to the ship's little orchestra.

Hannah had disregarded her living children while lost in her all-consuming bereavement for her dead daughter. Her husband too had escaped in his own way by throwing himself into his work and volunteering for extra shifts and extended hours in an attempt to blunt his tribulations. He took on the job of directing the rebuilding of the burned Mutual Rowing Club boathouse, thus leaving his wife and children to grope their way through their own desolation and find their way through that terrible time without the benefit of his guidance.

A photograph of baby Hannah occupied a silver frame on the chiffonier, and Johnny would spend many long minutes in front of it, staring, trying to remember her. Baby Hannah was disappearing from his memory. No matter how hard he tried he couldn't get the awareness of her back. He knew her face, he remembered her clumsy, animated toddle. But the remembrance of her essence and being, of who she was as a person, was fading away, and this terrified him. Because if she who were so loved could disappear, and be forgotten, what about him?

With the arrival of baby Daniel, Johnny turned all his attentions to him. Johnny recalled being ecstatic when his mother announced to all the children that she was going to soon have another baby. When the baby was just a few days old his mother sat with him on the sofa and allowed him to hold Daniel in his little arms He felt so grown up, proud that she trusted him enough to cradle this fragile little life. Johnny couldn't wait until Daniel was old enough to walk. He would be Danny's protector and personal tour guide through life.

As the days lengthened and warmed the family would go out after supper and sit on the little porch. They'd watch for the arrival of the Hamburgh St. streetcar to see who got off. It was like a parade — workers arriving for their shift across the street at the Buffalo Furnace Co., neighbor ladies coming back from shopping down on Elk Street, working men returning home from their jobs after a very long day.

Less than a hundred yards away as the little audience oohed and ahhed, the giant grain ships laden with the bounty of America's heartland labored to negotiate the severe bend in the river. Thundering horn blasts and acrid coal smoke blasted from the struggling tugs nudging the behemoths along. The fireboats stationed nearby exploded water through every nozzle of every water cannon each evening in an exciting play-out anticipated by every child. Neighbors hurried past, to and fro. Drunks stumbled out of saloons. The round-the-clock clanging and whooshing sounds from the furnace complex never ceased. There was much to see and hear and smell. When Hannah and Jim gathered the whole brood together on the stoop and a big pitcher of lemonade was at the ready, summer evenings could be no better.

Johnny sat on the bottom step where he would steady Danny while Nellie tried to teach him how to play jacks or pick-up-sticks rather than try and eat them.

Jim Jr. looked on, distant and removed, having dealt in his own lonely way with the death of his baby sister, not quite trusting himself to get too attached to the newcomer.

Then, unfathomably, at the same age baby Hannah was when she died, Danny died too. The baby who Johnny was coming to know, whose hand Johnny tightly held as he toddled and teetered in his attempt to navigate his little world, was gone as well, decimated by necrotizing enterocolitis. How could this be? What did this mean? Was it his fault? At night in his trundle Johnny felt his bed spinning as if tumbling uncontrollably through space. He held on tight to the mattress edges and prayed for it to stop.

Jim and Hannah reeled from the blow. Their two youngest children had now perished just when they'd gotten to really know them. Just when they had experienced the joy of hearing their first Mama and Papa uttered. Just when the babies had grown into the names they had been given and started to become true persons.

Hannah went to church. Jim went to Dalton's Saloon or retreated in the night to the darkened environs of the boathouse. Johnny couldn't sleep, but when he did manage to drift off he soon startled awake weeping and trembling. He was just a little boy. He didn't understand, nor could he.

The two youngest had died. He was now the youngest. Did being the youngest in this family mean that he might have to die now, too?

Seven year old Nellie, who had always been the carefree, alive, witty child, drew inward. Always good at school, she went from a B student to an A+ student, spending most of her evenings doing her homework meticulously, then burying her face in novels in an attempt to escape someplace else other then where she was. She didn't always understand her inherited volume of Innocents Abroad, but she liked it. It took her to Palestine and Syria. She walked in Christ's footsteps. And it made her laugh, a little.

Jim Jr. was eight. The eldest son was stoic and straight of spine, a replica of his father. He kept personal things in. He liked telling stories at the dinner table. The frequency of these tales diminished for a couple of weeks after they buried Danny, but soon, Jim Jr., having decided the family had gotten too quiet, took it upon himself to begin moving them forward, not always with their full cooperation. He kept at it regardless. They all must get on with their lives, he believed.

As the detective donned his uniform for the parade he thought back to the day not quite a year before when Danny had been laid to rest at Holy Cross Cemetery. He glanced out the window to see his four year old nephew Daniel next door, sitting on the Alderman's stoop with his brother Thomas, waiting to go to the parade.

Both of the Sullivans had named their sons after Daniel Halloran, their much-loved brother who himself had died far too young. Now, Jim's own son Daniel had died exceedingly young as well. Jim didn't believe in fate, nor was he superstitious, but he couldn't help but now be fearful a little bit for his nephew Daniel's fate.

The police parade would be the first big family celebration since Danny's funeral. Four hundred dandy coppers marched the city streets to be admired by the populace. Police Superintendent Bull, an ex-soldier, was seated upon a fine-looking stallion at the head of the column, appearing to be as proud as when he was commanding his military body. The annual procession was eagerly anticipated by thousands of enthusiastic citizens, and the fine appearance of the department drew praise from all sides.

A big crowd had gathered at the starting point and at two-thirty the big Arsenal doors swung open. The audience took a good long look. As the coppers poured forth, they looked as solemn as the event demanded, not daring to smile, not even at the pretty girls. Superintendent Bull was the cynosure of all eyes. He looked every inch the soldier in his splendid regalia.

The mounted platoon led by Capt. George Cable had the right of line and was easily the most popular feature of the parade, the men sitting bolt upright, high and proud on their spirited handsome steeds.

Powell's 65th Regiment Band followed, accompanying the coppers' march with popular airs of the day including Funiculi Funicula and Love's Old Sweet Song.

The parade moved up Broadway to Ellicott Street to Mohawk to Genesee to Delaware, to where Hannah and the kids waited proudly. They fidgeted, counting units until Company Ten came into view, and then they cheered their father. By this time in the parade the poker-faces had softened and the cheers and admiring comments of the parade-goers along the route of march were so enthusiastic and welcoming that the cops took to smiling and acknowledging those in the crowd.

Jim spotted his wife and children standing exactly where he'd asked them to, directly across from the former home of President Millard Fillmore, at Niagara Square. Hannah's new hat with purple orchids in the hatband was a beacon, and he caught sight of it from quite a ways off.

Johnny began jumping up and down with excitement and Hannah craned her neck to spot her husband. Nellie had recently begun to notice boys, and one in particular in the crowd became a rival for her interest in her father. Before Jim came into unobstructed view, first came the Band and their elegant uniforms with gold braid laid across their chests, fringed epaulets bouncing on their shoulders, and their spiked helmets with gold ponytails on top mirroring the movement of those on the steeds that were to follow.

Their wide white belts cinched the coats of their uniforms snugly at the waist, revealing not a single beer belly in the entire troupe. Saxophones, horns, cymbals, flutes, then drummers brought up the rear, splendid in their appearance and accomplished in their musical abilities. The parade viewers bounced and clapped to the oft-repeated popular and lively Funiculi Funicula.

Following the band came all the Companies in numerical order, the rank and file flanked at the outside of their line by their sergeants, each company marching with near-military precision. Some of the Companies marched with arms swinging in unison, others with arms stiff at their sides.

As Company Ten marched down Delaware Avenue, Johnny broke from his mother and ran to his father, who himself broke rank to hoist his son in his arms, planting a big kiss on his cheek, then scooted the boy back over to where Hannah, Jim Jr. and Nellie stood proudly at the curb. He placed him gently down in his original spot, kissed his wife as Jim and Nellie gave him a quick hug, and speedily resumed position to finish his march.

Johnny's eyes worshipfully followed his father until he was out of sight. He was brimming with pride, and rubbed his face where his father's heavy whiskers had brushed roughly against his cheek. Following the twelfth and last Company came the mounted officers riding their beautiful equines in lines that mirrored that of the men on foot, their configuration stretching the full width of the street in a double row.

Finally, the five patrol wagons of the department, each drawn up by a team of horses, came up the rear behind the mounted police. The wagons were shined to such a reflective brilliance that it caused onlookers to shade their eyes from the glare. Even the horses' reins had been buffed to a remarkable sheen.

At the rear of the City Hall the force halted. Mayor Bishop, Commissioners Jewett and Rapp and several of the aldermen, including John P. Sullivan, were standing on the curbing as the columns halted and faced about. Patrolmen Barrett and O'Connor were called out and happy to receive badges of meritorious conduct. The presentations were made by the mayor. Then he and Superintendent Bull, followed by the Commissioners and members of the Common Council in pairs, marched around and inspected the column while the band played.

After everybody had expressed being highly pleased by the showing, the parade wheeled around on Delaware Avenue and marched around to the front of the City Hall where it was publicly reviewed and praised by the Mayor and the different officials to the appreciation and cheers of the gathered multitudes. The parade then continued on its way with the crowd tagging along after; Franklin Street to The Terrace to Main to Chippewa to Delaware Avenue and again to Niagara Square to where the family waited. There it disbanded.

Jim ran to grab Hannah and his kids, then brought them over to introduce them to Captain Ryan. As Hannah smiled her sweetest smile and graciously shook his hand, she recited in her mind, "You dirty scum." Then the family was joined by Jim's partner, John Geary, and the recently-demoted and publicly shamed former Captain Michael Regan and his family, Hannah happy to have a kindred spirit in Ellen Regan with whom she could trade eye-rolls over the hypocrisy of it all. She and Ellen had gone through school together, united in their cynicism.

The families were then introduced to the exuberant Superintendent Bull, who was on top of the world with the great success he had just engineered. Finally then, JP showed up with Annie and the children. The Alderman's family had occupied places of honor on the steps of the City Hall.

Hannah had to admit it. Aside from the behind-the-scenes cunning and betrayal of it all, it sure had been a lot of fun. She was glad to be out and about again enjoying herself with her family. It was time to emerge as best she could from her mourning and move forward.

1894
Recalling Tom Sawyer

A few days after the Police Parade, Hannah was hard at work in her kitchen with her can of stove polish, perspiring from her obsession to keep the appliance gleaming. The window screens had all been in place on the open upper story casements since the end of May to keep the mosquitos and flies out. If only such a barrier was available to halt the soot and the industrial stink. It had been a hot couple of days and adding to the heaviness and the heat were the giant menacing black horse flies that buzzed loudly and frightened Hannah no end. They crashed into the window screens with a loud thump, causing her to cringe with each attempt at forced entry. If they landed on skin, they'd inflict a painful bite. She had always netted her babies whenever taking them outdoors for fear of their being attacked.

Coal smoke from screaming tugboats and laboring steamships mixed with the heavy sulphur stench from the Buffalo Furnace Co. across the way and the heavenly smell of roasting grain from the H-O Oats facility. Buffalo was the grain milling capitol of the world. While Manhattan may have had its forest of skyscrapers as its symbol, the Queen City had her towering grain elevators standing tooth and jowl, fencing off the waterfront's houses from both the lake view and its cooling breezes. Even when grain wasn't being roasted, its scent was always in the air.

The sun didn't set this time of year until almost nine o'clock. Consequently after supper the neighborhood was alive and humming with the resounding screams and laughter of children making the most of their extra hours of daylight. Six months from now it would be dark by 4:30 in the afternoon, so everyone took best advantage of the long warm days. Buffalo was a gray, wet, cold city that lay in wait all year long for its three brief months of warmth and light.

Nine year old Jim Jr. was a few blocks away on Katherine Street playing baseball at Travelers' Field. He enjoyed the camaraderie more than the actual game itself. His team mates could encyclopedically spout names and statistics of their favorite teams and players, which fascinated Junior, because the same lads couldn't apply a similar ability toward their schoolwork. He played the game, enjoyed his friends, and forgot all about it until the next game was organized. He gave away the sporting cards that neighbors saved for him, the ones that came with their tobacco. The neighbors believed he would cherish them, but the only ones he kept were those depicting cousin John L. Sullivan, world-champion bare-knuckle boxer. When John L. was in town, appearing in a vaudeville show at Shea's or some arranged exhibition, he was usually a guest of his father and uncle at an M.R.C. function arranged in his honor. It wasn't just the boys who worshipped John L. The girls too twittered and danced around him in coquettish fashion, vying for his attentions, which he happily showered upon them.

Eight year old Nellie had newly taken to asking her friends to call her Mary Ellen, her baptismal name. She thought it sounded a lot more grown up, but her friends wouldn't oblige. Clara Merrick, who spoke beautiful French because her father had emigrated from France, lived two doors down, and was her favorite friend. They and two other girls sat out on the front stoop. They played jacks as a clever diversion to cover their clandestine coaching by Clara in the art of French profanity.

Johnny busied himself directly across South street on the little pier with the neighborhood boys. Influenced by his father's bedtime readings of Tom Sawyer, they had inherited a raft that older boys had grown tired of, and with much less boat traffic on the still river after six o'clock, they could better imagine it to be the Mississippi. Johnny told his friends he'd be back in a few minutes. There was something he needed to see first. He ran into the house and sneaked up the stairs.

Jim was taking a intimate supper with Hannah in the kitchen before going back to work. The children knew that this was their parents' private time and were expected to keep away. They were instructed not to enter when the swinging door between the kitchen and the dining room was closed. "No" was all the encouragement that Johnny needed. He slowly crept up the stairs and stood silently behind the door. He pushed it slowly, slightly open, just a crack, so that he could see. His parents sat at the table, eating, leaning toward each other, speaking softly, smiling.

They ate braised beef and new potatoes; there were scarlet runner beans too, lightly boiled so that they still had some bite, with butter. The beans climbed along strings out back of the house in the garden and were so named because of the bright and beautiful red flowers that preceded the formation of each pod. Delicious green beans and beautiful flowers on the same plant for six weeks or longer. What could be better for those who loved to garden, like his mother?

After they finished eating, and the clock read close to departing time, they rose from the table. Johnny held his breath, because he knew what was coming. He had seen it before, and waited for his chance to see it again.

His parents stood pressed against each other tightly as his father held his mother securely in his embrace. His father's back was to him, and after a long, meaningful kiss, Hannah placed her head against her husband's, seeming to Johnny as if she were in some kind of trance. She moaned. He loved seeing them like this, because they never acted quite this way in front of the children. As he stared at his mother through the gap, the door creaked a tiny bit. She opened her eyes while still embraced and saw the sparkle of a little blue eye glisten in the shadow of the barely-cracked door.

She knew it must be Johnny.

After their eyes met, Hannah simply closed hers again, burying her face in her husband's neck, and stood with him motionless, savoring their intimacy. This scenario, which Johnny had viewed in secret before, deeply impressed him. He didn't know at his age exactly what to make of it, but he knew it was good. Very good. In a neighborhood where the mothers and fathers of his schoolmates were often at each other's throats, his own mother and father were still in love.

Johnny quietly, carefully let the door close fully and silently descended the stairs to the parlor, then went out the front door onto Hamburgh Street where he saw his friends on the dock already fighting over who would get to captain the raft.

Jim Sullivan hadn't even reached the station house when he had to turn right around and head back toward the Ohio Basin, which was six blocks from his house. He was responding to a report of a man's body in the Ohio Basin slip, the short canal that connected the Basin to the Buffalo River. John Spriggle from Mackinaw Street, who he knew from church, the father of five children, lay lifeless just under the surface when he arrived. Lieutenant Donovan was already there, assessing the situation, and rather than wait, Jim stripped off his clothes and waded into the water, then swam to Mr. Spriggle. He latched onto his belt and made his way the ten feet to shore where Donovan and a couple of passers-by helped pull both men from the water. Jim thought about Wilhemina Rapp's miraculous resuscitation of little Henry Zeller at the foot of Hamburgh Street when he was a young man, and considered for a second attempting that on John Spriggle, but it was obvious the man had been dead for at least an hour. He was a purplish grey color, and looked ghastly. Wilhemina told the crowd that day that after five minutes underwater, the procedure probably wouldn't work.

Jim and Lt. Donovan were assigned the regretful task of delivering the body home. Jim's heart pounded in his throat as the horses mournfully pulled the heavy dray up Louisiana Street to Mackinaw. Donovan turned the horses left, crossing the Mackinaw Street bridge that spanned the Ohio slip at the Basin's northeast end. They both dreaded what was coming. It occurred to him, that as horrific as it was for him to lose his children, how much more fearful it was for little children to lose the father who supported and protected them. Having had first hand experience with both scenarios, he felt he was qualified to conclude this.

The dray pulled up to the little cottage on the corner of Mackinaw and Chicago, where twenty children were playing in the street. They all froze in place. A police dray slowly pulling up to someone's house could mean only one thing.

Jim waited on the wagon as Donovan approached the front door. Before knocking, Donovan looked back at Jim for reassurance, then rattled the door. Jim watched solemnly as the lady who came to the doorway dropped the dish she was drying with her apron and screamed. Her children came running, and seeing their mother in such a state, began bawling and trembling, not knowing the reason why, but knowing something truly terrible was afoot.

The neighbors came racing out of their homes. The women ran to Mrs. Spriggle who was now crumpled in a heaving heap on the front porch. The men banded together and brought Mr. Spriggle's body inside to his family.

Back at the station, Jim was having the telegraph master notify the coroner, although a visit from him would not be required, as Jim and Donovan had determined that Mr. Spriggle had fallen in. Or maybe, weary of life, had jumped intentionally. Detective Geary exploded through the door and said, "Jim, something's happened at home. Hurry! Come with me!"

The boys drew straws to see who got to pilot the raft. Johnny lost, but that was okay. He was happy just to have a place on it. His friend Eugene Blair from right around the corner won the honor. They were the same age. Johnny's cousin Thomas Sullivan, the Alderman's oldest, was only six, and wasn't allowed anywhere near the dock. His father had whipped him good a few weeks previous for just sitting on the edge, watching river traffic with his friends. The

Alderman had been present long ago when they dragged little Henry Zeller out of the drink, and witnessed the miracle performed by Mrs. Rapp. A picture like that stays with a person. Forever.

Living right next to the river it was a challenge and a battle to keep one's children away from it. Many parents didn't even try, which disgusted the Alderman. He personally knew of parents who did not care to be parents anymore. Father O'Connor had confided in him in a moment of weakness that he had heard the confessions of mothers and fathers who wanted absolution from the sin of wishing their children dead, so that they could be free of the heavy responsibilities they endured.

Annie was eight months pregnant. She and JP had had already lost one baby to stillbirth, and the pain from that loss was so harrowing that he could not imagine what kind of parent would secretly hope for such a calamity.

So, their little Thomas, with rear end still pink and smarting, stood on the newly laid cement sidewalk in front of the corner saloon at Hamburgh and South. He wasn't allowed to step foot into the street. So he dawdled and watched with envy, hanging on to the South St.-Hamburgh St. corner sign post as the Toms and Hucks of the neighborhood squabbled and prepared to cast off from the dock.

The sun was low in the sky. It was around seven o'clock. Little Thomas had to shade his eyes to see his cousin and the other boys.

Hannah was at the kitchen sink, washing dinner dishes. She had sat with her brood before she and Jim enjoyed their private supper mediating their tiffs as they ate, then sent them out to play. She was thinking of that kiss, of the wonderful closeness of that embrace, body pressed to body. She looked down and saw the children playing. Nellie and her playmates had drawn a large hopscotch pattern on the asphalt of South Street and were busy completing their turns. The boys were on the raft and Eugene Blair was pushing off with a pole. And for no reason she could discern, one of the boys toppled into the water. She froze. The sun was in her eyes, and she couldn't see clearly. A woman screamed below, people started running toward the dock, and the boys on the raft shouted, "Johnny! Johnny!"

The intersection of Hamburgh Street and South Street forms an L. Hamburgh Street runs perpendicular to the river, straight to its edge. South Street runs parallel to the river, and ends at its intersection with Hamburgh Street. At the angle where the two meet is where the pier was built. Across from the houses on Hamburgh looms the Buffalo Furnace Co, where iron is made, and located between the Furnace property and the end of Hamburgh Street, is a slip that allows water craft to pull directly into the Furnace property from the river.

Furnace workers were standing on the edge of the slip and they saw Johnny fall in the water.

Immediately, two of the workers kicked their shoes off and dove in. They had to swim a hundred yards or so to reach the place where the raft was when the boy toppled. Their soaked shirts and canvas work pants slowed them down. The sun was blinding.

Hannah dropped her dish and ran headlong down the stairs toward the parlor, tripping and falling, and badly skinning her shin. She was oblivious, having but one thought in her head: No, no, no, no NO!!

She ran out the front door and down the few porch steps and toward the dock. The kids on the raft were screaming and pointing to the spot where they thought Johnny was. The water was black and murky with an oily sheen atop and the brilliant rays of the lowering sun in the evening western sky reflecting off the opaque water and the rainbow sheen of the oil made it impossible to see anything below the surface. It was seven o'clock. The workmen in the water were shouting, diving, gasping.

"Where is he? Where is he?" they kept screaming at the raft mates, who were all pointing in different directions. After falling in Johnny had surfaced briefly just once, then disappeared.

Johnny's sister Nellie stood paralyzed, enfolded in the protective arms of a neighbor who sought to prevent her from getting too close to the river's edge. Johnny's cousin Thomas stood terrified on the corner, glued to the sign post, not daring nor even wanting to cross the street to see what was happening. His mother Annie's worst fear had come true: his cousin had fallen in the river and now they couldn't find him. Annie had seen Hannah fly out of the house and had the presence of mind to grab the telephone. "Police Precinct Seven! Hurry, it's an emergency!" She screamed her terror into the mouthpiece as she saw Hannah teetering on the edge of the pier. She threw the phone down and ran. Annie shot from her house, holding her belly to keep her unborn child from being jarred as she bolted toward the river, and screamed at Thomas "You stay put!" as she passed him. She hurled her ungainly form toward Hannah, who was preparing to jump in. "You can't swim, Hannah!" Annie screamed. "You'll drown! Think of your children!" Annie grabbed Hannah around the waist to restrain her, but it took all her might, so overwhelmed was Hannah by the adrenalin coursing through her body.

"My baby needs me! Where is he? Why can't they find him?! Johnny! Johnny!" she shrieked, her unearthly wailing breaking and cracking as terror choked her voice with dread and helplessness. Annie shouted to their neighbor Jim Short to help her restrain Hannah, who was by this time entirely possessed with the compulsion to dive into the river to save her boy.

Other neighbors had heard the ruckus and ran from their homes along Hamburgh and South streets. One neighbor came running with a long ladder grabbed from the side of his house. Members of the Mutuals flew out from the boathouse with sculls in their hands and threw them into the river, nearly capsizing in their panic to get into them. Ed Stanton was one of these, and he cursed himself for having drunk too much beer. Hannah stood on the dock, rabid and raging. She had already lost two babies in less than three years.

This could not possibly be happening.

The fireboat William S. Grattan was on patrol a few hundred yards upstream, and at first hearing the commotion, turned and raced toward the scene. The workmen in the water were joined by a third man, then a fourth, and together they dove repeatedly, until one emerged, choking, "I got 'im!"

The others swam to him and together, exhausted, the team pulled toward the dock. A cluster of neighbors' hands reached down and grabbed the lifeless boy, while others pulled the heroic men from the river. The fireboat arrived and two firemen leaped onto the dock. Hannah snatched her son from his rescuers as they laid him on the boards. One of the firemen snatched him back from his mother and rolled the boy over onto his stomach and kneaded Johnny's back, forcefully pressing his full weight against it with the heels of his hands, trying to force water out of the boy's lungs. A bit did emerge, but Johnny had been under too long, and no one present thought about the obscure technique of blowing their own breath into his lungs. Johnny was unresponsive. Hannah, on her bloody knees, picked him up and shook him, screaming toward the sky, "Help him! Help my boy! Don't you dare take him from me! You can't have him!"

As soon as Jim Sullivan ran out of the precinct house, the desk sergeant placed an urgent call to the City Hall. The Alderman's secretary picked up the telephone.

"Is Alderman Sullivan there? This is Sergeant Meara at the Seventh Precinct! It's an emergency!"

"Yes," said the alarmed Emma Honan, "I'll put you right through, Sergeant."

Despite the late hour, the Alderman was still in a meeting in his office behind closed doors. He was discussing strategy with Fingy Conners and Alderman John Sheehan, the kind of scheming best scheduled for a time after most everyone else had gone home. The Alderman thought it best that few people as possible see Fingy Conners enter his office. Emma knocked on his door. He resented the intrusion.

"Yes!" he answered, irritated.

"Alderman Sullivan, you have a very urgent call from the police!"

JP picked up the phone.

"Yes, Alderman Sullivan speaking."

"This is Sergeant Meara down at the 7th, Alderman. Your brother's son has fallen into the river and may have drowned. Detective Sullivan just ran out of here to race home. I wanted to let you know."

The Alderman calmly said, "Yes. Thank you for calling."

He returned to his seat and picked up the conversation where he had left off. As usual, Fingy was incensed about the latest upset in his plans to rule the world. JP attempted to placate him and defuse the situation.

Emma had listened in on the call and was shocked and horrified to learn that the Alderman's nephew may have drowned. She stood outside the Alderman's door with his hat and cane at the ready for when he came racing out. She waited five minutes. Then ten. Then fifteen.

It would be a half hour before Alderman Sullivan ended the meeting. When he did finally emerge, Emma Honan was not able to look him in the eye.

The speeding dray driven by Detective Geary careened dangerously down South Street toward Hamburgh, barely missing crushing people in its path. Geary screamed at surprised onlookers, "Get the hell out of the way!" Hooves galloped furiously against the pavement as Jim stood upright in the careening wagon, almost falling out, trying to see, shouting with his voice breaking, "Hurry, Geary, hurry!"

Jim saw the crowd ahead assembled at the foot of the street, by the river's edge. They were gathered in a circle, nearly a hundred of them. The horses' reins were pulled up tight and Jim shot from the wagon before it could stop and barreled into the crowd, knocking people over. There he saw his wife, wailing over the lifeless body of their son. The eyes of the crowd were on Jim, crazed and horrified. Jim ripped Johnny from Hannah's arms, threw him on his back and opened his mouth. He sealed his own mouth tightly around his son's and blew, and blew again. A gush of fouled water shot out, covering his father's frantic face. Jim shook his son, then blew again. More water. Again, more water, but less this time. He kept blowing his life's breath into Johnny until no more water came out and his small chest rose as it filled with his father's oxygen, but still his son did not stir. Johnny's eyes were half open and a look of terror was frozen on his bluish face. For ten minutes Jim applied the breath of life to his son. Hannah grew silent, as did the rest of the crowd, as they viewed with awe and despondency a loving father's unstoppable desperation. Few had ever heard of this technique, and to some the act appeared to be incognizable; a drastic, futile, hopeless exercise on the part of a father who was not able to accept his child's fate.

Finally, dizzy and nauseated, gasping for air himself and feeling as if he would soon pass out, Hannah crying and wailing again upon accepting that the breath technique was not reviving her youngest child, Jim stopped. He buried his head in his boy's chest and sobbed, and with this act of surrender, Hannah lost the final shred of hope she had clung to, and screamed, cursing God. "You've taken three of my babies!" she wailed. "How could you do this to me again, you goddamned bastard?!"

Although all Catholics, nobody present seemed to be troubled by her ranting blasphemy, for at that moment they all wondered exactly the same thing. Indeed, what the hell was that bastard doing to this poor family?

Jim scooped his youngest into his arms and then stood, breathing heavily, trying not to pass out. Hannah held Johnny's blue face and stroked his wet hair still longing for any sign of life as the family walked the hundred paces back to the house. Geary supported Jim, his arm wrapped round his partner's waist. Annie supported Hannah for fear she might collapse. Annie's baby kicked again and again and she feared she might have injured it. "Thomas, go into the house!" Annie sternly ordered her son as the crowd passed him, he still remaining dutifully glued to the post supporting the street sign. Thomas ran home. The neighbors halted at the front gate and watched while Jim and Hannah carried Johnny inside, followed by Annie and Geary.

The crowd was not passive. As if one, every man, woman and child bawled and sobbed from their witnessing this catastrophe which had torn from their breasts their hearts still beating. They wailed together as family, all so much now the poorer, all having suffered their own personal calamities. This abomination they had together beheld proved only to further deplete their starved souls and vanquish their scant hopes.

The Alderman had informed Annie that morning that he needed to stay late for yet another political meeting. Annie, close to giving birth, told him that she had every right to expect more from him now, both as a husband and a father. He demurred, infuriating her with his indifference.

As she helped Hannah and Jim take Johnny into the house, Annie cursed JP for adding to the catastrophe by his not being home for the hundredth time when his family needed him most. She was sick and tired of his wrangling, fed up with the causes and concerns that had nothing to do at all with the family, yet consumed all their lives nonetheless. At that moment, again isolated and alone with the horror of this most recent tragedy, solely responsible for holding her family together in the Alderman's absence, Annie vowed, no more. The time had come. The Alderman would now receive his due.

Jim Jr. came racing down the street from his ball game, the news having reached him. Nellie stood forgotten on the edge of the gathering of neighbors, no one noticing her or offering comfort. She was sobbing with all the rest, lost, not knowing what to do, afraid to go inside.

Jim Jr. ran to her. "What happened, Nellie?" he cried to his sister.

"Johnny drowned in the river!" Nellie howled, and grappled her older brother for dear life. Jim Jr. struggled to free himself from her stranglehold, seized her hand, and dragged her through the parting crowd into the house.

Their father had lain Johnny on the sofa in the parlor, the same parlor where baby Hannah and baby Daniel had been laid out in their little caskets. Johnny's mother was kneeling on the floor, arms enfolding her dead son, sobbing uncontrollably into his chest. Annie was beside herself, helpless, useless, unbelieving, alone, imagining herself in Hannah's place. Annie felt her baby kick, its dreamy suspension jolted by the extraordinary circumstance and the stresses his mother was suffering.

Detective Sergeant Jim Sullivan, so composed when handling other people's tragedies, collapsed, sobbing convulsively, so defeated was he by this latest tragedy. At this moment he hated a God he had never believed in in the first place with a hostility and rancor he'd never before felt. There was no one else to blame, so for the time being Jim would allow this nonexistent bastard God to exist.

His entire life had been defined by loss. The people he loved most were continually being taken from him. Junior and Nellie were transfixed at first. They had never seen their father cry, let alone bawl uncontrollably. So frightened were they by this inconceivable event, they began to wail and bawl too, not just for Johnny, but for the emotional breakdown of their resolute parents. Their world was shattered.

Jim didn't see Junior and Nellie standing there at first, but when he did, he motioned them over. Nellie was terrified and didn't want to come any closer to her dead brother. She refused her father. There had once been five of them, and now there were just two, and she was now the youngest. Junior and Nellie each had the exact same terrifying thought at the exact same moment. Each wondered if they were destined to die next.

Jim Jr. would very quickly have a taste.

The next morning, in the Buffalo Express, right at the top of the page, centered, was the disturbing headline made all the worse by an unfathomable mistake.

DROWNED IN THE RIVER, it screamed.

Below the headline was a terrible blunder that rattled the family, none more so than Jim Jr. The Express' account of the tragedy claimed it was Jim Jr. who had drowned rather than Johnny.

LITTLE JAMES SULLIVAN, PLAYING ON A RAFT
AT HAMBURGH STREET, FELL OVERBOARD.

About 7 o'clock last night James Sullivan, the 7-year-old son of Detective J. Sullivan of the Headquarters staff fell into the Buffalo

River from a raft on which he was playing at the foot of Hamburgh Street.

Before he could be rescued he was drowned. He had been playing upon the raft with a number of other boys and accidentally fell into the river.

The body was recovered a short time later by some workmen employed in the vicinity. It was removed to the boy's house and Coroner Hanson was notified. The family live at No. 16 Hamburgh Street.

Jim Jr.'s friends, teachers and neighbors were all shocked by the report of his death, not realizing the newspaper had broadcast a cruel error. The misidentification compounded the grief and sorrow already devastating the family. Their dead Johnny was not properly acknowledged. Instead, grievous reports of his brother Jim Jr.'s death were reported city wide. All were saddened and confused, further challenged and heartbroken by having to continually correct the misinformation.

The irony and the eerie parallel could not be ignored.

As Jim Jr.'s father read the awful mistake in the Express, he couldn't help but recall his friend Mark Twain's story of Tom Sawyer, mistakenly believed by the townsfolk to have drowned in the river after falling from a raft.

Detective John Geary

The Eldest Child

Annie had been up all night long, keeping Hannah company until she was able to fall asleep. Then she quietly woke her children Thomas, Daniel, and Mazie, who were asleep on the sofa. She brought them home and tucked them into bed, then collapsed onto her mattress exhausted.

But she couldn't sleep.

JP had finally arrived home an hour and a half after they carried Johnny's body into the house. He spent the night there, with his brother, trying to console him. Annie needed him too, as did his own frightened and confused children. But on this particular night, Annie accepted that his brother needed him more.

Annie was determined that her two oldest go to school as usual the following day. They wanted to remain at home, but she knew they would just mope, or act rowdy and get on her nerves, so selfishly she put herself first. They'd all be better off with the children in school. The baby kicked inside her, still distressed.

She tried to keep herself calm. She felt like a fly some evil spider had wrapped in its silk tight as a mummy and left paralyzed and dangling at the end of twig by a single silken tendril, spinning, spinning dizzily in the breeze waiting to be consumed.

Instead of life becoming more homogenous and cohesive as the family grew and JP's business and political careers flourished, the opposite was true. His absence at the time of Johnny's death was the final indignity. He should have been home with his wife and family. Life was out of control. The last few years had produced one awful and frightening upset after another. Annie was over and done with shouldering all the responsibility.

The Alderman had proven exceptionally adept at exploiting the duties and distractions of his political ambitions as a way to justify the vacuum he'd left in the family, to block out what the rest of them were forced to confront head on out of sheer necessity by this absence.

He's not a husband, nor is he a parent, she concluded after much soul searching.

He's the eldest child.

The events of the previous four years had exacted a terrible toll on both Sullivan wives. The women had no such outlets as did the men; no convenient all-consuming self-important diversions, career, or social club or athletic contests to occupy them and redirect their pent-up energies. Hannah had no opportune surly criminal she could punch in the face as a release for her bottled up hurt and anger. The women had to just deal with it. The women were the only full-time parent. They were the ones left alone at home resolving problems both big and small while the fathers enjoyed the handy exit provided by their anointed station in society whenever things got too uncomfortable. At the same time they were provided a soap box from which to whine that they were the suffering ones, having to go out and support a family all by themselves and all.

It was the women who grew sick and exhausted from carrying developing human beings inside their wombs for nine months at a stretch, and then a few months later, repeating the ordeal all over again. It was they who actually raised the children, suffered the worst pain and loss, felt the deepest grief and bereavement, tossed and turned in the night, stayed up until dawn with their sick ones, suffered fear and embarrassment from what most recent foolishness their husbands might be up to.

JP walked into the house from his brother's. He announced the children were all still over there with their cousins and behaving themselves for now, but Annie had better go fetch them just the same. He said he was leaving immediately to go down to the ice house without so much as looking at her. He removed his shoes to change into his canvas Levis. As the result of his accident on the docks in his youth, one of his legs was inches shorter than the other. With his orthopedic shoe removed, and him trying to balance himself to change his pants, Annie took her advantage. She grabbed his arm with one hand while cradling the weight of her kicking baby inside her with the other.

"You sit down, you!"

She'd half-spun him around and pushed him down into the chair.

Thrown off balance, he sat involuntarily.

"You have played both ends long enough now John Sullivan, and since you have proven time and again you don't have the capacity or the maturity to make rational choices, I will choose for you. Your bloody political life can fall to pieces tomorrow for all I give a damn, because it has stolen my husband from me and their father from my children. Not anymore!"

JP was stunned by the shock of the normally subservient Annie's sudden attack. He blamed it on Hannah. That interfering bitch with her progressive ideas. At first he made light of Annie's outburst by the fact that she was, after all, a woman with child whose nephew now lay dead next door. Things would naturally be emotional for her right now.

He began to speak.

"Unh," was the partial syllable he managed to utter before she commanded, "Shut up!"

"Last year you came within a hair's breadth of being sent away to the Penitentiary for trading the answers to the police exam for ballots. And what the hell were you thinking back then, John P. Sullivan? You gave more than five hundred men the same answers to the test, and you thought nobody would take notice when every last one of them passed with flying colors? Were you even sober when you decided to do such a fool-headed thing? Did you even consider what outcome that might inflict on your wife and your little ones? What we would do if you were put in prison? How your children would manage with the shame and the taunts? How they would survive? Who would protect us with you gone? You, whose own father left his family to die in a bloody war, leaving your mother to fend for herself with you, just months old, in her arms? You, whose own mother went and married a convicted criminal so desperate was she that her children not end up on the street or in the poorhouse?

"Your children and I have stood enough of your fool's errands, your politics, your rowing club, your partners in crime! You were brought home to me just this last February half beaten to death on the street by assailants in the middle of the night, thugs you still refuse to identify to this day.

"What happens next time, JP? Should I go ahead and order your coffin now? Conners and Sheehan! That's who did it! Those vermin have bought and sold you like some street whore! Fingy Conners owns you no less than he owns the laboring souls of this ward that he has enslaved! And he even treats you like he owns you! Where is your respect for yourself, for your family, in that? What examples are you teaching your sons? To align themselves with criminals? To lie, cheat, to sell themselves, to literally steal the voter's ballots out of their hands as the only way to win an election? What kind of father are you who is never home? What kind of leader are you, scratching the backs of men who by all that is right in this world should be choking under the weight of your righteous determination as the elected representative of our people? You are the only voice that the hard-working men and women of this First Ward have, JP! They are crying out! And you are silent!"

JP's initial insult was quickly replaced by sheer paranoia. As she rattled on in her female hormone-induced dementia he looked around for any handy skillet or hidden brick that might be destined for his head. Hannah had been a powerful influence on Annie in recent months, but until this shameful tirade began he hadn't realized just how seriously.

"This all stops here, today, JP Sullivan! Right now. The rowing club, the political disgrace, breaking the law! You are coming home at night for supper from this day forward! I cannot force you to be a respectful husband to me, but damn you to hell JP, I will force you to be a father to your children! And if you force me to choose, so help me God I will be choosin' my children's future over your own. In a split second, I will!"

Annie Saulter Sullivan was never a woman to threaten, shout or curse, for that was not how she was brought up. She was a loyal wife who guarded well her husband's secrets. But now that push had come to shove, she was forced to use the only power she had. She had laid down an ultimatum. An unchallengable, immovable, moral, made-of-iron declaration.

"Annie Saulter, you will dare not threaten me!" spake His Honor, bending down to retrieve his giant shoe.

Infuriated, Annie kicked the huge orthopedic monstrosity out of his hand and across the room. It was so massive that she felt a sharp pain in her knee with the blow. The Alderman angrily stood up and paused to try and balance himself. She knocked him back down into the chair.

"Sit down!"

He felt fully diminished by her at that moment. Others had oftentimes made him feel less-than because he was a cripple. But Annie never had.

The expression that crossed his face as he absorbed that thought suddenly opened her eyes. She experienced an epiphany.

"Oh my God! So, that's it? That's the reason for all this malarkey of yours? Because you're crippled? "

JP just stared at her dumbly, wounded.

"That's why you kowtow to those men, those powerful men? To be accepted by them? You feel so inferior that winning their attentions means more to you than winning your own family's?"

JP had no response for that, neither lighthearted nor angry. He had been toppled right off his balance for the second time in less than a minute.

"You're so desperate for, for...what? Prominence? Respect? Legitimacy? That you engage in the exact opposite kinds of behavior to attain that? You lay down for these other men so they'll... they'll, what? Accept you? Like you?

They don't like you, JP! Isn't that obvious by the way they use you?"

Annie only realized then what she herself had just said. She stood there and raised her left hand to her mouth, covering it, the gesture indicating she had just fathomed something monumental. Why hadn't she surmised all this before? It was so obvious now.

A long uncomfortable silence filled the room. She stood there, thinking.

She surveyed the quarters for a brief moment, then went to the oaken corner closet, threw open the door angrily and gathered his three other orthopedic shoes from the shelves. She bent over the one she had kicked across the room and with some effort, picked it up. Then she opened the cracked window wider and threw the whole kit and caboodle out.

"You're staying home!"

She stalked out of the bedroom and slammed the door behind her so hard that the entire house reverberated.

A castrated John P. Sullivan sat in his little chair, hobbled by his wife's having had enough, and by her tossing his special shoes out the window.

He was forced by circumstance to sit there and think. To face his own mess.

His wife's valise was crammed to overflowing with all his crimes and indiscretions.

Not once during her tirade did Annie do the one thing—the first thing, in fact that he and all of his cronies would have jumped at in the same situation: threaten blackmail. He'd had a visceral urge to charge back at her, to defend himself, to justify his absences from the family by pointing out all the nice things he had procured for them. But as much as he wanted to challenge Annie, her words were in fact unimpeachable. He had been panicked for a time about the police exam scandal, it was true. When his name appeared first on the list of culprits printed in the New York Times... well, being exposed to that kind of public scrutiny could well have ended in total disaster. And then there was that midnight walloping he'd gotten.

He had long denied the truth to himself of his not doing right by his children. They were able to read the daily journals now. They were getting old enough to understand. Their little friends in the neighborhood were telling them what their own parents were saying about the Alderman around the supper table.

Annie could ruin him politically and legally, maybe even financially. But never once did she even hint she might do that.

JP recalled how he'd relentlessly pursued Annie Saulter, not simply because he fell in love with her, the girl who literally lived next door, but because she was uncannily similar in character to his own mother Mary. Strong. Good. Level-headed. Patient. Fair minded. Relentless in her convictions. Gentle as a lamb until pushed too far, then fierce as a lioness.

Like now.

John P. Sullivan himself possessed no such fine qualities.

Whereas Annie met challenges head on, he wheedled, evaded, negotiated, joked and connived.

Whereas she quietly went to church and kept her commandments, he grandstanded like some exalted pillar of the parish while breaking most of the ten.

Annie had a way of just standing there and telling people what she knew they needed to hear, whereas JP related charming parables with a wink, and scattered empty compliments around like so much cheap confetti before quickly walking away.

THE FIRST WARD I

Annie cared for the children's needs 24 hours a day, whereas he trotted the kids out periodically for public relations and photo opportunities.

The ice company, the Mutuals, politics...they consumed 95% of his time and energy, whereas the family was the beneficiary of 100% of hers.

He got up and with some difficulty steadied himself. He hadn't tried to walk without his special shoes in a long time. He limped out, past her, grotesquely, into the kitchen. She pretended to pay no notice. He took a block of wax from the gadget drawer and began waxing the tracks of the double hung windows that had been sticking since the weather turned warm. Then he limped slowly down the stairs into the yard and uprighted and shimmed the leaning T poles that supported the clotheslines and then gathered up his shoes from their landing spot. He laboriously made his way back into the house to sit on the step and put his shoe on. Then he stitched up the rip in the screen door. It would do the trick until he could get someone to replace it. Flies had been getting in. He picked up some petrified carcasses from the floor beneath the parlor windows and placed them one by one in his cupped palm. He tossed them in the garbage pail. Then he washed his hands.

Annie busied herself with dishes and kitchen duties, but her thoughts kept her spinning. JP came back in and thought about kissing her on the cheek or something, but he was still too angry and too chastened so he didn't. He had some more thinking to do. He didn't want a fight. Putting ultimatums of his own on the table wouldn't serve any purpose except to widen the chasm. A man didn't have to be a politician to see that much. And what would his ultimatums be, anyway? "Stop telling me the truth about myself, Annie"?

She knew him. She knew he had to chew on it a while.

"Why don't you go check on your brother again?" she said without looking up. "I'll be over there in a few minutes. Don't forget that your kids need you too now. They need their father to explain things to them. Go do that."

JP went to the bureau and pulled out a clean shirt, put it on, buttoned it in the mirror, put on his collar, combed what was left of his hair, and departed. Annie went into the bathroom and washed her face. The cool water felt good on her hot angry cheeks. She relaxed. She thought her outburst might have worsened the baby's agitation, but the kicking had calmed right down. Maybe the release of all her anger and tension had allowed the baby to relax as well.

She dried her face and brushed her hair. Even though troubled by her own fears and anxiety over the approaching birth of her child, she put these aside for the time being and prepared to go next door to help Hannah, her closest friend and confidante, make arrangements to bury her youngest child, yet again.

Emma Honan climbed the few steps to the front porch at No. 16 Hamburgh. She glanced down the street to see the normally lively little pier deserted. The guilty raft was nowhere in sight. She shuddered to think that the family would be forced to look at this scene every day, knowing their little boy died in that very spot.

People were lingering on the porch and in the doorway too, blocking it, trying to get some air. It was hot and sticky. There was no compassionate breeze. The Detective was exiting. Emma gently took his hand in hers.

"Oh, Detective Sullivan, I am so, so very sorry. If there is anything I can do, please just ask!" Jim didn't recognize her at first, but then realized it was JP's receptionist.

"Thank you. Please... can you go in and speak with Hannah? She's having a terrible time of it."

"Yes, yes, I will."

As Emma went inside, Jim went down the stairs and walked around the side of the house to where a leaf-shaded garden bench held its place at the foot of the porch. He wanted to be alone. He sat.

Emma tip-toed into the parlor where Johnny was laid out. Chairs ringed the room and people sat and talked in whispers. The choking scent of embalming fluid and too many gardenias displaced what there was of the room's limited oxygen.

Hannah sat by her Johnny, accepting condolences in a daze.

Emma paid her respects, and although Hannah looked at her directly as she spoke, her face registered nothing but vacancy.

Emma saw her boss come in. She dreaded having to pretend like nothing was wrong. Like she didn't know. The Alderman immediately occupied himself in conversation with his back turned to her. He hadn't seen her, so she slipped out unnoticed. On the porch, there stood Annie alone, arms folded, looking toward the spot in the river. She turned to glance at Emma and smiled a sad smile. Emma knew she couldn't just leave without speaking to her. It would look bad if she tried to avoid her.

They made small talk at first. Annie noticed that Emma was not looking her in the eye.

Emma Honan was close to fifty years old. Annie had never viewed Emma's presence in her husband's life as any threat, but her behavior was causing some suspicion now.

"Emma, is there something wrong?"

Emma looked at her, chewed her lip, then looked around to see who might be within earshot. She lowered her voice to a near whisper.

"Yes, Annie. Something is troubling me quite a bit," Emma confessed.

She had been consumed for two days with this, not knowing if she should say anything. But here she was now with the Alderman's wife, just the two of them, and impulsively, she decided she should tell her.

"What is it?"

Emma hesitated a few beats. Before she could change her mind, she choked out the first few words.

"The other evening, the police called the office to tell the Alderman that little Johnny had fallen in the river and was thought to have drowned. I listened in, Annie, I know I shouldn't have, I confess. But the police sergeant's tone sounded so urgent on the telephone that I felt I had to know what was the matter."

"Yes? Go on," urged the puzzled Annie.

"I jumped up and prepared the Alderman's things expecting him to rush out. He was in a meeting with Mr. Conners and Alderman Sheehan. I waited and waited. He didn't end that meeting until more than a half hour later! I was appalled, Annie! I know how close he is to his brother. Detective Sullivan visits the office several times a week. They do everything together. I couldn't understand why the Alderman didn't just come running out of his office in a blind panic immediately. I myself was in a panic over the news, and I don't even know the Detective very well at all. I didn't understand why the Alderman wouldn't just end the meeting instantly and run to his brother's side. It really disturbed me. I can't even look the Alderman in the eye now!"

Annie was struck speechless.

"I'm sorry I had to tell you, Annie. It's been a heavy burden for me to carry, seeing him respond in that way, or rather I say, not respond. I find myself uncomfortable even speaking with him now."

"Thank you for telling me, Emma," said the disquieted Annie. "You did the right thing. The Alderman hasn't really been himself these days," said the apologist. "You would know that better than anyone."

"Yes, ma'am, I do. Ever since that whole police examination affair he has been much more preoccupied and short tempered than before."

Emma searched Annie's expression for a clue as to what she should do next.

"I... I really should be leaving, Annie."

Emma wanted to get out of there, fearing that the Alderman had seen her speaking with his wife.

They said goodbye.

Annie watched her walk away, and took another long look at the river that claimed her sweet nephew. Then, after the baby kicked hard, she turned and went inside to sit by Hannah.

Detective Jim Sullivan sat paralyzed on the bench below the porch, hidden by the greenery. He'd heard every word.

As Johnny was being laid to rest at Holy Cross Cemetery, Annie Saulter was giving birth at the General Hospital. Sons Thomas and Daniel had been born at home, but the deaths of Hannah's children had instilled a new caution in her, and when her labor pains began, she demanded JP drive her to the hospital, rather than fetch Dr. Buswell.

Jim's fellow police officers arrived at Holy Cross Cemetery by the dozens, along with Michael and Ellen Regan and Captain Ryan. But he missed his brother's and Annie's presence. It couldn't be helped, even after hearing what he'd overheard. One child goes into the ground at the same time another comes into the world. He and Hannah were still subtracting while JP and Annie continued adding. He pondered that conundrum.

JP had committed to coming home to supper every Monday, Wednesday and Friday, and weekends. He was uncomfortable at first, sheepishly announcing to Fingy Conners and the Sheehans that he could not always drop everything when they needed him because his family needed him as well. Their expected arguments and backlash never came. They were family men too, but hadn't yet met wifely wrath in the same fashion that the Alderman had. JP was a little flummoxed to realize he could have made this his policy all along.

Things got better between Annie and JP. His wife's blowup coming on the heels of such recklessness on his part had knocked some sense into him. Some.

But there'd be no breaking with Fingy Conners, not without ending his political career. Annie was right about that: politics was what gave him his power, his validation. He was respected now. And even those who might hate him still deferred to him, at least in his presence.

He cut back a bit on his involvement with the Mutual Rowing Club. It was even harder dropping the aldermanic baseball team, since he was captain. But he did so for a year. As he began to let things go, one by one, and allow himself to think about what had occurred, what he had allowed to happen — a conclusion he had avoided reaching previously — he once again fell very ill.

JP had lost count of all the times he had knocked at death's door. He'd experienced more calamities of health than anyone else still around to talk about it. This time he suffered an attack of blood poisoning and inflammatory rheumatism and became extremely sick. He spent ten days in the General Hospital, then went home to recover.

The first morning at home he awoke to the most god-awful noise, well above and beyond the usual god-awful noise of the industrial surroundings.

The Buffalo Dredging Company was drilling holes to set dynamite charges in the river bottom. Explosions rocked the house, interfering with JP's recuperation. The Alderman placed a single call downtown to his colleagues in the Common Council, and immediately the racket stopped. For three days men stood idle and machinery floated silently on tethered barges, until Alderman Sullivan gave his permission for the expensive work to resume.

As he rested, JP paged though the latest Larkin Co. catalog, The Larkin Idea, choosing furnishings for the newly rebuilt Mutuals boathouse. This time around, the Mutuals had unanimously decided it was wiser to construct with brick. The Sullivan brothers from Alabama Street, Daniel and Jack, both Mutuals members and both bricklayers, insisted on it. He sorely wanted to add a pool table, the ideal winter diversion, and schemed about how to finance it.

He watched the clock so he could put the pillow over his ears when that goddamned noon whistle at the Buffalo Furnace shrieked, loud and long.

Jesus, it was awful. There was no getting used to it.

1899
Peter Newell Conners

Fingy's eldest son and heir-apparent, eighteen-year-old Peter Newell Conners, the polar opposite of his father in both looks and personality, lay in bed at Michigan's Orchard Lake Military Academy with a leg injury. In addition to the fracture he was suffering from a cold.

He asked that a telephone be brought to him. It took almost a half hour to secure a line through to Buffalo.

Fingy picked up the phone in his office at his most recent acquisition, the Buffalo Courier newspaper.

"Peter! What the hell happened there, son?"

Peter laughed, then sneezed.

"I tried to tell you, Pop! There are some regular Hankenschmidts and Sandows here on the football squad! If I didn't know any better I'd swear you arranged to sneak in a couple of your biggest longshoremen as ringers just to stir things up a bit here."

"Hey, now why didn't I think o' that?" Fingy laughed. "Listen, son. Yer doc is tellin' me it's a clean injury and there won't be no bad effects in yer future -- if youse jus' stay put! So listen t' me, Petie! You do exactly what the doc says, and heal up good 'n' proper. I already got one limpin' fool in my life I have t' keep close watch over. I don't need another. Hear me?"

Peter smiled broadly.

"Yeah, I hear you Pop! I've learnt my lesson. I'm not letting anything get in the way of my starting at Yale, so don't you worry. That nurse you hired for me sticks to me like – like Cheng to Eng! So I've got nothing better to do all day long except eat like a horse and study my lessons and speed this leg to healing up."

"Well it better be actual school books yer studyin' there, Petie, and none of that French smut I hear tell is circulatin' all about there! I understand the temptation, son. But there'll be plenty o' time fer malarkey once you get to where we need you to be. First things first, Peter. Business before pleasure."

"All right, Pops. Yale Bulldogs, make way! Here I come!"

Peter paused a beat. Then his demeanor took a serious and sentimental turn.

"I won't disappoint you, Father. You know that. You're my one and only. I owe everything to my Dear Pops."

Fingy choked up, then cleared his throat.

"Youse -- jus' take care o' yerself there Petie, and keep me informed. Telephone me anytime ye need to, son."

"Pop, you worry too much. I'm going to be good as new in no time. No — make that better than new. Tell Mary I was asking for her, will you?"

"Mary's plenty worried about youse too, Petie," fretted the boy's proud father. "She loves ye almost like she was yer real Ma. Ye be good, now."

"How bad can I be cooped up all alone in my bed?" he laughed. "All right. Goodbye Pops. I love you."

Fingy's eyes misted over as he gazed at the magnificent framed photo of Peter in uniform on his desk.

"Yeah. Me too son."

The First Ward was as tightly knit as a Aran sweater. Every man, woman, and child was deeply affected by Conners' rule. For nearly twenty years he had tightened the noose 'round the necks of the freight-handling longshoremen there. Now, after monopolizing the freight business it seemed only natural that he turn his attentions to securing the handling of the vast amounts of grain that passed through the city as well. And looking even further beyond that, to taking over the handing of ore, all in good time. When it became clear to the grain scoopers that Fingy was casting his net round them to completely control the grain contracting business, it proved to be the final indignity.

Up until Conners entered the picture the unloading of grain was controlled by boss shovelers who negotiated contracts with individual steamships to unload the vessel for a fixed price. That figure was then divided among their men on an equal share basis, or so it was promised. In reality the boss shovelers systematically padded their roster with a few phony names and pocketed for themselves the wages "earned" by these non-existent workers.

Conners approached the grain-carrying ship owners and began to gain their contracts one by one. He replaced the old boss shovelers with his own gangs of even worse thugs. With the Conners takeover, the scoopers' weekly wage took a devastating hit. But they soon found their weekly pay dwindling even further as Conners applied the saloon-boss system full-throttle to this new workforce, compelling workers to drink and eat—and even board—at his saloons. Additionally, the lucrative practice of padding the work crew with nonexistent workers was stepped up, Fingy divvying the take with his chosen boss shovelers.

In April 1899, defeated exhausted men stood in a long line outside 444 Ohio Street to receive their week's pay. Inside, Fingy handed the first man $9 cash and $3 in brass tokens.

Laborer Sean Clancey couldn't believe his eyes.

"What the...? What in buggerin' hell is this, Fingy?" Clancey demanded.

Kennedy approached Fingy and interrupted. "Boss, yer son's on the telephone."

Distracted and angry, Fingy barked, "Tell 'im I'm in the middle of somethin' and I'll telephone him back in an hour."

Fingy turned his attention back to Clancy.

"That's yer wage, Clancy. Take it 'n' scat! Get outa here."

"Me wage? Me wage is ten American cash dollars and two of yer bloody brass tokens — not $9 and three worthless slugs! Me kids can't be eatin' no brass slugs, you bungnipper!"

Men in line reacted violently to the explosive news of once-again lowered wages.

Before Fingy could even posture, Clancy's huge fist crashed squarely into Conners' teeth, Fingy erupting in a spew of blood. In a flash the laborers piled onto their hated boss with murderous fury. Hundreds joined in the riot. Fingy and his men hightailed it for their lives as workers exploded under pressure of two decades' pent up frustration and rage. They tore the saloon to shreds and stole all the cash, then set the building afire.

Minutes later fire steamers rolled up accompanied by police. Rioters scattered.

444 Ohio St., Fingy Conners' saloon and contractor's office.

Bells clanged. Horses screamed. A large group gathered down the block. Clancy addressed them fiercely.

"Fingy Conners' days of payin' us fer breakin' our backs with his no-good brass is over! We had our fill! We can't pay our rent with brass! Too many of our wives 'n' kids is sick 'n' sufferin' as it is. We can't live on $9! We have no choice but to go out on strike! Tell all yer neighbors and families! Tell yer priests! We're all slowly dyin' by Conners' hand anyways! Rather, we'll die fightin' fer what we're owed if we must, battlin' that carbuncle-faced bully-cock to his sorry end!"

Police swarmed, clubs drawn. Rioters pried cobbles from the streets and retaliated. The strike quickly spread.

Newspaper headlines shouted:

BANQUET FOR THE RATS
Grain Shipments Remain on Ships Anchored at the Foot of the Great Grain Elevators.
No Workers To Unload Them.

SHIPPING STOPS DEAD IN THE WATER
Ships From the Great Midwest Ports Back Up In Buffalo Harbor With Their Holds Brim-full. City Fathers Silent.

For weeks thereafter the lakefront was a battlefield between striking union men and gangs of thugs recruited from Chicago, Detroit and New York by Conners in his attempt to inaugurate a reign of terror.

Week after week the imported thugs cleaned out the resorts where the union men gathered. They demolished skulls as efficiently as they did saloons. Emotions ran so deeply that Fingy no longer dared show his face in the ward for fear of rock missiles, or more likely now, bullets.

Unfortunate Timing

The military academy's doctor did not need long to reach his conclusion. Peter Newell Conners was struggling desperately to breathe. Alarmed, the physician addressed the headmaster.

"Mr. Hull, you'd best have General Wheeler notify Mr. Conners, immediately. Tell him to come to Orchard Lake as quickly as he can!

"Yes, Doctor!" obeyed Hull.

The headmaster flew out of the room.

In Buffalo, a Western Union messenger rushed into Fingy's office as he blustered and berated his editors for not heading off the widespread condemnation of him resulting from the riot at his saloon the day before.

"Yer job is to tell a different story than what the strikers told — and what all the other newspapers printed! Why do I hafta explain youse that?"

"An urgent telegram for you. Mr. Conners!" said the breathless Western Union messenger.

"Yeah, yeah, they're all urgent these days! Just put it down there on the pile wit' all the others, boyo, an get the hell outa here. I'll get to it!"

"Sorry, Mr. Conners, sir," said Editor White. "How's about we say something to the effect of, it was a vicious crime committed by a few ungrateful anarchists against labor contractor Conners, who provides gainful employment for more than six thousand First Ward family men. We'll again restate that the entire economy of the ward depends on you employing these men, and how shameful this riot was. We'll have set history right and proper by this afternoon's edition, sir. You'll see! "

"No!" railed Fingy. "You'll see! You'll see the sidewalk at the end of yer nose if'n this whole t'ing ain't turned right around today in my favor. Now go. Git outa here and make this right!"

Fuming over Buffalo's other seven newspapers' account of the previous day's riot, especially the Catholic Union and Times, Fingy's brain was awash with various ways and means for preventing public opinion from getting in the way of his game plan. He angrily settled down to a flurry of work, forgetting the waiting telegram. An hour later, he got up and put on his coat.

"I got some business to do and I won't be back til after lunch, White!"

"Okay, boss," editor White replied.

An hour later the phone on Fingy's desk rang. White entered Fingy's unoccupied office to answer it.

"Buffalo Courier, Editor White speaking."

"Hello, Is this Mr. William Conners' office?"

"Yes it is."

"This is General Harris Wheeler at Orchard Lake Military Academy in Michigan. I must speak to Mr. Conners at once on an extremely urgent matter."

"Mr. Conners has stepped out. May I be of any help, General?"

"Sir, Mr. Conners' son Peter is dangerously ill. I sent a telegram many hours ago but have not yet received a reply. I was not able to secure a telephone line through to Buffalo until just this minute. Mr. Conners must come here to Orchard Lake at once! "

"Oh my!" gasped White. "I will go an fetch him myself, General. Right away!"

"Please hurry, sir. We fear this young man might not live through the night."

"Oh God, no! I will indeed hurry, General! Thank you!"

White frantically pored through the papers on Fingy's desk until he found the unopened telegram. He couldn't help but notice a copy of the book Hereditary Genius: The Science Of Eugenics by Francis Galton sitting there with a dozen bookmarks or more poking out of the pages.

White grabbed his coat and flew out of the office in a blind panic.

At the Iroquois Hotel, Fingy Conners paid his barber and put on his coat. He exited onto Main street where he nearly collided with Alderman Sullivan.

JP appeared to be quite visibly near the end of his tether.

"Fingy! I'm glad I ran into you!" said the discombobulated politician. "Listen, we have to talk about that riot yesterday afternoon! As the workers' alderman I'm under tremendous pressure to step in and do something for them! I'm not sure exactly what, though!"

"Not now, JP! I'm in no mood!"

Fingy rudely stalked off leaving JP high and dry.

Editor White vaulted down Main Street trying to locate Fingy. He ran into the barber shop at the Iroquois Hotel.

"Mr. Conners left here some twenty minutes ago," said his barber.

"Did he say where he was going after this, Mr. Tucci? It's crucial that I find him right away! His son is very ill!"

"He said something about the tailor, and cigars, and, uh – the diamond merchant, I believe."

White ran to Fingy's tailor, then to the cigar shop, frantically asking everyone if they had seen Conners.

While White continued rushing around in a frenzy, Fingy returned to his office. He sat down at his desk. Remembering the telegram, he rifled through the papers there. Unable to find it, he stalked out into the newsroom.

"Johnson. Where's White?" Fingy yawped.

"Don't know sir. When I returned from the pressroom he was nowhere to be found."

"Did youse touch anyt'ing on my desk, Johnson? That telegram? Where is it?" Fingy growled.

Johnson steeled himself in anticipation of another of his boss' explosive outbursts.

"Sorry, boss. Not me! I didn't step one foot in there!"

Fingy grunted and returned to his work.

Thirty minutes later, White flew into the newsroom gasping. He spotted Fingy at his desk, reaching for his ringing telephone. Terror filled Fingy's face. At the same moment White, dangerously out of breath and near collapse, ran into Fingy's office with the telegram in his hand.

"I was out trying to find you, boss! I looked every place!"

Fingy was frantic.

"Johnson! My boy is terribly ill! Get my wife on the telephone! Have Miller get my carriage ready immediately! White! Call Dr. Banta! Hurry! Hurry!"

Inside the dorm room at Orchard Lake, Peter's condition worsened. He shuddered with cold and was drenched in sweat. He struggled to breathe. As his doctor attended to him, headmaster Hull hovered worriedly.

"Pop! Poppa! Mr. Hull, where's... my Pop? Why isn't... my father... here? I need... my Pop!" implored the boy.

"Peter, your father is on his way. We telephoned him, and I am sure he'll be here any time now. Please try and relax. Getting overexcited only makes things worse!"

Peter seized the doctor's shirt in a death grip.

"I can't... catch... my breath, doctor. Help... me. Please help... me... breathe! I... want my...father! Papa, help... me!"

At Buffalo's Central depot Fingy was only just then rushing aboard a train with his wife and Dr. Banta.

"Did you arrange a car from Detroit to Orchard Lake, Jim?" his wife Mary reminded. "We can't afford to waste a single moment!"

Fingy didn't answer.

As Peter lay near death, wheezing, headmaster Hull paced furiously. He checked his pocket watch gloomily. He knew that 300 miles separated Peter from his parents. They would never make it in time.

Peter's uniformed mates sat by his bedside crying shamelessly.

At the same moment inside the Murphys' Blazing Rag saloon on South street the Murphy boys inspected the damage. The fervent unionizers scrutinized the newly broken windows in their tavern. Baseball bats at the ready, they were prepared for further trouble.

"Them was Fingy Conners' hired thugs wot done this, boys! If he t'inks this is gonna stop us from unitin' ag'inst 'im, that caffler's got another dream comin'," exclaimed the elder Murphy.

"It's high time we organize stronger, Pop," replied his son Jim, "and retake our manhood from that bastard! His aim's to ruin everyone who don't roll over fer 'im!

"Conners needs a good dose of Murphy family medicine!" threatened the youngest, John.

The train made its way across Southern Ontario at what seemed like a snail's pace.

Fingy and wife Mary sat bolt upright in their seats as the rocking train chugged along. Fingy cursed himself. The family doctor fretted over the frantic state of the couple.

The train slowed, then stopped.

410

"St. Thomas Ontario! St. Thomas! Five minutes!' cried the conductor.

"Damn it to hell Doc!" howled Fingy. "Every time this buggerin' train stops I wanna get out and push it meself!"

"Please, Mr. Conners," Dr. Banta beseeched. "We're almost halfway there. Making yourself sick isn't going to help your son. The train can't travel any faster than it's trying to. I beg you, for your boy's sake, remain calm."

Fingy looked out the window, his reflection in the glass doubling the deep affliction contorting his face. A messenger boarded the stopped train and walked down the aisle, calling out.

"Mr. Conners! Telegram for Mr. William J. Conners!"

"Boy! Here, boy! Right here!"

Fingy grabbed the telegram and ripped it open. His face collapsed into a mess of abject grief. He cried out.

"Oh! Oh my God, no! No, no no!"

Fingy's wife grasped the telegram as Fingy sobbed. Anguished, she read the mournful news.

The Detroit Free Press editorialized against Fingy loudly, for Detroit, like all the other great ports of the Great Lakes, was suffering mightily due to the strike in Buffalo:

> There are vessel owners at our port, members in good standing of the Lake Carriers' Association, who wonder greatly why the executive committee of the association continues to stand by "Boss" Conners in his present trouble with the grain handlers in Buffalo.
>
> They say if the association concludes to stick to its agreement with Conners to the bitter end, as their officers say they will, the money loss will not only be greater than the money saved on the shoveling contracts of the last three years, but will be greater than what would be saved for many years to come, no matter how low wages might go.
>
> The Detroit owners that kick on Conners say the association has every moral right, considering the failure of Conners twice to carry out his contract, to throw him overboard and concede to the scoopers.
>
> Conners has made desperate efforts to import grain handlers from New York and other places, but in every case the strikers and their sympathizers have induced the new men to go back on Conners on arrival. Conners claims he is working a full force of men at the elevators, but a glance at the elevators and the great fleet lying idle in Buffalo with its grain aboard shows this to be false.
>
> In the meantime, the grain carriers, the Detroit owners among them, are losing the chance to carry several cargoes in this, the best season the lakes have seen for ten years or more. Judging by all appearances, unless the Carriers throw Conners over, the strike is destined to last indefinitely, for the men in Buffalo are bitter against Conners and determined to oust him from the grain-handling business.
>
> But it is not only the Great Lakes Carriers who are losing. The Board

Of Trade at Chicago, Milwaukee, Detroit, Duluth and Toledo have been forced to close down all business on grain destined for Buffalo. The Erie Canal boatmen, the New York railroads, the ocean vessels that carry the stuff to Europe and the consumers on both sides of the Atlantic are being put to a loss that can never be made up and which is mounting into the millions.

No grain had left any Great Lakes port city since the strike began. Great ships laden full of the bounty of America's golden harvest sat at anchor, either in Buffalo or after returning to whatever port they had originally sailed from: Chicago, Duluth, Milwaukee, Toledo or Detroit. The ships lay idle, tied up and filled to the brim with their cargo, unable to do business with any other entity. It wasn't just Buffalo's First Ward families who were suffering under the domination of Fingy Conners any longer; the anguish was now spread far and wide.

The strikers were adamant about agreeing to any terms that did not include their foremost demand: the absolute abolition of the contract system and the firing of its founder, Fingy Conners. No agreement between the scoopers and the Lake Carriers' Association could be effected so long as Fingy Conners was part of the equation.

> From the very first, men followed him gladly, for no one would dare take a chance on walking in front, with his back to Fingy Conners.
> —Charles Forrest Moore

The scoopers knew well that unless the snake that embodied the diabolical saloon-contractor system lost its head, it would strangle them. Taking their scooper brothers' example to heart, the emboldened freight handlers now went out on strike as well. Ships clogged the harbor, and freight that had already been unloaded sat on the docks, rotting. The longshoremen watched the grain scoopers carefully, determined that whatever the scoopers got, the freight handlers would have as well. They were demanding a wage increase from 25 cents and hour to 30 cents, in addition to the silver-plattered head of Fingy Conners.

The harbor was at a complete standstill, choked with idle, laden ships. As the strike continued with no end in sight, the silence emanating from Buffalo's leaders in the Mayor's office and the City Hall Common Council chambers was deafening, most especially so from the alderman of the city ward most cruelly affected, John P. Sullivan of the First.

Even with the entire volume of public opinion turned up against him, Fingy Conners' ally remained shamefully staunch and silent, betraying the very workers he swore in each successive election to stand by. Not a single word about the paralyzing, months-long strike appeared in the Common Council's printed proceedings, despite its crippling the city's economy.

Even Buffalo Mayor Conrad Diehl claimed a "neutral" position on the matter, instead blabbing incessantly about the upcoming Pan American Exposition of 1901, which predictably, Fingy Conners was positioning himself to take charge of as well.

WILLIAM J. CONNERS, Buffalo

Fingy Conners

The Buffalo Star editorialized,
"During this crisis, what has our city government done? Talked Pan-American, while thousands of families struggle against starvation."

Negotiations persisted, but after many weeks of stalemate, the representatives of the Lake Carriers' Association stated that they had done all they possibly could to put an end to the labor trouble and were not successful in inducing the strikers to return to work.

On May 6th, the scoopers' union president P.J. McMahon addressed the strikers. "A fake proposition has been submitted to us by the Lake Carriers' Association," he said. "As it provides for a continuance of the contract system, I have rejected it on your behalf."

The men cheered and McMahon vowed to fight the matter out on the docks. That same day, the monthly men at the elevators and the coal heavers on the canal docks announced that they were joining the strike, adding 2,000 more men to the body of strikers.

Buffalo's Catholic Bishop James Quigley, longtime hater of Fingy Conners, stepped in to offer his services as mediator, confident that he could bring the two sides to an understanding—the understanding being that Fingy Conners and his saloon-boss system of servitude must go.

On May 7, Quigley's entry into the fray proved a turning point, bringing an army of almost universal condemnation to the front, in which every religious organization and virtually every newspaper and publication vilified Fingy Conners. After days of meetings and negotiations at his residence with officers of the Lake Carriers Association and Contractor Conners, he called for a rally with union leaders on May 10th at St. Bridget's Hall on Louisiana Street in the First Ward.

The awaiting throngs at St. Bridget's parish hall overflowed far out onto Louisiana Street. This time it wasn't just the scoopers showing up in a hunger-fueled rage, but with them came their rag-clad starving wives and children, and the handlers of freight, ore and coal as well.

Bishop Quigley had thundered and railed against Fingy Conners for years, and despite his exalted position in the now-predominantly Catholic city and his success at allying with Protestant and Jewish leaders in the cause, he felt stymied and impotent at having effected no change. More unfortunates now toiled under the tyranny of Fingy Conners than ever before.

Kennedy and David Nugent rose well before dawn to meet the train from Toronto bringing 200 Canadians to Buffalo to work on the docks as scabs. Nugent moved the arriving passengers quickly along.

"Come on, youse canucks!" ordered Nugent. "Hurry it up. Ye got plenty o' work awaitin' fer youse!"

The scabs were loaded onto wagons and drays and then driven off.

Thirty minutes later the Canadians arrived to an angry army of strikers outside the Dakota Elevator. They were forced to run the gauntlet of insults and rocks. At the same time, ore handlers from upriver marched in en masse to support the strikers. The Canadians had been provided no information on the situation.

They were unaware of the strike.

"Us ore handlers is one wit' youse scooper boys!" the predominantly Polish group shouted. "Let's give it to them scabs good!"

With a bloody melee threatening, Fingy's gang boss Sloak Slattery telephoned police headquarters.

Penance served and rank reinstated, Police Captain Mike Regan, in a foul mood, answered.

"Police Headquarters, Captain Regan speaking."

"Yeah, Mike, this is Sloak Slattery at the Dakota Elevator! We got a riot goin' on down here. The scoopers is attackin' our men! We need yer boys down here fast!"

"What "men" are you talkin' about, Slattery?", queried Regan. "Them scoopers are your men!

"No, Mike, I'm talkin' about the men Conners brought in from Toronto."

Regan paused a moment trying to make sense of what Slattery was talking about, then exploded.

"You mean, scabs? Fingy's brought in scabs?

Slattery fell silent for a few beats.

"Just git some coppers down here, will ya?"

"Slattery, you listen to me. There ain't one copper in this city who don't have a father, a son, a brother, or all three, workin' the docks! We ain't gettin' involved in your shit. Pay the piper! Take yer licks on yer own."

"Well, Boss Conners sure ain't gonna be happy hearin' youse say this, Mike!"

"Slattery," screamed the Captain, "ye'll soon be soon findin' out how foolhardy threatenin' a police captain is!

"Hey, I didn't — that weren't no threat, Captain!" panicked Slattery. "I was jist..."

Regan slammed down the telephone before Slattery could finish. The telephone quickly rang again.

"Headquarters, Regan here!"

"Regan, what's this I hear 'bout youse refusin' to send coppers down here t' break up this riot?" shouted Fingy Conners. "I'm here waitin'."

Captain Mike Regan became enraged.

"Me very own nephew's likely right there in the middle o' that skirmish, Conners! If I recall correctly, the last time I sent me men into the fray at yer request, it cost me all my stripes, half me wages, an' put me back walkin' the freezin' cold streets for a year and a half! I'll be tellin' you the same thing I just told yer stooge. You want t' import foreign scum into me city, don't you expect me to put me own men in the breach to be protectin' 'em! Yer on yer own in this, Conners!"

Regan slammed down the phone, then defiantly brushed errant lint off his captain's chevron, cursing Fingy Conners under his breath.

Fingy grew livid as he watched strikers attack his scabs in the shadow of the towering elevators. The Canadians scattered in terror. A scab fended off a striker's shovel and shouted, "But we never knew we was comin' here t' break no strike, lad! That Conners fella promised us all good payin' steady jobs at $2 a day, that's all! He put a big advert in the Star and the other Toronto papers!

Laborer Clancy stopped pummelling him.

"Ye mean youse canuck fellas didn't cross the border to come steal our jobs?" the surprised Clancy asked.

MICHAEL REGAN,

CAPTAIN OF THE FIRST PRECINCT.

Captain Michael Regan

"No!" pleaded the Canadian. "We woont do no such thing, mister! We're workin' men, jus' like yerselfs! Wit' families t' feed! Us workin' men's all got t' stick together!

Clancy began shouting to bring an end to the fighting.

"Hey, lads! Stop! Hold it! These here fine Canadian lads ain't no scabs! These're honorable Toronto boys wot Conners duped into travelin' down here on a barefaced dirty lie!"

The skirmishing halted. Men were helped up off the ground. They shook hands and brushed each other off.

Conners appeared in the elevator's office doorway, furious and red-faced. He howled, "Youse bastard canucks! I brought youse down here t' work fer me, not to be pickin' out no dance partners fer yerselfs! Youse can all go straight to hell now! If youse t'ink I'm payin' yer train back t' Hogtown, then yer just the bunch o' fools you look like! You fuckin' canucks kin starve! God damn all o' youse —and yer kids!"

Don't ye worry, laddie," assured Clancy. "Ye'll be comin' home wit' me after we're done here. Youse'll be eatin' wit' me family, 'n' stay long as ye need. We ain't got much, but ye'll have yer share."

Another striker named Lacey took up the cry.

"Yeah! Hey, all youse Toronto fellas! Listen! None o' youse got to be worryin' about havin' a place t' sleep! We take care of our own here in Buffalo! You'll all be comin' home wit' one of us!"

Men cheered. Newly befriended, the duped Canadians joined the strikers against Fingy in a raucous demonstration of solidarity.

JP pulled up to his home at No. 12 Hamburgh street in his carriage. Annie had called him at the city hall, distraught. He found his front porch crowded with agitated laborers milling about, just as his wife had described. Annie's alarmed face watched from a second floor window above as the Alderman approached the throng. She rocked a crying baby while their family dog Jack barked at the intruders. JP braced himself for a confrontation. He forced a smile.

"Well, hello th..."

A laborer named Jones interrupted.

"Alderman, things've rotted into a terrible state! Conners lowered our wage yet ag'in! We can't go on bein' worked half to death! Our kids is always sick and our women cryin' and miserable! We voted for youse last elections on account o' yer promise to improve workin' conditions, but ye haven't done a damn thing!"

"Oh, listen here lads," the Alderman defended. "I'm tryin' my best."

Laborer Dennis McLeary took over.

"Everybody here knows yer square in Fingy Conners' vest pocket, alderman, so stop yer connivin'! Yer not doin' nothin' 'cept just watchin' a bad situation go straight to hell! We're the ones who voted t' keep youse in office, not Conners. So youse better be standin' wit' us against that lyin' fucker, or else we'll put youse out!"

"Fellas," implored JP. "the poor man's just lost his son!"

McLeary scoffed.

"There's three men standin' right here on yer front steps wot's lost their little ones just this year, Alderman, and it's all because of Conners! We can't buy enough food, or coal! We been havin' t' send our kids to school even when they're ailin' – just t' keep 'em warm! We're scufflin' 'n' takin' our quarrelin' out ag'inst each other, when it's that bastard Conners who's the cause of all our troubles!"

JP inched his way slyly toward the front door as he spoke.

"Boys, I give you my word. I'm talking now to Mr. Conners on your behalf! You just need to trust me. It's a very complicated situation. I thank ye for voting for me and believing in me. I will do right by you! Please, just give me a little time!"

"Time is sumpin' youse already run outa, Alderman!" warned McLeary. "Mark me words! T'ings can't go on like this without a bloody awful turn!"

Completely surrounded by the barely controlled mob, JP quickly bulldozed his way into his house, slamming the door behind him. The incensed men stayed put, hovering about on his porch.

At St. Bridget's Hall a mass of throbbing humanity awaited. One thousand men jammed the inside and an even greater number spilled out along Louisiana Street. When the scoopers heard that the Bishop was on his way to the hall, they formed a double row from the hall, down Louisiana to Perry Street, and from there to the bridge at the eastern end of the Delany Forge Works. Through those lines of honor guard the carriage containing Bishop Quigley, Father Patrick Cronin, Daniel J. Keefe and John M. Hennessy passed. Every head was bared out of respect as the carriage sped along, the men's caps held over their grateful hearts.

It is on such occasions when vast numbers of men are roused to wrath by atrocious wrongs that the calming influence of a cherished man of God becomes powerfully evident. The Bishop approached to the cheers of the assembled out on the street, then made his way through the welcoming crowd toward the entrance of the modest clapboard meeting hall jammed with 1,500 men. As he entered from the street portal, a loud cheering rose up from the back of the annex, and the men in a wave from back to front rose to their feet, the tumult following the man and increasing in volume as he made his way to the podium.

At the speaker's stand he stood before them, their leader in the Church, and now their leader in the workplace as well. The audience remained standing, and would for his entire address.

When the cheering subsided, Bishop Quigley spoke.

"For fifteen years," he began "I have tried to abolish the evils to which you men have been subject, and at last it appears that these are going to be abolished. But the credit is due to new Local No. 51 for the glorious fight it has made for its rights. It is a subject I willingly would speak to you about for 24 hours, if certain restrictions had not been put upon me at the conference with the Great Lakes Carriers representatives held at my home.

"You and your families have suffered beyond human endurance for an entire generation now, at the miserable hand of Fingy Conners. You cannot feed or clothe yourselves. You and your children are sick. Many of you have lost babies directly due to the conditions that Conners instituted and fomented all these many years, and I say to you all gathered here today…this all ends now!"

A roaring cry arose from the masses as the decades of stifled rage were unleashed amidst the crude wooden rafters of St. Bridget's Hall.

Their mayor, Conrad Diehl, had proclaimed his neutrality in the matter.

Their alderman, the First Ward's supposed hero, John P. Sullivan, maintained an unshakable, unforgivable silence.

Their police, whose members' own laboring brothers, fathers and sons were currently suffering cruelly under Conners' control, and who knew better than anyone their anguish, understood that in the end, Fingy Conners owned the leaders of their department. If they were to keep their own jobs, they would have to do as ordered.

Only their Bishop possessed the self-righteous indignation, the courage of his convictions and the backbone to publicly raise up and confront the primitive and retaliatory fury of Fingy Conners. Despite the threats to his life and the continual reminders evidenced by Conners' enemies turning up floating dead in Buffalo's canals and slips, the Bishop boldly stepped out front to lead les miserables.

"You must vow to never again work for Fingy Conners!" shouted the Bishop.

Like a dam bursting, hunger-fueled outrage and hatred exploded from the depleted bodies of those tortured souls, most of whom could not recall a time when their lives were not denigrated by Fingy Conners' domination. The Bishop's remarks were interrupted by the wildest of cheering that followed almost every sentence he spoke.

"The era of Conners' rule of this ward is finished! Your politicians have refused to stop him. The law has refused to stop him. But you, my children, if you are willing to suffer just a wee bit longer, you can stop him!"

All it took to empower the powerless were a few well chosen words from a respected man with enough courage to stand up and claim leadership.

"By refusing to work, you castrate William J. Conners, like an old bull whose time had come and gone. By refusing to work, his power in this ward over your parents, over your husbands, over your children…ends!

"He has enslaved you just as clearly as the white men of the South enslaved the negro. You did not wear chains, but you have been bought, sold and traded as a commodity just as surely as the wretched negroes.

"White southerners stole negro children away from their parents. Fingy Conners stole the parents of the First Ward away from their children. Conners has stolen the future away from each and every one of you, and the law has stood idly by and allowed it to happen, year after year, decade after decade.

"Where is your esteemed alderman, John P. Sullivan, tonight, I ask you? Where is this Great Hero of the First Ward?" mocked the cleric.

"Where is this so-called champion of the ward, this former laborer with whom many of you present here today worked alongside on the docks? Where is this man who you have continually reelected to the board of aldermen for the past eight years to represent your interests? Sullivan is a friend and partner of Conners! He grew up with Conners, established the rowing club on South Street with him, established the Southside Athletic Club with him. It seems clear to me that your alderman's loyalties are not with the citizens of his ward at all, the voters who put him in office and kept him there all these years, but instead are with his saloon-boss Conners, for Sullivan has demonstrated that he is but yet another soldier in Fingy Conners' army of toadies!

"How can it be that your own leaders in government have completely turned their backs on you? How is it that the Mayor of the city of Buffalo himself, Conrad Diehl, has never uttered one syllable in support of you, his fellow citizens whom he swore under a sacred oath to God Almighty to protect from tyranny and lawlessness?

"How can it be that Sullivan has yet to muster the courage to face the Common Council with your plight, or to be quoted in the newspapers to say even one word in your favor?

"Sullivan won't do it! Diehl won't do it! But I know that you will do it!

"The time has come, my children, for you to inform Fingy Conners in no uncertain terms that his position in this city has been terminated!"

A fervor unmatched in the city's history erupted from the bottled-up torment and heartbreak set free within the clap-board building, unleashed by the truth at last spoken.

After a decade of inflamed anti-Conners rhetoric printed in his Catholic Union and Times, of which he was editor, and resultant threats to his life and limb from Conners and his thugs, Father Patrick Cronin was chomping at the bit to speak next. Cronin, a native of Limerick in Ireland, possessed in large measure the warm-hearted generosity and readiness to help those in need characteristic of his countrymen. He stood before the laborers and spoke passionately about his previous twenty years in Buffalo, having heard daily throughout, the outpourings of anguish from his flock.

"I have been outrageously abused by Mr. Conners' newspapers wherein he has had the hypocrisy to charge me with inciting the scoopers to mutiny and murder. Such outlandish charges made so predictably by Mr. Conners have become infamous in our city. I have counseled you to be law abiding and sober and you have heeded my advice. You have made me proud, and I want to assure you all of Bishop Quigley's fatherly interest in you and your families, and in your future welfare."

Father Cronin pictured the miseries and wrongs of the scoopers in eloquent language.

"It would be nothing but white slavery," shouted the Irish priest so as best to be heard, "to have the saloon boss system continued. The days of long ago, when the poor black in the South was driven to his work by the lash; when negro men, women and children were sold at auction for whatever they could bring; when husbands were separated from their wives, wives from their husbands, and children from their parents by men without scruples and without respect for man's rights or sacred liberties—those days could not have been worse than the slavery to which this man has made you subject for so many years.

"Riches and poverty are accidents. If, through a chapter of accidents a man becomes rich and powerful, his wealth and power do not make him any better than the poor man; they do not give him the right to trample over the poor man; neither do they give him the right to tell this man or that man where he shall buy or drink his beer."

Loud shouts and applause rose up from the legion of Irish drinkers.

"The money you have earned by the sweat of your brow has made this man rich and powerful, but it is blood money, and let no one ever fool himself into believing otherwise! The money has been spent for costly diamonds and other things. This state of affairs has been tolerated long enough—too long, in fact.

But we shall not stand it any longer.

"No one knows better than I, your confessor, what sorts of miseries and pestilence this tyrant has inflicted upon you and your families. I cannot begin to recount the number of sleepless nights I have spent during the last nearly twenty years caused by my tossing and turning over the evil doings of this despotic monster who has not only ruled over you and I, but the very government of our city, our county, and now even the State of New York itself!"

Father Cronin mocked Conners and his empty oaths and broken promises. He predicted God's curse upon the money wrung from the heart of labor by the infamous boss' saloon system.

"Mr. Conners no longer lives among those whom he persecutes. He now occupies a mansion far removed from the First Ward along Delaware Avenue, where his eyes no longer have to be offended by the evil and suffering he has caused, where his ears no longer need be injured by the vile curses he so richly deserves! He has surrounded his estate with a ten foot fence to stop the hurling of paving stones at his head and the dumping of chamber pots over his carriage. He drinks one hundred year-old brandy from France and eats foods prepared in New York's finest restaurants that are rushed here by railway car toward his gluttonous mouth. He wears custom made suits and Italian boots. He not only wears diamond studs in his shirts in place of buttons, but even more vulgarly, in his spats as well!

"When, whether you work for Conners again or whether you do not, let me tell you that his power is gone; his wings have been clipped. He has publicly announced that the saloon boss system has been abolished, but the fact that it was stated in the proposition made to your union by the Lake Carriers' Association that this evil would be abolished is proof that it still exists to this day. Mr. Conners is a bare-faced liar!"

So great a cry as could only be fueled by the recognition of truth filled the hall and flowed out the door and down the street.

"Throughout this struggle you have conducted yourselves like honest, law-abiding citizens. You have been quiet and orderly and thus have gained the sympathy and the respect of the public in general. The victory is yours!"

The hall fairly quaked with men cheering Patrick Cronin's words.

"But let yourselves know this above all things about Fingy Conners, my children," summed the Irish priest, his voice breaking from recalling their torment, "that the diamonds he wears are the crystallized tears of your own women!"

A mighty roar welled up from the deepest recesses of the men's souls upon hearing the gospel truth of the priest's statements, for no one suffered more at the foot of Fingy Conners than their voiceless women.

The men surged forward to shake the hands of the clerics who had boldly stepped down from the protection of their pulpits to enter into the fray of battle.

Together, it was now certain, with the aid of their crusading heroes, the workers would crush Fingy Conners.

A basic agreement was put into writing by the Lake Carriers Association addressing every major complaint to the benefit of the strikers; all that is, except one: Fingy Conners was still planted immovably at the helm.

The scoopers, having won every other point of contention except the only one that really mattered, refused to go back to work.

Another advertisement was placed in the Toronto Globe:

WANTED:
100 Laborers
Good wages, steady work.
—Peter P. Dalton
No. 444 Ohio St.
Buffalo N.Y.

Peter P. Dalton's official job description was "sub-boss" in the employ of Fingy Conners. Dalton had been elected inspector of elections in 1883 alongside John P. Sullivan. Dalton was a charter member of the Mutual Rowing Club and a recent president of that organization, and was a top-ranking henchman in Fingy Conners' gang. Dalton rode the rails back and forth to New York's Bowery to gather the most wretched and desperate souls from that place, and with empty promises and false oaths lured them back to Buffalo to break the strikers.

Conservative men who wielded great influence over the leaders of the grain scoopers lectured the laborers in newsprint that their demand for the complete abolition of the contract system was endangering the points of victory already secured by them, when in fact their only real demand was, and always had been, the firing of Fingy Conners.

Working conditions may have been poor indeed, but Conners' presence was absolutely intolerable, and he had to go. These so-called "conservative men" written of so ominously, especially in the Conners-owned newspapers, The Buffalo Enquirer and the Buffalo Courier, were of course in fact just one single man: Fingy Conners himself, speaking through his subservient editors.

May 8, 1899
The Buffalo News

Hannah put down the newspaper when she heard Jim stirring and began fixing his breakfast. She was heartened reading the news that 200 employees of Grattan & Lattimer at the New York Central freight house had walked out in sympathy for the strikers, even though they had no grievances of their own and their work had nothing to do with the unloading of boats. They read their statement to the gathered news reporters, then marched en masse up Louisiana street to St. Bridget's Hall to join the strikers.

Hannah wasn't the only citizen bristling over the city's many daily newspapers' cowardice in not identifying Fingy Conners by name in their blizzard of news stories about the strike.

"What is this all about, Jim?" she declared as she removed his toast from the hot iron skillet. She was forced to pause a few moments in silence before continuing until the Buffalo Furnace work whistle across Hamburgh street stopped shrieking.

"The newspapers are so afraid of Fingy Conners that they will only refer to him as "the contractor? Everybody knows who 'the contractor' is! Not printing his name is an affront, not just to the strikers, but to every law-abiding man and woman of this city. To each and every one of us. Everyone knows that devil's name! All this silly pretense must end!"

As Jim munched he nodded to appease her and continued reading the Buffalo News. Sipping his scalding coffee carefully, he offered no verbal response, instead concentrating on spreading Hannah's peach preserves thickly to the farthest edges of the hot crispy bread. But Hannah's pointing out this compelling oddity made him take notice that in the six strike-related stories published on this one single page of the News, not in any of them is "the contractor" referred to by the name William J. Conners.

The previous day Jim had arrested one of Fingy's City Elevator employees for pulling his guns on a crowd of strikers. Jim sniffed at not finding himself properly identified in the News' story reporting it:

HE WANTED TROUBLE
Contractor's Employee Flourished Revolver
Near Scoopers' Headquarters.

How admirably self-controlled are the members of new Local 51 is shown by the fact that last night 200 of them got out of the way of a single non-union man who was looking for trouble. The union scoopers retreated and left it for the police to take care of the aggressor.

About 200 scoopers of new Local 51 were standing about Nagel's Hall at Elk and Hayward streets, the Sunday headquarters of the union, when a young man, somewhat the worse for liquor, began parading up and down in the middle of Elk street. He was recognized as Michael Riley, a scooper who is not a member of the union, and therefore no one had anything to say to him.

Then he turned into Hayward street and drew two revolvers, which he began to flourish. Instead of attempting to disarm him, the union men withdrew and notified the police. Ten minutes later a policeman arrived and took Riley to the station house.

"A 'policeman'?" Jim uttered out loud. "They couldn't even get my rank correct?"

On the same page, stories of Fingy's chicanery ate up almost every column inch.

"Read the story about "The New Era Of Labor" if you want a good laugh," Hannah said, sliding two fried eggs onto Jim's plate.

A mysterious new entity, the "New Era Of Labor" had emerged in recent days, another of Fingy Conners' ruses. In an effort to recruit scabs to offset the growing loss of thousands of strikers on the docks, Fingy hatched the plan to rent office space in downtown Buffalo, well away from his customary hiring grounds of his saloons, and establish an employment agency there having the outward appearance of dignity.

Jim located the article and began reading.

An applicant had given his personal account to the Buffalo News:

"Last Thursday," said the man, his name withheld out of fear of re-prisal, "I saw an advertisement in the contractor's afternoon newspa-per stating that 600 men to work for $2 a day for a day of eight hours were wanted at the New Era Of Labor reading rooms, at Eagle and Ellicott streets.

"As I am out of work and have a family dependent upon me," he continued, "I called at 1 P.M. The man at the desk told me the New Era Of Labor required a fee of $2 for securing work for men, but the fee was not to be paid until the position was secured. He put my name down and told me to call again at 2 o'clock.

"At 4 o'clock I went in, and despite it being well past the time I had been told to return, I was told that the position I was looking for was now to be had. He told me there was a chance to go to scooping on the docks at $2 for eight hours work.

"I told him I was no "scab' and didn't want the place. He replied that police protection would be furnished and that steady work could be had all summer, but I wouldn't take the job.

"Last Saturday I saw an advertisement in the contractor's morning paper stating that 25 able-bodied men were wanted to work for $2 a day for a day of eight hours. The ad said that the applicants should call at 248 Main street. I went to that number and found that it was the contractor's newspaper building.

I went to room No. 1 upstairs and there I found the same man that I had seen on Thursday. He alleged that his former rooms had been so mobbed that he was forced to move. Said he: 'You are just in time to go to work on the docks."

There were 10 or 15 men around, and he pointed to those and said,

'Why, look at all these men. They are not afraid. You will have police protection'. But I refused."

The statement of the man were borne out by the published advertisements referred to.

"Interesting. You were right, Hannah," Jim said, finishing the story.

"Fingy demands these men pay him an entire day's wage as a commission for hiring them!" bristled Hannah. "The nerve! He places desperate men in a dangerous position as scabs yet demands a full day's wage paid back to him as a 'fee' for the privilege of getting their skulls cracked! Who else but Fingy Conners would have the audacity to even conjure up such a disgracious scheme!"

"Well, he's your cousin, not mine, Hannah. Maybe you can express all your furious opinions to your brother Dave. I'm sure he'll be glad to pass them on to his uncle-in-law," Jim smiled, trying not to laugh.

Hannah quieted right down at that, tormented as she was by Jim's reminder that, thanks to her brother, she and Fingy Conners were now family.

"All right, I have to get going, sweetheart. I'm late," lied Jim.

He was in no mood this morning for Hannah's rantings concerning the unjust world that tortured her ceaselessly. He kissed his wife and baby David and hollered his goodbyes to Jim Jr. and Nellie, then descended the stairs. He had to sprint to catch the Hamburg street trolley. He found a seat near the front and unfolded his newspaper for some peaceful uninterrupted reading.

At the next stop two teenaged boys got on in the midst of a fight. As they stumbled past Jim, one punched the other in the back of the head. Jim told the conductor to stop the car. He grabbed the two by their necks and tossed the puncher off. The extricated boy shouted his protests of innocence from the sidewalk.

"He started it, officer! He called my mother a whore!"

"Shut your filthy trap! There are decent people here! You can walk from now on! Don't you let me see you riding on my car ever again!"

As the car pulled away, stirring up a whirlwind of soot, the boy shielded his eyes.

Jim heaped his wrath upon the other boy still in his grip.

"If I ever see you pull a disrespectful stunt like this again, I'll brain you! You take your foolish battles to the park and have it out there. Don't you ever impose your anger on innocent people again, or you'll find yourself on this car riding with me all the way to headquarters where a jail cell in the basement awaits you. You hear me?"

The boy nodded with feigned remorse and sat down. No sooner did his butt hit the seat when Jim yanked him back out of it.

"You don't see these ladies standing up waiting for a seat? Where were you raised, boyo? In some polack pig sty in the east side cattle yards?"

The boy stood obediently and entwined his wrist in an overhead leather strap as the driver engaged the car forward. An elderly woman apprehensively took his seat. Jim nailed one final dirty look deep into the boy's eyes and sat himself back down, despite a couple of women standing adjacent.

He settled in and picked up the paper again. His friend and neighbor, M.R.C. member Peter P. Dalton's name caught his eye.

135 DESERTED
Contractor's Attempt To Import Men From New York
Was Very Unsatisfactory.

An effort was made yesterday to bring 150 men here from the Bowery in New York to take the places of the grain shovelers, but it failed. Pete Dalton, one of the chief lieutenants of the Buffalo contractor, went to New York and recruited the men. They were picked up around Harry Ryan's saloon at 49 Bowery and were the usual type of Bowery idlers. A number of them had just arrived from Europe and could not speak or understand the English language.

Out of the 150 men, only 15 went to work at the elevators and it was said about the docks this morning that not one of those 15 would go back to work today.

About midnight Saturday night Dalton started from the Bowery with his 150 recruits. Somehow the men had found out that they were being taken to Buffalo to take the places of men on strike and before he had crossed the ferry with his little army of workingmen the 150 had dwindled to 43. So Mr. Dalton loaded the 43 on the Lackawanna train and started westward.

There was no food and little sleep on the way up from New York, but the men say whisky was furnished in plentiful quantities.

Arriving at Bath N.Y. the men insisted on having something to eat and were each given 25 cents and allowed to leave the train and go into the railroad restaurant. Here again was a general desertion. Of the 43 who got off the train to get something to eat just 29 were on hand for Buffalo when the conductor called 'All aboard!"

The little squad of 29 came on to Buffalo and were met at the station by "Sloak" Slattery, radiant in a green sweater with a yellow border. Outside a bus was waiting. There were also two other vehicles. Two police patrol wagons loaded with patrolmen were in waiting. Slattery marched the men out and jammed them into the bus. But of the 29 who stepped off the train, 14 refused point-blank to get into the bus. That left just 15 of the 150 who originally started from New York. So with the small delegation the procession started for the docks. They formed in this wise: First, 'Sloak' Slattery with a sleek horse and a nice shiny little carriage that flashed and glinted in the sunlight. Second, the patrol wagon from the First Precinct. Third, the bus containing 15 men from the Bowery. Fourth, another patrol wagon with more policemen.

When the procession drew up at Michigan and Ganson streets, 'Sloak' Slattery bounded out of his little carriage and went back to let out the 29 men in the bus. Fourteen of them had disappeared. "Where's de udder guys?" angrily demanded "Sloak."

"Dey's quit de game," replied one of the number, and that was all there was to it.

The 14 who left the gang at the station walked up Main street and were taken in charge by some of the members of the new Local 51 and were taken to St. Bridget's Hall. The other 15 who stuck were taken to

Doyle's saloon on Ganson street where they were given a few drinks and something to eat, and were then taken to the Marine Elevator and put down into the hold of a vessel and put to work. The men complained bitterly because they had been given no chance to sleep and very little to eat since Friday night. Ten out of the 15 who went to work could not speak English. They had recently arrived in New York as immigrants.

The 14 men who left the Bowery contingent at the Lackawanna depot were taken care of by the members of new Local 51. They were quartered at Nagel's Hall and a collection was taken up among the scoopers to pay for their suppers. Today the Buffalo scoopers will call upon the Superintendent of the Poor to see if he cannot send the men back to New York. They sent a committee to Supt. Bull yesterday afternoon and that official told them he could do nothing in the way of sending them back because they all belonged within the State.

Last evening the Bowery men told their stories. They said Dalton had represented to them that there was no strike on in Buffalo. He told them there had been a slight difference between the scoopers and the longshoremen but it was all settled and now men were wanted to push the work as rapidly as possible. The men were promised ten hours' work a day at 25 cents an hour for seven months."

Jim now understood why all those strange Italian faces were in among the crowd of Irish at Nagel's Hall yesterday where Riley had shown up drunk with his revolvers drawn. The unfamiliar faces belonged to the men from the Bowery that the strikers had taken under their wing. Fingy had found out where they were, had gotten Riley drunk, provided him a pistol, then sent him in to take revenge on the deserters. Riley could have easily been killed carrying out this fool's errand for Fingy, his family left destitute to survive on their own. He was lucky, at least this time.

As he tied all these events together in his head Jim felt the emotion of shame surface. He bristled at how the Buffalo Police department, despite the disasters of the past. was nonetheless continuing in its capacity as Fingy Conners' private army. Of course Superintendent "Bullshit" Bull wouldn't intervene in aiding the scabs who'd deserted Fingy return to New York. Bull had been elevated to that office personally by Conners and wasn't about to bite the hand that fed him.

Worse, every copper had someone, friend or family member, who was a striker. And yet there they all were, packed into patrol wagons trailing behind one of Conners' thugs, ready and willing to bash in the heads of their own relatives, church members, and neighbors at the behest of "the contractor."

Jim felt the heat rise his cheeks. He got up and pulled the cord, then left the trolley on Main street to walked the last three blocks to headquarters so as to allow his mind to cool down.

May 11, 1899
The Buffalo Catholic Union and Times Editorial

No other newspaper in the city had the daring or the contemptuousness with which to speak the truth about Fingy Conners that Father Patrick Cronin's powerful Catholic Union and Times did. The newspaper editorialized:

Mr. William J. Conners, fatted prince of the late boss saloon system on the docks, must have been driven to desperation by this newspaper's exposure of his atrocious dens of robbery and degradation when he found it necessary to divert public attention from that infamy by assailing the Union and Times with a tissue of brazen falsehoods.

Mr. Conners declares that the editorial utterances in the Union and Times regarding the scooper troubles have been calculated to inflame to riot and rage the recusant grain shovelers and were of such a nature as to incite to violence and murder.

Mr. Conners is hereby challenged to verify this infamous charge, or else to stand publicly convicted as an atrocious liar.

Mr. Conners knows well—for we are told he can read—that the Union and Times had not only not incited to violence and bloodshed but it has counseled the exact contrary. To quote our very words, we applauded the seceding scoopers "for the admirable order, quiet, sobriety, and discipline they have maintained and we urge them to continue in the same peaceable and law-abiding course and to resolve under the circumstances to be inveigled into quarrels by any studied provocations."

Isn't this a queer way to incite to bloodshed and murder, Mr. Conners? After all, you are said to be an expert in such matters, so you therefore ought to know.

Isn't it notorious that the chief qualifications you require in a boss are his pugilistic accomplishments? Do you want the police records of the thugs who were sent out to provoke the seceding scoopers to violence?

Were not the gang of ruffians who demolished McMahon's Saloon on Elk Street for the purpose of inciting a riot to injure the scoopers' cause, your friends? Do you forget that the first shot fired during the scooper trouble was fired by one of your chief bullies from a ship at a group of scoopers and that this man has a police record that should make even the likes of you ashamed of him?

Such are specimens of the thugs and scoundrels who look up to you, Mr. Conners, as their friend, protector and patron saint. You know they ought to be in the penitentiary, if justice had half its due. And they would be there long since if not for the disgraceful "political pull" that has managed to keep them out.

Are these not the scoundrels who have terrorized the docks for years in your interest? Would not the record of their crimes fill volumes to the horror of the law-abiding citizens of Buffalo? And yet, Mr. Conners, it is generally believed that these are the unconvicted ruffians who are the instruments and tools of your vanities, ambitions and greed. Yet, in the face of these commonly believed infamous associations, you have the audacity to pose before those respectable people of Buffalo who do not know you as the embodiment of honest and chivalrous purpose and to lie in your throat by accusing the Union and Times of inciting to violence and murder the peaceful scoopers who were struggling to emancipate themselves from the dominance of your ferocity and greed.

Mr. Conners, if disgust could down, we should sincerely pity you.

Fr. Patrick Cronin

1899
Ways and Means

By 1899, Fingy Conners had acquired contracts at Buffalo, Chicago, Detroit, Duluth, and Milwaukee to handle business on the docks in these ports. He amassed a number of saloons in each of these places as well. The formula that made him fabulously wealthy continued to remain in place despite his public proclamations in his own newspapers that they were gone: workers continued to be hired out of, and were paid wages at, his saloons. Only those struggling family men with their many hungry mouths to feed at home who spent the most money getting drunk in his resorts were provided work.

Conners had amassed vast real estate holdings as well as contracts to pave Buffalo's city streets and parking lots for the new automobile. He owned the Magnus Beck Brewery, and through the renowned use of the persuasive methods that had served him so well in the past, convinced a substantial number of the city's more than 2,000 saloons to buy their beer exclusively from him. Conners owned two influential city newspapers, the Buffalo Courier and the Buffalo Enquirer, and used them to great advantage in both defending his methods and positions and demonizing his enemies. Conners had a gift for selling property for far more than its worth, whether it be his land to the city for the construction of new schools, or his personal yacht Enquirer, built for $75,000, then sold to the US Government two years later for $120,000 when war was declared with Spain, then bought back from the government for less than $20,000 after he war.

Fingy Conners had long had his four-fingered hand deeply planted in the ballot box as well, placing his friends in the most powerful positions in government and the police department. He paid for personal information on anyone who might be considered a threat or a rival for use in blackmail schemes. He made it his business to know which of the higher-ups were procuring the services of prostitutes and who kept mistresses.

Fingy Conners was a primeval creature having an insatiable appetite for total control, germinated from the seeds of the wounding abuses that had been sown deep within him in his youth. He possessed a limitless capacity for cruelty, directed almost entirely at society's most vulnerable souls: his own people. Because of his astonishing brazenness, relentless aggression and murderous ways, all were in fearful awe of Fingy Conners. He had learned at a young age a lesson that other despots had mastered throughout history as well; if you attack people suddenly, viciously and brutally enough, they will be so preoccupied with just fending you off that they will be too crippled to mount much of a counter attack.

By 1899 Fingy Conners had the lives of 6,000 dock workers around the Great Lakes in Buffalo, Chicago, Detroit, Duluth, and Milwaukee, under his boot heel, earning on average $4.00 a week off each man, for an approximate take of $24,000 a week. This was $24,000 a week that was not going into the stomachs of hungry children, or into local economies, especially that of the impoverished

First Ward and its struggling family businesses. Instead it went directly into Conners' bank account. His system by this time had been honed to such a fine point that only a bare minimum of his workers' pay ever made it past his saloon tills and into their pockets, most of it never reaching the desperate wives and hungry children of his toilers

.

1899
Like Grizzlies Protecting Their Cubs

On Monday afternoon May 15, John Nevels, a boss scooper in the employ of Fingy Conners, was mobbed by a gang of over 100 women and children on the street.

Nevels had been walking up Vincennes Street toward Sandusky when a group of small boys, mostly the sons of scoopers, but also including Thomas Saulter Sullivan, oldest son of the Alderman, tagged after him and called him a scab. Nevels drew his pistol and fired two shots at the children, claiming it was just to scare them.

The shots had a startling effect on all the mothers in the neighborhood, who swarmed from their homes en masse with brooms, clubs and kitchen knives, and joining forces with their children, mobbed Nevels and drove him to the ground. Thereupon he was roundly beaten with fists and the implements at hand. The women relieved him of his revolver, scratched his face and bit him, pulled out chunks of hair and tore his clothes. They had only just begun their fine work on him when two patrolmen unfortunately happened by and rescued Nevels.

He was taken to Police Station No. 7 where he admitted that he had fired two shots at the children. He claimed he did so only after the women attacked him, and that he had fired into the ground, rather than directly at the children. The women angrily countered that their children had been fired upon first, that it was the sound of shots that first alerted them to the attack on their babies. Nevels could not produce a permit for carrying a revolver, claiming "the women must have stolen it from me."

Fingy Conners quickly appeared at the station house, and Nevels was released into his custody.

John Nevels faced no charges.

The news of Nevels' shooting at his own child was the last straw. That so terrifying a straw was required to finally snap the Alderman out of his decade-long self delusion spoke volumes of his cowardice.

Thomas had run the three blocks home without stopping, and sprinted into his house like a shot, the eleven-year-old flinging himself at his pregnant mother for protection. Thomas told her what happened. Annie knew that Jim had not yet left for work. She grabbed Thomas and dragged him next door.

"They shot at my son with a pistol! One of Conners' thugs shot at my little boy!" screamed Annie to her brother-in-law.

Hannah embraced Annie and her nephew and trembled with furious indignation. She was beside herself. She'd long had dreams of clamping her hands around Fingy Conners' throat, going on ten years now. Jim had to physically restrain her. They listened to Thomas' tale again, together.

"I'll put an end to this Annie, I promise you I will!" pledged the infuriated Detective.

Satisfied that he would, Annie went home and placed a telephone call to the City Hall. Enraged, she screamed out the story to the Alderman. JP had to hold the earpiece six inches away, so startling was her volume.

After she hung up the telephone she developed a migraine headache, and needed to go lie down.

Later that night, at about half past midnight, a Fitch Hospital ambulance was dispatched to the end of Kentucky Street. Lying there in the middle of the road was the mangled form of John Nevels, both legs shattered into bloody splinters.

No one saw what happened.

🍀

May 18, 1899
Depew Avenue

Annie Sullivan peeked from behind her curtains cautiously at the men lingering on the opposite side of the street. As they huddled, all turned to look threateningly at the Alderman's house. She was frightened.

Hannah Sullivan had barely acknowledged the Alderman for years now, ever since the Sheehan scandals of six years previous. This proved quite a feat, since they lived next door to each other and family events abounded: graduations, first communions, confirmations, baptisms, birthdays, anniversaries. Then there were all the Mutual Rowing Club events, the list of which had grown to include a celebration for every conceivable holiday, always with some dance, tea, smoker, athletic contest, testimonial dinner, regatta or picnic scheduled.

Yet, despite this continual colliding of the two adversaries, year after year, they hardly attested to each other's existence.

But most recently, the Alderman's gross dereliction of his elected duty and his reprehensible denial of the suffering of the very people who voted him into office was to the point where Hannah was ready to break her silence toward him, if not his neck.

Hannah was fiercely determined that her children would not suffer any consequence of the Alderman's turning his back on his ward. As the scoopers' strike escalated fearfully, Hannah stopped allowing her children to attend any neighborhood event that included the Alderman or their cousins. She well knew the mood on the street and what desperation could do to a person. Her children were not going to be put at risk for the sins of their uncles, neither Jim's brother John P. Sullivan, nor Hannah's brother David Nugent. Every ward child of a freight handler or scooper knew that her children's uncle Dave was married to Fingy Conners' niece and was Fingy's right-hand man. And that their other uncle, the Alderman, was in cahoots with Fingy Conners up to his eyeballs, and always had been. The silence from the Common Council Chambers at the City Hall on the subject of Contractor Fingy Conners and the angry, desperate strikers was shocking, for the subject was never broached there. Commerce had come to a standstill around the entire Great Lakes, yet those in city government found other concerns with which to busy themselves. The strike was making international headlines, affecting grain supplies in Europe, yet the mayor, the aldermen and the supervisors spoke not a single word of it.

For the Sullivan offspring of both brothers, it was a time for laying low and keeping one's head down.

Jim first experienced new insight after Hannah's enraged reaction to the 1893 Police Exam scandal and the Sheehans' colonizers debacle. Then too, there was the overheard revelation that JP had more important matters to attend to than running to his brother's side after his youngest had drowned. Jim's relationship with brother JP had cooled and changed. They were still brothers, still close more or less, but Jim no longer jumped when JP called. He considered very carefully his relationship with JP, assessing each request for his cooperation with a new consideration, that of possible manipulation by his brother. When it was clear that JP was trying to involve his brother in yet another of his messes, Jim thought about it long and hard, and if he got involved at all, it was in a far more conservative fashion than in previous years.

This change in his brother was not lost on JP, for it coincided exactly with that of his own wife. As always, he chose not to confront what was placed directly in his path, but rather to just walk around it making as little consequence of it as he might be allowed.

Jim and Hannah's marriage was thriving once more, having struggled through enormous loss and disappointment. They had come to a better understanding of each other. Both had made changes in themselves in order to forge a stronger bond. As their relationship newly blossomed, so did their family. Whereas the deaths of their babies Hannah Jr. and Daniel had driven them apart, Johnny's drowning had the effect of cementing them back together.

Their newest child, David Nugent Sullivan, had been born robust and healthy on April 30, 1897. He was now two, however, and the apprehensive and increasingly superstitious Hannah could not escape the ghosts of her past. Baby Hannah and baby Daniel had both died at age two. Summer was coming, and along with it the dreaded cholera infantum that caused baby Hannah's death. This disease gave every concerned parent fits and nightmares.

As the warm weather approached it wasn't just disease that Hannah fretted about. The children would be playing outdoors more. She had never been more fearful that her children might be set upon by hooligans due to John Nevels' crazed shooting incident and the increasing public fury against the alderman. She believed her children were now seriously at risk, but certainly less so then JP's own brood of six. Annie was expecting her seventh child in less than a month and she too was afflicted with apprehension.

In his rousing speech at St. Bridget's Hall, widely reprinted in newspapers across the state, Bishop Quigley had shone the brilliant light of damnation on the alderman and the mayor. If JP felt previously like he may have been getting away with something by remaining silent, no longer was he so deluded. The change in attitudes toward him—on the street and in the council— from the moment Quigley's denunciations hit the news pages, was condemning. At long last, the wind had been stolen from the alderman's sails.

Hannah held her own share of accountability for tensions in both Sullivan homes as well. She was realistic about this.

She was forced by irrefutable circumstance to fully acknowledge to herself that her close relationship with her own brother David was every bit as much a factor in her fears for her children as were the sins of her brother-in-law the alderman, if not more so. She had even christened her youngest son with her brother's full name. Fingy Conners had insisted on attending the baby's baptism at St. Bridget's Church. He made a grand display of tucking a $100 bill into the baby's christening gown in full view of everyone's riveted eyes. Hannah felt humiliated by his manipulating her child's sacred day to his own benefit.

With tensions soaring and fear gripping the neighborhood, the two wives of the two brothers living side-by-side tiptoed around their own homes, dispatching Annie's servant girl Sophie to do the shopping for both families. Whenever the two visited each other they checked out the window beforehand to make sure no one suspicious was lurking about out front, then darted between their homes using the back entrance.

Jim fetched the children from school himself every day, in uniform. No longer were they allowed to walk home or ride the streetcar alone.

May 18 was an especially hot day, and pregnant Annie lay on the sofa with a splitting headache, troubled by the mutterings of the gathered men across the street, their angry inflections finding their way in through the open window. Her unborn baby was performing somersaults and her stomach felt deeply nauseous when suddenly a brick came crashing through the parlor window where their girl Sophie sat on the carpet playing with Genevieve, 4, and John Paul, almost 3 . All were showered with glass. Annie bolted, grabbing her youngest, while Sophie snatched up Genevieve. Annie flew to the telephone and screamed at the operator, "Quick, connect me to the City Hall!"

The brick had a note tied around it. Get out! was the message.

JP immediately rented a lovely big house on upper-crust Depew Street, far from the First Ward's chaos. The crew from the Sullivan Ice Co. was dispatched in company trucks to move the family's furniture. Afterward patrolmen were assigned to guard the alderman's abandoned home at No. 12 Hamburgh Street around the clock.

With Annie and all the nieces and nephews gone it was eerily quiet. Hannah felt quite isolated now, and newly vulnerable. Jim arranged for the patrolmen to keep a close eye on his own home next door as well, especially while he was away at work. Hannah had already asked her brother Dave to stay away until things resolved themselves. Events at the Mutual boathouse, even the Decoration Day picnic that had been the linchpin of the summer season for the past 18 years, were canceled. The historically close knit First Ward was now evenly split between those who despised Fingy Conners and those who were terrified of him.

Teddy

Bishop Quigley called a morning meeting with six representatives of the Great Lakes Carriers Association in the parlor of his Delaware avenue mansion.

Throughout the conference he steadied his feisty Jack Russell terrier Teddy dotingly on his lap.

"Gentlemen, this point is not negotiable!" exclaimed the Bishop in exasperation, stroking Teddy to help calm himself. "You have turned the business of hiring workers over to a veritable dictator! An enslaver of humanity who pays for the labors of family men in alcohol! Exactly what wrongs do you not see transpiring here? Boss Conners must go if you expect these men to return to work!"

"Bishop, sir," replied Harvey D. Goulder, attorney for the Lake Carriers Association, "you place us in an untenable position! Mr. Conners allowed my clients to flourish following decades of strife and turmoil on the docks. Thanks to him, business for everyone involved in the shipping industry is thriving. Customers are being well served and expediently so. Profits are up markedly. Many thousands of working men are gainfully employed. Do you really expect us to trade all that away? To go back to the way things were? You must suggest some other alternative!"

"There is no alternative, Mr. Goulder! Gentlemen, the present standards you operate under are inhumane! You might be thriving at present, but the cost for your personal prosperity is the enormous suffering and misery of thousands of men, women and small children! Thousands! Do you yourselves not have any children?"

The men huddled and conferred among themselves. Teddy, seeing his master upset, barked at the bad men.

Attorney Goulder stood and began gathering his things.

"Bishop, we quit. We will negotiate no further. If you wish to continue in your role as negotiator for your men, then fine, but you will have to deal directly with Mr. Conners himself. We are out of this."

The Bishop was dumbfounded as all rose to leave.

"Gentlemen, come to your senses! Stepping away from the table does not absolve you of your moral responsibility!"

The men simply shrugged, then exited. The Bishop's little guard dog followed after, yapping and scolding.

"Teddy! Teddy, you come back here, right now!"

Teddy stopped for a moment to gaze back at the Bishop, then trotted disobediently out the door, berating the departing guests from the top step until their carriages were well down the avenue. Quigley stood in the doorway and laughed at Teddy's spunk.

"That's it, Teddy. You tell those terrible men all about it! You and me, we're not going to let them get away with this quite so easily!"

Teddy jumped into Quigley's arms and kissed him thoroughly, causing the Bishop to laugh adoringly at his surrogate offspring.

At half-past noon Fingy dined with Attorney Goulder at the exclusive Buffalo Club. They sat beneath an oil portrait of Buffalo Club member Grover Cleveland. Goulder shared with Conners all the details of the morning conference he'd just conducted with the Bishop. Businessmen stopped by the table to pay their respects, mindful of Fingy's recent loss.

Soon after, JP entered the dining room in the company of fellow aldermen to enjoy lunch. Spotting Fingy, he excused himself and approached Fingy's table.

"Fingy, I need to speak with you," he said quietly.

Without looking up from his steak, Fingy replied, "I'm busy."

"Yes, I'm busy too," countered JP. "But things have gotten far out of hand. You won't return my telephone calls and you've been avoiding me."

Fingy expertly cut his rib eye, still avoiding eye contact with JP.

"We'll talk tomorrow, I said. As youse kin see I'm in an important meetin' right now. "

JP was being dismissed. Sheepishly he began to walk away. Then having second thoughts, he turned back and faced Fingy.

"No. We'll talk now. Do you mind Mr. Goulder?"

Goulder looked surprised. "Why, uh, no, alderman. I'll just..."

"Sit back down Goulder! I said tomorrow, JP!"

"No, Fingy! I've had it! My boy was shot at by one of your men! A brick was thrown through my parlor window and bloodied my baby! I have gangs of laborers menacing me, threatening me on my own front steps! I spent the whole morning arranging to rent a safe house in Central Park for my family to move into!"

Every eye in the elegant dining room was squarely upon the heated confrontation.

JP continued.

"I am under attack! The time has come for you to face this situation! Every religious leader in the city is screaming for my resignation – and for yours!"

"So, resign then. Go ahead," the disinterested saloon boss shot back. "What's stoppin' youse? Youse served yer purpose. As fer me, I ain't goin' no place. Now go. Get outa here. Yer weak. An' yer makin' a fool o' yerself."

Unruffled and calm, Fingy proceeded conferring with Goulder as if the alderman lingering there had disappeared and nothing out of the ordinary had just happened. He clearly ruled the room.

JP stormed out, infuriated.

Provocation

Hannah sat quietly at the kitchen table with a cup of coffee after the kids had gone to school. She peeked out the window to make sure the assigned patrolman was stationed there on his watch. She looked at the folded newspaper debating whether to open it. It only made her angry to read the news, but she was torn between needing to know what was going on and not wanting another knot tied in her stomach once she put the newspaper down.

She opened it and began reading. Fingy's apologists were quoted as justifying his saloon boss methods by explaining that Conners wasn't treating his workers or anyone else for that matter any worse than he himself had been treated when he was in their place.

"If that's his idea of a just and proper exoneration, now I understand why so many people who were beaten by their own parents feel it's defensible to turn around and strap their own kids!" sniffed Hannah out loud. "What sort of convoluted rationale is that?!"

Fingy Conners' world had for some time now been relocated to a glorious mansion among the city's most elite citizens, at 1140 Delaware Avenue. There was a photograph of it in the paper accompanying the article. The story delighted in telling of his wealthy neighbors deriding and mocking him: his vulgar speech, his vulgar attire, his vulgar mansion. Among his closest neighbors, the newspaper noted, was the residence and Chapel of James E. Quigley, Bishop of the Catholic Diocese of Buffalo. How remarkable that these two great adversaries would end up residing just a minute's stroll apart from each other.

"Interesting," Conners had been quoted as saying in response to the mocking Buffalo Times article about him after his Buffalo Courier editors had cleaned up all his bad grammar, "that people who were born into wealth they did absolutely nothing to earn feel themselves superior to those of us who acquired it through our own hard work and ingenuity."

"Hmmmph! Ingenuity! Is that what that little bulldog is calling the enslaving of good and honest people now?" she snorted upon reading the passage.

That same day a mass meeting was called for the strikers, and the hall was jammed with a feverish crowd. Bishop Quigley had been negotiating a contract on their behalf all day every day for a week, and was exhausted.

A scooper named Michael McNamara had been murdered on Elk Street for refusing to join in the strike. A boss-shoveler named Bill "Bishop" Kennedy, nephew of Alderman John Kennedy of the 19th, was shot through the lung in retaliation after answering a challenge to dare cross the street into the First Ward. Buck Skinner did the shooting though there were plenty of so-called eyewitnesses who swore he didn't. They claimed the shooter was instead a doppelganger of Skinner's. Kennedy died. Things were tense.

These kinds of altercations did not bode well for the plans that Conners was hatching for bringing in full trainloads of strike breakers from Toronto, New York and Cleveland.

The evening of May 14th at St. Bridget's Hall, the Bishop and Father Cronin, hoping to avoid any such further violent confrontations, persuaded the strikers to return to work the following day while final details could be hammered out in their new agreement.

The following morning, May 15, large numbers of obedient scoopers showed up to the various elevators with the intent to work, but were met with the demand to show "working cards" issued by Conners. None of the scoopers had any idea what was meant by this for they had never seen such a document. The scoopers later declared that the demand to present the card was made not just by the boss scoopers but also by the police, who, they declared, would not allow them on the docks unless they could produce one. This, and the fact they found there many men present who they termed as scabs working at the elevators, caused them to abandon the idea of going back to work.

The men walked peacefully back to St. Bridget's Hall, despite Conners' devising a situation clearly calculated to bait them to violence and hopefully win some measure of public opinion over to his side. At St. Bridget's they discussed the situation, and declared that Conners would have to fire all the scabs before he could hope for the return of the regular scoopers.

Union President McMahon reminded the men that it was stipulated in the Lake Carriers Association agreement that if the contractor, Conners, did not live up to the agreement, that the Lake Carriers Association would take the contract away from him.

McMahon said, "Let's wait and see what the Association does."

The strikers did not have to wait long.

Conners claimed that the scoopers refused to work without cause. He lied, claiming that he had fired all the boss scoopers as had been demanded, when in fact they were all still in their original positions, down to the last man. In a lifetime of lies and false accusations, these audacious distortions were most preposterous.

In frustration the Lake Carriers' Association promptly withdrew from the fray altogether, leaving Conners alone to fight it out all by himself.

Later that evening, Bishop Quigley headed up a meeting at St. Bridget's Hall. Caps came off and cheers went up as the Bishop entered with his dog Teddy on a lash and quickly took the podium. Teddy lay right down next to his master at the ready to protect him, to the amusement of the men.

"Gentlemen, I am very glad to meet you here tonight and to see that you are not discouraged at all by the occurrences of today. In fact it seems to me that you are more determined and steadfast than ever. I am not in the least discouraged, dispirited or disheartened in the face of the existing conditions.

"By reason of what occurred earlier today at the Great Northern, the Coatsworth, the Dakota and the other grain elevators, my position is very much stronger tonight than it was last night. This morning you uncovered another face of the situation to the public view, and that new face is of the greatest credit to you.

"You went to work this morning in accordance to our advice. When you reached the docks you found certain obstacles in your way which amounted to a rebuff and insult to you, and like honest, sober men, you walked away peacefully, back here to this annex to consult with one another, notwithstanding Mr. Conners' insidious provocation of you to cause trouble, which was great. You remained just as orderly and just as good law-abiding citizens as you had been before. God bless you for that.

"I won't ask you to go to work tomorrow or the next day, or the next. What we must do is establish as a settled fact that no man shall be employed there but members of your own union."

The men cheered him wildly.

James Quigley smiled.

"Now, isn't our position stronger today than it was yesterday? William J. Conners has driven me to take this stand and I'll take it and stick to it until the victory is won!"

The crowd roared.

"There will be no more men working on the docks whom you call scabs..." He was forced to stop until the cheering ended. "...as...as an obstacle when you go back to your work. You shall not go back to work until the trouble of the freight handlers and of all the other men who have stood by you is settled. With all these men united in one common cause, we will be so strong that nothing can defeat us. While we are settling your troubles, my representative Mr. Donovan will be down on the docks getting things ready for you. Behind us will be, as now, a public opinion which will be irresistible. It will be arraigned in our behalf in one solid wall of protest against oppression and injustice. Thank you."

The men stood and cheered and applauded fiercely for the Bishop.

Union official Mahany came to the front and spoke next.

"Contractor Conners broke practically every one of the provisions of the agreement today. I say, that when a trusted association like the Lake Carriers Association enters into a solemn compact affecting the welfare of 3,000 men and their families, as well as the prosperity of the greatest port on the Great Lakes, they should see to it that there is sufficient force back of it to make it valid.

"When a man tells the Lake Carriers Association that it can set for him and gives to it plenary powers to bring about by solemn conference the rectification of evils that are running sores in this community, and then breaks the agreement which the association makes, he writes himself as unworthy of the respect of the least honorable and least intelligent of the 100,000 persons who make up this community.

"Fingy Conners has gone looking for trouble from the beginning. He was looking for trouble this morning and he will find a full and plenty of it. What he has done will cause the people of this city to rise up as a unit to demand the rectifying of the wrongs which he has perpetrated upon the army of men upon the docks. Conners has precipitated the very trouble which has led us here today, that has led to the demand for the forfeiture of the charter of the old grain shovelers' union which will be made immediately. And if the commerce of this great port is disastrously affected, the blame will rest on his shoulders, and the public will know it. The public will realize, once and for all and without question that Conners places his personal and political interests above the welfare of 3,000 laboring men and holds those selfish interests paramount to the well-being of the entire community. He has without so much as a second's hesitation as to the dire consequences for all, placed the economy of the entire city of Buffalo in harm's way.

"I say that the solid wall of public condemnation which has been raised against Mr. Conners by his own act of violating his solemn pledges will result in your victory and his everlasting defeat!"

The Bishop was overwhelmed by the men wishing to shake his hand and pat

Striking workers congregate out front of St. Briget's Hall on Louisiana St. in Buffalo, May 1899.

his back. He stooped to pick up Teddy to prevent his being stepped on. Detective Jim Sullivan pried his way through the gauntlet with an urgent message. As the Bishop headed toward his carriage, Sullivan told Quigley the bad news.

"Bishop, it's about your cook, Mrs. Shea. She was run down by an automobile near the Chippewa market. She's been taken to the Sisters Hospital.

"Good God, no!" gasped the Bishop. "Is she expected to survive?"

"She's in a very bad state, I'm afraid. Her son and daughter are with her now. You must hurry and come as soon as you can to give her last rites.

"Yes! Certainly! What about the person who ran over her?"

"The automobile never stopped. We have a description, but it's not much of one."

"How much description is necessary, Detective? There can't be more than fifty automobiles in the entire city! It should be a simple matter to track down the scoundrel!"

"We're trying our best, Bishop."

"All right. I'll leave for the hospital as soon as I stop at home for my Viaticum. Thank you for coming here to inform me, Detective."

Quigley made a quick sign of the cross as his carriage sped away from the ebullient crowd. Teddy barked gleefully at all his new friends as they raced away.

Twenty minutes later the carriage pulled up to the Bishop's mansion. The Bishop quickly alighted. It was almost dark. He instructed his driver to wait.

"I'll be less than five minutes, Patrick. C'mon, Teddy."

As Quigley climbed the front stairs, housekeeper Mrs. Minehan opened the door. The porch light was out.

"Go pee, Teddy. I'll be right out. Go!"

Teddy trotted out onto the front lawn under the thickly-leaved maple.

"Why is that light not on, Nora?"

I -- I don't know, Your Excellency."

"Nora, Mrs. Shea has been in an accident. I am leaving again immediately for the hospital."

"Oh my God! What happened, Bishop?

"She was hit by an automobile, that's all I know. I will tell you more when I return."

The Bishop hurried toward his room. He threw some water on his face, then grabbed the handle of the small wood Viaticum cabinet and quickly headed out. At the front door he pushed the wall switch. The porch light did not respond. He stepped out onto the darkened verandah.

Quigley was suddenly halted dead in his tracks. The sound of faint squeaking and wheezing startled him. He spotted something moving on the floor in the dim light. Approaching cautiously, he saw Teddy. He saw blood. A huge puddle of blood. Teddy's throat has been slashed. He was gasping in the last throes of death.

Horrified, Quigley dropped to his knees and tenderly surrounded Teddy with his arms. His beloved dog stopped breathing.

"Oh, Teddy! My sweet, faithful, innocent little boy! Oh, dear, dear God, no!"

Quigley pressed his face tightly against Teddy's, kissing him frantically. Mrs. Minehan rushed out onto the verandah with an oil lamp in a panic. Seeing the horrific scene, she screamed and fell to her knees. Patrick, hearing their wailing, jumped from the waiting rig with a club in his hand and raced toward the mournful cries. Nora placed the lamp on floor and stroked Teddy. His nose was already cool to the touch.

"What in the name of God!" cried Patrick, before running back down the stairs to see if he could catch the murderer. He ran back toward the chapel where the darkness might best hide the culprit.

The oil lamp illuminated a flood of tears rolling down the Bishop's cheeks into Teddy's vacant eyes. Quigley loudly sobbed as Nora wailed in the ancient Irish manner.

Their grief for Teddy was naked and unashamed, as was their fear.

At Mrs. Shea's bedside, his clothing stained with Teddy's blood, his hands shaking, Quigley opened his viaticum. He removed the spoon, silver dish, a bottle of holy water, a crucifix, a set of thorns, candles and a box of absorbent cotton.

He set about performing the sacrament of last rites as Mrs. Shea's diminutive chest imperceptibly expanded with her final breaths. As Quigley uttered his last prayers, almost as if she knew she was now ready to enter heaven, her breathing ceased. Tears again filled his eyes. He stood as if paralyzed, transfixed both by the tragedy lying before him and the stains of the tragedy of the hour preceding.

The nurse, a stern, mature nun dressed in a white habit, pulled the sheet over Mrs. Shea's tortured face, turned to him and said, "You can't afford to be waiting around for God Himself to step in and sort everything out, your Excellency. He made you our Bishop for a reason."

Bishop Quigley

May 18, 1899
Out For The Bishop's Blood

Quigley stood before the jammed hall nervously, visibly shaken, and continued his address.

"...and thus, having said that, I will keep this visit brief. I know it may be difficult for you to understand the wisdom behind my newest plan, gentlemen, but I assure you that upon reflection you will come to see its prudence much more clearly. I am now asking you to accept the terms offered by Mr. Conners and hold yourselves in readiness to return to work as soon as Mr. Conners gives the go-ahead. Thank you."

For a moment a thousand men stood motionless in stunned silence. The Bishop quickly departed the podium. Bedlam erupted. Men rushed to confront him. Police intervened and cleared a path.

"Whaddya mean, return to work under Fingy Conners? What kind of rotten deal have you made with that living Satan in our name, Bishop?" cried one laborer.

"Traitor!" screamed another.

The men who packed the venue and those who stood outside on Louisiana Street could not believe their own ears. The Bishop, after all his inspirational exhortations and grandstanding, was suddenly urging the strikers back to work with their chief demand unmet — back under the unbearable yoke of Fingy Conners.

St. Bridget's Hall erupted in a primeval melee.

The crowd was infuriated by this about-face and blatant betrayal. Bone-weary bewildered men shouted out vulgar expletives at the priest who just days before they had been deifying. A few of the many who had brought pistols were tempted to draw them on the turncoat cleric. Then, when the angered and lecturing Bishop had the nerve to order the upset strikers, now cut off at the knees, to hold no further meetings, essentially calling an end to the strike without having settled it, it was a miracle the cleric got out of the Hall with his balls still attached.

Quigley had railed continually for almost fifteen years against Conners. He had lobbied the Protestant clergy and the Jewish rabbis to join with him in condemning Fingy Conners from their houses of worship for the evils he had created and continued to spread. And now, after thousands of men had gone out on strike to bring an end to the saloon-boss system once and for all, Quigley was telling them that accepting the contract that was being offered and going back to work for Fingy Conners was "the right thing to do for your suffering families."

"Who does he think he is, orderin' us not to hold no further meetin's, as if he's the boss of us? We're in this fight til the end!" shouted an irate laborer.

Loyal Catholics they may have been, but fools they certainly were not.

Fingy Conners had somehow gotten to the Bishop, the last person they had ever expected to be vulnerable to Conners' intimidations.

The laboring masses who had entrusted the priest with their future were enraged. Some were irrational. Sensing what ill might befall him, Father Cronin hurried the Bishop out of the Hall and into his carriage, and the two priests sped away from the boiling crowd.

As his coach raced in the direction of Delaware Avenue, the perspiring Bishop berated himself remorsefully over what he had just done. Over his lapse in character and leadership. About the fears he now had for his own life. These latest sins, the priest was aware, were a fear-induced reaction to the most recent threats against him, stemming from the aged sins that Conners had confessed to him almost fifteen years previous.

Quigley was well prescibed concerning the sort of monster Conners was. He had been thoroughly versed by the sinner himself in the details associated with the barbarian's past transgressions. He did not underestimate the levels of violence that Conners was capable of, for the evidences of this, which had kept the hospitals and county morgue bustling, had long gone unpunished. But now they had come home to roost on the Bishop's own doorstep. The details surrounding Conners' ancient confession and the revulsion it had instilled in him were now ruling the very direction of Quigley's life, and by default, his starving flock in the First Ward and those around the Great Lakes.

In his later recollections Quigley would recount that the very moment in which he experienced his greatest fear, he was jolted with the power of the Holy Spirit so violently that it nearly knocked him out of his speeding carriage. He had received a calling from the Lord Himself, as reminded by Mrs. Shea's nurse, who told him that this state of affairs must now come to an irrevocable end; that God had chosen James E. Quigley to end it.

The Bishop had spent his most recent months fearing the personal ramifications of Fingy Conners' confession of long ago. But now Quigley understood without question that Conners' confession — and he having been being chosen as the priest to hear it — instead of being a curse had truly been a gift from God.

Quigley, in a flash of exhilarating sacred enlightenment, determined that the very same catastrophe that had been controlling him must be now turned around to control the controller.

Any other priest suffering his predicament might have gone back to his church and locked the door behind him, consumed with foreboding. But Quigley wasn't any other priest. He took to his bed with a glass of warm milk infused with a shot of Canadian Club where he lay on his back with his arms wrapped around his pillow hypnotized by the lamp patterns dancing gaily on the ceiling until he drifted off to sleep.

The following day St. Bridget's Hall, the headquarters of the strikers and the private property of the Buffalo Catholic Diocese, was closed to the strikers and locked on orders from the Bishop.

Even though eighty percent of the strikers were Roman Catholic, a great number of them repudiated the Bishop thunderingly, vowed not to accept his advice any longer and to remove their headquarters to Fillmore Hall.

Shortly after 3 o'clock that afternoon, over a thousand mostly Irish scoopers formed a line in front of the Hall. There they were joined by more than a thousand Poles and hundreds of Italians. Their intention was to parade through the city in a show of strength. Police Superintendent Bull tried to put a stop to it, fearing it would incite a riot. Precinct Captain Martin halted the marchers at the Corner of Louisiana and Elk, demanding permits.

The marchers had none, so they turned and simply marched in the other direction, picking up thousands more supporters along their route as they proceeded downtown, through Niagara Square, up Delaware Ave. and past the mansions of Fingy Conners and Bishop Quigley.

The somber peaceful group, now almost bereft of hope, marched onward beneath the optimistic gaily colored banners strung across the city's main streets advertising the upcoming Pan American Exposition of 1901. As the marchers reached the mansions of Fingy Conners and Bishop Quigley, their pace slowed. Thousands of angry eyes riveted upon the palatial home of Fingy Conners as the Conners children hid behind velvet window curtains in fear, watching, Fingy having isolated himself from his offspring in his library.

Fingy too lurked at a window, apprehensively watching the barely controlled mob stalk past, paranoid that each set of eyes must certainly be memorizing his address.

Panicked, seven-year-old daughter Katie ran into the study without knocking in direct disobedience of her father's standing order.

"Oh Papa! Why are all those men outside shouting at us? I'm scared!"

So unnerved was he by his child's panicked intrusion that Fingy exploded.

"Bridget! Come in here now!"

The nanny soon appeared, looking white as a sheet.

"Bridget, take the children away from the windows! What's wrong wit' youse? Take 'em down to the basement t' the swimming pool."

"Yes, sir Mr. Conners, I'm sorry! I was just..."

"Shut up! Go!"

Bridget grabbed Katie's hand. As they exited Katie looked back beseechingly at her father. Hoping for a parent's comfort or some explanation of why they were under siege, she would receive neither.

Burdened and isolated, Fingy dropped heavily into his favorite leather armchair. He picked up a large exquisite album inscribed "In Loving Memory Of Peter Newell Conners."

The first page displayed a formal photograph of the handsome boy in uniform. Subsequent pages preserved news clippings, letters of condolence, and the cards that accompanied floral tributes.

On a card signed, "Theodore Roosevelt," a tear plopped down, smearing the ink.

Outside, Union President Pat McMahon headed the parade. He wore his signature eye patch. In his youth, as now, Skinny Pat was a good shot, only these days he was much better fed. A news reporter joined McMahon, scribbling in his pad as he tried to keep up.

"My men voted unanimously to refuse to work as long as Fingy Conners holds the Lake Carriers Association Contract,' spoke McMahon. "As their Union President I am officially stating that is our final word."

"What about Bishop Quigley, Mr. McMahon? What does he have to say about all this?"

With no lack of bitterness, McMahon replied. "You can tell the people of Buffalo that the scoopers are officially firing Bishop Quigley. In his utter uselessness and betrayal he can pack up his bags and depart this city for all we care. Perhaps Chicago's thugs in The Chute might wish to cut secret deals with him as connivingly as did Fingy Conners!"

"What do you hope to accomplish," countered the reporter, "marching this great army of yours past the homes of Boss Conners and Bishop Quigley, sir?"

"We are here to demonstrate our will and our determination, but even more persuasively, our numbers."

The massive river of desperate men finally disappeared from view outside Fingy's window, but he felt little relief. He secretly feared this might only be the beginning of the end of the unchallenged life he had known and cherished up until now.

Ultimately the parade headed back to Fillmore Hall where the men voted unanimously to refuse to go to work as long as Conners held the contract.

The public announcement that the strikers had officially fired Bishop Quigley was made. Amid the cheers there were also a few tears.

The original striking grain scoopers and freight handlers were newly joined by the striking Ore Handlers United, the International Union of Engineers, the waterfront firemen, and the coal heavers.

Work and commerce on Buffalo's riverfront ground to a complete halt.

Bishop Quigley's mansion and chapel.

449

Come, Take A Seat

The following evening the grain scoopers again amassed noisily, this time at their new home, Fillmore Hall, angrily restating an end to their association with the Bishop.

At the same moment, Fingy Conners, his henchmen the Kennedys and Hannah Sullivan's brother David Nugent all stood at the portal of the mansion that was the official residence of the Catholic Bishop of Buffalo. Fingy pounded on the heavy door with his meaty fist. David Nugent cast down his eyes to the spot where he had deposited the dying Teddy and noticed it no longer showed any hint of blood.

Quigley had been expecting Conners to call, unannounced as his visit may have been. The housekeeper answered the door.

"We wanna speak wit' the Bishop," Fingy demanded.

"His Excellency is in the sacristy," Nora Minehan spat out venomously, pointing toward the beautiful chapel neighboring the home.

She looked down to the place where Teddy had died, then fixed her eyes on Fingy.

"I cleaned it up so as not to worry yourself about havin' to leave here with blood on your hands."

Then she angrily slammed the door in their faces.

The men stalked next door and tried opening the chapel door, but it was locked. Fingy pounded.

They heard approaching footsteps having a familiar rhythm. The church door opened, and there stood Alderman John P. Sullivan.

"What a surprise, gentlemen. What may I do for you?"

The men were utterly taken aback, believing the element of surprise was to their advantage, and that their combined powers of intimidation could be used to persuade the Bishop to continue seeing things Conners' way.

The church door opened wider. From behind the alderman emerged his brother, Detective Sergeant Jim Sullivan, who locked his brother-in-law David Nugent in a gaze of contempt.

Then appeared Captain Mike Regan, the Crowley brothers undertakers, and finally, Buffalo's Mayor, Conrad Diehl.

"Gentlemen," nodded the mayor, somberly.

"Where's the Bishop? I wanna speak wit' him," dictated Fingy, in a somewhat more subdued tone than that of a few moments preceding.

"The Bishop has asked to speak with you, and you alone, Mr. Conners," the mayor said to Fingy. "In private. He wants the rest of us to leave and wait outside by the front curb."

Fingy's men all looked at one another.

"Shall we?" Alderman Sullivan invited, motioning the men outside.

Fingy nodded his agreement to his men. The mayor, the captain, the alderman, the detective sergeant, the in-law and the rest of the retinue all walked toward the curb to wait. Fingy stepped inside the church as the heavy wooden doors closed him in with an ominous thud. The Bishop was seated adjacent to the altar.

"Come, take a seat," Quigley invited, his voice echoing off the marble and stone.

Conners strode imperiously up to the altar, threw open the little gate, did not close it behind him, climbed a couple of steps, neglected to genuflect, and approached the Bishop, who remained seated.

"Remember that you're in the house of the Lord," Quigley cautioned, gesturing toward the chalice that sat on the altar. "Would you like to take communion, Mr. Conners?" asked the Bishop.

"No, I don't want yer fuckin' communion!" Fingy shot back, angrily. He remained standing, like a defiant little fireplug.

"Mind your language. You are in God's house!," scolded the Bishop.

The cleric extended his legs and admired the shine on his custom-made shoes, then began.

"One Saturday afternoon some years ago, Mr. Conners, I was hearing confessions at St. Joseph's Cathedral when a very drunk and disquieted man knelt on the other side of my partition and confessed things so appalling and shocking, that even a priest with my experiences in the slums of Naples was shaken to his core."

Quigley stopped for effect and to gauge the response in the face of Fingy Conners. Most all the Irish ruddiness drained from it. Involuntarily,   Fingy swallowed hard, though he tried his best to disguise his reaction. He had never determined the identity of his confessor of long ago.

"The following day, a very tall policeman came to my door and warned me that he had thrown a man having violence in his eyes into the gutter who was wanting to approach the church, and perhaps me in particular. I made my inquiries as to his identity, and I believe that same man is here with you tonight."

"Jus who do youse think youse are, priest?" All the hard-practiced diction Fingy had studied to allow himself more respectability flew out the window, and back flowed the repressed street lingo of the obscene dock-walloper.

"Do you know the penalty for interfering with the business of the Holy Catholic Church, Mr. Conners?"

"Can't be no more regrettable than youse interferin' wit me own business that don't concern the likes of youse, Quigley. Ye'll find out! An' youse think jus' because yer a West Point man, that impresses the likes of me?"

The Bishop paused for a moment and took in the sight of him, Conners with a wet cigar stump clamped between his teeth.

"Oh, but your soul, Mr. Conners! Your soul is my business! Surely you must know that, being the fine Catholic you are."

Quigley chuckled at his own sarcasm.

"I have been a priest for a long time, Mr. Conners. In my early studies in Italy I encountered people who, without any qualms at all, committed the most vile and egregious acts upon the weak, including their own children. The Church teaches that we as priests must forgive; that forgiving is our job as well as our duty. But as the years passed, and as terrible crimes against the weak continued to be re confessed to me by the very same men, over and again, I knew I had to make a difficult decision. I was at first deeply torn.

"The conclusion I arrived at was this: that God had created me in his own image. That literally, I, and indeed all of us, possess God-like attributes that He in his wisdom and generosity bestowed upon us. Among His many gifts was a wondrous and intelligent mind infused with the ability — dare I say, the responsibility — to judge for ourselves what is right and what is wrong."

"Youse git somethin' straight. Youse threaten Jim Conners and youse're gonna regret it ever happened."

Quigley wondered for a moment about just how much of an education this Conners creature had ever received, if any.

"Have you ever studied The Inquisition, Mr. Conners?"

"Ain't never heard of it."

"The Inquisition was a terrible event that lasted more than a century in its most heinous form. It was a reign of terror and extreme torture perpetrated on the citizens of Europe for the most minor of perceived slights in opposition to the Catholic Church, as determined by any local clergyman, purely upon his own whim. These same priests engaged in — relished, in fact — extreme methods of torture that were deranged in nature to say the very least. They committed these lunatic atrocities in a wholesale manner in the name of the Church. In the name of God the Holy Spirit.

"Religion, I'm afraid to say, has unfortunately throughout history provided a safe, unchallenged haven for the demented, even to this very day. Horrific crimes committed in God's name by these priests were not considered to be as such, nor were they punished. The worst degenerates in history have carried out their heinous deeds shielded beneath the cloak of religion.

"Yet nowhere in my many searches on the subject of The Inquisition in the Vatican Library did I ever uncover anything remotely resembling an apology by the Church, or even any direct acknowledgement of this barbarity and savagery committed in the name of Jesus Christ by the Church's own priests. This long, horrible, sorry chapter was hidden, not spoken of. As a young, naive, once-trusting Catholic priest, I found the Church's hypocrisy on this matter to be so extreme, so in opposition to what the Church claimed to stand for in my own mind, that I almost lost my faith over it, and I considered leaving the priesthood.

"I love my God, Mr. Conners, and I too love my Church. My God is perfect. But my Church is not. I realized that God put me on this earth not to do the bidding of other churchmen pretending to know better than I, but to do His bidding; to follow and spread His teachings, His laws...not the laws invented by a flawed Church ruled by errant humans. And so I made use of the God-given brain that He provided me to conclude that there were precepts prescribed by the Church that were clearly in opposition to the teachings of God. Some of these precepts were merely the inventions of priests seeking to increase their own power and wealth, such as the rule regarding eating meat on Fridays, for which the fish monger rewarded them richly."

Fingy tried to interject.

"Enough! Youse jus' git somethin' straight in yer head right now, Quigley. Continue pickin' a row wit' me and youse gonna regret it. Youse shoulda learnt yer lesson hard enough already only just recently!"

Quigley strengthened his voice and steeled his demeanor.

"One day!" the Bishop commanded, "... after a man confessed to me that he was beating and defiling his own daughters and sons, and that his daughters

452

were birthing his children, and he had begun also defiling those babies, I went to the Protestant authorities, who do not care much about the sanctity of the Catholic confessional. They apprehended this demon and threw his execrable carcass into the deepest dungeon that could be found in the region, and I relished the slow process of the diseases that rotted him there.

"What you have done in your past, Mr. Conners, is so vile and monstrous, that unless you relinquish your saloon-boss role in the contracting business — tonight — in front of those men waiting outside, and free your serfs from bondage, the world will immediately come to learn what has caused you to become the perverted and grotesque individual I see perspiring here before me now."

"Ha! Ye can't do it! A man's confession is sacred! We're standing right here in yer fuckin' Catholic church, priest, in front of yer fuckin' Jesus Christ, youse fuckin' fake!" spat the pugilist, taking a fighter's stance and raising his fists.

Quigley laughed heartily.

"I'm delighted to hear you profess that. That you believe so fervently in the Seal Of The Confessional. Because shortly after you came to my confessional on that fateful day long ago after you'd been shot, your shooter came to me as well. He told me how he waited in the shadows the previous night for you to emerge from your saloon. How he fired three shots. How to this day he still regrets only one bullet hit its target.

Fingy exploded.

"To this day? Who're youse talkin' about? Yer conversin' wit' this bastard still? You better tell me right now who shot me or I'll be comin'...

Quigley stood up in response to Fingy's accelerated threatening and motioned his hands in a manner indicating to Fingy to settle down.

"Tsk-tsk, Mr. Conners! Remember. You yourself just now stated you possess an unshakable belief in a priest's adherence to the Seal Of The Confessional. Anyway, you know full well that I cannot see the faces of those who kneel and confess to me in the dark! However I will provide you one intriguing clue from that confession. The responsible parties have never been absent from your life, are closer to you today than ever before, and in the future will most likely be closer still.

"Parties? There's more 'n' one? Who are they? I'll do away wit' all o' youse! When yer not expectin' it. When things have gone cold!"

Fingy moved forward fists raised as if to indicate he intended to hit Quigley.

"My, Mr. Conners! You're going to—how does your peculiar species put it, hereabouts—wallop me?!" The Bishop continued to laugh so loudly, that the men loitering out at the curb heard it echoing from inside the church, and looked at each other in puzzlement.

Quigley took a more aggressive stance, towering over the fireplug Conners. "Go ahead, Mr. Conners. Wallop a Bishop of God's Church! But first you just swallow this! God sent his only begotten son down from Heaven to save your soul, and you have rebuked him! And because of that, God took from you your only son, Peter, to punish you, to teach you a lesson which you have still neglected to learn! He took your son at the very cusp of his manhood, immediately before entering into your life as your apprentice and heir to your empire? This was no coincidence! It was God's plan! The timing was of His own brilliant choosing!"

Conners reeled, losing his balance so blind sided was he; so powerful was the blow delivered by this least expected of tormentors.

"God did not want another Fingy Conners defiling this earth, Sir!" bellowed the Bishop, his voice echoing in the empty chapel. "So God reclaimed your son and took your beautiful Peter to be with him in heaven before it was too late for the boy, before you could turn him into the same kind of monster that you yourself have become!"

No wallop, no pitching into the canals, no knife thrust that Fingy Conners had ever delivered to an unfortunate victim could ever approach the power of the blow delivered by the Bishop. No one ever spoke of his recently dead son in any but the most timid terms. No one dared even allude to his son's death as being anything other than a thoroughly unfathomable tragedy of leviathan proportions.

"All those laborers who have had to watch helplessly as their own sons and daughters died for lack of money and medicine due to your greed? God in his brilliance demonstrated to you that in spite of your millions, in spite of your considerable access to the finest doctors, that He could arrange for you the exact same catastrophe your workers have themselves suffered over and again under your mercilessness! The loss of your child!

"You and your entire family will continue to feel the wrath and power of God Almighty and of the Holy Church, Mr Conners. You will be set upon by the mobs in your own ward, as they tear apart your filthy saloons to get their murderous hands on you! There won't be enough of you left for even starving dogs to carry away."

William J. Conners, historically impervious to shock, was stupefied and muted by the holy man's brutal assault.

Outside, carriages arrived from the Buffalo Express and the Buffalo Star, carrying reporters. Alderman Sullivan caught their eyes, nodded and smiled and tipped his hat in welcome to the witnesses.

Inside, Quigley, towering over William J. Conners and staring down into his bulldog face, spat out, "And so it is written!"

The Bishop paused to take a breath.

"I have handed my account of your confession to me over to three respected individuals — men who by no stretch of the imagination might ever be mistaken for friends of yours, or of your corrupt police! They have made a vow to me that they will open and make public the contents should any harm come to me — whether it be because you presently appear to have a loaded pistol at the ready under your coat, or if I should so happen to be discovered at some point in the future — if I may quote a phrase I once heard in a confession of yours," Quigley mocks Fingy's diction, "floatin' in da Hamburgh Canal."

He paused, but Fingy did not speak. The timbre of the Bishop's voice changed from anger to grief.

"Priests are not allowed to marry nor to have children, Mr. Conners! We will never know the joy and the comfort such blessings bring. My Teddy was the closest thing I will ever know to having a child of my own to love and care for, and you stole that from me. Stupidly you thought that killing Teddy and poor old Mrs. Shea would frighten me away from my duty. But in fact these murders have made me determined to completely rid this city of you. They have even further tempted me to rid you from this earth as well. It's all I can do to refrain from snapping your neck at this very moment."

Quigley glared at Fingy with deadly contempt. He fired his final volley.

"You listen to me and listen carefully. All this ends now! You and I are leaving here at once. Either you will announce to the men waiting outside that you are immediately abandoning your saloon boss scheme, or I will recite for them the catalogue of your obscene crimes. And if you decide to shoot me with that pistol I see hiding there, make sure to have a ready explanation prepared for the group of news reporters who have been summoned to join our friends waiting out by the curb."

Quigley smirked victoriously and marched off.

Fingy was spooked by the claim of awaiting newsmen, unsure if Quigley was bluffing. Quigley violently flung open the sacristy gate with a loud clang and stomped angrily toward the exit half-expecting to be shot.

Fingy pursued him, his hand inside his vest fingering his gun, with only moments to decide his tactic. Fingy attempted manhandling the Bishop halfheartedly in an effort to prevent him from going outside. They tussled, the towering prelate easily sloughing him off.

Fingy again reached into his vest.

Out front by the curb the group had been freely passing the bottle, allowing them to rekindle the sorts of forgotten memories shared by boys who'd grown up together. Guard down, the familiarity of their lifelong friendships had begun to chip away at the more recent barriers that had been erected between them, and they commenced resurrecting the warm ways they used to know.

Jim Sullivan stood between his brother-in-law David Nugent and Michael Regan finishing his story, his arm wrapped around their shoulders, everyone engulfed in laughter.

"...and then, and then, Mike here says to my mother," recalled Jim, adopting an Irish accent, "but, but, Mrs. Halloran! I never intended to steal yer inexpressibles off the clothesline! I was just feelin' meself a bit of a chill!"

The distracted men were nearly on the ground from laughing when a loud bang startled them. They jumped at the sound of an explosive crack.

All looked in unison toward the church to see the chapel door had been powerfully heaved open, crashing against the granite exterior. Quigley and Fingy strode speedily toward them, as if in a race. Quigley turned to address the trailing Fingy Conners.

"This is for your taking my Teddy from me!

Verifying the presence of his competitors' news reporters, Fingy was visibly startled. The unrivaled master of the sucker-punch had himself been blind sided.

The men converged, all eyes on the Bishop.

Fingy had yet to break. He was faced with deciding between two life-altering choices within a matter of seconds.

"Gentlemen," began the Bishop, composed and dignified, "I have a revelation of overwhelming seriousness to share with you – news that may leave you flabbergasted. May I ask for your full attention, please? You will surely find what I have to say as shocking and unthinkable as it is staggering and upsetting."

All eyes were glued on Quigley. Reporters' pads flung open. Pencils flew across the page. Quigley did not pause, having already decided in a fit of high emotion to tell the world what he knows about Fingy, consequences be damned. He bulldozed forward quickly.

Fingy looked at the reporters writing speedily in shorthand, then at the Bishop, then back again at the reporters.

Quigley continued.

"This man you see standing here alongside me is responsible for some of the most..."

Fingy interrupted; cool as ever, he displayed no outward sign that he had been outfoxed.

"No, no, please! Allow me, yer Excellency," beseeched Fingy Conners. "Gentlemen, I'm announcin' here t'night that after weeks of soul-searchin' an' solemn holy prayer that I 'ave decided t' give up the saloon side of the contractin' business fer the time bein'. The saloons, I already figgered out some while ago, they been holdin' me back. I got grander ideas in mind fer how t' go about conductin' me affairs these days. An' I'm itchin' t' get started immediately. Good night."

Fingy smiled deceptively. The men on both sides were stupefied, but said nothing. Newsmen scribbled Conners' statement furiously.

"Mr. Conners!" called out a shocked reporter, "What caused you to change your mind?"

Fingy, ignoring the newsmen, turned and walked north. Kennedy and JP pursued him as the newsmen continued to question the Bishop.

"Wait, boss! I'll drive youse home," Kennedy called after him.

"Naw, it's only two blocks. I'll walk. I gotta look in on me girls. They're still a bit upset about that dirty parade they seen this mornin'. An' I got somethin' t' talk wit' 'em about. We might be travelin up t' Montreal."

The men gave no sign that they understand what he meant.

The newsmen hurried in departure toward their newsrooms to file the momentous story.

The old friends all shook hands with one another and prepared to go their own way. As the men said their goodbyes, Alderman Sullivan leaned in and said, "Bishop, I think we'd better get down to Fillmore Hall immediately to announce this, before that little shit changes his mind."

An hour later, an infuriated crowd began to shout as Bishop Quigley and Alderman Sullivan entered. JP was horrified at the venomous reception as the bishop gestured with his hands for the ruckus to quiet down. The alderman stayed close to the priest for protection, fearing the crowd might want to tear a politician apart.

The men quieted.

"Gentlemen," shouted the bishop, "one hour ago at my home... your former boss, Mr. William J. Conners resigned. You have won your battle! God bless you!"

A massive welling-up of jubilance roared from within the wooden walls of Fillmore Hall. Euphoric men spilled out onto the streets making themselves hoarse in celebration. The bishop and the alderman were nearly hugged to death by the emotional crushing assembly. Those in the neighborhood who had already gone to bed were awakened by the clamor of emancipated slaves banging metal barrels and shouting their joy to the heavens.

Bonfires were quickly built in the street as men, women and children celebrated. Fireworks being hoarded for the coming Fourth of July were brought out and put to a higher purpose, their meteoric exhilaration lighting up the sky. The news spread like wildfire to the city's other newspaper offices, their reporters speeding bleary-eyed toward the First Ward to confirm the laborers' victorious outcome.

The saloon-boss system was extinct.

Wives rejoiced at the prospect of having their husbands back home and sober for once and with extra money in their pockets. Children were made happy that their Pa would finally be coming home for supper after work, just like the fathers in the magazine serials.

Fingy Conners hadn't just been spouting hollow excuses earlier to save face or to justify his reversal. As lucrative as the saloon-boss business had been for him, the cunning primeval beast concluded he might just have bigger fish to fry. The saloon-boss system was a barrier he needed to cross over in order to enter his newest, more powerful phase in life. As he was soon about to prove in his latest reincarnation, Fingy Conners was once again in the right place at the right time. Buffalo's laborers believed they had defeated Conners, but little did they know what plans he had in store for them.

Although Fingy was made to understand only too painfully at this point where the balance of power lay between himself and the Bishop, "The Contractor" just couldn't help himself. He needed to puff out his barrel chest and make some blustery display regardless. He needed to exact a measure of victory and revenge in order to satisfy some unexplainable need in himself. His clever plan for immediate retribution was to ban the name of Bishop Quigley from ever again appearing in his two Buffalo newspapers, the Courier and the Enquirer.

This had the effect of tens of thousands of Catholic readers, no longer able to read news about their church leader in Fingy's newspapers, canceling their subscriptions and switching to the Times, the Star or the Evening News.

Fingy immediately commenced putting his heretofore secret Canadian scheme into action. Bottomless pit of vengeance that he was, Conners had planned a reprisal against his Buffalo enemies. Investing his fortune in collusion with investors from Chicago and New York, he would construct a super-terminal enterprise in Montreal that would entirely replace Buffalo for the handling of grain, putting thousands out of work and raining down deadly economic misery on the laborers of the First Ward, not to mention the entire city and beyond.

But for now, it was a time for celebration. The headline in the Buffalo Evening News exclaimed, GREAT VICTORY FOR THE MEN ENDS DOCK TROUBLES!, followed by a list:

Points Won By The Grain Shovelers:

Following are the points won by the scoopers. They include everything demanded excepting the absolute abrogation of the contract;

First—Rate of wages raised from 25c per working hour to $1.85 per 1000 bushels, or a rate of 49c per working hour.

Second—No high man's pay for the contractor, or a saving of from $15,000 to $20,000 for the men.

Third—The abolition of the saloon-boss System.

Fourth—Payment of the men in the offices of the elevators between the hours of 4 and 6 every Saturday.

Fifth—Appointment of time-keepers by the men themselves, so that the "dummy system" can be guarded against.

Sixth—The inspection of tallysheets and bills of lading, etc., so that no fraud can be practiced in the amount of grain elevated.

Seventh—The complete recognition of the new union and the exclusive employment of its members on the docks. The discharge of all non-union men.

Eighth—The suspension of the objectionable bosses.

Ninth—The practical supervision of dock labor by Bishop Quigley.

St. Bridget's Annex was filled with scoopers and the meeting called to order. Hon. Rowland B. Mahany, now former Congressman due to a campaign of hatred and revenge waged against him by Fingy Conners in the most recent election, spoke to the men.

"Take the advice of the Bishop, your truest, strongest and bravest friend," said Mr. Mahany. "Now that you have won the battle, now that you are about to secure concessions that make you great victors, return to your work. Return not only for your own welfare, but for the welfare of your families. You owe it to yourselves and to those dependent upon you. You owe it to this community, which has stood by you in this struggle; you owe it to the city now, to lift the blockade at this port." The men cheered Mahany ceaselessly.

The following morning, Fingy Conners was arrested by United States Deputy Marshal William H. Watts. The charge of violating the Alien Labor law was placed against him. Charles Richards was the complainant.

Richards alleged that he was brought from Montreal to work on the docks. He claims an agreement was made with him before he left Canada. Richards had worked but one day when he met some grain shovelers who persuaded him to quit. Inspector De Barry was notified and he investigated the case.

Fingy was taken before United States Commissioner Robinson and posted bail for his appearance May 31, at 10 o'clock.

At the time of Fingy's arrest, ten of Fingy's imported Bowery goons, brought to Buffalo by Conners to crack the skulls of the strikers, were arrested for demolishing a saloon at the Corner of Washington and Scott streets. They had stopped for drinks on their way to the Lehigh Valley depot as they were being sent back to New York. Reaching the depot, a brawl broke out, the police were called, and ten of the gang of fifteen were arrested. The others fled successfully. There were many injuries among Lehigh Valley employees and passengers.

The Bowery thugs were sentenced to the Penitentiary for thirty days.

June 13, 1899
Storming The Whaleback

Michael Werzlerski, also known as Mike Weir, secretary of the freight handlers' union, appeared in Police Court and asked for a warrant for the arrest of William J. Conners. His story was that he was standing on Ohio Street on Monday morning when Fingy abused him verbally and grabbed him around the neck with a hook of his cane and punched him to the ground where, Werzlerski alleged, Fingy Conners and Richard Nugent along with their henchmen continued to beat him. Richard Nugent, first cousin to Hannah Sullivan and her brother David Nugent, was a Conners thug.

Justice King advised the Pole to swear out a warrant for Richard Nugent rather than Mr. Conners. Werzlerski was satisfied with this and the warrant for Richard Nugent was issued.

The whaleback Mather, captained by John Park, pulled into Buffalo Harbor on Friday night June 9th and settled at the Minnesota Docks, laden of ore. Pat Crotty, the dock boss, didn't put a gang to work on her until the following Tuesday afternoon. At around 6 o'clock Tuesday, a gang of about 60 ore-handlers went into the hold to begin their work. There were Irish and Italian among them, but the crew was mostly Poles. About an hour later a half-dozen of them left their thirsty work to go have a drink at a saloon on Ganson Street near Louisiana Street. On the Turnpike Bridge they met a dozen men, many carrying pistols, on their way to the Northern freight house. They were led by freight boss David Nugent.

The two gangs fought. The row was precipitated, it was claimed, when two of the ore-handlers called Nugent's freight men "scabs." About 20 shots were fired, but no one was hit. The Polish ore-handlers were not armed. A few faces were bruised. Quickly the two gangs disengaged, going their separate ways.

Instead of proceeding on toward the Northern freight house however, the offended Nugent gang went looking for reinforcements, and returned with an additional 20 or 30 men.

Unnoticed by anyone who assumed their intention, they crossed the Buffalo Creek Railroad tracks near the Minnesota Dock office and made their way between freight cars and the traveling battering machines to the wharf where the whaleback Mather was moored. They climbed a ladder up the aft onto the deck and a dozen of them proceeded with stealth toward the open hatch near the rear of the vessel, where below in the darkness a dozen ore handlers were busy at work.

A dozen more of the attack party proceeded onward to the forward hatch.

The ore handlers were bending to their work, unaware of the approaching danger from above. The noise of their hoists, the clanking of the ore men's shovels, and the locomotives' whistles in the adjoining yards deadened any sounds made by the intruders.

David Nugent was the first to fire, getting off three rounds before being joined by others. In all, about 20 revolvers were discharged down into the two holds, with between 150 and 200 bullets flying downward toward the trapped ore handlers. Those in the attacking gang who were without revolvers threw stake irons and heavy rods down into the hold, hoping to spear a Pole. The marauders stood on the edges of the hatches and fired until the chambers of their revolvers were emptied. Some were so audacious that they reloaded and resumed their volley.

At the first sound of shots, the ore handlers raised their shovels over their heads against the rain of bullets flying from above, and scrambled for a safe corner. The bright light pouring into the hold blinded them as to the identities of the shooters. The projectiles sparked and shattered against their upheld scoops. Some workmen ran to seek shelter in obscure parts of the hold, diving behind piles of ore, screaming to their companions to run. As he tried to climb out of the hold, John Hanlon was confronted by a freight handler who put a pistol to his face. Hanlon quickly drew his shovel before his face and at that very instant a shot rang out and a bullet shattered a piece out of the end of his scoop. The force of the bullet slammed the shovel into Hanlon's face, breaking his nose.

The Mather's Captain Park hurried around from the front of the deckhouse upon hearing the fusillade, where he saw 30 or 40 men on deck. Some were firing into the hatches, and others were punching the foreman, Patrick Crotty. Ascertaining the determination of the attackers, Captain Park reached for the whistle rope and began sounding an alarm. He rang out three long ones and three short ones, and had only partly finished the SOS when half a dozen men rushed him, the barrels of their revolvers denting his face.

"Stop blowing that whistle or I'll plug you, you son of a bitch!" shouted David Nugent. He rested the barrel of his pistol on his forearm and looked down its length to take precise aim at the captain. Captain Park dropped the rope and walked around the deckhouse and out of danger. His chief engineer then appeared on deck and, not having witnessed what had just happened to the captain, grabbed the whistle rope. The gang pointed their guns and shouted at him to get the hell out. He did.

The ore handlers attempted to escape the depths of the hold. When they emerged on deck they were tossed forcefully off the boat. Those who resisted the invaders were knocked down and kicked in the head, their faces pounded with chunks of ore.

The shooters then tossed their guns into the drink, well aware that the several feet of gooey muck at the bottom would thoroughly swallow their guilty weapons. They then calmly gathered in a knot near the same ladder they had ascended just minutes before and got off the ship quietly and leisurely, not excited or perturbed in the least.

Dave Nugent waited until all his men were safely off the boat before disembarking himself.

Those Polish ore handlers who were not wounded swarmed out of their hold like infuriated fire ants and pursued their attackers down the ladder. 30 or 40 of them pounced upon and attacked the invaders in the rail yards. The attackers had disposed of their guns, so no more shots were fired. The ore handlers armed

The whaleback Mather unloads ore at Buffalo.

Ore men toil out of sight below in the open hatches of the whaleback Mather-filling buckets to be hoisted by cranes into railcars.

themselves with rocks, bricks and blocks of ore, all of which abounded in the rail yard. Blood squirted as scalps and faces were pounded and lacerated, and much worse would have transpired had not three patrolmen arrived on the scene. The attackers scattered, but some of them were apprehended by the officers.

Watching from close by, Sidney Diamond, chief office clerk of the Minnesota Dock Company, witnessed the start of the attack and immediately telephoned Precinct 7 for assistance, and then called the Fitch Hospital for emergency ambulances. Four minutes after the first shots were fired a patrol wagon arrived on scene, followed a minute later a wagon from Precinct 1 loaded with patrolmen, then another from Precinct 4. Two ambulances drew up and the officers fanned out. The Conners-owned patrolmen conferred with the Conners thugs for a while, who then went coolly strolling away down Ganson Street, with no attempt made by the police to arrest them. Instead, the besieged ore handlers were attacked by the police with clubs, thrown into wagons and arrested.

The Mather's Captain Park yelled at a police officer to arrest David Nugent. The copper laughed in his face.

Police swarmed the ship and descended into the hold, where they found John Malik unconscious, blood saturating the back of his coat, his shovel beneath him. A hoisting bucket was lowered into the hold and the injured Malik was lifted onto the wharf, where he was loaded into a Fitch ambulance.

Mike Smith was found sitting on a cross beam, bleeding badly, weak from fright and loss of blood. John Marek and Michael Metlinger made their way to the deck unaided, and were assisted into an ambulance. All of the men were rushed to the Fitch hospital. All of the men had young children at home.

Malik's bullet lodged near his heart, and he was hoped not to die as long as complications did not set in. However with a wound of such a serious nature, complications were the order of the day. Coroner Kenney arrived at the hospital to take an ante-mortem statement from Malik, as he expected Malik to die from his wound. Malik said he was one of the first to be hit as he bent over unaware of the attackers looming above. After he fell, two more bullets struck the ore around his head, just centimeters from his skull.

When the call came into precinct 7 from the Minnesota Dock, Detectives Jim Sullivan and John Geary were ready to go out on pickpocket detail at the Central Rail Station. Instead they crammed into the patrol wagon with thirteen other officers and rushed toward the docks.

Upon arrival, Jim was sickened to see the face of his brother-in-law.

"In trouble again, eh, asshole?" accused the detective. "You'll never learn, will ya, Dave?"

"They attacked us, Jim," exclaimed Nugent. "They stood on the ship and threw huge missiles of ore at us. Take a look at my head!" he cried, lying that the retaliatory slash he'd received from the Poles on the railroad tracks after the shooting was, quite to the contrary, suffered unprovoked beforehand.

"Who the hell are you kidding, Dave? Fingy sent you on another mission? Are you never going to tire of being his little bitch dog? You're not allowed by your own sister to even visit your niece and nephews anymore...doesn't that tell you anything about how you're behaving? Your own sister doesn't want you near them!"

"Fingy had nothin' to do with it!"

"What do you mean, Fingy had nothing to do with it? Every man I see here works for Conners!"

"You gotta help me get released, Jim. My young one is sick, and she might die!"

Hannah had fixed an early supper for Jim before he went in to begin his afternoon shift. As they ate together in the kitchen, the swinging door closed to the children to preserve the parents' private time, daughter Nellie lay moaning in bed with a belly ache suffered from joining her Nugent cousin in a gluttony of penny candy from Diggins' Store on Mackinaw Street after school.

"Serves you right, Nellie. I work all day to fix you a nice supper, and now look what you go and do," scolded Hannah. "That Mary Ellen Diggins should know better than to sell you all that junk!"

Jim leered at his in-law as if he were no more a higher life form than a slug.

"You know damn well that Molly's only got a stomach ache," countered the detective, "from all that candy she and Nellie ate, you liar. You got a little daughter at home, Dave, believing that her Pa is going to come home after work safe and sound, and instead you're up to these kinds of shenanigans? A pistol battle? Come on! We went and named our youngest boy after you! And you're actin' an idiot!"

In all, 75 persons were taken into custody and brought to Precinct 7. The Polish ore handlers and witnesses were allowed to leave after their statements were taken. Sixteen men, headed by David Nugent, all of them employed by Fingy Conners, were ultimately arrested.

Within minutes of his henchmen newly occupying their jail cell, Fingy Conners rushed in to Precinct 7 with fistfuls of cash to bail out his boys. He brushed by Jim Sullivan like he didn't exist. Fingy was told to go discuss the matter with Justice King. Conners had a conference with King, Police Superintendent Bull and District Attorney Penney. He was especially anxious to spring Dave Nugent, but they refused bail for all.

Early next morning, Fingy returned to Police Headquarters, demanding to be allowed to speak to Dave Nugent. He wanted to make sure his men had all gotten their story straight. Police Superintendent Bull refused him. Fingy was irked by his newly diminished status. The previous year Bull would never have refused him. Conners had put him in that job, handed it to him on a platter, for Christ's sake. But the grain scooper fiasco had knocked Fingy down quite a few pegs. Conners was still powerful, but for the first time in nearly twenty years, he was abruptly and routinely hearing the word "no." The police returned to the Mather and inspected the ship's hold. An idea of the fierceness of the previous night's fusillade was had by inspecting the interior. Spatters of lead were visible on the shovels that lay all about, on chunks of ore and on the sheeting of the hold. About 70 of these bullet marks could be seen. Splinters of lead lay all around. Captain Park estimated that 200 shots had been fired. The men in the hold said there was a constant flash and a bewildering spatter of bullets, but could make no estimate of the number of shots.

Over 1200 mostly Polish coal and ore handlers held a mass meeting at St. Bridget's Hall voting unanimously to remain away from work until they were promised protection by the police from the rejected bosses who were now employed as non-union freight handlers by Fingy Conners. The tide had turned. This time, the police stepped in on the laborers behalf, rather than their former boss'.

Fingy Conners rage was held in check by his cunning.

On June 14, Fr. Patrick Cronin's beloved Great Dane was kidnapped from the priest's yard. He well knew who was behind it. The bereft and infuriated Cronin rallied his troops immediately to quickly recover the animal, whereupon the fed-up priest began plotting revenge of his own.

On June 17, Detective Sergeant Jim Sullivan led the twenty three assailants from their cells into a holding room adjacent to Justice King's 10:30 court. King spent an hour disposing with a number of petty police cases before the gang was brought in. Jim had long been acquainted with every man, some of them members of the Mutuals, including Richard and George Dalton, as well as Jim's brother-in-law David Nugent and cousin Richard Nugent. All twenty-three bore themselves with perfect indifference, so assured were they that Fingy would get them released. Justice King called their names, had them stand up and read the charges to them. When asked how they would plead they answered "Not guilty!" in a defiant chorus.

The courtroom was jammed with laborers from the docks who were present to see for themselves whether or not they were to expect protection from the assaults of murderous thugs while engaged in their daily toil. Among them was Gus Wall, president of the dock men, who was assaulted by "Sloak" Slattery, and Michael Weir, who yet bore evidence of Richard Nugent's attack and Fingy Conners' caning of him in the form of a black eye swollen shut, and numerous bodily bruises.

All harbored serious doubts as to whether any of Fingy's gang would be rightfully and properly punished.

October 23, 1899
The Pan-American Bazar

A giant illuminated eagle glowed in warm welcome above the Armory's Connecticut Street entrance. The Armory had been built in the style of a Medieval castle. Once inside, Detectives Jim Sullivan and John Geary craned their necks up at the cathedral-like wood beamed ceiling of the brand-new home of the 74th Regiment and whistled at the amazing sight. Jim let out a long appreciative whistle.

"Quite impressive, I'll have to admit," he said.

Huge flags of all the nations of the Western Hemisphere, as well as bunting of stars and stripes decorated the immense arches high above them to thrilling effect, with the Bazar's participating countries' coats-of-arms at the center. Each of the 20 flags measured 50 square yards each. The glorious interior space stretched on forever, it seemed.

An entourage headed by Alderman John P. Sullivan turned heads as the extended family entered the Connecticut Street entrance, all agape at the reincarnation of a Bombay Palace glowing right before their eyes. The Bombay portal rose 60 feet high and 25 feet wide, flanked by golden minarets with all entablatures covered with translucent paper, behind which hundreds of electric lights transformed the palace into a glowing vision. Colored tinsel was used in every place in which an opportunity to produce a color effect was possible.

What with the Alderman's seven children, their mother, the Polish servant girl "Sophie Smith" — they couldn't spell or pronounce her real name, Grazyna Szczecin — Jim's wife Hannah and their three offspring, the group comprised an interesting attraction all on their own.

Hannah especially welcomed the diversion that the Pan-American Bazar promised, what with her brother currently on trial for shooting ore handler John Molik aboard the Mather. It appeared that neither he nor the slick Fingy Conners would be able to extricate him from this particular mess. She put it out of her mind for now and joyfully embraced the two and a half year old son she'd named after her shamed brother.

The group had briefly greeted Hannah's husband and his partner in crime prevention John Geary when they spotted them inside. Jim wasn't able to join his family in their fun. He had police work to do. Annie brought her new baby James with her, even though their girl Sophie was well trusted to remain at home with the youngest. The children of both families were thrilled by the Pan-Am Bazar's delightful pandemonium, as were their parents. This grand event was a preview of the scheduled mammoth Pan American Exposition of 1901, less than eighteen months away.

The Pan-American Bazar, which had been in preparation for six months, was enjoying its opening day. 10,000 people had been expected to attend, although 14,000 actually came through the doors, and yet there was still plenty of room to move about. The police correctly surmised that the widely publicized event would be a magnet for pickpockets near and far. The detectives had their work cut out for them. Already they'd spotted a few suspicious characters out on Niagara Street while assessing the crowds awaiting the doors to open.

The Armory's interior had been beautifully outfitted. Decorations overhead and along the walls were lavish, and brilliant effect had been secured by means of arc lights and innumerable bulbs. From the massive doors on the Connecticut Street side to the opposite end of the grand court, the picture glowed as perfectly as the skills of the electricians and decorators could possibly conceive it.

There were 300 girls in various costumes, scores of military in gaudy dress uniforms, and mountains of flowers. On the main stage a hand-painted curtain on which was pictured a golden-haired maiden being transported through space by a herd of harnessed butterflies soon parted to reveal continuous vaudeville performances and rousing airs presented by the 74th Regiment Band.

At promptly 9 o'clock the lights were dimmed, and Peasley & Schnoor, the famed aerial artists, thrilled the assembled with their break-away ladder. Fancy dancers Master Raymond Kimball and Miss Winnie Spanner delighted the crowd, followed by a boxing contest courtesy of the Battlestone Bros. Finally, scheduled to close the show at 11 o'clock were the Philippine Girls, showcasing a performance of fancy drill.

An impressive reproduction of the 1893 Chicago World's Fair Peristyle measuring a full 200 feet in length, with its arch reaching 28 feet in height, dominated the space. On the second floor mezzanine, in a room 60 feet square, a reproduction of the Bremen Rathskeller, with nine of its arches faithfully reproduced and rows of wine casks displayed, featured refreshment tables arranged exactly as they stand in the original Rathskeller in Germany. The Apostelkeller, one of the divisions of the Bremen landmark, was reproduced with 12 enormous casks in a room 20 feet wide by 45 feet long, adjoining the main room. Modern science served to make the reproduction more cheerful than the original through the use of suspended chandeliers and clusters of electric lights.

Hannah and Annie wanted to sit and enjoy a glass of sherry, so the Alderman and the servant girl Sophie took charge of the rest of the brood to witness the nightly Storming of San Juan Hill, reenacted by handsome Regiment men who had been drilling for the event since August. The women relaxed beneath the Rathskeller's chandeliers. Toddler David lay peacefully asleep in his mother's lap, likewise did Annie's baby James in hers, and the women sipped their glasses blissfully.

Hannah and the Alderman had come to an unspoken agreement to tolerate each other's presence in a civil manner, for these days neither wife was kowtowing to her husbands' periodic overbearing displays. As a result, the exhibition of the men's imperious behavior had diminished from the day a few years back when the women decided together to no longer tolerate it.

"It's just downright insulting," Hannah had said to Annie, who readily agreed.

"If they can't speak to us any more politely than they do to the servant girl, then we'll just stop speaking to them," replied Annie. And they did. Once their conspiracy to snub had been relentlessly exercised upon the men, a new atmosphere of politeness began to be enjoyed in both homes.

The bazar's fantastic reproduction of San Juan Hill measured 30 feet high by 110 feet long. Under San Juan Hill a grotto was constructed, as well as an ice palace and 30 booths. Every government in the Western Hemisphere was represented here: Peru, Chile, the Argentine, Brazil, Mexico and all the other young and weaker republics occupied booths over which presided men and women attired in the costume of the country represented.

The children braced themselves as screaming bugles echoing through the rafters signaled the charge up San Juan Hill. The assembled thousands cheered and roared as the regiment stormed upward. Hannah and Annie were able to look down upon the choreographed spectacle from their perch in the mezzanine. An immense number of palm trees and other tropical plants decorated the hill for an authentic effect. Only the most lush greenery of such size guaranteed to impress the unimpressionable was used. A blockhouse was built atop the hill's summit, its architects having been assisted in their work by a number of Regular Army men.

Great cheers welled up from the throng as the spectacle deafened and thrilled, then ended in a celebration of victory. All the Sullivan boys were left fully ablaze with the glory of battle, eager to reach the age when they could join the cavalry.

After the reenactment they visited the grotto beneath the Hill, where a breathtaking cascade, a model for the grander version planned for the 1901 Pan-American Exposition, fell in great sheets of water, gushing and crashing into clouds of spray, behind which electric lights were placed for an ethereal effect.

Scores of guides helped the public find their way among the cornucopia of delights. The Midway presented demonstrations of Marconi's wireless telegraphy and of the X-ray. A large model of a planned flying machine was suspended from the rafters, spectators laughing and shaking their heads at the folly of such a ridiculous idea.

At about 10 o'clock while in the thick of the crowd that was assembled in front of the vaudeville stage transfixed by the aerial performance, Detective Jim Sullivan spotted a stylishly outfitted young man, very handsome in looks.

"Look, Geary, I think we're onto a live one," Jim quietly whispered, nudging his partner.

The young suspect displayed no odd behavior nor any outward sign that he might be up to no good, but the practiced instincts of the detectives diverted their attentions to him. The young man pressed his way through the crowd, then lingered directly behind an elderly well-dressed woman. As a distraction he dropped his umbrella, apologizing to the woman graciously, so that as he jostled her she would not think it an affront to herself.

The Detectives immediately drew closer and observed his sleight of hand as his digits slipped effortlessly into the elderly woman's pocket while he righted himself again. The move was so skillfully performed that had they not been watching for that exact motion with their eyes fixed upon him, even the seasoned police officers might have missed it.

Sullivan stepped up to the man's left and Geary to his right, and without any commotion, arrested him. No one watching the aerial act realized what had taken place until Jim interrupted the victim to ask if her purse had been stolen. A cautious lady, she had in fact been holding the purse in her hand against just such a possibility.

The detectives brought the thief into brighter light, and immediately Jim recognized him as the famed thief, Kid Morgan of New York City. Morgan denied his identity and insisted that he was a traveling salesman. Sullivan and

Geary took him to Police Headquarters. Asking around, they learned that earlier he had been seen in the company of a well-dressed young woman, and they at once set out to locate his accomplice. They found her in a lodging house on Elm Street.

The proprietor had a key and let them into her room without knocking. With the opening of the door they happened upon a lovely young lady, completely naked, lying on her back in the bed, legs wide open and pleasuring herself. She was dreamily enjoying the inhalations from an opium pipe. She did not seem disturbed in the least by their presence.

She identified herself as Mrs. Nellie Morgan. The detectives directed her to get dressed so that they might take her to Police Headquarters to join her husband. She was in such a dazed and happy state that dressing herself took quite some time, but patiently and without rushing her, the detectives sat observing her leisurely progress.

Nellie Morgan was known to be a pickpocket of professional ability. The couple was charged with vagrancy.

While the detectives performed all their good work, the Sullivan cousins sat at the bazar's Cafe Français and enjoyed vanilla ice cream and gâteau de beurre and Coca-Cola. It would later prove difficult the get the children down to sleep, even long after they'd reached home, so excited were they by the evening's thrills, and so wide awake from all the sugar and cocaine they'd been allowed.

October 31, 1899
Dick Nugent Takes The Stand

The testimony of Richard Nugent's version of what happened involving his cousin David Nugent aboard the whaleback Mather on June 13th took up four columns of space on the Buffalo Express' front page. The trial was the talk of the city.

Dick Nugent was known to his cohorts by the nickname "Weasel." At less than five feet five inches tall, Dick Nugent always felt he had a lot to prove. Eager to win the approval of the tough guys, he followed his cousin David Nugent around like a lovesick puppy. Dick Nugent was indicted along with his cousin David and fifteen others for rioting in regards to the Mather shooting.

Detective-Sergeant Jim Sullivan escorted his wife's cousin from his jail cell into the packed-solid courtroom, and as Dick Nugent would tell it, his cousin Dave not only did no shooting, but heroically tried to stop his men from attacking.

Dick Nugent claimed his cousin Dave was a saviour.

Others in the room seemed somewhat skeptical.

Dick swore what he was expected to swear. He swore he himself didn't do any shooting and that his cousin Dave didn't do any shooting. He swore that he and his cousin Dave went aboard the Mather to protect their men and to prevent trouble. He swore that both he and cousin Dave seized men who were doing the shooting, took their revolvers away, and put them off the ship.

Conveniently, a mysterious missing man by the name of Scotty Fullerton, who somehow "got away" right after the shooting, along with a now-dead man named Albert Powers, and a nameless "stranger" were the only ones that had been doing any shooting.

Dick Nugent testified:

"I am 23 years old. I live at No. 73 Tennessee Street. I keep a saloon on Ellicott Street. I opened my saloon seven weeks ago. Before that I was a stevedore employed by W.J. Conners. I am a first cousin to David Nugent."

After telling some instances of violence growing out of the strike he said "On the day of the shooting Mr. Conners had some trouble on the dock with a Pole named Mike Weir, a walking delegate for the freight handlers' union. Weir pulled a gun on Mr. Conners and said to him, 'You mick asshole...' Oh, can I say that?"

He was assured he could.

"'You mick asshole, we'll get you off the dock!' Mr. Conners had a cane with a big crook on it. With that he hooked Weir around the neck and pulled him to himself and struck Weir and knocked him down.

"Weir got a warrant for my arrest and I was arrested at Police Station No. 7 that afternoon. Mr. Nugent, my cousin, bailed me out. He and I then went to Billy Watt's saloon next door to the station house and had a cigar. Then we went down to Mr. Nugent's Hotel at 444 Ohio Street where I heard some of our freight handlers telling about the trouble they had had with the Polish ore handlers a

470

little while before that. They said the Poles had thrown something at them.

"Then I went next door to the hotel to Mr. Conners' office and talked with Mr. Conners about the warrant that Weir swore out. Then I went back to Dave's and he told me he was going to the Northern freight house with the men. He asked me to go along with him and I went.

"Dave and me walked along about 300 feet behind the gang. Suddenly the men turned off the path and made for the ore dock. They climbed up on the boat and I says to Dave, 'These fellows are up to something wrong!'

"We followed them on the boat and I saw a man standing over a hatch and shooting down into the hold. He was a stranger to me. I ran up to him and pulled him back and asked him what he meant by doing that. I looked down in the hold and saw Molik stooping over to pick up his coat. I guess he had dropped it. I don't know who shot him, but I saw him straighten up, then fall on his back.

"Then I saw Scotty Fullerton and I yelled to Dave, 'Stop that man! He's got a gun!' Dave ran up the boat and I saw him grab Fullerton and tussle with him. He knocked the gun out of Scotty's hand and kicked it out onto the dock. Then Dave began throwing men off the boat. I helped him. We hustled them off as fast as we could."

The attorney for the defense, Mr. Shire, asked, "Were you ever attacked by Poles before this trouble?"

"Yes! One time fifteen of 'em pitched in one me."

"Did you fight them?"

"I did the best I could."

"What did you use to defend yourself?"

"Nothing but my fists."

That was all the testimony Mr. Shire desired just then, and District Attorney Penney began his cross examination. Dick Nugent assumed a defiant attitude and declined to answer some questions bearing on his story about Mike Weir until Judge Emery instructed him to answer.

"After this Mike Weir had spoken to Mr. Conners, as you say, and you knocked him down, didn't your gang jump on him and beat him up?" asked Mr. Penney.

"No."

"Didn't you in fact hit Mr. Weir before he ever pulled out a revolver?"

"No."

"Didn't he try to get warrants for others when he got one for you?"

"I don't know."

Mr. Penney drew out the information that Dick Nugent had spent much time drinking in various saloons on the night of June 12th, and that on the day of the 13th he and Terry McLaughlin, another of the indicted men, had been drinking at the Tifft House, Hurley's, Forrestal & Streich's, Watt's, and a number of other saloons.

"When you heard these freight handlers in Nugent's Hotel telling about their trouble with the ore handlers, did they tell you that they had fired shots at the ore handlers on the Turnpike Bridge and that the ore handlers had thrown chunks of ore at them?" asked the District Attorney.

"No, I didn't hear them say anything about shooting and they didn't say what the ore handlers threw at them."

"When Dave Nugent asked you to go with him, what did he say to you?"

"He said that he didn't feel like going to work that night because they'd had trouble with the ore handlers."

"What business did you have with that gang?"

"Oh, I wanted to go with Dave."

Dick Nugent swore under oath he didn't pick up Scotty Fullerton's revolver after Dave Nugent had knocked it out of his hand and that he didn't toss it overboard. Perhaps the fact there was no such person as Scotty Fullerton meant that in this case what he was swearing was the truth.

"Fullerton was pointing it at the captain of the boat, who was pulling the whistle, when Dave pulled him away and knocked the gun out of his hand!" lied the witness, dramatically.

"Was that the same gun with which he shot into the hold?"

"I don't know."

"Did you hear Dave Nugent say something to the effect of, 'God damn you, stop blowing that whistle' to the captain?"

"I don't think I did."

"Will you swear that he did not say it?"

"I will not."

Mr. Penney next asked about the curious nameless stranger that Nugent claimed fired shots into the hold. Dick Nugent swore that Scotty Fullerton, the mysterious missing man, fired one shot, the nameless "stranger" fired two shots, and that he did not see Powers, the dead man, fire any shots.

Mr. Shire, attorney for the defense, took another turn.

He asked the witness about certain assaults to illustrate the troubled times that prevailed on the docks last spring and summer during the Scoopers Strike.

Dick Nugent related that on one occasion he was in charge of a gang of sixteen men unloading wet grain when a Pole came aboard the boat and began to talk to the men between decks.

"I put him off the boat and told him not to come back again," said the diminutive Dick Nugent. "There was a big Irishman named Joyce on the dock, a big six-footer, and he tried to put the Pole up to come aboard again, and I told that Irishman that if he wanted anything himself, he could have it. So the Irishman started to come aboard with the Pole. As he was coming up the ladder I knocked him down. He came at me again. The Pole and another Pole joined him. The Irishman pulled out a revolver. I grabbed up a piece of dunnage or scantling and went at him. They pressed me close and I ran up the hatch to the upper deck and picked up an axe and stood there and told them to come on. Meanwhile one of my men went down into the hold and fired three or four shots from his revolver just to scare them. The Irishman and the Poles then got off the boat."

"How many men were out on strike last spring?"

"About 2500."

"And there was more or less trouble going on between them and the men who took their places, the scabs, wasn't there?"

"Yes."

"Now, on the night of the so-called riot on the Mather, what was Scotty Fullerton's condition on that boat?"

"He was pretty drunk."

"Did you have any difficulty in throwing him down?"

"Not at all."

Mr. Penney cross examined the witness again.

"You say that Mike Weir had a revolver when he confronted Mr. Conners on Ohio Street the day before the Mather incident?"

"Yes, sir."

"You hit him and took the revolver from him."

"Yes."

"You weren't afraid of him, his being over six feet tall, or his weapon?"

"Well, I took a chance."

"And you did him up. Hmm. Impressive. Now, Nugent, have you ever had any trouble in which you got the worst of it? Or did you always come off the victor in all of your fights with all these six-footers?"

Laughter filled the court.

"Oh yes, I have been done up," said Dick Nugent, flustered.

"This Joyce fellow, the big Irishman. He was six foot tall, you say?"

"Yes."

"Yet you still dared him and the Pole to come aboard the boat?"

"There were two Poles besides Joyce."

"And you dared all three?"

"No, just the Irishman."

"This Pole that you put off the boat, was he a six-footer too?"

"Pretty nigh that."

"And though you are barely five feet, five inches tall, you put him off the boat?"

"He was drunk."

"Is that the way you do up all your six-footers—tackle them when they're drunk?"

"No."

"You say you grabbed up an axe and stood at the top of the hatch with it?"

"I did."

"Would you have killed any of them had they dared to come up?"

"I probably would have used the axe." replied the witness.

"You, in fact, started that particular fight, didn't you?"

"Oh, I don't know."

"Well, haven't you so testified? Haven't you sworn that you first put that Pole off the boat?"

"Yes, I suppose so."

"And when the police arrested you the night of the so-called riot aboard the Mather, they told you that you had already made more than enough trouble for them, didn't they?"

"No. They said I'd caused them trouble before."

A tall, lean fellow named Gallagher was called to the stand. He said he was staying at 71 Louisiana Street and that he was a lake fireman. His manner and his answers caused some laughter in the courtroom.

"I was down on the dock, looking around for to ship on some boat. My brother was working on the Fryer, tied up behind the Mather, and I was aboard the Fryer when I heard shooting. I saw a man come running down the dock with a pale face and I hurried down on the dock and went over to the Mather and saw men getting off her."

"You heard gun shots, yet you ran toward them rather than away from them?"

"Oh, yes."

"Then what did you see?" asked Mr. Shire.

"I seen this man," Gallagher said, pointing to Dave Nugent, "shoving men off the boat. An' I seen him stop another man from shoving a man into the river. Then I heard this man," he said still pointing at Nugent, "say, 'you oughtn't done no shootin' in amongst the crowd.' Then I saw a man pick up a chunk of ore to hit another fellow, and this good man," pointing again at David Nugent, "pulled him away and told him not to do that."

"You don't work for Mr. Conners, do you, Gallagher?"

"No, I never did."

"And you don't know David Nugent?"

"No, sir, I don't."

District Attorney Penney cross examined the witness.

"Where have you been today, Mr. Gallagher?"

"Uptown," said Gallagher.

"Did you stop anywhere?"

"Yes, in a saloon on Main Street, near the foot."

"Who did you see there?"

"A man. I don't know his name."

"How many drinks did you have?"

"A glass of beer and a cigar."

"How many saloons have you visited today?"

"I don't remember."

"How many drinks have you had?"

"I don't remember."

"Oh, give us some idea."

"I don't remember."

"Who's been loading you up today?"

"Nobody, as I know of."

"Who paid for your drinks?"

"I don't remember."

In reply to further questions, Gallagher offered that he had been wandering around town during the morning and that he had been drinking with two or three men.

"But you can't remember how many drinks you've had, eh?"

"Couldn't have been over two or three drinks. I don't look very drunk, do I?", asked Gallagher, slurring.

The courtroom erupted in prolonged laughter.

"I'm not talking about your appearance," said Mr. Penney.

"Well, I'm not a distillery," said Gallagher, smiling.

Mr. Penney brought out that Gallagher was recently from Cleveland, just a few days ago.

"How did you witness anything on the Mather back in June if you just arrived a few days ago?" asked the District Attorney.

"I travel. I am a salesman, and I was here in June last."

"Didn't you talk at length to your brother about this case?"

"No, sir."

"You knew your brother was a witness in this case, didn't you?"

"He might have been."

"Well, don't you know for certain that he was?"

"Yes, but I didn't tell him any details or anything like that, I kept what I knew a secret."

"What did you keep secret, may I ask?"

"Uh. What secret?" asked the witness with great surprise, after pausing for a second to catch himself.

"You just said that you kept what you knew secret," said Mr. Penney.

"You're the one that spoke about secret. I didn't say anything about secret."

"Shall I have the stenographer read back the testimony?"

"Sure."

The stenographer read Gallagher's testimony.

"No, that's wrong. I never said that," he sniffed, wiping his nose.

"Now Gallagher, how many drinks have people bought you today?"

"I don't have to have people buy me no drinks!" he shouted with a show of indignation. "I've got money right here in my clothes." And with that he felt his trousers pocket, but did not withdraw his hand.

"Oh, I don't doubt that at all. Not at all, Sly. I daresay you've got lots of it," chuckled the District Attorney.

At this, Gallagher leaned far over the railing, thrust his face out challengingly, and said, "What do you want to bet I have?"

Laughter filled the courtroom.

Mr Penney replied, "That would be betting on a sure thing."

"Well, there's where you lose!" exclaimed the witness emphatically. "I ain't got a damned cent!"

The court officers were compelled to pound on the floor vigorously for a full minute before they could subdue the laughter that followed this sally.

Once Gallagher staggered off the stand, a string of character witnesses followed, eager to tell the court what an upstanding and fine young man David Nugent was. His sister Hannah and brother-in-law Detective Sergeant Jim Sullivan were not among these.

James Ryan came first. Ryan was former Police Commissioner, had served as Alderman in the First Ward for six years, Water Commissioner for eighteen years and was presently Grade Crossings Commissioner. He said he had known Dave Nugent for 14 years.

"What kind of man is he?" asked another defense attorney, Mr. Hoyt.

"A perfect gentleman," stated Mr. Ryan with a theatrical flair.

Mr. Penney objected and the answer was stricken out.

"I want to know, Mr. Ryan, what is David Nugent's reputation, on the speech of others?"

"Good—the very best," replied Ryan.

"I mean in regards to his reputation for peace and quiet."

"Well, I mean for everything," Ryan replied.

Renowned attorney Edward Coatsworth came next and testified for Nugent, stating that, "His reputation has always been the best, so far as I know."

Various others, local grocers, hardware store owners, all of varying nationalities, followed one another and swore to the absolute goodness of Dave Nugent.

By contrast, on the following day the testimony given on the stand was very unfavorable to the defense. David Nugent's attorney Hoyt made very effort to shake the evidence, but the witnesses held to their accounts.

"Now, Captain Parks," began Mr. Hoyt, "isn't it a fact that David Nugent said to you when he asked you not to blow the whistle that the other men would shoot you if you didn't?"

"No," replied the Captain, dripping with loathing for the attorney. "When a man stands with a revolver aimed directly at your head and you see his eye along that barrel, it doesn't look as though he's telling you that some other person is going to shoot!"

Some of the witnesses, including the captain, were bitter against the police for their unusual display of partiality in favor of the gunmen.

Captain Parks testified that on the evening of the riot, he was in his cabin and was aroused by the sound of shots. The second mate came running in and called him to the deck. Men were firing into the hatches and others were punching Crotty, the foreman. The Captain testified that he saw the defendant, Dave Nugent, attempting to hit Crotty.

Pointing to Nugent, the Captain said, "That man there, after cursing at Crotty and trying to strike him, he ran to a hatchway and fired shots down into the hold. He then went to the other hatches and fired down those as well.

"I ran back and blew the whistle for assistance. Nugent then came up to me and ordered me to stop, covering me with his revolver. 'Stop blowing that whistle or I'll plug you, you son of a bitch,' he said. He rested his pistol on his arm and aimed it carefully at me and I stopped. He stayed on the boat until all his men were off."

Joseph Madden, fifteen years old, followed the Captain on the stand and testified seeing Nugent shooting through the hatches.

Michael Metlinger, who was shot while down in the hold of the Mather, went to work the night of the shooting at 5:30 o'clock. He worked at the hatch with the badly wounded Molik. "I heard shots," he said. "I looked up the hatch and saw men running around. That man there," he said pointing to Nugent, "said, excuse the language, 'Come out you fucking polack or I'll shoot you dead,' and he fired and I took a shot."

The witness was positive that Nugent was the man who shot him.

"Did you not tell the police that it was Denny Shea who shot you?" asked Hoyt.

"Yes, sir," responded Metlinger, "but I was mistaken in name and not in face. That man there was the one who shot me," he said, pointing directly at Nugent.

"What policeman did you tell?" asked Hoyt.

"I don't know," said Metlinger.

"That's strange," said Hoyt.

"I wouldn't say that," interrupted District Attorney Penney, "they're your friends in this case."

Frank Kenefick of No. 212 Mackinaw Street, hatch tender on the Minnesota Docks, identified a number of the shooters by name, having known them previously. He stated that he saw Nugent fire down the hatch and saw him atop the captain at the whistle.

"There were 8 or 10 men around the hatch, No. 3 hatch, and I saw four shoot. I saw the smoke but not the flashes. I saw Nugent fire three times with about a quarter of a second between each shot."

District Attorney Penney asked Kenefick if he had seen one of the accused shooters, John Dalton, since the shooting and what was said at the meeting.

"Why," responded the witness, "I met Dalton on Louisiana Street and he said to me, 'Do you want to send those fellows to prison?' and then he asked me if

I would not go light on the prisoners. He said his brother George was on the Mather trying to prevent the men from fighting."

Hoyt asked Kenefick, "You say Dalton asked you to go easy on the accused men?"

"Yes, sir."

"You told him you intended to stick to your statement? Why would you do that?"

"Because I am not willing to perjure myself." Kenefick responded.

"Did Dalton ask you about the statement?"

"Yes, he asked what I had said. I told him it was none of his business and walked away."

John J. Flynn of No. 31 Ganson Street, an engineer at the dock, was present at the shooting.

"What did you see?" asked District Attorney Penney.

"On the night of the shooting I was standing on the dock and I noticed Mike Hanavan coming along at the head of a gang of men. He had his left hand in his pocket and a revolver was half sticking out. He went aboard the Mather. Then followed a man I don't know. The third man was George Dalton and the fourth Dave Nugent. When Hanavan got aboard he told the hoisters to quit and they did. As soon as Nugent climbed aboard the shooting started. Nugent was the first to fire a shot. I distinctly remember he went to No. 3 hatch and fired down it. Molik was taken from that hatch."

"Who shot first?" asked Penney.

"That man right there," reiterated the witness, pointing to David Nugent. "He yelled, 'Come out of there you sons of bitches,' and fired."

"What did he do then?"

"The gang moved forward, firing down the other hatches. Those that hadn't revolvers threw heavy rods of iron and stake irons down onto the men below. The captain was blowing the whistle and Nugent and Hanavan went aft, leveled pistols at his head and told him to stop."

"Did you see Nugent try to stop the fight, put any of his men off the boat, or prevent any of his men from getting on?"

"I absolutely did not!" responded the witness emphatically. "I saw just the opposite!"

On November 2, 1899 David J. Nugent was found guilty of second degree assault in the shooting of John Molik, with the jury recommending leniency. The penalty for his crime, assault in the second degree, was a $1000 fine and 5 years in prison. Nugent's attorney W. B. Hoyt immediately moved for a new trial.

Nugent remained free on $5,000 bail.

❧

December 25, 1899

Annie Sullivan was at long last in her element. In a city exploding with growth and new wealth, Central Park's Depew Avenue was the au courant residential neighborhood in Buffalo. It was located well north of downtown far afield from the smoke and stink of industry, away from thugs and ruffians, removed from the smelly river and the horrendous racket of iron manufacture, screaming boat whistles and the flotillas of chugging engines belching coal soot.

The homes were large and beautiful with generous lawns and yards, and although the structures varied from one another, there was a unifying element of dignified wealth that united them, the result being a distinguished cohesive urban haven. The Alderman's family was compelled to move out of their stately rented house before the New Year, back to dirty old Hamburgh Street in the First Ward. An alderman was required by law to live in the ward that he represented. Annie resented that rule. This is where she belonged.

The Alderman had made a promise to her in bed one recent night, soon after the strike was fully settled and things got halfway back to normal on the waterfront. He promised that the very day he left political office he would bring her and the children back here to live in a fine home on Depew Avenue or adjacent, this time to stay forever. For a few moments this made her gloriously happy until she concluded that the only way the city was ever going to get rid of this particular Alderman was if he died. She recognized that aside from his family that politics was his reason for living. The Sullivan Ice Company brought in the money, she naively believed, but it was the Common Council chambers that made him spring out of bed every morning, singing.

Annie decided that the best way to wind up their wonderful half-year on Depew Avenue would be to have a giant Christmas tree with electric lights and to host an elegant holiday dinner for the family and a few close friends.

She had her heart set on a blue spruce, a tree that grew abundantly and perfectly symmetrical in many people's yards, but was rarely available in the Christmas tree lots. She told JP about it. He said he'd arrange it, but found the task challenging. Oldest son Thomas volunteered he knew where to find one, and asked for $10 to acquire it.

"Ten dollars!" his mother exclaimed.

"Ma, if you want a Christmas tree as rare as the blue spruce, you're gonna have to pay for it."

A perfect seven foot specimen appeared on December 18th, carried in by young Thomas and two new friends he had made in the neighborhood. The tree came from the Christmas tree lot on Main, he said, and was the only blue spruce they had. It was set in a tub with rocks and stones piled around its trunk to keep it upright, the tub filled with water to keep the tree fresh.

"Spruce are really thirsty. It was cut recently, the man said. So we need to add water every day," instructed Thomas.

Annie extravagantly tipped each of the three boys a quarter, and they instantly headed off to the soda fountain.

Later that same day she met Hannah downtown to shop and have lunch in Hengerer's department store tearoom. Hannah couldn't conceal how much she missed Annie. She had been rough on her, too rough at times. Annie didn't think so. Quite the opposite, in fact. Annie believed that without Hannah she may have never woken up and stood her ground with the Alderman. It took a brutal shaming to shake her out of her perfect housewife's fantasy, and she was, all in all, very grateful to have Hannah in her life.

The Wm. Hengerer store's lavishly decorated windows along Main Street had become a tourist attraction with each succeeding Christmas season. Torontonians and Hamiltonians descended on Buffalo each holiday season for the wealth of American goods not readily available in Canadian emporiums and to see Main Street's dry goods stores' holiday window displays. Buffalo shoppers reciprocated, in Hannah and Annie's case at least twice a year, by hopping the train that crossed the International Bridge to Toronto for treasures from England, Ireland, Scotland and France found in handsome shops and stores along Yonge Street. The Eaton's store and the Eaton's Annex were their favorite Hogtown destinations. They were excited to learn that a tunnel connecting the two Eaton's emporiums was being built under James Street that would allow shoppers to check their heavy winter woollens in the store and go back and forth between the two at will in even the worst weather without having to go outside or risk crossing the busy street. It seemed a splendid idea, they thought, one that Buffalo should consider copying.

The two Sullivan brides went from floor to floor sampling Hengerer's winter season temptations, lusting after cashmere sweaters and Japan silks, forgetting for a while that shopping for others was the reason for their visit.

In Tinsel Towne, Hengerer's Christmas decor department, they both purchased the new colored electric lights for their Christmas trees, something Hannah had not fully appreciated until awed by the spectacular effect of the electric display lavished on the decor at the Pan American Bazar.

Annie had hired additional help to aid her in pulling off her holiday soiree. Sophie was entirely assigned to the care of the children, and Mildred and Patricia Driscoll, mother and daughter, known most famously for their culinary skills, were brought in for the month of December. They would prepare the feast, ready the house, and help the family pack up for the move back to Hamburgh Street after Christmas.

Hannah had only seen the house once, back when the Alderman's family first moved in at the end of May. Now she stood in appreciation of Annie's skills in turning this rental into a warm and welcoming home. Hannah thought to herself, if I knew I was only going to be staying here for six months, I would never have put all this work into it. Hannah's hat was off to Annie.

Annie had splurged on having new Arts-and-Crafts style frames custom made by her talented friend Elbert Hubbard for some watercolors she had purchased when the women attended the Academy of Fine Arts sale years ago. These beauties had just sat in a drawer waiting for display until now. New photo portraits of her children filled the gleaming top of the grand piano, the property of the home owners. She had tried to play the instrument, curious if she might be one of those gifted souls who could play by ear. She wasn't. She had the front hallway repainted and the mahogany floorboards buffed in the downstairs rooms, and the porte-cochere swagged with welcoming evergreen boughs and red bows.

The house smelled of Christmas through and through; of a crackling log fire in the brick fireplace, of fresh cut spruce, roasting turkey, baking cookies, cinnamon-scented candles in the water closets, the perfume of the women. It was a magical wonderland that Annie had created, and what most impressed Hannah, more even than Annie's talent, was her lack of vanity about it. As if practically anybody who chose to could pull this off.

The families gathered noisily around the massive dining table; the Alderman's, Jim and Hannah's, and the newly reconciled Uncle Tom Nunan and his wife and kids. Annie asked to say grace before they began to eat, something none of the families normally did. She thought though that it was appropriate, for she was feeling very grateful for the blessing of having lived in this house.

In the middle of their exquisite turkey dinner there was a loud knock at the door. Jim got up to answer it. It was the police. His cohorts seemed surprised to see him standing there amid such grand surroundings.

"Oh, Detective Sullivan, hello. Merry Christmas. Uh, we have a report that a young boy who lives at this address had cut down a prized blue spruce tree from your neighbor's yard over on Woodbridge?"

The detective turned around without hesitation and boomed, "Thomas! Come here!"

December 28, 1899
Regrets

Judge Emery heard the argument of Attorney Hoyt on the motion for a new trial in the case of David Nugent. In a power move, Hoyt and Nugent waltzed into court an hour late. The judge neglected to address this, or to scold Hoyt, despite the blatant disrespect this showed toward everyone involved.

Hoyt presented a laundry list of complaints. He stated that the special grounds on which he would move for a new trial were that the verdict was clearly against the law and against the evidence, that the verdict had been decided by lot and by means other than the fair expression of the jurors, that an error was committed in the court in refusing to appoint a commission to examine two witnesses living in Chicago whose evidence the defendant considered essential. That the court had erred in refusing to set aside jurors challenged for bias and that the charge of the court was contrary to law.

District Attorney Penney challenged these points, arguing that the trial had been more than just properly conducted, given the notoriety and public interest.

The judge gave Mr. Hoyt until January 3rd to submit his papers. Afterward, he would make his decision pertaining to a new trial.

Meanwhile, Hannah Sullivan hadn't quite found God again, but was reexamining herself and her attitude. Her brother David's murderous behavior and Fingy Conners' all-out assault on the legal system in his attempt to get Nugent freed were weighing ponderously on her.

She had always protected her younger brother, shielding him from harm, excusing his terrible decisions, blaming their convoluted upbringing and the unstable conditions at home. Their mother Mary was unbalanced, and unable to care for her children. Hannah was placed with her cousins, the Shea family, for much of her upbringing. David was a problem from the start, greatly affected by the instability at home, with no competent male adult to lean on nor to learn from, so preoccupied was their father Jeremiah Nugent in coping with his wife's illness and his own coterie of personal demons.

Hannah recognized in herself the very same over-compensating behavior that she had demonized her husband for. The very same enabling of their younger siblings, based on their thin justification that their brothers had each in his own way gotten a raw deal in life.

Hannah had read with horror the awful accounts in the news journals of the ferocity and audacity of her brother's vigilante attack on the Mather. But worse, she cringed at the result. Michael Molik was now a cripple, and Nugent's bullet would remain lodged close to his heart. It was too dangerous to try to remove it. Molik had four children, all under the age of eight years. The family had nothing, as was evidenced by a visit paid to their apartment by a news reporter. They were subsisting on the kindness of friends who possessed little more than they themselves did. Hannah Sullivan felt guilty for what her brother had wrought. For perhaps if she had been more strict, expected more from him, encouraged him to overcome his childhood problems rather than use them as ongoing excuses for all his sins and wrongdoings, then maybe David Nugent wouldn't have turned out to be the kind of man who stages a vigilante attack on a ship with his gang of thugs and shoots at helpless men hard at work trapped in their hole like rats. It was an incredible act of cowardice, she concluded. In confession her priest told her she was not at fault. She asked God's forgiveness anyway, and for His help for the Molik family, Catholics like themselves.

Hannah kept silent on the matter, but secretly wished her brother would soon begin his prison sentence, or there was no telling what he might do next if allowed to get away with such a terrible crime. He had shamed himself, his sister, his entire family.

But no, actually, that was not quite accurate, for his real family was Fingy Conners. Fingy was the father that David never had, their own father Jeremiah Nugent so detached as he was.

Hannah had come to the difficult decision that David Nugent was not fit to be around her children any longer. She had thought at first she'd keep him away just for the time being. But now, after all that he'd done and all that was made so painfully public in the courtroom and the newspapers, she saw him for what he really represented. She never again wanted to find him sequestered in whispered conference with her sons out back during family events. God only knows what kinds of ideas he may have planted in their impressionable heads already. She worried about what he may have suggested to them. She thought many times of asking Jim Jr. about it, but was afraid of the answer.

That night in bed she told Jim about her decision.

"All right, Hannah, but we can't keep the kids away from each other. We can't punish David's Molly for what her father's done," said Jim.

"My concerns are with our own children first and foremost, Jim. Molly and Nellie go to school together and play together, and that's fine, but I don't want Nellie or our boys going over to their house. His Molly is always welcome here, but he is not."

"So how do we explain this to the kids?" Jim asked.

"With ours, we'll just have to be forthright, and tell the truth. 'Uncle Dave did a terrible thing, something he doesn't regret. And because he isn't sorry, he isn't welcome here any longer.' It will be a valuable lesson for them, don't you think? About responsibility, and the results that come of our actions?"

"I don't know Hannah. Maybe it's too much for them to take in. And then, what about David's? What do we say to his kid when she asks why their cousins can't visit?"

Hannah just shrugged.

"All right Hannah. I'll agree mostly. But I'm not going to shun him or Molly. They need us right now, right or wrong. We're their family. All of us. I've seen too many instances of good kids going bad over something of this nature," counseled the detective, citing experience.

"I haven't figured that out yet," countered Hannah, "exactly what to say to Junior or Nellie. How to explain it. But they read the newspaper, and they certainly hear all about it from their school friends. They know what happened, no matter what story David might wish to tell them. But if I know my brother, my guess is he hasn't told his Molly a thing about it yet. Everything that little girl knows or doesn't know she's getting only from the street."

"All the more reason why we have to include her. Mark my words, Hannah."

"All right. I'll figure something out. Let me sleep on it, Jim."

Hannah lay there unable to fall asleep as Jim snored softly. She regretted the day she slammed her husband with the cast iron skillet, and what that might have done to their family had she injured him seriously. She shuddered. She believed that at that moment she may have perhaps been literally insane. That even though at the time she felt as dismissed by and as invisible to Jim as her own father had made her feel while growing up, she could have handled the problem in a more satisfactory manner.

She had success encouraging Jim to create a friendly distance between himself and his brother, and Jim seemed to be the better for it. Less stressed. Less put upon. Now she was reciprocating by doing the same with her own sibling. Certainly their family would be better off with neither brother's interference. She didn't regret engineering that. But she did regret her own blindness about her flawed relationship with her brother, it being no healthier than Jim's was with JP.

She decided she should own up to this to Jim, to say the words. To sincerely apologize.

December 30, 1899
The King No Longer Reigns

After more than a quarter century on the bench, Police Justice Thomas S. King concluded that the end of the centenary would be a fitting date to finalize his long career, to retire, and to give himself, as well as Mrs. Justice King, a well-earned rest. His last day on the bench would be the last working day of the century, Saturday, December 30, 1899.

He was a fixture in Buffalo history and his name had appeared daily in the newspapers, decade after decade, but now he looked forward to some well-earned peace and anonymity.

The retiring magistrate's last day in court featured a docket lighter than usual. New Year's Eve 1899 fell on a Sunday, so he was just barely escaping the flood of revelers and criminals who take most advantage of that holiday to misbehave. He was happy to be leaving.

His first case stepped forward. The Justice was in good humor and not inclined to be quite as withering in his comment as usual. Carrie Norton, a negro, who tried to kill herself by taking laudanum several days previous, was arraigned on the criminal charge of attempted suicide.

"Did you take laudanum?" asked the justice.

"Yes, sir."

"Well, why didn't you take enough?"

"I tried, Your Honor."

"Well, go along. Do better next time. Case dismissed."

The mother of ten-year-old George Rausch of No. 107 Herman Street appeared in order to have her son sent to a reformatory because, she claimed, he was incorrigible and was liable at any time to kill her and her husband.

"Again, the boy has got to suffer for the negligence of his parents!" said the justice. "Why didn't you and your husband take care of this boy as you ought? You are to blame, not he. But he is bad, I have no doubt, and I'll send him to the Rochester Industrial School. Some people ought to be punished for having children. They ruin them and then expect the country to take care of them!"

Thomas Murphy, Harry Montgomery and Gerald Callahan, youths of eighteen, were charged with stealing a horse blanket from a shivering beast that stood on Washington Street. Murphy pleaded guilty, the other two pleaded not guilty.

"I was drunk when I did it," whimpered Murphy.

"Well, then, take the pledge for a year. Nice thing for a boy to be drinking hard liquor almost before he's weaned. Swear off!"

Murphy took the pledge.

"Now pay a fine of $3."

Murphy asked that Montgomery and Callahan be discharged because, he claimed, he had committed the theft unabetted by them. Justice King granted the request, saying, "That's an old trick, Murphy. Together you've got the means to pay only one fine, so one of you agrees to shoulder the blame and all pitch in their money to save him from the Penitentiary."

George Murphy's was the last name on Justice King's final docket, an interesting coincidence being that the justice who would be taking King's place was also named George Murphy.

When the business of the court was disposed of, Jim Sullivan and a number of other detectives and officers approached the bench to shake hands with him and extend their best wishes.

"No hard feelings, eh, Sullivan?" Justice King said as he leaned over to take Jim's hand.

"None," replied Jim with a forced smile.

Jim Sullivan had stood before Justice King himself in his younger days, after beating his stepfather and Eliza Beatty. Jim had tangled with Justice King on countless occasions since as a police officer due to King's extremely lenient treatment of gamblers, in contrast to his harsh punishment for lesser offenses. But all in all, Justice King had been just, and he was tough on those who were the worst offenders. That's what mattered, Jim thought.

Hanging back behind the detectives was a plainly clad old man, who once the others had cleared away, extended his hand to Justice King.

"Judge, your leaving this court must mean a good deal to you, but it means fully as much, if not more, to me. And I'll tell you why, if you can spare a minute or two."

"Why certainly. Go on. I've seen you around here for years, but I don't know you from Adam."

"Yes, I've been around a good many years. I started visiting your court eighteen years ago when it was over in the old building on The Terrace and I've been a constant visitor ever since. Except for sickness I haven't missed three days here in the last ten years. It has been the only regular feature of my later life. I have found more entertainment in being here than I could have found in any other way and I don't know now just what I shall do. I can keep on coming, of course, but when you go, this court loses its peculiar individuality.

"I used to be in the West when it was pretty wild and I must say, and it should not displease you, that in your court there has been a flavor of the old frontier courts. Its disappearance takes out of my life its chief element of diversion, of enjoyment, and I will be lost from now on. So you see, your retirement means probably as much to me as to you."

"We'll shake anyhow," said the justice, accepting his hand.

A few minutes later the queer stranger was standing in the outer hallway talking in a reminiscent manner to several persons who stopped him.

"Some of the funniest things I ever saw in my life," he said, "I have seen in this court right here. I remember a few years ago a tramp who had all the external characteristics of his type was arraigned before Judge King. He pleaded guilty, he said, to anything on the calendar, but chiefly to being a tramp.

"Well," said the Justice, "you're no good to anyone and no good to yourself, are you?"

"No, sir, Your Honor, I am not."

"Then, I've got a remedy for your case. You take a boat out of here and on some dark night steal up on deck and jump into Lake Erie. Will you do that?"

The bum thought about it for a moment.

"I don't mind the killing of myself," replied the tramp, finally, "but I object to the method. Suggest something else that hasn't got water connected with it."

"The Justice was so amused at the man's droll humor that he let him go. Another incident I recall occurred when the court was over at The Terrace. A negress named Rachel King who was one of the toughest women in the city and who had been arrested innumerable times, one day was arraigned before Justice King on the charge of assault, third degree. The justice knew her by sight and by name, but in an unconscious sort of way he asked for her name, whereupon she replied, 'Rachel Sweeney.'"

"Rachel what?" asked the judge.

"Sweeney."

"No, you can't fool me. Your name's King."

"No Judge, I've married two days ago."

"And you're charged with knocking down a man who struck your new husband?"

"Yes, Judge."

"Well, you're discharged from the word 'go'. No one can assault a man who was so kind as to save my name from everlasting disgrace. I'll protect this man Sweeney. I've got no better friend."

The old man was thoroughly enjoying holding court of his own with the reporters.

"It isn't easy to recall on the spur of the moment many particular incidents. Moreover, special occurrences aren't what have made the court famous. It has been the general tone of the place, the continual outbursts of the judge, either humorous or scathing.

"I recall one time about five years ago, a wealthy man in the city caused the arrest of four poor boys for picking up wood from his premises. On the day of the arraignment the wealthy man, who was also prominent, went up behind the justice and whispered to him. Then he started out. He had got part way to the door when the magistrate's rage burst in all its fury, and a royal rage it was too.

"'Here, come back here, you rich scoundrel! Officer! Stop that man and bring him back here!'

"The rich man turned around and faced the judge and this is what he heard:

"'Why, you curmudgeon! You miser! You'd shake hands with the devil and act as his agent in a virtuous community if you could make a cent off it. And you ask me to fine these boys heavily? I'm going to let these boys go and if you even come sneaking around here any more as you've done today, I'll have you arrested on the charge of being a public nuisance.'

"The rich man turned red and white alternately and sneaked out of the room. That illustrates the fact that the wise, the illiterate, the poor, the rich, were all subject at times to the both the justice's wrath as well as his generosity."

December 31, 1899
A New Century Cometh

The country was in a state of great excitement at entering the new century. It was a landmark, the 20th. Just the sound of the number when spoken aloud soared with the melody of a modern future. Why, just twenty years ago there were no telephones, no X-rays, no automobiles. And now look! The new century held astonishing promise as progress accelerated at a dizzying speed.

The Sullivan cousins were excited about being witnesses to the landmark event and partaking in all the related celebrations.

Hannah and Jim's precocious Nellie was boring her brothers to tears over her fascination with the 1900 Paris Exposition. In this day's Buffalo Sunday Express, the illustrated edition, there were many large photographs of the various and astounding constructions, such as the gorgeous Pont Alexandre, the connecting link between the two sides of the exposition across the river Seine, and the Monumental Gate at the Place de la Concorde. But most of all, Monsieur Eiffel's breathtaking tower that newly dominated the Paris skyline. She thought it wondrous and imaginative, and was thoroughly perplexed that many Parisians stated they found it an abomination, and vulgar.

"The French!" she exclaimed in dismay at their lack of taste.

"I thought your cousin Molly was coming over, Nellie. Did she change her mind?" asked Hannah.

Nellie went silent.

"Nellie. I'm speaking to you."

"Mother, Molly is angry and doesn't want to be around me. She told me her father is innocent, and I told her she was wrong, that everyone knows he did it. Everyone at school calls her names, like 'murder's daughter' and 'jailbird' and such."

Oh, God, said Hannah to herself.

"Nellie, Molly is going through something terrible right now. She does not want to believe her father could do such a thing. No child ever would. I want you to not talk with her about her father anymore, do you hear? She needs you. No matter what your uncle did, Molly is innocent, and frightened. She needs all the friends she can get right now. She needs her cousins especially."

"But mother, you told me that Uncle Dave did a bad thing."

"Yes. I did. And he did do a bad thing, Nellie. But imagine how terrible and embarrassed Molly feels right now. If the children at school are making fun of her, then she is suffering. Very much so. You are her cousin and you must be especially kind to her right now. And that means, with everyone else talking about her father, that you cannot. Do you hear me? Your job is to be Molly's family, and help her. This is a very cruel time in her life."

"Nelllllieeeee!" came a shrill voice from down on the street.

Molly was outside calling. Hannah opened the window a crack and hollered,

"Molly, come on up, Honey, we're making cookies. Hurry up out of the cold."

A smile spread across her reddened face, and with great relief, Molly ran up the porch steps.

"Go down and make sure she doesn't leave her wet galoshes on the carpet, Nellie," encouraged Hannah.

"All right Mama."

The New Year's Eve party at the Mutual Rowing Club boathouse had been in busy preparation for a week. The event was always a highlight of the club calendar, but the turn of the new century called for an achievement to outdo every previous effort. Hannah didn't need to, but she wanted to bake sugar cookies, twelve dozen of them, for the guests.

The Alderman and his family were now entirely moved back into their house at No. 12 Hamburgh Street, what with the scoopers strike settled and everyone's emotions cooled down. Perhaps people might even begin to forget their elected representative's disappearing act as they fought tooth and nail to take back their very lives from the sucking tentacles of Octopus Conners.

The Alderman's kids were certainly happy to be back home with their cousins and their friends, although Annie had effortlessly acclimated to the good life on Depew Avenue. Part of her hated returning to Hamburgh St. Part of her didn't mind. She'd had her taste of the future, and was reluctant to return to the past. She was tired of the filthy river, the choking smoke, the acrid outpourings of the foundries and factories. But by dictate they were required to live in the Ward, and there was nothing even remotely like Depew Avenue in the First.

Even more so she had quickly become friendly with her new neighbors, who were certainly of a better class than those surrounding her on Hamburgh Street, no offense. They respected her because she was the wife of an alderman whose name they all knew, one of the city's most witty politicians. Unlike Hannah at times, they did not look down on her, or make her feel like a ninny. She felt special—and respected—on Depew Avenue. She'd had time to consider some things while living removed from her relatives. On her own, out from under the family shadow. It was like a vacation. She adored it.

Annie stood in front of her closet, still unable to decide between two dresses, both brand new. But no matter. Whichever she chose, she'd outshine every woman there.

December 31, 1899
New Year's Eve

The Alderman had not been feeling well for days now. He tried to hide it from Annie, but she could see the signs.

"JP, you need to see the doctor."

"I saw him this morning, Annie. He told me to just take it easy and not exert myself. I'll be fine. I am not going to miss this party."

The family's servant girl Sophie took charge of sitting with the youngest children, Anna, Genevieve, John and James, as well as Hannah and Jim's youngest, David. Annie was still uneasy about leaving her new baby, but their houses were situated directly around the corner from the boathouse. In fact, from the boathouse's upper parlor windows she could look right into her own brightly-lit rear windows, which she would find herself doing numerous times as the minutes ticked toward the new century.

Hannah had been making a special effort to lose some weight and pay closer attention to her appearance, and she wanted to look especially attractive for this party. She didn't want anyone to see what a burden her brother's crimes had put on her.

Annie looked spectacular, having gone downtown to a Delaware Avenue beauty parlor, where she spent over 3 hours and more than fifty dollars. She dared not tell JP that. Her dress was a brilliant sapphire blue silk satin, and she glowed like the jewel itself.

The club had hired the band of the popular colored fiddle player Rufus Jackson, and the numbers they poured out alternated between the rousing and the sublime. There was no let up in the music, for the most part, unlike previous bands the club had engaged that demanded numerous lengthy breaks. This ensemble cost more, but they were worth it. A large Christmas tree glowed with electric lights and dripped heavily with glittering lead tinsel, painstakingly applied one strand at a time. The boathouse was artistically decorated with evergreen swags and holly, colored streamers and many bouquets of flowers. Overhead in the most public places were hung opportune bunches of mistletoe, so that unsuspecting couples might be trapped and forced to kiss in front of all eyes.

Hannah had not rested easy the entire time Annie had been living away from Hamburgh Street. She was surprised at how much she'd missed her. Their relationship had for years alternated between something that was a source of irritation to them both, and their being just as close as real sisters. Hannah feared that with Annie away and having her first real taste of the good life that she might just be lying in wait for the opportunity to slam her with a full accounting of her brother's sins, as well as her own denial about the trouble he'd long been heading for. She knew she deserved a good dressing down, and was prepared for it. She'd take it like a man.

But Annie was not of that sort. Annie believed that in time Hannah would come to realize the part she herself played in the upheavals she blamed others for, and she was right.

At the party the wine flowed freely and both women let down their guard and had enormous fun together. They happily reconnected with each other as well as with the other wives and their children, many of whom they had not seen since the Valentine's Day party almost a year ago, before the scoopers problems had shut down everyone's social lives.

"Oh God. I knew this night was too perfect. Take a look, Hannah."

Carol O'Hara was there. After Michael Moriarty had grieved his dead wife for nigh on to five years, he finally got around to listening to his M.R.C. friends' advice and began seeing someone. The problem was, no one ever dreamed he'd aim so low his first time up at bat, especially after all these years. He had initially brought the terribly insecure Carol O'Hara to the Valentine's Dance last February, and she proceeded to antagonize every woman present. She'd made a catty observation about Annie's hair and Hannah's posture, Ellen Regan's lack of style, Catherine Stanton's shoes and God knows what else.

Now here she was, at it again. The word had gotten back to Annie that O'Hara had pronounced her beautiful new fur jacket "pretentious", obviously because O'Hara possessed no such thing of rare beauty herself.

Annie was fuming.

"What makes a woman like that so nasty, Hannah?" she scowled.

Oh, Annie! She's jealous! That homely little battle axe looks twice her age! Like she's been dragged through town by a team of runaway horses, then stepped on."

Annie couldn't stop laughing.

" One truth in life, Annie, that has yet to be disproven, is that whenever we hear anyone criticizing another, they are always telling us far more about themselves than they are about the person they're lambasting!"

Carol O'Hara sauntered by at that moment, ignoring the Sullivan wives.

"She's a mouse, Annie, and she knows it. You, my sister, are a princess. She knows that too. Just make her invisible, because in reality, she almost is."

The two giggled at that.

"What do you keep looking at?" asked Hannah after noticing Annie peering out the window.

Annie laughed. "Oh, I'm checking on the house, to see that the baby's all right." At that very moment Sophie could be seen next door in the window, waltzing with the infant and laughing.

"I think I'll run over quickly just to check on things," said the nervous Annie.

"Wait, I'll come with you. I need to use the bathroom, but not the one in this place. Too many men have been careless, if you know what I mean. And you shouldn't go out alone anyway. It's New Year's."

Uneasily they negotiated the icy walk and the piles of shoveled snow at the corner a little woozily, stepping carefully so as not to slip. Hannah dared not look at the place in the river where her Johnny had drowned. She didn't want to be sad tonight.

They entered the house. It was warm and cozy, and Sophie had everything in order. The young ones were all asleep, except for the waltzing baby. The Christmas tree was lit, and Sophie was playing music on the Victrola. We Three Kings.

"He was fussing, and if I dance with him he calms right down," giggled the twirling Sophie in her heavy Polish accent.

When the women were satisfied that all was well in Sullivanland, they headed back around the corner to the party. The air was exceptionally frigid, so they hurried along, trying not to fall. As they rounded the corner, they halted in shock. Up ahead in front of the Mutuals' boathouse they could not believe what they were seeing.

The elegant, genteel Annie looked around frantically, dressed in her gorgeous sapphire gown and fur jacket, and spotting her prize, bent down and seized a metal pipe leaning up against the wood fence with her exquisitely gloved hand. She wore a beautiful wide rhinestone bracelet on the outside of her glove, and it sparkled incongruously in the light of the electric street lamp as compared with the rusty heartless pipe she grasped.

Both elegant ladies had the exact same idea simultaneously.

They charged, screaming like banshees, Annie brandishing her pipe ferociously at the parked sleigh, next to which stood the Alderman involved in a loud and angry exchange with a belligerent Fingy Conners.

"We're comin' inside JP!" commanded Fingy. "I am one of the founders of this club! Wit'out me..."

Fingy glanced up just in the nick of time to sidestep the metal post connecting with his skull. Annie was out of control, insane, rabid, swinging the pipe wildly. The Alderman tried to obstruct his wife and nearly got clobbered in the process.

"You goddamned animal!" spat Annie. "I'll kill you for shooting at my boy! My family had to move out of our home because of you, you pile of horse shit!"

Hannah jumped on Fingy at that same instant, blessing God for providing her this grateful opportunity to finally have at the bastard, her best frock be damned. She scratched at his face as Annie, now disarmed by her husband, punched and bit the savage pitbull of the First Ward. Fingy's companions lunged toward the brawling trio, but four party guests including Ed Stanton who had come outside to have a smoke jumped in to block Fingy's Hessians and safely pull the women off.

The whole scene only lasted a few seconds, but long enough to draw Conners' blood. The women would not be subdued. Their infuriated shrieks and flailings continued, drawing a flood of guests swarming out of the building, and setting eyes upon the execrable Fingy Conners, most were agape at the nerve of the man, showing up here of all places.

The prettified mob moved forward. Angry shouts arose and Fingy jumped into his carriage, pushed up into it by his companions, Hannah's brother David Nugent, and old Dennis Hurley, he of the glass jaw.

Hannah caught her brother's eye and seethed with venom at his choice of loyalties.

"Don't you dare go with him, David! We're your family!" screamed the outraged Hannah at her brother, her hair unpinned now and hanging down in her face. She labored to catch her breath.

As the sleigh sped away, David Nugent at the reins, Annie bent over and picked up the pipe again and fired it with all her fury at the departing vehicle. The missile smashed a lantern and pierced the metal carriage shell, impaling itself there horizontally.

The Alderman was on the ground.

"JP!" exclaimed Annie, thinking her husband had slipped on the ice.

He tried righting himself, but collapsed again, and fell hard.

"Call the ambulance," the Alderman said weakly. "You'd better call the ambulance."

Midnight church bells rang joyously and firecrackers popped simultaneously with the clamor of the Fitch Hospital's ambulance roaring up.

"You go with him, Annie. I'll go check on the house and make sure everything is all right there," assured Hannah.

Annie knew that she should be with her husband, but was apprehensive about leaving the baby.

"I promise you, Annie, I'll leave right this second and stay with the baby," pledged Hannah as she stooped to pick up her evening bag off the ground.

Jim said, "I'll follow you to the hospital Annie. You just go with him in the ambulance, I'm right behind you."

As the ambulance raced off with the detective not far behind, the noises of street celebrants, firecrackers, bells and buzzers and horns, drunks shouting their slurred Happy New Century! to whomever was within earshot, and pistols being fired into the sky all melded together and mixed with the Alderman's delirium. He was hallucinating.

"Where's my Pa?" he asked. "Pa!"

Annie felt his forehead. He was burning up.

"Oh, God," said JP, returning to reality for a moment. "What a way to begin the new century."

As the seconds passed, Annie grew alarmed over whether this was indeed a new beginning, or the beginning of the end.

She made the sign of the cross.

"Hurry, please!" she begged the driver.

q

The Saga continues in
The First Ward II:
Fingy Conners & The New Century

More books by Richard Sullivan

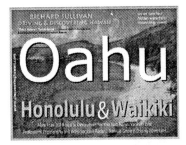